A NOVEL

Manufactured in the United States of America.

Book cover design by Sherman Cammack, from original drawings by Tony Tiscareno and aircraft artwork by Sydney Jordan. Final detail artwork completed by Karen Cheadle.

Dedicated to:

My family and friends

and

Clifton “Gene” Gent

Acknowledgments

To my friend and mentor, James Dalessandro, who taught me the Art & Science of professional screenwriting, later backed me on this different path and adventure of writing this novel, always my deepest and most profound gratitude.

To Lynnea Laux and Carol Fink, who helped me endlessly with my research in Key Largo and the Keys as a whole, who adopted me as their "Little Bro."

To Ian "Kobe" Cooper, my man in Israel, who aided me most kindly with my many queries here and there.

To Gail Francis-Tiron in Gibraltar for her kind help in my dedicated research of the "Rock."

To Jim Irwin of Aircraft Spruce & Specialty Co., for his thoughtful assistance and research to my questions.

To the George T. Baker Aviation school in Miami for their kind assistance.

To Dexter Turner for his help when I needed it, in all things avionics.

To Reece Howell for kindly sending me the Pilot's Operating Handbook (POH) for the Mitsubishi MU-2 for my research.

To Craig Sjoberg for giving me my first ride in an MU-2!

To Cotronics Corp., Inc., and Mohawk Innovative Technologies, Inc., for the use of their names and actual products, though used fictitiously.

To Kelley Dupris, my friend and first editor, whom I know drove nuts with this manuscript of epic proportions, requiring him to do his editing on three continents. Awesome job!

To Jonah Tice, my friend and second and fourth editor. It is with massive appreciation that I thank you for your tireless, selfless, and faithful help.

To Michelle Straube, my third editor and adopted big sister from decades ago, whether she wanted the job or not, who gave the specifics of editing and a woman's point of view. You have my endless thanks, always.

To Peter Friedman, my friend, supporter, and depthless source of resources and information in aviation, politics, and most anything else needed throughout this story.

To David Friedman, my friend and valued technical source for anything aviation, and else what.

To James "J.D." Newman of Infinity Aerospace for his exposure and resources to the kit plane world over the years.

To Jerry Grove, who gave me some hands on experience with kit planes and much knowledge.

To Sherman Cammack, my friend and gifted graphic designer, who got the artwork right the first time. Well done, sir!

To Karen Cheadle, my hero, who came on board here at the end and finished my artwork.

To Sydney Jordan, my old and dear friend, one of the founding fathers of science fiction, who took my drawings and created the beautiful original artwork and storyboard work for the original screenplay version.

To all, my greatest level of thanks and appreciation in helping this lonesome writer achieve a dream!

February 22ND, 2022

To my friend and sister -
Sharon Edwards -
May you enjoy the read,
as you travel, journey, and
experience something new
in the human experience!

Tony Tiscareno

Part 1

"All things wicked start from an innocence..."

Ernest Hemingway

Chapter 1

Finca Vigia—Havana, Cuba
23°4′3.87″N, 82°17′47.1″W

January 1, 1959

The powerful hands drove their meaty fingers in relentless pounding until the hunter was satisfied that his quarry was completely subdued. He wouldn't let slip anything from his grasp that would undo his image as master of his craft. In his mind, the prey would hang on the wall where many of nature's fiercest creatures found their immortality. But now, his fingers began to ache, and the knęes that had supported him through two world wars as part correspondent and part soldier were getting wobbly.

Ernest Hemingway looked out the window of his bedroom/study, gazing at the ferns and palms interwoven among the foliage that encompassed his home and surrounding grounds. He took a deep breath and stepped back from his typewriter, which sat on a dictionary atop a waist-high bookshelf. He looked at the gazelle's head mounted on the white wall above his typewriter. He gave the gazelle a wink.

His latest work would be similarly stuffed and mounted, he thought. Then he realized the days were gone when he could sit at his desk just beyond his bed, thoughts well ordered, pounding away on his portable Smith-Corona, creating works that eventually gained him a Nobel Prize. For a long time, he had done all of his writing standing up as Dickens did. Wounds sustained during World War I and two plane crashes in Africa many years later made it too painful to sit. He was past his prime and slowly, painfully coming to grips with that fact. Some thought he had written himself out by 1934, the year he published his last book of short stories. Now fifty-nine, he had years of depression, alcoholism, and repeated head injuries from various accidents tallied against him. His more charitable friends attributed Hemingway's accident-prone nature to his chronically poor eyesight. His less charitable friends pointed to his endless drinking as the probable cause.

He needed a drink now. He pulled the page from the typewriter, collected it with the others, and made his way to the living room.

Hemingway's Cuban home, Finca Vigia or "Lookout Farm," was a white stucco country home built back in 1886 that Hemingway bought in 1940. It had been his one true home ever since. It was a simple, seedy, but somehow still elegant place located a few miles northeast of Havana. A constant reader, Hemingway had about nine-thousand books in the house. Animal heads, trophies from his African safaris, and hunting trips in Montana festooned the walls.

Here and there, animal skins were draped over furniture or spread on the floor.

The pessimistic feeling that had swept through Hemingway just now as he was quitting work for the day eased once he had taken a deep sip of rum. He tried to clear his thoughts. Then he shuddered as he heard a thump outside, which turned out to be a Cadillac pulling up the hill past his house. It was his mobster neighbor Julian Sanders. He was perhaps coming home from his casino-nightclub—as he did every morning, probably accompanied by his young son Roman, always made to ride in the backseat, even if just the two of them.

The automobile, purchased new and delivered to Sanders, was showing signs of battle with the salt air. Sanders tried to befriend Hemingway, inviting the author to his casino-nightclub occasionally, but Hemingway looked to maintain his distance.

Gambling did not interest Hemingway, especially, except for cockfights, a common blood sport in Cuba. He liked to go into Havana, where he enjoyed the cockfights and the occasional lover's spat. He was often found at his favorite bar, the Floridita, holding his signature drink, the Mojito, a Cuban cousin to the American Mint Julep.

The mob was still a powerful presence in Cuba. Hemingway wondered how long this would continue. Even now, as American and foreign tourists and wealthy Cubans were waking from a night of celebration in every hotel and nightclub in Havana, President Fulgencio Batista y Zaldivar had loaded his wife and children into an airplane during the night to flee the unstoppable political force coming his way. Not even the mob, busy running its casinos and pouring drinks, was aware of any of this. At least the mob pretended not to notice.

Hemingway expected the announcement soon that Dr. Fidel Alejandro Castro Ruz was the new leader of Cuba. Most of the support for Batista had withered. Hemingway put the tumbler back down on the glass end table and went back into his bedroom to deal with other business.

Chapter 2

The Riviera Hotel (Havana)

January 1, 1959

"I hope you are all sober enough to know what's going on here," said Meyer Lansky as he fell back into his office chair. Meyer Lansky was clinically too sharp to believe that another banana-flavored cowboy riding in to reform the Cuban government would be another soft sell as Batista had been. The founder of the National Crime Syndicate, parent to the modern Mafia, may have built a big organization, but he did not take Castro lightly. He was a Polish Jew who grew up on the streets of New York City and was known for understanding the Sicilia mind better than the Sicilians. His childhood friend, Charles "Lucky" Luciano, was heard to say, "You may have had a Jewish mother, but somewhere you was wet-nursed by a Sicilian." Lansky understood Latin bravado.

In the 1920's he teamed up with another childhood friend, Benjamin "Bugsy" Siegel, in a rise to power, which would brush aside the old line Mafiosi who stood in their way. Lansky considered himself a businessman of genius, and many in the world of organized crime agreed. Although their admiration was generally alloyed with degrees of resentment common in both the criminal and legitimate business worlds. When Lucky Luciano spent nearly a decade in prison, only being released to help the U.S. track down German and Italian spies along the New York City waterfront, he said of his right hand, "Listen to Lansky."

The quiet man was always thinking and always about one thing: profits. His gaming establishments were now under threat. Lansky's Batista connection had made Havana, Cuba, the gambling capital of the world. And as the U.S. was only ninety miles away, it had become a playground for America's eastern states. Now things were coming apart. Lansky had brought a clean game to the casinos of Cuba, and it had paid off. His operations in Cuba were bringing in fifty million dollars each year.

His hotel, the Riviera, lay along the Malecón, the stone built-wall that rose high from the beach that ran the city's length along its northern coastline. To some, it was a long stone bench to sit and watch the sky and sea by day. To others, it was the place to stroll amidst the glow of sunset with lovers walking hand in hand in the salty air.

The Riviera stood apart from the other hotels and casinos at the edge of town. The seventeen story, three hundred fifty-four room high-rise with its curved balconies was renowned for its panoramic views of the city, beach, and ocean.

The phone rang. "Yeah," Lansky said. His men listened to his end of the short conversation. "We'll play it cool. See what happens," he summed up and put the phone down.

"So, boss, we won't be packin' up too soon, will we?" his right hand asked.

"Castro plans to leave for Havana soon. Problem is, the people are all jazzed about it. I don't like an ego I can't control. We'll go about business as usual tonight." For the first time, Lansky felt claustrophobic in his stylish office. He knew it was time to get out.

***

Julian Sanders dropped the phone harder than he should have. It startled his son Roman. Sanders bounced back into his chair. He looked around the office. The Hotel Malecón Viejo was his. All his. He looked at his two right hands, both savvy men and ruthless if need be. Sanders had fought long and hard to establish his presence in Havana. "Castro may be in power, now, but I ain't gonna run like I did back in forty-six. No-siree-bob!"

Julian Sanders grew up along the docks of New York City, running the streets as a hoodlum. He gave up the streets somewhat and began working on high-rise construction projects, becoming a foreman at twenty-four and then a project manager. Later, Lansky brought Sanders into work on the syndicate's new project in the growing town of Las Vegas: the Flamingo.

The project began with Hollywood Reporter publisher W.R. Wilkerson in 1945. But postwar material costs and Wilkerson's gambling addiction halted the project. The syndicate saw potential and offered to help, entering into an agreement with Wilkerson. Everything ran smoothly until Benny Siegel took over. The hair-triggered mobster was known to beat up a man for mistakenly calling him "Bugsy" to his face. Siegel had no sense of business, especially the construction business. The mob had only so much patience, and going over budget by six million dollars for a two million dollar project made them anxious and suspicious.

Siegel had Wilkerson run out of town. Wilkerson retaliated the best way he could. He reported the gross overruns of the casino-hotel. Julian Sanders knew that Bugsy and his girlfriend, Virginia Hill, were skimming off construction funds. Hill was a party girl and courier for the mob, a singer, dancer, and former hooker who was put in charge of decorating the Flamingo. It was rumored that her many trips to Europe were to stash funds in numbered Swiss accounts. It became impossible for Sanders to do his job with constant conflicts from Siegel. It came to a point when Bugsy ran Sanders out of town at gunpoint. Sanders went to Havana and spoke to Lucky Luciano himself, who had sneaked back into Cuba, despite the U.S. imposed exile to his native Sicily. In each of the three meetings that the bosses had, Lucky called for the death of Bugsy.

The hit was carried out on June 20, 1947. Lansky's deputies took control of the Flamingo from that moment forward.

Sanders' loyalty and integrity was rewarded. He would own and run the Malecón Viejo. Out of spite, Sanders called his nightclub the Flamingo Room. The nine-story, sixty-two room, six suite hotel had been his life for the past ten years.

"You're going to hear it from me first, boys, I ain't gonna ever be run out of town again," Sanders pounded.

"You know, boss, we have to be careful. We have power like all the bosses, but this Castro has an army. I figure living up in the hills for as long as they have may have made them a bit, you know, cranky. Same thing happened to us when the Japs moved in on us in Guam, and we had to take our base back from the hills. We was cranky," said his right hand Mickey.

"And cranky is cranky, boss," added Georgio. "It's been nice here with mostly nice people looking for a good time. Even if they come cranky, they go home happy."

Sanders studied the two men. "I know what you're saying, boys, but I have my life here. I got my kid here now." Roman looked up at his father with a slight smile. Whatever Roman didn't understand about his father's business, he knew that his father loved him.

Sanders, for the first time in a long time, saw some life in the little boy's eyes. He wanted his boy to be tough but also to have compassion when safe to do so. "Son, would you go down to the restaurant? I'll be along soon."

Roman got up and went out quietly. Sanders watched the closed door for a moment. "Look, boys, I finally got my son away from that two-bit whore. The one thing he needs right now is stability."

"Look, boss," Georgio said. "Everyone loves the kid. And we all want him to come out of his shell, run, and play with the other kids. He's starting to come around with that Cruz kid."

"Ernesto," Sanders interjected.

"Yeah, that's him. His father has spent a lot of money here. And we have taken good care of his clientele. The sugar business has been good to our business."

"And it will continue to do so."

"Yeah, but, boss," Mickey chimed. "Suppose it goes sour, and we have to go. Natives might get restless, and hey, we still have Vegas."

"I ain't ever going back to Vegas! We have our own entertainment right here. We've kept our noses clean. Good family environment if you are of age." Sanders looked at his men. "I ain't gonna be run out of town ever again!"

Chapter 3

Pan Am Clipper "Pride of America"
Miami International Airport
25°47′36″N, 80°17′26″W

January 8, 1959

The main landing gear rotated forward up into the gear well of each inboard engine nacelle. As the gear doors closed over the aircraft's last connection to the earth, the Pan Am DC-4 climbed skyward. Once leaving the runway at Miami International Airport, the aircraft turned in a southwest direction as warm red rays of a setting sun washed over the nose of the shiny metal skin until the tail was caught in the same reddish glow.

The passengers wondered what the short flight would reveal when they landed in Havana. For some, it would be a changed Cuba from the one they left just days ago. Perhaps, it would be unrecognizable. Two stewardesses rose from their folding seats and began serving drinks as cigarette smoke curled and tumbled up from several seats.

Francisco Javier Cruz swung a freshly lit Cojiba cigar scissored between his chubby fingers in rapid gestures to aid his points of the conversation. "So, Castro is a Socialist. Money still is the lubricant of enterprise. You think now that he has reached Havana, he will live as he did in the mountains?"

Hugo Valdivia stirred in his seat. "That is not the point, Javier."

Cruz shrunk back in his seat, taking a quick puff of his cigar, releasing the aromatic smoke upward in a long exhale. He had great respect for Valdivia, a thirty-six-year-old tobacco farmer and businessman. "Dr. Castro is for the people. We are some of those people, Hugo."

Cruz took another puff, more leisurely this time, enjoying what he thought was the checkmate to the conversation that started four days ago in San Francisco, amid nervous tobacco and coffee buyers, over the régime change and their profits. Ease spread over Cruz as his lips widened into a smile. He looked over at his friend, whose strength in body and mind was both envied and admired. Hugo Valdivia wore the finest clothes yet worked the fields with his workers come planting and harvest time. He still taught the fine art of rolling tobacco leaves upon the thigh as his father taught him. He had a large home in Miami, yet none of his workers lived poorly. He shared his wealth. Cruz was sure that Castro could not help but admire Hugo Valdivia. "Hugo, one way or another, we'll be okay. Trust me."

Valdivia settled in his seat. His eyes stared ahead, slowly working their way shut as his thoughts matched the rhythm and rumble of the engines.

Up front, first officer Martin Rio pulled the throttles back to a cruise speed of 190 knots and adjusted the mixture levers as the captain watched. The captain was a former "boat skipper" who had cut his teeth on the Boeing, Martin, and Sikorsky flying boats of two decades ago.

Though considered a Cuban national, Martin was born and raised in San Francisco. His family owned land in the fertile Pinar Del Rio province, west of Havana. Martin started a flying service between Miami and Havana in an old Cessna T-50 "Bobcat" twin, which caught the attention of Juan Trippe, who did something similar in 1927 at about the same age. Trippe was impressed with the young pilot and appreciated his sense of business and adventure. He wanted him in his organization. Martin was honored to meet the Pan American World Airways juggernaut and world flight route innovator who bridged the world. Martin finally earned his way in the co-pilot's seat of the company's DC-4 and DC-6 fleet. Naturally, he had his eye on the newly heralded Boeing 707, the flagship of Pan Am.

"I suppose you'll drop this old tin can like a hot rock once you build enough time in the company," the captain huffed. "For me, of course, I wouldn't trade the real golden era of flying. Nothing like the Boeing Three-Fourteen. Nothing since will ever be like that sweet old lady. You know we could pull off a mini tune-up in flight on those beauties."

Martin let go of the large pretzel-shaped control wheel as the autopilot took over. His thoughts drifted to his wife Amanda and their four-month-old son Lance. Since he started flying with Pan Am, Martin moved his family from Pinar to Havana to be closer to the airport. Martin knew that Amanda had grown up living a hard life on a farm in Oklahoma and craved the urban life. She put her teaching credentials to work in an elementary school.

Pan Am Clipper "Pride of America" lowered its landing gear. They were cleared to land at Jose Marti International Airport. The runway was well lit. It widened as the aircraft came closer. Martin felt tense yet made a smooth landing. He prided himself on his professionalism.

The aircraft pulled off the active runway and rolled along the connecting taxiways to the gate area, where the engines muffled to a quiet stop. The ground crew moving in unison, rolled the airstairs up to the aircraft. A stewardess opened the door of the plane. The cool tropical breezes blew scented air into the stale, smoke-stained cabin, reviving many and reminding them they were home.

Amanda Rio cinched up her arms. Baby Lance had gotten heavy during the long wait for Martin. She scouted out a fresh group of passengers and crewmembers with differing uniforms until she spotted a black uniform and white pilot's cap worn by a nearly six-foot-tall man. Martin spotted Amanda and didn't slow his stride until his arm was behind her in an embrace.

They were soon in their Chevy sedan and heading for home. Martin could relax after a long day in the air and get a sense of the mood of the country. After talking to family and friends on the telephone, Martin was convinced that Castro could be a blessing, if for nothing more than the ousting of Batista. With the U.S. government acknowledging the new Castro régime, albeit begrudgingly, perhaps there might come a balance to the island nation, one that had never existed in Cuba during his lifetime or for a long time before.

***

The car pulled up to the departure area of the Jose Marti International Airport as it had done routinely for the past twelve months—since Castro took power.

Martin Rio kissed his wife Amanda and son Lance goodbye. He stepped out of their car and, with a smile and wave, entered the terminal building. He had an eight-thirty a.m. flight to Miami, then on to New York. On his return trip to Miami, he would be meeting with a realtor about a house in either Miami or Key Largo. It took little convincing now that they might possibly have to flee Cuba and abandon their house and belongings to the state—to Castro.

Martin cleared his mind as he entered through the gate to his plane. He would be flying the larger DC-6 today on its two-leg journey. He gazed at the aircraft named Clipper Splendid. It had the new logo paint scheme. A blue circle on the tail accented with white lines; one down the middle, three curves up, and three curves down. Between the curves: PAN AM.

Martin noticed that all the window shades were pulled down when he entered. The cabin was empty. As he turned toward the cockpit door, he heard rustling behind him.

Two well-dressed gentlemen stood up. They were Cuban, both in their forties. They had a business look about them. They approached Martin with care and respect. They knew the ex-Army sergeant had taught hand-to-hand combat and was a judo expert.

"Hola, Señor Rio," said the first man. He stepped forward into a better lit area by the door. "It's me, Rafael Dominguez, a friend of your father's. How is he these days?"

"Packing, or at least I wish he were," replied Martin.

"That is what I and my friend here wish to speak to you about. Do not worry. We are booked on this flight. We just wanted to talk with you before the others come."

"What about?" Martin said. The two men came closer. They avoided the opened door as much as possible.

"This is Señor Guzman. We want to talk about a solution to Castro." Martin studied Guzman's sterile gray eyes.

The luggage handlers drove up in their wagon train luggage cart. The driver caught a glimpse of the angry first officer speaking to two men. It was enough to make him suspicious, given the atmosphere in the Cuban capital, one of raging paranoia.

The conversation ended abruptly when the flight crew came on board. Veronica, a vivacious blonde stewardess, originally from Scotland, led the other crewmembers.

"Gentlemen, if you'll find your seats," Martin said, holding his stare until their frowning faces were tucked behind the fourth row. Martin moved up to the cockpit.

***

Martin was on his return trip home. The DC-6 would be on the ground in ten minutes. Martin's concentration was broken by the two men who spoke to him on the flight out two days earlier. They would be labeled as Batista loyalists, or Brigadistas, and consequently traitors to the Revolution. He could be considered in league with these men just by talking to them.

They asked him to stay on the island and act as an agent. They had to be with the forces that had been carrying out dozens of bombings, destroying many tons of sugarcane, tobacco, and dairy to hurt Castro, but Castro wasn't suffering.

Martin returned his focus to the present. The captain noticed several plumes of smoke rising in the distance.

The captain grinned. "Looks like too many backyard barbeques gone awry."

Martin looked at him. "Captain, those are bombings."

They were cleared to land.

As they landed amidst a rocking explosion, Martin noticed a piece of aircraft aluminum jammed tight into his side window, sticking into the cockpit by an inch. He accepted that the blood on it was his own, which he confirmed by feeling his right temple and then seeing the blood on his hand. Flames from engine number 4 flashed. The stalled engine's propeller was wrapped up with a piece of the wing. Martin spun around, but the captain had already pulled the fire suppression handle. A mist enveloped the flames inside the engine cowling.

Veronica rushed into the cockpit. "Captain, what happened?" She saw the blood on Martin's hand and the side window.

"We're okay, Ronnie," the captain said.

"Veronica, would you bring me a damp cloth after you settle the cabin?" Martin asked. She nodded. Taking a couple of deep breaths, she turned back inside the cabin.

"We need to get you to a doctor," announced the captain.

The captain parked the aircraft and shut it down. Martin held the cold compress to his right temple. His thoughts were of his wife and son.

***

"Vegas," Meyer Lansky responded to the voice on the phone. He was at his home in Miami. "Vegas is now America's playground. Jules, listen to me. I would have thought those couple weeks in jail would have you packed and gone when they released you."

"Meyer, Castro has lost a lot of revenue by shutting us down. He's been rethinking things," Julian Sanders replied.

"So far, you've managed to keep out of jail because you're kind of unnoticeable, which is good right now, but you have the Reds crawling all over the island like rats, Jules, and that ain't good."

"So, I have to tuck my tail and run again?"

"No. We do like we always did when we ran our card games. You know when we was kids. When the heat got too much, we packed up and went to another street corner."

"I'm grateful to you, Meyer, but I ain't gettin' pushed out again."

Lansky fell back in his chair. "Jules, why do I have this problem with you? I just learned that Castro nationalized the Riviera yesterday. That makes me sad, but there is nothing I can do about it. The Riviera was my baby. I only had a year of operation before I had to leave. Do you think your investment and your loss is heavier than mine? You have to think smart about these things. It's time to move to a new street corner."

"You know, Meyer, I hear tell that the CIA—that maybe they might be in a position to whack this guy. You know, maybe we might take care of it ourselves. I hear rumors."

"Jules, you have to quit distressing me like this. I don't want to hurt your feelings, but you ain't the best shot. Fidel's goons are like the SS or the Stasi. Think about your boy. Think about Roman."

Meyer Lansky looked around at how peaceful his Miami home was, where the troubles of Cuba no longer reached him, except for his old friend Julian Sanders, one of the few to remain behind. Lansky said goodbye and hung up.

***

They were calling it Operation: Peter Pan.

Martin leaped out of the car, holding several dollar bills. The driver's face was leathery but kind. "Do you want me to wait, Señor Rio?" he asked.

"No, Miguel. Get back to the farm and look after my folks. Keep them safe."

Martin entered an old colonial home. He heard no noise from below, not even from the housekeeper. He went up the stairs to the master bedroom.

Amanda was packing several suitcases. Martin relaxed. "Where's Perla?"

"I sent her home with some extra cash for herself and her family. How are your parents?"

"Managing, like the rest of us."

"Well, we aren't going to manage under Castro any longer. He wants to send our children to Russia. I won't have that. No politician is going to tell me how to raise my child."

He took her by the hands and pulled her close. "He won't."

"It's really bad, Martin. The principal closed the school down only two hours ago. All of the parents have come to pick up their kids. They're all heading to the airport."

Martin pondered for a moment. "They'll need visas. That'll be tough."

"What about us? What can we do?"

"Let me get cleaned up and changed into my uniform. I have an idea. Keep packing, but stick to essentials."

He looked out the French doors that led to the veranda and the beautiful ocean view beyond. He would never have such a view as this again. Perhaps this was why he never bought that home in Florida. Now things were different. Five thousand dollars in their savings account in a Miami bank would fund their new start.

Martin carried three suitcases out to the car and placed them in the trunk. Amanda carried baby Lance out to the car. Martin started the car and backed out of the driveway. He and Amanda had one last look at their home. The tough Okie, as Martin's father called her, couldn't hold back her tears. Martin's eyes teared for a moment. He put the car into drive.

He pulled onto the main thoroughfare and headed east to Jose Marti International Airport.

Martin showed his employee pass to the guard at the gate and drove into the parking lot. The lot was mostly full, but he soon found an empty spot. They locked up and grabbed the luggage. Martin put on his white cap to complete the look of a Pan Am pilot in uniform.

In the terminal, Martin spoke to a ticket agent who produced one ticket despite the restless crowd in front of her. Martin thanked her. He tried to keep a professional demeanor, but the gratitude in his eyes betrayed him. She smiled and then took the next in line.

Martin came to the waiting area where Amanda and Lance sat. Amanda kept the police in view. "Let's go," he said.

The Rio family strode past two policemen. They arrived at their gate, but the lounge area was packed solid. Martin found a single seat for Amanda and Lance. It was heartening to see their rescue vehicle, a gleaming DC-6 through the large glass window that had incurred the nickname: the Fish Tank. This secret exodus of Cuban children was new to him, but he had seen a few other families torn apart here. A detained parent watched helplessly through the window as spouse and children boarded the plane. The state police routinely questioned Martin, like others that traveled to and from Cuba. His best alibi was his flight schedule and his uniform. No surprises, but probable suspicion.

Martin made his way up to the counter and pulled the gate attendant aside. Amanda watched nervously. She took slow breaths as her judo training had taught her.

Martin was making his way back. As their eyes met, he gave her a casual smile that seemed to calm her.

The gate attendant announced Pan Am flight 442 to Miami in English and Spanish.

Martin helped Amanda and Lance up, taking their place in line. The gate agent carefully studied each boarding pass. Maybe she was a Fidelista. They were everywhere. It was now commonplace for neighbor to spy on neighbor. Amanda thought how several in her neighborhood had been questioned by Castro's secret police. Some never returned home. Some of her young students were taken away to live with other relatives when their parents didn't return for them.

There was a sudden rumbling behind Martin, then a tap on his shoulder. He turned around to see two armed policemen. "Step aside, por favor," the first police officer said. Martin turned further to his right as he moved out of line, pushing Amanda forward. "You too, Señora." Amanda moved out of line as a couple fumbling with their boarding passes pushed past her.

"Why are we being detained, officer?" Martin asked.

"We have reason to believe you are a saboteur. You will come with us."

"What? I fly for this airline. I live here."

"The pilots are already aboard the plane, Señor. What are you going to do, serve the café?" The second policeman smiled thinly as an aftereffect. He probably didn't speak English.

"I'm on a jump flight. Out of Miami to New York." Martin looked at his watch. "In three hours from now. You're not going to make me late for work, are you?"

"What about your wife and baby? She is not a stewardess, and the baby is not a co-pilot."

"She's going to visit her family in the States. They haven't seen our son yet. Now, may we go?"

"You may go, but if you are not back, all your property will become the property of the state."

Martin feigned confusion. "Why wouldn't I come back home?" He put his hand on Amanda's arm and guided her back to the gate.

The two police officers snapped to attention when Captain Manuel Ricardo del Toro marched up with two state security officers.

"Wait!" he shouted. The room went quiet.

"Now, what's wrong?" Martin demanded.

"You have been seen with counterrevolutionaries," del Toro declared.

"Listen, Captain, I have not, or have I ever conspired against the Revolution. I am merely going to work. I don't know how to be any more clearer than that."

"You are a Cubano…"

"I'm an American citizen."

"Sí, your place of birth is San Francisco, but you are a Cubano. Your parents are Cubano…"

"I grew up in San Francisco. My father is from Mexico, originally."

"But you live here. Your mother is Cubano, Sí? And they own a plantation here. You are Cubano."

Martin sighed. "Why am I having all this trouble?"

Del Toro smiled. "There is no trouble, Señor Rio. Your wife and child may board the aircraft. But you are under arrest."

Amanda was horrified. "Martin?"

"It's okay, honey. Go see your parents. Say hello to Uncle John and have a nice trip." Amanda nodded. Martin fought a growing urge to attack and run. "I'll get things cleared up and join you later," he said reassuringly. He ached to hold his wife and child one more time, but they had to go. Amanda fought every instinct to stay. The little hand that wiped a tear from her cheek set her priorities straight. She walked through the gate and out to the tarmac without looking back. Martin watched, like so many others had before, through the glass-lined political wall.

***

The plane made a slightly bumpy landing at Miami International. Amanda leaned back in her chair. She noticed the little boy and girl across from her, peeking out the window. They had stains of chocolate on their clothes. There were no adults with them. She pictured their parents enticing them on the plane with candy. Amanda resolved that they were coming with her.

The children's names turned out to be Carina and Anthony. Carrying Lance, Amanda led them off the plane. A priest came up to her as she entered the terminal. He was tall and rugged with visible scars that time hadn't quite blended into a wrinkled face. "I'm Father Michaels. I'm here to collect Carina and Anthony."

"Oh, thank God," she said.

Two men approached, holding out badges. A third man came up, a Pan Am representative by his uniform. He had an air of competence about him. He moved through the last set of passengers to reach Amanda. "Mrs. Rio, I'm Felix Lima. I'm the head of operations here for Pan Am." He pointed to the gentlemen next to him. "I talked with Mr. Trippe just moments ago, and Special Agent Ted Bache here of the FBI and Mr. Brian Schaffer here from the State Department are also here to help you."

Amanda shook involuntarily. She hugged the two children and said goodbye, hopeful for them. They looked back at her as if they were leaving their mother all over again. Amanda's eyes welled up. She was about to collapse. Lima had an arm around her immediately, supporting her as her trembling hands clutched his arm.

"Let's go to my office, Mrs. Rio, and see if we can work things out to get Martin home."

***

Wood had its own resonance, a hollow flat thwack sound in its pitch and echo. Martin stumbled a few steps, finding himself on his knees. He stood. The first strike to the back of his head hurt and numbed him. He stumbled again, but surprisingly to the guards, didn't waver much. The second blow to the back of the head, however, shook him harder. The guard made sure he put more wrist action into his second swing, dropping Martin to his hands and knees. The wooden stick then came down on him with the hardest crash yet, sending him flat on the stone floor. Martin's thoughts flashed in and out of waves of consciousness. The next sound was not discernible by echo but by feel. His interrogator's boot rammed into his side. The sound of cracking ribs coursed through his body. Another boot kicked him in the stomach, driving the air out of his lungs.

It had been less than two hours since he had been placed in a military jeep and sped through the streets of Havana to the State Security building.

Martin was jerked off the truck and hauled in, officially booked, and then led down below for interrogation. The rumors of torture were already well known to resisters of the Revolution. A year ago, this place of torment was a school.

A French priest, Marcellin Champagnant, had founded the Brothers Marist, a Roman Catholic institution, in 1817 when he opened his first school. Villa Marista opened its doors in 1903. The building housed promise for education, both secular and spiritual, to the children of Cuba. Now it served a different purpose.

The room of stone was dark. The floor was damp and cold. He was being reeducated. The student's desk was a wooden crate, too small to stand up in or lie down. Martin wasn't resisting. He was abandoning. He smiled, comforted by the fact that his wife and son were safe. His interrogators now left him alone. He took solace in the echo of military boots growing dimmer as they marched up the steps and the quiet of his surroundings allowed him a respite, where he need only argue with his pain.

Chapter 4

Langley, Virginia

38°56′47″N, 77°9′32″W

April 3, 1961

The United Fruit Company was the linking of bananas and trains. The bright yellow fruit was unknown in the United States until 1870. By 1899, the Boston Fruit Company and the United Fruit Company merged to become the largest banana company in the world with plantations in Colombia, Costa Rica, Cuba, Jamaica, Nicaragua, Panama, and the Dominican Republic. Within a few years, Americans were consuming over sixteen million bunches a year, making UFCO a commercial and political empire. It stood as nothing less. It controlled most of the politicians as well as the farmable land and railways throughout Central America and the Caribbean. None more so than in Guatemala, its headquarters in the region. It tolerated no rivals—not unionist nor politician. It had at its disposal a private militia—the United States Army.

In 1954, when Guatemalan President Jacobo Arbenz sought to expropriate the unused land of UFCO with the idea of portioning it out to the poor of his country, he offered what United Fruit considered an "unacceptable" price for its land. The U.S. government judged this as communism in action and labeled the government a "Soviet satellite." The irony was that Guatemala had been a democratic country for the past ten years. The CIA nonetheless arranged the overthrow of the Arbenz administration and replaced it with a controllable dictatorship. A year earlier, in 1953, the CIA had been successful with a similar action in Iran.

Allen Welsh Dulles reflected over these triumphs of seven and eight years ago. He was proud to uphold American interests abroad and felt an obligation to the United Fruit Company. He was a principal shareholder in the company and sat on the board of trustees with his brother, former Secretary of State John Foster Dulles.

Dulles fidgeted in his chair behind the dark wood desk, which he had sat in for the last eight years as Director of the Central Intelligence Agency. There was uneasiness to this Black Ops scenario, neatly stapled and freshly placed on his desk, revised almost daily, it seemed. Executive Action was a plan created to remove unfriendly foreign leaders from power. Fidel Castro had so far proven to be a much tougher nut to crack than Arbenz.

The current plan lacked specificity and cohesiveness. The political ramifications should it fail would be enormous. He hated President John F. Kennedy's indecisive nature and was sure if Eisenhower were still in office, the plan would have flowed as smoothly as when it was first put together nearly two years ago. Dulles would wrestle with his thoughts throughout the night and beyond as orders for the operation would be given, then canceled and given again, changed, and modified from a strategic to a political point of view.

Chapter 5

Havana, Cuba

April 17, 1961

Martin Rio was pleased to have food and to be out of his small jail cell. He had a bit more room than the wooden crate in which he had spent his first two weeks, months ago. He felt more like a man when he could look out through iron bars instead of wooden slats, lying in his feces and urine. He might have had to stay longer in the wood crate, but he kept kicking it apart until the beatings proved to be too painful for such displays of defiance. He had convinced himself that it was worth giving up the struggle, for now, just to have the feces and urine washed off of him before being moved to Villa Marista's proper jail cells.

Martin was cleaned up and given a change of clothes for transport to an official prison labor camp down south. He wasn't told precisely where. What he did hear was of an impending invasion by the United States. Martin hoped so. Regardless of what happened outside, this was a good day for him. The legal and political pressures had worked to his benefit this time. His name had come up too many times before Castro in communications from the State Department, Juan Trippe, his attorneys, and Amanda's letters, pleading for his safe return.

Martin lifted one shackled leg, bowed his head, and slid into the back seat of a car with an armed agent next to him. He nervously clinked the chain restraints around his wrists. The agent dropped his hand hard against Martin's wrists to quiet him down. Martin just nodded. The car sped down the southern road instead of the main highway toward the south, which surprised Martin. Castro's paranoia had permeated throughout Cuba.

Martin could see smoke rising from what he guessed was the San Antonio de los Baos Air Base. Then he heard the low pounding rumble of Pratt and Whitney Wasp engines of World War II aircraft.

The four men inside the car instinctively ducked as a B-26 Marauder bomber flew over. Martin could just see it arch up in a climb to the right, then disappear. The driver looked frantically for more aircraft. The agent in the back with Martin turned to look out of the back window. Martin sat back calmly. Another B-26 roared overhead at treetop height, rocking the car. The three Cuban agents ducked again. Martin didn't. The agent next to Martin stooped lower to look out of the right rear door window. Martin turned his body to the right. He swung it hard to the left, jamming his elbow upward into the man's nose. The agent flew back, spasming and then collapsing. Martin flung his cuffed hands forward, roping the chain over the head of the agent in front of him, nearly pulling him into the backseat as the chain cinched around the man's throat. With a snap of his left leg, Martin kicked the driver in the back of the head. The car swerved left, then right, bouncing violently until it slammed into a palm tree. The instant stop flung the agent in front of Martin through the windshield, the inertia dragging him from the back in one sharp jolt over the front seat.

Martin came to a moment later. He could feel the pain in his abdomen and outstretched arms. With a moan, he pulled the bloodied body back enough to get his chained wrists over him and fell back into his seat. He lifted his shirt to see bloodstains from a large abrasion. Martin rifled through the pockets of his backseat companion until he found a key and the man's pistol. The cuffs were off.

Painfully, he pushed his way out of the car. He stood and walked down the road as casually as possible, then collapsed. His final thought was that this was still his day.

***

Castro was screaming over the report that several of his limited number of fighter aircraft were destroyed. Fortunately, some of the aircraft were decoys. He still had at his disposal T-33 jet trainers equipped with .50 calibre machine guns, a few A-26 Invader bombers, and a few remaining Hawker Sea Furies. Intelligence reports shot into Castro's office quicker than he could don his eyeglasses. It was just unknown when and from where the attack would come. How many soldiers would line the shores of Cuba if the attacks were by sea or descend from the mountains? Would they be American soldiers or comprised of his rebellious countrymen? Fortunately, the Yanquis didn't get all of his fighters. His army would repel the invaders with every last drop of Cuban blood!

***

Martin opened his eyes to see a cockroach scampering by. The thought of eating another one sickened him. Prisoners were mostly starved for food. The rations they did get were often shared with malnourished guards. Soon the madness of hunger left him. The tropical scents of open-air replaced the stale cold air of his incarceration and invigorated his palette for the desire of fruit. He let the insect continue on its way.

The road was somewhat isolated. Even Castro sympathizers, mostly common people, wouldn't necessarily stop to investigate for fear of involvement. The roadblocks he worried most about were his injuries.

Martin stumbled down the road as the sun continued to set behind the lush green trees that surrounded him. He felt weaker than when his day began, but energies from within kept him going. He needed to see a house, farm, anything where he could find refuge. Martin felt his spine stiffen and fear roll over him. He was caught in the headlights of an approaching vehicle. Martin stopped.

The vehicle stopped. “Hey, Señor, where are you going?” the voice called out from the cab of an old Chevy truck.

“I need help, Señor. Please,” Martin begged. The man got out and helped Martin into the cab of the truck.

***

Castro paced the floor of his office. He yelled orders at his brother Raul and to Ernesto “Che” Guevara. He was shouting about countermeasures.

When the attacking B-26’s landed in Miami with Cuban pilots emerging from the planes to claim asylum, Castro knew it was a ruse. The U.S. ambassador to the United Nations, Adlai Stevenson, could deny any U.S. involvement. This was retribution for Castro’s nationalizing of American companies. This was Cuban soil. His soil. His land. He would continue the fight against the Americans. He swore they would not do to him what they did to Jacobo Arbenz. Let them come. He would take them on, defeat them at their own game, crush any rebellion and prove to them and the rest of the world the unifying power of La Revolucion!

***

11:45 PM. Mariano Mustelier, head of the militia post in Playa Girón, was stationed near the mouth of the inlet known as Bahia de Cochinos, the Bay of Pigs. He noticed a red light out in the dark horizon of the sea. Reaching the beach with a fellow militiaman, he observed signals from what was now clearly a boat. Cuban fishermen probably lost, struggling to find their way back to land. Jumping into his jeep, he helped them by flashing the headlights. Gunfire was heard over the roar of the waves. Both headlights were shot out. Mariano jumped out of the jeep, pulled up his rifle, and began shooting back into the blackness. “The North Americans have arrived!” he yelled out to his men, ordering a retreat and radioing Santa Clara. The call was never made. Men rose from the sea and took out Mariano and his men, but the sounds of gunfire reached the ears of other militiamen nearby up the road, announcing their arrival. The invasion was on.

Castro was awakened from a restless sleep. He half expected the Americans to come from the mountainous regions of the north, the logical entry into the country. The mountains were his strength during the years he waged guerrilla warfare against the Batista régime. But the Yanquis were coming from the south, from the ocean, and through the swamplands. He had a battalion of nine hundred men stationed at the Central Australia Sugar Mill along the road to Playa Girón, plus several platoons of militia-men stationed in the area. He wasted no time ordering the battalion in the Northern Province of Matanzas, east of Havana, to hurry down to Girón. He also ordered the mobilization of three other battalions in the Las Villas Province to get down to Girón to protect the other two main roads through the swamplands. Castro couldn't suppress a grin when he thought how stupid the Americans were for invading from the mud. He gave orders for the remaining operational aircraft to take off at dawn.

***

Martin shivered and jerked to consciousness as a radio crackled in the other room. He had slept longer than he wanted, but it was the first time he slept stretched out since his incarceration. He worked the covers off himself and bent forward only to find it very difficult. He fought his way into a sitting position. He heard the window next to the bed rattle lightly. He stood up, painfully, slowly, stepping toward the narrow light that sliced through the door. Martin stumbled his way into the room. He recalled the small room with a kitchenette toward the corner. The walls were of cracked plaster, the floor of old and worn oak hardwood.

***

Juan Garcia, a kindly man, virile in stature despite his seventy-years, noticed Martin. "Ah, mi amigo, Marteen. It has begun. The invasion, it has begun. Maybe you go home soon."

"You mean the Americans have invaded? Martin asked, trying to gain his focus. The partly broken clock on the small table indicated that it was four a.m. He made his way over to Juan Garcia, who sat at his table fine-tuning an old radio.

"I am tuning to Radio Swan. They will tell us."

"That's just a propaganda station."

"I know, but they will tell us."

"Where have the U.S. forces landed?"

"They have come from Playa Girón."

"What? That's only a few miles from here."

"We are safe here. We are off the main road to Playa Girón and eight kilometers from the bay." Martin took a seat at the table just as the house shook. He hurried across the room, ignoring the pain of his sudden movements. He looked out the only window in the front of the house that continued to shake. Several heavy vehicles rolled by in the near distance.

The static cleared, and a high-spirited voice in Spanish came out of the speaker. "Take up strategic positions that control roads and railroads! Make prisoners or shoot those who refuse to obey your orders! All planes must stay on the ground. See that no Fidelist plane takes off. Destroy its radios. Destroy its tail. Break its instruments. Puncture its fuel tanks..."

Martin went back to the table and sat with Juan Garcia. It was apparent that the American invasion was coming from the sea.

***

At the San Antonio Air Base, Captain Enrique Carreras snapped to. He listened intently to Castro bellowing out new orders over the phone. "At this moment, a landing is taking place at Playa Girón. But I want you to sink those ships! Don't let those ships go!"

Captain Carreras ran out to the few surviving aircraft. The pilots slept lightly under the wings of their planes. Hearing a shout, they scrambled to attention.

***

Martin sipped his first cup of coffee in many months. It was mostly old coffee grounds. Juan Garcia apologized for not having milk or sugar despite sugarcane fields and a dairy farm nearby. Martin assured him that the coffee was perfect. He put the empty cup on the table just as the recognizable rumble of vintage aircraft sounded overhead on their way to meet superior U.S. jet fighters.

***

Pablo Samora wiped the sweat from his brow; his eyes fixed upon the airspace outside the cockpit of his British-built Sea Fury fighter. He didn't know what damage he could inflict on the enemy, but once the American jet fighters caught him on their radar, he and his aircraft would disappear. Two other pilots flew in formation with him. As soon as the mist covering the ocean and beach dissipated, it would yield a clear shot. Pablo saw two Landing Craft Infantry—LCI amphibious assault ships unloading soldiers and tanks on the beach. His fellow countrymen were holding back the invaders. More were coming down the Playa highway to join them. He looked up and around. There were no enemy fighters to engage. He lowered his nose for a strafing run.

Daniel "Dano" Orozco, a strong, stout man in his late thirties, who just two years ago lost his car dealership and auto repair garage to Castro, pushed his way ashore with the rest of the Cuban exiles that made up *Brigade 2506*. He was glad to see what looked like air support. Then he realized that something was wrong.

Pablo Samora squeezed the trigger on his control stick, firing his four wing-mounted 20 mm cannons, followed by the other two Cuban aircraft.

The exiles jumped to the ground. They watched as several of their fellow Brigadesmen were torn apart. Orozco jumped as the Sea Fury flew by. He turned to see that the LCI had taken a direct hit. Dark red swirls of seawater filled the pockmarks in the sand. In an instant, the dead were all around him. He noticed that his uniform had rips and blood splotches over the legs and torso, but he could move. He heard the sound of metal scraping and turned to see both LCI craft backing up. The flat metal ramps at the bow scraped against the sand as they retracted to make the vessels watertight.

Pablo knew he had hit many of the invaders in his first strafing run and had damaged the LCI's. He flew past the beachhead and climbed skyward over open water where he got another pleasant surprise: the armada that the Americans had raised was just a handful of boats, a couple of cargo ships off the coast, and the landing crafts he just damaged. Pablo engaged the rocket select and drew a bead on the first cargo ship in his sights. He fired his rockets. He hit the ship with enough accuracy to do it damage. His fellow pilots were now following suit. It was a good day for Cuba and a good day for the Revolution. Pablo swung around to attack again.

***

Castro was happy at the news of a successful first strike against the Americans. Better, new intelligence spoke of them getting stuck in the marshes of Zapata. An ever-mindful tactician, however, he now worried. Where were the American fighter jets? Where were the Marines? Perhaps it didn't matter. The American plan was doomed.

***

Martin needed to get closer to the action but knew he was too weak to risk it. He didn't have much energy for dodging bullets or shrapnel. He was, moreover, in a comfortable setting. He thought about his wife and son. He felt certain he would return home to them, whether in Havana with the end of the Castro régime or in Florida.

Chapter 6

Washington, D.C.
38°54′17″N, 77°00′59″W

April 21, 1961

Incompetence led to humiliation, which in turn led to political fallout. JFK was in trouble. If he didn't do damage control soon, his own party would turn on him. And few knew it, but the president was not well. His body couldn't produce cortisol, the "fight or flight" hormone that he supplemented with prescription pills. He was in a fight and had nowhere he could fly.

The Bay of Pigs invasion would be known globally as an American failure, especially this morning, with Cuban anti-aircraft fire having brought down an American B-26. Papers found on the dead pilot's body identified him as Leo Francis Bell from Boston, Massachusetts.

Kennedy picked up the piece of paper just delivered to his desk. It was a communiqué from his Russian archrival and a further dose of humiliation.
It read: *It is not a secret to anyone that the armed bands that invade that country are trained, equipped and armed in the United States of America. The planes which bomb Cuban cities belong to the United States of America, the bombs they drop have been made available by the American government...As to the Soviet Union there should be no misunderstanding of our position: we shall render the Cuban people and the government all necessary assistance in beating back the armed attack on Cuba. We are sincerely interested in a relaxation of international tension, but if others aggravate it, we shall reply in full measure.*

Nikita Khrushchev

Every time Kennedy read the letter, his heart pounded. It still shocked him and caught him by surprise, but acceptability was a moot point now. Kennedy had other problems. He didn't need to have to deal with the Soviets now. He sent a reply to Khrushchev, which stated that the United States had no intention to intervene militarily in Cuba, but *"should an outside force intervene we will immediately honor our obligation under the Inter-American system to protect this hemisphere from external aggression."*

Neither man knew how well their resolve would be tested a year and a half later.

JFK stood before the media for the planned White House press conference. Composed, as usual, he said, "There is an old saying, 'Victory has a hundred fathers, while defeat is an orphan.' What matters is only one fact; I am the responsible officer of the government."

As the president continued to put his best spin on the situation, more Cuban exiles were running away. Most ran into the muddy swamps, where they made easy pickings for the Cuban army. Others who knew the territory moved inland toward less occupied villages.

Chapter 7

Playa Girón, Cuba

22°04′N, 81°02′W

April 22, 1961

Dano Orozco was operating on adrenalin after landing on the beach five days ago and hiding out from the enemy—his fellow Cubans.

He thought of family and friends. Perhaps some of the soldiers still scouring the area had been friends before the Revolution. Maybe he sold them a car. He had one of the best reputations on the island for fair trade and looked after all of his clientele equally. Could that win him some favor if he were captured? Orozco fell to his knees. He flipped over, grabbing his knee and rolling on his back. Tears came. He let go of his knee, and his left leg dropped. His body went limp. He was at peace for the moment.

Martin Rio, a little stronger, moved further from the comfort and relative safety of his host's home to the main road. Martin guessed that he was less than half a mile from the main road that went to the south to Playa Girón or north to Havana—to Castro, but also to his family. No one knew whether he was alive or dead, and that information needed to get out. A cool breeze wrapped around him. He needed to head back to the house. Juan Garcia said he had a surprise for him when he got back. He took a last look at the road, still littered with rifle shells, potholes and soot from the heavy artillery fire of a few days ago. Martin tried to move quickly, but his joints and leg muscles were still too stiff and weak. It didn't matter. His focus was on getting back to the house.

Orozco felt leaves and twigs give way under the weight of feet as their echo vibrated through the grass. He stumbled and fell to the ground. His arm moved slowly down his leg until he felt the butt of his rifle. He slowly moved his hand up the stock. Once he located the trigger guard, he slipped his stiffening finger inside and around the trigger. He felt cold and clammy. He didn't know if he should keep the rifle aimed in the direction it was or move it up toward his head. Instinct worked along with his eyes; the rifle barrel rotated toward his head.

He stopped as he heard voices. They were sharp and harsh one moment, nervous and apprehensive the next. They were soldier's voices. He worked his left hand out from under him and grabbed the steel barrel, slipping his hand underneath and around the stock. The voices came closer. He raised the rifle best he could, but suddenly someone stepped on it.

"Don't move a muscle," said the voice in English. The man leaned over Orozco. "I heard you, and it's possible these clowns did too. There's four of them," Martin whispered.

"Who are you?"

"Someone like you who needs to get the hell off this island."

"Get off? I want to come home."

Martin noticed that Orozco's English was quite good. "Well, I have a beautiful wife and a beautiful little boy, and that's now in Miami. I no longer have a home here."

"Look, mister, I have, or had, a really nice car dealership in Havana. I sold Chevies."

"What else would you?" Martin mused. "Which dealership?"

"Why do you want to know?"

"You might still owe me a tune-up."

Orozco grinned. "My name is Orozco. Daniel Orozco."

"Well, there goes my free tune-up."

"Don't tell me that you bought your car from Javier Cruz? He's a crook. He's had his big fat fingers in too many pies in Cuba, and I tell you he will try to wrap even Castro around them."

"Doesn't matter now. Can you move? You look pretty banged up, and I'm not in much better shape."

"Yeah," Orozco said as he stirred from the grass. He tried to lift his head and then his torso with new expressions of pain. He let go of the rifle with his left hand and moved his arm back under him, prying himself up on his elbow. "If you could pull a bit more por favor."

Martin pulled up on his right arm. At least the house was only a short hobble away. Martin pulled as Orozco pushed.

Then they heard voices. Martin dropped on top of Orozco, covering his mouth. The voices came closer. The sound of trampling on brush and grass came closer. Then the voices separated, creating confusion as to where they were going or where they were coming from. Then it became clear. The voices were coming straight in their direction. Orozco had resigned himself to the fact that this was probably the end. His mind was clear, but his body was without force. Martin had resolved that he would die where he lay. He would not be able to travel the two hundred yards to the house.

The trampling stopped. The soldier who stood in silence just a few feet away, Martin thought, was no doubt enjoying the easy shot. Martin was getting a spasm in his back. He regretted that he would not be able to thank Juan Garcia, so he spoke the words anyway: "Thank you, Juan Garcia."

"You are welcome. But how did you know it was me?" Martin rolled off Orozco, breathing easier. "I see you have a friend," Juan Garcia said. "Is he a prisoner too?"

"No, he is one of the soldiers from the liberation forces," Martin replied, slowly regathering his wits. "Where are the soldiers? I know Castro's goons were running around."

"I told them there is no activity around here, and their search would be better down south, closer to the ocean where rescues were more likely to take place. I must tell you, Marteen, you, I don't mind helping, but he is with the invasion forces."

"We have to help him, Juan Garcia. We can't leave a man to die. Not when he was trying to help us."

"Come then, let us get you up on your feet first." Juan Garcia took hold of Martin and lifted him up with little difficulty. He then raised Orozco, who groaned with pain.

***

The hour's drive from Miami to Key Largo, along US 1, was uneventful, yet Amanda Rio clutched the steering wheel tensely. She finally had some peace from the media and government about her husband's imprisonment. She had her son Lance to think about now.

She turned the Oldsmobile sedan off the main road and up her street, where a pair of tall palm trees marked the entrance to the semi-circular driveway. Another pair stood at the other end.

The house was a two-bedroom, one-bath bungalow. The locals called them *Conch Cottages*. The whitewashed, lime-green trimmed home was nestled inside a quarter-acre lot of mangroves and gumbo limbo trees.

With some help from Pan Am founder Juan Trippe, Amanda was able to move back to the climate and lifestyle she so much enjoyed. Her next few days would be arduous, especially settling in and securing her new job as a schoolteacher at Key Largo Elementary. The school year was nearly over. She would not have time to acclimate to the small island, the largest of the Florida Keys.

Amanda pulled into the open carport, which was connected to the house by a breezeway. Lance sat in the lap of Betty Drake, Amanda's new neighbor from across the street and her landlord. Betty was Jamaican, tall, in her mid-thirties, with long chestnut hair.

"Well, we're here. Perhaps permanently," Amanda said.

"Honey, don't make it sound like Devil's Island. You're in the Keys now. Have fun. Enjoy a bit of life. Heaven knows you deserve it." Betty put her hand on Amanda's shoulder. "You're a tropics girl. This is where you belong."

"I know. Well, let's go in, and I'll make us some lunch." Amanda got out of the car and flipped her seat forward. "Come on, young man, let's go get you something to eat." Amanda reached into the back seat and pulled out Betty's five-year-old son Roger. Lance immediately ran around the car over to Roger. Amanda was amazed at how quickly the boys had drawn so close. Roger was protective of Lance. Lance would always see Roger as his big brother.

Amanda opened the side door off the kitchen and went in. The boys followed, with Betty closing the door behind her. The kitchen was larger than Amanda thought it would be when she first entered the house three weeks ago. The home had been remodeled as a vacation rental. Amanda placed her purse and shopping bag near the sink on the Formica countertop.

"You know if the rent is too high," Betty said, "I can talk with Rodney, and we could drop it a few dollars more."

"It's fine. You may have to have us over for dinner more often, but I'm happy with everything."

Betty's husband had given her a dream life, but she now had a companion with whom she could talk girl talk, which helped them both.

Amanda and Betty went out of the kitchen, sat in two wicker chairs, and placed their iced tea glasses on the small table between them. The boys were out front playing. Amanda nestled herself back into the chair. It wasn't like her beautiful home in Cuba, but for a single mother, it was fine.

***

The smell of rotten flesh was unmistakable. Orozco had severe gangrene throughout his leg and hip, poisoning him. He had been more lucid when they found him a week ago; now, he was delirious most of the time. He kept trying to tell Martin and Juan Garcia something, but they could not make sense of his rants and ravings.

"I have seen this too many times," sighed Juan Garcia. "He will not last much longer. The gangrene is too strong."

Orozco's eyes popped open. He shook violently. Martin and Juan Garcia grabbed hold of him. "Havana," Orozco said. "Mercedes. Wife. Get out. You-get-out..." He stopped breathing.

"Sí! Sí!" Juan Garcia exclaimed. "Comprendé!"

"I will find Mercedes in Havana. I promise," Martin said.

"He knew we understood him. He is at peace," Juan Garcia said, closing Orozco's eyes.

"I think he was telling us of a contact, a way to get off Cuba. I will make sure you go with me, Juan Garcia. Don't worry," Martin said.

"Leave? I do not want to leave. This is my home. You have a young wife and son waiting for you in America. You must go."

***

Martin Rio, stronger and healthier now, rode silently as Juan Garcia tried to keep the Chevy truck on the road. The worn tires made any attempt of a wheel alignment impossible. The truck jerked to the left every time they hit a pothole. The older man's nearsightedness was evident from his lack of control along the curves of the highway. Martin wished he could relax more, perhaps even take a nap. But his mind was too active.

The landscape changed from rural serenity to concrete and brick, honking horns, the rumble of jet aircraft. It was also where the heaviest concentration of political repression and control was exercised over the populace of Cuba and where Castro's power was unmatched since his victory at Playa Girón.

Martin watched a Soviet MiG-15 take off. It was true. The Russians were here.

"If we had only used just one—just one jet fighter, Juan Garcia, the outcome would have been different. I would be home. Here."

"It's okay, we are here now, and someone will help us."

Juan Garcia merged with traffic as he headed toward the northeast end of the city to Old Havana. They were heading for what had been Orozco's car dealership.

The truck turned the corner and headed down the street, where luxury items could once be found. They drove past the car dealership. The name of Orozco Auto had been painted over rather poorly. The letters still showed through.

The former auto palace was now a military depot, servicing jeeps and tanks. There would be no shiny new cars with optional leather seats available here. Martin saw several soldiers moving about, trying to look busy, but he knew they were just killing time.

A jeep with an officer pulled up behind them. Juan Garcia sped up to keep his cruise down the street as casual as possible. Martin noticed a woman in what had been the glass-lined showroom floor walk across it to nearby offices, and then they were down the street, out of view. "Juan Garcia, pull over. I need to go back." The truck pulled to the curb.

"I think there are too many soldiers, Marteen."

"Just hang around somewhere, and I will come back in a few minutes. I need to see this woman. I think she is Dano's wife, Mercedes."

Martin headed back down the street, and Juan Garcia drove up to the next, turned, and parked.

Martin's steps slowed from a quick pace to a more casual one. He walked into the showroom and headed to the offices. In the cubical-sized offices, once used to pressure people into buying a car, Martin opened the door to find an attractive woman in her thirties seated behind a table. Paperwork was neatly arranged around her. She stopped and looked up when she saw Martin.

"Hola, Señora," Martin said. "I would like to know where I can go to get parts for my truck. We live in the country, and it's not so easy to come up to Havana." He paused. "Are you Señora Mercedes?"

"What did you say?" she asked.

"Could you tell me where to find her?"

"Mercedes is an automobile. I am Carmen Orozco. Can you read, Señor?"

"No, I cannot read."

"But soon you will learn, mi amigo," the voice behind Martin said. It was the voice of Captain Manuel Ricardo del Toro. Fortunately, del Toro did not recognize him. Martin was no longer wearing a Pan Am uniform but was dressed like a peasant and bearded.

"The Revolution will give you this and more," del Toro said. "Are you a supporter of our beloved Fidel and of the Revolution?"

"Sí. But I need some car parts, and I do not know Havana well."

"I need those reports, now, Señora Orozco," Captain del Toro insisted. He smiled at Martin before he left.

"I would say it was the look of being rejected," Martin said in English.

She wrote down an address on a piece of paper, quickly torn off one of the reports. "My husband, Dano?

"Dead," he said with a hush. "I was with him when he died."

She lowered her head for a moment. Tears welled up in her eyes. "Call by tonight."

"Thank you. And I am sorry about Dano."

He left the building and walked toward Juan Garcia's truck.

Martin got back into the truck. They drove off.

"Hungry?" Martin asked.

Juan Garcia drove down two streets and then made a left turn.

"Did you find this Mercedes woman?"

"Yes and no. Mrs. Carmen Orozco, yes. Her Mercedes Benz, no. I need to make a phone call. I'll tell you where I hope."

The Chevy truck turned down a narrow cobblestone street and Juan Garcia parked by the curb. Martin had always enjoyed this part of Havana, with its colorful three and four-story buildings. Large arrays of pastels, pinks, and oranges, blues, and greens were everywhere. Even the limestone had a coral hue to it. Cuba was the only place in the world that Martin knew of that had such a perfect balance of color and décor that could rival nature.

The two men got out of the truck amidst Cubans working perfunctorily at the few shops on the street. Elderly men and women sat in front of their homes, a few doing the same on the verandas above. Ribbons of freshly laundered clothes lined second and third-story balconies.

Martin followed Juan Garcia down four rows of homes and then stepped up a flight of stairs to the second floor. Juan Garcia knocked a couple of times and then waited.

"Sí?" an older woman's voice said from the other side of the door.

"We need to use the phone," Juan Garcia said. There was a long pause. The phone rang from inside. It was quickly muffled.

"The phone no longer works. You have to go to—to..." the woman's voice paused. "To the Bar Floridita. They have the only working phone I know." Martin heard steps moving away from the door.

"I could use a drink," Juan Garcia said.

"And a new transistor radio," Martin added.

"Yes, I live in high hopes of listening to FM radio one day."

Martin followed his benefactor down the stairs.

Juan Garcia leaned against the wall, rubbing his right knee when Martin came out to the street. "Are you okay, Juan Garcia?"

"My knee is hurting again. An old battle wound from long ago."

"What war were you in?"

"Name one." Juan Garcia straightened up and made his way toward the truck. Martin held on as Juan Garcia maneuvered the truck through traffic, heading further north. They drove past their destination in search of a place to park. Juan Garcia worked to squeeze into a spot barely big enough for the aged Chevy to fit, but a run-up on the curb and a smooth reverse fit them in nicely.

The harbor was within a short walking distance. Martin saw a cargo ship being pulled by a tugboat, moving slowly between some of the centuries-old buildings of Havana. The vessel was Russian.

They entered La Floridita, home of the daiquiri and one of Hemingway's favorite places.

Martin stopped at the entrance, his hand on the door. Parked two cars down was an early fifties blue Mercedes-Benz with a tan interior. The license plate frame had "Orozco Auto" on it. Martin moved cautiously inside.

Martin and Juan Garcia went to the mahogany bar and waited for the bartender to take notice. Then a firm hand landed on Martin's shoulder.

"Come join me at my table," the voice said in clear English. It was a familiar voice.

"Bartender, two beers," Martin said. The bartender wiped the bar top with his white towel out of habit, flung it back over his shoulder, and brought up two bottles. With the caps removed, he slid them in easy reach. Martin and Juan Garcia moved toward the bench seat booth, where Mr. Guzman waited for them. He was impeccably dressed as usual. Juan Garcia slid in first, then Martin.

Martin took a drink of beer. "I could kill you, Guzman."

"But I am the one they sent you to find," Guzman said, smiling thinly.

"I've done nothing wrong."

"You have spied for me."

"That was trivial, superficial information I gave you."

"Nonetheless, you have killed," the voice dropped to a low delicate whisper, "or perhaps murdered is a truer word, three of Castro's security agents."

"My hand was forced."

"I want you to do something else for me, Martin, and then I will see that you get to Florida, to Key Largo, where your wife and son are."

Martin's heart sank, but he kept quiet. Juan Garcia kept both hands on his beer bottle, not even taking a sip. He got a sense of the conversation. He did not trust this well-dressed negotiator. He could tell he was the type who never got his fingernails dirty.

"What do you want now, Guzman?"

"Do you like rum? Bacardi has a tradition here in Cuba that goes back just one year short of a century. Meet me down at the Bacardi building at midnight. You should know the place. But come alone, with all due respect to your friend here." Guzman nodded a gentleman's smile and then got up. Martin stared at the booth behind his. It was Papa's booth. No one but Hemingway could sit there. But he would not be returning to it. He was dead since last month from a self-inflicted shotgun blast to the head.

***

Martin crossed the street to the abandoned Bacardi building, where Juan Garcia had dropped him off over an hour ago. The building, built about 1930 as an office for the rum company, was an eclectic display of *art deco* and formality. The building was long but tiered somewhat like the White House. It had square and rectangular cuts to it, like a French palace, but with Cuban zest.

Martin came up to the main entrance and took a pull on the door. Nothing. Then he heard a click. The door moved slowly forward. "Come in. Quickly," Guzman's voice said in an intense whisper. Martin pushed himself through.

Inside, Martin was greeted by the residual orange glow shining on Guzman's face. The flashlight's beam was at least half its normal strength. "There hasn't been any proper electricity here since the company had to evacuate, and I'm afraid my work has used up my stock of batteries for the time being, but if you follow closely, we shouldn't stumble on anything."

"Okay, I'm here. What's going on?"

"Certainly, my friend. No need to waste time. I am funded by certain benefactors…"

"Who? The CIA?" Martin gazed around the darkened interior, which with its open center floor design, gave it a cathedral look. "The Bacardi family? They put a banner out on this very building, welcoming Castro when he rode into Havana two and a half years ago."

"True, but that was before Castro betrayed us, betrayed you. Look at your loss."

"Others have lost worse than me." Martin wasn't in the mood to be patronized.

Guzman walked away from the door, towards the back. Martin followed carefully with the thought of Guzman being a shield to anything that might pop out of the darkness.

Martin heard the rattling of keys and saw the door open in front of Guzman into further darkness. Guzman disappeared into it. Martin followed, looking for the orange glow of the flashlight.

"Close the door behind you," Guzman's voice rang out in a soft tinny echo. They were in a stairwell. The orange glow of the flashlight moved upward, in rhythmic bobbing with each quiet step up. Martin stumbled on his first encounter with the concrete steps but then was in sync thereafter with Guzman.

***

Julian Sanders was fed up with the Russian invasion. He had accepted that the days of well-groomed gentlemen with gorgeous gals hanging off their arms, cocktails in hand as they strode into his casino—were over. He missed American banter, nightclub shows, and high-stakes gaming. Now he catered to drunken Soviet soldiers, who laughed at what the capitalists had to leave behind. The thought of these people enjoying themselves off of American enterprise made him sick to his stomach. Other than the occasional British tourist not smart enough to go elsewhere for his holiday travels, it was Russians everywhere.

Mickey lumbered up to Sanders, who winced at the sound of another Russian winning at the craps tables. "Same as every night, boss."

"You think it's time to go? Pack up?" Sanders asked.

"Castro don't look to be going nowhere."

"We go back to Vegas?"

"Where else, boss? We held out, but this ain't us."

***

Martin followed Guzman through the double doors. He knew they were on the eighth floor, presumably the penthouse. The full moon did little to illuminate the large room, which had a stale smell, mingled with a sickly sweet flavor of old rum.

"Rum," Guzman said. "Rum, my dear Martin, is the true flavor of rebellion and revolution. Only in the past several decades has oil arguably replaced rum as the great global elixir."

"You forgot coffee, sugar, and slave trading," Martin quipped.

"No, no thought of leaving out the other great tools of industrialization. Given the recalcitrant nature of man, one should have an idea of what one is fighting for. It was rum for several centuries. But at the end of all human conflict, it still comes down to land. Who owns the land?"

"Your point?"

"Those who have fled had the most to lose. The poor naturally ebb and flow with no real change. Even you, with your life here stripped from you, have had little choice. But now you do. You can join us and regain what is yours."

"And I only have to do what?"

"There is an old but working Cessna T-Fifty like you used to own. In two days, Fidel will give one of his long-winded speeches in the Plaza de Revolucion. You will fly over, and we will drop napalm on him."

"Homemade, I suppose?"

"It will do the job. Four—twenty-litre jerricans will be filled with diesel and gasoline. A brick of plastic explosive and a detonator will be strapped to each." Martin had the image of them stealing four of the rectangular-shaped gas cans off military jeeps. For some reason, he found the idea amusing. "You will glide in quietly as possible, and one of our men will push them out of the aircraft."

"And then?"

"You keep flying northeast to Florida. That's it."

"What about Castro's aircraft?"

"There are only a handful of operational aircraft since the Bay of Pigs invasion."

"Is that what they're calling it?

"It sounds better than failure, blunder, military fiasco. Regardless, it's a part of history now. But we can create a better historical turnout with your help."

The lights came on, causing blind spots. Martin shut his eyes, but it was too late. He heard a crowd of men rush in behind him.

"So, Señor Rio, where will you fit into history?" del Toro asked as he entered the room.

Martin looked at Carmen Orozco in front of him. The darkness hid her, but her fear was quite exposed. "As a man that just wanted to go home to his family, Captain. Nothing more."

"Lo siento mucho, Marteen." The voice of Juan Garcia felt like a chilled knife in Martin's back. He tried to grasp the logic of betrayal.

Martin turned to the apologetic old man behind del Toro. "You betrayed me, Juan Garcia? And you're sorry?"

"Do not be upset with him. The good general still has your best interests at heart," del Toro said. "But you, Señor Guzman, you are a different story. You are a spy, a saboteur, and I am finally glad to meet you. We have much to talk about."

"General Juan Garcia?" Martin asked. "Juan Garcia Obispo?" Martin snapped his fingers and pointed at Juan Garcia. "You are General Juan Garcia Obispo. You served under Batista. You fought for the United States in World War One and Two. If you were a Batista loyalist—I don't get it. Why?" Martin repeated the words in Spanish, still confused.

"You are mistaken," del Toro said. "Juan Garcia's valor served him as well with Batista, as it did with the United States. As you have seen for yourself, he has had little to show for it until Presidente Castro expanded his land. His loyalty is to this new nation."

"Land he can't use. He wants a transistor radio. That's what he wants."

"Then get him one. I will see that he gets it. Come. You can go home."

***

Julian Sanders loaded the magazine into his Beretta semi-automatic pistol, chambered a round, and placed it inside his coat. "Where's Roman?"

"He's out in the casino, boss," Mickey said.

"Okay, it'll be a last look before we go. I just wish we could blow this place up when it was full of Commies."

The phone rang. Sanders jumped.

"Easy, boss." Mickey patted Georgio on the shoulder, and the two men moved out of Sanders' office.

Sanders picked up the phone. "Yeah. Javier. Where are you? We're ready to go. Please tell me we'll make our flight."

"Just be out front, and my car will be by to pick you up as arranged," Javier Cruz said.

"Good." Sanders put the phone down and left his office, leaving the lights on. Castro could pay the light bill from now on.

Sanders continued his fast pace until they reached the lobby, where he slowed to a stroll. The two-story waterfall was running normally. He saw the four suitcases by the front door and continued past them. He looked outside to see if Cruz's sedan had driven up. The last scheduled Pan Am flight that the Castro government would allow was only two hours from departure.

Two muffled beeps of a car horn got the four of them moving toward the double doors and outside to the waiting car.

Mickey spotted the nervous driver of a black Lincoln Continental Town Car jerking to a stop under the porte-cochere from the semi-circular driveway. The trunk lid popped open. Mickey threw in two suitcases.

Georgio dashed out, tossed the other two suitcases in the trunk, slammed it shut, and opened the right rear door. Sanders and Roman hurried out. Sanders pushed his son into the back seat. Georgio ran around to the left rear side of the car. Mickey grabbed the right front passenger door.

The army jeep bounced slightly in the air when it hit the upslope of the driveway just before it came to a screeching stop underneath the porte-cochere. Del Toro, riding shotgun, grabbed the top of the windshield frame and stood up. "Halt!" he commanded.

Two soldiers stood in the back of the jeep, rifles up. They jumped out. Before they hit the ground, Georgio had hold of a Thompson M1 Paratrooper sub-machine gun. He fired. The two soldiers, riddled with bullets, fell backward to the ground. Del Toro wedged into his seat as low as he could go. He knew it was futile to stay where he was, so he stood up to see the two men holding two Thompsons on him. He noticed that Georgio stood posed, the folding buttstock fully extended and braced against his armpit. Georgio fired a single .45 calibre shot from the Tommy Gun through the jeep's windshield, killing the driver.

Two more jeeps plowed through the parking lot and headed up both ends of the semi-circular driveway. Georgio spun around to the front entrance while Mickey took a bead on the jeep coming up from the rear. Both men opened fire on the two jeeps closing in on them until they clicked empty.

Del Toro pulled out his gun and fired at Mickey but only ripped his suit coat as the bullet lodged inside the door. "We have to go now!" yelled the driver. Mickey maintained focus, dropping out the old stick magazine and pushing a new one up into the bottom of the weapon, chambering the next round. He jumped from inside of the open passenger door as the jeep rammed into the Town Car. He opened fire on anything moving.

Sanders had his Beretta aimed at del Toro, who also aimed his weapon at Sanders. Del Toro smiled. "It looks as if we have a Mexican standoff, amigo. What shall we do?"

"It's your call, Captain. We can leave, and you have yet another fine hotel free of charge," replied Sanders. "Go inside; make yourself comfortable."

“The problem is, I cannot allow you to leave.”

“It’s no problem. Everyone lives, or everyone dies. You choose.”

“I must then concede to you, Señor Sanders, though you are the one in peril here.”

The thudding echo of boots covered over the backs of the three mobsters. Mickey and Georgio pivoted and opened fire, dropping several soldiers. A bullet shot through the windshield of the Town Car, killing their driver. Georgio grabbed him and pulled him out. “Come on!”

Mickey wormed his way around the door and plopped into the front passenger seat. Georgio put the car into drive, holding his foot on the brake pedal.

Sanders never took his eyes off del Toro, even when another jeep came barreling into the parking lot from the street. “Gotta go, Captain.” Sanders shot del Toro in the leg, then got into the now moving car. He hopped up, one hand on the roof and the other on the door with his left leg inside. Sanders spasm, yelling out. Del Toro’s bullet had severed his spine. The power to support his weight was gone. Slumping lower, he looked at his son. “Get my boy home. Go! Go!” As Georgio pounced on the gas pedal, Roman grabbed hold of his father and fell out. It sickened Sanders’s trusted men to leave their boss behind and his only son. Another jeep came around from the front to block them. Georgio braced himself as he collided with the jeep. The impact from the full-size luxury sedan knocked the jeep over on its side. The Town Car sped away.

***

Martin Rio stepped aboard the Pan Am aircraft. It was his first taste of home. His emotions were mixed. General Miguel Juan Garcia Obispo, a man he had come to love, should have been on this flight. But he was nothing more than another Cuban refugee. “Thank you, Juan Garcia.” Martin leaned back in his seat.

Mickey and Georgio took their seats. They felt relieved to learn that Francisco Javier Cruz had Roman in his care within the hour and could soften del Toro’s anger with money. They were amused to learn that young Roman had attacked del Toro, breaking his nose, taking two soldiers to pull Roman off him. But their boss was dead. They would meet up with Lansky back in Miami and inform him of events.

The first of the four engines sputtered to life, interrupting Martin’s thoughts of what kind of transistor radio to get for Juan Garcia.

Chapter 8

Washington D.C.

November 1, 1962

President Kennedy took no great solace in repelling Soviet ships that neared Cuba just over a week ago. October 22nd would stay with him for some time to come. The world had come to the brink of nuclear war.

For now, it left Jack Kennedy with no desire to fight. Then he smiled, for it dawned on him that Nikita Khrushchev, no matter how many times he had flipped off his shoe and banged it on the podium at the Kremlin, or the United Nations, had to feel as he did—relieved. Kennedy was not anxious to hear about any more plots against Castro.

"Operation: Mongoose is dead, Bobby," he said to his brother, the attorney general. "Let's keep it dead for now."

Not the president's cabinet, the CIA, nor the war department understood why support for Castro was so strong. It seemed all so logical, so plausible that the citizens of Cuba would have run side by side with the Cuban exiles as they made their way to Havana and Castro himself. Why would they not want that? It left the president drained and Castro with a tighter bond to Khrushchev.

President Kennedy picked up the file and took a last look at the operation. The great irony is that when Operation: Mongoose was created nearly a year ago, it was meant to culminate in October 1962 with the removal of Fidel Castro. "The Cuba Project" was the primary program under Operation: Mongoose, which outlined several tasks that would range from political, psychological, military, sabotage and intelligence operations inside and outside of Cuba, with even proposed attacks on key Cuban leaders.

Kennedy flipped through more pages, catching General Edward Lansdale's notes that outlined four different ways for the United States to proceed:

A. Cancel operational plans; treat Cuba as a Bloc nation.

B. Exert all possible diplomatic, economic, psychological, and all other pressure to overthrow the Communist régime without overt employment of the U.S. Military.

C. Commit U.S. to help Cubans overthrow the Castro Communist régime ...including the use of U.S. military force if required at the end.

D. Use a provocation and overthrow the Castro Communist régime by U.S. military force.

Kennedy directed the development of Option B.

As he stared at the page, he found himself chuckling when he remembered a scheme to create a rumor that Jesus Christ would not return to Cuba in his second coming until the Communists were gone.

He stopped laughing when he recalled one scheme proposed under Option D, which called for the sabotage of a Mercury rocket just after lift-off, even possibly killing the astronaut, then blaming Cuba for using a radio beam to throw it off course. "Who thinks up this stuff?" JFK said, shaking his head.

Part 2

**“Do not put your trust in nobles,
nor in the son of earthling man”**
David

Chapter 9

Pan Am Clipper "Pride of America"
JFK International Airport
40°38′23″N, 73°46′44″W

August 25, 1973

Captain Martin Rio stepped aboard the Boeing 707-321C cargo plane. The airliner had its crew but was missing one passenger. He frowned. He made his way forward to the cockpit after a glance aft to confirm that the various pallets of equipment destined to Tehran, Iran, for the Standard Oil Company, were secure.

Martin moved through the cockpit door, where his first officer and flight engineer were already situated. "Morning, Captain," said First Officer Dave Stauffer, a forty-year-old from Pittsburg, California. It was a mid-sized town located in the San Francisco East Bay Area. Growing up in San Francisco and moving back to the City two years ago, Martin knew of the industrial and bedroom community town.

"Hi, Dave," Martin said, pleased to see Stauffer. "Glad to have you on this flight. How's the family?"

"Good. This is Jerry Dunbar. He's manning our fuel gauges."

Martin held out his hand to the young flight engineer. "Nice to have you aboard, Jerry."

"Thank you, Captain."

They began the pre-flight checklist.

A Pan Am Boeing 727 pulled up to the gate and shut down its three engines within a few seconds of the man on the ground crossing his two wands above his head. The jet bridge rolled close to the fuselage. The door was opened.

Inside the terminal, a Pan Am attendant observed the flow of passengers coming off the jet bridge. Finally, the attendant's vigilant search rewarded her. She hurried toward a fast walking teenager.

A man watched for the same fifteen-year-old boy. The man was Latin and typically well dressed. He still had a distinguished nature, though gray-headed and somewhat balding. He watched the Pan Am attendant pull the boy aside and take him over to the gate counter. The attendant handed him a phone. He watched the boy's eyes light up as he spoke over the phone. The man waited until the boy left the gate counter and then hurried across the flow of passengers dashing by in both directions to intercept him. The man called out. "Lance. Lance Rio."

Martin laid down his clipboard and turned as he heard a familiar voice say: "Hi, Dad." Lance entered the cockpit and leaned in past the center console. He and his father embraced.

Martin planted a kiss on Lance's cheek. "Hi, son. You have a good time with Roger?"

"Yeah, we did a lot of scuba diving and kicked around the Keys a bit."

"And how are the Drakes doing?"

"Betty and Rodney, Sr. are good. I also worked with Rodney, Sr. in construction. He says I'm a natural."

"Okay, we'll catch up later. We need to get in the air. It's warming up, and it's already going to cost us six hundred more feet to get airborne." Martin nodded toward the empty seat behind his that had a headset placed on it. "Go ahead and take a seat."

"Before I do, Dad, there's this man waiting to talk to you. I think he's with the government."

"Wait here." Martin moved his seat back, climbed out, and moved through the narrow cockpit door.

Martin turned the corner. Guzman flashed a delighted smile. Martin stopped, then came up and grabbed Guzman throwing him off the plane. Guzman landed hard on the jet bridge.

"Dad, what are you doing?" Lance exclaimed.

"Go back inside, son. And close the door." Martin looked at the gate attendant. "Pull it back. We're clear."

The jet bridge rolled back from the aircraft as ordered. The gate attendant left.

Feeling pain as he stood up, Guzman collected himself. He managed to smile as he faced Martin. "Maybe I should have anticipated your reaction more carefully."

"I don't know why you are still alive, but whatever the reason is, I don't know you."

"You misunderstand, my dear, Martin." Guzman stepped forward.

"What do you want, Guzman?"

"Your family in Cuba is truly at a loss. And now, with the hostile takeover of the family business in San Francisco, you have no further ties to the business your father began so many years ago. Only its debt."

"Tell me something I don't know."

"I have been a silent partner with your father. You would not know this, of course. I had a vast interest in his success. But thanks to Castro, it is nearly gone."

Martin shook off any look of surprise. It would probably turn out to be the only honest thing this man ever had to say. The family business that had thrived in the import and export world was nearly dead after a decade of the U.S. trade embargo on Cuba. The company once employed forty-six people. The number was now down to seven.

"And you're here to collect a debt?"

"If I may, I will meet you at your home in San Francisco after you are back from this flight. Be careful in Tehran. Tensions are building there." Guzman limped up the jet bridge.

Chapter 10

U.S. Airbase Saigon, South Vietnam
10°49′08″N, 106°39′07″E

August 26, 1973

The U.S. Marines UH-1N Huey helicopter shook lightly as the main rotors spun up to idling speed. The pilot waited for the necessary warm-up time and then rolled in the throttle. The aircraft rose. Soon there was nothing beneath it but dense green jungle.

The Huey slowed to a hover as it flew past the last bit of jungle to a clearing of what was a small village that had once farmed the nearby rice paddies. Now it was nothing more than a charred reminder of a successful military operation.

"Okay, sergeant, we're at three hundred feet," the pilot reported.

"Good, hold it here," said Sergeant Roman Sanders.

"Why are we here, Roman?" asked Petty Officer Scott Ensor. "And why do we have this family with us?"

"You wanted to come along, Scotty, so just sit back and let us conclude a little business," Sanders replied.

"We have a time limit, Sanders, and we're on the Navy's time."

"It says U.S. Marines on the side of this chopper. You're just a passenger."

"Got news for you. We own the Marines."

Sanders grinned. There were three other Marines in the helicopter. "You see any action, sailor?" Ensor pointed to the Special Warfare badge on his chest. Ensor was a Navy SEAL.

The two large doors of the Huey were slid back. "What are you doing, Sanders?"

"Like I said, just finishing up some old business. Isn't that right, General Vu?" Sanders turned to a Vietnamese man who sat with his family. "You know what I want, Vu. Be straight with me, and you and your family get to live. Think of your wife, your little boy, and baby girl."

"I am just a farmer," the frightened man said.

"No! You're V.C.! I can smell Commie on you!"

Vu said nothing.

"Fine. You need some convincing. That's cool." Sanders nodded to the Marine on the little girl's right. He grabbed her. Ensor's lunge was met with a pistol to the side of his head. "No, no, sailor. You stay still." The Marine grabbed the little girl with one hand and swung her outside of the helicopter. She screamed. The Marine's left arm was in a wrestling match with the panic-stricken mother. "Come on, General Vu, this is your baby girl. No secret is worth your daughter. I know you understand me. I'm listening."

"I know nothing. I am not this V.C.," Vu said.

"Guess I was wrong." Sanders nodded to the Marine. The Marine let go of the little girl. Her screams faded as she fell. "Now, you know how so many fathers and mothers felt when you butchered their children. Look in my eyes, General. Like you, I am beyond compassion."

Vu looked at Sanders with the painful realization that he was seeing himself. Vu's attempt to hide amongst the South Vietnamese had failed.

The helicopter tilted to the left as it made a small circle around the lifeless little body lying face down in the rice paddy below.

"Give me something, so I can spare the rest of your family. You ever spare anyone, General?" Sanders watched his eyes. Vu wiped tears from them and looked at Sanders with hatred. "Give me something, so you can continue to enjoy the generosity of the United States."

"War is over. I am farmer," Vu demanded.

Sanders frowned. Then he gestured for the little boy. Vu held tight to him. The Marine seated to his left elbowed Vu in the face. Vu's hands went slack. The Marine to the right reached over and grabbed the little boy and pushed him to Sanders. Sanders took hold of him and moved him to the opening.

"War's not completely over, General. Not for me. Now, farmer or soldier?" Sanders watched Vu, studied his body language. There was no yielding. With a subtle push, the boy was at the edge. The rotor wash dragged him outside. Vu instinctively reached for him. The mother saw her son drop as she came to consciousness. She screamed at Vu. Sanders shrugged. He twisted the gun up against Ensor's head to keep him still. He nodded to the Marine, who grabbed the mother and yanked her out the other doorway. Her scream of terror was heard for a couple of seconds. Then only the ambient noise of the hovering helicopter was heard. Sanders looked at Vu. "You're no use to me now, Vu, so go," Sanders said with a nod to the doorway. Vu stood up. The small-framed man was nearly able to stand erect but hesitated as he looked down upon his dead family. "Come on. I don't have all day." Sanders raised a leg and gave him a boot forward. The flaying arms of Vu did nothing to keep him inside. He fell.

Ensor shot his right arm up, scraped the gun out of Sanders' hand, and took aim at him. "Why? With his kids?"

"It's the Chicago way."

"What are you, a Marine or a gangster?"

Sanders grinned. "Both."

Chapter 11

U.S.S. Kitty Hawk (CV-63)
18°43′03″N, 106°46′12″E

August 27, 1973

Captain Townsend rubbed his face. It was just after midnight, and he had been up for twenty-one hours. He hoped that the COD transport would be landing shortly.

An inquiry had been launched into an incident in which Petty Officer Scott Ensor, whose SEAL team was currently assigned to the Kitty Hawk, got into a fight with Marine Sergeant Roman Sanders. Both were experts in hand-to-hand combat and had beaten each other badly, leaving shed blood, bruises, and broken bones.

Lieutenant Jeffrey Ralston, the ship's JAG officer, stepped into the captain's office six hours earlier in the wake of the dust-up between Sanders and Ensor. The tall naval lawyer reminded Townsend of Napoleon Bonaparte. He had the same dauntless eyes, dark and observing. The nose was long and aquiline that flared out to large nostrils. It was an aristocrat's nose. The coarse black mane of perfectly coiffed waves fit in with military specs yet defied it.

"Can we afford another embarrassment, given a year ago, Captain?" Ralston questioned. "I would recommend against an Article Thirty-Two hearing." A year earlier, a race riot broke out on the Kitty Hawk.

"And what do you propose I do, Lieutenant? Send them to their rooms? These are serious charges against these men."

"So you're going to let this baby killer off?" Ensor growled.

"Petty Officer Ensor, you're in no position to do other than ordered. If an Article Thirty-Two hearing is convened, you will face brig time and more than likely be dishonorably discharged thereafter," Ralston replied.

"That's about how it would be, son," the captain said to Ensor. He turned to Ralston. "Now, what I want from you is a recommendation."

"Very well, sir. Both men will need some time to recover, naturally, but then I recommend thirty days in the brig, a letter of reprimand, and two month's loss of pay for both, and then a return to duty. If we agree, I can submit the paperwork."

"Fine. I'll endorse your recommendation." Townsend turned to Ensor. "You're getting off light. Damned light. Dismissed."

Ensor rose, eyes forward. "Aye-aye, sir." Townsend nodded to one of the MP's to help Ensor out of the room.

Townsend turned to Sanders. "I want you off my boat, mister."

***

"Captain's on the bridge," called out the Executive Officer. Townsend entered and looked out of the bridge's large angled windows. He saw navigation lights in the distance. His transport plane was nearly there. He followed the lights until it entered a downwind entry for landing.

"XO, you have the bridge. I'll be down on the flight deck," Townsend said.

***

The C-2A Greyhound made its approach to the back end of the carrier. The pilot worked the aircraft down over the threshold until the main gear hit. The C-2A's tailhook touched down between wires 2 and 3, a perfect landing.

The Greyhound wouldn't settle long. Ensor came down on the flight line. Even in the middle of the night, the flight deck was still an active place. Ensor was happy to hear that Sanders was ordered off the ship. He thought for a moment what would happen if he ever saw Sanders again. The man was a psychopath and didn't belong in the military.

Sanders begrudgingly allowed himself to be led by two MP's to the back of the C-2 transport. They would accompany him to the naval base in Yokosuka, Japan. The aft end ramp was lowered for the injured man to walk more easily into the aircraft.

Sanders came to an abrupt stop on the ramp, catching Ensor's glare. The MP's pushed Sanders inside the plane.

The C-2 had two small circular windows toward the back of the aircraft, one on each side of the fuselage. The windows were dark.

The C-2 spooled up its engines for takeoff. Ensor noticed a flicker of light from the lone side window. Sanders lit a cigarette and then gestured his farewell toward Ensor.

The steam catapult shot the transport down the runway and off the ship, as ordered.

Chapter 12

Key Largo, Florida

25°6′24″N, 106°25′48″W

October 16, 1973

Lance was happy that the school day was over. This being a Friday, the weekend meant earning some extra cash by working for Roger's dad in construction. Plus, some scuba diving on Sunday, if his dad didn't insist that he attend church. He had no use for church. Lance reasoned his going to church was his father's way of thumbing his nose at Castro and Karl Marx.

Since the move back to Key Largo from San Francisco a month earlier, his father had become distant and obsessed now that his brother had been sent to prison. Lance felt terrible that he never met his Uncle Ignacio, "Nacho," as he was called.

"Ah, young Lance is home," Guzman said.

Lance recognized those same sterile gray eyes and immediately felt uncomfortable. "I'm going over to Roger's for a while."

"What about your homework?" Amanda asked.

"Don't have any." Lance walked through the kitchen.

"Now," Guzman's voice lowered, "we will have forces ready. All you have to do is the flying end of it. And I appreciate your taking a leave of absence from work. It will be worth your while. I will see to it."

"I still don't know why you haven't spent the last dozen years in a Cuban prison," Martin said flatly.

"I'm much more valuable to people out of prison."

Guzman placed a photograph of Martin's brother on the table. He was shackled along with several others, with armed guards interwoven among them. "Listen, my friend, this is about your brother, now, and for Cuba, soon."

"I'm not doing this so you can bring the mob back to Havana, Guzman. Get that straight right now. I happen to approve of Castro throwing them out."

"Oh, yes, Fidel was all so noble. Now he's the big mob boss. He does what every Communist leader does. He skims the cream off of the top for himself and then tells the people to share what's left and calls that social equality. Hardly. Let us save your brother and deal with Fidel once and for all."

Lance knocked on the screen door. Betty Drake answered the door. "Lance, you know you don't have to knock if the door's open."

Roger was in his bedroom watching Speed Racer on his television. Lance just caught the theme song intro. "Hey, you know what they need to make? A Mach Five," Roger said without looking up.

You mean like a Chevy Mach Five?"

"Yeah, you know, good on gas, you know with the Arabs screwing us on oil and all, but with some horsepower. Of course, it would be an instant chick magnet."

"There's no back seat."

"Dude, you can do it in an MG Midget."

Lance let it go. Roger was the ladies' man. All of the girls went for him. Even their jealous boyfriends thought he was cool. Roger had everything going for him in life. His goal of playing football in the Coast Guard Academy would be a reality next year. He had his private pilot's license since summer.

The evening air blowing through Lance's hair, accompanied by another beautiful setting sun over the horizon, made him feel better. He and Roger were riding along in Roger's MG Midget. "I don't like this Guzman guy, Rog."

"He's not a politician?"

"Oh, he's a con man, all right."

The MG Midget pulled up in the driveway, where Lance looked over his shoulder and saw that no lights were on in his house.

Roger and Lance entered the living room, where they heard Martin and Amanda speaking with Rodney Sr. and Betty at the kitchen table. They seemed somber.

"Let's go home, son," Martin said. "We need to talk."

Lance found himself now sitting at their kitchen table with his parents. "Sometimes, we have to do things in life that we don't want to do, but …"

"Dad, you and mom aren't spies or soldiers. Not anymore. You don't have to do this."

"I have to at least try and help my brother, son. Do you understand how badly it hurts me that you do not know your family because of Castro?"

"You can't leave me! Mom?"

"We're not abandoning you, honey. We would never do that, but your uncle needs our help," Amanda said softly.

"I thought this is what the CIA and the army are supposed to be doing. Why don't they go get him? You both have been out of the army for nearly twenty years."

"Don't worry. We're not busting him out of prison. We're just flying in, or I'm just flying in and flying him out. It's not as big a deal as you think, son." Martin and Amanda put their arms around their only child.

***

Five nights later, Martin turned into Key Largo's Ocean Reef Airport. Martin drove up to the tie-down area, where several general aviation aircraft lined up wingtip to wingtip. Looking at the luminous dial on his watch, he saw it was just past two in the morning. Amanda had left three days earlier, posing as a German vacationer. She became fluent in German while stationed in Berlin during her army days. Letting Lance know that his mother worked for a time in Army Intelligence and even behind the Iron Curtain as Greta Fuchs brought a coy grin to their son. Mom was a spy!

A black Cadillac pulled up. The right rear window lowered. It was Guzman. "Follow me, Martin, if you would."

Martin started up the dark green Karmann Ghia and followed Guzman down the tarmac to another line of parked aircraft.

The Caddy pulled up next to a white van with three men prepping an aircraft. Martin recognized it as a Cessna 337 Skymaster, a twin-tail boom, twin-engine aircraft with one engine in front and the other straight behind it at the aft end of the short fuselage.

"I understand that you have quite a few hours of flying time in this aircraft," Guzman said as he approached Martin. Moving closer, Martin realized that this aircraft was not white, but a khaki tan color, with two ordinance hardpoints under each wing. This was not the civilian model, but the military version: O-2. He watched Guzman's men attach four small bombs to each pylon. "As per our agreement."

"Understood," Martin said. He opened the upper part of the pilot's side door and then the lower airstair part of the door, gaining entrance to the aircraft.

A man came up to Martin. Guzman took note. "This is Raoul. He is your co-pilot. You will do as he says. That is, he will instruct you on where to fly. I give you my personal guarantee it will all go as planned."

"Let's get on with it then." Martin brushed Raoul aside and entered the aircraft. He felt for his Colt .45 semi-automatic inside his light windbreaker, giving it a comforting tap.

***

Lance needed to sleep but couldn't. He watched the minute hand sweep continuously around the softly backlit face of Roger's alarm clock, now past three in the morning.

"Roger," he called out sharply, his voice trailing into a whisper. "Roger."

"What?"

"Roger, get up," Lance said as he sprung up.

"Why, what's wrong?"

"We have to go. I need to get to my dad."

"Yeah, okay."

The two boys slipped out the front door and into the MG. Once they were clear of the house, Roger drove fast.

He hung a left turn northbound onto U.S. Highway 1. The town was quiet. Lance gazed out on the ocean side of the island, where the water lay still due to miles of coral reefs. As with most of the Keys, the landmass was narrow, barely over a mile wide in most places. Key Largo, the largest of the Florida island chain, was no exception.

The minutes ticked by. Roger continued speeding. They passed the Jew Fish Creek Bridge turnoff, where Highway 1 continued onto the mainland. Roger avoided the turn to the left and kept straight through to the 905. The tiny car sped the two boys northeastward, where the ambient lighting grew dim quickly, and darkness was all that lay ahead of them.

Lance looked forward into the darkness beyond the reach of the headlights. His mind wandered for a moment. Then he was suddenly jerked forward. The car skidded to a stop. "What happened? Why did you stop?"

"Look!" Roger demanded. A crocodile was crossing the road. The headlights bathed the pinkish-white mouth and gullet, exposing some of the reptile's sixty-six teeth. Croc crossing signs were posted like any other traffic sign, but this was the first time Lance ever encountered one.

"Just honk your horn and go around it."

"Man, it ain't no damn squirrel!"

Lance spun his legs over the top of the door and dropped onto the road. The crocodile swung its tail and arched its head at Lance, highlighting its teeth.

"Lance, what are you doing? Get back in the car!"

"Just get ready to go."

"Go? I'm ready to go back to bed. Get in here!"

"Come on. Get ready to go." Lance never took his eyes off the croc's teeth. He lunged at the croc and then jumped back. The croc charged Lance. Lance fell backward but rolled back up on his feet before the crocodile was on him. He jumped over the body of the animal and ran to the car. "Go!"

Roger hit the gas as soon as Lance landed back inside the MG. The crocodile turned and ran off the road, back into the swamp.

The MG continued along Gate House Road, which blended into Anchor Drive.

Roger made two tight turns and drove on a road that ran parallel with the runway. The sound of not just one but two aircraft could be heard doing a run-up.

Martin taxied into position. He told himself that this was a good plan, and it would all be over by late morning. He brought the twin throttle levers up to full power.

Roger swung tight onto the runway, where advancing light wrapped the tiny car in luminous peril, pushed from behind by the strength of over four hundred combined horsepower.

Martin yanked the twin throttles back to idle and hit the brakes. The sports car stopped about twenty feet in front of him. A crackle over the radio brought Martin back to the mission. "What's going on?"

Martin keyed his mic. "Nothing. It's fine. Just a short delay." Martin looked over at the second Skymaster, still on the narrow taxiway.

Raoul paced back and forth, smoking a cigarette and then throwing it down in protest. He kept some distance from Martin and his son. He understood. Despite being upset, he thought that the two boys acted with courage. But he wanted to get back to his own family by day's end.

"Dad, don't go. If you go, I feel I will never see you again. Like last time."

"I have never taught you to hate, son. Ever. But this man is different. Never forget what Castro did to me, to our family, and other families. You hate all the evil this man stands for. Now go with Roger. I'll see you after school." Martin hugged his son. He put his hand on Roger's shoulder. "Look after your brother."

"I always do, sir."

***

Martin felt in tune with the aircraft and the mission. The other Skymaster posed as the one traveling through Cuban airspace. It was still dark, but the plan called for the two aircraft to fly closer together as it got lighter.

The Cuban air traffic controller responded to the second Skymaster pilot's request to enter their airspace with a "Welcome."

Martin followed the lead aircraft. He would have no contact with the other aircraft. It was up to Martin to keep and maintain a proper distance, not too far and not too close. It would only be another fifteen minutes before they were actually over Cuban soil as they were now tracking to the radio navigation signal from the Varder VOR radio station.

Martin saw the lights of Varadero in the distance. It was a tourist town located about eighty-three miles east of Havana. Its Spanish name, Playa Azul, meant Blue Beach. Martin had enjoyed many trips there to scuba dive or just relax on its pristine beaches as a young man. Now it was foreign soil to him.

Raoul focused his red-tinted penlight. He mentally followed the lines he drew on his chart. His head bobbed slightly as he looked first at his stopwatch and then at his chart, calculating time and distance down to the second. "Now."

"Roger." Martin pushed the yoke forward, pulling back on the throttles. The Cessna dropped out of the sky. The aircraft rumbled. They could feel the air buffeting around them.

The two men rode the aircraft down to where Martin leveled off three hundred feet above the ground. The sun was just coming up, and he would enjoy one of the great pleasures of night flying: night giving way to morning.

Raoul noticed Martin's attention on the eastern sky. "I imagine you get to see this all the time." Raoul studied his chart. "Now."

"Turning to heading one four zero," Martin confirmed.

As the morning rays brighten, Martin studied the landscape below. Raoul looked up from his chart and stopwatch. "Do you know where you are?"

"I remember."

"Cheer up. You are above the road this time."

Three red flashes shot up from the flora-lined road below. A couple of seconds later, three more red flashes. Martin reached for the landing light rocker switch, which he flipped on for one second only. Three more red flashes came as a reply, and then the plane was over and past the area. They were to land at the small airstrip at Playa Girón. The landing site of the Bay of Pigs invasion was now a tourist site. Despite how smoothly things had gone, they were still just twenty-five miles from the third largest airport in Cuba, in Cienfuegos, which it shared with the Cuban Air Force.

The Skymaster came in and settled quickly on the runway. Martin pulled off of the runway and taxied over to the desolate parking area. He shut down the engines.

"Excellent, my friend. Now we wait, but I think not for long," Raoul said.

It had been just over an hour since they left Key Largo. Martin wasn't the nervous type, but he felt a tingling in his arms. This would be the last time he would ever do anything like this again. He pulled out his Colt .45. Raoul raised an eyebrow. "Let us hope it doesn't come to that."

Martin released his seat harness. He opened the clamshell door and stepped out. Raoul did likewise, lighting a cigarette. He strolled around the nose of the aircraft. Martin gave serious reflection on where he was and what was involved. "Tell me something, Raoul. What did my brother do to deserve your help?"

"I can't discuss it right at the moment. Let's just say in his paranoia, Castro has locked up many people that otherwise should never have known prison. Like with you."

"I didn't ask you what he did to get thrown into prison. I asked you what he did to deserve your attention."

"I told you before, nothing." Raoul looked away.

Martin grabbed Raoul and pinned him against the aircraft. "Answer me!"

"You don't want to take me on."

"I will if you don't answer me."

Martin let go. Raoul sighed and stamped out his cigarette. "Back in nineteen-sixty, Castro proclaimed that education and science were the future of Cuba, which led the way to higher education in science. Your brother, with his advanced degree in agriculture, was asked to become part of CENIC. You are familiar with this?"

"Yes, CENIC is the National Center for Scientific Research here in Cuba. They do biological research. My brother specialized in crop protection."

"And in pathogens." Raoul paused. "Your brother became infected with Dengue fever. He tried to infect Castro when he last visited the facility. Thus his incarceration. We planned to try again ourselves but needed your brother's help."

"Dengue is rarely fatal. You can do better than that."

"After this, we will not need to bother you or your family again. Let it go at that."

Martin heard a car coming down the road. "Let's get back in the plane."

The vehicle was an old ambulance with a white cross on each front door.

"Okay, we're in business. Let's get ready to go." Raoul jumped back outside.

The ambulance came to a halt. The two men upfront, dressed for the part, hurried to the back and opened the large door. They helped Amanda and Nacho outside and over to the plane. Then they removed one of the bombs, shuttling it back to the ambulance. Amanda helped Nacho into the aircraft, but he stopped, coughing. He pulled down his mask and spat up a blackish substance that looked like tar. Martin knew it as *Vomito Negro*. Black blood. His brother was hemorrhaging from inside, on the cellular level. There was no cure, and there was no vaccine. Amanda helped Nacho in behind Martin. She gave her husband a quick kiss and took her seat.

"Hi, baby," Martin said. "Glad to see you both."

The two Cubans came and removed the other three bombs.

Moments later, they brought out a hexagonal-shaped canister, some five feet in length. It was not a bomb, Martin was sure. It was too light. They secured it to the inner hardpoint under the wing. They ran back and came out with another canister and attached it to the inner hardpoint on the right-wing. Martin noticed they were more nervous with the canisters than the bombs. It caused a restudy of the modified Armament Control Panel in front of him. Raoul hopped into his seat and closed both door sections. He saw the puzzlement on Martin's face.

"Do not worry. You did your part. Let's go, please."

Martin started the front engine as the ambulance drove off, followed by the rear engine.

The O-2 followed a brief northwest course. Martin rolled in a turn to the northeast for the short flight over Cuban soil. Raoul stopped the turn. "What are you doing?" Martin questioned.

"Keep on this course," Raoul insisted.

"What? We'll fly right over two air bases and right over Havana."

"I know."

"You want us to get shot down?"

"Just stay on this course," Raoul said, holding a pistol. "Give me your gun. Carefully."

Martin wiggled out his gun. They were now being hijacked.

"Martin," Amanda said with great concern. She had rolled up Nachos' right shirtsleeve. There were a dozen red marks on his arms. She opened his shirt. A dozen more red spots covered his chest. They were mosquito bites.

"What did you do to my brother?"

"We did nothing. However, this is a small sacrifice to right a great wrong. We may still come out of this alive."

Amanda put her .25 Berretta up to Raoul's head. Martin took both guns from Raoul.

The canisters were now obvious. Martin moved his hand over to the armament control master switch. Raoul shot his hand out and slapped it away. Martin elbowed him in the side of his head, banging it against the side window with a chop to the throat. Raoul groaned and slumped over. Martin turned on the armament controls to the hardpoints and activated the left mounted canister. A six-sided cylinder popped back, where hundreds of mosquitoes flew out into the air stream. They were packed into thousands of tiny cells. Martin immediately closed the cylinder. He reasoned that each bug carried what infected his brother. Each one was meant for Castro, a plague to be released over the Cuban capital. Whatever happened to anyone else was unimportant and collateral.

The O-2 continued northeastward, flying over the peaks and smoothly dropping down to continue following the terrain. The ocean was now in sight. The rising sunlight shimmered on the water. The worst was behind them, and in just a few more minutes, they would be out over open water and soon in international airspace. Martin turned back to his wife and brother. "When we're halfway over open water, I'll drop the canisters into the ocean. That should take care of it."

"Martin, why the mosquitoes?" Amanda asked.

"To spread Dengue fever. They suckered us into doing their dirty work—again! As much as I would love to see Castro bitten by one of these bugs, I won't start an epidemic."

"I don't have Dengue fever," Nacho said.

"What do you mean? What do you have, Nach?"

"There is no name for this disease. Cuban soldiers in Africa contracted it, but we managed to isolate it. It is like Dengue, but it's many times worse. Always deadly. No cure."

"Does that mean we're contaminated now?" Amanda asked nervously.

"We think it is spread by the mosquito bite only. But you should probably stay back."

"Honey, how much longer?" she asked.

"We're safe now."

They sped out over open ocean. Martin's remaining thoughts were whipped into unconsciousness as the fireball and shockwave struck him from behind.

Chapter 13

Opa-locka Executive Airport, Miami
80°16′27″N, 80°16′42″W

October 22, 1976

The Cessna 172 was still twenty feet above the runway. The nose was too high, and the plane was about to stall and drop when Lance Rio took over. Lance added power and lowered the nose, arresting the plunge to the runway directly below. He gained enough airspeed to work the aircraft into a decent flare and landed with minimal squeaking of the tires.

The Cessna rolled to a manageable taxi speed, turned off of the runway, radioing the tower they were "*clear of the active*," and taxied back to the flight school ramp.

The man grabbed his clipboard. "Sweet, Lance. Congratulations, you passed," the flight examiner said. Lance Rio was now a CFI, a Certified Flight Instructor. Lance had passed the oral exam easily, although the examiner made it as tough as he could.

Lance settled in a chair in front of the examiner's desk. The examiner ducked under a model of a large-scale B-17 that hung down from the ceiling. "Well, Lance, if you have a goal, I would say you are on track. Do you still plan to go for your ATP?"

"And my A and P. I will start the next trimester as long as the money holds out."

"Well, if you get your A and P, I mean having an aircraft mechanic's license is a good thing, but if you want to become an airline pilot, you need your ATP rating."

"That's another thousand hours before I can go for my Airline Transport rating."

"Don't rush the process. Anyway, you can now supplement your expense by instructing. But I think you should go to college. Airlines like college grads."

"I understand, but I want my A and P first. Then maybe I can get some aeronautical engineering under my belt."

The examiner reached across the desk to shake Lance's hand. "Keep up the good work."

Lance gathered up his things and left the small office. He came out to the MG Midget, bequeathed to him by Roger, who had been in the Coast Guard Academy for the last two years.

Lance didn't mind the long drive from North Miami back down to Key Largo. He blended in and moved through traffic.

It was early evening. Lance slowed as he came nearer to the Drakes' house, his home for the last three years. He pulled up and stopped. He could see what was once his home in the rearview mirror. He felt a great emptiness.

Betty finished with the last bits of preparing dinner. She heard the MG drive up.

Betty came out of the house and went around to the driveway where Lance still sat.

"Lance. Are you all right, honey?"

"Yeah, I'm okay."

"Did you pass?" Betty asked as she came up to the car.

"One hundred percent on the written, and I passed with flying colors on the check ride."

"Well done. Knowing how good you are, I wasn't that worried."

She understood that Lance had bottled up his feelings since Martin and Amanda's death. She remembered him falling apart when he first got the news and Roger grabbing hold of him.

"I wish my dad could have been with me. That's all."

"I know, baby. Come on, let's go inside. It's near dinner time."

Rodney Sr. was eased back in his recliner, reading the paper. The TV was on. Lance went down the hallway to his room.

Lance dropped his flight bag next to his bed. He turned and sat on it, taking a good look at Roger's empty bed. He missed Roger.

Lance came into the family room and sat on the sofa. Rodney Sr., still semi-reclined in his easy chair, turned the top of his newspaper down. "I'm proud of you, Lance." He shook Lance's hand. "Like I said before. Flying is a great hobby, but hobbies take money. I signed a new contract today to remodel a home down in Marathon. I want you with me on it. You're my best painter. And you will probably be doing the tile work. All marble."

"That's fine, Rodney. But I want to keep my goal in aviation, because—"

"I know. It's in your blood. Same with Roger. But flight instructors don't make much. You have a real talent in construction. You can't make the money in aviation you can make with me. Roger will learn that one day too. He'll be flying someone else's plane instead of owning two like me. Why do you think I keep the big Cessna around?"

"Tax write-off."

"Well, yes. And that's why I don't have you fly it when we take clients on our little aerial tours. It looks good when clients see me flying them around. It builds their confidence in me as they also get a look at how beautiful the Keys are and get an idea of how great it would be to have a home here. And then they see my home and my boat, and all, and that makes them want to live here that much more. We profit from that. I want to share my gift with you." Rodney Sr. leaned toward Lance. "Now, I fronted you a lot of money for your training, which I was happy to do, but we need to see eye to eye here."

"I paid you back from my trust fund. And you got money from the life insurance. Well, what the lawyers didn't take. And I have worked a weekend free for you every month for room and board for the last year."

"I understand all that. But I need to count on you."

"I want to go for my A and P come the start of the next trimester in January."

"Go where?"

"To the Baker Aviation School in Miami."

"Fine." Rodney Sr. picked up his newspaper. "You want to swing a wrench instead of a hammer and paintbrush? That's your call. But don't expect me to front any more money for your flying. And Roger is gonna want his car back real soon too."

Lance knew dinner was going to be a silent affair. For the first time, he felt like an uninvited guest who had long overstayed his visit.

Chapter 14

George T. Baker Aviation School
Miami, Florida

August 22, 1977

Lance wheeled the MG Midget through traffic, almost losing his focus as he noticed a Pan Am Boeing 747 in the near distance on final approach into Miami International Airport. Lance didn't see a future with Pan Am, or any airline, though it was always his childhood dream to be a Pan Am pilot. Maybe if his father were here, however, he knew to keep his focus on planes instead of girls, even though at age nineteen, biology and aviation seemed to play tug-of-war with him. The airliner slipped from view behind several buildings.

Lance turned northbound onto NW 42nd Avenue, which also became Le Jeune Road, and headed up the street until he turned into the main parking entrance to the school. He grabbed his books and binder and headed to the front entrance, smiling at the school's mascot: an actual 1950s RF-84 jet fighter out on display.

Other than math, most of his education had been easy for him. He had completed two trimesters and an additional evening class. This morning's class, which was the start of a new trimester, would concentrate on his passion: Turbines! If all went well, he would take his FAA written exam in January and be a certified A & P—Airframe and Powerplant technician. He would also start his avionics course.

He padded down the hallway, turned into classroom 206, and made his way to a front-row desk. Wesley Gent, the chief instructor, wrote on the blackboard. Lance soaked up everything he had to say. His experience as an aircraft mechanic and naval aviator went back to World War II and Korea. After twenty years in the Navy, he retired and flew F-104 Star-fighters for the Air National Guard before applying his knowledge to teaching.

Gent continued writing on the blackboard. Then he turned around to see his favorite student. "Lance, you're here. Good." Gent came over and shook Lance's hand. "Congratulations on your next instructor's rating."

"Thanks, Wes."

"Listen, I'm thinking about building another kit plane. I thought maybe you advanced students would like to help me work on this one too."

"Which kit?"

"I'm thinking maybe a Rutan Vari-Eze. I can buy the plans and get some of the parts from a couple of companies that make parts, so it won't drag on."

"But, what about the BD-Five? We haven't finished that one."

"We've gone as far as we can without the driveshaft system."

Lance thought about how the Bede Aircraft Company went bankrupt before many of the kit plane customers had all of the parts they had paid for. Gent kept his BD-5 fuselage and finished wings up against a wall in his garage. The twelve and a half foot long, all-metal, bullet-shaped aircraft was designed to fly at 200 to 300 miles per hour, depending on the engine.

"I was thinking, Wes, why don't we turn it into a J model?"

Gent smiled sheepishly. "Make it a jet?"

"Why not? What we could do is turn it into a turbofan, build a front fan for it. I'm thinking maybe we could take the first-stage compressor wheel off of a T-Fifty-three turboshaft engine and modify it for the engine."

"You're talking about a lot of work, Lance. Re-engineering—and a lot of work."

"I'm willing to do the work."

"Let's have you pass this course, get your A & P, and then come next year, we'll talk about it. Okay? Tell you what. Come over tonight, and we can talk about it."

"Can't tonight. I have a student after my second class today at Opa-locka. Then I have to meet some lawyer back home who's interested in lessons. Maybe this weekend, if I'm not painting this house down in Tavernier. We've almost completed the remodeling on it."

"When do you sleep, Lance?"

"At night."

Gent pivoted away from Lance with his eyes rolling, heading back to his desk. "Oh, to be young again."

The door opened and two teenage boys, followed by a man in his thirties, filed into the classroom. Then a cute brunette came in. Lance turned to see who had entered, and his eyes fixed on the girl's dazzling blue eyes. She noticed him noticing her.

***

Lance had just finished spraying out the inside of the house with two other men following him with paint rollers. He sprayed—they back rolled.

Lance could now remove his dust mask and cap and pull the spray sock off his head. The airless paint sprayer had been drained and was now being flushed with water. Lance aimed the spray gun away from the thin plastic sheeting that protected the glass-paneled French doors. As he pulled the trigger, the plastic sheeting would lift off the glass that it naturally clung to and was sucked into the spray stream. When Lance released the trigger, the plastic would float back and cling to the glass panels. Lance watched it again. This was aerodynamics.

"Boy, what are you doing?" Rodney Sr. huffed.

"Cleaning up."

"Well, finish and get the equipment stowed. I still needed you badly on a job down in Marathon. I need you hanging drywall and possibly doing the tile work in the kitchen."

"I can't make that one, Rodney. I have too much going on."

"What? What did you say to me? As good as I treat you, you're going to stab me in the back like that? You owe me."

"Owe you? I don't owe you. I've paid my debt to you several times over."

"Okay. I see how it is. Then maybe it's time we go our separate ways."

***

Roger came home for Christmas to learn that his father had kicked Lance out of the house. "Why?" he demanded of his father. "I don't like coming home to hear this, pop. He deserves better than this. Lance is family. You made your choice in life. Let me make mine and let Lance make his. We haven't forgotten the hand that fed us, but you have to do right by Lance. He's been through enough in life. We're all he has."

"He's living up north now, in Miami, somewhere in Hialeah," Rodney, Sr. said indifferently.

"I graduate soon. I want him there with you and mom."

Rodney, Sr. frowned. "He won't come back. But I'll make my peace with him. I'll even help him out if he needs it."

"That's good, pop. Just face it, Lance was meant to fly."

Chapter 15

New London, Connecticut
(United States Coast Guard Academy)
41°22′22″N, 72°06′06″W

May 25, 1978

Roger took the silver dollar and his first salute as a U.S. Coast Guard officer. He was now Ensign Drake. He looked for his family after the ceremony was over.

"So, I guess you'll be going into their aviation program?" Rodney, Sr. asked.

"No. I want to go into the law enforcement area, pop."

Betty stepped forward. "Son, are you sure you want to do that? Wouldn't you want to put your engineering degree to better use?"

"No, mom, it's where I've applied. You know I'm a hands-on kind of guy. It's what I've been training for."

His father shrugged. "Well, I guess you're too much of an athlete to be sitting at a desk. Do what you think is best, son."

Lance approached with a cute, hypnotic blue-eyed girl at his side. "Rog, this is Keri."

Roger embraced them both. He stood back. "Keri, it is nice to finally meet you. And thank you for coming to my graduation."

"Thank you for inviting me," she said.

"I hear you and Lance are inseparable these days."

"Not as inseparable as you two are from what I hear," Keri said.

Roger caught the glaring looks of his girlfriend. She was tired of holding their three-month-old baby, David Anthony Drake. "Lance, we'll meet up later, okay?"

"Sure, Rog. We'll see you later."

Emily was indeed angry. She often was anymore.

"You might have come over to your own family first, you know," she snapped.

"Don't start, Emily. Not here, not now." He looked around.

"It's all fine for you. You've got your career. What do I get? I get to stay home and raise your baby is what."

"You'll get back in later. You only have one year to go."

"No, I will have to make up this semester, and *then* I'll have a year to go. That is if they let me back in, to begin with. Here, take your son." Emily thrust the baby into Roger's arms and walked away.

Chapter 16

Miami

25°46′31″N, 80°12′32″W

August 19, 1978

"Fast-what?" Wes Gent asked. It was the first time he had ever heard the term.

"Fastglass! It's made out of fiberglass, and this puppy will do about one hundred sixty knots, about a hundred and eighty-four miles per hour true airspeed. Hence, fast—glass."

"Oh, the things you come up with, Lance."

Gent enjoyed being with Lance. Having the twenty-year-old around was like having a son to do things with again. Over the summer, Gent and Lance poured a concrete slab and built a prefab metal shop in the backyard that faced a side gate since his wife booted him and his planes out of their garage.

The Vari-Eze kit was not quite a kit but a set of plans purchased from Burt Rutan's company. The Rutan construction method left the builder to do everything. Fortunately, as the kit plane world had begun to standardize and industrialize, prefabricated parts were becoming available through such companies as the Aircraft Spruce & Specialty Co. in Southern California and Wicks Aircraft Supply that once built pipe organs.

The Vari-Eze design was a basic fiberglass cloth embedded with liquid epoxy resin, creating a matrix that was then laid over a medium-density polystyrene foam core cut to the shape of whatever part was to be glassed. Some joked that they were making little more than flying surfboards. The retort to that was metal planes were "*spam-cans*." But the design was strong and could handle high g-forces. It was also a way for many pilots to have an affordable aircraft of their own.

"Fastglass. Very sleek, very sexy, very visual. That's how we should promote it," Lance said as he laid a large block of polystyrene foam on the long worktable.

Lance had cut out the wing templates from plywood by laying the drawings from the plans over a piece of plywood, where he sanded lightly and painted them white. Following the marks Gent drew on the polyfoam block, he nailed the templates in place with small lathing nails. The templates had small numbered slash marks from one end of the template to the other.

Gent grabbed the foam wire cutter, a simple wooden frame with a thin wire stretch between the two ends. He swung the other end to Lance. He turned up the current on the small transformer until the wire glowed red-hot. The two men then leaned over and positioned the wire to the number 1 mark on each template. The hiss and sizzle of the wire melting its way through the high-density polyfoam material was the initial sign of success.

"Okay, just like before. Position one," Gent called out.

"Position one," Lance responded.

Gent moved carefully upward, letting the heated tungsten wire do all of the work. He called out position 2. Lance, at position 2, gave the reply, "Position two." It was satisfying to see the wire slide its way through the foam block, vaporizing it into a useful form.

Gent and Lance completed the cut. Lance studied it, looking for defects. "Looks good."

"You have a real talent for this. Why don't we break for lunch and cut the last wing section afterwards?"

"Okay. I'll clean up the shop." Gent patted Lance on the back on his way out as Keri walked in. Lance turned and smiled brightly at the love of his life.

"So, this is my competition?" She strolled around, looking.

"Why would you say that? You have no competition."

"Maybe." She kissed Lance. "Can a plane compete with that?"

"Depends on the girl."

"I thought you were going to say, depends on the plane."

"No, it's the girl." Lance kissed her back.

***

Kerilynn drove her little yellow Ford Pinto through the main entrance of the Everglades Mobile Home Park, then down Gator Lane, one of only three streets in the small community. She pulled into the carport of a mobile home. She was holding back tears.

Lance saw her car out the window. He slipped into his black dress shoes and grabbed his sport coat. He wanted to look his best for tonight. Keys in hand, he went out the door and came around as Keri was easing her way out of the driver's seat. His smile dropped when he saw her tear-stained eyes.

Lance grew angry. "You're never going back home there again."

***

"That whole family is—I don't know the word, dysfunctional. And her stepfather is an ogre. He keeps that whole family under a dark cloud. That's no way to live. I won't let her go back there."

"Are you two going to get married?" Gent asked.

Lance clasped his hands on the dining room table. "Well, I'd like us to."

"It's a big step, you know?"

"I do." Lance grinned. "See, I have the two main words down already."

Gent smiled. "Still, it is a big step, and frankly, I don't think you're ready. You still have all of these goals. A wife would demand more of your time than you would probably want to give right now."

"This is getting complicated. She can't go back home. I won't let her. And the next time her stepdad smacks her, I'll call the police."

"Where will she stay? At your trailer?"

"Well, I was going to ask…"

"Yes, she can stay here for a while, but then you'll have to work out other arrangements."

The front door opened. Sybil Gent and Keri walked in. Wes Gent was concerned on multiple levels about the future of the two youths.

***

The year 1979 began quietly but with new questions for Lance to ponder. Lance drove his little red Mazda pickup truck carefully around the parking area and to the back of the school building. The school was closed on the weekends. Gent got out, went to the chain-link fence, and unlocked the gate. The rotary engine revved up, and Lance drove through.

Lance backed into the school's shop. Jesse Del Monte strolled up to the pickup, gazing at what the large painter's drop cloth was covering. He released two straps.

His walrus mustache danced when he spoke. "Hey, Wes, didn't our boy here pass his written?" Del Monte called out to the other side of the drop cloth. "I go away for winter break, and nobody tells me anything."

"He only missed one question on the powerplant portion. Guess he still has his mind set on what he thinks a turbine engine should be instead of what it is," Gent relayed.

"Well, looks like our boy here is on his way to being Super Pilot."

With the drop cloth off, the fuselage of the Vari-Eze stood on two fixed legs that stood on a piece of plywood strapped to the open tailgate. The nose of the aircraft rested on the roof of the truck cab.

The three men carefully lifted the lightweight aircraft and placed it on the shop floor. Lance reached inside the cockpit and grabbed what looked like a window crank, and turned it as fast as he could. Slowly from underneath, the nose gear appeared.

Del Monte grinned. "Looks like you're building up a full head of steam there, Lance."

"We should have a test flight sometime this spring. And then I can get married."

"Married? To Keri, our receptionist?" Del Monte blurted out.

"Yeah, why?"

"It just caught me by surprise, Lance. That's all." Del Monte said nothing further.

Chapter 17

Langley, Virginia

May 26, 1982

CIA case officer, Jeffrey Ralston, stepped out of the elevator. He was on time for his meeting with the Director of Central Intelligence.

Admiral Stansfield Turner rose from his chair and shook Ralston's hand. The two men smiled at each other, a professional courtesy. Ralston smoothly undid the button on his coat. With both hands, he pinched the front of his trousers as he sat. He considered Turner an ethical man in an unethical business. Turner had tried to rid the agency of bureaucratic walls that kept one person from sharing information with someone just down the hallway, let alone other agencies.

"Well, Jeffrey, you've done very well in your eight years here at the Agency. I gather you don't regret leaving the Navy?" Director Turner stated.

"No, sir. I'm where I was meant to be," Ralston affirmed.

The director looked at Ralston's opened file on his desk. "Well, in both of your overseas assignments, you've shown initiative and tenacity."

"I've done the best I could, sir."

"We know we have to grow with our technical environment. It was our interception of the Soviet signal that alerted us to this recent KGB activity in Angola."

"Still, I've yet to see a satellite read a man's heart."

"Your father, Harold, served in the O.S.S. during World War Two. He worked with Wild Bill Donovan. Before we became the CIA." Turner nodded emphatically. "Old school."

"Admiral, it was my asset in Germany that put us on the path to what was going on."

"The Turkish baker in Munich?"

"Yes, he was formerly Turkish Army Intelligence. It's all in my report."

"But your asset in Angola was killed. Aerial surveillance could have shown us the Cuban convoy."

"We wouldn't have known where to look before the weapons were delivered. It was unfortunate that a rival faction showed up when they did. My Angolan asset was simply caught in the crossfire."

"Are we taking care of his family?"

"We are. As you can see in my report, the Cuban army stationed in Angola brought in a shipment of arms. We blew them up, convoy trucks and all."

Turner read the report but liked hearing things straight from his office's mouths as long as they kept to the point.

"Yes, it looks like the Soviets are none the wiser. Good." Turner took a few seconds to look over the file again. "Your wife has done very well in her overseas assignments. Yet, you both have requested assignments back here."

"Maggie's spent nine of the last eleven years overseas, sir. And we have a young son now."

"And you want to head your own separate task force?"

"To capitalize on this latest KGB situation and undermine their efforts as much as possible. Who knows, we might even get another shot at Castro."

"I'm sure heads are rolling back at the Kremlin." Turner closed Ralston's file. "Your family lost a lot of money after Castro nationalized everything."

"Many people did, sir. And if I find a way to correct matters, well..." he trailed off.

Turner sighed and leaned back in his chair. "Well, I don't want to hold up your career."

"Thank you, sir." Ralston rose. With less than a decade in the CIA, Ralston would have his own team—and an office to go with it.

Chapter 18
Miami

August 30, 1982

Blood never seemed as bright as when it oozed out from greasy black fingers. Borax soap and a bandage would get him back to work before the boss found out. Lance had a jet engine to get back up and running and quickly. When you kept a multi-million dollar business jet down, you were often dealing with people who had more money than sense and as little patience. The expression: "*You'll be hearing from my lawyers*" sprang up more than once just outside of the shop floor. Such as it was working for *Spencer Aviation: Jet Mecca*.

Lance would rather be flight instructing on a permanent basis, but now he was a married man and took a steady job with a steady paycheck.

Lance cleaned and bandaged his injury and went back to work on the Learjet 35. He looked up from his work and noticed his boss walking toward him with what he hoped was a pizza box. Arland Spencer was a hefty man in his fifties. His reddish-brown hair was at that stage where it was lined with honey-golden stripes that gave him a crown of gold before their luster would tarnish to silver.

"Are you being careless?" Spencer asked, noticing Lance's bandaged finger.

"No, but these pilots are. This combustor is going to fail. It's being overheated."

"You don't buy a Learjet to fly slow. Here's your part." Spencer lifted the lid of the box he carried to reveal a new High-Pressure turbine blade wheel assembly. No pizza.

"Now, get it on today. I want this plane up and running by morning."

"Yes, sir." Spencer put the box on Lance's worktable and went back to his office.

***

Lance drove up behind Keri's Toyota sedan and parked. It was almost nine o'clock. He was tired and hungry.

Lance had remodeled the house. It didn't look like a mobile home on the inside. The living room was open and flowed into the kitchen area as one large room. Lance had added a peninsula to turn the countertop from L-shape to U-shape. Two cushioned stools provided a place to sit and eat. Lance had taken off the fake dark walnut paneling and replaced it with drywall, which he textured and painted. The place now had a certain elegance and charm.

His hunger pangs sharpened as he smelled tomato sauce. Keri had made stuffed cabbage rolls for dinner, one of his favorites. He put his lunch box on the counter. But just then, a sharp thud from the back of the house shook him.

He knew that sound. It was expensive metal being thrown around. Lance looked at his wedding ring. "I tried to call you twice after five o'clock," he said. Keri came from the back of the hallway into the living room. "I had to finish an aircraft by tonight, or I would lose my job. Do you understand? I'll probably lose it anyway, just so you know."

"Why?" Keri asked, fighting back more tears.

"Because I refuse to sign off on an engine that I know will blow its combustor in the near future."

"Why is that your fault?"

"Because I'm the one that worked on it." Lance took pause. "Whatever you've got bad inside of you is tearing us apart. I'm not your stepfather. I'm your husband. I'm sorry he made your family sit in the back at our wedding. I'm sorry he made your life miserable. But I didn't. I'm trying to make it better."

"Fine. I'm crazy. You married a crazy person."

Lance shrugged. As before, there was no point in talking further.

Lance took the hot glass pan out of the oven and set it on the stove. Keri came into the kitchen. "I'll do it. You can go wash up."

"I'm already washed up."

"Let me do it," she snapped. Lance backed away.

***

It was seven a.m., and Lance had the Learjet 35 out on the ramp. The plane's engine was running. So far, it looked good. He shut it down, waited until the dull whine of the engine was low enough, opened the hatch, and stepped out.

Pete Gorman, a fellow mechanic, strolled up to Lance. He could see Lance looked tired. "You been fighting with the wife again?"

"Almost packed my bags last night. But you know what? I didn't do anything wrong. Not one blessed thing, Pete. Nothing."

"Women. You don't need to do anything wrong." Pete followed Lance back into the hangar.

"I emptied my locker."

"What? You're still not going to sign off Gold-fart's plane?"

"Goldfarb."

"Whatever. This guy is only going to get you fired. Just sign it off. It's not worth your job."

"It's not worth me losing my license and having the FAA down my throat either when it fails. And it will."

"Come on, Lance. Goldfarb is nothing more than a flying ejaculate."

"Ew, Pete. Gross. Do you always have to talk like that?"

"Like what? No, seriously. He flies his two Lears around delivering racehorse and prize bull semen to breeders."

"Well, still."

"Whatever, dude. Anyway, the guy can't stand the smell of a farm, but in most cases gets his samples in person, and up, up and away in his two Learjets."

"I guess we're in the wrong business."

"Well, if you don't sign off his jet, you'll be out of business. Come on, Lance. We're buds. Don't abandon me to a life with just the stupids around here."

"Cowboy" Jim Benchley, a former Air Force pilot, strolled up to the Learjet with his co-pilot. Benchley didn't belie his nickname, Lance thought. The maverick pilot patted the aircraft's fuselage as if it were the flank of a horse. He opened the clamshell doors and stepped in for a peek.

Lance and Pete made their way back outside to the tarmac, pushed forward by Spencer, who wiped from his mouth saliva that seemed to gather every three or four sentences. The three approached Benchley, who sat on the floor of the plane with a cowboy boot on the airstair lower step. Benchley smiled, but Spencer wasn't smiling. The two mechanics looked like a couple of teenagers on their way to the dean's office. Benchley looked at Spencer. "We have a problem?"

Benchley listened to Lance and Arland arguing. Lance still refused to sign off on the Lear.

"Look, kid," Benchley said, "I get you want to cover your butt, but Mr. Goldfarb will be here any minute. What am I going to tell him?"

"Well, can't semen be frozen, you know, in liquid nitrogen, or something?"

"That's very funny, kid. Do you know how much prize bull semen is worth? And that's just a side business. We mainly fly donated organs across the country. We save lives."

"I understand, sir, but you're riding this plane too hard."

"I was flying Thunderchiefs and Phantoms when you were still in diapers. Besides, you don't buy a Learjet to go slow."

"You're overheating the engines. You're running them too hot, too low. Wait until you are up high, at least if you're going to put the pedal to the metal."

A black limo pulled up near the Learjet. Benchley swore a couple of times and then focused on Lance. "Sign off the damned airplane so we can get back to business."

"Can't do it, sir. Sorry."

Desmond Goldfarb stepped out of the limo. He moved like a puppeteer controlled him. Every step seemed to convey impatience. His eyes were narrow.

His eyebrows were naturally angled up. Goldfarb slouched and spoke with an upturned head, tilting to whatever side the conversation took him. "We have a problem, Mr. Benchley?"

"The kid here won't sign off the airplane so we can put it back into service." Goldfarb studied Lance. "Young man, I would gather that you are a new mechanic with minimal experience, and you don't understand flight all that well. I mean, what a pilot has to go through."

Spencer tightened his jaw. "Lance is just being overly cautious, Mr. Goldfarb. The plane runs fine, but he feels that he can't sign off the plane because of a feeling he has about other parts wearing out too fast, because of the previous damage."

"And you tested everything? Nothing else was broken?" Goldfarb asked.

"I didn't get to do a couple of tests that I wanted to do," Lance stated.

"Because of time, sir. We knew you needed to be fully functional by this morning."

"Then, Arland, you can sign off the aircraft so we can take it?"

"Well, I suppose, but Lance did the work."

"Look, it's simple. Fire him. Sign off the plane. And we're on our way. Or I find another shop to care for my planes."

"Yes, sir. Lance, you're fired," Spencer said.

"And I'll see to it that no one else employs you around here," Goldfarb added.

"Just for the record, Mr. Goldfarb, I have taught thirty-four students," Lance stated.

"Students?"

"Yes, I'm a flight instructor and an ATP. I teach instrument and multi-engine instrument flying. I've built two kit planes. Obviously, I'm an A and P. I'm also a certified avionics technician. I've logged over two thousand three-hundred hours in the air." Lance looked at Spencer. "Thanks for the support, Arland." Lance walked away. "Oh," he said over his shoulder, "you'll be hearing from my lawyer."

***

It felt like a long drive home. Lance pulled into the carport. He wasn't in a hurry to go inside. He unloaded his toolboxes one by one and put them in his shed.

Keri stepped out of the side door. "Did you lose your job?"

"Yeah," he said in quiet shame.

"That's just great, Lance. What do we do now?"

"I don't know." Whatever proud moment Lance had in confronting his boss, Goldfarb and Cowboy Jim with moral integrity and aeronautical expertise was now gone. Keri slammed the door behind her.

Keri prepared lunch. She noticed Lance outside of the kitchen window talking with their neighbor, Juan Alvarez Bertrand. Bertrand was a Puerto Rican native who had lived in Miami for most of his life outside a few years in New York City. Keri found him to be a braggart, carrying on in conversations about accomplishments where she had seen little proof. His time in the Marine Corps Special Forces, fighting in the Korean War, was uninteresting to her, but Lance seemed to go for it, no doubt adding to the judo he learned from his father. Juan and his wife, Isabella, had a parental influence on him. Juan was a bit shorter than Lance but stout with a big gut. His accent was too thick for her liking, and she always felt he was overly friendly with her. She stared a bit longer at them. Lance came inside.

"I suppose you're telling Juan what a bad person I am," she said sharply.

"No! You never came up. I was telling him about what happened with my job. He said I should rent the hanger across from him and start my own business." Lance felt that trembling that rose up in him when she was this way. "Give it a rest. Please!"

"Fine." The phone rang. Keri headed for it. Lance snagged the phone off its hook. "It might be my mother," she barked.

"And if it is, I'll give you the phone straight away," Lance replied. "Hello…Rog!"

"Oh, great," Keri said, turning back toward the stove.

"What's up?" Lance said. He listened. "You want me at a police auction? Where? New Orleans."

"You're going to New Orleans now?"

Lance covered the phone. "Rog will be by in a couple of hours. Hey, it's a job. They need someone who can fly an MU-Two."

"Yeah, I know. We're still paying for those lessons too."

Lance took a quick shower, packed, and ate. Then he spent a solid hour making love to Keri. He left her in bed. He dressed and set his bags by the door. By the second honk, he was kissing her goodbye.

Chapter 19

Lakefront Airport, New Orleans
30°02′33″N, 90°01′42″W

September 1, 1982

The Lear 55 "*Longhorn*" banked to the left, turning south so that Lance could no longer see Louis Armstrong International Airport. For several hours before they left for New Orleans and the hour in the air since Lance had met with DEA, FBI, possibly CIA, and two Coast Guard officers, one of which was Roger. Lance wondered what he got himself into, but he was confident that Roger would not let anything happen to him.

The Learjet flew south and descended. They would be landing at Lakefront Airport. Lance had the opportunity to take his more advanced students there, usually in a twin-engine Piper Seneca on cross-country IFR flights from Miami to California.

The jet came over the threshold. Lance could feel his view tilt-up as the plane flared for landing. The mains touched, and his view was level again as the nose gear touched down. Gravitational forces pushing from behind demanded they continue in acceleration until the forces of flight withered away, and the aircraft settled down into a slow taxi off of the active.

The aircraft parked near the front of the *Million Air* hangar, where all of the action would take place tomorrow. Lance could see many other jets and turboprop aircraft out on the ramp. His competitors, no doubt.

A black van pulled up. Its driver shuffled the passengers into it and drove off.

Lance rose from a deep but disturbed sleep. Roger, who had slept in the bed next to his, was up, having a cup of hotel coffee. He was dressed in a medium gray suit. "Morning, Sunshine."

"What time is it?" Lance asked.

"Six-fifteen. Time to get up."

"Okay. Give me a minute." Lance looked around the room. He noticed Roger's bed was to the right of him. "It's like when we were kids when I would sleepover."

"Yeah, but this isn't my room, and we aren't kids. So come on. Be ready. These guys downstairs are going to drill you some more."

Lance nodded but was still puzzled. "Why me?"

"This thing literally fell into our laps all last minute. I came in straight from Columbia, picked you up, and back on a plane to here. You're the only one I know that can fly a Mits. It's too tricky an airplane."

"Well, it's not. You just have to remember it thinks it's a jet."

"Anyway, you can fly it, and you're here. So come on, your star is about to shine."

Lance and Roger were met in the lobby by the two federal agents who had traveled with them the night before. The black van was waiting for them outside.

The van pulled onto the airport grounds and out onto the tarmac. It stopped short of the Million Air hangar facility. DEA Agent Mike Neeley looked nervous.

"Agent Neeley, this is an FBO," Lance said.

"FBO? FBO? What's an FBO?" Neeley said nervously.

"Mike, relax," Roger said. "FBO just means Fixed Base Operations, which means this is a facility where you can buy fuel and have service done on your aircraft. Usually, they have flight instruction and a pilot's lounge. That's all. Lance just means you will have a lot of activity on or around the ramp and hangar. He's cool with it."

"Okay. FBO, Fixed Base Operations. Got it."

"One thing I have always taught my students, Agent Neeley, is that *panic-equals-death*," Lance said calmly. "Remember, I've been to a few of these auctions."

"Okay. I'm cool."

"This is about Lance now," Roger said. "We're his team, his backup, so let's focus totally on Lance."

The auction was already underway. A cheer went out from about two hundred people all gathered around. A man standing in front of a Bell 206 JetRanger helicopter was jumping up and down, his hands raised in triumph. This happened to be Lance's favorite helicopter. He wondered what the man paid for it.

The auctioneer moved his small wooden platform over to several strapped wood crates and read off item numbers. He began sequential rapid-fire pricing of the items. Many of these crates only contained parts of aircraft or aircraft engines. One crate had pieces of a helicopter electrical system, yet there were at least a dozen bidders. As items were bid upon and won, the crowd thinned. Lance followed along with the auctioneer and crowd, now noticing that he was alone. He didn't know where Roger was other than he was near—somewhere.

The morning air was warming faster than Lance would have liked. It would not be good to have his upper lip sweat much more, which could make his false mustache fall off in the midst of heavy bidding. His wig was also getting uncomfortable. He was afraid to scratch it. The wig was long, tied in a ponytail with a gold clip. The CIA had fitted him with a sharp $600 Italian suit. Sharkskin. Just like James Bond. Lance was a spy, if only for the day.

Lance followed about forty men and eight women past the glass-lined steel doors that were now sliding open. He counted about a third of the men as being Latin. "*Log Jam*, this is *Eager Beaver*, over."

"Who's Eager Beaver, and who's Log Jam?" Agent Neeley called out. "We didn't authorize these names. Come on now."

"Lance, why are you using these names?" Roger asked, chuckling.

"Because it just dawned on me that we didn't have code names."

"Code names? Screw the code names. Just do your part. Is he kidding me?"

"Lance, we don't need code names here," Roger replied.

"How can you have a covert, undercover operation and no code names? That's unspyworthy or something like that." Lance heard someone else chuckle over his earpiece.

"Okay, Eager Beaver, this is Log Jam. They're going inside, so get in there," Roger said.

It was time for Lance to earn his pay. The hangar was huge, with twenty-two thousand square feet of space. It was built in 1939 when the airport was called the "the Air Hub of the Americas."

Lance moved past a tall man, poised and polished in dress and demeanor, who nodded and smiled at him. Lance realized that it wouldn't be hard to fit in as long as he maintained the normal, nonchalant American attitude of it being okay to be in debt. He had a limit set by the Feds on what he could bid. Roger told him to have fun with it.

The hangar had seven high-end aircraft lined up in a semi-circle behind the auctioneer. He started with a Cessna 340 twin-engine pressurized aircraft to his right. A Beechcraft Queen Air, also a twin-engine piston-powered aircraft with pressurization, followed the Cessna. The stakes went higher to turbine aircraft. The item now up for bid was a Rockwell Aero Commander 690 turboprop. The twin-engine turboprop was indeed a prize.

Lance was shoved around as the crowd bumped past him for its bids to be acknowledged by the auctioneer. Lance was sweating more here, inside, than out on the ramp. The cheering for a won item was much more sedate than earlier, more of an "ahh" than anything else related to emotion. Lance moved back from the crowd. It was not his time to bid. He noticed the tall man, still in the same place, he first saw him. The man even nodded and smiled again at him when their eyes locked for a moment.

The sixth item, an older Lear jet 23 model, failed to meet the auctioneer's beginning bid, so it was passed over after several attempts.

The final aircraft was the one that Lance had secretly coveted since he first saw it: the Mitsubishi MU-2 *Solitaire*. It had no equal in its category. It was almost as fast as Cessna's entry-level Citation jet. Lance loved its stout fuselage, which reminded him of a great white shark. The high-wing aircraft could do slow takeoffs and landings and then high-speed flying. No wonder it was a favorite of drug smugglers.

Lance moved back as some of the crowd came to examine the aircraft. The auctioneer dropped his platform in front of the Mits and stepped up.

"Now, ladies and gentlemen, this is a two-year-old Mitsubishi MU-Two Solitaire, item number..." Lance listened as the man read down the list of options and capabilities of the aircraft. "Do I have a starting bid of one hundred fifty thousand dollars?"

A hand went up. "Do I have a bid of one-seventy-five?" Another hand went up. "Do I have two hundred thousand for this splendid aircraft?"

Lance could tell by the way the auctioneer's eyes moved that the next hand was raised right behind him. "Two hundred and fifty thousand dollars," a voice said from behind. It was the voice he had listened to over and over again, the voice on the tape recorder. The second most notorious drug kingpin in the world was standing three feet behind him—Enrique Rojas.

Lance raised his hand. "Three hundred thousand."

"We have three hundred thousand from the gentleman over here," the auctioneer said nearly in praise.

"Three hundred fifty thousand," Rojas countered.

Lance had been told not to go above three hundred thousand. However, he knew that Rojas, who risked coming in the first place, had to outbid him. "Four hundred thousand."

Lance could hear Agent Neely screaming over his earpiece.

"Okay, don't get carried away, Eager Beaver," Roger chuckled.

"We have four hundred thousand for this remarkable aircraft," the auctioneer called.

"Señor, leave your bid at four hundred thousand," Rojas said. Lance felt a sharp poke in his back.

"Okay," Lance said without turning around. "The plane is yours. No argument." Lance lowered his voice. "If you are listening out there in TV land." Lance waited. He remembered and applied his own rule of thumb, his motto: Panic Equals Death.

"Five hundred thousand!" Rojas shouted. There were no other bids.

Just as the auctioneer bequeathed the Mits to Rojas, Lance felt a wave of commotion from behind. "If so much as a single drop of his blood is on the end of your knife, I'll blow your head off. Comprendé?"

Lance never heard Roger sound so deadly. It unnerved him. He found it hard to turn around, but he did. Rojas held up the stiletto knife. Roger took it. Rojas was handcuffed and escorted out.

The auctioneer looked at Lance. "Well, sir, I guess you have the winning bid at four hundred thousand. Unless—do I hear four-twenty-five? Going once. Going twice. Going—"

"I withdraw my bid. This is a drug smugglers' plane."

"I assure you, sir, this aircraft is legal to sell, even if it is from a drug seizure."

"Yeah, well, obviously, they want it back."

Lance had withdrawn his bid, and the audience was beginning to leave. The auctioneer went back to work. "Do I have one hundred fifty thousand dollars, do I have one-seventy-five?"

"Two hundred thousand," a voice from behind said. Lance knew that voice as well. It was a recent voice—a voice of abusive affluence that just caused him needless suffering.

"Lance, are you coming out?" Roger asked.

Hearing Roger's voice gave Lance the impetus to act. "Rog, listen. You missed one. This guy is a spermicidal maniac."

Agent Mike Neeley's voice rang out. "It's Rico Suavé! Get him!"

It took everything for Lance to get his wide grin down to serious. "He's wearing a medium-blue suit, about six feet tall, a long head, sandy brown hair. Hurry!"

The auctioneer continued. "Okay. Two hundred thousand going once. Going twice—" The Feds surrounded Desmond Goldfarb. They cuffed him and led him out of the hangar. "What's going on here? What is this plane cursed or something?" What was left of the crowd hurried out of the hangar in unison, except the tall man in the back. He was still there. "People, please. Come on. This is your day to own the finest turboprop in the skies."

Lance came up to the beleaguered auctioneer. "I don't think today is that day, sir."

"No, it's not. What are you, the FBI, DEA, CIA?"

"No, sir, just a civilian helping them out."

"Well, it was their aircraft up for bid."

"Sir, would you take a bid of whatever amount I have on my Visa cards? It's all I have. I'm checked out to fly the MU-Two. I apologize. I don't even begin to have the kind of money to buy it, but you'll at least be rid of it."

"Then whose money were you bidding with?"

"The feds. In a pretend sort of way."

"Pretend?" The auctioneer eyed Roger approaching. "Who are you?"

"Coast Guard. And his best friend."

"Why wasn't I told about this?"

"We couldn't risk it. We just grabbed Enrique Rojas. After Pablo Escobar, he's the most dangerous man in the drug business."

"Yeah, yeah, I know the name. But why did you arrest Desmond Goldfarb?"

"You know who he is?" Lance asked.

"He won a bid on a Learjet twenty-five from us a couple of years ago. So, what did he do?"

"He got me fired yesterday."

The auctioneer grinned. He looked at the Mits, then out past the hangar doors where Goldfarb was yelling at law enforcement people. He looked back at Lance, who was taking off his mustache and pulling off his wig. "Today's your lucky day, kid. Give me what you got on plastic, and the plane is yours."

"You can't sell this plane like that," Roger said. "It has to go back on public auction."

"Look, Captain, Admiral, whoever you are. You put it up on legal public auction. I auctioned it. Or tried to. He…"

"Lance Rio," Lance said, shaking the auctioneer's hand.

"Mr. Rio, here, just gave the winning bid. And look! No one is cuffing him."

Roger grinned. "Way cool, Lance. Unofficially, of course."

"Glad you agree, Commodore." The auctioneer looked at Lance. "Let's do some paperwork, and you can fly her home. She's fueled and ready to go. I'll settle up with the feds later for my commission."

Jeffrey Ralston, having stood in the back during the operation, walked over to a Gulfstream II bizjet nearby. Everyone from Neeley to the FBI partners in the operation protested as soon as he was within range for letting the MU-2 be given away. "Let him have it. He earned it." Ralston had his intrigue. He stepped inside the aircraft.

Roger came up to the port side of the MU-2. The large one-piece door was open. Lance sat in the opening. "What a day, Rog."

"Yup. And you got a nice suit out of it too."

"That was quite a coup you pulled off today, Mr. Rio," Goldfarb said, walking up from underneath the left-wing. "Let's be realistic. You couldn't possibly afford this aircraft for longer than a month. But you could captain her for me."

"I will never sell this plane, especially to you," Lance glared.

Goldfarb frowned. "Well, if it's any consolation to you, my Lear did lose its port engine today. We put just eleven hours on it since yesterday, and boom, it's stuck in Cincinnati at the moment."

"I tried to say."

Goldfarb grimaced. "You're a bright young man. Perhaps we can still do business. I had hoped to use this for an air ambulance service within a thousand-mile radius of Miami. We could work out a leasing agreement. You'll have to use it in some sort of charter business or lose it."

"I don't think so."

"You don't have to like me, Mr. Rio. It's just business."

"Call in a week from now, Mr. Goldfarb," Roger said.

"Here." Goldfarb took out a business card. "When you are done patting yourselves on the back, sometime next week, give me a call. I'll be expecting it." Lance took his card.

"And in the meantime, you can think of a way to make it up to me," Lance said smugly.

Goldfarb shrugged. "I just did." He walked off.

"Wow, he put me straight," Lance said.

"Never mind him. You did good today, babe."

"Thanks for looking out for me, though."

"Hey, since we were kids. Come on, let's go."

Lance and Roger climbed inside the aircraft and took their seats up in the cockpit. Lance let it soak in for a moment and then spent nearly an hour going over the pilot's operating handbook with Roger. The whine of the right turbine engine being awakened with the breath of life quickly spun up. Lance watched the needle on the engine EGT temperature gauge spike up past the 770° Centigrade mark, then dropped down to its idle temperature. Lance lit the left engine a minute later. With the props biting into the air, Lance added a little power, and the MU-2 began its first taxi under its new master.

A "cleared for takeoff" came over the radio. The stout turboprop shot down the runway. The runway disappeared underneath as Lake Ponchartrain's glassy surface greeted them. With the gear up and the full-span flaps retracted, the sports car of turboprops sped home.

Roger smiled as he looked out over the horizon in the direction of the setting sun. "Red skies at night…pilot's delight."

Chapter 20

George T. Baker Aviation School, Miami

September 2, 1982

Lance taxied across the ramp that took him from Miami International Airport property to that of the school. Wes Gent was now standing in front of him, hands on his hips, shaking his head. Jesse Del Monte was flagging Lance in for parking with his hands but gyrating his hips like he was disco dancing. The two men waited until the propellers stopped rotating and then got aboard the plane.

Del Monte flopped into one of the tan leather seats. His walrus mustache flexed with content. He grabbed the phone nestled on the cabin-long drink rail and put it up to his ear. No dial tone. He replaced it in its holder.

Lance maneuvered the small gas-powered aircraft tug up to the MU-2's nose gear. He reached up under the nose gear and disengaged the upper torque link from the lower torque link on the nose gear strut so it could swivel freely for towing.

He turned the aircraft around, backing it into the shop. Gent held up his hand and gave a loud "Good." Roger put the wheel chocks around the left main gear.

The sun had dropped below the horizon. "Good timing, Lance," Del Monte said.

"I appreciate you letting me keep my plane here. Wow, my plane. I still can't believe it."

"That's okay, Lance. But our new semester starts in a few days. You'll have to park her somewhere else by then," Wes said.

"I should have her out of here by Sunday. I just have to figure out where."

"Well, let's lock up, and I'll give you guys a ride back up the road," Gent said.

"Okay, but I want a ride soon," Del Monte said. "In…what shall we call her?"

Lance smiled. "What else? Miss Solitaire!"

***

It was a beautiful Sunday morning, but Keri remained unhappy.

Three nights before, when Lance told her about the airplane, she called him stupid, a fool, and said that he needed to grow up. Was he insane? It didn't matter how much he tried to explain the logic of his move. It was pointless. He said he could always sell the aircraft if it came to that. She demanded he did. He refused, setting off another argument. They lacked for nothing. She didn't work. He had rescued her from a loveless home.

They woke up peacefully, but then it started again. Wanting to maintain the peace, he rolled over and wrapped his arms around her. "It's simple. What's it going to be, love or war?"

"What do you want to do?" she asked.

His hands weren't caressing her to make war. She hadn't told him she decided to come off the pill. Arousal pushed the thought into the back of her mind.

***

The short drive to the Gent's was pleasant enough. Lance hoped that peace could be maintained. They pulled into the curved driveway. Lance had his arm around her as they walked to the kitchen entrance. Dinner was always good at the Gents. Lance felt he was in a good place. Sybil asked Keri to help her clean up after dessert. After two large pieces of peach cobbler, Gent invited Lance to follow him out back to the shop. It was time to show him something new.

Lance noticed a couple of new posters hanging on the back cabinet doors, next to a poster of a 1950's Lockheed F-104 *Starfighter*. The words *Pan American* caught his attention on the first new poster. It was from the golden era of flying, the late nineteen-thirties, and depicted a Pan Am flying boat ascending over a palm tree and island. The other poster showed the Wright brothers' workshop and a wing rib that undoubtedly found itself part of the historic Wright Flyer.

On the far right side of the shop was a homemade wind tunnel. Lance had done most of the fabrication. The wind tunnel was made from plywood and Plexiglas and rested on a wood frame supported by four caster-wheeled metal legs. Four *Pressure Tap* holes were drilled on top along the length of the Plexiglas part of the wind tunnel at one-foot increments and marked PT1 through PT4.

Gent brought over a small airfoil, a mini-wing from the cabinet. Lance recognized the airfoil as the one he made a few days ago. It was a piece of sheet aluminum wrapped over a foam core, with two pins sticking out on each side. Gent placed it inside the wind tunnel. He worked the pivot pins through the mounting holes. The thumbscrews were left slightly loose.

Lance opened the back door. A blower unit from an old central air conditioner was attached to the front end of the plywood box. Wes rotated a black knob that brought the squirrel cage fan to life. Lance could hear the sound of air moving through the chamber. He reached around the open back end to feel the air blow on his hand. The airfoil developed a series of small vibrations. Then it fought against the faster-moving air, and then it flopped downward. "Wait. Something went wrong," Lance said.

Gent shut off the blower. "I thought you said you balanced it."

"I did. It was perfect. I don't know why it dipped down like that."

"There should be nothing wrong unless you made a mistake."

"Wes, you saw me build it."

"And you just saw what it did at a wind speed of just eight miles per hour. Here, let me check it out." Gent popped open the clear plastic lid and looked inside. "Okay, I'll set it up at an angle of five degrees. Let's see if it's you or something else."

Gent closed the lid. He turned the blower back on. "Okay. What's happening now?"

Lance saw the small wing begin to vibrate and flutter again. Gent turned up the airflow. The wing fluttered and then dropped again.

"I don't get it, Wes." This was beyond puzzling.

"I just don't think you did it right, Lance. It's simple aerodynamics. We have to start over."

Logic did not jive with what Lance was seeing. "Wes, I assure you it was perfectly balanced. For whatever reason, I don't know why this thing keeps dipping down."

"It's not your fault, Lance. It never was. It's the fault of aeronautical engineering as wrongly interpreted by Daniel Bernoulli, who wrongly interpreted this thing we call fluid, gas, and pressure."

"Wait. What?"

"What's happening here is that instead of splitting the air stream in two, with a low pressure on top and a higher pressure underneath, as taught in aero engineering, is that more correctly the air is hitting the blunt cambered surface, and…"

"Builds high pressure. It's so obvious now. It has to."

"I'm sorry I was so dramatic, but I needed you to see and reason it out for yourself. Not many do."

"I don't know what I've reasoned out exactly." Lance knelt to look at the small airfoil in the chamber.

"Turn the airfoil upside down and remount it." Lance didn't ask why. He did just so. Gent cranked up the blower. Lance watched the tiny wing shiver and shake as before, then flop up. "If Bernoulli were correct, could you fly upside down?"

Lance kept puzzling the pieces together. "Well, I'd have to fly it at a higher angle to maintain level flight when I'm upside down, which isn't Bernoulli, but —Newton! Equal and opposite reaction!"

"Exactly! It's no different from you sticking your hand out the car window and changing the pitch of your hand to make it go up or down. It's the deflection of air that gives a wing lift. Not a phantom low pressure going over the top of it."

"But, has anyone else come up with this idea?"

"Behind you." Gent gestured to the poster of the Wright brothers' workshop. Yes! The wing ribs! The top and the bottom of the wooden wonders had no camber but curved slightly down to a thin edge.

"So, the Wrights were right? From the start?"

"Yes. If they had used a cambered airfoil, the Wright Flyer would never have flown back in nineteen-o-three. The air accelerating over the wings would have pushed it into the ground as soon as it left the launching track. Let me show you." Gent had a manometer mounted on the wall. The silver-gray plastic box measured pressure. He bought it at a Boeing auction sale for twenty-five dollars years ago. He ran a thin rubber hose with a short piece of brass tubing on the end from the manometer and stuck it into the PT3 hole. "Here, hold this." Lance held the tube as Gent turned on the blower and ran it up to a wind speed of fifteen miles per hour. "What you don't want to do is mistake siphon pressure for low pressure. Now notice the reading with the tube flush with the interior wall of our wind tunnel. No change in reading. Why is that?"

"Surface friction. It's because it's reading stagnant air, the boundary layer."

"Exactly. That thin layer of air is not moving. It's static. But now notice what happens when you move the tube further into the main airflow."

Lance pushed the tube slowly inward. The scale on the manometer showed a definite reduction in air pressure. It was siphon pressure. Lance thought of his construction days with Rodney Sr. The same set of physical laws that drew the plastic film from the wall into the spray stream of the airless paint sprayer were at work here.

"You've just learned what Boeing has refused to learn even with their million-dollar wind tunnels. They should know better. You need to test the air pressure outside of the boundary layer. Let's do that." Wes went to the cabinet and brought back more flexible rubber hoses, plus a two-foot-long brass tube.

"What's that for?"

"My star pupil can't figure out an airspeed indicator?"

"Okay. I got it." Lance took the tube and the rubber hoses. He took an old airspeed indicator off the wall, flipped it around, and pushed the end of each hose into the back of the unit. He took the shorter hose that had a small brass tube in it and stuck it into PT3—flush. This would serve as a static port. The other end of the long hose was stuck on the end of the long brass tube. "What wind speed am I measuring?"

"Good question. Hold on." Gent opened up the lid and put the airfoil back right side up. He twisted the thumbscrews on the bushings tight. "I don't want it to move on this next test." He closed the lid and locked it. "Stand to the side." Lance went around to the back. He could feel the airflow go from a breeze to a blast in seconds. "You're going to measure wind speed around the airfoil."

"Okay." Lance stood to the side as much as possible so the air wouldn't be deflected off his torso and disturb the free flow of air exiting the wind tunnel. He slipped the tube in from behind but above the back end of the airfoil.

"What is the airspeed indication?" Gent shouted over the rush of air.

"It's reading about twenty miles per hour."

"Okay. Good. Now, move the tube just like you have it, but underneath. What's the airspeed reading?"

"Well, it's…" Lance waited for the needle to move to a lower setting. It did not. "It's about the same."

"According to the Bernoulli principle, the air should be moving faster over the top. Yet, you're seeing that this is not true."

"Next, you're going to tell me that there's no such thing as a venturi."

"There's not."

"Come on, Wes."

"Look, the cambered airfoil is considered to be a venturi cut in half, right? Well, where's the higher speed, lower pressure over the top of it? You're holding the tube and taking the readings, not me!"

Lance removed the brass tube and came away from the back end. Gent shut down the blower. "Well, obviously, I can't dismiss your findings. But why haven't you brought this information out?"

"Let me show you what you are up against." Gent gestured toward the wind tunnel. "Take the airfoil out of the chamber." Gent went back to the cabinet and slid open a lower drawer. Lance freed the airfoil.

The airfoil in Gent's hand was the weirdest thing Lance had ever seen. It was nearly flat in front, then curved with a heavy camber along the top and down to a thin tail.

"This is the Roof Top airfoil. It was never built, let alone tested. But I did."

It was the same as before. Lance not only watched but also had a firm hand in the systematic destruction of his religion, of canonical law that governed his life and beliefs in aeronautics. And how simple it all was. All accomplished with a sheet of plywood, clear acrylic panels, and scavenged parts.

"I'm sure you're wondering what the answer is."

"Yeah, I'm hoping here for a revelation."

Gent smiled. "Let me show you."

Gent pulled out another mini wing. It was different. The edges in front and back were sharp, and it had a shallow even curve along the top and the bottom, similar to the Wright brothers' design. "This is the *Accelerating Airfoil*." Lance had his revelation.

"So, what do we say now about Bernoulli?"

Gent shrugged. "He was wrong. His premise was wrong. He published a paper in seventeen-thirty-eight called *Hydrodynamica*. Which is Latin for?"

"Water. From hydro, and—it's water dynamics, basically."

"Correct. But we're dealing with air here, not water. Air is compressible. Water is not. In nineteen-seventy, I duplicated Bernoulli's experiment as best I could because some of what he wrote wasn't quite clear. But as you have seen, his premise of a fluid losing pressure the faster it moves is simply false. His premise of the venturi is also wrong."

"Yet planes do fly, and they've gotten more fuel-efficient," Lance remarked.

"Then compared to how an airfoil should be shaped, they have only improved on a flawed design. Their airfoils would be more efficient if they turned them backwards and flew them upside down." Gent paused. "I'm not saying that the accelerating airfoil is the be-all and end-all, but it's certainly in the right direction. If you cut your drag in half, you increase lift, and you would need less wingspan, and…"

"I get it, Wes."

Lance picked up the Roof Top airfoil and turned it sideways. "You know, if you put a fluke on it, it'd look somewhat like a sperm whale. And I would put a hole right here." Lance pointed at what would be the whale's head.

"A pressure tap?"

"No. A blowhole."

Chapter 21

Gulf of Mexico

23°37′40″N, 78°52′11″W

December 22, 1982

Being a winner didn't mean you'd won. Lance was heading home to Keri and to who knew what. He was completing a round trip to and from the Cayman Islands for a group of lawyers that he came to think little of, except for the firm's owner, Hector Cobian, a former student and friend.

The controller greeted Lance over the radio as he entered Cuban airspace and was cleared to fly through the *Maya Corridor*, as filed; one of three corridors allowed transit through, for a fee.

It wasn't long before the Cuban coastline had vanished, and Lance could relax, once clear of Castro's airspace. However, this area was where his tension was always the highest. He wondered as he looked down if this area might be the final resting place of his parents.

In minutes, the MU-2 was over the island stringed pearls that were the Florida Keys that marked their final descent into Miami.

The aircraft taxied up to the tan-colored corrugated metal hanger. The sign above the hanger doors said: *RIO DESTINATIONS Air Charter Services*. Lance parked his aircraft.

He stood by the aircraft door as three attorneys stepped out and thanked Lance for another smooth, profit-laden trip. As they walked to a waiting car, a look of disgust tightened across his face.

"Does that include me?" Hector Cobian asked as he stepped off the aircraft.

"What?" Lance said, tuning back in.

"You've become more aloof, less sociable, these past few trips."

"I've watched you destroy a man's life, Hector. And then celebrate it."

"I begged him to leave it alone."

"What did you want him to do? It wasn't your client's intellectual property. It was his! He proved it, but you twisted everything around. You did your little smear tactics. You vilified a decent man. Especially when he couldn't afford his lawyer anymore and had to go at it Pro Se. I watched you commit perjury to win. I can prove it. I can prove that the first judge, in this case, committed Abuse of Discretion. What about the doctrine of *Stare Decisis*, Hector? Huh? That judge allowed him to amend his motion. He did. The judge accepted it. Then that crooked judge went back on his word and sanctioned him. Illegally!"

"How do you know all these terms?"

Lance took the question as absurd. "You've been letting me read motions, research in your library when I'm at your office and ask your paralegals any question I've wanted. I know a lot of terms. In Latin. The language of the Inquisition."

"Yes, I forgot what a research hound you are. But, Lance, look, the law is a very complicated thing."

"No, it's your application. That's what's convoluted. Okay, yeah, you have tens of thousands of laws on the books that no one can keep track of, especially a judge. I've observed repeatedly. Law needs to be simple, straightforward, so you can understand it. I mean, how many laws do you need to say 'thou shalt not steal'?"

"Come on, Lance. It depends on the situation."

"No, Hector. No! Taking someone else's property, whether intellectual or physical—is stealing. See? Simple. You can't expect people to respect a law they can't understand, or worst, think they can get around. Which I know is where you come in." Lance's expression saddened. "Is this what they teach you at Harvard Law, Hector?"

"You're just young and idealistic."

"I'm not idealistic. I've been through the legal gauntlet before over my parent's estate. Remember? When I actually was young. And I don't want to be a part of this anymore."

"Now, wait a minute. We have several trips booked with you. You know we need the agility you provide."

"Oh, yeah, we've been able to hit three courts or law offices within a five hundred radius on a good day because of me. All those billable hours."

"Don't talk to me like that. You are well paid, and we've been throwing in bonuses. We're professionals. You should act like one."

"Really? Did you know your so-called professionals ganged up on the plaintiff outside of the courthouse and threatened him, insulted him, belittled him, and laughed in his face? All nicely planned. I was there. I saw it!"

"When was this?"

"Three trips ago. When you had court here and couldn't make it upstate."

"I'll take care of it."

"Why bother? Damage's done. You have a system so rigged, Hector—it's unreliable. It's untrustworthy. You people do more damage than any terrorists could ever hope to do. And I hate it!"

"Lance—" Hector said, searching for a thought in his frustration. "I get your strong sense of justice. If you don't like the system, change it."

"Become a politician?"

"Why not? You obviously got the moxie for it."

"That's everyone's pat answer. And I would have to become a lawyer first."

"Yeah, so?"

"Hector—a lawyer is the larval stage of a politician."

Hector pointed his finger at and then behind Lance. "Keri, you try and get through to him!"

"Oh, I will," she said, hardened and spiteful. Lance noticed she was dressed in clothes he had not seen before. Again.

"I'll talk to you later, Lance. When we've both cooled down."

"What about all of your golf clubs?"

"What?"

"Your golf clubs. After you took that man's timeshare, before his wife could take it, now that he's going through a divorce, you celebrated with a round of golf. That was the purpose of this trip."

"I'll get them later." Hector stormed off, got into the car. Lance could hear him yelling at his colleagues as the limo drove off.

Keri glared. "How can you be so stupid? We're barely making it, and you want to be self-righteous."

"What do you mean we're not making it? We've paid off the plane in the three months we've had it. We have operating funds. And we're building a saving account now."

"We're spending more than we bring in."

"How is that possible? We're making a profit."

"Sure. Blame it on me. You want to do the books? Go ahead."

"I'm not blaming you for anything."

"I can't take this anymore."

"What can't you take? What's so hard? Look, can we talk about it at home?"

"Talk all you want. I won't be there." Keri stormed off, got in her car, and drove away.

Outside of his hanger, Juan Bertrand stood watching. The drama outside put a slight grin on his face. He turned and went back inside his shop. To him, Lance was a boy, and what Keri needed was a man.

Chapter 22

CIA facility: undisclosed location

December 27, 1982

The moment Ralston entered the cell, Enrique Rojas sprang from his cot and attacked. He had been locked up since September. With two quick moves, Ralston sent Rojas crashing to the floor.

"I could leave you here, in the dark, and never give you another thought," Ralston said.

Rojas crawled back to his bunk and sat. "What is it you want of me?"

"Fidel Castro." Ralston snapped his fingers. A blue velvet jewelry box was handed to him. Rojas could see that it contained a small two-inch long electronic device.

"If I refuse?"

"I leave you here without giving you another thought."

"Where does this device go?"

Joshua Wilson, the newest member of Ralston's team, stepped forward, removed a protective cap from a round metal tube, and stabbed Rojas on the outside of his left thigh. Rojas yelled, grabbing his leg. Soon, the wound site went numb, but not his trepidation.

"What happens if I fail?"

"Failures happen. Betrayal? That's another matter. In that case, and on my order, the device will inject you with ricin. As you know, it's one of the deadliest poisons known to man, and you would be dead within a few very painful days. And there is no antidote."

The elegant ruthlessness of this CIA man told Rojas he was dealing with his equal. His only recourse was to comply.

Chapter 23

Miami

February 2, 1983

Lance woke. He had dreamt about Keri and then about the accelerating airfoil. It had not been a restful night.

Lance wandered into the living room and kitchen. He hated coffee but needed a caffeine boost. He drank a cup of Keri's leftover coffee and then enjoyed a cup of his own Earl Grey tea.

Keri was probably at her mother's. She had not said where she was going. He wished he knew where she was. Goldfarb told Lance that he might have two flights today, which would have him home by early evening.

***

Lance flew a heart transplant patient from South Carolina to Newark, New Jersey, where a heart packed in ice waited at Newark Beth Israel Medical Center. It was his longest flight to date for Goldfarb. The air ambulance helicopter had just landed, rocking the Mits. The flight nurse Dave and Paul, the paramedic, removed the gurney with the patient strapped to it and wheeled him over to the helicopter. Two flight medics stepped out, and in concert, slid the patient onto their litter and into their aircraft.

It was at least forty degrees colder in Newark than in Miami. Lance zipped up his leather flight jacket, which had belonged to his father. He had it tailored to fit.

Lance had an epiphany. He went over and spoke to the helicopter pilot, who was unsure of the request but agreed. He ran the twin turbine engines up to full power. Lance looked up at the whirling mass above him. Not so much as a breeze did he feel. It left him with no choice but to deny Bernoulli completely. His culture of belief was firmly destroyed. So be it. He was a truth seeker. Satisfied, Lance stepped away. The rotors of the A109 helicopter bit into the air, and it lifted skyward. The harsh rotor blast of chilled air stiffened him up. He hurried inside to the warmth of the pilot's lounge.

He tried to call Keri, but there was no answer. Then he called Goldfarb, who at least was happy with Lance's work. He told him so. Goldfarb said to be ready to fly again in ten minutes; a medical package awaited pickup.

***

Lance was sure he could smell chocolate inside the aircraft. They were flying over the "sweetest place on earth" for traffic to Harrisburg International Airport, right over the factory of Hershey Chocolate.

Lance taxied near a waiting van with a *Penn State Medical Center* logo on its side. A technician slid back the side of the van and jumped out with a mid-sized cooler.

The technician handed Paul the paramedic the cooler and then gave him a bag. Dave, the flight nurse, grabbed the bag and looked inside. "Hey, chocolate!"

"Compliments of Mr. Goldfarb and our medical center," the technician said. "You guys need to hurry. Have a safe flight."

Lance popped two more Hershey kisses into his mouth. He advanced the throttles and sped down the runway.

***

It was just past six o'clock on a still mild evening when they returned to Miami. Lance guided Miss Solitaire back into the hangar and left the aircraft tug connected to the nose gear. Roger drove up and joined him.

"Saw you come in. Long day?"

"Very long day, but I'm glad to see you. We had a nice perk today. Chocolate. About five pounds of it." Lance reached into his side pocket and pulled out a few Hershey kisses.

"Cool." Roger untwisted the tops and popped the candies into his mouth. He helped close the big hangar doors.

***

Lance parked in his carport. Keri's car was gone. He decided to keep his truck close to the exit end of the carport. He got out and went to the front door.

He turned on the lights. The living room and kitchen seemed normal, as did their bedroom. He slid a closet door back. Her side was empty. He checked the dresser. Her drawers were empty. He hurried into the kitchen. He grabbed the phone off of the wall and dialed.

"Audrey, it's Lance. May I talk to Keri?"

"What makes you think she's here, or she even wants to talk to you?"

"Where else would she go? Come on. There's no reason for this."

"Yeah, hold on."

"Lance," Keri said sternly.

"Are you coming home?"

"Why? You don't want me."

"Stop this. You know that isn't true."

"You don't care about me."

"You're what I live for. Stop it."

"No. You live for that plane. That's all you care about."

"The plane is our livelihood. It's okay to enjoy your livelihood. We're in a hole because you keep spending. You keep charging, buying clothes, buying gifts for your family, which they don't appreciate. You can't make up for a bad childhood that way."

She hung up.

***

Lance couldn't sleep any longer. It was pointless. It was after three in the morning. In his grogginess, he made his way into the bathroom, hoping a shower might wake him up.

By four a.m., he had pulled up outside his hangar. He worked both hangar doors open and guided the tug to bring the stout aircraft from its nest. He unhitched the tug and ran it back up to the hangar. He parked his truck in the hangar and slid the two doors closed.

Fortunately, he only had a medium-short flight this morning to Grand Cayman. Lance began his preflight check, turning the props, checking gear oil levels, and control surfaces. He checked the rudder when a voice hit him from behind.

"Señor, I wish to hire you for a quick flight." It was the stiletto laden voice of Enrique Rojas. He could almost feel its poke in his back with each word.

"I'm sorry, but I have a six-thirty flight this morning," Lance said without turning around. He reasoned that Rojas had escaped and somehow found out that he had the Mits. Miss Solitaire was a mistress caught between two men, each seeking to possess her.

"I will pay you five thousand dollars cash to take me to the Bahamas. You will not pass up that kind of money."

"I'm sorry. I can't." Lance walked back to the hangar. Rojas followed.

"You will take me now."

"And what if I tell you I don't have enough fuel to make it that far and the fuel trucks don't run until six, about an hour from now?"

"Then I will believe you. Just as I tell you that I have a gun, and you will believe me." Rojas paused. "I trust that you have not let so much as a scratch come upon my aircraft since you got her. So I will trust now that you would not let her end up in the ocean. Now, close up, and let's go. Vámonos!"

Rojas watched Lance go through the start procedure. "What are you, eighteen, nineteen years old?"

"I'm twenty-four. Twenty-five in August. Or would've been."

Lance pulled around to the end of the runway and lined up. "I don't have my passport."

"I do not believe you."

“It was worth a try,” Lance shrugged.

Rojas laughed. “Just be as smart as you are clever.”

Lance upped the throttles, and the plane was off.

***

Lance followed a Learjet in landing on Runway 14 at Nassau International Airport. He taxied to the customs department. Now his fatigue was combined with stress. The authorities must be coming around the aircraft, Lance thought. The door opened. The answer was no.

“Ah, Miguel!” Rojas shouted as he wiggled out of the co-pilot’s seat and nearly fell into the cabin, reaching for his brother. They embraced. “This is Lance Rio, Miguel. Our pilot. Come, Lance, you can freshen up.”

In the restroom, Lance considered his alternatives. They made sure he didn’t have anything to write with and had even stripped him of his wallet, keys, and loose change.

Lance came back to the MU-2, escorted by the Rojas brothers. “Now, I want you to plot a course for Cartagena. It will be just you and I,” Enrique Rojas said.

The engines were running, and the taxi lights were on. Lance watched the dials and instruments. He would play his ace card soon. The threat of danger kept his head clear.

They took off. Rojas was satisfied with him so far. Lance didn’t look at him as he lowered the cabin air pressure slightly. “I’m still prepared to crash this plane. I’d rather go that way than by one of your Colombian neckties.”

Rojas laughed. “You watch too many movies. The drug business is like any other. We would not be in business if there was not a demand.”

“That’s just marketing.”

“Are you going to tell me you’ve never gotten high?”

“I have never so much as taken a hit off a joint.”

“Never? Really?”

“Never. Probably the one thing I’ve never been stupid enough to do.”

“I am impressed, mi amigo. But you are bad for business.”

The MU-2 continued up, passing twenty thousand feet. Rojas was now more sedate. Lance had to make sure he didn’t succumb to his own ploy. The effects of hypoxia were settling in on him as well. His vision was narrowing. The cabin looked half as wide. But he could still think. He turned the transponder to 7500, the *hijacking* frequency, and hit the *ident* button. He knew he could handle the thinner air better than Rojas. “So, Enrique, what do you plan to do when we get you home?”

“I. I am…I see the…children…” Lance noticed the bluing of Rojas’ lips. He then noticed his fingers were developing the same blue-gray coloring of oxygen starvation. Lance ignored the radio call from Miami Center, requesting an answer.

"What's your favorite food? Do you know what two plus two is?"

"I..." Rojas looked at Lance, who smiled and adjusted a dial or two. Lance's fingers were turning blue. He fought the temptation to raise the cabin pressure. Rojas slumped back. Lance instantly donned the oxygen mask that hung ready on his left side. He took deep breaths. A minute passed. The view of the instrument panel widened. Colors were less faded, becoming more vibrant. His head was clearing. He looked over at Rojas, who was becoming a deeper shade of blue. Lance upped the cabin air pressure slightly. He took two more full breaths and then reached over and undid Rojas' seat harness and re-strapped it over his arms snugly. Lance looked out ahead. He could see the Cuban coastline coming up. Lance clicked the microphone button on the control wheel. "Miami Center..."

Rojas was only slightly blue now. By the time they were over Florida, he was merely pale. The landscape was getting its morning dusting of orange glow as the sun rose from over the Atlantic horizon. Lance had a straight in for Opa-locka Airport. He slowed, dropping the landing gear right after the flaps came down, cleared for Runway 9 Right.

The slight jolt on landing aroused Rojas from his oxygen-deprived sleep. He seemed to sense trouble and struggled instinctively against his bindings. Lance headed for the Coast Guard station hangar.

Aircrew and aircraft technicians scattered as Lance rolled inside the hangar. He could see the lieutenant who had been tasked with the capture of Rojas screaming at him. Roger came out instinctively set to fight at the commotion. His eyes widened in disbelief.

Lance grimaced at Roger as the engines lost their muscle to paddle the air. He fell back into his seat. He was safe.

Chapter 24

Langley, Virginia

February 3, 1983

Ralston had planned to be at CIA headquarters for only part of the day to clear up some paperwork once it was confirmed that Enrique Rojas was back in Colombia.

He turned on the morning news. But, just as *Good Morning America* had begun, ABC SPECIAL REPORT flashed upon the screen. GMA host Charlie Gibson sat poised.

"What now?" Ralston thought, sipping his first cup of coffee.

"Colombian drug lord Enrique Rojas was captured after a jailbreak in Florida early this morning…" Gibson intoned.

Ralston burnt his lip. He felt life evaporate out of his body. He looked at the television set with a sense of atheism to what he was hearing. He moaned: "There is no God."

Chapter 25

Marathon, Florida Keys
24°43′34″N, 81°03′05″W

February 5, 1983

Lance taxied off the runway. He hadn't been to Marathon Airport in a long time. The island itself wasn't called Marathon, but the unincorporated town sat on seven different islands or keys. The airport was on Vaca Key, the largest of the seven islands. Lance called it *Cow Island*, or *Moo Island*, in jest, as *Vaca* meant cow. Roger sat in the co-pilot's seat beside him.

Lance parked close to a Gulfstream II jet, which he recognized as the one that had belonged to the Feds when they nailed Rojas nearly six months earlier. Just as Lance brought his plane to a stop, a man in a dark suit approached the aircraft's nose and motioned him to follow. Lance did so, swinging around the front of the business jet where the man was standing by the left-wing. He signaled Lance to stop. Lance shut down the engines.

Roger climbed out of the co-pilot's seat. "Let's go meet some new people." The tall man that Lance remembered in the back of the hangar during the auction stepped down to the tarmac. It made Lance a bit nervous meeting these people again. He felt unmistakably ambivalent about this meeting but trusted Roger.

"Lance, this is CIA operations chief, Jeffrey Ralston," Roger introduced. "And Mr. Ralston, this is my friend, Lance Rio."

Lance and Ralston shook hands. "How do you do, Mr. Ralston?"

"I must say, Lance, it is a pleasure to finally meet you. I want you to come to work for me."

Lance was taken aback. "You want me to be a CIA agent?"

Ralston smiled at his innocence. "I will teach you. You will learn."

Ralston stepped inside of the MU-2, taking a seat. Lance sat in a rear-facing seat. "What I am looking to do, Lance is hire you as a contract pilot for us."

"You mean exclusively?"

Ralston nodded. "Yes. I would want you exclusively for us."

"I don't know, Mr. Ralston."

"I know you have debts to pay off, and incidentally, you have my sympathy regarding your divorce. We can help with all of that."

"I still have a student to finish up within the next few weeks."

"Your thirty-seventh student, I believe. That's quite an accomplishment, and that's fine. I don't want to confine you, Lance. I want to expand you."

Ralston let his words sink in. CIA case officers were salesmen, and Ralston knew he was getting near to the close. "I will pay you five thousand dollars a month, outside of your operating costs. To sweeten the pot a little more, I will liquidate all of your loans."

"For how long?"

"For as long as you wish."

"What will I be doing? Who will I be doing it with? I need to understand that. I don't want to be running drugs or transporting drug lords. I won't do that."

"Do you question your clients now about what they do?"

"If I knew they were bad people, I wouldn't take them across town. And I certainly don't want to kill anyone."

Ralston shrugged. "Most of us don't even carry firearms. I just want you to fly for us and keep an eye out for anything you might observe. That's all."

"I have one condition. I want Roger to work with me."

"The Coast Guard might not go along with that, so don't count on it. But I'll see what I can do."

"When would you want me to start?"

"Now," Ralston said, motioning someone. Enrique Rojas stood at the door of the aircraft. He smiled and winked at Lance. "Take Mr. Rojas back to Cartagena, stay overnight, and come home tomorrow. That's all you need do. Someone will be there when you arrive. Don't worry. And Roger is coming with you on this flight."

"No hard feelings, amigo," Rojas said.

Ralston moved to the door of the plane. "He has his orders, correctly understood this time, Lance. Just like you."

***

Hector Cobian and Lance walked up the steps of the Miami-Dade courthouse. Lance wore the same suit that the government had given him. The same government that had him up for the last twenty-one hours with various flying duties. He still could not believe that Keri had filed for divorce. He had been numb since the process server dropped the envelope into his hands several weeks ago. He wanted to object but found it somehow pointless.

Hector and Lance entered the lobby. They turned a corner that entered a long corridor. There was Keri, her lawyer, her mother, and the man he treated like a father, his neighbor Juan Bertrand. Lance stiffened.

"Never mind," Cobian said. "Come on. Let's go in." Hector took Lance by the arm and led him inside the courtroom.

The courtroom was filled with men, women, and their attorneys. A few children were present. "This is routine," Cobian told Lance. "And don't forget, I'm here for you."

All were commanded to rise. The judge entered the courtroom. The courtroom was quiet now, with only the voice of the judge addressing the players. The judge was a woman in her fifties.

Case after case went through the clerk's hands until they finally called Lance and Keri's names.

The judge waited for all to be seated. "It is very sad to see a young couple fail to make the sacred trust of marriage work."

"Your honor, I didn't want this. I swear it," Lance voiced.

"Mr. Cobian, please instruct your client not to speak," the judge ordered.

"Yes, your honor," Cobian said, giving Lance a stern look. The judge ordered counseling and then a review in six months. They were dismissed.

Lance followed Cobian outside the courthouse. Juan Bertrand approached Lance. "Let me ask you something…"

"Lance, come on. Right now," Cobian said. Lance obeyed his attorney, following him down the steps. Lance looked back at Juan and Keri. Juan looked smug while Keri looked guilty.

Lance arrived home and pulled his car around to the far side of the house as he usually did. He saw Isabella Bertrand outside watering her plants. He moved to the steps but stopped and went across the street.

"Are you all right, Lance?" she asked.

"I don't understand, Isabella. Why was Juan at the courthouse with Keri?"

"He what? I don't know. That is, I didn't know he was."

He left her to finish her watering, but as he stepped up onto his deck, she flew into the house and then back out with her car keys in hand.

It had not been an hour since Lance got home. He showered and ate some toast. He was on the phone with Sybil Gent when a pounding on the door jarred him. He could see through the window that it was Bertrand. Lance answered the door. Juan looked at him. "Step outside." Lance did. "Look, if you think you're gonna cause problems in my marriage—I kill you!" Lance heard that with absolute clarity.

"I only asked her why you were at my divorce hearing. That's all."

"It's not her business. Your wife needed help, and I was there to support her."

"I don't understand. What help? She has no reason to leave me. I haven't done anything wrong."

"I don't care about that. You have twenty-four hours to clear this up."

"Clear, what up?"

"You want to play the man's game? I play for keeps." The thick fingers wrapped around each arm and pushed Lance up against the wall. Then Juan's left hand wrapped around his throat, while the right hand drew back into a fist. Lance's eyes were bulging. Everything in front of Lance blackened. "Come on, show me what you know."

"It's not my way."

Juan dropped his grip on Lance and stepped away in disappointment. "Remember, twenty-four hours." Bertrand walked away.

"I treated you like a father!" Lance yelled at him.

Juan Bertrand turned and pointed at Lance. "And I treated you like a son."

This was not how a father treated a son. But fear had done its job.

Chapter 26

The Caribbean

19°36′56″N, 78°20′56″W

February 17, 1983

In the back of the plane, two men of dubious quality sat. One of them was on the phone for some time. Were they CIA? Latino drug lords? They spoke with Latin accents and wore expensive suits. Lance's thoughts were not at his twenty-nine thousand foot altitude but on Juan Bertrand. His hangar was one hundred feet from Juan's, about the same distance as his home. He contemplated moving. Maybe back down to the Keys. Maybe Marathon.

"Excuse me, pilot. We have to land at Grand Cayman," one of the men said. Lance moved his right ear cup off so he could hear him better. "We have to make an adjustment and land at George Town. And we must stay there."

"Sir, I have to be, absolutely have to be back in Miami today, without fail."

"Un momento," said the man on the phone. He stood up as far as he could and spun backwards into the right side rear-facing seat. He leaned to his right at Lance. "Let me be clear. You do as I say. This comes from my people."

"I understand, sir, but I have to be home tonight. I have to be in court tomorrow. I simply cannot miss."

"Okay. I understand." The man grabbed Lance by his hair and yanked him over as far as he could, knocking off his headset. The man grabbed the left shoulder harness and pulled it across Lance's throat. Lance felt neck muscles pull. "Grand Cayman. Now! What we are doing is bigger than anything you have going. Comprendé?"

Lance wanted to crash the plane. Instead, he struggled to reach the cabin pressure knob. The man saw that Lance was turning purple, his eyes bulging and gasping to breathe. He released his grip. Fear had done its job.

Lance rubbed his neck, wiped his eyes, and tried to calm his nerves. This man also played for keeps. He took deep breaths in the thinning atmosphere. He donned his mask. Pure oxygen refreshed and calmed. He heard his attacker hang up the phone and then talk to his friend. Soon there was no sound in the cabin. Being mugged in his own aircraft was the final straw. He looked back into the cabin where both men were turning blue. Good. He was now again captain, not captive.

Lance set up for a very steep descent of six thousand feet per minute. He thought of Desmond Goldfarb and Hershey chocolates and of the kinder people he had enjoyed. All he had seen and felt in this world was the brutality of men.

Ralston would have to understand he wasn't the ruthless type and didn't belong. He would repay the CIA the balance of their investment.

Lance dropped the landing gear. He saw three greens lights and knew the gear was down and locked.

The aircraft slowed. He was cleared to land on Runway 26 at the Owen Roberts International Airport in Grand Cayman. He made a left base turn for the runway and lined up.

The aircraft was down, and Lance had the prop reverse kicked in to make the second exit off the runway. He taxied to the parking ramp, where two waiting police cars sat. He shut down the engines. The police officers removed the two men before the props had stopped spinning. At least he had the satisfaction of watching those men drool on their pricey Italian suits.

***

Lance had hoped that Keri and her attorney would be intimidated by such posh and executive-level surroundings of Cobian's law offices. She wasn't. Lance hid for most of the day after getting back and locking up the MU-2 in the hangar. He had changed the locks and the codes on the alarm system. He just couldn't deal with any more bad people. It was tough enough to take Keri's glare.

"Now, there is the matter of the aircraft. A Mitsubishi MU-Two turboprop, I believe," her attorney said, looking over his file. Hector Cobian could see Lance tighten up. Keri's attorney more or less skimmed over their assets, which didn't amount to much. The prize was the plane. She berated him so many times for buying it. Now, she was looking to cash in on it.

"What about my plane?" Lance said defensively.

"Lance, please," Cobian said.

"Well, actually, it's both your plane, Mr. Rio. Mrs. Rio is part owner and entitled to half of its earnings or half of its value. I had the aircraft appraised for roughly half a million dollars."

"You're not getting my plane!"

"Lance, ease off," Cobian admonished.

"That's all you care about is that stupid plane!" Keri shouted.

"No! But, it has never failed me. And has always been faithful to me."

Cobian reasoned that Lance's getting a loan could be tricky. However, he was more concerned with getting Keri out of his life, no matter how painful.

"I think it would be fair that we have some time to come up with options with respects to the aircraft. It is, after all, Mr. Rio's current means of making a living," Cobian said.

"Fine. We'll expect some word from you by next week."

Both attorneys stood.

"That's it?" Keri pounded. "What about my money? What's owed me?" Keri rose from her seat. "And we'll have to discuss child support too."

"Why?" her attorney asked.

"Because I'm pregnant."

"Why wasn't this disclosed before?" Cobian shouted.

"This is the first I'm hearing of it," Keri's attorney said. "Are you saying Lance is the father?"

"Who else?"

Her attorney dropped his head. "I'll have to confer with my client and get back to you. Let's go, Keri." He felt sorry for Lance.

"We agreed on five years before having children. You agreed to this!" Lance yelled.

"Well, I thought it would bring us closer. Guess I was wrong."

"That wasn't your call to make alone!"

"Come on, Keri," her attorney said. He stood. "Let's go."

***

Lance drove to his home, stopping just inside of the carport as usual. As he got out of the truck, he saw Juan Bertrand standing by the tailgate. Lance looked for something to defend himself with, being trapped between his truck door and the side of the house.

Juan Bertrand held up his hands and shook his head. "No violence. No violence. I just want to talk. That's all."

Lance didn't move. He had just come to realize that he was in a semi-fighting stance. Juan backed up clear of the truck. "I just want to talk with you."
Lance came out of the shadows of the carport. "About what?"

"I'm sorry I get so angry at you."

"I'm learning there are a lot of bad people in the world. I'm just not very good at avoiding them."

"Look, you have to take responsibility and be a man," Bertrand insisted.

Lance had no idea what that meant. "Look, I will stay out of your way. It's that simple."

Chapter 27

Langley, Virginia

February 21, 1983

It was a tense Monday morning for Jeffrey Ralston. He still couldn't find his missing link, his pilot: Lance Rio. He knew the plane was locked up inside of his hangar, but Lance had gone off the grid over the weekend.

Ralston's team sat around his desk, twiddling thumbs, while the rest of the CIA staff continued in its beehive of activity throughout the offices and corridors that surrounded his. Ralston was under pressure from the top to work on Soviet countermeasures in the Middle East, mostly in Israel. His German connections were able to ease some of the pressure, but the KGB was relentless. Still, he had his operation in the Caribbean and the best shot of nailing Fidel Castro as any number of black ops missions had presented themselves in years. It would be the highlight of Ralston's career to kill Fidel Castro.

Joshua Wilson, his right hand, sat directly in front of Ralston's desk. To Joshua's right was David Nance, the newest member of Ralston's team. To Joshua's left was Mike Castro. Mike was a handsome young man of thirty-two. His semi-dark Latin features often worked to Ralston's advantage, as when Mike had disguised himself as a Saudi businessman a year earlier. The success of that operation gave Mike his first big promotion since joining the Agency five years earlier, but like most of the CIA's successes, it was seldom discussed.

Ralston's phone buzzed. He picked it up and listened. "Where are you, Lance? You've caused us some huge delays." Ralston leaned back in his chair. "All right, Lance. I'm listening." Ralston frowned. "You're quitting? I hardly think so. There is no quitting now. I don't need you to reimburse me, plus interest. All right, all right, calm down."

Ralston could sense that the young man's heart was racing. He could hear it in his voice. He was scared, and remediation was necessary. "I don't want you to feel you're alone. Look, I am sending someone down to you today. He's on his way. His name is David. You'll like him." Ralston covered the phone and looked at David Nance. "David, how soon can you get packed and on a plane?" Ralston turned his attention back to Lance. "Lance, give me your contact information and hold tight. We're on our way." Another light lit up on Ralston's phone. "Lance, I need you to hold on. It's my other line. Relax and keep your head. Everything will be fine. I promise." Ralston looked at Joshua. "Our assets mistreated my pilot."

"I'm on it," Joshua replied.

Ralston pushed the first button at the bottom of his phone and continued writing a second note. “Yes.” He tore the small sheet of paper off his notepad and handed it to David. “Put Lieutenant Ensor on the phone and tell Captain Sanders I’ll be with him in a moment.” This was the closest he wanted these two ever to come to meeting again.

Chapter 28

Miami

February 24, 1983

Lance and David Nance hit it off right away. David had eased Lance's troubled mind somewhat. However, upon coming down and meeting Lance, David was troubled by the ligature marks on Lance's neck.

David drove up to Lance's hangar. Lance had gotten used to David ferrying him around during the past few days, and he didn't want to let go of that feeling of security.

"I know it's not the CIA's responsibility, but it doesn't look like I can get a loan. Keri doesn't believe me. So, she won't settle," Lance said.

"Have you told Jeffrey about this?" David asked.

"No. He doesn't want me whining about my personal life. Just my mission readiness."

"You're wrong," David scolded. "You should have told us about this. We are depending on you. Look, just focus on the mission, and I'll speak with Jeffrey about it immediately."

David's portable phone rang. It was Ralston. David related the incidences and then listened. "The mission is a go, Lance," he said when he hung up. "You need to be in Panama City by seven tonight, their time." David looked at his watch. "Which gives you two hours. I have to leave, but your friend Roger Drake is there..."

"Roger's there? He's going with me?" Lance's eyes lit up.

"I thought that would bring a smile to your face. He's been there for the last three months. Okay, so you need to do your pilot thing and plan a flight to Omar Torrijos International Airport…"

"Formerly Tocumen International Airport."

"Good. You know the place. You will pick up Roger there and a Navy man. He will identify himself as Captain Jack. Refuel, then fly directly to Cayo Largo, Cuba. Stay overnight and be ready to depart by nine a.m. with Roger and Captain Jack to Cancun, refuel, and then straight to Galveston, Texas, where I'll meet you."

"Why not fly back over Cuba? It's shorter."

"No! Do just as I am telling you. No deviation under any circumstances."

"Yes, sir. I understand." Lance still didn't know what the nature of the mission was, but he was beginning to suspect that it might be an assassination. He said nothing. Lance opened the car door and shook David's hand.

David looked poignantly at Lance. "See you in Galveston this time tomorrow."

Lance gave a wave as David drove off. He went into the office. He felt good inside for the moment and was happy he would be seeing Roger in about five hours, but now, he needed to get his mind in gear. It was time to *plan his flight*—and *fly his plan*.

Lance wheeled the Mits out of the hangar. He would be airborne in fifteen minutes. A van pulled around the left-wing and stopped. Juan Bertrand strutted around the front. Keri's window lowered. Her smug look told him she had found her sugar daddy. "Where are you going with that airplane?" Bertrand asked.

"Excuse me?" Lance couldn't believe his audacity. "I have a trip to fly, and it's not your business."

"You can't ignore your wife's right to her share of the assets."

"Juan, this is not your business."

"She asked me to help her. I'm only trying to look out for her."

"Yeah, I can see. Whatever. I have to go."

"You're not going anywhere with this plane."

"You can't stop me from using my property."

"You are going to do right by Keri. That's final," Bertrand said, moving in closer to Lance. Lance backed away.

"This is illegal. You can't stop me from flying my plane. I'll call the police."

"You go over and talk to your wife and get it settled. Right now."

Keri turned her head and looked down her nose at Lance. Her lips barely parted. "And you will respect me."

"I better not hear of you disrespecting her anymore."

"When did I disrespect her in the first place?"

"Because of you, I'm going through divorce now. I sleep on my couch in my office. I've had it."

"I had nothing to do with it."

"You a liar," Bertrand said.

"What's wrong with you people?"

"This is my plane as much as it is yours," Keri said. "So is this business and the hangar. Everything is as much mine as it is yours. And I say I want the plane to stay here."

"And it's gonna," Bertrand added. "I don't care about me, but she deserves you to be a man and do the right thing."

"I have to go," Lance insisted. Bertrand stepped in front of Lance. He jumped back. "I'm calling the police. This is harassment."

"You think I care if I go to jail?" Bertrand said as he pulled out a holster with a small semi-automatic pistol inside. "Think I won't blow you away? I told you, I play for keeps."

"Then I'm going to put the plane away," Lance insisted.

"Leave it. I'll put it away," Juan said.

"It's not your plane! It's mine!"

"It's hers too!" Bertrand shoved Lance. "And if you call the police, don't let me find you."

Fear had done its job again. Lance ran off.

Chapter 29

Omar Torrijos International Airport, Panama
9°04′17″N, 79°23′01″W

February 24, 1983

A black sedan drove past the gate and onto the tarmac near the area where general aviation aircraft, private and corporate, usually settled for the night. Neither Lance nor an MU-2 was among them. Roger got out of the car, puzzled and in need of answers. He removed a bag from the car and shut the door. The car drove off. The sun was setting.

Another car drove through the gate. Its headlights were on and caught Roger in their beam. Roger checked to make sure that his gun was just inside his windbreaker. He clicked the safety off. The car came close and stopped. The Navy man he was set to meet stepped out and came toward Roger.

"Ensign Drake?"

"Captain…?"

"Jack," Lieutenant Scott Ensor said, extending his hand.

"Call me, Roger."

"Call me, Scotty."

Both men stood the same height, were built muscle hard and lean. Ensor went around to the rear of the car and opened the trunk lid. He removed three bags, one a little bulkier than the other two.

"Where's our ride?"

"Should have been here by now," Roger said. Ensor grabbed two of his bags and moved them over toward the small terminal to the pilot's lounge. Roger grabbed the other. It had some weight to it.

Roger put the bag down. He studied the bag for a second. "LAR Five rebreather?"

"Yeah."

"SEAL?"

"From what I hear, you should've been a SEAL."

"I'm good where I'm at. Should make lieutenant in the next couple of years."

They waited for two hours. Roger was worried not about the mission but Lance. His thoughts raced. Where was Lance?

Chapter 30

Cayo Largo, Cuba
21°38′00″N, 81°28′00″W

February 25, 1983

Captain Roman Sanders, a Marine Corps reservist and now in his fourth year with the Agency, sat in a folding chair that rocked gently in the light breeze. He watched a few tourists walk by on the dock above the fishing boat he chartered exclusively for the last several days. Two days ago, he even had a fishing party go out for the day with some nice catches. His presence looked nothing out of the ordinary. It was as peaceful and scented a place as the Caribbean offered. It had a calming effect upon him that he had not felt for some time. It felt like home.

As part of the S.O.G., the Special Operations Group, the CIA's paramilitary wing, he staked out the airport. He was looking for Russian aircraft but saw an old DC-3 instead with a faded Cubana Airlines logo land and taxi. The vintage aircraft turned out to be the Cuban equivalent of Air Force One.

He spotted Castro, with cigar in hand, step down from the angled aircraft. His bodyguards exited the plane and created a loose circle around him. He was here to scuba dive.

Sanders had taken his boat out about three hours earlier, following Castro's dive boat moored four berths down. A quick look at his watch told him that Castro's dive party should be returning soon. Sanders took the small transistor radio in his hand. Within it was a transmitter that would set off explosives put in place by a Navy SEAL. Sanders got the privilege of detonating it.

Sanders heard a twin-diesel-powered boat pull into the harbor. He could hear the engines rev and water churn, which meant it was turning and backing up. Sanders smiled. It had been over twenty years since the death of his father. He was just minutes away from sweet revenge and justice.

The boat backed into place, with a young crewman jumping off onto the pier to secure a rope. Castro, with his entourage, laughing and puffing on cigars, stepped off the boat. Sanders pressed the hidden transmitter button on his radio. Nothing happened. Something was wrong. Sanders sat up. He pressed the button again. Nothing, again. The mission was scrubbed.

Sanders stewed for several minutes as Castro, and his party walked past him. Castro gave Sanders a wave with his cigar and a hearty grin when he strolled by. The Cuban cat with nine hundred lives had won again.

Chapter 31

Miami

February 26, 1983

The black van drove around the corner of Lance's hangar. The hangar was closed and locked. The van continued and turned left around the next row of hangers where Bertrand Aviation Services was located. Bertrand was closing his hangar door. Josh Wilson spotted what looked like Lance's MU-2 inside his shop. Why would it be there? They drove on.

It was near eight p.m. Lance wandered aimlessly around the airport, much of it in a daze. Everything that he owned and loved had been taken from him. He felt that he had no dignity or self-respect left. Since Juan had taken his plane and his wife, he had nowhere to go. And he didn't know how to face Jeffrey Ralston, which terrified him. He couldn't remember exactly how his night went, other than his wandering. He thought he had slept up against a building somewhere but wasn't sure. He didn't even know if he had left the airport grounds. He hadn't eaten since the morning before. He continued to walk along the road. As he came closer to a hangar, he recognized it as his. He could hide out there. He had some food in the small refrigerator. There was a bathroom with a shower, and he could sleep on the small sofa in the office. Tomorrow, with a clearer mind, he could figure out a course of action.

Lance heard a vehicle approaching. It sounded like Juan's van. Lance ran. Just another one hundred feet to go. The black van's large side door slid back. Joshua Wilson jumped out and slugged Lance in the face. Lance dropped. A black hood was thrown over his head as he was dragged into the van, where a hypodermic needle awaited him.

***

Lance didn't know where he was, other than that it was a high-rise office building, where he sat alone on a stiff leather sofa. Glancing out the window, he recognized the Miami skyline. He didn't know what time it was, only that it was dark. The room was dimly lit, but he could see four silhouetted figures standing in an arc around him. He kept his hands clasped between his knees and look at the dark cherry wood coffee table in front of him.

"Well, well. Our wayward aviator," Ralston said as he, Roger, and Ensor entered. "Do you have any idea of what damage you've caused? Do you? Do you understand the gravity of the situation you—and I, for that matter, are in? Of course, you don't. Nearly ten million people will remain in captivity, thanks to you." Lance kept looking at the coffee table in silence. Ralston was seething, and he wanted answers. "Well, what do you have to say for yourself?" Lance continued to be silent. "Answer me!"

"I…I took my plane out and was good to go, but they wouldn't let me." Lance looked up. "I don't know how to fight these people," he said, trembling. And then his anger flared, "I don't know how to fight any of you!"

"Fight who, Lance? What are you talking about?"

Roger's eyes widened. He tensed when he saw the large bruise on the side of Lance's bloodied face. "Who did this to him?"

"He's damn lucky that's all I did to him," Joshua Wilson said.

Roger moved forward. Ensor caught him by the arm. "Cooler heads prevail," he said in a whisper. Roger stood down.

Wilson moved around to the front of the coffee table. "Where were you, Lance? Huh? Speak up, boy! Do I need to slap you around some more?"

Ralston realized he needed to observe. He channeled his anger to one side as things didn't add up to Lance's nature. He considered for the first time that outside forces might be at work. Regardless, there would be hell to pay.

Wilson shook his finger. "Tell us where you were!" Wilson bumped into the coffee table, shoving it into Lance's legs. It triggered something in Lance. Energy exploded through his legs, and he kicked the table, bashing it into Wilson's shin, knocking his legs out from under him. Wilson dropped on top of the table as Lance went airborne, grabbing the coffee table, pulling it out from under Wilson, and bringing it down on top of him. He then swung it wildly at the awestruck silhouettes. Two figures came at Lance. Lance hit one of them, chasing the other back into the shadows.

"I didn't do anything wrong! Do you hear me? I didn't do anything wrong!" Then he crashed the table on the floor, where he cracked a leg and then, with a growl, flung the table at the large window, breaking off a leg. The window partially shattered. "I tried to come, I did, but I was scared, okay? I was scared. I'm a coward and not cut out for this work. I told you that. I can't deal with bad people. Why can't I just go home?"

"No, Lance. You are not a coward. But you do have a fear of man that will have to be neutralized. And I will help you," Ralston said calmly. He stepped forward to the brighter spot in the room. There was a settling element to his voice, a compassionate tone. Lance still held the broken table leg. "I want you to tell me what happened. I am not angry with you."

"I just wish Roger was here. If Roger were here, everything would be okay. I just need Roger."

"All right, Lance." Ralston waved his hand.

"I'm here, Lance. Rog is here."

"Roger?" Lance scanned all of the silhouettes in front of him. Roger stepped forward. It tore him up inside to see Lance in such a beaten condition and on the edge of going psychotic. Roger held out his arms. Lance dropped the table leg and hugged Roger with all his strength.

"It's okay. Rog is here." Ralston approached them. Roger held onto Lance with his right arm as he turned to Ralston. "Lance is through, Mr. Ralston. He's had enough."

"On the contrary, Roger. Lance is just beginning. If you would, please find out what happened so that I can take the appropriate action."

***

It was just after midnight when the fifty-two-foot yacht pulled away from its berth. *Miss Lynnea* motored quietly out of the harbor. Once Roger had explained all that Lance had gone through, Ralston felt sorry for his young hire but looked upon this experience as basic training.

The yacht headed for open water. Once past the breakers, the twin-diesel engines pushed it through the waves at twenty-five knots. Ralston came out on the deck, comfortable with the summation of the situation, even before its finale. The missed opportunity to take out Castro would gnaw at him for some time, but what he lost in political correction, he gained in new capability. That rare, brief glimpse of an adrenaline-charged act of survival caught even him off guard. It happened so fast. Ralston now saw great potential in Lance Rio.

The yacht came to a quiet roll upon the waves as the engines went silent. Ralston noticed that the moon was still nearly full. It made for an enchanting evening with guests. He wrinkled up his nose in disgust when he saw he was standing close to two five-gallon paint buckets strapped to the left corner of the stern. He waved his hand. Two men dressed in black brought a hooded Juan Bertrand out onto the rear deck from below. His hands were cuffed behind his back. Ralston leaned up against the deck railing. He waved that the hood should be removed. Juan looked harassed, angry, and confused. "What is this? Who do you think you are to do this to me? I will sue you."

"No, Mr. Bertrand, you will do nothing of the kind. In fact, your options are rather limited at the moment," Ralston replied. "You see, I also play for keeps."

Bertrand grinned. "Lance, he hired you to get back at me because I take his wife. Because he's not man enough to do it himself."

"You seem to have an odd idea of what a man is. But to the contrary, Mr. Bertrand, we hired Lance. And it is we who are getting back at you." Ralston tried to maintain a sophisticated demeanor, but the thought of this man only evoked anger. "I don't care whose wife you took, but you destroyed our operation. You have no idea, not so much as a clue of the damage you have done. And I am man enough to make you pay for it."

"You, the government? I not a scared of you."

"Good. Then you'll see things from a pragmatic point of view."

"I have rights! I am a veteran. You better believe me I will sue you."

"Again, you are persistent in wanting to bring lawyers into this. Very well." Ralston waved, and underwater lights came on, illuminating an area around the boat's stern and sides. One of his men marched over to the two paint buckets. He wore long rubber gloves and unhooked a rubber strap. He popped the lids off of the buckets. The smell of fish chum was overwhelming. The man took the ladle inside, scooped it, and tossed it over the side of the boat. Ralston nodded. The man took the other bucket and tipped it over the side, spilling its contents overboard. A look of understanding on Bertrand's face brought a smile to Ralston. Fear had done its job.

It wasn't long before thrashing was heard in the water. Several fins broke the surface. Some zigzagged erratically in the slick of fish oil and blood. One shark breached the veil of liquid into the realm above to chomp down on pieces of fish still floating on the surface.

Roger responded to a wave from Ralston, bringing out on the rear deck a hooded Keri Rio. She didn't know it was he that guided her to her finale. Roger, feeling little sympathy for her, ripped the hood off her and shoved her forward. "Mrs. Rio, I need your full attention. It's critical you pay very close attention to what I am about to say to you and your boyfriend," Ralston stated.

"Who are you?" She asked, defiance still resonating in her quivering voice.

"They're CIA," Bertrand said. "And what they are doing is illegal."

"What you have done, Mr. Bertrand borders on treason."

"You a liar," Bertrand said, tightening himself against the two men holding him.

"Really? Lance's plane is in your shop illegally, and I am sure we can tie you to drug smuggling. Your first choice is obvious." Ralston's words were timed to another ladle full of chum tossed over the side. Bertrand could hear the light splash of the bloody fish stew hitting the water, followed by renewed splashing by the sharks. "Your second choice is not as simple, but one you have to agree to now. You and your little girlfriend here have to leave Miami tonight."

"I have a business here. I am not leaving my business. You go to hell!" Bertrand shouted as he struggled harder against the two men holding him.

"You'll be given fifty thousand dollars to relocate. Your tools and supplies will be shipped to you once you are settled elsewhere. Just not in the state of Florida."

Bertrand broke free and charged Ralston. The stout man rammed into Ralston, knocking him against the teak wood railing, cracking it. Ralston was seized with pain. His legs collapsed. Bertrand tried to free his cuffed hands, but they held. Ralston sprang up and brought a rigid hand down on Bertrand's neck, dropping him to the deck. Ralston righted himself and brought his large shoe up into his face. Ralston wasn't satisfied. He brought his foot into Bertrand's ribcage, cracking a few. "Throw him overboard." Bertrand found himself teetering on the gunwale. "Both of them."

Roger grasped Keri harder and moved toward the side of the boat. By his reckoning, it was simple. Lance deserved justice. He tilted her over the side.

"Roger!" Keri exclaimed in shock and horror.

"That's right, girlfriend. Now I know you can never harm Lance again. And I can live with that."

Keri screamed. She struggled. "What about Lance's baby? Will you kill her too?" Roger stopped. The back of Keri's knees were wrapped against the inside of the boat as tight as she could squeeze. She was about three feet from the water. A large silhouette arose from the depths into the lit surface. The tiger shark broke through the waves, snapping its jaws. Roger pulled her back up onto the deck.

"Okay. Okay. We'll leave. We take the offer," Bertrand said, catching his breath.

"That's very sensible, Mr. Bertrand," Ralston said.

"What about Lance's baby? I want Lance to have his child. Not this mental case," Roger said sternly.

"I don't care about that, Roger," Ralston said.

"Well, I do." Roger still had Keri by the arm.

"This is my baby. And no one else's." Keri shook Roger's grip from off her.

"I'll be the child's father. I will adopt her," Bertrand said as he stood up.

"I'm not letting this maggot raise, let alone touch this baby!"

"That's not your call, Roger." Ralston turned to one of his men. "Head back to shore."

"Lance will never see this baby, Roger," Keri shouted. "What do you think of that? Explain that to Lance. This baby will be Juan's."

"Then..." Roger was at a loss. He could only come to a single, bitter conclusion. Roger looked at Keri with both shame and resolve. "God, forgive me. Lance, forgive me." Roger drove his powerful arm upward. His fist made contact deep into her belly. The impact lifted her petite frame off the deck. She dropped into a fetal position. Lance was free of her—forever.

The engines were started. The yacht headed back to shore.

Chapter 32

Langley, Virginia

March 11, 1983

Lance made his way along the road. A road map lay folded on the front passenger seat. He drove a car left for him by the CIA. It seemed to give a sense of mystery and intrigue. Uncle Jeffrey, as Lance came to refer to Ralston, was definitely a schemer. Flashes of the past couple of weeks erupted in his mind. Keri and Juan were gone.

Lance pulled up to the main gate of the Central Intelligence Agency. After showing his I.D., he was directed to the parking facility. Lance cinched up his tie, realizing that he was wearing the same suit, tie, and shirt that the CIA had bought him last year.

Lance entered the main lobby wearing his Visitor's badge. He stopped in front of the CIA shield on the floor. It was quite impressive. Lance studied it.

"It's sixteen feet in diameter," Ralston said, standing at the edge of the granite circle. Lance looked up and smiled. "The eagle, of course, is our national symbol. The sixteen-point compass star represents the convergence of intelligence data gathered from around the world to a central point—here. Both going out and coming in. The shield is naturally a symbol of defense." Lance went to the center of the granite emblem to meet Ralston. The two men stood in the middle of the compass star and shook hands. "Welcome, Lance, to the headquarters of the Central Intelligence Agency."

With only a passing thought to whom Ralston was talking to, a dozen people walked past them on the emblem like any other day.

"Come. Let me show you around," Ralston said as he put his arm around Lance and moved him to the Memorial Wall. It was a large sheet of white marble, with two and a half-inch sized dark stars chiseled into it. Lance estimated that there were between fifty and sixty stars. Most of the stars were faded from black to charcoal gray. But a few were still black.

"If you think about the thousands of men and women who have worked here over the last four decades, it's a small number of stars compared to other agencies and the military, but I take each one personally. The fact that a star exists here doesn't mean they failed, but gave their life for the success of the mission, which saved countless other lives."

Ralston took Lance on a tour of the building. In many ways, it was like a college campus, designed for groups of people to intermingle. He learned about the white noise that was generated down corridors to keep what was said inside—inside.

Lance was ushered into Ralston's office. Ralston stayed back to talk with his assistant out front.

Lance wandered over to a wall decorated with several glass-framed pictures of a younger Jeffrey Ralston in a dojo, wielding a samurai sword. He wore a hakama, the traditional wide pleated trousers of an Aikido practitioner. Another photo was taken with Ed Parker, Grandmaster, and founder of American Kenpo. Ralston was a pilot, as photos of his standing by various aircraft suggested. He was a naval officer and a Harvard lawyer. Yuck, Lance thought. Two framed letters, in particular, caught his attention. The first was handwritten in French, dating back to 1808. The other was handwritten in German.

Ralston entered and shut the door behind him. "The first one is a letter to General Clark from Napoleon Bonaparte."

Lance looked at Ralston. "I could see you as a Bonapartist."

"Oh, how so?"

"It fits you. My father once drew a contrast between him and Castro when I said that Bonaparte was a dictator, as we learned in school. My dad said that was the British perspective, and they had no right to talk. He said Napoleon had to rule with an iron fist, but it was inside a velvet glove. He had to get order back into France, but quick! But he was fair to all. Nothing like Castro."

"Firm, tough when necessary, but never ruthless. Your father was very insightful. There is so much to learn from the man's life that I require it of all my people." Ralston then drew Lance's attention to the second letter. "Bertolt Brecht. Do you know who he is?"

"He's a German poet or playwright. Something like that."

"He was both. While I lived in Germany, I came across this paper of his most famous quotes. Why? No one knows. Perhaps it was in quiet reflection as he went from Nazi Germany to being stuck in Soviet-controlled East Germany."

"What does it say?"

"The first one says: *Intelligence is not to make no mistakes, but quickly to see how to make them good.* The second one says: *The finest plans have always been spoiled by the littleness of them that should carry them out. Even emperors can't do it all by themselves*. The next one down says: *Because things are the way they are, things will not stay the way they are.*"

"That's because when you forget what you revolted against in the first place, you just sponsored the next."

"Interesting thought. And below that says: *It is easier to rob by setting up a bank—than by holding up the bank clerk.*"

Lance chuckled.

"But the final one is what hits me as most pertinent. It says: *Do not rejoice in his defeat, you men. For though the world has stood up and stopped the bastard, the bitch that bore him is in heat again*."

"I would say we need to get her fixed."

Ralston grinned. "That would be the trick."

"How do you stop her then? Do we know who she is?"

"Some say the devil," Ralston said as he came around his desk.

"That's a copout. There's no such thing as the devil. It's just an excuse to act badly."

"If you say so."

Lance sat in front of the desk as Ralston reclined in his chair. "Lance, this is my goal. To suppress what is bad in men long enough to let what is good in them flourish. There's no trick to understanding that. As you have seen here today, we're just people. Our job is to gather intelligence and present it to our elected officials to help them make informed decisions."

"I wouldn't lead with that if you are trying to recruit."

Ralston grinned. "Point taken. However, it's the way we operate."

"By hook or by crook?"

"As with all things that deal with dangerous people, we need to be resourceful. It saves lives. But our work isn't all cloak and dagger."

"I'm impressed with your facility, but I don't see myself as a CIA agent."

"The first thing you need to understand is that there is no such thing as a CIA agent. Not if you are employed here, draw your paycheck from here as a federal employee of the United States government. We are officers. The general term is *Case Officer*. What we do is seek to employ someone from the country we are in and have them gather information for us."

"I see. You recruit them. To spy on their own country for you."

"In essence. They are then *agents* of the CIA."

"I get it. You hire them, pay them, and help them…"

"And we've helped many. We have our spy planes, spy satellites, phone taps, bugs, etcetera, but the best intelligence gathering is still human intelligence. It all comes down to people. You need to be a people person to do well in this business. And you are. One of the best suited I've seen in a long time."

"That's kind of you."

"I'm not looking to be kind. I'm looking to recruit, to enhance this facility. And I am certain you belong here with us."

"So, I have to go out and find agents?"

"Assets. We call them assets. And it's not like selling door to door."

"Is that what I will be to you, just an asset?"

This sour note put a smile on Ralston's face. He leaned forward. "You come work for me. I will teach you—you will learn. Then in a year's time, you tell me who is the asset?"

"I don't ever want to back down from the likes of another Juan Bertrand. Ever."

"You won't. I will train you myself in addition to the standard training you will receive. It will demand more of you, though. A lot more. It will be between us. A gentlemen's agreement."

Lance understood the opportunity before him. "I will do everything you say to do, sir."

"Good. But remember this going forward, Lance. The greatest judo you will ever learn—is that of the mind."

Chapter 33

The Farm

37′19″48″N, 76°40′12″W

September 27, 1983

Lance knew it was still Tuesday. He waded through the waist-high swamp water. He could still hear shouting in the distance, punctuated with machine-gun fire, unmistakably from an AK-47. They shouted in Swahili.

Lance and Tara Abbott had been on the run for two days straight. The water lowered as they neared the shore. Lance grimaced as another swarm of mosquitoes waited at the edge of the water for them. "Boy, can't get a break from you, females," he said. Tara stumbled, sucking in air. More shouting in Swahili came from the other end of the swamp. "I gather they are still looking to make your acquaintance?" Lance frowned at their predicament.

"You don't want to know," Tara said. "You're too much of a gentleman."

"I'm sure it's nothing I haven't heard before on a construction site."

"Probably nothing you haven't thought of doing yourself, flyboy."

"Don't be ridiculous. What I've thought of you wouldn't mind at all."

"You think?" she asked with a cocky grin. "You ever make it with a black woman?"

Lance swept her up, carrying her as he pushed the last few feet to shore. "No. This is about as close as I've come."

"That's okay. This is as close as I've come to being swept off my feet."

Lance ran through the mosquito swarm as Tara flayed her arms to ward them off. He hurried past the shrilling buzz until he found a spot of soft grass and a tree to lean upon for a respite.

He dropped to his knees and carefully put Tara down. They began slapping their arms and each other's faces until the tiny intruders were gone. Tara caught sight of one more and caressed more than slapped it on Lance's face. She wiped it away. Lance's smile was warm and gracious. She pulled herself to him. Her lips covered over his, gently prodding them to respond. His lips moved in unison with hers. She could feel his hunger. She pulled away. "Now, you've been to first base with a black woman."

"With a woman—period."

"You married too young."

"Still am—technically."

"I will respect that." She pushed herself back against the tree. Lance untied her boot. "One day, she'll regret what she did, and that's on her. Regardless, you need to keep going forward with your life, my young man."

He slipped the combat boot off and rolled the sock off. Her ankle was swollen. "Unfortunately, we don't have ice to put on it, but I'm going to bandage it tightly so we can stay mobile." Lance took off his shirt and cut the sleeves off with his knife, making long strips. She admired the newest set of muscles that seemed to develop weekly on his body.

Bandaged and redressed in her boot, Tara tried to walk without Lance's assistance. The best she could do was hobble. She fell into his arms. "It's no good, Lance."

"Here." Lance took off his backpack and put it on her. "Now, jump on." She didn't hesitate as Lance lowered himself. With her secure, he pushed forward.

Lance had no idea how far he carried her through the brush and trees. But the clearing up ahead suggested at least six kilometers, according to their map.

They came upon a dirt road that should lead to an airstrip. It was just after six p.m. local time. The sun's rays were giving notice that twilight was approaching. Lance stopped. He heard a military truck racing nearer from the darkened end of the road. Lance rushed behind some heavy brush and dropped to his hands and knees, rolling Tara off him. He helped her to remove his backpack. "Lie flat. Stay still," he said as the rusty olive drab World War II-era troop truck howled by them. Lance could see several armed men standing in the back. Once gone, Lance hoisted Tara up again on his back, which was aching, and followed the road from the brush.

Lance stood on the edge of the forest. He found the airstrip. It was an asphalt-paved runway. The truck had stopped in front of a quaint little building that had the characteristics of an airport terminal. A large hanger was next to it. He dropped down so Tara could slide off. A Bell 206 JetRanger helicopter sat on the tarmac near the runway. A lone guard, armed with an AK-47, stood by the chopper. Good, thought Lance. They needed a weapon.

"Do you know how to fly that thing?"

"I have six hours in helicopters," Lance stated as he dropped back to the ground.

"Is that enough?"

"Ah, sure. Come on."

Lance headed around the forest's perimeter, keeping an eye on the guard. He had to get them out of there. The pain was getting too much for Tara. Packing Tara through the forest and swamps had worn him down to a systemic ache. Lance dropped to the ground and rolled over. Tara slid off. "I know you're hurting, sweetie, but hang in there, and I'll get us out of here."

"Well, be careful."

"Hey, we're shadow warriors, remember? And I have this swashbuckler gene thingy that won't leave me be."

"Anyone ever tell you you're one in a million?"

"My mother. Never got that one, though. Anyway, get ready."

Lance sprang up and moved closer to the helicopter. The guard came around the front of the aircraft, turning left down its side. Lance jumped down on the back of the guard's right knee, slipping his arm around the guard's neck and squeezing. The guard dropped two sharp elbow jabs into Lance's hardened stomach with no effect. The guard went limp.

Tara hopped and limped her way to the helicopter. Lance picked her up and put her in the left front seat. He dashed around to the pilot's seat. He moved several toggle switches on the overhead console and one under a red metal guard on the instrument panel and pressed the starter button. The loud clicking of the igniter preceded the hollow whine of the engine spooling up. Lance watched the N1 tachometer that said *Gas Producer* on the gauge. At 13 percent rpm, he rolled the throttle open. The deep throaty sound of combustion completed the musical orchestration of the aircraft coming to life. The main rotor began its track around them. At 62 percent rpm, he moved his hand from the starter button. "Come on, baby. We need to go!" Lance rolled the throttle to full power. Lance raised the collective and moved the left pedal forward to counteract the torque effect of the main rotor. The helicopter felt lighter. Dust blew up, blanketing his view. At that moment, several men burst through the veil of dust. One was blowing a whistle, his face bulging red. He frantically waved the helicopter back down. Lance put weight back down on the skids and rolled the throttle back down to idle.

The head instructor of the CIA training camp, Randy Michaels, a brawny Texan, ripped open the door. "You are not a helicopter pilot! What the hell do you think you are doing, mister?"

"Evading capture, sir. I wasn't going to actually take off."

"This is not part of the exercise."

"Sorry, sir, we, I, got caught up in it all."

"I pushed him on it too, sir," Tara added, winching in pain.

"Sir, Tara has a severely sprained ankle. She needs medical attention."

"All right. Just get out of the aircraft."

"Engine still needs to cool down first."

Michaels stepped away, signaling for the other instructors to assist Tara.

Two of the instructors helped her out. She reached her hand back in toward Lance. Lance held her hand for a moment. She looked at him and winked. "One in a million."

Steve Truxel, the instructor, posing as the enemy guard, came around. "Not bad, Lance. I think we need to get you your helicopter rating." Truxel scanned the instrument panel. "Okay, it's cool enough. Shut it down." Lance pushed the idle release button and rolled the throttle closed. The engine immediately spooled down. Only the swish of the rotor blades mildly disturbed the tranquil setting of the Virginia landscape.

Tara was helped into a waiting van. "Bye, Lance. Had fun, see ya soon." Lance was a bit sad that he would be without his training partner for a while.

Randy Michaels came back over. Lance looked worn. "Well, you two had quite an adventure. We need to take care of you too." The van drove off as the rusty old troop transport rumbled up to a stop. One of the instructors came up behind Lance and popped a black pillowcase over his head. Michaels drove the butt of his rifle into Lance's stomach hard enough to drop him to the ground. Lance forced himself up quickly but was met with a kick to the back of his legs and another butt to his stomach. He was grabbed and dragged off.

They drove for miles in the troop truck, with Lance lying on the floor of the truck bed, his hands bound behind his back, and someone holding him down with their foot on the back of his neck. Lance felt every bump, which added to his new bruises.

He was inside—somewhere. The pillowcase was ripped off as a foot pushed him down into a waiting chair. Lance's head cleared, and his vision caught sight of the six others of his training team, also held captive. "Admit it, you are CIA," the masked voice of the guard said in a Middle Eastern accent. "Your comrades have already given you up. Anything you say will all be lies. But speak. We love to hear American lies."

Tara Abbott, on her way to the infirmary, was missing out on POW training. Here in this classroom, the lines between simulation and reality blurred the most. No one would leave with their dignity that intact, but there was an inherent pride in the accomplishment that the training factored in. It would be challenging, but in retrospect, no one would trade the experience.

The ability to calculate days from nights and how many had transpired was lost on everyone. Lance and his team endured endless sleep deprivation, insults used to warm up another set of interrogations, both vulgar and repressive. When put outside, it was with the disorientation of wearing their pillowcases as they crawled through the slimy mud. Lance only made the mistake of raising his head once while crawling through the gooey mess. A rifle butt to the head taught him to keep it low. Any weaknesses set the masked guards on a trainee like wolves on a lamb. The stick and carrot of compliance with their captors was a cookie, a peanut butter cookie. Lance hated peanut butter cookies. He was determined not to break for anything less than an oatmeal raisin. The motley training team ranged from a divorced wife, Tara Abbott, to an Army Ranger looking for a more liberating career than the military. They were all at the end of the Paramilitary or PM training. It was priceless as far as Lance was concerned.

A truck convoy rumbled their room. The guards dropped their weapons and ran outside. Instructors with familiar faces like Steve Truxel and Randy Michaels rushed in. Lance and the team were ushered out single file. The bright sunlight was overpowering at first, but they soon adjusted. They were all just happy that they made it through. It was a welcome sight to see the white van with the large sliding side door. Each took a seat. Randy Michaels' radio crackled to life. He put his hand on Lance's shoulder and pulled him back. "Not you."

Lance was confused. Two instructors cuffed his hands behind him and put that filthy pillowcase back over his head, dragging him back into the cement bunker.

Lance was shoved back into the same chair that had made his acquaintance days earlier. Randy Michaels entered. "It's real simple, Lance. This is not a training exercise. It has just come to our attention that Cuban nationals paid you off—not—to fly to Panama. So that makes you a traitor. Mr. Ralston will be on his way shortly. We should just kill you now instead of wasting taxpayers' money on room and board in Leavenworth."

"No. That never happened. Jeffrey knows perfectly well what happened. I don't know any Cuban nationals. I'm not a spy."

"No? What do you think you're doing here? You're training to be a spy! For who, Lance? The Cubans? No, the Russians. They got to you first. You plan to report back to Mother Russia about what you've seen at headquarters, huh? Tell'em how we train around here?" Michaels kicked Lance backwards in the same chair. The instructors left. They weren't instructors now—they were interrogators. Lance couldn't understand how they got their information wrong about what happened. How would he convince them otherwise?

Every two hours, he was roused and interrogated. Was it the weekend still? He didn't know. He was pulling rabbits out of hats, creating information that sounded good. Whatever he could scheme, but he couldn't be sure if his interrogators accepted it. Every four hours, a foot to the chest knocked him and the chair over.

By now, Lance only heard echoes of voices. Randy Michaels came in. "Come on, Lance, you're going to jail. The FBI will take over now. But, if I had my way, you wouldn't leave here alive." Lance instinctually obeyed. He stood up from the chair he had been strapped to only to collapse on feeble legs. They snatched him up and marched him to the door.

Three vans waited outside. The blaring sunlight was burning his eyes.

Ralston, like the rest of his training team, including Tara on crutches, stood in front of him. His cuffs were removed. He was marched forward.

"Now," Jeffrey Ralston said in a very emphatic tone. "Let Lance Rio be an example to you all."

Lance's team was dressed in civilian clothes. Their PM training was over. But he would find himself back in that devilish world he had come to hate: the legal system! His life was over. Being innocent of these charges had nothing to do with getting a fair trial. Lance's eyes cleared enough to see Ralston. There was that smile on Uncle Jeffrey's face. His eyes cleared further. Ralston had a smile of sincere warmth and a gesture of not containing himself any longer. Ralston broke out in applause. The others eagerly followed, from his teammates to all of the instructors. Even chief instructor Randy Michaels was grinning from ear to ear as he clapped.

Ralston opened the door to his van. "Come on, Lance. Time to go home. This portion of your training is over. Except for your written final, of course."

Tara, having perfected her crutch-supported stride, came up to Lance. "Well done, flyboy. Like I said, you're one in a million." She didn't care that he stunk and was covered in filth. She gave him a kiss on the cheek. "Come on. Let's get you cleaned up."

Michaels came over and put his hand on Lance. "You did good, son. I'm proud of you and proud to have trained you this far. You're one tough cookie."

"No, sir," Lance said. "Resilient. I've always considered myself resilient." Lance climbed into the van.

Lance was back at the barracks, what had been their home on the Farm these past several months. He was shaved and showered and back in civilian clothing. He planned to enjoy what was left of his weekend, starting with a proper meal. He made his way to the dining table and sat opposite Tara. "Shame you missed out on the P.O.W. experience. It would have made a man out of you."

Tara grinned. "So, are you saying you'd like to lock me up in a dark room and interrogate me?"

"Maybe you two should get a room and spare us," Milton Cohen said.

Lance could almost hear the Harvard upper crust flaking off his vowels.

"You should know better than that, Uncle Miltie," Lance taunted.

"Will you quit calling me that?"

"Or you will kill me a million times," Lance said in his best Milton Berle impression.

Despite the few quips here and there, the team had become quite cohesive. It was inherent in the training and Lance's ability to teach the art of cooperation over competition.

Randy Michaels came into the dining hall toting two bottles of merlot. He placed the wine bottles on the table. "Well, kids, summer camp is over. Next, we start the tradecraft course. And in short order, there'll be drinking. A drunk spy is an asset to the enemy. So watch getting snockered."

"Ooh…" Milton said, taking hold of one of the bottles. "Live ammo."

"And Lance, Jeffrey wants you to get the Mits and bring her down here while you continue your training. Speaking of which, Jeffrey will see you for some one-on-one in an hour."

"Seriously?"

"Seriously." Michaels looked at the others. "I would like all of you to know that we've never put someone through the P.O.W. exercise quite like we did with Lance. Definitely never as long."

The others enjoyed the wine as Lance trained with Ralston according to their gentlemen's agreement. Lance gained more knowledge along with more bruises. He didn't mind.

Chapter 34

Grenada

12°03′00″N, 61°45′00″W

October 26, 1983

"*The Spice of the Caribbean*" is how Lance knew the beautiful small island nation of Grenada. The United States government had a new name for it: *Operation: Urgent Fury*.

The coup of 1979 that had installed pro-Marxist leader Maurice Bishop into power had now assassinated him. With the help of Cuba, the new coup ruled in his place. Pleas for help finally came the day before with the dawn raid of the Marines from the north and the Army Rangers from the south. Many U.S. citizens, mostly college medical students at the university, were trapped.

Lance had to leave the Farm, his current training, and fly to Grenada. Ralston showed wisdom in making the Camp Peary airport the home base of Miss Solitaire while Lance trained there at the Farm.

The morning rays of the sun bubbled up off the eastern horizon as Lance caught sight of several U.S. Navy ships below. The radio crackled. "High Five, this is Flotilla, over."

"Flotilla, this is High Five," Lance radioed back.

Lance turned toward the island, which he would traverse to the west side in a matter of minutes. He slowed down but kept to his ten thousand foot altitude. Lance caught a shadow over on his right. A Hercules AC-130 gunship came up parallel with him. He rocked his wings and then gave a wave to the aircraft's skipper, who waved back. "Good morning, High Five, this is Mother Hen, over."

There was some intimidation, but more so a strong sense of security with the fellow high-wing big brother next to him. "Good a.m. to you, Mother Hen. Ready to follow your lead."

"High five, then follow us in for some good karma, over."

"Mother Hen, just keep me tucked under your wing," Lance said. He always got a kick out of call signs' somewhat countrified radio talk. It reminded him of his CB radio days. His handle in 1975 was *Secret Squirrel*. Who knew?

The larger aircraft turned and dropped in altitude. The Mits followed but from above the AC-130. Lance could see flashes of light, fire, and smoke below in one place after another. If he hadn't gone through explosives training, it would have been more unnerving than it was. He felt for his pistol, which he carried in a new shoulder harness.

"High Five, jump back up to ten thou!" the skipper ordered. Lance watched for a moment longer as the AC-130 fired its side-mounted Gatling gun. It cut a path for what he assumed were American and East Caribbean forces to move through. The ominous sound of a bullet hitting his aircraft woke Lance up from the live-action diorama below. "Come on, High Five, get'er up there! Too many unfriendlies down there throwing rocks."

"Roger that. High-tailing it outta here," Lance said as he went for full power and maximum rate of climb.

Lance made it back up to ten thousand feet and watched the gunship make its way over the narrow band of land to the west side, to St. Georges, the island's capital. Lance was over water again and slowed his aircraft down. He circled. Four Huey Cobra helicopters came down the coast and then turned inland. He could see a swarm of rockets fired from them.

"High Five, LZ at the airport is no good. Your pickup can't make it there. Stuck in St. George's. Need an alternate pickup."

"Roger, Mother Hen. Understood." Lance studied the nooks and crannies of the coastline as he flew alongside it.

Lance could see no place to land until opportunity jutted out to meet him. "Mother Hen, this is High Five, over."

"High Five, go ahead."

"Get my people out to the port authority cruise ship terminal. I can extract them there."

"There's no place to land, High Five."

"I think there is. Please just do it. High Five standing by."

Lance circled slowly for better than an hour. His thoughts of fuel burn weren't far from the top of his list of concerns.

"High Five, this is Mother Hen. Do your pilot thing."

Lance dropped the airspeed to just a few knots above stall speed. He only added a little power when he saw that he was drifting below the edge of the pier. The moment he touched down, he snapped the thrust reverse into action and made use of the powerful brakes. The pier wasn't much wider than his thirty-nine-foot wingspan.

Five people stood at the end of the terminal building. "He won't have anywhere to turn around. We'll never get out of here!" a woman cried.

Lance saw how tight it was going to be. He never parallel parked an aircraft before. He taxied to the left as far as possible and then swung the Mits hard right. Continuing in an arc, he turned hard left until he saw his right wingtip nearly touching the terminal building. He engaged the thrust reverse, backing up while tapping on the right brake pedal. The aircraft backed up and turned more toward the pier. He taxied forward. He stopped. Full thrust reverse again. He stopped.

He moved forward and was lined up with the pier. It worked. He set the brakes and jumped out of his seat. He opened the door and stepped out.

An army soldier ran up to him. "Sir, we just took this area, but some unfriendlies are trying to take it back."

"Understood. Get my people over here," Lance said. He could hear explosions over the sound of his engines. The soldier waved for people to come. Lance held the door open. He saw a couple of women, followed by a man dressed in a suit, with two other men dressed in suits, who had their hands on the first man. Maybe a politician or some high-ranking mucky-muck, he thought. Lance funneled everyone inside. "Everybody, just get in and grab a seat."

"Wait!" a woman shouted. "The lieutenant's not here yet."

"We have to go!" Lance stepped in, shut the door, and pushed his way back up front.

"Wait for the lieutenant. He's here," the woman shouted. The door opened and then closed quickly.

"Go, Lance. Go!" Lieutenant Roger Drake yelled. Lance grinned and amped up the engines. They shot down the pier.

There were screams. "We've been hit!" There were a few thumps on the right side of the fuselage. Mist fingered its way into the cabin. Roger pushed his way forward and knelt. The stout aircraft cleared the pier and trouble behind it.

"We've been hit," Roger yelled. Lance noticed a light dusting on Roger's face.

"How are our passengers doing?"

Roger looked behind. "About two lines by now."

"Coke?" Lance said as he noticed that Roger was rather wide-eyed himself. "Take a seat and put your mask on. Quick. Hey everyone. Cover mouths with something." Roger took the co-pilot's seat and donned the oxygen mask. The cabin had a light powdery haze to it. Even Lance had a heightened sense of euphoria. "You're the Coast Guard liaison officer here?"

"Was. Last two months. Stinking Cubans had to ruin my vacation."

"Yeah, they're good at that."

***

Roosevelt Roads Naval Air Station, Puerto Rico, was still a beehive of activity since Lance had landed there three days earlier. Ralston wanted Lance to get back to the Farm, to class, as he was missing valuable training, though he had faith his protégé would catch up. The DEA and U.S. Customs teams gutted the MU-2 under Lance's insistent guidance. The insulation had a strong Mylar film on both sides that kept the coke powder hidden within its fiberglass layers.

All told, they recovered nearly three hundred pounds of uncut cocaine. Lance shook his head. "It's no wonder they wanted the plane back."

Ralston approached. "Lance, you still figure on flying out of here today?"

"In about two hours, Jeffrey."

"And you're flying back with Roger?"

"Yes, Jeffrey, back to Florida to drop me off," Roger said.

"Well, new skins and other replacement parts are on order."

"I'll work on it on weekends."

"That will be fine, Lance. But don't forget our training. You still have much to learn."

***

One of the provisions the CIA provided for its trainees at the Farm was a small fleet of bicycles. It was their chief means of transportation. It also provided relaxation with leisurely rides along the dirt and paved roads of the ten thousand acre woodlands of Williamsburg, Virginia.

Lance pedaled down from the main training center, where the dorms, cafeteria, and classrooms were, to the Camp Peary airport. He coasted up to the hangar and stopped. The hangar was open. "Hey, Lance!" Eric Pitts yelled out.

"Hey, Special!" Lance called back. Lance had given Eric Pitts his nickname because of the famous Pitts "Special" aerobatic stunt biplane—a kit plane. The tall, girthy, country gent with a beard and wavy reddish-brown hair had a mountain-man look about him.

The MU-2 was finally airworthy, and he couldn't wait to get her up into the air. It had taken all winter to drill out rivets, remove damaged skins on the fuselage and part of the left-wing. Some of the interior panels and windows were replaced to complete the repairs.

Lance put up the bike. Pitts had already attached the tug to the nose gear. It was time for *Miss Solitaire* to spread her wings.

Chapter 35

Washington D.C.

July 4, 1984

The Wednesday afternoon was filled with the smell of grilling meat. Jeffrey and Maggie Ralston always put on a first-rate spread every Fourth of July. It was a family tradition that catered to friends, colleagues, and political ties.

The Tudor-style house was of brick and stone and sat on extensive grounds. Of the dozen trees spread around the back, half were fruit-bearing. Raspberry and blackberry bushes lined the back fence. In smaller circles of the intelligence community, Ralston was known for canning fruit preserves. It was his outlet for calm.

Lance came out of the small guesthouse, his occasional domicile, since shaking hands with Ralston over a year ago. Lance moved past several of the seventy-six guests. He discerned that Washington D.C. was like Hollywood. In Los Angeles, you didn't have to go far to find someone who worked in the entertainment industry. D.C. was similar. It was the government industry here. It left a sour taste in Lance's mouth to think of it in those terms, but this is what he saw firsthand. On the whole, he didn't care for these people and looked to mingle with more familiar faces.

He found Milton Cohen sipping on another glass of wine. "Oh, Lance, Lance, my dear friend, what a special gathering, don't you think?" Lance was sure his affable nature was alcohol-induced.

"Have you seen Tara? I wanted to tell her some news." Lance's scan roved around the backyard and garden area.

"Great news of her own, don't you think?" Milton rolled back.

"What news?"

"Of her new assignment. Didn't you hear? Anyway…oh, there she is." Milton waved.

Lance cut through guests and across the lawn to get to Tara. "That boy has had way too much to drink," she said as Lance approached.

"But he's friendly for the moment." There was a warmth, a glow to his presence that took her mind from Milton. "I heard you are leaving. Is that true?" She turned and walked back through the garden, away from the others. Lance followed.

She stopped by the koi pond. Alone, away from the others, she turned to him. "That's true. I will be leaving on the sixteenth, Monday morning, for Africa. I've been assigned to the American Embassy in Swaziland."

"I see." He had been out of contact with her and the others after graduation as his advanced training kept him down at the Farm while the graduates took up positions back at Langley.

"My dear, Lance, we did have a spark, but that was a summer ago."

"I don't believe you. I know you care about me."

"Listen, my young man, yes, I care deeply for you. But what kind of romance or life could we have together. The agency has no need of sending you to Africa when your greatest asset to them is in the Caribbean and this part of the world."

"I understand that, but—"

Her finger touched his lips. "There are no buts. I won't want to leave you if I let myself fall in love with you. We have great new beginnings. You need this time and space to grow. I'll only slow you down. Any woman will."

"Yeah, but—"

"No buts. You need time to grow. And this is your time to do so." She kissed him, having to feel his lips once more. "You are still one in a million." Tara left by another path in the garden.

Ralston was manning two large barbecue grills. Roger sat in a lounge chair, sipping beer. Ralston reseated himself in a chair next to Roger, taking hold of his glass of white wine.

"I don't know all that you did, Jeffrey, but he's not the same Lance," Roger said.

"He's still the man you call brother. We just made him resistant to the ills of the world. That's all." Ralston took a long sip of wine. He set his glass back down on the small glass table between them. "Your commitment with the Coast Guard is about up. And frankly, I'd love you to come be a part of us."

"I appreciate that, but here's my thing. I've finally made Lieutenant."

"I understand."

"I'd have to start all over. I have nine years invested in the Coast Guard. I'm finally getting to enjoy the fruits of my labor."

"Well, keep it in mind."

Roger saw Lance come from the garden area. He lifted his sunglasses and saw that his friend was upset. Ralston took note as well. "Jeffrey, keep him busy."

"Oh, I have plenty for him to do."

"I mean, keep his mind busy."

"What do you mean?"

"Fastglass."

"Fast—what?"

"Have him build a plane. You know, between assignments."

"We just got the Mits back up and running."

"No, I mean, have him build a kit plane."

"You mean one of those things you build in your garage? I hardly think that's where his energies should be put."

"Jeffrey," Roger said, sitting up. "Lance took a TRS-Eighteen turbojet engine that's used in the BD-Five 'J' model, the jet version…"

"Yes, I know what the BD-Five is. It was in the latest James Bond movie, something or other. And the TRS-Eighteen is a French-made turbojet engine used in the Cruise Missile."

"Exactly, but Lance turned that little turbojet engine into a turbofan engine. No joke."

"Really? Then, I will certainly explore it."

"No, sir, exploit it!"

"All right, Roger. I shall delve even deeper into all that is Lance Rio."

Chapter 36

Colombia

4°35′00″N, 74°4′00″W

March 19, 1986

The bronze metal skin reflected the glory of such birds of prey as the golden eagle and the red tail hawk, awakening to the rays of a new dawn. The MU-2 traversed the mountainous peaks and valleys of Colombia, heading for a landing at Guaymaral Airport, north of Bogotá.

Lance carried on with the theme of rebirth from the ashes of his past. The aircraft's new paint job reflected that mindset.

Roger woke. "Where are we?"

"About twenty minutes out," Lance answered.

Roger smacked his lips as if the action would relieve his dry mouth. He looked around and then looked back into the cabin, wincing in the meantime. "You need to put a lavatory somewhere in here."

"Use your range extender." Roger reached down for the red plastic portable urinal between their seats. He shook the Little John at Lance, intimating it was full. "Here." Lance pulled a small sealed plastic packet from his side panel and handed it to Roger.

"You carry pee packs?"

"Disposable urine bag…for those who drink too much coffee before a long flight and sleep on through anyway. And you better do it now if you want to do the landing."

"Okay," Roger said. More and more, there was a telling difference in Lance, a professional pedigree to his darkening nature that Roger had yet to fathom. Lance didn't need his protection anymore. Roger's demand that Lance grasp the realities of a hard and cruel world saw its realization in the man he had become.

Roger held the Mits smoothly over the threshold of Runway 11. Lance made sure he kept power in as the runway was 8,478 feet above sea level. The mains touched, and the aircraft settled. Roger snapped in the thrust reverse levers.

"Not bad for a high altitude landing. Take the next turnoff," Lance said, scanning.

Lance drove the rental car around turns and bends of the road to the 8 Autopista A Tunja from the town of Chia to Bogotá, where they had an appointment.

"Lance, tell me something. Honestly."

"I'm always honest with you."

"Were you a virgin when you got married?"

"Barely."

"I get it. A man's urges are a powerful thing."

"I had to do the honorable thing by her. She needed that."

"You remember that," Roger pointed. "No matter how it all turned out. That's what counts. Not like me. There's too much resentment on Emily's part for us to ever work things out."

"She'll be someone else's, Rog. Your son will be raised by someone else."

"Well, I gotta tell you, babe, that's already happened."

"What? No."

"We moved on a year ago. She found somebody else. He's a good guy, so it's cool."

"Remember what my mom used to say to me? And us?"

Roger dropped his head. "Yeah. Don't let twenty minutes of pleasure give you a lifetime of misery."

"Doesn't matter now, I guess."

"No. They're good words to live by. Trust me."

Lance turned into the ground station parking lot on Circunvalar Avenue. Roger watched another of the bright red aerial trams leave upward, clutching onto the overhead steel cable that ran to the top of Monserrate Hill. The top of the hill was another seventeen hundred feet above Bogotá, putting their final destination over ten thousand feet.

Lance parked near the road and backed in so he could face the platform. Lance checked his Walther PPK .380 semi-automatic and replaced it in the shoulder holster inside his flight jacket. Roger gave a similar reassuring inspection of his Berretta 9 millimeter and then wiggled it inside his waistband.

"Okay, there's three ways to the top. By aerial tram, or up in the funicular," Lance offered.

"The Fa—what?"

"The funicular. It's like a train car that rides up really steep tracks. Or we can walk up the pathway the faithful take on their pilgrimage to the sanctuary."

"How long is the pathway to the top?"

"I've done it in about nineteen, twenty-minutes."

"Cable car, it is."

"You've gone soft, dude," Lance said as he opened his door.

"Yeah, well, I could kill you over our code names."

"Hey, I have a flair for code names."

Lance followed Roger into the gondola along with many other people. Roman Sanders filed in with the rest and stood at the back. The doors closed. The tram squeaked with the upward pull of the overhead steel threads that suspended them above the lush greenery of the mountain slope. Lance enjoyed the trip up with its breathtaking beauty. They rolled through the white steel frame of the first tower that stood partly out of the thicket. Roger looked apprehensive as they neared the top.

"Don't worry. There are more with us than with them," Lance assured.

"You're quoting scripture now?"

"Thought I was quoting Jeffrey."

The tram slowed and then stopped, nesting itself in the platform. The passengers exited. Lance and Roger moved through the tram station and along the large flat stone walkway. Ahead was the Sanctuary of Monserrate. The clean, whitewashed monastery stood with a grace that its surroundings could only enhance. The four-hundred-year-old building stood atop the hill, where it looked over the city of Bogotá like a watchtower. Lance moved toward San Isidro's House restaurant, a white colonial-style house perched on the edge of the hill. Roger continued toward the path that led up to the sanctuary. "Lance, I need to make a quick stop."

"Now, you're feeling religious?" Lance said, looking at his watch.

"It's been a while, so, yeah."

"A waste of time, but whatever."

Roger went up the path that led to the steps of the sanctuary. Lance followed.

Roger stopped to look at the figure of Jesus that had him lying on his side, supported by his forearm and elbow as with his right hand nailed to a cross that laid flat. A towel-sized red and gold embroidered tapestry lay across his loins.

Lance came up to Roger. "You know I never understood why they always have Jesus looking so anemic. He was in construction, like us. He should look a bit tougher."

"What do you know? Look at the pain, the anguish on his face. He died for our sins."

"It's not like people appreciate it, Rog. Anyway, did you get your mess blessed?"

"Yeah, I'm good."

"Come on then. We have a job to do."

The two men came back down the pathway and over to the restaurant.

The restaurant was renowned for its French cuisine and touted as the best in the city. Its dark warmth wrapped its guests in the soft glow of candlelight that illuminated each table, along with sconce lighting and a fireplace that set the mood for quiet dining. Lance continued through the main dining room out onto the glass-lined terrace with a panoramic view of the city below. They took a table in the back. They were the only two there. Lance could see part of the steel cables that stretched past his view to the tram station. A cable car emerged from the trees. Lance figured that his mission was on board that car. He took off his sunglasses and placed them on the table. Roger kept his sunglasses on.

A few minutes later, Enrique Rojas came out onto the terrace. Lance noticed an elegant walking cane in his hand that tapped the terracotta floor with each painful step. With Rojas were three other men; two were his bodyguards and his younger brother Miguel.

"I gather you are Peaches, and you are Cream?" Rojas said, amused.

"He's Peaches," Lance said, nodding toward Roger. "I'm Cream."

Rojas pulled a small sealed sandwich bag from his right coat pocket and tossed it on the table. He pulled back the chair and sat opposite Lance. His grin was smug. "I had this removed three hours ago. Your GPS satellites, your orbiting necklace of death, can no longer track me. I am no longer your puppet."

"I see." Lance picked up the blood-stained baggie with the homing device inside.

"What do you say about that, Señor Rio?" Rojas said with a slap on the table.

Lance took in a deep breath and let it out slowly.

Rojas leaned in. "This is my world. I pull the strings!" It was apparent that Rojas had planned this for some time and that the Agency's unsettling suspicions were correct.

"You disappoint me, Enrique. This is hardly our only means."

"You think I fear you, boy? Your CIA? I fear only God."

"No, you don't."

"I go to pray every day. My priest, he prays for me. And God listens to him."

"Wow. Premeditated forgiveness. How sincere."

"We will leave here, go back to the airport, and fly to where I say. We will load four hundred kilos of product on board—my plane."

"And I fly it back to the U.S.?"

"I don't have any need for you after that. The plane can fly straight into the U.S. without being searched."

Lance was annoyed. "That's unfortunate, Enrique." Lance stood. One of Rojas' men whipped out his pistol. A light clink preceded a flash of red on his shirt. The man turned to see a neat bullet hole in the large glass window. He collapsed.

"Come on, Peaches, we're outta here." Lance pocketed the plastic bag.

Miguel Rojas fidgeted, nearly reaching inside his waistband. "You are dead. You hear me? There is no place you can hide. You are dead!" He grabbed Lance by the arm. Roger's reaction time was a half-step behind. Lance snagged Miguel's arm in a lock and snapped his forearm.

Lance looked squarely at Enrique Rojas. "I play for keeps now."

Roman Sanders, hearing every word, disassembled the sniper rifle and fitted it into his backpack. He came down from the hill above the restaurant and made his way through the tourists to the cable car station.

Roger and Lance hurried to the station. Sanders came up behind them. "Get your butts back to the plane and get out. Mission's aborted. But great work, kid."

Roger and Lance came to the car. Lance hesitated. Cautiously, he dropped down into a pushup pose. A small bomb attached underneath. He pushed himself back up. "Nope, no black star for Lance today."

"You serious?"

"As a heart attack."

A black Mercedes-Benz sedan pulled around the corner and jerked to a halt. The driver's window came down. "Get in," Sanders said.

With Roger and Lance inside, the black sedan sped out of town and back to the Autopista.

Sanders hung up his satellite phone. "Okay, here's the new setup. Our mission is to take your plane down to Rojas' private hangar in Cartagena and get the drugs. We're sending a new message."

Sanders drove to the airport parking area of Guaymaral Airport. The Mits was gone. "Where's my plane?" Lance moaned.

"I think I know where they towed it," Sanders replied.

Sanders drove past the Metropolitan Police's Aviation area, where they kept airplanes and helicopters, usually provided by the U.S. in the *War on Drugs*. He pulled to the side of a row of hangars and parked the car. Sanders pulled out his Beretta and checked it before replacing it in his waistband.

The three men padded down the back row of hangars and came around to the front. The hangar doors were open. Sanders heard some men inside conversing in Spanish. He took a quick peek. He turned to Lance and Roger. "They're taking out the bench seat." Sanders screwed a silencer onto the end of his pistol. While Lance and Roger contemplated their next move, Sanders slipped around the corner. A couple of quick *thwack* sounds of metal parts moving and the tinny sounds of brass casings hitting the concrete floor, and all went silent. Sanders popped back around the corner. "Well?"

Roger dragged one man back without hesitation. He knew the drill. Lance knelt and grabbed the other man. He figured they were mechanics. They wore light tan coveralls. Both men had their pistols in their hands at the time of death.

"I'm going to get the car and bring it inside. It's pushing two o'clock. Something should happen anytime now," Sanders said.

It was past four o'clock in the afternoon. A black Range Rover pulled around the row of hangars and drove straight into the darkened hangar.

The pilot hopped out of his car, taking his flight bag with him. He smiled. There was pleasure in his gait as he advanced toward the aircraft. The pilot looked inside of the left side window as he patted the plane. He came around the left engine and moved to the door. He opened the door. Lance aimed his silencer-equipped PPK at the pilot. "Hola."

The sun was setting across the airport grounds. "This is a VFR only airport. It doesn't even have runway lights, despite having a control tower. And it'll be dark soon," Lance said.

"Understood," Sanders replied. "Okay, let's clean up and get airborne. We have maybe a ten-minute window."

They were sequenced into the traffic pattern and cleared to land at Rafael Nuñez airport. Roger brought in 20 degrees of flaps that made the small thin wing fan out into a large wing. The MU-2 came over the breakers. Roger caught a glimpse of the waves brushing up on the white sands below before it was replaced with the view of the road with headlights shining in both directions. Then they were over the fence at the end of the runway. Lance eased the power back as he flared for landing. Sanders contemplated his upcoming egress.

The Mits slowed near a row of hangers. Sanders jumped out and crouched behind several aircraft.

Lance pulled in front of Rojas's hanger and shutdown. It was quiet except for an Avianca 707 taking off. The hangar doors opened. A man, standing on the back end of a Lektor electric tug, sped out to the MU-2. He hooked up the nose gear in the bucket. Lance checked his gun and worked his way out of his seat. Roger followed. The Mits was towed inside.

A gruff-looking man bounded his way over. "Where is Luis?" he said in Spanish.

"Tied up, back at Guaymaral, I should still think," Lance said in English.

The slobbering man pulled out his gun. "Okay. I speak English. You talk. Where is the pilot?"

"I am the pilot. I have that arrangement with Enrique."

"You have seen El Patrón?"

"Yeah, I had lunch with Papa Rojas earlier today. So, load me up." Lance hoped it was going to be that easy. Sometimes it was. Perfunctory motion often overshadowed caution.

Roger let his eyes shift. The slobbering man noticed. He shifted his eyes momentarily. Lance had a firm grip on his hand and the gun, twisting both to induce pain. He took the gun. “Turn around and walk back inside.” The man turned around to see armed men dressed in black move inside of the hangar.

Lance called it a mini-coup. It was a message about to be sent to Rojas. The Special Operations Group had quietly taken down the drug operation inside the hangar and captured all present. They were bound, gagged, and blindfolded. Lance loaded the cocaine carefully. It was in one-kilogram bricks, double-wrapped in plastic. He filled the aft baggage compartment and then began filling the cabin.

“Whoa!” Roger’s voice rang out. Lance stopped and went to where Roger stood near several oil drums. Roger pulled off the lid of a second one.

Sanders came up to Lance and Roger. “More coke? Okay. Get it on the table so we can see what we have.”

One of the S.O.G. men took off his hood. It was Joshua Wilson. He secured his MP-5 submachine gun. He and Lance had since become good friends. “Lance, how much weight can you carry?”

The answer an hour later had put the Mits takeoff weight with full fuel, seven hundred pounds over maximum. Lance had to think of it in terms of doing a ferry flight where overweight takeoffs were calculated with temperature, weather, and lots of extra runway. They had been going since four in the morning out of Florida. It was just past eight in the evening with another four hours plus of flying left to the mission. There was only one thing he knew he had to do as distasteful as it was to contemplate. Lance didn’t know if cocaine or coffee was the worst stuff to ever come out of Colombia.

Lance brought up full power. The MU-2 humped itself forward. The aircraft left the runway when it was ready to fly. Lance bumped his elbow against a wall of cocaine, reaffirming that he and Roger were trapped up front in the cockpit. The cabin was packed with one ton of pure cocaine. They would fly with oxygen masks on for the entire trip, keeping the cabin nearly unpressurized. This left more air for the engines to make horsepower. The cabin class twin never felt so small, so claustrophobic as now.

Roger finished calculating their E.T.A. “We should be in Nassau about one-fifteen this a.m. or so. I figure it will take them about half an hour to dig us out of here.”

Lance managed a decent landing and a quick exit off the runway to the Nassau BizJet Center, a legitimately run air charter and FBO that the CIA operated covertly. Lance’s eyes were getting blurry. He finally found relief in seeing the Agency’s Gulfstream jet parked nearby, and a man waving lighted wands snapped into view, motioning the Mits to continue forward inside of the hangar just ahead. Lance shut down the engines, falling back against his seat.

Shortly, the two props stood motionless. The metallic rumble of the large hangar doors being slid shut reverberated around the cockpit. Lance heard the aircraft door open, some voices, and then the movement of the cocaine being removed. He could only think of the massive vacuuming the interior was going to get.

It was over half an hour before Lance and Roger could escape the confines of the cockpit and finally get out and stretch. Ralston was there to greet them. "Well done, boys. I need you both to get some sleep. You launch back to Colombia in five hours. We found Rojas' cocaine farm near the Venezuelan border. We'll have her ready to go, but go get some rest for now."

Lance was past the annoyance of being woken out of deep sleep and aimed back toward the Mitsubishi turboprop. "Oh, Lance, by the way," Ralston said, "when were you going to tell me about your run-in with Pablo Escobar?" Ralston watched Lance come to a halt. He knew in the two years that Lance worked in Central and South America, he came across many interesting people. Even, it seemed, the number one drug kingpin in the world.

Lance turned back to Ralston. "I wasn't, Jeffrey."

"All right, Lance. But tell me, who are you protecting?"

"You, Jeffrey." Lance re-aimed himself toward his aircraft.

***

Lance maneuvered the Mits over the tightly knit patchwork of green below him, where he followed the serpentine flow of the River Cauca. He was near his marker to turn north, left of a small village on the right side of the bank. Traveling inland, they flew past the town of *La Gabarra*. It was known to the CIA that Enrique Rojas employed about forty peasants to grow, harvest, and prepare the coca leaves into cocaine. This was a typical operation throughout Colombia.

"Lance, do a three-sixty," Sanders called out. Lance immediately took stock of the area and then let the right-wing drop. Halfway through the turn, he heard Sanders swear.

"What is it?"

"The FARC," Sanders said. "About twelve clicks from our LZ and headed our way."

A chill went down Lance's spine. The grimace on Roger's face told him he suffered the same foreboding thought. The FARC, the Revolutionary Armed Forces of Colombia, the military wing of the Communist Party, was diametrically opposed to the leadership of the Colombian government.

"Those guys are bad news," Roger said.

"I narrowly missed them a few missions ago, and I want to keep it that way," Lance added.

"These guys are like the Siafu. Ever hear of the Siafu, kid?" Sanders asked.

"Yeah, they're a species of army ant or driver ant in Africa. They lay a path of destruction wherever they roam."

"I've seen a Masai tribesman take a Siafu ant and let it bite both sides of a wound to act like sutures. They tear the body off, and the jaws hold the gash shut. Best, we avoid them."

Lance brought the MU-2 down onto the dirt strip surrounded by trees and brush on three sides. A minute later, he shut down the engines.

The three men stood outside of the aircraft and loaded up. They each carried a short barrel variant of the M-16, designed for close-quarter jungle use. Each man grabbed a small bag, each containing ten incendiary devices. Lance locked the door, and they headed into the thicket.

They moved swiftly through the heavy foliage and then down through the grassy knolls, down to where the small farming community was, a mile away.

Rows of turned earth, supported lively green foliage, placed in another setting could be grapevines, but these were cocoa plants, and their yield was of a contrary nature. The villagers were simple, humble people that served the likes of Enrique Rojas as nothing more than farm implements. Small huts a couple of hundred feet away from the cocaine orchards were where the leaves were processed into cocaine, and the villagers lived. A lone man could process about three hundred and seventy-five pounds of cocaine a day. Lance studied his surroundings.

A wooden pole, fairly thick, stood up about eight feet high, placed between the orchard and the huts. As Lance approached, he noticed that it was tattered with many dark red-stained divots. A white circle of rocks lay around the pole. The Inquisition, for some strange reason, came to mind. The sight of this torture stake unnerved his sense of morality. It angered him.

Lance planted eight of his ten thermo-bombs along the rows of cocoa plants, some of which towered two feet above his head. Roger and Sanders were doing similar at the other ends of the field, but Lance had a more pressing agenda. He had to get these people out of there. Not because of the bombs alone, but because the FARC was by now only three miles away. These people had no power to save themselves, and they had suffered enough.

Sanders spied out one of the huts that had sleeping women and children inside. He let them be. He headed to the boundaries of the farthest field to set up his contingency plan.

Lance came upon another hut, the largest one in the compound that had long tables inside. This was the processing lab. Several men worked in unison to take the leaves at one end of the hut and convert them to cocaine powder, which was then wrapped in plastic and weighed. It meant survival to them and their families. Lance was sure they had no idea of the destructive impact their livelihood had on the world's societies outside of their little village. Lance entered, his M-16 poised. The shivers of fear, culturally anticipated, crept through the men. Lance waved them to one side of the room. He set his last explosive device by the fresh leaves on the floor. He could smell the kerosene used with water and sodium bicarbonate to soak the leaves for their first step in producing the drug.

Lance hated these moments when he needed to communicate effectively in Spanish. Consistently to Ralston's dismay, he could not understand why Lance was not fluent in Spanish by now. He ushered the men outside into the arms of the village priest. This was a problem. Lance sighed. "Padre, habla inglés?"

The weathered old man had bright eyes, yet Lance felt indifferent to him. The priest might try to stand in the way of completing his mission. The priest seemed to sense a disjointed response from Lance. He looked at Lance. He wasn't impressed either. Perhaps he thought of Lance as just another armed troublemaker.

"FARC, coming here, aqui, comprendé?" Lance said animatedly. Several men spoke in rapid-fire Spanish to the priests, but Lance got the gist of it. They understood their lives were in danger, and they needed to flee.

Lance caught through the priest's string of questions the word "Dónde." Lance pointed south-southwest and then moved his hands in a brush-off motion. "Ándale. Hurry—go—go!" Then he heard the low tree-hidden rumble of a piston aircraft engine east of their location. "Roger! We have company. I bet it's Rojas."

Sanders came from down the road. His glaring disposition unnerved Lance. "Why did you alert the villagers?"

"To save them from the FARC. I won't let innocent people get hurt if I can help it."

"Learn this here and now, kid. There's no such thing as innocent people!"

"Nonetheless, I'm sure Rojas is here."

"Okay. We use the villagers for a contingency while we circle back to the airstrip."

Lance, Roger, and Sanders ran the villagers into the jungle.

Rojas stepped into view from the small surrounding of his men. Eight men dressed in combat fatigues flushed the villagers from the high grassy jungle.

The priest came up to Rojas, bowed down, and kissed his hand. "Isn't that supposed to be the reciprocal?" Lance said.

"Power makes you the kissee, not the kisser," Roger remarked.

"Let's move," Sanders ordered. The three men backed away carefully.

Upon arriving back at the airstrip, two Cessna 207 Skywagons were parked, one behind the other behind the Mits.

"Grab a strut," Sanders said, as he and Roger each grabbed a strut of the high-wing aircraft and pushed with a couple of strong heaves, rolling the plane backward off the dirt runway.

Lance pushed from the propeller and then ran to the MU-2. Inside, he dropped into his seat with the key in hand, which found its place in the master switch lock.

"Courageous attempt, Mr. Rio. But you are not leaving," Enrique Rojas said, breathing rapidly.

"Need a breather, Enrique?"

"Enough of your wit. Come out."

Lance stepped outside.

Lance, Roger, and Sanders had their fingers interlocked and behind their necks on their march back to the village.

Miguel Rojas entered through the circle of armed men. His glare gave Lance a certain amount of satisfaction. His plaster-encased arm, hanging from a sling, snagged one of the men, whom he shoved out of the way. "I am going to kill you!"

"Kill me? You can't tie your shoe." As hoped, Miguel went to backhand Lance. Lance blocked it and dropped Miguel Rojas with a single strike.

"Enough!" Rojas shouted. "Get my brother up."

"Rojas, we need to make a deal," Sanders said, reaching carefully for a cigarette.

"No deals."

"Sure?" Sanders pulled out his gold lighter and lit his cigarette. He took a puff.

"No deals."

"That's too bad." Sanders moved his thumb along a slide switch twice. A wall of fire and thunder encapsulated everyone. Lance, Roger, and Sanders dropped to the ground, covering their necks and ears.

One of Rojas' men jumped out of the lab hut, engulfed in fire. Lance watched him inhale flame. He flung his arms spasmodically and fell writhing on the ground. Another of Rojas' men went for his gun. Through the heavy smoke, Lance caught sight of Sanders whipping his wrist. A small tube popped out. Sanders took hold of it and fired the single round into the man's chest. Sanders took hold of his AK-47 and wiped out three of Rojas' men with a squeeze of the trigger. He tossed another assault rifle to Roger. Lance moved his hand to rub

his face as it tingled. Burnt skin came off in his hand. It was then that he noticed that Sanders and even Roger both had burnt flesh. Looking back, he saw Rojas rise from the dirt, with flesh hanging off of his face and neck. Burnt flesh from the back of his hands hung over the end of his sleeves. Screams of panic rifled through the villagers as they scattered. Lance saw them first. Like sharks drawn to distress, the FARC hurried to the sounds of war. Sanders flipped open the cigarette lighter and moved the slide again. Dust, flame, and smoke blew up around the FARC guerillas, igniting Sanders' contingency plan to keep them at bay. Two FARC soldiers were instantly consumed by fire. The wall of fire kept the other soldiers back, but bullets shot freely through the intense flame.
The rest of the FARC would only be ten minutes away.

Lance felt blunt pain across his back that knocked him against the Inquisitor's pole. It took his breath away, yet the raw energy of survival pushed him up against the smoldering edifice. The bright eyes of the priest were hard varnished emitters of fury. He raised the still burning piece of wood at Lance's head. Lance still had the Walther in his hand, but his arm wouldn't bend up. The priest brought his weapon down with all his force. Roger leaped in and blocked the fatal blow, knocking the priest off his feet. Roger gave Lance a couple of slaps.

"I'm here." His arm bent freely now. He pointed his gun at the priest.

"Never mind him. Let's go," Roger said as he grabbed Lance.

The priest rolled over and raised himself with an outstretched arm. He rattled off several deep throaty words in Spanish. No, it was Latin. "Damnare, infernus, aeternus" were the words Lance picked up on.

"This fool just cursed me! Cursed me to hell!"

"Okay, spooky. But, let's go!"

Lance, with Roger and Sanders, ran across the carbonized cocoa field and back into the thicket. Every vine and branch painfully reminded them of their raw wounds.

Enrique Rojas struggled to move but gained mobility with each painful elongation of his body. "Miguel. We must hurry. We will make a deal. They will have to take us then."

"Enrique. They won't take us." Miguel forced himself to sit up. He felt new shivers of pain running down his arm in the broken cast that once held his arm in place.

Roger joined Sanders in moving the second Cessna again, rolling it off the runway.

Lance quickly tunneled up to the cockpit. Momentary fumbling found the key, and the aircraft had life once again. Engine No. 2 spooled up first. There was combustion. Engine No. 1 spooled up. Lance moved the throttled to the reverse mode. Then he felt no nose gear steering. Roger jumped inside. "Roger, the torque link is disengaged. Rojas must have done it."

"Okay, got it." Roger stepped out and ran up to the aircraft's nose. He grabbed the back of the torque link mechanism and snapped it back in place. Roger stood and gave Lance a thumbs-up. Lance looked down and moved the rudder pedals. He could steer. He shot a thumbs-up back to Roger. Roger jerked and fell on the nose of the aircraft. He pushed himself up, but as his eyes rolled up, he slowly slid down. Lance had no breath. He could see a beaming Enrique Rojas maybe one hundred feet away. Lance flew out of his seat. He came out and scooped up Roger. Roger tried to speak, but it was too noisy, and he had gone into shock. Then Lance saw the blood on his hand. Lance stood and aimed. The Walther PPK delivered Lance's regards just left of center of Rojas' forehead. He watched the drug lord fall back. He saw Miguel and aimed, but he dropped down into the grass.

"Great shot, kid," Sanders said.

"Help me get Roger on board," Lance said with panic in his voice. Lance reached down for Roger.

"Go do your pilot thing. I got your buddy," Sanders said.

Lance was no sooner in his seat than Sanders rolled Roger out on the bench seat and seat-belted him in best he could.

Lance had the engines in reverse thrust. There could be no wasted motion. He augmented the thrust to complete the half circle and then hit full forward power. Sanders knelt between the two rear-facing seats and held on as g-forces intensified. He kept a watchful eye as they rolled past the two Cessnas. The FARC came out of the tall shoots of grass that lined the edge of the dirt runway. Sanders' final contingency detonated the two aircraft. Lance pulled back on the yoke to escape their terrestrial confinement. It was two hundred, twenty miles to Cartagena. Lance intended on making it there in forty minutes flat.

***

Lance eyed the Company's bizjet, following it into the night sky as he held a bag with Roger's bloodied clothes. He threw it inside the Mits. He stepped up and was dragged back by his hair and slugged on his jaw. He dropped.

"Boy, I told you what to do and where to go! You cost us all a lot of money by taking out Rojas. You could have popped your cherry on someone else," growled Karl Frick.

Lance raised himself and turned, facing a Vietnam-era Colt .45. Karl Frick stood tall with a full mane of reddish-brown hair and a long, though sparse mustache. He looked at Lance's burnt face and neck and his right gauze-wrapped hand. "Get a bit singed, did you? Good."

A Colombian named Eduardo Bolivia, a bit taller than Lance, with thinning hair, puffy eyes, and lips, shook his head. "We have to make an example of you, Lance. Or, you resign and working under our control."

"I'm not your *mule*," Lance said stanchly.

"Cool with me," Frick said, cocking the hammer on the .45.

Frick felt a gun barrel push up firmly against his left temple. "Un-uh, friend. Give me the gun," Roman Sanders insisted. Frick moved slowly. Sanders pushed the gun barrel with more intensity. "C'mon." Sanders looked over to Bolivia. "You too. You okay, Lance."

"Yeah, I'm okay." Lance looked at Bolivia. "He said, you too."

Bolivia grumbled, pulling out his gun, slowly at first and then with a jerk. Lance caught his hand gripped around the pistol, and twisted it with a kick to the head. Bolivia tensed for a second, and then his hand dropped from the gun as he did from standing.

"Nice, Lance."

Lance looked at Sanders, quite somber. "Is this all I have to look forward to, Roman?"

"You have it all wrong, Lance. These men are your neighbor."

"My what?" Sanders watched the pained expression, one of recognition, roll across Lance's face. "You mean—Juan?"

Sanders nodded toward Frick. "They are the same people."

Sanders backed away from Frick and walked toward Lance. "Whoever they are—complete the mission." Sanders stepped inside the Mits and sat in the right rear-facing seat.

Frick flashed a sinister grin. "You wanna play my game, kid? I play for keeps."

Lance's jaw tightened. "Just get in the plane."

"Nah, man, you ain't throwing me at the feet of Jeffrey." Frick whipped his hand to and fro a couple of times until the *balisong*, folding knife blade was pointing at Lance. Frick lunged. Lance kicked the knife up and out of his hand.

"That kid has some of the fastest feet I've ever seen," Sanders said, grinning. Yeah, hi, Jeffrey, we have a contingency," Sanders said over the air phone. "We'll need you in Miami. Hold on," Sanders said, leaning forward. Sanders winced when Bolivia grabbed Lance from behind in a chokehold. Too many seconds were going by. "Jeffrey, hang on!" Sander dropped the phone and moved to the door, pistol in hand. He stopped—witnessing the explosive nature and training of Lance kick into action. Bolivia flipped back over Lance's left leg as he took a hit in the face from Frick. He let go of Bolivia and blocked, grappled, and blasted Frick with innumerable punches. Frick fell back; in panic, he turned and crawled toward the Mits. He stood up only to be met by a foot that kicked him into the aircraft. Sanders pulled his feet back as Frick flew inside.

Frick looked up at Sanders. "Come on, man. Stop this. I'm all busted up inside. I think my jaw is broke. He's nearly killed Eduardo."

"Hey, you wanted to stir the hornets' nest," Sanders said.

Lance went back and grabbed Bolivia off the asphalt. Then he marched him angrily toward the Mits. With each step, though, Lance forced composure by the time he stood at the door. He looked up at Sanders. "You and Jeffrey hit harder." He pushed Bolivia inside. "I don't like being like this, Roman."

"The best of us don't."

"But that I have to share this planet with them, whether next door or not—I have no escape."

Sanders pulled the cap off the first of two syringes. "I don't know what to tell you, Lance. Other than, when they cross your path, they don't escape you."

***

Lance sat next to Roger's bed in the low-lit private room. He was safe in a Miami hospital. It agonized Lance to watch helplessly as Roger lay there.

Rodney Sr. and Betty Drake rushed into the room. They froze in horror, magnified by seeing the red, burnt, and bruised face of Lance.

"What happened?" Betty asked.

"Lance can't talk about that, I'm afraid," Ralston said. "I'm very sorry, but it's classified."

"Who are you?" Rodney Sr. asked.

"Jeffrey Ralston, CIA. We are doing everything possible for your son."

"When did this happen?"

"Two days ago. I have to tell you—Roger's been shot," Lance admitted. Betty weakened in her knees. Rodney Sr. steadied her.

"Lance, no details," Ralston admonished.

"I don't give a damn what's top secret. Why didn't I know my son was injured?"

"Rodney, Betty, Mr. Ralston made sure Roger has had the very best care."

"Lance got him to a hospital in time, and we medevacked him here this morning. He's healing very well now," Ralston offered.

"Who shot my boy?"

"I took care of it, Rodney."

"You a tough guy now, Lance? Was it your fault? You tell me, boy!"

"You know I'd put his life before mine, Rodney. You know that!"

“Come with me, Lance. Leave Roger with his parents.”

Lance let the night air refresh him somewhat. He and Ralston took a seat on a bench.

“I know you think your world is crashing down around you, but the spirit you evoke is praiseworthy,” Ralston said.

“Keep your medals, Jeffrey. I don’t want them. I don’t want any of this anymore.”

“I won’t underestimate your sacrifice. But you did take out the number two drug lord in the world. And before that flew the number one drug lord back home—Pablo Escobar.”

“He insisted on a ride home. I insisted he pay for gas.”

Ralston once again appreciated Lance’s coolness under pressure. “And?”

“He laughed and took the gun out of my face. On the flight to his home, Hacienda Napoles, I told him that my father was the co-pilot on the Pan Am flight that took Meyer Lansky off Cuba before Castro got to Havana. He thought it was a good omen. He refueled my plane and gave me five grand in cash.”

“I’m happy about your perk. But why was I not informed?”

“Coffee. Which I hate even more now.”

“Does this have to do with an associate of Escobar’s, Eduardo Bolivia, a coffee broker?”

“And arms and drugs dealer.”

“What? We have no intel on this.”

“You do now. We’ve been his competition.”

Ralston was growing impatient but knew to listen. “Go on.”

“Bolivia has also been running guns into Nicaragua for the Contra rebels. He cornered me back in Colombia and threatened to expose me for violating the Boland agreement if I didn’t do his bidding.”

“Did you deny anything and everything?”

“Naturally. But he knew, Jeffrey. We were outed. You by name.”

Ralston frowned. “By whom?”

“It’s funny how coffee is second only to oil in world exports. Hence, people will kill for it. Even betray their country and friends for it. You need to be more careful whom you invite to your Fourth of July barbeques.”

Ralston tied the pieces together. “Are we talking about Karl Frick?”

“He met me at last year’s barbeque. It’s a small community we operate in when you get right down to it. Frick served six years in the Air Force and eight years with us, notably with Air America, where he no doubt honed his illicit skills.”

“Yes,” Ralston sighed. “And he’s very well connected politically. He’s also an asset. We use his coffee import business as a cover from here in Miami.”

"No, Jeffrey, we're the asset. He's been shipping more than a cup of joe with Bolivia."

"When did this all happen?"

"Three weeks ago. But I took care of it."

"Oh, Lance, what did you do?"

"Two diabetics shouldn't be threatening me. That's all."

Ralston jumped up and paced. "I don't want you back in Colombia. Or anywhere near Latin America again."

"Why?"

"Because you should have told me about this immediately."

Lance stood his ground. "It had to be this way, Jeffrey."

"Plausible deniability? Is that what you are going to tell me, Lance, me of all people?"

"Yes! At least for the interim. I had to keep your name out of it. I owe you that. For the first time in my life, I had the power to stop evil and protect someone I care about. I wasn't helpless, and it was awesome!"

Ralston calmed. "Then, I thank you for that, Lance. Where are they?"

"At Frick's girlfriend's condo. Tied up in the garage. But I think Frick's wife will beat you there."

Ralston accepted with this revelation that he would have to orchestrate a whole new paradigm regarding Lance.

He sent Lance home.

Ralston came into Roger's room. Roger opened his eyes. "Jeffrey."

"Well, you are among the living. We needed some good news. "

"Listen. You need to keep my family safe, and Lance. You keep them safe from Rojas. He'll want revenge. Promise me."

"Consider it done. And what will you do for me?"

"I just died for you." Roger closed his eyes.

***

Rodney Sr. was a stubborn man. He left Lance standing as he directed the cabin cruiser away from the pier. Betty Drake held the urn. Lance was resigned to Rodney Sr., blaming him for Roger's death and denouncing him as ever being part of his family.

Part 3

"The heart is more treacherous than anything else and is desperate. Who can know it?"

Jeremiah

Chapter 37

The Farm

May 14, 1987

Lance had a new plane: a Cessna Citation SP-I. The single-pilot bizjet was beefed up with higher thrust engines and capacities by Sierra Industries. Lance had them modify the wing to an accelerating wing—somewhat. It looked like any other Citation jet, except the wings had a sharper leading edge, which also featured a glycol wing de-icing system. Down-turned winglets fitted to the shortened wingtips and a wing fence along the top gave improved performance in lift, speed, and range.

The two front seats to the Citation were out on the hangar floor. Lance looked up out of the side windshield. There was his MU-2, "Miss Solitaire." She was safe. He was safe. Ralston kept him mainly at the Farm and training extensively since the Iran-Contra Gate scandal exploded into a media circus.

Currently, a new radar system was being installed in the Citation. Eric Pitts squirmed his way out from under the instrument panel.

"Here, it'll be easier for me to get under there than you, big boy," Lance said.

"Hey, be my guest," Eric offered.

"I'll have the same radar they're using in U.S. Customs' citations. I really will be a high spy," Lance mused.

"Well, I don't miss being out in the field. I'm glad I'll finish out my time right here. Home every night with Gina and the kids."

Lance and Eric sat at the small table. Eric had even brought out a nice bottle of wine that complimented their beef stew.

"I know you feel like you're in limbo, but given all the mess politically right now, keeping you out of sight is a good thing."

"Guess you can't do good things for bad people, and it not come back to bite you."

"One thing I know about Jeffrey is that he understands."

"I hope he doesn't plan on me hanging out here for the rest of my career."

"I don't," Ralston said, entering. "Thus, it's time for a change of scenery."

Chapter 38

Munich, Germany

48°8′00″N, 11°34′00″E

May 19, 1987

"There can't be any direct connection between you and the CIA ever again. Including this plane. So it's yours." Ralston had occupied the right seat since they departed the Camp Peary Airport at the Farm for the North-Atlantic. Now they were several minutes past the French-German border. They would soon start their descent from 41,000 feet into Munich-Riem International Airport.

"Jeffrey, you think now might be a good a time to explain what's going on, you know, like before we land?"

"I suppose. First of all, I appreciate your trying to defend me—and, more importantly, the Agency. You were put into an incredible bind by some very powerful men." Ralston still marveled at what he saw a year ago. "Though you had them tied up helpless in chairs epoxied to a garage floor."

"I screwed up, didn't I?"

"But you learned from it. Never go it alone."

Lance thought of the Iran-Contra Gate scandal that occupied the news at the moment, with Oliver North and his people set to appear before a congressional hearing. By issue, he could or perhaps should be sitting next to Uncle Ollie in a trial that was politically motivated. Lance knew he would be chewed up and spit out. It was a disquieting thought.

"So, how long do I hide out here?"

"We have disavowed your existence with the CIA, Lance. We had to."

Lance's gleaming new reality darkened. "I'm burned? I no longer work for the CIA?"

"Au contraire. Yes, your four years as a government employee are over. But you will now be a contractor. The CIA will contract privately for your services but at triple the pay with perks and bonuses."

"So, now I'm just an operative? And I have to have a handler like I'm a circus animal?"

"Oh, for the love of…Lance, don't be so blasted melodramatic all the time! You report to me. Outside of a new location and employment status, it's all still the same. Better, in fact."

"Wait. How long will I be in Germany?"

"It's your new home."

"Come on, Jeffrey. I can't live here."

"I admit I had to work out some logistics, all off the cuff, and call in a few favors."

A Lufthansa pilot, sounding young and arrogant, shot out his landing request in German.

"See, I didn't understand a word he said. And he's supposed to speak in English. I'm screwed."

The Lufthansa pilot insisted on responding in German. It was irritating the other pilots set in the landing queue that Lance was quickly approaching. Ralston was unnerved that everything he had put into motion was about to crash and burn. He had a troubled son to get back to, a wife to calm, a country and spy agency to calm, but immediately he had Lance to calm.

But then, the British came to the rescue. Lance caught sight of a British Airways Boeing 757 on an intersecting course to Munich-Riem. He could plainly see the *Speed Bird*, the long thin red line that ran most of the length of the fuselage that had a thicker sharp down angle near the nose. The name served as British Airways' call sign. The Speed Bird captain shot back at the Lufthansa pilot via communications with Munich control on everyone's behalf.

"We are in Germany. Why do I have to speak in English?" the Lufthansa pilot argued.

"Because you lost the bloody war!" the Speed Bird captain radioed in response.

Lance roared in laughter. Ralston barreled out in laugher himself. It broke the ice and did what careful planning had not. Ralston was grateful that circumstance had smiled favorably on him when he needed it most.

"We could give it a try?"

"As you wish, Jeffrey."

Lance was focused on the landing, but in his peripheral view, he saw the outlining of his new life.

After the Cessna bizjet had secured itself from flight mode to taxi mode, he rolled past an island of general aviation aircraft, somewhat in the center of the tarmac, toward a wall of buildings that went from Nazi-era art deco that looked impressive still, to a more modern look, to sheet metal skinned buildings. The brick-red control tower looked like a Lego block. It looked cool.

Ralston pointed to the *Alpine Execujet* hangar in the middle of a row of large hangars. A man in his sixties, Lance was sure, with a pleasant smile, stepped into view just inside of the hangar entrance and waved Lance inside. He cut the fuel to idle stop and coasted the last few feet inside. The quieting of the engines coincided with the hangar doors rumbling close and it going dimmer.

“Lance, the moment you step out the door, you are no longer Lance Rio. And you’ll need this.” Ralston reached inside his right breast pocket and pulled out a *Reisepass*. His new German passport. Lance saw his photo. It was decent, he supposed, all proper and in order. Then he saw his new nom de somebody, his new alias.

“Manfred Bosch?”

“I picked it myself,” Ralston said proudly. “You also go by the nickname of Manny.”

“Am I related to the power tool company Bosch’s?”

“No. Well, fourth or fifth twice removed, I believe I’ve designated.”

“Do I even look like a Manny?”

Ralston frowned. “It was that or Fritz.”

Lance acquiesced. “Manny, it is.”

The door opened. “Hello, my nephew. Welcome home!” the voice said with a German accent.

“Hello, Uncle. It’s nice to be back. Wow, my very own uncle. And he loves me?”

“Like a son,” Ralston affirmed.

Chapter 39

Washington, D.C.

September 28, 1987

It was after three in the morning. The wind blew lightly against Ralston's bedroom window. Specifically, an uncut branch from the maple tree in the front yard. Life was at a monotone. Voices weren't too quiet to raise suspicions, nor were they so loud as to drive him to distraction. Work and family life were simply at a steady expression of contentment. His mind, though, drifted to that of the goings-on of Lance. He hadn't spoken to Lance in over a month. It was sad in a way that Lance wasn't in the fold, like before, but he was too valuable to lose because of a former traitorous friend and to the bureaucracy that would have swallowed him whole before he had a real chance to blossom. Ralston found his robe and went downstairs to his office.

Ralston settled himself at his desk and dialed.

"Hallo," Lance answered.

"Lance, it's Jeffrey. How are you?"

"I'm fine. Is anything wrong?"

"No. I just have some things on my mind, and I need to pop over and discuss them with you. And it's time to check up on you anyway."

"Well, come on over, and I'll buy you a beer."

Chapter 40

Munich

October 1, 1987

Oktoberfest. The yearly *Wunderkind* of events, as Lance thought of it, now that he was part of the crowd in the world's largest *Volksfest* or *People's Fair*. As massive as the amounts of beer there was on hand, there were as many people to drink it. Most of the attendees were Bavarians, but it drew people from all over the world. Lance enjoyed the whole feel of it with its traditions of *lederhosen*-clad men and, of course, *dirndl*-clad women—every man's fantasy that had ever watched a Hammer horror film.

Werner Pick, Lance's newfound uncle for the past four months, brought a beer toting Jeffrey Ralston over to their table. Werner's daughter, Anja, accompanied them. She was a dazzling German beauty with large crystal blue eyes. The blonde hair was full and luxurious. She stood nearly as tall as Lance. Being athletic and an avid skier kept her goddess-shaped figure taut. She bested Lance by a year. Anja left the men to talk.

"Hello, Lance. I'm glad to see you acclimating," Ralston said as he sat.

Lance smiled with a nod. "Let's just say it was a good thing you weren't here for the first month in my abandonment."

"I left you in kind and capable hands," Ralston replied, taking a swig of his beer.

"So, you did. So, *was ist los*? What's up?"

Ralston raised an eyebrow in light offense. "*Nicht— wei geht's es Ihnen*? Not, how are you?"

"You have a large beer in your hand. It's obvious how you are."

"So I do. You were in Berlin for the president's speech back in June?"

"Yes, I can say that I personally witnessed President Reagan tell *Gorbie* to "*tear down this wall*," Lance said in a reasonably good Ronald Reagan impersonation.

"And we want to help Mr. Gorbachev do just that. There are changes on the horizon, and I need you to be ready. I need you to keep building your roots here as you continue to expand." Ralston enjoyed a few quality swallows of his beer. "I also have been thinking that it's time for you to build one of those kit planes for us."

It was early evening when Lance drove up to the hangar with Werner and Ralston. Ralston observed Lance's movements as he drove. They were second nature. Good.

The three men entered the hangar. There was the Citation as Ralston had remembered it. It had a new registration number: D-BDEE. D for Deutschland. It inspired Ralston to see the physical manifestation of his handiwork. "So when can you build one?"

"Let me get fluent in German first."

"All right, Lance."

"What would you like?"

"Surprise me. Just make sure it's—what's that nickname of yours? Oh yes, Fast Glass."

"Fastglass," Lance corrected.

Ralston had gone back to his hotel. Lance set time aside to practice Kenpo. He ran through forms, making sure each and every one was accurate, smooth, and powerful. A bottle of water and his white towel sat on the Citation's wing. Lance wore black gi pants, no shirt, and traditional shoes.

Anja watched from the doorway connected to a small hallway that led to the company's offices where she worked. Lance finished a set and headed the few steps to his towel and water.

"Come in, Anja."

"How did you know I was here?"

"I better know who is sneaking up on me." She came closer. Her beauty was emitting rays of energy that hit Lance stronger the closer she came.

"You have a black belt?"

"I have two." He now realized he needed to put a shirt on.

"So, you could teach me how to flip someone?" She grabbed his arm and twirled inside of it, resting her body up against his. Lance felt he just went from black belt to yellow belly.

"Yes, but not now. I have an early flight tomorrow, and I need to go to sleep."

"I can stay with you tonight?"

"No, Anja. You need to go home. Bitte."

She turned inside of his arm. She kissed him. She pulled away. "Are you truly sure?"

"Now is not a good time, Anja." There was a pleading to his voice and expression. She took a half step back. She nodded.

"Do you ski?"

"No."

"I will teach you." She kissed him tenderly on the cheek. Anja left through the door she entered. Lance touched his cheek.

Chapter 41

Peshawar, Pakistan

34°01′00″N, 71°35′00″E

November 19, 1987

Lance had carried some interesting people on flights all over Europe and the Middle East in his Citation and with pilots on other aircraft that Werner owned. Some were arrogant Arabs, Germans, and once an Italian CEO who thought himself the Pope. The biggest kick to date was faring a fun lovin' half-drunk Texan to Pakistan. Lance wouldn't let him smoke in his plane, but the Congressman made up for it with drink. Lance hoped he had slept most of it off as he didn't stir once during a refueling stop. The Congressman finally roused himself to life "in need of a pee."

Lance was finally glad to be on the approach to Runway 30 into Islamabad, Pakistan International Airport.

The Cessna jet slowed enough upon landing to make a big U-turn as the runway also served as the only taxiway. A 747 was holding short. Lance cleared the runway and was directed to parking.

Two small white vans, dirtied by years of wear and neglect, pulled up. Ralston stepped out of the right side, sliding door in the front van.

"Well, it looks like your ride is here, Congressman," Lance said as he pulled out his bag.

"Look, son, you got to call me Charlie. Everyone does, ya know."

"Lance, lock up and grab your cold-weather gear," Ralston said.

"Jeffrey, he's one of yours? I should'da known."

"No, Charlie. You shouldn't."

The van left, followed by the other.

Three hours later, Lance could step out and stretch his legs. It was cold. The warm air inside the van was quickly dissipating. Zipping up his coat and donning gloves were in order. They were in the city of Peshawar. Peshawar meant: "City of Flowers." It was like any other city in the region in that it had a bustling citizenry going about its business. Lance noticed that only the main streets were paved, making them like the rest of the town on the dusty side. Most buildings were no taller than five stories. This city of flowers had a more ominous reputation for being the cloak and dagger capitol of the world. Whether that was true or not, it did draw a lot of skullduggery.

Their rest stop and a bite to eat did little to unsettle Lance as to why he was there. It was reasonable that Ralston wanted Lance involved to whatever extent in the largest covert operation that the CIA had ever orchestrated. Political motive was simple: make Afghanistan the Soviet Union's Vietnam War. Lance spent his time in the region flying over the Afghanis, where their plight was abstract to him. Clarity was only a short drive out of town, about thirty-five kilometers southeast, and the trigger for the whole operation.

The envoy stopped at the *Jallozai* Afghan refugee camp. Lance's first impression was a valley of tents. There were thousands. Upon closer inspection, he noticed they were makeshift. Some were staked with tree branches or any wood or metal available that could make a pitch. The tent covers were blankets or blue and purple plastic liners. Any cloth material that could be placed over the frame. The small pup tent-sized habitats were packed with an entire family. Then the smell of human waste hit him, supported by the smell of rot. His sinuses broke open, and he felt drainage build and flow making him nauseous. He had to spit. But every new breath brought in kept the cycle going. Lance put his handkerchief over his nose and mouth.

"Yeah, Lance, I tell ya, the first time I got a good whiff of this, I about puked my guts out. Takes a bit of getting used to," Charlie said.

"You can never get used to this!" Lance said venomously. "This is an atrocity! What's wrong with mankind?"

Lance focused on the people, mostly women and children. What men there were in the camp were either old or infirmed with marginal abilities to care for themselves. Hatred for the Soviet empire was a fire in him now. The smell was of secondary concern as Lance went further into the camp. Even though the grime on their little faces, he could see that the children were beautiful. Lance felt a yearning that only a father could know. He couldn't keep tears from shedding when he came upon a little boy that had his legs blown off. The bandages were soaked, not with blood but with the stain of gangrene. The woman that held him never looked up but gently rocked her dead child. Lance did not know what to do. Should he go back to the van and get a shovel or walk on indifferent to the wake of death that permeated the camp?

Ralston and Charlie grabbed Lance and moved him down to the other end of the camp, where a dusty, somewhat rusted white Toyota van stood. Two people were giving medical aid to the ever-growing queue. Lance watched them. They were like the living dead in a zombie movie, staggering, shuffling foot by foot, with blank looks on their faces. They were like convicts with long prison sentences. These people were institutionalized. They had shut down mentally and emotionally. There was no hope, no reason, just an ever-dwindling need to survive. Death was their release.

"I know we can do something about this, Jeffrey."

"What would you suggest, Lance?"

"Bring in mobile water treatment units. Build them some showers. Wash tubs for their clothes. Soap. Thermo blankets. I can pack a load of stuff in the plane and drop it off here. I mean right here. I can land over there." Lance pointed to a flat spot out of the way. "Or get a C-One-Thirty in here. How much trouble could it be? Really?"

"And would you like them to have Charmin toilet paper while we're at it?"

"That's out of line, Jeffrey. You know where you can go!"

"Watch it, buster!"

"Lance, I have to tell ya, I appreciate your passion about it, but it's just not that easy. Believe me, Jeffrey knows," Charlie said.

"How much more palm greasing would it take?" Lance asked.

"Lance, think of it as political logistics. Screwed up as that sounds. In addition to the Soviets, there's this big ol' tribal thing going on."

"I don't care. This Hatfield and McCoy's—Crips and Bloods foolishness has to go."

The congressman looked over to Ralston. "I think we need to get on the road before it gets dark."

Lance was numb. He couldn't get the stench of human misery out of his nostrils. They had driven only a small fragment of the way into the Khyber Pass, the famed road that historically linked Pakistan to Afghanistan, where caravans carried goods across Asia, and even Alexander the Great once trekked through with his army. The Khyber Pass had also been traditionally one of the most dangerous roads to travel. Even more so with the Afghan-Soviet war in progress. They drove further north to cross on mountain roads that were safer along the Hindu Kush mountain range, where they would cross over into Afghanistan. It was vast, barren, and cold. Snow had fallen, which also led to lower combat activity.

It was a moderately clear day, though, as they ascended, they were met with fog and drizzle. They had to don respirators for the two-mile drive through the *Salang Tunnel* as it had no working ventilation system. The driver turned on the headlights. A man walking next to his mule, pulling a cart, was appreciative of the brief glimpse of the road in the pitch-black tunnel. Finally, they came to the end of the tunnel and exited as a Soviet troop truck passed them. It unnerved Lance.

"They have more to be nervous about than us. The Mujaheddin are known to ambush the Soviets when they come through the tunnel. Oddly enough, it was the Soviets back in nineteen-sixty-four, in an agreement with the Afghans, that built this tunnel," Charlie said.

"That's very neighborly," Lance remarked.

Further along the mountain road, they finally started to descend, where Lance's first glimpse of Afghanistan came into view. Sharp echoes bounced all around them. Lance recognized it as gunfire. The driver pulled over. Heavy vibrato echoed everywhere, shaking the van. A Soviet Mil-24 "Hind" attack helicopter pounded the thin air just above them. Ralston scanned the area with binoculars and saw a faded beige Suzuki Ravi pickup truck. The tiny three-cylindered vehicle moved the two men in the cab and the four in the truck bed slowly along the mountain road several turns back. One of the men raised a shoulder launcher, but the Hind caught sight of them and strafed the truck with machine-gun fire before the man could aim and fire the stinger missile. Ralston thought it unfortunate.

The two vans continued and then turned off the dirt road to a muddied pothole-laced road. The van came to a small clearing. The Mujaheddin came out of the rocks and crags surrounding the vans with AK-47s raised. Comfortable, they lowered their weapons with a more casual approach to the vans. Behind a few large rocks was a cave.

Lance helped with the unloading and unpacking of supplies. The Afghans were more interested in the six new stinger missiles brought to them than with necessities and hygiene. Lance shook his head.

"Hey, Lance, look at it this way," Charlie said. "It's like you have this neighbor, and you're all friendly and caring, but then he comes in and invades your home; takes your wife and kids. But you aren't able to fight back. You're helpless. Then one day, someone doesn't like the way your neighbor is treating you. He steps in and makes him stop. Then he shows you how to stand up to your neighbor on your own. You know what I mean?"

"You just summed up my life in a couple of sentences." Lance walked off.

Lance was somber and quiet. Snuggled in his bedding, he leaned against a rock. The temperature was below freezing outside the cave and not much better inside. Lance understood the need for sleep. He had had a long day and needed to recharge. With another clear day tomorrow, the Soviets would be back out on the prowl.

Morning came.

"Lance, you need to get up. We have to get going back down the mountain," Ralston said.

"Okay. Give me a minute."

Lance came out from the cave to see Ralston and Charlie packing the van. The other van had left. He turned in anger when he heard two Afghan men quarreling. Their words turned to action, and blows were exchanged. Lance jumped in the middle and threw both men down on the slushy ground. "Enough!"

The two men on the ground yelled at him, both scrambling to their feet. One Afghani charged him, but Lance grabbed his hand, locked his wrist, and flipped him over it, landing him back on the ground. The other man pulled his knife. Lance kicked it straight up and lunged forward to grab it on its descent. A single kick to the gut sent the aggressor to the ground, where Lance dropped on him, grabbed his beard, and positioned the knife to his exposed throat.

"Lance, leave him alone," Ralston ordered. Lance stood. The knife wasn't balanced for throwing, but he made it stick into a log on its second rotation.

"Rival tribes. Your Hatfield's and McCoy's," Charlie said.

"I was thinking Army-Navy." Lance jumped into the second row of seats by the congressman and slid the door shut.

Ralston's attention was drawn to the thumping echo down the mountain pass. A Hind was on the prowl. He looked at their driver. "Thank the chief for his hospitality. And remind him that my young friend here was upset because the real enemy is not in the camp but coming."

The driver spoke those words to the chief. The chief applauded and said he would have Lance come back and fight with them.

They began the drive down.

Lance was happy to be back to his jet. Ralston and the congressman would be returning in the Agency's Gulfstream jet. Ralston approached Lance. "Is there anything you need before I leave?"

"I plan to stop off in Baku as you wanted. But if you could get me an Aircraft Spruce and Specialty Company catalog?"

"It will be waiting for you when you get back home."

Lance followed the Gulfstream to the runway and into the air, following some of the roads they took two days earlier into the mountains. They would have to turn soon to stay out of Soviet-occupied airspace. Lance could see two Pakistani F-16s on patrol over the mountain range. Then something caught his eye. Rapid flashes followed by streams of dark smoke that shot across the mountain gorge and smoke billowing up. Anger gave way to the security of altitude.

Ralston bolted upright in his seat when he saw the Cessna jet drop out of the sky and dive into the ravine, and then disappear as clouds covered his window.

The Mil-24 attack helicopter hovered like a giant dragonfly. The two-man crew watched from inside their bulbous canopy, obliterating several of the Mujaheddin. Two small trucks lay as burning rubble along the mountain road.

Only one man was able to jump out of the back before it was destroyed. He took a stinger launcher with him along with much shrapnel. He was hurt but dared not move or would reveal his position. Some rocks and snow-covered shrubbery kept him hidden for the moment. They knew he was there. He saw no alternative and turned on the launcher's electrics. He fought to stand and face his enemy. The Russian sitting higher in the back seat waved, laughing at him. The Afghani pushed the launcher to his shoulder, but his leg gave way, and he slumped back down.

A soft, buzz saw hum came through the pass, echoing between each side of the ravine. The hum grew and then roared as a large white flash pulled up underneath the helicopter, startling it from its hover. The pilot over-corrected in reaction to stabilize the flaying aircraft. He rotated back to hover toward his prey. The Afghani smiled and squeezed the trigger. The flying monster held its hover inside of the fireball and then broke apart, dropping a thousand feet to the bottom of the ravine. The man weakened and dropped to his knees, his life force leaving him. He wondered if the man in the jet was the one that had his knife to his throat. He praised God for sending him.

Chapter 42

Munich

November 25, 1987

Lance rose from his bed after sleeping a rare nine hours straight. He put on sweats and went to the stairs that were more like a ladder from his studio apartment below.

He opened the trap door, as he called it, and came up into the small foyer, adjacent to the kitchen, where Werner and Anja were having breakfast. When his eyes met Anja's, their instant attraction burned through the last remains of his grogginess.

"Guten Morgen," Lance said. He spoke only in German as his current knowledge allowed. Anja rose to get Lance his morning tea. Lance took his seat at the table. He saw the Aircraft Spruce & Specialty Co. catalog on the table, waiting for him as promised. The picture on the cover was of the Rutan Voyager aircraft that flew around the world non-stop almost a year earlier.

"What are you planning?" Werner asked.

"Design and build a kit plane. I need to outfit the hangar with equipment, if I may?"

Werner moved a yellow notepad in front of Lance. "Tell me what you need? Go on, write it down. You will have it if we don't already."

Stirrings from the back of the townhouse drew Lance's attention. A four-year-old little girl came out. Ute was the spitting image of her mother. She crawled up onto Lance's lap. His arms held her. He placed several kisses on her. Anja's heart melted. She went to the refrigerator. Who was this man that had come into their lives and held all of their hearts?

Lance settled on the leather sofa in the living room, looking out the large glass windows. He watched the snow rock gently to the ground. It was peaceful, and he let its calm wash over him.

Werner came in and sat on the sofa. "I have watched you closely ever since you have come here, Lance. I find you a man of great character. Trustworthy. A man who cares for others. My girls are quite taken with you."

"Werner, you must know that Anja and I have not been intimate."

The crystal blue eyes, deep-set within the folds of aged skin, widened with his smile. "Despite her attempts. Yes, my daughter and I are very close."

"It would be bad manners with her up here and me a guest down in the studio. Despite my screaming loins."

Werner chuckled. "I understand. You are a man. She is a woman."

Lance looked around. "By the way, where is Anja?"

"She has taken Ute to see her father—Urs. You can speak freely."

"You are wondering if I could love Anja and my little Ute as my own."

"The truth is you already have."

Lance didn't smile lightly at being revealed but for a telling sign of recognition. "You're an *Ostler*. East German. Aren't you?"

"What makes you ask that?"

"I've been here long enough to detect an East German accent. Given your age, I would say it was dear old dad, Harold Ralston, who helped you out of East Germany once upon a time." Lance saw the look of capture flexing within the wrinkled brow. "Perhaps you were—Stasi."

"Clever boy. I was like my brother Otto, an aeronautical engineer. We worked for Messerschmitt forty-three years ago until it was discovered that our mother was a Jew. Though our father was Roman Catholic."

"I'm so sorry, Werner."

"We both ended up in the camps. Otto was sent to Auschwitz and I to Belzec, both in Poland. I have not seen my brother since. I barely survived as Belzec would unload the unwary off of the trains straight into the showers."

"You mean the gas chambers."

"One and the same. I became of one of the *Sonderkommandos*."

"That's the SS, isn't it?"

"It's misleading. Sonderkommandos means "Special Unit." We were the Jews that unloaded the dead bodies out of the showers and from the railcars for those that died in transit to the camp. Usually, the Sonderkommandos were killed off every few days, weeks, or months as routine. We knew too much and would be replaced by another and another after that. I found myself swallowing gold teeth, earrings, even a gold watch once just to have something for barter. I survived for nine months. Until the end of the war. Something unheard of in that camp."

"Your rescuers were the Soviets, and now you were under the loving care of Stalin. Out of the frying pan into the fire."

"You could say. My brother was sent to Russia to work for the Miko-yan-i-Gurevich Design Bureau."

"Yes, the MiG Aircraft Company."

"I denied any knowledge of aeronautics to stay in Germany. Unfortunately, the Stasi recruited me. However, I set out to be an informant to the West. It was Harold Ralston that first contacted me. And planned our escape in nineteen-sixty-six."

"Well, Uncle Werner, I am glad you are here and my friend." Lance paused. "Would you teach me about the ways of the Stasi?"

Werner looked at Lance with puzzlement. “Such as?”

Lance smiled evenly. “Everything.”

***

“If you want a relationship with Anja, keep doing the quality of work you are doing, and you’ll have my blessings,” Ralston said quietly.

“And build your plane when I’m not running back and forth to Pakistan.”

“Yes. But as it’s your one-year anniversary here, I thought we would spend a little time together. See how things are going.”

“Except we’re in Berlin.”

“I like all my people to experience Berlin. Especially East Berlin.”

Lance caught another silent flicker of a newspaper peripherally from a patron sitting across the busy *Café Adler.* The famed café sat diagonally on the corner of *Check Point Charlie*, the portal through the Berlin Wall that Werner and Anja as a young girl once were smuggled through. Lance found it satirical to see two guardhouses stationed 100 yards opposite each other on the same street. On top of each guardhouse was a large poster. On the Soviet side, a charming soldier there to greet you. On the American side, when leaving the Soviet sector, a young American soldier with the same angelic expression. Lance found Berlin to be a quasi-nervy place once you understood that it was an oasis deep inside the Soviet desert. It was a geopolitical anomaly. The city was apportioned into U.S., French, British, and Soviet sectors after World War II. Yet, all of Berlin was encapsulated within East Germany.

Their breakfast came. “It’s like we’re the cowboys, and the Indians are circling us,” Lance said.

“Some equate it to being in the water, and you’re contending with circling fins.”

“I like my analogy better.”

“Why is that?” Ralston said as he enjoyed his first bite of scrambled eggs.

“Easier to shoot back.”

Noteworthy about the Café Adler, it was truly a denizen for spies. Lance observed without be observed if someone read a newspaper while their food got cold. Only one man acted smooth enough to pull it off. Lance noticed that the man in a medium brown sport coat had the look of a spy. He could have been a former Nazi party member, now Stasi. There were nuances he had learned to pick up on back in his training, further refined by Ralston and Werner. Lance was maturing into a very savvy spy. His anal nature was an asset.

Lance followed Ralston out of the café. The man Lance thought the smoothest with the old peering over the newspaper trick uncrossed his legs and folded the newspaper, laying it on the table. Franz Heckler, a tall, lean man with gray hair parted on his right side, left payment on the table, and stood up. He followed them out on the street. It was a personal and professional triumph that he never let a query about someone go unanswered.

Herr Heckler lost sight of them until they drove past him and headed to the checkpoint. They were going into the Soviet sector—his turf. He looked up the street and gave a short but sharp wave. A car parked three rows up started and pulled out. Heckler jumped in. His driver cut off another car only to be held up by the American guard at the checkpoint as prearranged. Ralston wanted nothing to interrupt the next five days of training.

***

Seven months of work and a completion date were enough to ferry Ralston over to Germany.

Ralston entered Lance's hangar. He was shocked at what was a relatively large hangar was now lined with more tools and machinery than he ever would have granted. His eye caught martial arts training equipment against the wall and large mats folded next to them. This part, he immediately approved.

Eric Pitts came down from the upstairs apartment. "Okay, Lance, now that Jeffrey is here, let's get this over with. My jetlag ain't gettin' any easier."

Ralston appreciated that Eric Pitts had been dragged repeatedly back and forth over the Atlantic to help Lance.

A large thin canvas covered what Ralston expected to enchant him. Lance took one end, and Eric took the other and peeled it back from nose to tail. Ralston stood intrigued with the tandem two-seater. "Were you trying to build a spaceship?"

The kit plane was of the *canard* family with the main wing in the back and the smaller wing or foreplane in the front. It had a crisp, lean shape about it, where the fuselage and the wings flowed into one another, and the canopy flowed seamlessly into the flat wedge-shaped nose. The aircraft was beautifully accented in a light blue-gray two-tone paint scheme. It looked late twenty-first century.

"Well done, boys. Tell me, what kit plane manufacturer did you go with?"

Eric looked confused. "What's he talking about?"

"None, Jeffrey. It's our design. You are looking at the prototype."

"Oh, lord, Lance, all I wanted was a fast composite kit plane. You're not aeronautical engineers."

"Jeffrey, do you see an aircraft in front of you?" Lance growled. He waved his hand toward Eric. "He's a mechanical engineer! He grew up helping his dad rebuild Stearman bi-planes! This is not our first kit plane. There are four innovations on this aircraft that'll knock your socks off, which is not what I want to knock off right now!"

Ralston ignored Lance's flaring nostrils and dagger glare, giving casual eye contact to the plane as he strolled around it. The wings were on the short side. The end of the wings had large chevron-shaped winglets that also served as rudders. Ralston moved the right rudder as he came around. The three-blade propeller caught his attention.

"Innovation number one," Lance huffed.

They looked nothing like he had seen before. They were thin and curved like the front fan blade of a turbofan jet engine with small end plates on the tips. The base of each blade was round and fit flush with the hub. Ralston pushed the propeller blade at the top with two fingers as if not impressed. He could feel the slight drag from the souped-up 360 horsepower Mazda rotary engine. He came around the left-wing, noting the sharp leading edge.

"Your accelerating airfoil insistency, no doubt."

"No doubt. Call it innovation number two."

"Impress me more. I'm not feeling the buzz."

"The aircraft is eighteen feet long with a wingspan of twenty-one feet. It's built around a light-weight chassis. Gross weight is two thousand three hundred pounds with sixty-gallons useable. And-it-is-fast!"

Ralston looked inside the cockpit. He expected an amateur setup, but to his surprise, he saw a very sophisticated instrument panel. It had a military-style side-stick control mounted on the right armrest. "Innovation number three."

"That's not an innovation, Lance."

"Yeah, it is, Jeffrey," Eric said. "It's our vacuum-assist system. Works on siphon pressure. You'll really be able to crank this baby all over the skies. You're looking at the prototype.

"That's only three innovations."

Lance sighed. "Didn't you notice how wide it is, Jeffrey? Twenty-eight inches. Though that's not innovation number four."

"All right, Lance. Roomy is good. When will it be ready?"

"We start test flights next week."

"Good. There's work for you two to do."

***

Simply put. This was fun! It was the kind of flying that Lance thrived on the most, high-g turns and dives. All he had to do was keep a proper supply of airsick bags onboard. He was never so self-absorbed that he forgot about his passenger in the backseat. Flight instructing had made him intuitive that way. After Lance burned off the first fifty hours of flying time with no mishaps, Ralston ordered another fifty hours before accepting a ride in the new aircraft. Once accomplished, Uncle Jeffrey blessed the new winged wonder and put it and Lance to work. This was his fourth run at pulling out a deserving Ostler from the East for whatever purpose the CIA deemed necessary.

Professor Ingrid von Stickel, a Germanic Amazon, nearly blew out Lance's eardrums with a dirty, husky laugh that exploded into an almost operatic shrill every time he dipped, bobbed, and weaved his way through the fifteen-minute run inside Czechoslovakian airspace. In her forties, she was a rather handsome woman with a fun-loving nature. It was apparent she had been locked up in a Soviet-controlled laboratory way too long.

Lance watched the rising sun throw its warm solar caress on the snow-capped Alps that lay ahead by still another forty miles. Another innovation, the double muffler system housed inside the near soundproof engine compartment, made for a quiet ride. The *Shadowhawk,* as Lance was inspired to call her after his second sortie behind the Iron Curtain, turned out to be one slick little sport plane.

Lance was now only ten clicks away from the welcome mat when off to his left, he spotted a Czechoslovakian Albatross L-39 tactical jet fighter-trainer. Even though Lance could max out an impressive speed of 352 knots, or 405 miles per hour, the L-39 still had nearly a 100 mile per hour speed advantage. Lance had the edge in maneuverability with 12-g tolerant wings.

Lance watched the rising sun throw its warm solar caress on the snow-capped Alps that lay ahead by still another forty miles. Another innovation, the double muffler system housed inside the near soundproof engine compartment, made for a quiet ride. The *Shadowhawk,* as Lance was inspired to call her after his second sortie behind the Iron Curtain, turned out to be one slick little sport plane.

Lance was now only ten clicks away from the welcome mat when off to his left, he spotted a Czechoslovakian Albatross L-39 tactical jet fighter-trainer. Even though Lance could max out an impressive speed of 352 knots, or 405 miles per hour, the L-39 still had nearly a 100 mile per hour speed advantage. The climb rates were comparable. Lance had the edge in maneuverability with 12-g tolerant wings.

Lance kept a focused eye on the L-39, watching it turn toward the east when he heard cooing from the back seat, and then a strong hand came around his seat harness and rubbed his chest. "Liebchen..." she said. He could feel her warm breath as she pushed her head around his seat headrest. "Liebchen mach mir den Hengst."

"Make like a what?" Lance said in English.

"Ah, du bist an Amerikaner? Ja?" she said in greater delight. She put her full wet lips on his neck and bit. The plane jerked up. Ingrid was thrown back into her seat. Lance tried to relax his grip on the tightly held control stick, as he was certain he just suffered a stroke.

"Put your belt back on!" he yelled in German. "How did you fit up here anyway?" he yelled in English.

Lance watched the L-39 make a slow turn to the left, but then its turn rate sharpened. It spotted him. Lance shook off his temporary nerve damage and shoved the Shadowhawk into a dive. He knew the L-39 was armed and would shoot him down if he got a clear shot. Lance was determined to stay a blur.

The Shadowhawk pegged over 400 miles per hour. It pulled out of the dive and skimmed along the grassy knolls, climbing toward the fringe of the Alps where he could better yet blend into the snow-covered peaks. If the L-39 pilot thought clearly, he would welcome this intrusion into his airspace as the Soviet Union has lessened its grip on his country. However, like any predatory creature, the Czech jet would instinctively chase what ran from it.

The L-39 pilot recognized the aircraft as a kit plane he had seen only once at an air show. His prey intrigued him, and he pursued.

The Czech pilot was forced to keep higher power settings to stay up with the nimble, strangely shaped aircraft. He had seen a pirated Czech-dubbed version of the first Star Wars movie. He was chasing a *Tie Fighter*, but he could see the whirl of propellers on the backend. The aircraft turned inside of him and was gone.

Lance pulled up sharply, losing the bigger aircraft, but felt a thud rock the aircraft. "Do you have your seat harness back on?"

"Almost," Ingrid said with some panic in her voice.

"Hurry! Your actions could get us shot down. And grab the airsick bag in the pouch next to your left leg. You may need it."

The L-39 rolled upside down and pulled a high-g half loop to change directions as quickly as possible. Lance saw this and pulled up into a high left turn to stay above the jet. He rolled out of it and headed back toward the Alps. He was only a minute away from the border.

The L-39 rolled out of another tight turn to see nothing ahead or below him. He knew that he had to head to the borderline to find the elusive aircraft. He turned and climbed in the direction of the German-Austrian border and brought in full power. The first half-minute yielded nothing. Then out of his right eye, he caught movement. The pursuit was over. He wouldn't be out-flown. The Czech pilot dropped the nose and turned toward his prey.

Lance needed more speed. Nothing else would do. He caught sight of the L-

39 just off his left flank. He rolled hard left and then yanked the aircraft to a hard right turn. The G-meter tagged 9.9 g's. The invisible force of gravitational weight was tremendous. His vision narrowed. He forced his head up to see that he had thrown off his pursuer once again. He pushed forward on the stick and leveled out. Ingrid blacked out.

Two new fighters dropped down off the left side of the Shadowhawk. Lance felt tension relax when he saw the Iron Cross on the F-104's fuselage. They were West German interceptors.

The L-39 pilot came close off Lance's right. He gave a wave to Lance. Lance gave him a salute and then in a bit of charades, tipped his partially closed hand to his lips. He pointed to the Czech pilot and back to him. The Czech pilot gave Lance a salute and peeled off back into his airspace, thinking, yes, it would be nice to have a drink someday with this adventuresome pilot.

Lance was on final, the runway moments ahead. The sun was up and shining at just before seven in the morning. He engaged the fourth innovation. The full-span ailerons slid back and locked, operating now as flaps. The unique flaps system cupped the air. Roll control was now by spoilers. The Shadowhawk came over the threshold at 80 knots indicated, slowing to just above its stall speed of 55 knots as it smoothly touched the ground. Lance stepped on both rudder pedals, which pushed the rudders outward as speed brakes. Lance and passenger were safely home.

Lance taxied off the active and down to the end to where his hangar was. He taxied right into the open doors of the hangar. The engine came to a silent stop, rolling the last several feet into the waiting arms of Jeffrey Ralston. The electrically operated hangar doors closed immediately. Ralston had a sheepish grin on his face. Lance remembered that Ralston could hear everything in the cockpit as it happened. He popped the canopy up, and with the release of his seat harness, stepped out. He opened the back canopy and shook Ingrid lightly to wake her. She mumbled something in German about needing "mouth to mouth."

"No-no-no. You'll be fine in a moment." Lance helped her out of the aircraft. "I think we need to cool it for a while, Jeffrey."

"I would say we've thoroughly worn out our welcome on this last run. The Stasi must be going ballistic. Go enjoy your day, Lance."

***

The *Marienplatz*, the town square in the middle of Munich, was where Lance liked to come and just be one of the people. It drew many from all over the world as it had since the Middle Ages. Lance held onto Anja's hand as they strolled through the square. It was nearly noon, and Lance stood facing the new town hall. The huge edifice, fashioned in Gothic revival architecture, had a 260-foot tall tower that housed a clock up high, and below it was the center of attraction—the *Rathaus-Glockenspiel*. It brought most of the town and tourists to a halt. Thirty-two life-sized mechanical figures dressed in medieval costumes came to life after the bells began chiming. Lance could hear the mechanism that rotated the figures along a track, which told the story of the marriage of *Wilhelm V*, the *Duke of Bavaria,* to *Renata of Lothringen*. Lance waited as the joust began. This was his favorite part of the show. Upon the second time the knights on horseback came out from behind the stage, the Bavarian knight knocked the French Lothringen knight back, winning.

Anja cuddled up to Lance. "Are you my Bavarian knight?"

Lance's mind drifted. "Anja, what does the word *Hengst* mean?"

"Kind of what I just asked you. Hengst means stallion. Like the horse."

Lance chuckled. "So, Liebchen, mach mir den Hengst, means, make like a stallion?"

It dawned on Anja that the small, light reddish rash on his neck was not a rash. "You have been a stallion to another woman!"

"No. It was an air to air attack!"

"You are a liar. I know a hickey when I see one!"

"Anja, I would never lie to you." He pulled her to him. "And you should know you're the only woman I want to make like a stallion with." His kiss, so deep, so passionate, calmed her body and mind. His gaze reached into the depths of her being.

"Okay, I am listening," she purred.

Lance sat Anja down on a now available bench. He held her hands. "Our relationship has to be honorable. And what you agree to—keep. That's very important to me."

"Liebchen, I understand you don't want to be hurt again."

"It's more than that. What you vow—keep. Be sure I'm the one you want to be with."

"I've lived with you for over a year. I know the man you are. So you're not a big mystery to me. Other than how you will make love to me."

"Well—it has been said of me that I am like a velvet glove—wrapped around a freight train."

Anja jumped up and straddled him, kissing him madly. "You just said the wrong thing to me, Herr Rio, Mr. Rio."

"Help! Rape! Save me."

"There is no one to save you. You are mine!"

He pulled her back, sat her to his side, and turned toward her. He watched the light dance in blue shimmers in her eyes. "Then, Anja, my darling, will you marry me?"

"Yes."

"When would you like to set a date?"

"Now." She plunged her lips back into his.

***

Lance wondered how they made it home in one celibate piece.

"So, you are asking my daughter's hand in marriage?" Werner asked conservatively. The three of them had sat at the table for over an hour. Werner didn't want his daughter to lose the best happiness she had ever come to know. "But to leave her a widow would bring great devastation to us, Lance."

"I know, Werner, I know. That's why I have said to her that I need to finish what I've started. Fulfill my obligation to Jeffrey. That's only right. After that, I'm what I was meant to be. A family man."

"I must talk with Jeffrey about this. You have to register with the *Standesämt* for a legal marriage to be recognized here, as you are falsely a German citizen."

"Anja will marry Lance Rio. Not Manfred Bosch."

Lance sat on his bed, down in his room. He was somber. Everything seemed too good. He had another chance at love with a woman that was a dream girl. And he could give his heart to a little girl that stole it over a year ago. He would have as a father-in-law a man that had come to treat him more like a son than a fictitious nephew.

The hatch to the staircase opened up. In tight pink sweatpants and a matching top, Anja came down with a bottle of wine and two wine glasses in her hand. She faced Lance. "You could have told me it was your birthday today."

"August the eleventh, nineteen-eighty-eight. Wow, I made it to thirty."

"In ancient Jewish culture, today, you are a man."

"Oh, is that all it takes? Make it to thirty. Good thing, my name is Lance and not Logan."

"Don't be cute. At least not while you're on a bed, and I have a full bottle of wine." There was a part of Anja that was the optimistic and frisky schoolgirl, and then there was the mature woman that understood life and its complexities.

"Maybe you should sit in the chair. Over there," Lance suggested.

"I'm fine where I am." She handed him the two wine glasses. She poured. Then put the bottle down. "I know you will hate me for saying this, but I wished we just lived together."

"We do."

"Very funny. I'm up there, and you are down here. Or you are gone for days or weeks. Or at your other home at the hangar."

"Be patient, Anja. You will always be the girl that taught me how to ski."

Chapter 43

East Berlin

52°30′52″N, 13°29′15″E

March 7, 1989

The *Ministerium für Staatssicherheit*, MFS, the *Ministry of State Security*, or *Stasi*, the official secret police of East Germany, upheld no rule of law but was the shield and sword of the ruling political power. A power waning with each new day seemed to bring further destabilization to Mother Russia. Control of all her satellite countries was doctrinally challenged. The word: Freedom was no longer whispered behind closed doors but with some relevance on the streets.

Franz Heckler drove up to the front of the MFS building and screeched to a halt. The Mercedes-Benz diesel car rattled for a few seconds and then went quiet. He considered this automobile to be the moniker of style and success. Beige was the color to exemplify his status in the world best. The moment he took to compose himself before he headed inside betrayed his insecurities. The Stasi employed some ninety-one thousand people to keep watch on a population of nearly sixteen and a half million. One in fifty citizens were informants. The morass his department found itself in from the endless bureaucracy that always hungered had threatened him personally.

Heckler stood on the large red rug that covered part of the hardwood flooring of the Minister's office. Erich Mielke, a man that stood behind thick-rimmed glasses, waved Heckler to sit in one of the two blue cushioned chairs that faced each other in front of his desk. Like Heckler, the eighty-one-year-old Mielke was a troubled man, having served as Minister of State Security since 1957. "Go ahead, speak, Heckler. How did another one escape?"

"With help from the West. But, this time, we know that Professor Anton Krexa was flown out."

"How?"

"Oh, not by any ordinary aircraft. They have made us a laughingstock for the last time."

"I assure you, Moscow is not laughing." Heckler placed a few enlarged but grainy photographs on his superior's desk. "What is this? We are chasing UFOs? They are the ones abducting our scientists?"

"Nein, Herr Minister. It is a spacecraft driven by a propeller. It is a kit plane. A do-it-yourself-built aircraft. It is very fast, particularly stealthy, but we will catch it."

***

A day earlier, Lance grabbed his sixth person of interest for the CIA. He had to change direction to egress out of hostile territory with MiGs coming from the south and a thunderstorm waiting for him from the west. Every time a lightning bolt let loose, Lance thought of it as Mother Nature's phaser. It was high-energy weaponry in its purest form. He gave it its customary wide berth. He made mention of it to his passenger. A conversation started—then a controversy of ideas. His passenger suggested he should stick to flying.

Lance had only been back in West Germany hours earlier, before this midnight run, with just enough time to ready the Shadowhawk and himself for the mission. He had yet to let Anja know he was back. Their phone conversations were strained over the last few months, but Lance kept admonishing her to be patient. Now, all he yearned for was to be back with her. Shortly, he would have *laser specialist Professor Anton Krexa* back with his family, whom he had not seen in over twenty-five years. The man was soon to be free.

***

Lance was home. He came in through the tunnel entrance to his flat. He secured the alarm and entered through the steel door. His room looked the same. He put down his bags, went into the bathroom, and turned on the shower. It was nearly eight in the morning. Soon he would transverse the ladder-like stairs, pop the lid that separated abodes, and enjoy a cup of Earl Grey tea, which started his mornings. The last seven months of very demanding training and intelligence work was finally behind him.

Lance came upstairs clean and refreshed. He sat with his cup of tea and looked at the morning's newspaper, the *Münchener Merkur*, a local newspaper that Lance had come to enjoy, along with the other newspaper that Werner read, the *Süddeutsche Zeitung*. Both papers had an article on Iran breaking off talks with the U.K. over writer Salman Rushdie's new novel, The Satanic Verses. "Whatever," he shrugged.

He heard a bedroom door open. He was surprised that anyone would be home.

"Papa?" Anja called out from the hallway. She was still in her PJs. Her hair was a mess. Her stomach was somewhat nauseous. She rubbed her tummy in hopes it would calm. She pulled up her top, exposing the tanned midsection that had become a medium-sized mound. Her eyes came into focus as she stepped toward the kitchen. She saw Lance's glowing brown eyes go dark and lifeless. "Oh, Lance," she said, dropping her top.

They stood looking at one another for moments that seemed beyond the day. Lance controlled his shaking and went up to her and wrapped his arms around her. He knew of nothing else to do. She embraced him with her whole being, pulling him tighter to absorb the energy of her shaking body.

Lance sat her down. "I know you must hate me," she sobbed.

"I was thinking how much I loved and missed you. What happened? Tell me the truth."

"You won't want me now," she said, lowering her head.

"I'm entitled to know what happened, Anja. Please tell me."

"I missed you so much. Though I knew you were coming back to me, to us, I was so depressed without you. It was December, and Christmas time was coming, and I was alone. I took Ute to see her father."

"I see," Lance said.

"No, you don't. I didn't plan on this. I didn't want to be with him."

"Did Urs force himself on you?"

"At first." She watched Lance tense up, and it frightened her. "No, not exactly."

"Which is it, Anja? He did, or he didn't. There is no in-between."

"Lance, please, I don't want to lose you."

Lance rose from his chair. "What you want is now irrelevant. It's now about your baby."

"But what about you?"

"I'm irrelevant too." Lance went to the stairs and closed the lid over him.

Chapter 44

Munich-Riem International Airport

48°08′16′N, 11°41′25″E

October 20, 1989

Lance found he enjoyed it when he worked out in his hangar to run, jump, and land on the wing of his Citation jet in full lateral splits. He had this level of flexibility since he was a teenager. It only added to his prowess.

It was late Friday afternoon, and he had plans to spend some time with Anja over the weekend to get her out of the house since giving birth to a little wonder named Sophia Jolie Pick.

Lance had come to terms with the fact that he could only be a friend to Anja. He reflected on how he spent three weeks at his hangar home before he could face her again. "Humans make mistakes," he told her, "but they have to live with the consequences of those mistakes. And—so does everyone else around them." His love for her would painfully dry up and wither away over time, and if approved, helped by distance.

Lance slid off the wing, letting his legs come together before his feet touched the concrete floor. Ralston walked in through the door at the other end of the hangar. "I assume you aren't developing some new fighting system to duke it out on a wing?"

"Yes, it's called Wing-Fu."

"Cute. But we have a new development." The door to the hangar opened again. Lance saw another man come in with Werner. Ralston noted the stack of five broken concrete bricks on the workbench. He grimaced. Lance could now break them open palm. "I need you to be the consummate professional. Like now."

"Lance," Werner called out. Lance looked casually troubled. His cover I.D. name Manny was not used. Lance sniffed the air. He could smell cigarette smoke on the other man from forty feet away.

"Ah, karate," the other man said enthusiastically. "I also do karate. Perhaps I could teach you some moves."

Lance smiled thinly, looking with disinterest over to Werner.

"Does this gentleman need transport to somewhere, Werner?" Lance asked in German.

"Ah, you are not Manfred, Ja? You are *Ame*," the man said in English using the shortened form of the word *Amerikaner*.

Ralston stepped in. "Lance, Werner's brother, Otto has been retired from his work at the MiG manufacturing facility in Russia and with the relaxing of rules is moving back to Germany. East Germany. We need to bring him back here to his family. Our intelligence is sketchy at the moment, but we do know he has the latest knowledge on the new MiGs in development."

"It has been so long since I've seen my brother, Lance." The memory of pain drew tightly on Werner's face. "If he could be brought here, I would be remarkably grateful."

"So—you just waltz in and waltz right back out, Ja?" the man said, taking off his aviator sunglasses and placing them in his black lambskin flight jacket. Lance remained the consummate professional, as requested.

The *Bundesnachrichtendienst* or BND, the German version of the CIA, the *Federal Intelligent Service*, knew who Lance was, but only by a few. Manfred Steiger, the other Manny whom Lance flew with from time to time, was BND. The other pilots at Alpine Execujet joked that when they shared a cockpit, they were the M&M flight crew. (Manny was Plain, and Lance naturally was Peanut).

"Lance, this is Agent Urs Von Jäeger with the BND. He's been assigned to us," Ralston announced.

It was too late to retract his hand. Lance was committed to the social act of a handshake. The slightly larger man with his larger hands tried to squeeze hard. It confirmed what Lance thought of him. The German was in his early forties, but the stench of cigarette smoke that poured off him had created a craggy landscape on his face. Lance's grip was stronger. Lance smiled lightly. His dark eyes proved to be the more intense over the German's light blue.

"Perhaps, Agent Jäeger, you could wait for us out in the lobby while we bring Lance up to speed," Ralston motioned.

Urs smiled charmingly as he pulled out a pack of Davidoff Classics and placed a cigarette in his mouth. The lighter came out as the cigarette pack went back inside of his jacket. He gave the cigarette a couple of puffs to ensure its activation. Urs watched the smoke rise, and Lance's nostrils flare a few times.

"Of course, Herr Ralston. That will be fine." Urs took a deep draw on the cigarette and then expelled it. "This should be interesting, Ja?" He turned and left the way he came.

Lance thought he heard a chuckle out of him when he went through the door. Ralston knew Lance by nature didn't like confrontations, but it had become routine, part of the job. He had long hardened. Anyone's ability to ever intimidate him was non-sequitur.

Lance threw his towel on the white laminate countertop that served the upstairs apartment as his eating nook. Three barstools complemented the counter along with German stainless steel appliances on the kitchenette side. The other side had a bed against the wall and a small sofa and lounge chair.

"You knew before I said anything," Ralston stated.

"That he knocks up Anja as a hobby."

"I'm sorry, Lance."

"Doesn't matter now, does it?"

"Forgive me, Lance, but in my enthusiasm, I went to Urs. After receiving this postcard from my brother." Werner pulled out the frumpled postcard and gave it to Lance. "This is how I have ever gotten correspondence from Otto." Lance saw it was addressed to Werner Pick and not his real name August Mieneke.

"I need you to work with Urs," Ralston directed.

"Sure. I'll work him over," Lance sassed.

"Keep it professional. Coldly and objectively, not personal."

"Fine." Lance picked up his towel and rubbed his ever-tightening neck and shoulders.

"Are you in pain?" Ralston asked.

"Yeah. I now have a case of heck-a-neck."

"And where are you going?" Ralston asked, his temperament waning.

"I'd like to have a shower if you don't mind. And I don't ever want to see that man in my hangar again, or it will be personal."

Lance headed to the bathroom. Ralston nearly corrected him on whose hangar it was but thought the wiser of it.

Chapter 45

Dessau, Germany

51°50′00″N, 12°15′00″E

November 8, 1989

Otto Mieneke rose from his chair after having lunch with a stranger, a man whom he quickly learned to treat as an old family friend, to stem any intrigue that might be suspected by neighbors. He saw the man to the door and said goodbye for a second time. For a second time, he rejected the notion of leaving his home. He had not been back to Dessau, the town of his birth, since the end of World War II. When the Soviets gleaned the fields of German talent after the war, it was only a fortunate few that made it to the West. He was not one of them. He sat back down and took the bottle of Schnapps that the visitor brought him. Otto took it as an inducement to come to the West. It was his favorite Schnapps at that, *Himbergeist*, or *raspberry spirits*. It was a simple pleasure he had not enjoyed since before the Soviets took him from his homeland. Otto held the bottle of clear liquid and deliberated whether he should twist the cap and break the seal when there was a knock at the door. It startled him. He moved to the door as fast as his worn hips would let him. He opened it. It was a young woman, very attractive and somehow familiar.

"May I enter?" she asked.

"Yes, of course. Forgive me. Please." Otto stepped back and let the woman enter. He closed the door. Was this the abrupt pickup?

"Thank you, Uncle Otto."

He stared. The faded pictures of the young girl he never met now stood before him as a grown woman. "Anja! My darling niece," Otto said, hugging her with trembling hands. "How did you get here?"

"By train. It's not too hard to get a travel visa these days. It's been wonderful to come back to our home."

"But, you are taking such a risk to come here."

"Uncle, our whole lives have been nothing but risk. But things are changing. We need to take a little walk."

"Will we return after our walk?"

"No, uncle."

Their stroll to the tram station was casual. They caught up on family. She told him about her two girls and regrettably losing a very special man.

The beige and red-trimmed city tram seemed to float around the corner. It stopped. The doors slid apart with the hiss of air being expelled. Otto moved his cane in first with slight hesitation but was gently prodded inside by Anja.

A man stepped into the rear of the same car, hidden by a small rush of passengers. The corners of his lips curled up. It was all going to plan. Each element had taken the bait, which would lead to the big fish. At least the one he was interested in bringing down. Though he was loyal to the East, coming back was something he held with contempt. He was too used to the refinements of the West. Every crossing was a portal back in time to the stagnate and bland perfunctory motions of an obsolete hierarchy. He removed his *Ray-Ban* Aviator sunglasses and pocketed them in the black lambskin leather jacket.

As the sun dipped below the horizon, a Volkswagen Beetle drove on the old tarmac. The mosaic of cracks that sprouted tufts of grass once led winged innovations skyward. Now it was a place for a father to teach his son how to drive.

The navy blue 1970 *Bug* revved up. The father praised his son for smoother shifting. The car came to a stop with less jerking this time. The son started again, shifting according to the small indicators on the speedometer. An intense beam of light lit up the inside of the car. "Halt!" the harsh voice said over a loudspeaker. A Russian-made Army Security jeep pulled alongside them. One of the security policemen kept shining his flashlight in their eyes. By the time their vision had cleared of spots, the two policemen had a hand on each door handle. "Step out of the auto," one said to the father. "What are you doing here?"

"I am teaching my son to drive," the father said.

"In a western auto?"

"The car belonged to my aunt, who died last year, and she gave it to us. It is allowed."

"I will tell you what is allowed. Show me your papers," the policeman demanded. The father produced their documents that entitled them to remain slightly above suspicion. "I could charge you with being spies." He looked closer at their papers. "You are not worth the bother. Go." The father took the wheel and drove them away.

The jeep drove around with the policemen scanning the blanket of darkness before leaving the area.

A lone figure came out from behind the trees. He raised his handheld radio. "Deep Need, this is Ground Fault, you are clear to visit." Joshua Wilson looked through his pair of night vision goggles. He waited.

A minute went by. Josh looked again, scanning the different shades of green that filled his view when an angular green blur shot past him.

Lance landed with barely a squeak of the tires and quietly taxied to Josh Wilson. He and Josh pushed the Shadowhawk back toward the trees.

Lance took note and reflected on the very ground he stood. A few relics remained of Hugo Junkers' factory, where the first all-metal airplane was born and the legendary Jumo 004 jet engine. Lance chose this place because it was time that someone socked it to the likes of Kaiser Bill, Hitler, and the Soviets who raped and stole from this man of great vision and peace. Plus, it was just outside of town.

Lance checked his Glock-17, 9mm. His trusty Walther PPK was stationed in his ankle holster for backup. Lance and Josh headed the short distance back to the trees.

Lance gave a quick leg up, and Josh was up and climbing. He waited until Josh was perched. "See anything?"

"No, not yet," Josh said in a clear whisper. He continued to scan. "Wait. Someone is coming." Lance pulled his Glock and threaded the silencer on the end of the barrel.

Lance could hear Anja. "Only a short distance more, uncle. We are almost there."

Lance moved silently toward them. "Anja," he whispered.

"Lance. Where are you?"

"Right behind you."

"Do you have to do that, Mr. Ninja man?"

Otto saw the future of aviation on this hallowed ground. "Is that our aeroplane?"

"That's your ride out of here. You're going to love it." Something caught Lance's attention. It was more than danger. It was a rival. It caused his nostrils to flare. "Josh, we have company."

"I'm not seeing anybody," the voice said from up the tree. Anja and Otto looked up into the dark foliage but saw nothing.

"You have someone up in the tree?" Anja asked.

"A squirrel. Stay quiet. And get behind those trees." Lance moved forward toward the Shadowhawk and dropped low. He pulled out his small radio. "Ground Fault, anything?"

"Negative, Deep Need," Josh replied.

"Deep Need, this is Shallow Giver," Ralston radioed.

"Come in, Shallow Giver," Lance acknowledged.

"What is your time of departure?"

"Just making sure we're clear."

"Understood."

"Deep Need—run!" Josh exclaimed over the radio.

Lance ran with all his worth upon hearing the launch of escaping high-thrust gases, followed immediately by the flash and pounding explosion of his aircraft being destroyed.

The bright flame rendered Josh's night vision goggles useless, other than seeing Lance get knocked flat. He looked down at Anja and Otto. "You two go hide." They looked up at the foliage above them, this time partly seeing their phantom ally amongst the leaves with the added brightness. "Please hurry! Go!"

Lance moved slowly. His ears were ringing, yet he heard military vehicles surrounding him. A spotlight bathing him in light finished off his night vision. Several sets of booted feet surrounded him. One pair stopped in front of him. He could smell the acrid cigarette smoke reach down to him. "That's twice you've blown smoke in my face, Urs."

"Come, my dear, Lance," Urs said delightfully. "You have much to tell me."

The ride was rough on Lance's shaken and burnt body. Anja and Otto were in another jeep. Yet, he knew he was the main catch.

They arrived at a local police station. The Stasi operated in a separate section of the building. The two services had nothing to do with one another. Lance followed Urs with two armed security soldiers at his side. Anja and Otto followed under armed escort.

The three were seated in front of a desk. Lance hated that they found his Walther, but it was not unexpected. Urs sat down and rocked in triumph. He opened a folder. "Do you know what this is, my friend?"

"A file on your humiliations?"

"Nein! It is case closed. I can close this file now that I have you."

"Tell me, Urs, does being a double agent really compensate for being a deadbeat dad?" Lance pulled a flat pin out of his sleeve and quietly unlocked the handcuffs from behind him.

"Keep your clever words to yourself. I could have you shot."

"There's not much left of the Soviet Union or East Germany worth shouting about, let alone shooting anyone over. Anymore. It's all about to become just a bad memory."

Urs came angrily around the desk. "No. You arrogant, stupid American spy." Urs grabbed Lance's Glock off the desk and aimed it at him. "I will shoot you with your own weapon."

"And you won't get away with it, you stupid German backwater peasant." Lance needed to push him. "Take a look around, sunshine. German unification is on the lips of everyone..."

"Not everyone, Herr Rio," Franz Heckler said, entering the room. He came around and sat in his chair. "In spite of Hungary opening their borders, and—"

"And—it must truly be tiresome, having to come back to your little archaic, vacuum tube society—and report?"

"I appreciate you are a clever man, Herr Rio. But all the rants and raves of the likes of Lech Wałęsa, stirring up the people of Poland and now Hungary opening up its borders, will not deter me from my work."

"You live very well, Franz. That is when you are in your apartment in the West. Your time of shoving all of this drudgery on your people is, I repeat, is nearly at an end. The people are rising up, babe, more and more. They can taste their freedom."

"Freedom," Heckler said caustically. "An overused word in America."

"True. But not here. Here, it's fresh and exciting!"

"And here is where you offer me asylum if I let you go?"

Lance looked at him deadpan. "I don't want you in the West."

"Yet, you are obligated to offer me a deal," Heckler said smugly.

"And I, my dear Lance, will be back in Munich tomorrow, regardless," Urs said, pulling out his cigarettes.

Lance smiled at Urs. "And they will be waiting for you slick."

"You are a liar. They have no clue."

"Of course, we do."

"I know you would kill me if you could," Urs said, lighting his cigarette. "Not over this so much, but Anja."

"She was mine to lose."

"Yet, she has only ever known me." Urs looked down at his seated prisoner and blew smoke in his face. He watched Lance contort his face, flare his nostrils, and turn his head.

Lance stood. "That's the third time you've blown smoke in my face."

"What is it you Americans say? Third times the charm."

"Now it's three strikes, and you're out." The blur dazed Urs as he fell back hard against the desk. The moment Lance had weight on his foot, he took his weapon as Urs slumped to the floor. The door flew open. Josh Wilson rushed in and put down the two soldiers before they could train their Kalashnikovs on Lance. Lance aimed at Heckler, waving him from behind the desk. Then he looked down at Urs. He would end the pain and tyranny this man had caused. Lance hesitated.

"Lance, kill him!" Anja shouted.

"I—I can't do this to my girls. I can't be the one who kills their father." Urs moaned as he stirred, finding himself sitting on the rug. He looked up snobbishly at Lance. Lance kicked him again on the side of the jaw, knocking Urs over and out. He then reached for Heckler. "Come on, let's go."

Lance walked Heckler out of the front of the building. Several of the local police stood awed. "This action is against Herr Heckler. Do not interfere."

"Get them!" Heckler yelled. No one moved.

"Get used to it. They hate you Stasi that bad."

They moved along a row of cars. "Give me your keys," Lance said. Heckler slowly moved his hand in his pocket. "Quickly!" The Stasi agent pulled out his key ring.

"My auto isn't here," Heckler said with a certain praetorian smugness.

Lance saw that it was a Mercedes-Benz key. He looked around. A beige Mercedes-Benz was parked a few spaces up from them. He could hear the tinning and cracking of hot metal still cooling in the cold night air. The key opened the passenger door.

"Come on." Lance waved everyone inside the car.

At that moment, Stasi agents and Army Security soldiers poured out of the building. "Here," Josh said, tossing Lance a small dark canvas bag. "You may need this."

"Here! Over here!" Heckler said, jumping up and waving to them. Lance spun and kicked him against his car and finished him off with a chop to the neck.

Josh spiraled two grenades toward the rushing enemy. There was no movement after detonation. Lance seated Anja and Otto. They sped away. Josh drove off in a different direction.

Only two Stasi had some life to stand. They came and picked up Heckler.

With some distance, Lance pulled out the small radio from his cargo pants pocket. "Shallow Giver, this is Deep Need. We made a break for it."

"I know. Ground Fault brought me up to speed. Go to our safe house in B-Town. I'm leaving now," Ralston said.

"Roger. See you between checkpoints."

Lance continued to head out of town and onto the motorway that would lead to Berlin.

Lance checked the odometer. They had driven about 40 kilometers, about a third of the way to Berlin.

More travel brought a realization. "We need to dump this car and pick up a clean one. Let's try Belzig."

Anja was puzzled. "Lance, how do you know these places?"

"Where do you think I was for five and a half of the seven months I was gone?"

Lance followed the motorway for a while longer until the turnoff for Belzig came up, which put them on a more rural road.

They entered the quiet town. Lance bore in mind that only a fraction of East Germans could afford a car, and those who could often have a several-year wait. Finding one could be difficult.

Deep Need, this is Shallow Giver, over."

"Go ahead, Shallow Giver," Lance replied.

"I'm airborne. What is your situation?"

"Looking for another auto. Just passing some church."

"It's not some church. Martin Luther preached there. I remember it from when I was a little girl."

Lance frowned. "William Tyndale was my hero of that era."

"Never mind, Deep Need. Proceed to destination. Over and out."

Lance couldn't tell much about the church other than its Romanesque cobblestone and brick construction. He drove around the corner and then suddenly pulled over to the curb.

"What are you doing?" Anja asked shakily.

"Picking up another auto." Lance hopped out of the car with his canvas bag.

She saw a Trabant a few meters up ahead. She watched Lance go to the driver's side door, manipulate something small in his hand, open the door, and duck inside. A moment later, the car started with a puff of smoke from its two-stroke engine. Lance popped back outside the vehicle, waving to her. Otto hobbled too much for his liking. There was nothing he could do except getting him out of East Germany. Anja helped her uncle into the backseat of the small, squat car. Lance thought of blowing up Heckler's car for blowing up his aircraft, but quiet in and quiet out was best. He settled for stabbing all four tires.

Lance seated himself and stomped on the accelerator of the gutless wonder, bringing all twenty-six horsepower that the engine could muster to life. The car accelerated from 0 to 60 m.p.h. in 21 seconds flat, he remembered. "Great. We're off like a herd of turtles."

At least they were back on the road in a different car.

***

The freezing night air didn't take long to penetrate the car's interior before all three were awakened. Lance sparked two wires together until the two-stroke engine sputtered to life. In a few minutes, they would have warmth flowing inside the car again.

Lance pulled back onto the road on the outskirts of Berlin, hidden amongst trees in rural countryside that didn't invite the Stasi to come looking. In town, though, he would have to navigate through shark-like infested waters.

Lance drove down the broad avenue of the *Karl-Marx-Allee*, where the *Frankfurt Tor*, domed, twin-towers greeted him from both sides of the street. It was quiet, nearly four in the morning. Anja was nervous. "Do you know how far we can go?"

"Well, technically, until we—*hit the Wall.*"

"Funny you are. I meant until we could get stopped."

"*Schlag die Wand*," Otto said, chuckling. Even with limited English, he got the joke.

They turned down another street, and shortly they were on another avenue, the *Unter den Linden*. Lance turned left again down the *Friedrichstraße*, which she knew led to the crossing. Could it be that easy?

Lance pulled over to the curb in front of an apartment building. He spoke in German. "Listen. Someone is going to take you up to our safe house. The apartment is bugged by the Stasi, which is next door and a floor below. They bug everything and everyone. So, don't worry. Travel documents are being prepared. You'll be fine. Just do exactly as I say. Okay?"

"Okay," Otto said in English. A man came up to the car. It startled Anja.

"Go with this man," Lance said.

"Will I ever see you again?" Anja asked grievously.

"It's possible," Lance said distantly. "But if not, take care of yourself."

Anja watched the love of her life drive off. He turned the corner and was gone. She stood, unable to leave.

Minutes later, a man came down the street. Anja trembled.

Lance strolled up to Anja. "Fancy seeing you again." She wrapped her arms around him. "Come. We need to go inside." She grabbed his hand as they trotted up the stairs.

Morning came for Lance about eight a.m. He stirred on the small sofa. Hans Ziegler, a perennial aide to the destruction of all things Soviet, stepped out of the small kitchen. The dark, curly-haired fifty-five-year-old greeted an awakening Lance. "Ah, Lance, you have risen."

"I wouldn't go that far, Hans." Lance looked over at the white radio that showed a red light on the dial. The Stasi wasn't listening at the moment.

"How about some breakfast?" Hans offered.

"Perhaps when the others are up."

"We're up," Anja said, coming out of the second bedroom. She wore a blue bathrobe that had seen better days. Lance could hear Otto creaking on the other twin bed in the room.

It was just after nine a.m. when the radio dial went from *red* to *green*. The Stasi were listening. Everyone sat around and read or caught up on their fictitious lives. A woman by the name of Gretchen lived next door. Once, Hans overheard her tell one of her friends that their superior was a Soviet whore. The best counter move to his informant neighbor was a romance. She was a possible ace card that might play out in the future. The future was coming quicker than anyone thought.

Evening came.

The four of them took the car down to the *Café Moskau* for dinner, a popular hangout for the East German and Russian elite. It was an elegant restaurant and bar that Lance had come to enjoy. He figured one last meal before he made his escape back home through the Iron Curtain. They sat down at a table near the large open glass wall. Lance thought it a fitting place for Hans and Otto to enjoy the best the restaurant had to offer. Below, on the ground floor, Soviet military mucky-mucks sat around the bar, toasting their stature. It unnerved Lance to walk past them. It just never showed. Once they were seated upstairs, he relaxed when his meal came. One thing he had learned to do was enjoy his meal, no matter what, no matter where.

There was a commotion down below as they ate. Lance excused himself and took the stairs down. He could hear a woman, only catching the end of what she was saying. "*Gefälle!*"

"What fell?" Lance wondered to himself as he hit the bottom of the stairs.

The woman yelling was a waitress, in near hysterics about what was on the television set.

Lance gathered around casually with others at the bar. He recognized the East German propaganda minister, Guenter Schabowski. He was addressing members of the international press at the GDR International Press Center, particularly someone from the Italian press agency ANSA. Lance missed part of it, so he paid more than the usual attention, especially when the words "*—that regulates permanent exit, leaving the Republic*," echoed into his ears. He felt an energy that warmed its way through his chest. "Therefore, um, we have decided today, um, to implement a regulation that allows every citizen of the German Democratic Republic, um, to um, leave the GDR through any of the border crossings." Lance felt his heart pound madly. Listening to Schabowski's many word whiskers amplified certain trepidations in the minister's voice as he read from a paper. Life just changed for Germany and the world.

"When does this go into effect?" the crowd of reporters called out.

"Without a passport? At what point does the regulation take effect?"

"What?" Schabowski asked.

"At once? When?" the press shouted out again.

Schabowski scratched his head. "You see, comrades, I was informed today." He put on his glasses, "that such an announcement had been um, distributed earlier today." Lance felt a cold sweat roll down his back. "—The responsible departments of passport and registration control in the People's Police district offices in the GDR are instructed to issue visas for the permanent exit without delays and without presentation of the existing requirements for permanent exit." Schabowski tried to soften what he just said with a tone of temperance.

"Without a passport?" the press asked.

"...I cannot answer the question about passports at this point."

Lance could tell that Schabowski did not realize what groundwork he was laying.

"When does this come into effect?" the press called out.

Schabowski looked through his papers. "That comes into effect, according to my information, immediately, without delay." Lance realized it was over. The cork had just been popped from the genie's bottle—forever! He rushed back upstairs.

"How are we doing? Enjoy your meal? Finished?" he asked.

"Oh, it was wonderful. Danke, Lance," Hans said, full and content.

"It has been a long time since I enjoyed such a meal, my friend. I thank you truly," Otto added.

Lance looked for a waiter. He flagged one over. "Why the rush?" Anja asked.

"There's been a change in plan. We have to go."

"Where are we going?"

"Home."

"Now? Without our papers?"

"We won't need them. I think."

They left the restaurant. Before getting into the car, Lance looked at the Café Moskau once more. On the corner of the building was a mockup of Sputnik, the first satellite to ever be launched from Earth. It sat at the end of a long metal pole. He saw the letters: MOCKBA lit up in neon red color.

His radio buzzed. "Go ahead, Shallow Giver."

"Deep Need, do you know what just happened?" Ralston's asked.

"Affirmative. Heard it on the tele firsthand."

"Good. Standby. This may get easier in a day or two. We're here now. Over and out."

The Trabant turned the corner to Hans' apartment building. The moment, which lasted only a second, seemed to freeze in time. Franz Heckler stopped from entry into the building and turned to see Lance clearly at the wheel. His eyes widened for a second and then drew down into angry blue slits. "Halt! Halt! Come back here! They are out here!"

Lance floored it, cursing the tiny car's kinetic limitations. He turned off the lights as he turned the corner.

Lance circled around, making a right turn and coming back down Friedrichstrasse, where he just caught Heckler's beige Mercedes-Benz turn right down at the end of the street.

Lance answered his radio after it buzzed twenty minutes later. "I have a heckler in the audience. Over."

"Understood," Ralston said.

Lance turned onto *Mohrenstrasse*, two streets before the border crossing. Trabants were parking anywhere and everywhere. Families were piling out of them and heading to the border crossing. "Okay, we're on foot," Lance said.

"To where? The Stasi are breathing down our necks," Anja exclaimed.

"Anja, aren't you getting what's happening here? Come on, let's go."

It took some time to make their way down to the border crossing due to Otto's slow gait.

More crowds gathered, expanding by the hundreds with each new minute into a single mass. It was beyond impressive. It was awe-inspiring. What was extraordinary was that similar crowds were gathering on the west side of the Wall.

The more that gathered on the east side of the Wall, the more cheers rang out from the west. "I think we are about to be part of history," Lance said, still trying to take it all in.

The mass of human beings continued to swell into the tens of thousands. Cheers erupted as people from both sides of the Wall waved to one another. Beer and champagne were waved from outstretched arms. The four of them found themselves at times squeezed by elated men and women that ebbed and flowed around them. The ratio of citizens to guards expanded exponentially by the second. It was a sea of humanity, a tidal wave of hope that no gun or tank could now suppress. And then the longed-for singularity in their history happened.

"They have raised the gates!" a man twenty meters ahead of them yelled. Lance had not heard such a roar since he went to a soccer game and witnessed the winning score.

Fireworks lit up and sparkled the night sky behind them from the area of the *Brandenburg Gates*, a two-hundred-year-old monolith that would now symbolize an opening to the West and the rest of the world. Lance was concerned about Otto getting hurt with the intensifying crush of people. "Otto, how are you holding up?"

"I am refreshed, my young man!"

Lance looked at Anja. She nodded, sinching up her arm in his.

Lance moved through the crowd to get a closer look. The crowds were pushing on the crossing gate, yelling at the *Grepos*, the border guards, to raise it. He saw one guard frantically on the phone inside of the guardhouse, asking no doubt what to do. The other Grepos were dumbfounded. There was no way on this night that any of them would have the stomach to shoot. "It's over," Lance said, barely able to hear himself.

A flurry of people crowded out his view. But, above them, he saw the end of the red and white striped gate swing up. Another soccer game-rivaling roar erupted. The area in front of Lance thinned as people flooded through the perimeter of their former Soviet-imposed zoo.

Lance caught sight of many dashing across from the American sector into the middle to meet their East German brethren. He saw East Germans climbing up onto the Wall itself, ushered on by cheering friends and family, drinks in hand. Lance took a final look at the mingling crowd in between the two gates, inside of the "Death Strip." There were no shots—only shouts—of joy that echoed in the onetime aptly named: "No Man's Land." No more would families be torn apart by a heartless ideology that never held their spirit to begin with.

The border guards were trying to check passports or any documents but just gave up. Lance's radio buzzed. "Lance, where are you?" Ralston asked.

"About a hundred meters from the American gate," Lance estimated.

"We're here, on the other side. Can you cross over?"

"There's no one to stop us now."

"It looks that way. We're standing by."

"Come on, let's start walking," Lance said. "And—we're off to see the Wizard...," the others joined in, "the wonderful Wizard of Oz, because—because—because—of the wonderful things he does..."

Anja took the cue to link her arms with Lance and Otto. Hans linked his arm with Otto to help support him.

They walked past the East German checkpoint and out into the Death Strip. Freedom for Otto and Hans was moments away. The success of the mission for Lance and Anja was within the same footsteps.

They approached the guardhouse with the MP's standing alert. Lance caught sight of Jeffrey smiling proudly. He came forward with Josh Wilson and David Nance. They made it. Ralston pumped Lance's hand, patting him on the back. It hurt a little, it still being a bit raw.

More West Germans rushed past them, mingling with new people. Then Lance turned when he heard a Westerner call out to someone in the crowd inside of the Death Strip. The Westerner, a young man in his twenties, called out, "Vater." He was calling out to his father. A man in his fifties made his way through the endlessly cheering crowd to his son. The son ran to his father and embraced him with all his might. The tears, the joy of reconnection to his family, brought a tear to Lance.

"Otto!" Heckler yelled out. Lance caught sight of Heckler aiming his gun at Otto. "Your secrets die with you!" He pulled the trigger. The bullet caught Anja to the right of her left shoulder blade as she covered her uncle. She slumped. A man busted a beer bottle against the back of Heckler's head, dropping him. He took his gun, pocketed it, and rejoined the festivities.

Lance knelt, holding Anja. She was moving into shock. Ralston quickly called for medical help. "Lance, bring him in."

Lance watched Heckler work his way up from the ground. Some of Heckler's team had now joined him. Lance kissed Anja and then marched toward the middle of the Death Strip. Heckler's team seemed to get the idea of placing distance between him and the enraged American. New flurries of people crisscrossed between them, obstructing Ralston's view. Then Ralston, Josh Wilson, and David Nance caught sight of Lance grabbing Heckler by the arm and striking him once in the chest. Then turn and walk away. Heckler struggled, staggered, and collapsed.

Ralston questioned for the first time, teaching Lance the darker arts of death that he apparently had mastered.

As history would probably never record—Heckler would be the last man to ever die in the Death Strip.

Chapter 46

Berlin, Germany

52°30′26″N, 13°8′45″E

October 3, 1990

The term: *New Länder* meaning *state* or, in this case, *states* as the reunification of Germany was now complete at the stroke of midnight. The five states that comprised East Germany were reincorporated back into the fold, and now all ten states made up one Germany.

Lance held his arm around a wiggling Anja as she cheered with the thousands that took part in the last great hurrah. Lance was her best friend. He looked after her when she was in the hospital and then at home. Lance was forced to acknowledge one of two thoughts. Leave or surrender. He turned her toward him. Her eyes tearing and heart-melting once again by this man, she opened to his embrace. They kissed with a flood of passion and need that drowned out the cheers around them.

Lance held both her hands. "Anja, my darling, will you marry me and be my wife?"

"Yes. My answer has always been yes."

"With all of the ups and downs of life?"

"Yes," she said reassuringly. "I am never letting you go again."

***

It seemed complicated initially, but Lance had a marriage certificate dated October 15, 1990.

Lance stood in a navy blue suit, with a vibrant pink tie displayed against a white cotton shirt. Anja wore a white silk dress with a pink scarf. The registrar handed the signed document to Lance, shook both of their hands, and went onto new applicants. In Germany, this was the only recognized form of legal marriage. Lance and Anja were a married couple. A ceremony could follow, but they agreed upon a reception. Lance would not go into a church but did offer a compromise come their honeymoon.

Werner arranged a small reception in Lance's hangar. David Nance stood up as Best Man. Ralston, Josh Wilson, and Mike Castro stood as immediate family. The Citation was ornamented in a *Just Married* sign and ribbons, serving as a backdrop for photos. But it would be staying. "Darling," Anja whispered into her husband's ear and then nipped the lobe. "Shouldn't we get going?"

"Anja—don't do that. I'm already making like a station."

"Then, I need to get you to our honeymoon suite."

Lance looked at his watch. "Jeffrey, we need that lift around the corner."

Ralston stepped out of the black sedan first. It amused him to see his protégé love-struck, but he would wish it on no one better. Ralston allotted a week's holiday.

***

The flight out of Munich-Riem was on time and uneventful, except for Lance. There was no such thing to him as an uneventful flight. It was special every time. Anja turned to Lance as he watched the ground fall away. "Tell me, Mr. Rio, how are your little horsies doing?"

"Now that you made me think of it, they're racing in place."

Chapter 47

Kerkyra (Corfu)

35°39′00″N, 19°52′00″E

October 15, 1990

After their flight to Athens, they boarded another short flight to the Greek island of Corfu. There wasn't much sunlight left. Due to the time of year and where Corfu was geographically, the air cooled quicker than in the southern areas of Greece. Anja didn't care. It didn't take long to drive across the narrow width of the island along one of the only two main roads.

"I have always wanted to come to Greece. And now I am here with my own Greek god," Mrs. Rio said.

"I'm not Greek," Lance mused.

"And we'll see about the other," Anja said with a raised eyebrow.

"Woo, pressure."

The beautiful greenery of the landscaped flowed into the bluish-green seascape as the sun shimmered along the coast and then far out to sea.

"It's beautiful, Lance. It's so beautiful," she said appreciatively.

"You're the only beauty that fills my sunsets now."

She smiled, touching his face. He took her hand and kissed it.

Lance parked at the resort, which featured luxury apartments. It wasn't long before they were in their suite. Alone. Aware. Anticipating. On the small table by the door was a bottle of champagne, set to chill. Chocolate-dipped strawberries, exotic fruits, and nuts rounded out the complimentary setting. Anja was at ease and felt like this was home. She unpacked her bag and then noticed that Lance was still wrestling with the bottle. She knew he didn't like most champagne. This was deeper. There was trepidation. She came over to him. "Lance, darling. It's okay. There's no need to be nervous."

"I just want this to be special."

"It is special. We become lovers tonight. It's the most special." She loved his boyish nature and looked forward to their lovemaking shortly, but more so their life together.

Anja sat on the bed in white lace. Lance brought two champagne-filled flutes over to her. He handed her one. He took a sip as she did. She put her glass down and took his, placing it beside her on the nightstand. She opened up her arms, which drew him to her. Her caress unraveled any tensions he had.

"Are you ready to make like a stallion?"

Anja woke with a stir, feeling to the side for her husband. It snapped her to full consciousness when he was not there. She sprang up. Lance sat in the chair at the small table by the door. She got out of bed and walked to the bathroom. "You were supposed to make like a stallion. Not a freight train."

He grinned.

She came up to her husband, still lost in thought. "Are you alright?"

"It's just that as hard as life is, I never thought I'd be living a fairy tale."

Anja smiled, nearly tearing up. She pulled at his hands.

They would make love and then sleep a little longer.

The newlyweds made their way into the village for lunch. The outside seating was inside a stone patio that overlooked the cliffs and ocean. From there, Lance saw his next destination and, by decree, in compromise, one that would make his wife happy.

The journey by car was pleasant, no matter where they drove. The scenery was beautiful and did what such a view did to newlyweds. It encapsulated the newness of their lives together.

The main road took them through the village of Krini and down the steep road to the bottom where they parked.

Lance took Anja's hand after she settled the camera around her neck. "Ready?"

"For the last three years," she replied.

"So you were. Then to make it officially official."

They began the long walk uphill.

The ocean served as a fitting canvas through the viewfinder that enshrined Anja. Lance snapped the picture. It compelled him to pull her close and kiss her. They stood embraced and didn't care what part of the world went by.

They walked the final steps up through the small archway to the top of *Angelokastro* or *Angelo's Castle* and stood close together amid the ruins. The view was spectacular. The thousand-foot sheer cliffs of the Byzantine castle made clear why this was a *city on the edge*, or *extremity*, an *acropolis*.

Anja spotted the stone-built little house on the citadel's highest point. "Is that it? Is that the Church of the Acropolis?"

"I believe so." Lance took her hand and strolled to the shed size stone church, and entered.

A thin dark cross hung on the back wall that was part of a simple altar. Two dark wood kneeling posts stood side by side. He took her hand, and they knelt.

Lance vowed: "As I stand before you, I also stand before God. And with this very breath, I now take, I vow to love and cherish you through all happiness and adversity that may come before us. And with this breath I now take, I promise before you and the institutor of marriage that with my final breath, my love for you will never waver nor grow dim. I seal this vow with a kiss upon this ring that I have placed upon you before man and God." Lance kissed her wedding ring.

Anja vowed: "As I stand before you, I also stand before God, and with this very breath I now take, I vow to love and cherish…and…"

Lance raised an eyebrow. "You owe me."

"Fine," she pouted. "And obey—through all happiness and adversity that may come before us..." He pulled her close and kissed her. Her arms tightened around his neck as she felt forever locked in all ways to this man. And she got her church wedding. Sort of.

Lance noted her gleaming face. "Now, we are officially official.

A flash broke the ceremony. "That was beautiful," the woman said. The man next to her at the church entrance flashed another picture. "Are you two kids on your honeymoon?"

The woman was in her late forties. She sounded Midwest American but had a Slavic look to her. It was the same with the man, but he was older. He raised his camera again.

"That'll be enough with the pictures if you don't mind. I'm still seeing spots," Lance said as he pulled Anja behind him. They walked out of the church.

"Oh, I'm sorry, I forgot." Lance took Anja's camera from her and headed back inside.

Lance aimed the camera at the older couple. He saw both of them turn away but not in time to stop the capture of their objecting expressions. "Oh, I'm sorry. I forgot to snap a picture on the inside, you know, to show the family back home. If you would smile." Lance snapped another picture. Both of their hands went up. "Oh, I'm sorry. I'll wait until you two do your visiting, and then I can get a picture of the altar."

"Don't worry, son, we'll step out of your way," the man said. The couple left the church but didn't go far from the entrance.

Anja came back in. "Is everything alright?"

"I didn't want to share our private moments with anyone else. That's all."

Lance snapped a couple of pictures of Anja in front of the small altar. She took his hand and strolled back outside with him.

"Are we leaving?"

"I have a confession to make. I miss our girls, so I know you must. I want to go call them." Lance saw relief roll across her face.

"I didn't want to say. I thought you would be angry because we are on our honeymoon."

"We're family, my wife. That's first. And if you feel something, always tell me. Now, let's go call our girls."

Anja walked down the way she went up, holding onto her husband. All she could think about was the phone call home and then to be lost in love with her husband, making love the rest of the day.

They used the payphone at the restaurant, near the car park. Lance used nothing but coins to make the call. The phone rang. Anja nearly bounced in place as she spoke in excited German to her oldest daughter. Anja handed the phone to Lance.

"Hallo, my sweetheart," he said. He listened to a day in the life of his little girl. "Baby, put Opa on the phone." He could hear Werner about to take the phone.

"I love you, papa," Ute said.

"I love you too," he said quietly. "Hallo, dad. I need to speak to Onkle Gottfried if he is there."

"No, he is not here at the moment, but I can call for him," Werner said in a slight quiver.

"That would be lovely if you could find him. Yes, we're going to be resting for the afternoon, after a bite to eat. Here, let me put her on the phone. I need to put in more coins. Hold on." Lance put more coins in the phone, stepping back to glance around. Anja thought it strange he used no names but wanted to speak to Jeffrey Ralston but then spoke happily with her father.

"Is everything okay?" she asked.

"I want to see if I can extend our honeymoon."

Her arms went around his neck. "I believe our room beckons."

They drove back to the resort. Lance paid extra attention to any car behind him. He kept it as casual and carefree as possible.

The newlyweds sat at an outside table. A Greek man of solid stature came and sat at their table. "Hello, Lance. Good to see you again. I only just found out you were here visiting."

"Andre, you must forgive me, my dear fellow. I'm on my honeymoon."

"Yes, Uncle Genos only told me an hour ago."

"Yes, we have a close kinship."

"Yes, we're all close-knit."

This man knew the code. Lance extended his hand and shook Andre's hand. Andre scraped his hand back, now holding the roll of film. Lance took a sip of his water.

"Not to worry. I'll see you soon." Andre bowed slightly as he rose. He made his way through the tables to the stone steps that led to the parking area.

"You make a lot of friends, don't you?" Anja stated.

"And now I have my best friend."

"Well then, friend, take me back to our room—and be friendly."

Lance held his wife for a moment as they finished dressing, secure in the pleasure they just gave to one another, a completeness in their affection neither had known before.

"You make everything about my life have meaning."

"It was good then that I came along," she said.

The phone rang. "Lance," Ralston said. "Get out!" The phone went dead.

"We need to leave, Anja, right now." He said calmly but with a sincerity she knew not to question. She grabbed her light jacket and headed to the door. "Stop!"

Lance looked out the window. A flower bouquet hung on the doorknob. "We'll go out through the veranda."

She immediately thought that they were on the second floor.

Lance pulled the bed sheet off and cut it into strips, tying them together. He dropped their bags over the side of the veranda to the ground below. Anja slid down the makeshift rope to the bottom. She was safe. He had enough line to tie it to the doorknob. He turned the doorknob. He unlatched the lock above it and backed away out through the French doors and over the side. As soon as his weight pulled on the bedsheet rope, the door popped open. An explosion sent flame and debris out over the veranda as Lance dropped down to the ground below.

He ran to Anja. She was shaking. He held her. "We have to go."

"I wished you had killed him. Ute and Sophia would understand," Anja said as tears filled her angry eyes.

"You're my only concern right now." They grabbed their bags and went around to the front of the parking lot.

Fire and smoke were billowing from their room. Guests and resort personnel scattered from the burning building. It saddened Lance to see such evil at work. The gas torches and mood lighting had just come on to tie in with the setting sun's own romantic glow. The notion of a romantic dinner was no longer a consideration. He scanned the area and saw the couple from the tiny church. Then, he spotted Andre in his car and hurried over. Lance had their four pieces of luggage in the boot, and he and Anja were quickly inside. The couple saw them. "Andre, get us out of here!" Lance pulled out his gun, wishing it was his Glock and not his smaller Walther.

Andre moved quickly from the resort grounds and drove southward. The couple followed. Andre pushed every last ounce of power the engine could deliver to the wheels. The couple followed and continued to gain.

"Move, baby," Lance said, jumping into the back seat. He looked upfront. The road climbed upward to higher elevations. "Andre, there's a couple of sharp turns coming up. Slow on the second one."

Lance put down his window. Andre took the first turn fast enough for the tires to squeal. The other car was gaining. Andre hit the second curve twenty seconds later and hit the brakes. The first bullet hit the driver. The other six were discharged into the right front headlight, grille, and tire. The pursuing vehicle jerked to the right, smashed into the guardrail, and went over the side. Lance suffered a moment's remorse. He popped in a new magazine.

"We've been compromised. I don't know how, but..." He couldn't wrap his mind around it. "Anja, did you tell anyone where we were going?"

"No, you said not to. Of course, I understood that."

"Did you call anyone?"

Lance had to go back to basics. Simplicity was at the root of all things complicated.

"I had a call put through to home last night when you were in the shower to let papa know we were here and safe."

"Oh, baby, you compromised our location."

"I didn't say where we were."

"You didn't have to."

"You're a beautiful couple. I am sorry, my friend," Andre consoled.

Andre hurried to the northern end of Corfu International Airport, where private aircraft parked. A Hawker bizjet just landed minutes earlier, set for immediate takeoff once Lance and Anja were aboard.

The honeymoon was over.

Chapter 48

Munich

October 18, 1990

Jäeger meant *hunt* or *hunter*. Its definition now meant only one thing to Lance: *hunted!* Pride and arrogance were powerful fuels for evil. They blindly moralized heinous things that man continued to do to his fellow man. At this level, there was no discussion about it. It all had to be destroyed. All Lance could do now was support his wife and family.

Anja tore from his arms and screamed at the burning building. Both the first and second floors were engulfed in flames until well-aimed water jets won out. Now only ominous charcoal-gray smoke billowed out from what was their townhouse. Werner grabbed his daughter and held her. Lance looked at his watch. It was just past six in the morning. The firefighters had been fighting the fire for the past three hours. They brought out the first body bag. It was Otto. He gave his life that Werner and the girls would survive.

"Werner, please take Anja to the girls," Lance said.

Anja ran back and embraced Lance. "I am so sorry. I love you. I love you so much."

Lance took her by the hands. "As long as you and my girls are safe. That's all that matters. Go be with them." Anja nodded and left with Werner.

A group of security people blended around them that Ralston and David Nance emerged through. The press and news vehicles were thickening. Spies and reporters didn't mix well. Ralston thought it best to leave. "I know, Lance, you understand the inevitable. And I am so sorry."

***

The black saloon came through the gate and turned the corner of the hangar complex, its headlights going dark. It parked near Lance's hanger. The driver took note of a Hawker jet poised for flight. The phone buzzed. "Yes, one moment. It's the call you've been waiting for, Herr Ralston."

"Thank you." Ralston picked up the phone in the backseat. "Hello, Graham, Jeffrey here. I need a favor on short notice, I'm afraid. I need you to look after someone very special to me."

Lance loaded the last bag of his earthly processions into the Citation and brought it outside the hanger with the aircraft tug. He disconnected it from his aircraft and rode it back inside. Ralston entered the hangar. He approached Lance with empathy. "They will be here in a few moments."

"I know," Lance said, hitting the close button and walking outside for the last time.

Two black vans pulled up near the Hawker jet. Werner stepped out of the first van, holding Sophia. Joshua Wilson and David Nance hopped out of the second van, orchestrating the loading of luggage and passengers without delay.

Ute was still asleep inside the van. Lance took her from David and carried her to the Hawker. Lance kissed his sweet Ute softly several times and handed her to Werner at the aircraft's door as its running lights came on.

Anja watched Lance take a bag from Ralston and put a bag inside his aircraft. It confused her. "Lance, aren't you coming with us?"

"No, my wife. I won't be going with you."

"Why do you put it like that? You are my husband." She lunged her shaking body at Lance, wrapping her arms around him. "No. I can never lose you again."

"Anja, listen to me. You have to leave Germany and never come back. It's too dangerous for you and the girls. We've already lost Otto."

"Why can't you find Urs and kill him?"

"It's not that simple."

"But you have to come with me. You are my husband. I am your wife."

"No, darling. You need to understand that our marriage never happened. Come tomorrow, there will be no record of it anywhere."

"No, the Russians can't destroy me twice in a lifetime!" She weakened. He held her up. "Please, Lance. I can't live without you."

The Hawker's right engine spooled up.

"Yes, you can. And you will. You need to raise our girls with all the love that we promised them. You will always be in my heart, Anja, but you must go to a safe place where you can be free from all this."

"Lance, please. Don't leave me! I beg you!" she screamed and held tighter as he pushed her away.

"This, you have to obey." He kissed her trembling lips. "I will always love you. Wherever I am, always know that my love is with you. But now, you have to go, my wife. Every second you are here puts you at risk. I—I have to send you away now."

Lance nodded to David and Josh. They came and escorted Anja inside of the plane. The aircraft door was pulled up and locked. Lance turned away as the Hawker's second engine came to life. He had to.

He boarded his aircraft, where Ralston had already taken the right seat.

With the Citation set for travel, Lance radioed for a taxi request. He was cleared to taxi to Runway 25L via Intersection C. He would follow the Hawker.

The Citation held short of the hold lines that preceded the runway. Lance watched the Hawker jet rise into the night sky until it disappeared into the moonlit clouds. They were gone. Lance looked back. The ALPINE EXCUJET sign had been taken down. It, too, was as if it never existed.

Lance taxied onto the runway for his final departure.

"Citation Delta-Bravo-Delta-Echo-Echo, you are cleared for takeoff. Please expedite," the tower instructed.

"So many fond memories I have had of this airport over the years," Ralston said as he looked out the side window at what was his goodbye to Munich-Riem International Airport. "We shall never return to her again. But, onwards and upwards. Speaking of which, shouldn't we be rolling?"

Ralston kept his view out the window. It would be the only bit of nostalgia he would allow himself.

"Citation Delta-Echo-Echo, please expedite. We have traffic on approach," the tower said in a more urgent voice.

"Come on, Lance. What's the holdup?"

Ralston turned around. Lance shook uncontrollably. His eyes were streams of tears that lacked any sensory acuity. He looked as if he was in anaphylactic shock. Ralston put his hand against Lance's chest to force calm.

"Citation Delta-Echo-Echo, please expedite or clear the runway."

Ralston advanced the throttles and rotated the aircraft into the realm of flight. It had been a long time since he piloted a bizjet and had just over an hour to bring Lance back from unfathomable depths before they reached their new destination.

Chapter 49

Thames Ditton, England
51°23′41″N, 0°20′28″W

November 2, 1990

Thames Ditton was about ten miles outside of Central London. The city bordered along the serpentine path of the Thames River.

Clear of his dreams, Lance stretched once more and then sat up in bed.

Lance made his way downstairs to the kitchen, where the aroma of thick-cut British slab bacon was cooking. He looked forward to a proper cup of British tea—his new vice.

Graham Rye was busy over the cooker. Graham stood just over six feet tall, which the brawny man usually enhanced with the wearing of Texas-made cowboy boots. He had a wide cruel mouth that curled into an endearing smile. He had dark eyes like Lance that glowed brightly when he smiled.

"Good morning," Lance announced as he slid into one of the mahogany wood bench seats at the picnic-style breakfast table.

"Hey, good morning, Master Lance. You all right, mate?"

"Yeah, I'm fine."

Graham put a plate of food down in front of each of them. He slid down on the opposite bench. He looked at the lightly tear-stained eyes of Lance and grimaced. He put a hand on top of Lance's and squeezed firmly. "Listen to me, mate. My heart bleeds for you. But I can tell you're the type of bloke that will pull through."

"Do you get over missing your wife and your kids?"

"Simply put, mate, I miss my wife like smog and my kids like oxygen." Graham held a sustained grin. "So, tell me, young Jedi, what do you want to do with your life? Do you want to go back to the States?"

The thought of humor dropped from Lance's face. Soberness filled his gaze. "There's nothing to go back to."

"You sure?"

"Yes." His eyes darkened. "And I have to punish a rather nasty man."

"And persuade the Russian mob to cancel the contract on you and the Mrs. That won't likely happen."

"I have every faith in my powers of persuasion, Graham."

"Could be interesting, but I need to tell you, I've been contracted to find Urs and spank him abusively. The lads are out scouting for him now."

"I'll tell Jeffrey that won't be necessary."

"Look, mate, I can put that on the back burner for now. This idiot Saddam

Hussein will arrogantly keep defying the U.N. resolutions and—"

"Understood. I need to get back to training anyway."

"Right. You can join us for an upcoming two-week training trek we do several times a year. I have some property down south by the coast where we get away from it all and have a sort of training camp set up there. We use live ammo and all that. But we will also be training on location in Tunisia for about ten days after that."

"Wow. I get to train with the famous SAS."

"Retired, mind you. But, you do get to train with SECTOR. It'll be good for you. Put some hair on your chest or thereabouts. The lads will be back in two days anyway. We can kick around town, as they say. Go up to London if you'd like."

"Great. We can go to my favorite Greek deli and have kebabs for lunch."

"What is it with you and kebabs? You're like a bloody addict. Of all the things to remember England for."

After leaving the British army, Graham and three other former team members formed their own private security company—S.E.C.T.O.R. *Special-Executives* for *Counter-Terrorism-Observation* and *Rescue*. They had no sign on the door and were not mercenaries, but strictly to help people in need of help. Naturally, their more significant contracts were from the British and American governments. They had a contract to assist in Iraq if and when the U.K. went to war. They already had two reconnaissance missions in Iraq since the invasion of Kuwait for the British government. Lance understood the level of professionalism that surrounded him and the quality of a new and caring friend.

***

Lance didn't know whether to throw up the contents of his means of survival or wait with the hope of keeping it down. He was dehydrated enough. Even with the winter solstice approaching, the Sahara Desert was unforgiving. "*Bla-dee-ell*," he yelled out in his most aggressive cockney. "Struth!"

The other three of Graham's security company stood watching. Lance trained to the same rigors of the Special Air Services—the S.A.S., notably one of the most elite Special Forces units in the world. They were, in fact, the first. First created by Colonel Sir David Stirling in 1941. They became a model for every other Special Forces unit ever to follow.

Barry Salmon, call sign: *Sushi* was not S.A.S., but S.B.S., or Special Boat Services. They were the British equivalent to the U.S. Navy SEALs. James "Jamie" Squirrel, call sign: *Acorn*, and Nigel Garlick, call sign: *Sulfur* waited for Lance to calm down. Graham was *Bishop*. Lance suggested with a name like

Rye; his code name should be: "Dough." Graham chuckled, and in turn, gave Lance the call sign: *Kebab*. Lance was not impressed.

Lance leaned against a set of rocks that seemed to mark the end of the Sahara sand and the beginnings of the Atlas mountain range. They were still without water, and the little they could get from creative survival techniques was not enough. All this while carrying a backpack, which in British Army terms was called a *Bergen*, and what you put into it was your *kit*. They weighed in at 55 pounds. And Lance was back to wearing army boots. He hated army boots and hadn't had to wear them since his training days at the Farm. He modeled himself after the Ninja more than a soldier. Extreme stealth. Light on the feet in lightweight shoes.

The order came again. "Look, mate, you have to drink your pee," Graham said.

"No, no more. Yuck!" Lance countered.

"Come on, you know we're down to it now."

"It's not bad enough I get stung by a scorpion and nearly die."

"You weren't going to die, exactly, and the anti-venom worked. I did tell you to keep your boots on and check them carefully out here."

"I'm still sick from it."

"Just don't ever get stung by one again. Turns out, you're highly susceptible to its charms."

"And then you made me eat it."

"You'll live. Now, come on, mate. You need to rehydrate yourself, all kidding aside." Lance sniffed the mouth of the canteen. It repulsed him.

"Come on, mate, take another swig."

"I'm getting there. What about you, blokes?"

"Our concern is for you. You're not as used to this as we are."

"Fine." Lance took another full swig and choked. His face wrinkled up in an exposé of emotional disgust and condemnation. He took another swig. He had reached his limit and threw the canteen down. All that had happened to him in the two past months was now summed up with the taste of his own urine.

"Drinking your urine is something you can do about once. After a while, the body will hold onto whatever water is left, and you won't be urinating, actually. None of us now are even sweating that much and need to. But, it will keep us going a while longer until we can find some water. We should be able to find some traces of water as we cover over the rocks. Let's load up and keep going," Graham said.

"What about you, guys? Aren't you going to drink up?"

"Oh, right," said Nigel. "Mates."

Graham, Jamie, Barry and Nigel, each reached into their Bergens. They pulled out a tall can of Guinness Original Stout. Cold. It was cold. After days out in the heat of the Sahara Desert, their beer was cold! Lance snarled.

"We have special coolers that hold some dry ice. We had them specially made for us about a year ago," Nigel added.

Lance fell back, laughing. He was just initiated. He picked himself back up and bowed. "Oh, I could go for a Sector sandwich about now."

"And what's that, mate?" Graham asked, bemused.

"That's where you slice up some Salmon, Squirrel, and Garlick and put it on some Rye and chomp down on it."

Graham patted Lance on the shoulder as he took the lead up the hill. "You chomp away, matey. Just do it with love."

Night had fallen where the ferocity of the desert heat was only matched by the frigid desert cold. The SAS didn't light fires. All of their meals were eaten cold. It followed the five basics of camouflage: *Shape*, *Shadow*, *Shine*, *Silhouette*, and *Spacing*. But on training missions that didn't involve threats, it was comforting to huddle around a campfire. Lance studied the desert blackness in the moonless night. Graham was content with the warmth of the fire. He saw Lance change expressions with every dozen or so flickers. He looked lost. Then he looked calculating. "You're a tough cookie, matey," Graham said.

"Resilient, G. I consider myself resilient," Lance said with a smile, though his gaze was still off into the unseen desert landscape.

Chapter 50

Baghdad, Iraq

33°20′00″N, 44°23′00″E

January 16, 1991

Lance came through the rather sedate hotel lobby of the Babylon Hotel, where guests and those that catered to them all were politely on edge. Lance had observed many journalists from ABC News, CNN, and the BBC, ready to cover what seemed inevitable—war. To them, he was just a German charter pilot asking questions.

The night air was still, foreboding and full of tension. You could feel it within your solitude or mingling within the citizenry of Baghdad. The military was on high alert, and that was of concern to Lance. There were many players within the crux of the operation, each with its own code name, depending on the country involved. Lance knew it best as: *Desert Storm.* Within that operation was his own. *Operation: Personal Justice.*

Lance stepped into the waiting black Mercedes-Benz.

Lance had been in the ancient city for the last four days. He familiarized himself with the locations and landscape of the *Cradle of Civilization.* He delivered several U.N. workers and medical supplies to Iraq with Mike Castro, posing as an Iraqi businessman. Lance hadn't worked with Mike for some time. Since the U.N. sanctions went into effect, the embargo was strangling the economy and the temperament of the nation. Lance was sure, though, that Saddam Hussein wasn't missing any meals.

Mike Castro drove over the Al Jumhuriya Bridge, crossing the ancient Tigris River that would yet see another edition of human intrigue set to plan as it had done for millennia.

"Hope you had a catnap, Lance. It's going to be a long night," Mike said, shaking off the sleepies himself.

"I'm too amped to sleep," Lance responded.

Mike turned off the bridge and headed down Haifa Street, where it paralleled the Tigris. Lance looked at his watch. It was just past 10:30.

"The plane just left Mother Russia. So, we're a go," Mike said.

They moved onto the Matar Sadam Al-Duwali Road and headed west.

Ten miles out of central Baghdad, Mike followed the loop around, which then ran north, up the main airport drive that ran over two miles up the center and looped around the airline terminals and back down again. Their turnoff came sooner, where airport guards met them at a gate. Both men pulled out their passports. A flashlight lit up Lance's face. They saw that Lance was dressed in a pilot's uniform. Mike spoke fluent Arabic in three flavors: Iraqi, Egyptian, and Saudi. Lance was ready with his Walther, having attached the silencer moments earlier. The guards stated no further flights were allowed tonight. Mike responded in some urgency that his business partner was in a terrible accident and had to leave back to Egypt and was awaiting an answer to his request from a government official. The guards shrugged and let them through.

They came around where several bizjets were parked in a row. Mike drove up to Lance's Citation. Lance opened the door and went inside. Moments later, he came out and began to take off engine covers, unchock the wheels, and get their means of escape ready. Mike stayed in the car and continued to take care of business on his satellite phone. Lance finished outside and went back inside the aircraft.

A half-hour later, Mike came into the aircraft. It was dark, quiet, and eerily still for some reason. He moved past the first row of seats. He could see a silhouette in the last row of the right seats. The silhouette wiggled a couple of times. Mike reached over and raised the window shade, which put some light into the cabin. Lance was asleep. Mike sat opposite Lance and leaned back, closing his eyes. A few extra winks were a good thing.

A security car drove up and parked. The headlights flashed inside, stirring Mike out of a sound sleep. He saw two security guards looking around. "Lance," Mike said quietly.

Lance stirred. Then trembling, he reached up with his hands to grab hold of something not there. Tears leaked out of the tightly held eyelids.

"Lance," Mike said sharply. Lance sprung upright. "Hey, we've got company." Lance opened his eyes, wiping them. Mike knew the pain of those dreams and gave his friend needed moments to compose himself. "I'll go outside and talk to them."

Mike stepped outside. He approached the two guards. His hands lowered, and then he snapped his fingers. Mike went around to his car and opened the trunk. He pulled out two boxes that had new laptop computers in them. He gave them to the two guards who showed appreciation at first, but after tossing the boxes into the backseat of their car, they took a tougher stance with Mike. One guard raised his voice and then his pistol to Mike. Mike raised his hands. Two muffled puffs silenced their aggression.

"If they had only taken their gifts and left," Lance said coldly.

Lance sat in his pilot's seat. He turned on the master. He watched Mike drive the security car away. He turned on the radio master switch. Radio number 1 was tuned to the tower's frequency. He listened. The voice of a Russian *Aeroflot* pilot called the tower. The tower gave the transport landing instructions, clearing it for Runway 33R, which was on the civilian side of the airport. It wasn't long before Lance could see the night-hidden, high-wing, four-engine turboprop descend below a row of large hangars in front of him.

The Antonov An-12 *Cub* turned midway off the runway. Lance switched to radio number 2, which was tuned to ground control. As expected, the aircraft was cleared to taxi around past the airline terminals and down to Echo Ramp, where it shut down about three hundred feet in front of him. Lance watched from his ringside seat. "Kebab, you copy?" Mike said over the radio.

Lance had one earphone set to their scrambled private frequency. "Go ahead, Sandman."

"I'm hanging back between the hangars. Stand by."

"Roger that. Standing by," Lance said, knowing that Ralston was listening half a world away.

Two medium-duty cab-over trucks came from the military side of the airport. The first one pulled behind the aircraft, backing up. Light cut through the upswept tail section of the Russian aircraft as the clamshell doors opened inward. Lance watched the activity with his night vision binoculars. He could make out Sulfur in amongst the crew. Nigel jumped down off the back end of the transport as the truck backed up closer. Others jumped off the back end to begin unloading the aircraft.

"Kebab, this is Bishop. Over," Graham radioed.

"Bishop, this is Kebab. Go ahead," Lance replied.

"I'm under the second truck. Acorn is under the one being loaded. Our presents are set and gift-wrapped. Just waiting to get clear."

"Roger that, Bishop. Standing by." Lance could see Nigel handing another crate to the man standing on the backend of the truck. He watched the operation unfold and go as planned. He looked at his watch. It was just about 3 a.m. Outside of the activity in front of him, it was quiet. Peaceful. There was nothing to go bump in the night.

A lone figure, stepping out of the cargo plane's front hatch, lit up a cigarette. He sauntered to the rear, past the last truck. Then stopped, looking Lance's way. His movements became erratic and nervous. He stretched fore and aft, zeroing in on the Citation jet.

Lance turned off the master switch and dove between the crew seats, squirming from the cockpit to the cabin, crouching behind the first seat behind the door. He could hear the door latch turn slowly. The door flew open, and the man jumped in, swinging his gun aft and then forward toward the cockpit. It was the wrong way to look. He felt his right ear nearly rip off as he was yanked back, and a gun barrel pushed into his right eye. "Hallo, Urs."

“Ah, my friend, Lance Rio.” Urs raised his arm at the elbow, holding his gun flat in his open hand. Lance took it and tossed it on a back seat. “I have come to learn a great deal about you, my friend. Perhaps you should have stayed a flight instructor, which I understand you were very good at.” Lance pushed his gun further into his eye socket. It created trauma to Urs’ nervous system causing him to flinch. “Though you are quite gifted in this area.”

“As you are finding out, my Stasi friend.”

“What? No.”

“Then, KGB.”

“They are both old relics on their way out. The true power has always been the corporations. You should know that. In ancient times they were the traveling merchants, the ones that established trade routes around the world. It is no different today. The kings and priests have always blessed their exploits, for a cut, naturally.”

“I am aware that the mobs of the world try to legitimize their existence in business.”

“Try? They succeed. Products you and I count on come from them. I understand you tried to come between a man and his coffee business once. I hope with age you have become wiser. You don’t fight, you join, and then you profit.”

“So, how do we resolve this, Urs? There’s the matter of a contract on Anja, family, and myself. I have no reservations about killing you now. I would enjoy it!”

“I have respect for you, Lance. We can come to terms of mutual benefit.”

“I scratch your back and you scratch mine?”

“Ah, you have caught on. I understand that since you had to leave the CIA, you have been on your own. But you still work for them.”

“I work for whoever pays.”

“I see. Then you could work for me if I pay, Ja?”

“I’m not seeing that happening.”

“Don’t worry. I can cancel the contract—naturally.”

Lance pulled his gun back from Urs. He was on a mission, and personal issues had to be put aside.

“I can’t just let you go—naturally.”

“I understand that you know your way around Afghanistan and this part of the world. Good. That will come in handy.”

“Something like that.”

“Then it is down to business. And you owe me twice.”

“Twice?” Lance asked flatly.

"This operation, the reason you are here. The armaments which are being unloaded as we speak, I assume, are only moments away from being a write-off."

"And second?"

"You shattered my jaw. I had to have it wired shut for nine weeks. And cadaver bone used."

Lance kept silent about his heart and soul being shattered. He smiled emphatically. "Then we have a deal. And to seal the deal—" Lance brought the blade of his hand down on the back of Urs' neck. Urs flinched once and then went still. Lance then hit him with an auto-injector. The drug would keep him out for hours. He dragged Urs to the back of the plane and put him in the right rear seat, strapping the belt over his arms.

Lance moved up to the cockpit. He turned on the master switch and turned on the radio. The first truck headed back to the military side of the field. His plane buffeted from a strange vibration. There was a flash in one place after another, miles away. And then the air raid sirens blare. The workers all stopped. He watched Sulfur wave off the second truck driver. The propellers on engine number four began to spin on the Russian transport. The whine of turbines spooling up filled the air. Lance turned on everything and put his headset on. He opened up the frequency to Ralston. "Mother, this is Kebab. Come in, over."

"Kebab, get out of there! The war just started."

"I gathered. Nice of you to let us know."

"Never mind. Just get out of there. Now!"

Lance flipped to another radiofrequency. "Guys, abort! We have to go. Now!" Lance said as he powered up engine No. 2.

The An-12 taxied out while the third engine was just spinning to life. He listened to the Russian pilot call for immediate takeoff. It was granted. That was their cue to go ahead of them. Lance watched the four-man team of S.E.C.T.O.R. and Mike Castro ram inside the plane. Lance had ignition on engine No. 1. Lance got the Citation moving to the left to do an intersection takeoff. He could see a couple of jet fighters on the other side of the runway starting up. The An-12 was at the end of the runway already and had begun its takeoff roll. Lance could see tracers from anti-aircraft gunfire blaze across the sky with brilliant flashes of light and manmade thunder.

"Kebab, go! Get out of there! An F-One-Seventeen just dropped its load above you!" He could hear the panic in Ralston's voice that matched his pounding heart. Lance shoved the thrust levers full forward. The jet shook with a jolt as it rushed along the taxiway that merged with the military's runway about halfway up. Lance pulled the throttles back when the tires squealed in opposition to nearly being pulled off their rims in the tight turn. A flash and a second flash from across the field told him that the two trucks would never deliver their Russian arms to the Iraqi military. The runway grew brighter. The Russian transport was only moments away from crossing their position. Lance had no choice. He hit full power and held his jet as much as he could in the turn onto the runway. The Cessna jet was bathed in the An-12's landing lights.

The co-pilot of the An-12 pulled back the throttles as they nearly hit the tail of the bizjet. "No, you idiot! Run it down! Go!" the captain said as he pushed the throttles back up to full power.

Lance pulled back on the yoke at 85 knots indicated airspeed, and held it until they were in ground effect. At 120 knots, he pulled back sharply on the yoke and sent the Citation jet into a steep climb upward.

The first bomb hit just behind the An-12, blowing a hole in the runway. The second bomb exploded a second behind the transport. The blast tore off the tail. The Russian plane tipped forward and plowed into the runway, tumbling and igniting into a fireball on the third spin, landing with a crash. Across the field, more bombs rained down fire and destruction.

"Kebab, head out northwest on a heading of two-niner-five. We just took out an anti-aircraft battery up ahead of you, so it's your safest way out. Call me when you get to cruising altitude. I'll meet you back home," Ralston said and then signed off.

Lance leveled off at 40,000 feet with a flight plan into Bucharest, Romania, to refuel and then back up into the flight levels and home to the U.K.

***

Lance passed over the English coastline for a straight-in approach to Shoreham Airport on Runway 2. The landing was typically smooth despite a very tired shadow warrior. His clearance to turn off and taxi to a private hangar, where a Gulfstream jet stood, gave him a settled feeling, but also one of angst. It reminded him of saying goodbye to Anja all over again.

The hangar doors opened as Lance cut the engines and rolled inside. Everyone piled out and stretched. Gladly.

Urs was awake but wobbly. Lance took Urs by the arm. He saw a pleased Uncle Jeffrey.

"We made a deal," Urs said quietly, nervously.

"And we're good," Lance replied. "I still have to hand you over to those that paid me. Just give them what they think they want. You know how this works."

Chapter 51

Helmand Province, Afghanistan

31°00′11″N, 64°01′02″E

October 1, 1991

The *Papaver Somniferum*, the *opium poppy*, was like other poppies in that it had beautiful flowers. But in their immature state, they were green egg-shaped pods, somewhat unearthly, cresting in several folds at the top. Eerily, Lance stood in the middle of a poppy field, where pop culture contributed to the notion that if he looked down upon the plant, it would open up, and a *face-hugger* would spring out and inject an *Alien* fetus inside him. In a sense, the monster had already burst out of his chest, taking his heart with it. He followed observantly. Several Afghan farmers moved systematically through the poppy field, placing slits on the sides of each pod.

"Now, notice the white milky substance oozing out," Urs said. "This latex will dry into a dark, reddish-brown resin. Later, they come back and scrape it off, and that is the raw opium. It is from this base that we get morphine. However, with a few more steps, we turn that into heroin, about three times stronger and far more irresistible. Irresistible is our bread and butter. And naturally, our repeat business."

"Interesting," Lance said. And it was.

"We, of course, harvest a portion for medical purposes, but obviously, the more lucrative aspect is on the streets." Urs gestured toward a long wooden shack set away from the fields with a rusty corrugated metal roof. "Come. We can see the final process."

"Ironic isn't it that in Islam, they are prohibited from using or selling intoxicating substances," Lance said casually.

"The greater irony is that this is a better cash crop than wheat, considering they don't have enough food to eat. But that is how our world turns. So, we turn with it."

Lance followed Urs inside. It was all low-tech but well organized. Somewhat rusty metal vats with a fire underneath boiled the resin in water and other ingredients to create heroin. Urs smiled at Lance. "I gather you wouldn't care to try the product yourself?"

"I've never been that stupid."

"Only with women," Urs said, laughing.

Lance rode in the back with Urs in a shot-up Russian troop truck, secured by the Mujahidin that backfired now and then. Nestled around them were five hundred, one-kilogram plastic-wrapped bricks of raw opium and crystalline heroin. Lance rubbed his hard callus hands. "You seemed to have a lot on your mind, my friend."

Lance looked up at Urs. "If you were me, wouldn't you?"

Urs slapped his knee laughing. "If I were you, my friend, I wouldst be a heroin addict."

***

Lance followed a medium-haul An-26, twin-turboprop cargo plane on final approach into Kerki Airport in Turkmenistan. The runway was paved, but the lines between the asphalt and the ground were rough and uneven. It beat the pothole-laden dirt road from his last trip in the drug smuggling trade. The name: *Kerkiçi* was a Turkified pronunciation of the original Persian name: *Karkuh*, meaning "Deaf Mountain." Somehow it made sense to make this place a drug stop.

Lance settled his aircraft in a slow taxi. Another smuggled shipment of opium and heroin saw its way northward. This had been the way of things for Lance over the past six months.

A long taxiway that angled off from the other end of the runway took them to a large, mostly barren ramp, where Lance shut down the aircraft. They took off their headsets.

"Now, we make money," Urs said.

Lance realized in clear and perceptible terms; cooperation was the first ingredient in making a double agent. Urs had it down to an art form, and Lance was learning from a master.

A small weathered Russian van pulled up to the side of the aircraft. Urs and Lance stepped out. The Turkmen driver, in his fifties, came up to Urs and spoke to him in Russian, which slightly surprised Lance. Lance was intrigued by the man's ethnicity. The Eurasian man could pass for a Native American Indian or an Eskimo. Lance remembered that he was a people person and enjoyed the diversity of his fellow humans. If just for this moment.

Urs turned to Lance. "Ready to go?"

"As soon as the fuel truck gets here."

"No. We leave your plane here and go in the Antonov that just landed."

Urs pulled out a black cloth hood.

"You're kidding."

"For the moment, yes. When we arrive in St. Petersburg, I'm afraid not."

***

A stout Russian knocked on the double set of oak wood doors. They opened, and he entered, followed by Urs and a hooded Lance. Urs helped Lance to a chair and pulled off his hood. A man in his seventies, thickly set, heavy-faced, sat behind a desk. Lance stayed casual, turning to see the room, and smiled in acknowledgment of the others around him. The room was well appointed with expensive coverings. Bookcases lined one wall. There were two draped windows where Lance could hear the traffic below. Lance sat in one of two leather chairs that matched a sofa placed peripherally around the large rosewood desk. Two large Russians stood to the side of the head of the Uspensky Bratva or brotherhood.

Ganandy "Daddy" Uspensky smiled at Lance, tossing him a wrapped stack of American dollar bills over the top of the desk. Lance caught it. It was a stack of $100 bills. Ganandy snapped his fingers, and the large Russian to his left picked up a small attaché case and opened it on the desk. "One hundred thousand American dollars," Ganandy said.

"Make it one hundred and fifty," Lance countered.

Ganandy reached into his top desk drawer and tossed two more stacks into the attaché case. "Twenty thousand more. I give more if you fly for me more."

"You've been more than fair. Thank you."

Ganandy found Lance Rio surprisingly different. There was no arrogance or ruthlessness to his nature. "What is your connection with the CIA?" Ganandy asked bluntly.

"Nothing more than what you have been told. Like you, I'm former CIA as most of you are former KGB."

Ganandy grimed. "You flew another aircraft in the United States. Where is it?"

"My Mits? I sold it to buy and enhance my Citation. I decided to try someplace else after my divorce if you're wondering what I'm doing in your neck of the woods."

"Then, we must keep you happy, so you want to stay here with us."

"But, make it three weeks from now."

"Why so long?"

"I pulled another bug from my plane just before this flight. Let's just say that the CIA are poor losers. I need some time and distance."

"I would be poor loser too if you were found to be untrustworthy."

It was odd that with his life on the line so many times in the past nine years, it didn't seem to faze him with Ganandy's not so veiled threat.

"I am never untrustworthy to my friends. Now, I would like to get cleaned up from my travels if I may." He smiled respectfully to Uspensky.

Many things popped into Lance's mind. His continuing to master Russian with a St. Petersburg accent was paramount.

Chapter 52

London

51°30′60″N, 0°7′47″W

April 13, 1992

The day started with pockets of sunshine, but Lance didn't know if the increasing clouds would let loose with rain. Regardless, this would be no Monday Morning Blues. He looked forward to this day with great eagerness. A well-polished black limo pulled up along Oxford Street, in front of the Dionysus Greek Deli. Lance opened the door and seated himself inside. The car merged back in with London traffic.

Lance found himself nestled in a rear-facing seat. "Lance, this is Sir Trevor Rees with S.I.S. or MI-Six," Graham said as if introducing royalty.

"Sir, Lancelot. Your reputation delightfully precedes you," Sir Trevor said.

"I hope that's a good thing, Sir Trevor," Lance said, shaking his hand.

Trevor looked to be in his late forties with well-coifed salt and pepper hair. His hazel eyes were clear and observant. He looked a man of breeding and style, who would have his suits tailored exclusively on *Savile Row*. He was, after all, knighted by the queen for some deed of valour.

"You've managed to cram a great deal of knowledge and expertise into a relatively short work experience of under ten years. But, more importantly, you are a trusted and loyal friend to those you call a friend. I hope we will become such friends."

"That would be most welcomed, Sir Trevor."

"Now. I about had a proverbial cow when Graham told me of your plan. In confidence, of course. I must tell you that I know Jeffrey Ralston very well. Would I assume that Jeffrey knows nothing about this?"

"No, he doesn't. Nor do I plan for him to know. For now."

"You understand that there are several more thousand syndicates and gangs after this."

"One crisis at a time, Sir Trevor."

"Right. Well, we aren't the police, Lance."

"Oh, yes, we are! We may not be out issuing traffic citations, but our job is to serve and protect. You know we do a whole lot more than just gather intelligence, Sir Trevor. In the end, we stop selfishness."

"I don't follow, I'm afraid."

"Sir Trevor, all criminality, whether speeding, pushing drugs, or invading another country, are all acts of selfishness."

"And you want to make selfishness unprofitable?"

"And painful."

Sir Trevor took a breath. "I want to be sure your motives are in balance, Lance. Are you doing this because of your wife? Are you looking for revenge?"

"How up are you on history? The Napoleonic period specifically."

"I studied history, as I read law at Oxford, with much interest in the Napoleonic period."

"Do you know why Napoleon invaded Russia?"

"At that time, England ruled the seas. Napoleon ruled the Continent. Napoleon wanted a united and peaceful Europe and nearly had it."

"Except—"

"The moneylenders. With the likes of Barron Nathan Rothschild and Sir Francis Baring holding England and much of Europe hostage as debtors, naturally, they were diametrically opposed to the peace and prosperity Napoleon brought to the Continent."

"Correct. Rothschild and Baring held the largest deposits of gold and silver." Lance shrugged. "Typical bankers."

"They funded revolt after revolt. Napoleon, who distributed gold and silver to a country that he conquered so they could continue to function, got savvy and took it back, forcing bankruptcy after bankruptcy, nearly breaking the bank, so to speak."

"All that you say is true, but what was the catalyst?"

Sir Trevor was puzzled as to what answer Lance was trying to draw out of him. He was thinking too clinical. Then a wry smile came across his face. "Then, enter Marie Walenska that some say was the 'Polish Esther' who captivated Napoleon. Her plea was for him to rescue Poland that had been divvied up between Prussia, Russia, and Austria. Without her influence on the emperor…there might not be a Poland."

"Anja. My wife pleaded with me not to let the Russians destroy her life twice in a lifetime. Unlike Napoleon, I was not successful. But we can save others."

"That's most noble, Lance, but complicated, very complicated."

"We're in a complicated business, Sir Trevor. But my plan is simple. By the way, for a Brit, you're quite sympathetic to Napoleon."

"Any true historian would have to acknowledge that Rothschild and Baring used the media of that time to smear Napoleon. And, besides, my mother was French, who escaped a trip to the concentration camps by the French Resistance, who in turn joined them, and—once saved a British pilot shot down behind enemy lines—my father."

"Well, Sir Trevor, I am no less compelled than *mum*."

Trevor grinned knowingly. "I see Jeffrey still insists on all things Napoleon in the curriculum. Very well, Lance. You'll have your tactical support. Off book, of course."

***

It took a lot for Lance to come back to the same Munich government building where he and Anja received their marriage certificate. He remembered the blissful day tenderly until a stabbing pain of anguish brought him back.

He was in the passport office days earlier, bearing the name: *Martin Rolf.*

The same anxious, overworked clerk who seemed to sprout more gray hair since he last saw her gestured him to her station. She took the application, noting the name: *Anton Fuchs*.

Digging in long-abandoned files as the deftly trained spy was used to doing finally yielded the results he sought—a birth certificate—his—that was part of a cover name his mother used forty years ago during her two years in Army Intelligence. "Thanks, mom," he whispered.

Lance walked out of the passport office with a light smile across his face. He would shortly have two passports, both sent to his new Munich address. *Rolf* meant *Wolf*. *Fuchs* meant *Fox*. To do what he had to do would require the ruthless savagery of an attacking wolf and the patience and cunning of a fox.

Chapter 53

Beqaa Valley, Lebanon
34°00′32″N, 36°08′43″E

May 4, 1992

Lance shot out smoothly, rolling on his back as he fell one foot to the Antonov's near three feet of forward motion. The rear loading ramp had almost closed, cutting off the interior lights that kept the aircraft from staying silhouetted against the backdrop of the night sky. It wouldn't be long before he fell through the frigid and unbreathably thin atmosphere to warmer, denser air below.

Five hours earlier, Lance had another flight change from Daddy Ganandy. Instead of flying into Kerki and staying there, he refueled and flew into St. Petersburg International Airport. After parking and shutting down, he was surrounded by Russian maintenance people who stripped the plane of every bundle of heroin, like piranha. Then, escorted by Urs to a waiting Aeroflot An-26 transport that departed within the hour, he was bound for Rayak Air Base in Lebanon. Just as tactical support had informed him. Lance expected crates of munitions, not the three full-sized military pallets loaded inboard, blocking his path. He knew they weren't just from a gun and drug-running Russian mobster but in arrangement with the former Soviet government.

"You know, Urs, running drugs is one thing, but running munitions into Iraq is another," Lance recalled saying.

"Lance, my dear fellow, one man's embargo is another man's black market. Pretend it is like your prohibition era. You know, the Roaring Twenties."

"Yes, a good time was had by all. I guess Daddy Ganandy is...Al Ca-pone?"

Urs chuckled. "Exactly. Now you have caught on."

"And we're Bonnie and Clyde?"

"Oh, Lance, your sense of humor. Don't forget this is no different than your Iran-Contra affair that you were personally involved in. Everyone wants to survive, my friend. Now, we must board the plane." Lance grabbed his backpack and followed Urs into the aircraft.

The Antonov An-26, with its four across seating, separated by an aisle, could carry forty passengers or six tons of cargo, or a mixture of both. This arrangement only had three of its potential ten rows, giving it the appearance of civilian activity. Lance sat in the front row, left side. A security guard the row behind him, and Urs on the right side. There were only three windows on each side of the cabin, spaced several feet apart. The three pallets were behind a heavy beige curtain. Once they reached Lebanon, they would be off-loaded and trucked through bordering Syria into Iraq. Embargo or not, moving arms into Iraq would continue to be a cash cow for the newly minted Russian government.

Just over three hours into the flight, cruising at twenty thousand feet, Lance rose from his seat. A large hand grabbed him by the neck. In a moment of fury, Lance wrapped his arm under and over the big Russian's arm, locking it and snagging him over the top of his seat with a breaking chop to the back of his neck. Urs scrambled up from his seat. "Halt!" he shouted at gunpoint.

Lance looked at the motionless Russian slumped face-down over his seat as calm and clarity came back to him. "Sorry. I have this thing about neighbors grabbing by the throat. I just wanted to use the lavvy."

"Perhaps. But I must remember you are unearthly in the art of killing. Is he dead?"

"Dunno."

"Check him," Urs ordered.

Lance lifted his head off the floor. Nothing. Lance pulled him up, pushing him into a seat. Nothing. He shook him violently; slapped his face.

"See, you killed him!"

"Come on, mate, wake up!" Urs moved closer. Close enough. In one smooth motion, he twisted the gun in Urs' hand. With a jerk, he had Urs over the seatback, snapping his arm.

Urs lunged at Lance in anger. Lance sent two striking cobras to intercept.

Lance rolled over and held his hands funneled over his mouth to take in several chilly high-pressured breaths, which also gave him a view of his proximity to the ground below. He rolled back on his back. In the faint distance, he saw a flash and then a spray of elongated fireballs that trailed like meteorites streaming in rhythmic arcs over the horizon.

Lance thought back to moments ago how he had to struggle past the first pallet that left no room over the top of it or much on either side. He had managed to slip in a gas canister in the flight deck, but there was so much cigarette smoke he was sure the flight crew never noticed the nerve agent. He had to tear open two crates that revealed mortar shells, grenades, plastic explosives, the standard fare of AK-47s, which he moved to get him and his backpack through. He braced himself as he moved the control levers that lowered the ramp, causing rapid decompression. When the ramp was halfway open, he moved the ramp controls back to close and let himself be sucked out. It had to look like an accident on an otherwise routine flight.

In this unique position, as he looked up at the stars that filled the heavens with a clarity he had never experienced before, he truly wondered for the first time if someone was watching. It was in this oddly existential moment that he contemplated if his actions caused a pawn to move to a new square on some deity's chessboard.

Lance rolled over and pulled the ripcord. The backpack released the hidden parachute. His descent slowed. He finally saw several flashes of green light. He responded with three green flashes of his own. Closer, he aimed for the steady green light below.

***

"It's a shame we can't stay longer, Graham," Lance said as he enjoyed his final sip of wine that accompanied a first-rate lunch.

"Yes, the romance of wine, women, and song. Or poetry, I should say, does adorn the beauty of the red-tiled roofs set amongst the vineyards of the hilly terrain. But, it wouldn't do for you to be seen running about sightseeing—now that you're dead," Graham counseled. "Another time, mate. You started this mess."

"No. Evil did."

"A shame, nonetheless. It is beautiful here. Very peaceful for such a turbulent region. But that's our world. Sometimes a living hell."

Lance looked in a southerly direction across the valley. This was wine country, which seemed incongruous within an Islamic nation. Yet, most of the area was Greek Catholic, culturally.

"Do you really think there is a hell, G? You know, a place of eternal hot and bothered?"

"Dunno, mate. You're probably asking the wrong guy."

Chapter 54

Miami, Florida

May 22, 1992

Lance sat glued to the television with Wes and Sybil Gent. They watched as the remaining moments of a thirty-year dynasty came to a close.

"*And so it has come to this: I, uh, am one of the lucky people in the world; I found something I always wanted to do, and I have enjoyed every single minute of it. I want to thank the gentlemen who've shared this stage with me for thirty years, Mr. Ed McMahon...Mr. Doc Severinsen...and...you people watching, I can only tell you that it has been an honor and a privilege to come into your homes all these years and entertain you—and I hope when I find something that I want to do, and I think you would like, and come back, that you'll be as gracious in inviting me into your home as you have been. I bid you a very heartfelt good night.*"

"And I guess that's that. No more Johnny Carson. Well, time for bed," Sybil said, rising off the sofa and heading into the kitchen.

"Can I see you out in the shop," Wes whispered to Lance.

Lance followed Wes to the shop they built more than a decade ago. He opened the shop door and turned on the two rows of fluorescent lights. Lance frowned at the wingless BD-5J and the dull dust-covered wings still in their cradle. "I know a little about the spy world, Lance."

"I'm fine, Wes."

"You had a good time in the Everglades? Enjoyed the wildlife?"

"It served its purpose."

"Yes, I feel you are not here just for a visit. Just be careful."

"I am."

"When I say be careful, I mean more in you losing your way. If you find yourself so callous, so indifferent, so bitter…get out!"

Chapter 55

Western Siberia, Russia

60°58′40″N, 66°14′02″E

June 22, 1992

Lance studied the activities of the oil refinery crew carefully under the moonless night. He and Graham sat perched on a lone hillside above the refinery.

The *Usconeft Oil Company* was Ganandy's entry into free-market big oil. He was a small player compared to other newly formed industrialists.

With the fall of the Soviet empire, the *Greed Machine,* like the proverbial genie in the bottle, was released. What was black market was now storefront shopping, but the capitalistic mechanisms that moved the western world were still held up by the "Khrushchev Effect." The shoe-pounding, close-minded visionary's legacy, coupled with overly proud policies of the new Russian government, was still run by the old guard. The former Soviet satellite counties had fared better than Russia itself in readapting, once out from under the thumb of Mother Russia. In short, the Russian oil business was weak, adolescent, and flaky. They needed the know-how of the West but didn't want to be under its control. The West wanted stability, especially in contract agreements and taxes. Otherwise, the West was reluctant to invest in a losing proposition. Yet, the vast untapped oil and natural gas reserves of Russia were simply too massive to ignore.

Lance, with his night vision binoculars and Graham with his, spotted Nigel in orange coveralls. Nigel came from a third-generation oil working family. His perfect Russian and refinery skills let him glide effortlessly inside the fenced-in plant. The refinery itself was the lackluster design of earlier Soviet technology from the 1950s and slapped together in an array of towers of various sizes, fed by a chaotic highway of pipes, pumps, and valves that seemed to wander endlessly around the plant. Yet, the plant was fairly productive, considering its age and small size. The plant was commissioned in 1962 but fell into disrepair and finally shut down in 1984. Under Ganandy Uspensky's influence, the dormant plant was reopened four months ago, much to the dismay of several Russian businessmen. Ganandy was in the way of progress. The plant was labeled a joke. It needed major renovations just to be safe. A railroad line served the backend of the refinery. This was the means of shipping in crude oil and then useable petroleum products out. There were no pipelines to and from the plant. The current system wasn't efficient or cost-effective by western standards, but then this was Russia.

Two men followed Nigel. They were Daddy's henchmen. "Looks like it's all going to plan," Lance said.

Nigel stopped by two large pumps that came off of the fractional distillation tower. The scale and rust were clearly seen even through the green-tinted night vision binoculars. These men, like several of Daddy Ganandy's goon squad, were always on hand, day and night, to keep the workers focused. Nigel came up to the first pump and pointed. Lance could just spot the explosive device stuck on the side of the pipe ahead of the pump motor housing. The two men quickly huddled around it nervously.

"Nothing his goons can do about it," Graham said.

The two men hurried off. Several orange-clad workers soon huddled around the bomb. It took only seconds for them to recognize the situation and disperse. The plant alarm rang above all other noise.

"Not-a-thing," Lance added.

The small explosion cut sharply through the night air. The plant was now on fire. Satisfied, Lance left back to the *Moskvitch* sedan they had nearby.

Lance sat in the back with the door open. His mind wandered for several uncountable minutes. Then he smiled contently. The word on the streets would be that the Leopold Kovalenko syndicate in St. Petersburg and the Yuri Petrenko syndicate in Moscow were behind the sabotage. But the courageous refinery workers would stop the fire with minimal damage. Blood would spill in gangland Mother Russia. Daddy Ganandy's ruthlessness would be put to good use. Another source of evil would be stabbed in the heart after a stab in the eye.

"Ah, Lance. Hey mate, we've got a problem," Graham called out. "They haven't put out the fire yet. I don't think they can."

"What?" Lance jumped out of the car with binoculars in hand.

"It looks like they can't open a valve to the waterline."

Lance rushed up to Graham, sliding down on his knees. He couldn't see clearly from all of the bright white-green imagery in night vision mode, so he flipped it to normal vision. He had some depth of color now and could see the moving blackness that fed the fire. Another pump was still pushing heavy molten crude oil on the ground right into the fire. Lance watched in desperation. His plan was going very wrong. The pump motor finally seized up from the heat. Lance sighed in relief as the flow of crude stopped. The second pump seized up more violently, cracking the housing that leaked flowing black residual material on the ground that caught fire immediately. It didn't take long for the flames to work up the side of the old distillation tower that was full of lighter distilled gas oils and gas vapors. Lance had a sickly feeling in his stomach. Destruction was imminent.

The plant emptied of its workforce in clumps. Trucks, cars, anything that would run was jumped on and driven as far away from the plant grounds as speed would allow. A large truck ran right through the guard tower gate. A dozen vehicles followed after it and then passed it on the road. More cars and trucks raced from the refinery.

"Ah, we need to go. Now!" Lance said. They ran flat out back to the car.

Lance had the driver's door opened when the distillation tower blew apart, sending the rapidly expanding fireball upward as a wall of flame and smoke ripped out from the flash. It hit the railcars, tearing them open and adding to the inferno. Lance and Graham dived inside the car as the heat and shock wave hit. The windows cracked. Lance cleared, burning fragmented window glass from his head. The smell of rotten eggs penetrated the air. It was the smell of death.

"Can you drive?" Graham blurted out from the backseat.

"Yeah," Lance said as he pulled his handkerchief over his nose and mouth. He attempted several starts, then the small car revved to life. The windshield wipers cleared some of the dust away, but it was like looking through a mosaic of individual glass pieces. He moved the car for all it's worth.

Lance and Graham came upon the scattered throng of oil refinery workers. They mingled the little sedan around the various other cars and trucks. Graham caught something off the peripheral to his right. "There's Nigel."

Lance turned toward their arm-waving teammate. Then he saw someone else.

Lance went predatory. He jumped out of the car, past Nigel and jumped up in the air, and came down on Brutus Uspensky. Lance stepped off the big Russian. Brutus came to his feet in a fighting stance. Lance kicked him in his left thigh, dropping the big man to his knees. Lance grinned. He wanted to play.

"Come on, Lance, we've got to get out of here!" Graham yelled.

Brutus charged Lance, who stopped him in mid-stride and hammered him with several blows. Brutus fell on his face. "Not without our Plan B."

Brutus struggled. He made it up on his knees, pulling a knife. Lance recognized it as a *Spetsnaz*, Russian Special Forces ballistic knife. The high-tension spring-loaded blade came flying out of its handle. A bullet from Graham knocked the knife blade off its trajectory and the handle out of Brutus' hand. The big Russian charged Lance again, catching Lance around the waist. Lance worked with his energy as the big man dropped Lance to the ground. Lance brought his knees and feet up and carried Brutus, rolling them both over until Lance could let their weight drop down on the Russian's neck. Brutus went slack.

"Done playing?" Graham asked, annoyed.

"For now. Let's put him in the boot. Nigel, the needle."

Lance and Graham picked up the weary Russian. Nigel lifted the trunk lid and popped Brutus in the neck with an auto-injector. A few struggling seconds later, Brutus slumped inside the trunk with minimal guidance from Lance. Another massive explosion from the refinery lit up the night sky.

"Smell the sulfur?" Nigel warned. The advancing dingy yellow hue of death would kill every living thing in its path. It was time to go.

***

In Moscow, for most Muscovites, it was the start of a new work week, at a quarter to seven in the morning, but for Lance, it was the continuation of his operation. He exited the office building down to the street below. A Russian gunman named Fedor Agapov, wounded and bleeding, staggered out the door after him. Lance had a large, rather Aquiline prosthetic nose, hazel-colored contact lenses, and dark rusty hair.

Lance came around the car and slipped into the front passenger seat. Brutus sat in the driver's seat, hardly able to move. Graham sat in the back. Fedor Agapov saw Brutus behind the wheel and cursed him. He stumbled down the steps, clumsily aiming his gun.

Lance gave Brutus his Makarov. "It has a single shot, and your old prison buddy Fedor is aiming at you." The Makarov delivered the only choice possible deep into the chest of Fedor. Brutus shook with anger and tears. "Oh, come on. Don't be such a poor sport." Lance's mock chastisement turned genuine. "But then, I still shake with anger and tears."

Two more Russians came out shooting. They recognized Brutus. They cursed him and opened fire. Graham put down one and wounded the other. Brutus took a bullet. Lance reached over and opened the door and brought up both feet, and kicked him out. With a hop in the driver's seat, Lance started the sedan and drove off. It was onto St. Petersburg.

***

The *Waldorf Astoria* was a grand hotel. For the moment, Lance enjoyed his palatial surrounding. He was exactly one floor below Ganandy's suite. The final battleground would be in five-star luxury.

Ganandy operated with thirty-three people that were his inner circle. The rest of his organization was spread out over several hundred peripheral members. Only a handful had he ever met. His top three lieutenants were all family. They, in turn, controlled ten subordinates each.

Ganandy shook as he lifted the tumbler full of vodka for the fourth time. He lamented: forty-seven, including thirty-one immediate members, were dead or missing. The death toll had spilled over into seven other syndicates. Their loss was severe but unimportant to him. But like them, his plans and visions of the future—were now fully evaporated. He couldn't put his finger on the combustible scenarios that had played out, other than it was a single-minded force behind it. He would soon have no clout to keep his home at the Astoria. The terrifying thought of ending up as one of his faceless members shattered through the numbing effects of the alcohol. Night had fallen long ago, and he was hungry. He called for food.

The elegant buffet cart preceded the hotel worker out of the elevator. It turned down the long hallway to the last suite. The young man knocked on the door. Mishka and Oleg, Ganandy's bodyguards, stood at the door. They studied him, his pale blue eyes, the somewhat slicked back reddish-brown hair neat and trimmed as any employee of the Astoria would have represented. Oleg lifted the silver lid, revealing rare, golden Oscietra caviar on a bed of shaved ice. The serving spoon was mother of pearl, which was said not to taint the flavor of the caviar. Some water biscuits accompanied the delicacy. The young man waited for orders. Mishka waved him inside the suite when a young blonde woman—distraught, pushed her way through Oleg and Mishka, nearly spilling the cart. The young man immediately apologized. They looked at him with further disinterest and waved him inside.

The young man pushed the cart down the red-walled, gold-lined foyer and into the dining room. There was an assassin's sound behind him, the streaking thud of a silencer-equipped pistol being discharged. "We're clear," Graham said in a low voice.

"Roger that," Lance said quietly. He pushed the cart into the dining room.

"Hello. Mr. Uspensky. Room service," Lance said in perfect Russian. He wasn't quite fluent yet but spoke like a native. Daddy wasn't in the crystal and gold-lined eating area.

"Bring it in here," the dour, soft, rumbled voice said. Lance wheeled the cart into the study.

It was the room Lance was first brought to with Urs. He didn't look around but wheeled the cart up to the side of Ganandy's desk that the troubled man sat behind. He looked tattered and worn—just the way Lance wanted him.

"I was told to apologize, Mr. Uspensky. We haven't received our order of the Beluga caviar, but with the compliments of the management, we have Oscietra caviar." Lance lifted the lid of the serving platter. "It's the very rare golden caviar. I am told it has a nutty, creamy flavor, like mature Brie. We hope you will accept this with our compliments."

"Proceed," Uspensky said. Lance noticed him puff up, prideful as if authority had been restored to him. Lance served him a plate with the manner befitting an employee of the Astoria. It was pride before the crash. Uspensky ate happily. He added more Vodka to his tumbler.

Lance leaned down behind him and spoke in English. "You know one man's caviar is another man's bait?"

Ganandy drew in a strangled breath and choked. Lance popped him on the back. He gasped but settled down.

"Better? Good." Lance hit him in the arm with an auto-injector. Ganandy yelled and grabbed his arm.

Graham popped his head into the study. "All good?"

"Just hit him with a little bit of Americana."

"Right. We'll cleanup out here and check back in a bit." Graham disappeared.

Lance held up the auto-injector. "Eastern diamondback rattlesnake. I milked them myself last time I was in Florida. Just for you." Lance replaced the injector into his pocket. He could tell that the pain was radiating outward from the injection site. "We don't have much time, so let me get to it."

Lance sat in the very chair of his first introduction to Uspensky. He crossed his legs and held his hands together, flexing the fingers of one hand with the other in a reflective pose as Ganandy went into spasms.

"Anja was the love of my life. I value her far more than you could acquire in thousands of lifetimes. So now, I have forced us to trade what is most precious to us."

Lance removed his wig and fluffed his hair. He checked on Ganandy before removing his contacts. It made his eyes water, but he kept his target clearly in sight. Ganandy reached under his desk. Lance was around the desk and had the semi-automatic pistol out of the shaky hand and safely into his.

Lance pocketed his contacts. "I don't know how people can do the contact thingy, but then I guess you get used to it. We humans have to get used to a lot of things we shouldn't."

Ganandy looked up at Lance Rio. It was him. Lance prepared a spoonful of caviar on a biscuit and sat back down. He ate with delight. Then, his eyes went narrow, black, and focused. "I don't know why people like you have to be on this planet, but like Urs, you are about to be ripped from it."

Lance looked at the gaunt, sweaty face, the glassy, dilated eyes that swelled with each blink, and the dry gaping mouth that looked to form words.

"The venom inside you is digesting you, breaking you down into harmless flesh. I have destroyed your organization and crippled others. In a moment, you will no longer exist. Don't worry, more like you will follow. For a time."

The more Uspensky fought the effects of the venom, the more quickly it worked. Lance heard steps come from behind.

"All cleaned up?" Lance asked confidently.

"All but one," Graham said.

Daddy Ganandy Uspensky saw it as a reflection of himself as his life force faded. Lance continued to enjoy his slow, painful demise when he felt an auto-injector drive its potion into the base of his shoulder. He jumped up and spun around, knocking the chair over. Graham took Lance by the shoulders. "I have your back, mate. Do you understand? I need you to understand."

"Yes. I understand. I went too far, didn't I?"

"Just a bit," Graham replied kindly.

"I see—you die—first," Ganandy said out of his drooling mouth.

"No, mate, you won't," Graham said firmly. "We just need Lance to calm down now. He's safe and secure. No worries. But you're done." Graham aimed the silencer-equipped Makarov Lance had carried around for so long and put two into Ganandy's chest. It was the last complete imagine he saw. Lance turned to Graham as his eyes shut. He fell forward. Graham caught him. "Don't worry, mate. I got you."

Chapter 56

The Atlantic

58°00′00″N, 58°00′00″W

July 3, 1992

The heavy layers of sleep that covered him were peeling off. It was getting easier to swim through the blackness and into the light of consciousness. Flutters of light made their way through, where Lance saw a foggy image of his mentor.

"Well-well-well. Look who's still alive," Ralston said.

Lance stirred and realized he was on a bizjet. "Pussy?"

"Very funny," Ralston said tersely. "You have no idea of the damage you've caused or cost us, do you?"

Lance sat up. His vision continued to clear. He saw Ralston sitting in a rear-facing seat. Sir Trevor was sitting on the opposite side rear-facing seat with Graham standing behind him.

"And you think this action will reunite you with Anja?"

Lance focused. "And why shouldn't it?"

"We had to scramble a lot of resources to tidy up your reckless behavior."

"There was nothing reckless about it. It was all precision and ridiculously easy to pull off," Lance countered.

"You are not a master spy—yet!"

"Do you think I've invested these past nine years to be adequate or mediocre?" Lance leaned back in his seat. "Hardly."

"An entire town had to be evacuated, buster."

"Evil was stopped. Killed dead. Several times over, in fact. And it was beautiful!"

This flippant attitude of Lance hit Ralston like a raw nerve. He felt betrayed and dishonored. Ralston leaned forward. He wished this particular moment with Lance was private, but he couldn't suppress his anger any longer. He spoke in quiet harshness.

"I went to Anja to tell her of your death. Even I wept over you. Something I wouldn't do for my own son." Ralston leaned back into his seat. "Treachery burns bridges, Lance. Is that where we are?" Ralston watched Lance's insolence weaken.

"No," Lance said, lowering his head.

"To Anja, you will stay dead. She's soon to remarry anyway."

"What?"

"You didn't expect her to wait around to a memory, did you? In the meantime, we must give thought to how you will make amends."

Lance had no emotional pulse. “Whatever you say, Jeffrey.”

“Exactly. But for now, I have my barbeque to attend to.”

Overall, Ralston would forgive. The Lance he first mentored had returned to him.

Chapter 57

Washington, D.C.

July 4, 1992

The annual Fourth of July barbeque at the Ralston home had its official start with the rise of the ceremonial smoke permeated throughout the patio, backyard, and garden area. The restful odor of grilling brought several conversations to a halt or at least slowed some down before talk of politics, religion, and business resumed. The talk of the day had no interest with Lance. Ralston manned his two grills with his glass of chilled white wine—as usual.

Graham came up to Lance, a bit apprehensive, but like the trained soldier he was—he marched forward. This was about friendship. "You know I always had your back?"

"I know," Lance said, somewhat deflated.

"Any further, and it would've been viewed as an outside attack in short order and not just a bunch of inside mob hits. The Russians would've gotten wise, and we'd be in a real mess with them all over again."

"He's right, Lance, I'm afraid," Sir Trevor Rees said, approaching.

"Sir Trevor, I would think you'd feel out of place being here on Independence Day."

"Not at all, my dear fellow. The small band of fellow British subjects that rallied against the crown set up a precedent that we British have come to enjoy down to this day with the monarchy in its rightful place."

"You mean as a tourist attraction?"

"That's not what I meant. I see your wit and sass are still intact. You have a friend in me, Lance. You may not see it now, but you do. I'll leave you with that." Sir Trevor left.

"You're bad," Graham said, raising an eyebrow.

"I know."

"Silly bugger," Graham added.

"We cool, G?"

"Always were, mate."

"I know Jeffrey stocks various ales. I'm sure there's a Guinness in there somewhere."

Lance was happy to see his friend David Nance, who was there when he once trembled before men of an aggressive disposition.

David and his friend Raymond broke away from their group and came over to Lance. Raymond was urbanely polished and groomed. He was a political aide by profession Lance was informed. "I want to introduce you to some other friends that I invited," David said.

Two steps toward the conversation Lance heard: "I've said time and time again, abortion providers are saints. Abortion is not a tragedy, but a means to our own liberation and empowerment," the woman cleric at the center said. He had walked past their earlier conversations, which centered on gay rights, gay marriage, and the absolute necessity that a democrat take the White House. "And at whatever the cost, we have to protect a woman's right to choose!"

"Lance, why don't we go over here?" David said, aiming him elsewhere.

"No. Let's say hello to the good Reverend."

Lance approached the woman they all centered around. She was a plain-looking woman in her thirties. He could tell she was used to commanding attention. Several other women, one who looked the socialite and head of one of their women's activist organizations, smiled and nodded with every word the lady cleric spoke.

Lance moved in through the middle of them and the conversation. "What about the baby? Why doesn't the baby count?" Lance asked politely.

"A fetus, or an embryo, is not a baby. It's not even a person. So, it cannot have rights. It's up to the mother only," the lady cleric said.

"I see. So, even though a three-week-old embryo has a heartbeat and the promise of laughter, it's just the removal of an odd bit of tissue?"

"And you are, sir?"

"Just a concerned father. But, I am surprised given that you are a man of the cloth. You are the man in the relationship, aren't you?"

"Now, wait a minute."

Lance hammed up his puzzled look, interrupting. "So what you are saying is that the womb is like being in outer space?"

"Now, you're just being silly. How can you compare a womb to outer space?"

"Well, it's like in the Alien movies, when the creature is about to tear apart a human. What's the tag line?" Lance looked at David. David's eyes widened. "Oh, yes. In space, no one can hear you scream."

"As you can see. As long as the *Right* refuses to be progressive, our work is not done."

David and Raymond followed the flock of women away. Lance held up his hands. "What'd I say?"

"Lance, come over here," Ralston summoned.

Lance strolled toward the grills. "You rang?"

"Should I have fed you raw meat first before allowing you back out into polite society?"

"Just making conversation, Jeffrey."

"Yes, well, I'm still working out your penitence. For one thing, I expect you to keep mastering Russian. And by the way, harden your R's. I want you sounding American."

"I haven't been an Amerikaner in five years."

"Well, start now." Ralston removed another rack of ribs onto the cutting board.

A senator from Georgia with a couple of his party associates sauntered up to Ralston. "You know, Jeffrey, we need to nip this democrat nonsense in the bud. You know they'll push for universal healthcare."

Lance widened his smile. His eyes fixed on a new target. "Why so selfish, Senator?"

"Excuse me?"

"You heard me."

"And you are?"

"A concerned citizen who considers healthcare a right, not a privilege."

"Look. You *liberals* will never get it. Government can't run anything efficiently. It's a bureaucracy that fails," the senator said with a disgruntled huff.

"Are you saying that our government, the greatest in the world—is that inept?"

"Over the private sector, absolutely."

"But, Senator, you *are* that government."

Lance suddenly found himself holding a paper plate of ribs. "Go, eat!" Ralston ordered.

Some left the barbecue less happy than when they arrived, but it gave Jeffrey and Maggie the evening to themselves. Lance had come out on the patio and sat quietly with a couple of ribs and a glass of Merlot.

Ralston came and sat opposite Lance, placing his tumbler on the round glass patio table.

"They would have been tastier, but being called out of the country suddenly as I was—they weren't marinated quite as long."

"On the contrary. I can taste the love in every bite."

"Naturally, you've worked up quite an appetite beating up and offending my guest all afternoon."

"The truth only hurts the humble. It offends the haughty." Lance gnawed the remaining meat off the first rib.

"They were my guests, not yours."

"You didn't know half these people, Jeffrey. They were invites of people you knew. And hardly anyone who came here sat and just enjoyed themselves or made the endeavor to get to know one another. They huddled in their own little polarized groups. Some left without ever thanking you for your hospitality. That—was what was rude."

"All this tells me is that I need to keep you on a shorter leash."

***

It was a quiet early morning at the Camp Peary Airport. Lance rolled the Citation jet out from the hangar as Eric Pitts walked alongside the aircraft. It had a new color scheme and a new German registration number. "Hey, Lance, how much longer do you plan to be in the spy biz?"

"I don't know, Eric. However long it takes me to do my seven trials."

"I thought it was twelve."

"Hercules was twelve. I'm barely able to handle two. Why do you ask?"

"You know, I've been working for Uncle Sam since I was eighteen. Here and in the Navy. I figure another year or two, and I'm done."

"And you plan to go back home to San Diego?"

"Yeah, just around the corner in El Cajon. Gillespie Field Airport is there. Gina and I are from the area, so it's a no-brainer where we'll end up. You know how we talked about creating a kit plane company of our own?"

"I do."

"Well, depending on how long you're back overseas and all, maybe I could get it started. We have the Internet now, so we can stay connected anywhere. You know, life after this."

"Life after this. Interesting concept."

"You could have a new start. Maybe get Anja back."

"That won't happen. She's married with a new baby."

"Ah, Lance. You're breaking my heart." The big man wrapped his arms around his friend.

"It's okay, Special. It is what it is."

"Are you sure? "

"I'm sure. Look, go on in. I have to wait until Jeffrey gets here."

"Hey, you listen, man. If you ever need me—anywhere, anytime."

"Just look after the Mits."

"You got it."

Eric gave Lance another hug and went back inside the hangar. Lance rubbed his arms. He was feeling the late November frost.

Ralston drove up and parked just to the side of the hangar. He walked up somberly to Lance, handing him a file. "In your treachery, the one good idea you did come up with is Onyx Aviation Services. Get it established, but in Germany."

"I live in England."

"Germany. Before you move onto your new assignment."

Lance frowned, stepped up into the doorway of the Citation, and grabbed the door. "Auf Wiedersehen, Jeffrey."

Part 4

"A stone was cut out not by hands, and it struck the image..."
Daniel

Chapter 58

Jerusalem, Israel
31°47′00″N, 35°13′00″E

July 4, 1993

Lance was trying to calculate if the many moments of the year so far were auspicious or audacious and which had the higher tally.

The new year fostered in a new presidency in the U.S. Other inaugurations followed from Ghana to the Czech Republic and Slovakia, once the same country. The Internet now had real purpose as of April 30th with the availability of the World Wide Web. The cell phone industry reproduced new models with a sort of technological mitosis. Lance thought it funny that in the U.S., it was called a *Cell*. In the U.K., it was a *Mobile*. In Germany, it was called a *Handy*.

Audacity certainly had its place. Come February 26th, six people died in the World Trade Center bombing in New York City. A thousand more were injured. In Bombay, India, a bomb attack killed two hundred fifty-seven people, with many more injured. The IRA had detonated two bombs in England, killing two children. The Middle East and Africa were an undeniable mess and the main reason for Lance's new directive.

Onyx Aviation Services had four jets, with a fifth possibly being added to the line. That could be construed as auspicious, but audacious was winning out at the moment. Lance pulled back the thrust levers—again, for an approach into Atarot Airport. He could see Israeli soldiers finally driving off several Palestinian boys or young men from the wire fence. Twice they had thrown rocks, bottles, and other debris on the runway. If this attempt to land wasn't successful, his third try, he would divert to Tel Aviv as his alternate.

Lance brought the jet down with a harder than normal landing and stomped on the brakes as the thrust reversers did the rest to decelerate rapidly. He cleared the runway before anything else could happen. He taxied toward a group of hangars and a man standing in front of an opened hangar. Lance knew the routine.

Lance hit the fuel cutoff levers. A loss of forward energy was immediately noticed as the jet coasted fifty more feet. Lance hit the brakes when he knew he was inside the hangar. The hangar doors closed, darkening his new surroundings. He continued to shut down the aircraft and then make his way to the door. He didn't expect fanfare when he opened the door but had hoped someone would be on hand to welcome him. There was nobody. He lowered the step and stood on Israeli soil, in the dark. Lance felt for his Walther. The lights came on. He heard sure-footed steps coming toward him. The steps came around the nose of the aircraft, and finally, a man with an amiable smile came near.

"Welcome to Israel, Lance Rio."

"And you are Uncle…?" Lance asked brightly.

"No, I'm afraid, no uncle. But you may call me Danny. Danny Sharon."

The man was tanned, Lance's height, lean in build, with larger hands that he shook. He was mostly bald and had a goatee that was nearly all gray. He looked to be in his late sixties or early seventies. "Gather your bags, and we can go."

It was a bit cloak and dagger, but maybe this was how auspicious played out in the Holy Land.

Lance thought about Ralston rising shortly to begin his preparations for his locally, world-famous barbecue but figured this year would be with less politically agenda-driven invitees. A bounce in the road snapped Lance back to Israel. Danny Sharon drove his 1977 Series III Land Rover with new ownership pride down Route 60 to the heart of Jerusalem. The sheen on the vehicle's beige exterior had long faded to blend in with its limestone surroundings. There seemed to be more attention to detail and care on the interior, but time and adventure had worn its imprint there as well.

The diesel-powered four-wheeler rumbled down the main road that separated modern Jerusalem from the smaller walled-off *Old City*. Lance had only seen it from the air a few times and usually at some distance laterally. The Dome of the Rock was now before him. As the road descended, Lance found himself hunting for it around Danny's head.

Danny smiled. "Don't worry, my boy. You will see it up close, along with the other attractions. But first, we must stop so that I may show you your new digs."

"New digs? I'm not going to a hotel?" Lance figured he would be here for two or three weeks and then head back to England.

"I see Jeffrey didn't tell you, which means he has confidence that you will adapt."

"Yes, well, I'm going to have to get him to quit living so vicariously through me.

The main road lowered with the golden dome dropping out of sight. They yawed to the right as the road split in two, and Lance found himself on a café lined street. He caught a glimpse of the street sign EMEK REFAIM.

"It means Valley of the Giants," Danny said.

"Sounds like an old TV show I used to watch."

"Emek Refaim is considered the Rodeo Drive of Jerusalem. I am sure in time you will have your favorite haunts to frequent."

Lance scoped out the various cafés and restaurants that whizzed by and then Danny swung the old Land Rover into a tight right turn onto RACHEL IMENU Street and then another right turn onto RUTH Street. The street was short.

Another tight turn put them in a driveway. The house was old, though modern white vinyl-clad windows encased everywhere there was glass. Lance recognized that the majority of the trees were Date Palms with a lone pomegranate tree. Lance stepped out of the Land Rover and felt a moment of relaxation as he walked on the evenly worn cobblestones.

Danny led the way to the front door. The heavy oak door had large hinges across it that served more for looks to authenticate its heritage than anything structural. Lance followed Danny inside.

Lance looked around. The walls were an inviting, stonewash white finish. The floors were clear maple hardwood, with modern euro-designed furniture lightly spaced in the living room. Copious amounts of books lined a wall-to-wall bookcase.

Danny put down the two bags he carried on the polished marble floor of the foyer. "As they say back in the States, Mi Casa es Su Casa."

"That's very kind of you, Danny, but, if you don't mind, I would feel more comfortable knowing that I am not being an imposition."

"Let's just say that I owe Jeffrey, imposition or not. Now come. If you go upstairs, you will find your room to the right. And you have a private lavvy as well."

With his bags in tow, Lance headed up the rather steep steps, which seemed fashionable in many homes in many countries a century ago.

"Oh, I stocked the refrigerator for you."

"Thank you. I'll be back down in a moment."

The first thought to enter Lance's mind is that Danny wasn't staying. Perhaps he owned the house but didn't live here. Or it was a vacation rental—for spies. Lance grinned at the thought of time-share intrigue. He moved as one with his luggage up the stairs.

The door to his room was slightly ajar. Lance laid his bags on the queen size bed. He was pleased with his new accommodations. The maple hardwood floors extended upstairs, but under his bed was a large Persian rug. Lance took off his windbreaker. He removed his Walther and placed it on the left side nightstand. Then he removed the shoulder holster, wrapping the straps around it. To the left of the bed was a window. He moved the linen drapes out of the way, seeing the backyard below. It was a lush blend of trees, ferns, and gray cobblestone walkways, and low walls. Danny rushed away from someone as if he just dismissed him. The man, larger, gray-bearded, grabbed Danny by the shoulder and spun him around. Lance swept the Walther into his hand in quick stride.

Lance came down the stairs in three stealthy steps, moved through the living room and into the kitchen. It was as he hoped. The kitchen had a patio door that led to the backyard. He unlatched the door and slid it open carefully. He listened. They spoke in Hebrew. The man unknown to Lance spoke tersely. Danny spoke calmly yet matter-of-factly. Maybe it was nothing. Lance backed away and turned his interest to the kitchen. The small euro refrigerator held his attention. He looked inside to see what Danny stocked in it. Lamb. He envisioned lamb kebabs. He decided that his official entry into Israel was now auspicious. And then there was some other meat of equal size wrapped in white butcher paper. Lance pulled the piece of cello tape back and unrolled the package. It caught him off guard for a moment, but the seasoned flesh would also be enjoyed come morning.

"What is it with people?" The other man started yelling again. Lance placed the Walther in his back pocket and went outside.

"Problem, Danny?" Lance asked firmly.

"Who is this?" the man asked.

"He is my guest come to visit. Lance, this is my brother Ezra."

"How do you do, sir?"

"It's Rabbi," Ezra Sharon growled.

"Rabbi, then." Lance waited. Nothing cordial came to pass. "My name is Lance Rio."

"Lance will be staying here for a while, Ezra."

"He's another one of your gentile spy friends? What are you, boy, English, American?" Ezra turned his soured expressions back to Danny. "What about your own?"

Lance marked the day back to audacious.

"I told you, Ezra, I have no interest in this foolishness. Now, it was good to see you. Come up to the ranch sometime, and we can share a meal."

"I will never come to that pigsty!"

Lance reasoned that the rabid rabbi had gone looking for a fight and wasn't happy with the outcome. He could see bluish-purple bruising peering through his beard.

"Rabbi Sharon, I think you need to calm down," Lance said.

"And what would you know, Christian? We come from a long line of scholars, scientists, and statesmen. The very embodiment that stands before you. What do you know, boy? Nothing!"

"Ezra! Enough!" Danny ordered.

"It will never be enough! There was a reason God said to have nothing to do with them, so we would not be polluted by them."

Lance had enough himself. "Perhaps, sir, you should leave. Outside of venting, you have achieved nothing. You haven't given me a stranger to your land, a favorable impression."

"Go back to your triune god and leave us."

"Sorry?"

"Ezra, leave," Danny demanded.

"What are you, boy, Catholic?" Ezra said.

"For one thing, I'm a man. Second, I belong to no religion."

"Don't test me, boy! We existed two thousand years before your priests. Now, get out of my sight before I curse you to the very presence of Satan himself."

"You first!"

Before Danny could take a single step, Lance had his Walther drawn. Ezra didn't blink. Venomous words in Latin spewed from his mouth. Each word hit Lance like spit upon his face. Lance felt some peripheral assurance that with slightly more pressure on the trigger, it would immediately stop the vile incantations that summoned unearthly judgments against him.

"Lance!" Danny shouted. Lance backed away. His thumb gently nestled the hammer back in place. He sat down in a patio chair. His hand and gun rested on his lap.

"They always fall for their superstitions," Ezra mused.

"Leave, Ezra. I won't ask you again."

"Then go to your guest, Daniel. Ask his Jesus for forgiveness. Let him place his golden phallus around your neck like a noose."

"Maybe we should all ask Jesus for forgiveness," Lance said contritely.

The scourge ended. Ezra pushed his way back through the foliage. Danny pulled out a chair and seated himself.

"I have no explanation, Danny. If you would call me a cab, I'll be packed in a moment."

"I see. But, first, I must know the man that has stood up to my brother."

"I can't be the first."

"No, but you're the first to pull a gun on him."

"Seriously?"

"My brother has pulled that damnation ploy before. Take no heed of it."

"Your brother—is a very bitter man."

"We lost our families during the Six-Day War in nineteen-sixty-seven. Except for Ezra's wife. After the war, she wouldn't stay…"

"And he wouldn't leave?"

"No. He became hardened, extreme."

"And misjudging. I have no phallus or cross to hang around my neck."

"You know what that is?"

"It's a symbol for the male sex organ. Long before Christianity. I've always been into history. And museums. And castles. Any castles around here?"

"Ah, I see. But tell me, what made you say we should all ask Jesus for forgiveness? I have my intrigue."

"Given your brother's words and attitude toward you, I figured you were either a progressive or secular Jew. Or I don't know, a Jew for Jesus."

Danny chuckled. "Interesting. Anything else?"

"Well, that and the fresh slab of bacon in the fridge."

***

Sweat couldn't cool Lance off quick enough as he struggled to find a way out of the endless rocky caverns that glowed red hot—so hot that the rock itself burned with fire. It would have been more bearable to stand behind a jet engine than continue trudging through the limestone pathway with no way out. Lance could hear laughter up ahead in the dimly glowing end of what looked like another tunnel. He could not dream up the lost feeling of abandonment somewhere deep inside of the famed Judean hills. He knew of the harsh surroundings outside of the hole he was dropped in, but he had no training to handle this type of heat and hopelessness. The thermal activity of the cavern was overheating his shoes. The neoprene rubber soles that were great for gripping rock were now melting against them. Lance hurried toward the laughter. A cooler environment had to be there with their jovial banter.

He recognized it as a large crowd that had massed together, where he could now hear cheers. And then it hit him in a sickly sort of way that the cheers were the kind you hear at a sporting event. But this was no football game. This was sinister. A man stood up on high. He looked like Nero. He turned toward Lance. A Machiavellian laugh burst from the sardonic grin. Heatwaves produced a rippled appearance. Nero raised his hand toward Lance. The cheers and boos of the unseen crowd rose to ear-deafening levels, and then the thumb-prone hand twisted down. The verdict was in. The ubiquitous cheers shot away from the glowing rocky walls of the cavern and whipped by and behind Lance like red-hot wisps of superheated steam. Burning, stabbing pain of being impaled dropped Lance to his knees, which the oven temperature ground seemed to eagerly wait for this moment. Lance felt the burning impalements pull from his body, searing his lungs. He was dying for cold air to breathe. He turned, trembling, unable to understand why as he saw his blood boil to a scab on the three tines of the trident, wielded by a two-foot-tall, burning red demon. The lava red bat wings flapped rapidly to keep it in place. Lance didn't have the power this time to swat at it.

Lance woke. He wrangled in sweat-soaked sheets. The night mountain air that gently blew in from the open window chilled him as he sat up. He could smell smoke, but it was the sweet burning smell of meat. Bacon. He knew where he was. He was safe from the nightmare. One that hadn't terrorized him since the death of his parents. Lance reached for his jammy pants and pulled his tee-shirt over him, and left the room. The day looked to pivot back to audacious.

Lance walked into the kitchen, still dazed but aware of his first morning in Israel. The kettle boiled.

"I heard you stirring upstairs, so I reheated the kettle," Danny Sharon said brightly. Too brightly for the hour, Lance deemed.

"Thank you," Lance thought, he said. He felt like death warmed over and imagined he looked it. He sat at the small round table.

"You seem to be suffering jetlag, my boy."

"No. You're only three hours ahead of Germany. I'm just glad it's the bacon sizzling."

"Meaning?"

"I'm back to audacious."

Danny sat a proper cup of British tea down in front of Lance with a few pieces of thick-cut bacon.

Danny sat and leaned forward. "What do you believe, Lance? I have my curiosity."

Lance tuned in enough to see the green digital clock on the oven. It was 4:42 a.m. "You mean besides the need for more sleep?"

"Yes, besides that."

"I'm—more of the—what *no*t to believe in type."

Danny gestured. "Please."

Lance let a few sips of tea realign his thoughts. "Look outside and up. What do you see?"

Danny turned and looked out of the glass sliding door. "The obvious. Stars."

"Now, if true, that everything was created in only six literal twenty-four hour days, you would step outside on a clear dark sky—and see the *star*," Lance said with a lilt in his voice. Danny chuckled. "Technically, you'd see the light from only six thousand light-years away as that would be the only light to reach us from the furthest star, and that would have to be the very first star. I base this on the six thousand years thingy. That jives with human history. I give it that. But in no way the universe."

"Interesting hypothesis."

"It's not a hypothesis, Danny. There could physically be no star past six thousand light-years from Earth. The speed of light is constant. We would not see our galaxy or any other—because there'd be none! That, of course, is not the case. The universe is obviously older than six millennia. How much older? No human knows."

"What you might find interesting is that the Hebrew word for day is *yohm*. And it does not always mean a twenty-four-hour period."

"You mean like when someone says 'back in the day,' like that?"

"Precisely. A new day has dawned. Meaning a new beginning in life. Not tomorrow."

"Then why not clear up the confusion? You know, take the stupid out of it."

"Traditions. Deceptive reasonings. Things too strongly entrenched. But continue."

The bacon was exceptional. Lance let it go down with a final sip of tea.

"When I was actually in the CIA, we had a special class on nuclear bombs and the physics behind it. They brought in this nuclear physicist who liked to hear himself talk."

Lance got up and went to the drawer. He returned to the table with a pen and pad.

"Okay. So our instructor starts writing—."

Lance wrote: 1, 000, 000, 000, 000, 000, 000, 000, 000, 000, 000, 000, 000. He counted to make sure there were thirty-six zeros in total.

"Then he says this number is the force or pressure in pounds of weight holding a single pound of matter together. It blew my mind! I exclaimed, 'no way,' he said, 'way.' I tried to put it into some kind of perspective so I could wrap my head around it. I came up with an aircraft carrier. Something at one hundred thousand tons displacement or two hundred million pounds. So I divided two hundred million pounds into thirty-six zeros. I came up with the number fifty with twenty-seven zeros behind it."

Danny studied the math. "Close, it's five with twenty-seven zeros."

"Oh, okay, thanks. It's still an astronomical number. That's why nuclear fission is so difficult to achieve and why when a nuke goes off, minimal destruction of atoms actually occurs in spite of the mushroom cloud and all that. I could see a string of U.S.S. Nimitz class aircraft carriers tipped up and stacked end to end strung out into outer space, millions of miles—all resting on this one-pound piece of meat, like a ribeye steak. I knew then and there that evolution was impossible, at least from the standpoint of life coming from nothing. The amount of energy needed to produce every single pound of matter in the universe would be off the scale. Unimaginable. It would take an ultimate being with unsurpassed intelligence and unfathomable power."

"Why not consider the facts of evolutionary biology?"

"You can't have one without the other. Building blocks first. And, all this energy wasn't just lying around the universe and somehow coalesced into matter. Law of inertia. And for another thing, energy is always generated."

"True, but it can be stored."

"After it's generated."

"Point taken."

"If you study the atom, you realize, for lack of a better term, it's a manufactured item. With moving parts! If you unraveled a DNA molecule—it would be as long as I am tall—all tucked neatly inside of a cell—which you could fit some ten thousand of them on the head of a pin. You're asking an awful lot of nothingness, Danny."

"Perhaps."

"When I lived in Munich, I made friends with two scientists that worked for the Max Planck Society. I'm sure you know the Max Planck Institutes are some of the premier science research facilities in the world. Really, you don't get better than them. Wolf and Leon lived a few floors up from us. Wolf works in plant breeding. I found Wolf to be equally frustrated and awed by his work. He taught me how plants and flowers grow from spirals. It's called the *golden angle.*"

"Yes, it's based on an angle of approximately one hundred and thirty-seven-point-five degrees. It's a number from the series called the *Fibonacci sequence* by the mathematician of the same name."

"Yes, that's right. Now, I see spirals even in my cauliflower."

"So, you are neither creationist nor evolutionist."

"I look at it this way. They've spent hundreds of millions of dollars over a solid century trying to prove evolution and yet can't. By intelligent scientists no less."

"Another valid point."

"However, science, nor religion, seems to satisfy the big "Whys" of life."

"Such as why are we here? Why all the conflict and suffering? Why a burning hell?" Lance's eyes widened slightly. Danny took note.

"Yeah," Lance said somberly.

"I tell you what, my boy. Today we will be tourists," Danny sparkled. The place he had in mind for Lance was not on the usual tourist map.

***

By late morning they drove the short distance to the Old City.

“Okay, get out,” Danny said bluntly.

“All I said was that you have a big hole in the wall.”

“Yes, opened in eighteen-ninety-eight for Kaiser Wilhelm of Germany to be allowed a royal entrance into the Old City. And that he didn’t want to get out of his carriage.”

“I can’t follow in the steps of Kaiser Bill?”

“No. We must make your first steps into the Old City—auspicious.”

Lance hopped out of the Land Rover and dodged around another car. He walked through the angled, narrow entrance of the Jaffa Gate. The mini-maze portal kept soldiers from centuries ago riding full charge into the city’s interior. Lance entered into ancient Jerusalem, stood, and then hurried back into the Land Rover as Danny entered.

“Straight ahead is the Muslim Quarter. To our left is the Christian Quarter.” Danny said, making a quick right turn. “We are about to enter into the Armenian Quarter, and down this way is the Jewish Quarter. Where my brother lives.”

“Got it. Jewish Quarter—Ezra—the plague—avoid like.”

Danny chuckled. “Oh, Lance.”

The Old City was relatively small compared to the rest of Jerusalem, a sprawling metropolitan area of well over half a million people. Like any other metro area, it was packed. Lance observed everything his tired eyes could take in on their first pass.

“I gather I will be learning Hebrew?” Lance asked casually.

“This is your new domicile,” Danny replied. “Tensions aside, you will enjoy living here.”

Danny parked.

Lance rested his hands on the stone railing as he looked down upon the Western Wall, or Wailing Wall, the most sacred site for Jews. Many different peoples, from the religiously minded to tourists, wandered below. It was a wide-open plaza. The Wall itself made up the side foundation of the mount where the Dome of the Rock stood.

“Tell me, Lance, what do you see?”

“A wall. A big one. And, I see…” Lance observed darkly dressed men in their hats and curly locks, bobbing only inches away from the face of the wall. “Hasidic Jews. Some are placing their paper prayers in the cracks of the wall. What do you see?”

“Fools. Like my brother. They wail or lament over the destruction of the Temple by the Romans in seventy C.E. and yet fail to learn from it.”

Lance thought Danny’s tone rather stern. “I think we’re back to audacious.”

"You must forgive me, Lance. I have seen much bloodshed over this mass of stone and the buildings upon it."

"I get it."

"Let me explain."

"No need. People still fight over the interpretation of a stop sign."

"Yes. Well said."

They pounded a beat through all four quarters. They finally stood at the Golden Gate. Danny was tired but offered: "It is believed that the Messiah will come through this gate."

"In spite of it being walled up?"

"Sultan Suleiman I, in fifteen-forty-one, walled it off. Then the Muslims placed a cemetery on the other side."

"Yeah, that'll keep him out."

"Superstitions abound. Tell me, do you believe you will go to hell?"

"That seems to be the consensus."

"I must show you something, Lance. I would be remiss not to share it with you."

***

They drove past Emek Refaim, their turnoff, and descended into the lower valley. Shortly, Danny pulled over and parked. Amongst cobblestone walls and limestone hills, there was a small park that looked tranquil with its own splendor and charm—a place to relax. Danny ushered them out.

"What's this place?" Lance asked as they walked down.

"My getaway from time to time. For you. Freedom."

Puzzled but game, Lance followed. "Your little slice of paradise?"

"The word paradise in Greek is *para'dei·sos,* meaning a beautiful park. Or park-like garden," Danny addressed.

"Why do you use Greek instead of Hebrew?"

"Like the Greek rendering, the Hebrew word *par·des'* means similar. A park."

"I thought paradise was in heaven."

"No." Danny watched confusion turn to frustration. It meant Lance was thinking, which meant he was listening. He was reasoning it out. "They are strictly an earthly reference. Biblically speaking."

"That doesn't make sense."

"It will. Come."

They walked deeper into the park, past a set of trees where two couples enjoyed wine and song. One of the men played his guitar.

They continued until Danny stopped at a large tree. "What you must do, Lance, is think back across the millennia, two thousand years ago, back to the time of Christ and then further back to the time of such kings as Ahaz and Manasseh."

"Who were they?"

"Kings. Apostates. Vile men. We are in the Valley of *Hin·nom′*."

"Yes, I saw the road sign when we drove down here."

"Where we are now is believed to be the area that was known as *To′pheth*. Child sacrifice took place here." Danny watched as Lance's face contorted slightly. "King Ahaz was instrumental in making even his own sons and daughters pass through the fire, sacrificing them to the god *Molech*. They would play the *tup·pim′*, the tambourines to drown out the screams of their children as they burned to death. The same with Manasseh."

"How could someone be so sick and twisted?"

"A vile business, I know. But, King Josiah condemned the action when he became king decades later and made this area a wasteland."

Danny could tell his words had increasing value. Good. "Now, we move up to the time of Christ. By his time, this area was a garbage dump kept burning day and night."

Lance drew a hardened look of recognition. "By fire and brimstone?"

"Well, by brimstone, or sulfur, that being the fuel source. Of particular note, and please do note this, a criminal that was deemed unfit or unworthy of a proper burial after his execution was thrown into this fire heap."

"To burn forever and ever?"

"Bear with me, here. Now, at the time of Christ, this place was known not only as *Hin·nom′*, but *Geh Hin·nom′* or, in Greek, *Ge·hen′na*. What you must know is that Greek was the internationally spoken language at that time. As English is today."

"And?"

"Christ, in symbolic language, referred to Gehenna as the *Lake of Fire*. The *Second Death*. He meant that this divine judgment would render a person in complete non-existence—forever. Forgotten. As if that person were never born."

"What are you saying to me, Danny?"

"Lance Rio—welcome to hell."

"No!" Lance dropped to the ground. It startled Danny.

"It's okay, my boy. You are now freed in the knowledge that hellfire is a lie. You have reasoned it out. Good! Good!"

Lance growled. "He had no right. You don't do that to a child."

"Lance, please, tell me. I am your friend." Danny took hold of Lance's shoulders. He gazed into the tear-filled eyes.

"The priest, my father, made me go to. Once, during confession…"

"You must say it! To free yourself!"

"He. He began to undo my trousers. He moved me around, and I—I flipped him! He cornered me in the confessional booth. I said that my dad would kill him, and the police would arrest him. He slapped me. And then he spoke harshly at me in Latin. He cursed me, Danny! He was the pervert, and I get the curse! He told me that if I ever spoke of this, he would hand down a curse of eternal damnation on me. No escape. I was a kid, Danny. For God's sake!"

"But, now you are free of him! You are free of the lie!"

"He gave my parents' eulogy. He said as long as I stayed silent, they were safe in Purgatory and would go to heaven when he did. Is that a lie too?"

"Lance, your parents have never been in any such danger. Come. Let us go home."

"But, what to believe."

Danny raised Lance to his feet. "Your choice is simple, my boy. You can believe either what the ancient Israelites truthfully wrote of this place and of death. Or you can believe what the ancient pagan nations that surrounded here wrote. There are no other choices."

Chapter 59

Baghdad, Iraq

33°20′00″N, 44°23′00″E

July 9, 1993

Lance was cleared to land. The chaos since the ouster of the inspectors a few days earlier had calmed and gave a chance for Ralston to get intel gathers back inside.

Lance had his own turmoil still brewing inside. Danny had shown him in a copy of the Catholic Douay Bible, in the book of Jeremiah that spoke of Topheth as being a detestable place for passing their children through fire. He read that God himself said that such a thought had never even come up into his heart. Lance now accepted it as truth. He was free, though bitter.

The great lie that held him hostage to a priest he had not seen in two decades was now moot. Further, Danny told him where his parents were—*She'ol* the common grave of mankind or gravedom. It was not an individual burial site or a particular grave but a condition of the dead from which the word hell emanated. The Hebrew word *qevu·rah′* referred to an individual grave.

These were not the words in Hebrew that Lance imagined learning first.

Danny topped it off with the word *ne'phesh*. Nefesh came from a root word, meaning *breathe*. In a literal understanding, nefesh was a breather, the person. The word *soul* came from nefesh. This was all dinner conversation that kept Danny bouncing up and running over to his bookcase between bites for reference material. For Lance, it was strength in truth and knowledge. Lance did not know what was more egregious, a pedophile priest running around or the centuries-old lie he told to cover his bad behavior.

Lance followed the lineman around to the right-wing after the left-wing was topped off. The Iraqi man was nimble in how he threaded the fuel hose out from the truck and around to the fuel cap. Lance leaned against the wing. "Did you know that animals, like man, *are* a soul?"

"Yes, thank you very much," the Iraqi said. His limited English aside, he was very focused on his job. Lance would throw him a few Iraqi dinars as a tip.

Lance spooled up engine number two first, and it lit off. It had been a sixteen-hour day. The trip home to Israel would be short, fortunately. He was tired and still had several thousand questions waiting for answers.

Lance proffered to Danny that perhaps the Bible and religion were not on the same parallel course—as most believed.

Chapter 60

Israel Museum, Jerusalem
31°46′21″N, 35°12′16″E

July 25, 1993

Lance looked upon the fragmented parchment that was the book of Daniel, or one of eight copies on display from the original Dead Sea Scrolls, which were dated between the third century B.C.E. and the first century C.E. In all, nine hundred seventy-two documents were recovered from eleven caves, from 1947 to 1956 and housed in the *Shrine of the Book*, a wing of the museum.

This was Lance's fourth trip to the museum. Danny entered the room, looking at his watch. He spotted Lance, who had walked from the house.

"You are like a child in a candy store, Lance," Danny stated. "You have become too obsessed."

"Obsessed?" Lance snapped. "You have set me free!"

"But you must be balanced, my boy." Danny's concern was warranted. Lance was both enthralled and angered at the same time.

"I know we need to leave."

"Yes. But, my concern is, have I awakened a sleeping giant?"

"I don't know about that. But I will never, ever! let a *man* chain me to a lie ever again!"

***

The drive up the inner coastal route and then through the observably narrow mountain pass was a pleasant distraction for Lance. In the three weeks he had spent in Israel, he finally came to terms this was home. This land excited him. There was new knowledge of a new land and a new language to learn and its people. Jeffrey was still on him to develop a new kit plane superior to the Shadowhawk. Despite whatever dramas, such thoughts were never that far off.

The beautiful patchwork of the agricultural quilt that was the Jezreel Valley was breathtaking. The dusty Land Rover came out of the narrow pass of the mountains to a stoplight at the intersection of *Megiddo Junction*. Danny signaled a left turn.

Lance poured over a map. "You know, we aren't that far from Nazareth, where Jesus grew up." He looked up and saw a large hill that was less than a hundred feet in elevation from where they sat. "Is this a biblical site?"

"This is Israel. Everywhere is a biblical site."

The light turned green, and Danny made his left turn.

"I get that. I mean, is it significant?"

"Only Armageddon."

Lance spun around as they drove past the onetime hilltop fortress.

"Actually, it's called Tel Megiddo. The word *tel* you might as well learn means hill or mound. It was a one-time fortress, and many decisive battles were fought here. There's a small airport nearby here, by the way."

"Armageddon Airport?"

"No, Megiddo Airport," Danny said bemused.

They drove around the tel of Megiddo and northward on Route 66. Lance appreciated the flat agriculture landscape that invoked the term: God's Country. Homes were spaced generously throughout the land.

They didn't drive that far from Megiddo Junction before the less than faint smell of livestock entered the Land Rover. "Ah, we are near my Kibbutz," Danny said.

"That's a type of commune, isn't it?"

Lance wrinkled up his nose at the smell of—Pigs! He was surprised to see pigs inside of the roadside fence. Danny made a right turn and drove down a long narrow asphalt driveway.

"You have pigs in Israel? I never would have thought."

"Never assume, my boy. I call this a kibbutz, but it's a working farm and ranch. About nine hundred hectares."

"Okay, about twenty-two hundred acres."

"A bit over. My father bought this land back in nineteen-twenty-two. Jews had been buying land here back then since the eighteen-forties. Most of the land out here was owned by the Sursock family."

"Yes, a Greek Orthodox family from Lebanon. They were partners in the Otis Elevator Company."

"Yes. This particular bit of land, though, was owned by an Egyptian Mufti who considered it worthless swampland and laughed all the way to the bank."

"I guess in the end, you had the last laugh, given what you've done with it."

"In the end, no one is laughing."

"Then, if your Arab brothers didn't want you living here, they shouldn't have sold you the land in the first place. And taken better care of their own, the *fellaheen*."

Danny grinned, shaking his head. "You have done your homework."

"Required by Jeffrey. Naturally."

They drove through a black, somewhat rusty wrought iron gate with a curved archway and up a long road. Lance focused on a good-sized ranch-style house as they came into a circular cobblestone driveway. Danny stopped the Land Rover in front of the porch.

"Nice place," Lance said as he continued to scan the landscape.

"You might say this is my Ponderosa."

"Kibbutz Ponderosa?"

"You could say. We're organic here. All our dairy here is raw, unpasteurized. You'll notice the difference."

For the first time in hours since their long journey from Jerusalem, Lance stood outside of the Rover when he noticed an Arab man running toward them. Danny called to him in Hebrew. The man slowed, throwing his hands up and then dropping them in utter defeat. Lance felt a nudge between his feet. A small white pig had wedged its way between his legs.

"What is this?" Danny asked. "Ah, you have made a new friend. And how did you escape, little one? Bassam!" The man stopped and explained himself. "Lance, this is my right hand here, Bassam."

Lance walked back toward the man and extended his hand. The little white pig walked in step between his feet.

"I am sorry about the little piggy, Mr. Lance," Bassam said as he bent down to grab the pig, but the little pig squealed and jerked back, staying between Lance's legs.

Lance knelt and put his hand under the jaw of the frightened animal. "What's the matter, little guy?"

Two hours later, Lance sat opposite Danny outside at the patio table, with the little white pig resting comfortably under Lance's chair. "This little porker isn't going to want to sleep with me?"

"Probably. Pigs are quite a clean animal. Besides raising some for food, we raise them for medical research and as sentries. They have a tremendous sense of smell that can rival a bloodhound. We train them to smell explosives. Especially on a terrorist."

"Would that be predicated on the idea that a terrorist smells like a truffle?"

"Oh, Lance," Danny chuckled.

Lance woke to the stirring at the end of the bed. He looked at the small pig rolling on its back, obviously in hog heaven. "Come on, truffle hound. I need a cup of tea."

The pig followed Lance through the Great Room that stood center of the house. The motif was a gentle blend of cream white walls, limestone, and lightly stained wood paneling.

Lance traipsed over the oak floor that went to tile once he entered the kitchen.

Lance braced the large legal-size pad against his lap as he made sketches of his next aircraft design. It was bolder than any before. He had his milling machine back in Germany in storage. He thought about how he would need Eric

Pitts as a second mind and pair of hands to build it. Special had retired from the CIA and moved back to El Cajon, California, just east of San Diego. He rented two hangars and began a business manufacturing custom kit plane accessories. Landing gear systems, military-style control stick, and throttle grips with different control button features.

Danny walked into the kitchen. "Good morning." He noticed the doodling on several pieces of paper. "Your next project?"

"Hopefully."

"I appreciate you have a lot on your mind, but wondered if you would care to help with the animals today?"

"Sure. I can help milk the cows if you like. I've done it before."

"A man of many talents. And now a milker of cows added to his accomplishments."

Chapter 61

Jerusalem

August 11, 1993

"May I remind you that half a year ago, Islamic terrorists attacked the World Trade Center," Jeffrey Ralston propounded.

"I need to go back to school. I have ideas, and I need more knowledge. I don't need a degree," Lance said.

"Why would you go to school and not get a degree?"

"I just need the added knowledge on some things. I have enough accreditation to hang on my wall."

"All right, Lance. We at the CIA encourage continued education. Though you are not in the CIA, per se, you are still family. But, if I need you, you need to be airborne in short order."

"Yes, why no degree. I've checked out Megiddo Airport and plan to set up there as well. I have a truck I bought to get around with."

"A little restructuring in one's life is a good thing from time to time. I'll even pay for your first year's tuition. Do you plan to attend down here in Jerusalem?"

"No, in Haifa. At Technion."

"What?" Ralston sighed. "Very well. What classes are you looking at taking?"

"Higher math, of course. I'll get a tutor on that one, though I have Danny."

"For one, as logical as you are, you'd think math would come easier. What else?"

"Intro classes to electrical engineering and material sciences. I want to study up on ceramic technology, and they teach it there."

"Seems a little ambitious. However, as you wish. I have some meetings with Mossad officials here in about an hour. How is your Hebrew coming?"

"I have the alphabet down, but writing square-squigglies from right to left is weird."

"You'll get used to it. Oh, and happy thirty-fifth."

"Today is your birthday? Why didn't you say something, Lance?" Danny begged.

"It's just another day."

Ralston and Danny realized that Lance wasn't celebrating life, cake aside. Ralston knew to keep Lance happy was to keep that mind of his engaged. The land of Israel would serve both of their purposes, it was turning out.

Danny led Lance upstairs to the attic.

A flick of a switch lit up the highest point of the house. It displayed the immediately recognizable red, white, and black Nazi flag that nearly covered the opposite end of the room.

"A little souvenir that came with the house," Danny said with a small sense of pride.

"A Nazi owned this house?"

"He was a descendant of the German Templers that first settled here."

"Like the Knights Templars?"

"No. The German Templers were a so-called Christian group that moved to Israel in the eighteen-seventies and built eight colonies here. After Israel came under British control, those living here during World War Two were rounded up and expelled from the country as many had joined the Nazi party. During my Nazi-hunting days in the nineteen-fifties, I tracked the previous owner back here to this house—"

"—and it came furnished." Lance brightened. "When were you going to tell me that you were with the Mossad?"

"I was one of the founding members."

"I see. Where are you from originally?"

"New Jersey. I came here a couple of years after the war."

"It's nice to have a place to call home."

"And now you do too. Ruth Street and Megiddo are your home."

Lance was touched by this elder man's kindness. Maybe here, he would not be chased away.

Chapter 62

Haifa, Israel

32°49′00″N, 34°59′00″E

September 24, 1993

Many trees and shrubbery surrounded the campus buildings of the Technion—Israel Institute of Technology.

Lance came early enough before his math class to meet his new tutor waiting for him in the math lab. Lance made his way into the empty room where a lone figure sat. She turned around, her blonde hair flying outward like a model's. She was very pretty with a gymnast's body. She was also the daughter of Ganandy "Daddy" Uspensky.

"Hello," Lance said, pushing forward past the infirmaries of negative thought. It wasn't purely out of goodwill that his first year of tuition was covered by Uncle Jeffrey in one of the best technical schools in the world.

"You are Lance Rio?" She raised her hand cordially.

"Yes. I'm here to be tutored in algebra. I have to stay ahead of my other classes that are all math-heavy."

"This will not be a problem. I will instruct you," Katya Semjonova said in a cute Russian accent addressing the slight concern she registered in Lance's voice.

Semjonova was Katya's mother's maiden name. He learned later that she was estranged from her father for some reason with no intel as to why. But here she was in Israel and now his tutor. The matter was problematic for Lance.

"Are your math skills weak?"

"Probably. I'm going to need a lot of help, Miss Semjonova."

"You can call me Katya. Now, let's get started."

"Then please call me Lance." Maybe it was the blonde hair, her honey-brown eyes that had a captivating effect on him. He accepted that she was the tutor, and he was the student. A spy had to live his camouflage. At a minimum, his math skills would increase.

Chapter 63

Kigali, Rwanda

01°56′38″S, 30°03′34″E

April 9, 1994

The order to evacuate was clear. Three days earlier, a Falcon 50 jet carrying Rwandan president Juvénal Habyarimana and the president of Burundi, Cyprien Ntaryamira, was shot down, killing all twelve aboard. Ironically the private jet crashed in front of the presidential palace. The incident was blamed on the Tutsi rebels. The Hutu-flavored government backed by the militia and supported by the Hutu prominent populace began killing their fellow citizens because they were Tutsi, all within the hour of the plane crash.

Lance was clear to land into Kigali International Airport. He was in his second semester at Technion and learning what he needed to know. It was peaceful in the northern part of Israel, away from the conflicts that plagued Jerusalem. He had enjoyed a growing friendship with Katya outside of his math tutoring. So far, there were no snags in his advanced education.

Overnight, a thousand French and Belgian paratroopers arrived without U.N. approval, taking control of the airport. Their only mission was to get ex-pats out of the country. They cleared Lance to go into town and provided transport for him to the U.S. Embassy. The air was thick with unrest. The only other place in the world that he ever literally felt such tension in the very air was in Belfast, Ireland, where once a British soldier pulled a rifle on him.

Lance thanked his driver and stepped out of the jeep. After his I.D. check, he was waved inside. Lance made his way to the front entrance and was met by an African woman inside the lobby. He didn't notice who she was. He was still too distraught by seeing ordinary men walking along the roadside of their neighborhoods carrying machetes, looking for a neighbor to slaughter. He caught sight of a man hacking another man in the neck midway down a suburban street.

"Not even a hello?" she asked. He recognized the voice of someone very special.

"Tara?" Lance found himself immediately rocking her in his arms. Tara kissed him on the cheek. She was as lovely as the last time he saw her. "Oh, it is so great to see you, but we need to get the assistant to the Ambassador and his wife out of here. That's my specific orders."

"That would be me. I'm the wife of the assistant to Ambassador Rawson. I'm now Tara Reed."

"David Reed is your husband?"

"For the past six years," Tara said. "David is stuck in Gitarama, about sixty kilometers from here. It's our second-largest city."

"Well, then, I have to get you out of here."

"I can't leave without him. I thought you were out of the CIA."

"Officially. But, you know, still family."

Lance sat in her husband's office. He had had his fill of the hate monger on the radio that Tara translated for him from Kinyarwanda, the official language of Rwanda. "Cockroaches, he calls the Tutsis. Where is this radio station?"

"You can't just pop over and put a bullet in this guy."

Deadpan, Lance looked up at her. "That kind of hate never has a place on this planet."

"Same old Lance. One in a million." It brought a smile to him.

"How long have you been stationed here?"

"Four years. The intelligence work here can be on the slow side, but the beauty of this place more than makes up for it. It's a shame you weren't here for a trip into the mountains to see the silverback gorillas. Nothing will bring you closer to God."

"So far, nothing has."

The phone rang. She answered it and hung on every word spoken. Her expression told him to fish out his gun and shoulder holster from his backpack and be ready for action. "I'll be ready to go." Tara hung up the phone. She was distressed. "The Interahamwe militia is on the move."

"Do you have your field box handy?"

"Yes. It's right here." Tara pulled out a metal box and worked the combination. She opened the box and removed the nine-millimeter pistol. She inserted the magazine and chambered a round. She moved the safety to lock.

"When was the last time you fired a gun?"

"It's been a while. Not much need out here, but I can use it if I have to."

The drive out of the U.S. Embassy was nerve-racking at best. Intermittent gunfire in the background surrounded them as they headed toward the airport. It was the unmistakable sound of AK-47s, the machine gun choice of slaughter. A swarm of neighborhood militia marched up the street Tara drove down. A rock came through the jeep's windshield. Lance whipped out his Glock. They were armed with machetes, and a few had small hatchets. They backed off when Lance aimed at them. They drove on as Lance flung the glass cubes off of him. They hurried down another street.

"Stop!" Lance yelled out. He saw a small boy, all of eight years old, run from a large man with a machete. He lunged up, but Tara dropped her body across his lap.

"No, Lance! I know. I know."

"I cannot watch this and do nothing!" Lance dropped back into his seat in defeat.

Lance noticed that many of the street signs were French-designated RUE. The streets were paved in asphalt with a light dusting of the earthy salmon-colored dirt from the side of the roads. The rich volcanic soil was the reason the geography was so beautiful. Rwanda was the *land of a thousand hills*. Now that beauty was marred by the brutal ugliness of genocide.

Tara's jeep took gunfire and sputtered to lifelessness, coasting to the roadside.

"We have to run for it!" Lance grabbed his backpack. He ran with Tara to a house. He heard the sound of several military vehicles racing down their street. They fired again at them. Lance kicked in the door. Tara ran inside. Lance returned fire, hitting the two front tires and radiator of the lead vehicle. With one vehicle down, they stood around in confusion. They weren't that sophisticated, but they were focused.

Lance and Tara ran out the back of the house with barely anytime to notice the dead family inside. "Over the fence," Lance ordered. He pushed her up and over the high wall and then hopped over. Tara came down on a dead man causing her to sprain her ankle.

"Oh great, déjà vu," Lance said, grabbing hold of her ankle, rubbing it. They heard soldiers on the other side of the fence burst into the backyard.

"I can make it." Tara shot up and ran to the side yard with Lance quickly behind. Lance knew they had to cross another street and then hide before the soldiers wised up and came around the next street.

They crossed the street and worked their way over another set of fences.

Army vehicles did just as he expected them to do. They came over to the next street. But they were surrounding the house they just left.

"Thank God," Tara whispered.

Lance wondered if they should have stayed in the jeep, got kicked around by the army militia, and then ordered out of the country. Except the militia fired on them. Perhaps they thought a white man was trying to save a Tutsi woman. The paramilitary organization Interahamwe had disarmed ten Belgian U.K. peacekeeping soldiers and then killed them. Lance had no reason to assume that they, in this scenario, would just let them go. It would be getting dark soon, and they could move under its cover toward the airport.

They moved inside of the house, where the rotting smell of the dead awaited them. They came upon a dead mother and two infants that had been hacked to death. The same would no doubt be carried out up and down these streets. They moved toward a back bedroom and rested. Lance cut strips of a bedsheet for a bandage that he wrapped tightly around Tara's ankle.

"You want to know a bit of ironic intelligence gathering I've done?" Tara asked.

"Sure."

"A certain Mr. Robert Kajugo—is a Tutsi. His father acquired Hutu papers for his family. He's also the president of the Interahamwe. The Hutu machinery set to exterminate the Tutsi."

"Doesn't surprise me. They say Hitler was part Jew," Lance said, grabbing his backpack. He took out his satellite phone.

***

Jeffrey Ralston sat glued to his desk at CIA headquarters. "Lance, do what you have to. You and Tara are our people on the ground. As soon as I can, I will get you hooked up with the U.N. peacekeepers there. They should be able to get you out."

"We're probably about ten-kilometers from the airport, but I don't see getting out of here by air right now. At least not tonight. And we should try and help as many as we can, Jeffrey."

"That's not prudent, Lance. The truth is there is no real U.N. support over this."

"What? Oh, come on, Jeffrey! These people are being slaughtered on sight. Please, I'm begging you, do something, anything!"

"My immediate concern is getting you and Tara out safely."

***

Lance describe his new aircraft design to Ralston. "I call it the *Sparrowhawk*. It's a thirty-foot-long, tandem two-seat jet-powered dream machine. The unique thing about this design is the wings. The Sparrowhawk will have what I call tandem bi-wings. That is, it will have two sets of identical wings. One set in the mid-forward part of the fuselage and the other set at the rear. Each wing will be over six feet long. The two front wings will have the elevators and handle pitch control, while the rear set of wings will have the ailerons and handle roll control. I plan to modify a G.E. T-Fifty-Eight turboshaft engine used in helicopters by using the engine's core and turn it into a turbojet engine, which some kit plane enthusiasts have been doing. But, I want to go a step further and add a nineteen-blade front fan to the engine—thus making it a turbofan engine. It would be quieter, more fuel-efficient, and more powerful."

"Very ambitious, Lance. Well, you have my support. I look forward to the fruits of your labor on this one. And well done. You continue to impress me," Ralston said.

Lance shuddered and stirred to consciousness. His body was sore from another uncomfortable night on an old broken-down cot. He felt a hand on his arm. It was tender, reassuring. "You okay?" Tara asked.

"Yeah."

The church was dark and dank with the humid and squalid fill of refugees. Lance sat up. He felt his whiskers form something of a beard. He hadn't seen the business end of a razor in nearly two months. Nor anything closely relating to a bath either. He saw the nun, the single force that ran what he flippantly called St. Michael's Hotel and Hospice. How they ended up in a church, he didn't know. It was more Tara's doing.

A man wielding a bloodstained machete pushed through the church doors and demanded all Tutsis come outside. Lance eased his Glock from under his pillow and screwed on the silencer. The nun approached the man. "What are you doing going around killing people? Don't you think about Christ?"

"Yes, sister. I do this in the name of Christ." The man went up toward the front of the church and knelt, pulling out his rosary beads. Lance observed him. By the time he was through his fifth of ten prayings of Hail Mary, Lance was up and shoes on. The man crossed himself and stood up. He looked at the nameless faces that hid as best they could between and underneath the pews. "I will be back for all of you."

He scurried across the floor and out the door. Lance was seconds behind him. The nun heard the muffled "thwack" for a second time since Lance and Tara showed up five days ago. She waited by the door. Lance came back in with his gun holstered and the machete in his hands.

"Mr. Rio, you cannot keep killing these men and adding blood on your hands."

"Sister, if you did a better job at teaching the gospels, I am sure my actions would not be necessary. And don't talk to me about blood. The Church has so much blood on its silent hands once again; I'd be a millennium in line waiting for any divine punishment." Lance had no mood to say anything more. He went back to Tara. "We need to leave and take another shot at getting north of here."

Lance thought about how their position geographic-wise was smack in the middle of the country, and it was a long way on foot to the northern border where the rebel Tutsi Rwanda Patriotic Front, the R.P.F. was located and safety. It was the same scenario to the south in Burundi, where U.S. Marines were stationed. They could appropriate another vehicle, but that was riskier than advantageous.

Lance, as a white man, could function more effectively without Tara. She was a black woman that was darker in skin color than most Tutsis, which had helped preserve her life so far. The Tutsis tended to be lighter in skin color than the Hutu, but this was not a guaranteed measure of identity or safety. It was as reckless a pattern of thought as genocide itself. For some odd reason, Lance thought of the original Star Trek episode: *Let This Be Your Last Battlefield.* The character of Commissioner Bele, who was black on the right side of his face and white on the left, was chasing after a felon named Lokai, who was white on the right side of his face and black on the left. They were the very last two inhabitants of their planet. Genocide had left their world dead. To a strong degree, Lance was living that episode.

Lance and Tara walked outside of the church doors. It was calm, almost blissful until whiffs of death attacked their sense of smell, followed by visual cues of dead bodies lying on front yard lawns and porches. In some cases, the bodies were stacked waist-high. Lance set off on foot with Tara by his side to the east, and then they would head north.

They headed away from the suburbs on less-traveled roads that would lead out of town where they could head up into the hills. Lance had scavenged a few cans of food from homes that now served as mausoleums.

"How are you holding up?" he asked.

She smiled thinly but proudly. "Still by your side and keeping up, my young man."

He put his arm around her and gave her a squeeze. Lance was a fast walker by nature but slowed his gait to stay by Tara's side. She meant a lot to him in the past. She had a husband he mandated would be reunited with her. A wife belonged with her husband. The pain that cold-hearted politics and ideologies had on destroying families would not happen to Tara.

They heard a large vehicle coming around the bend from below. They took cover in roadside brush. The Glock was poised to fire. The canvas-covered army truck rolled past them, its engine growling to move the five-ton vehicle up the steep road. Regular army, no doubt, filled the covered back of the transport.

Lance felt relief flush through him. Their calm was short. A high-revving smaller truck was heard working its way up the same hill. Lance took out the long tube and screwed it onto the end of his pistol. The faded red Toyota pickup pulled over after one of the men in the back slapped the top of the cab with his machete. There were six men in the bed and two inside the cab. No wonder it crawled up the steep road. The man standing placed his machete on top of the cab and then faced the precipice.

"Get ready to move," Lance said.

Lance crouched low and moved through the brush like a big cat on the prowl. The standing man finished his business. Lance put one right between his shoulders. He tumbled off the truck and down the hillside. Lance sprang from his roadside camouflage and finished off the other five.

The driver tried to put the vehicle in motion, but Tara stood between him and escape. Staring at her weapon, poised to fire, caused him to stall the engine.

"Tell them to get out of the truck and move to the back if they want to live," Tara spoke to the driver. He and his passenger stepped out with their hands held more forward than up. "Tell them to throw these dead men over the hillside." Tara related Lance's words.

They were scared, as they should be. He saw two blood rusted machetes in the cab of the truck. An insensibility rose up in Lance. There were no superlatives to throw at the situation. The last body was thrown down the hillside. Lance wished it burned with *sulfur*.

"Now ask them where they came from and where they are going."

Tara spoke to them. "They came out of Kigali. They were following the army truck to find more Tutsis trying to make it north to where the R.P.F. are holding the line and safety for Tutsi and any moderate pro-Tutsi Hutu." Lance had seen such Hutu held as traitors and killed right along with their Tutsi neighbor.

"Do you think there is anything else to get out of these men?"

"No, not really," Tara said. Lance aimed the Glock.

"No—no—wait—wait!" the driver said.

"Is that what your Tutsi neighbors said before you hacked them to bits? Begging for mercy doesn't work too well around here. Does it, mate?"

Lance put a nine-millimeter hollow-point slug center mass into the driver. Before Tara could say a word, Lance dropped the other. Both men fell back and tumbled down. It was more than Lance's accent that had changed over the years, Tara thought. He was a trained killer, an assassin. It unnerved her a little to be with him.

"Tara," Lance said softly. "Get in, please. We need to go."

The small truck continued up the hill.

Lance shook the satellite phone. "No, Jeffrey, there's no way for me to get to the Citation and make a break for it. And we're too far north."

"I need you and Tara out of there," Ralston directed.

"All I can do is keep heading north. But you tell Mr. Reed, with my dying breath, I will get his wife back to him."

"I think he knows, Lance."

"No! You tell him, Jeffrey, these words."

"All right, Lance. I will tell him."

"I'll contact you in a few. I need to conserve my batteries. Let alone my mind."

"I know this is hard on you, Lance, but I also know you have the gift to compartmentalize it."

"Okay. Over and out." Lance turned off the sat phone. It was time to move.

The road down along the Nyabarongo River was rough, but now it turned bumpy. Lance drove slowly with only the parking lights on. He stopped. It felt like pothole after pothole. "What in the world." He opened his door and looked down. "Oh my God!" he said, alarmed. Tara opened her door.

"Oh, my God! Lance, get off them! Drive over there!" Tara said, bouncing in her seat.

"I'm trying! Hold on!"

Lance turned on the headlights and hurried the truck forward until there were no more bumps and the road was flat. He turned the headlights off and stopped. His heart was racing. His stomach was nauseous. Tara was shaking. She broke down and cried into her hands. "I can't take any more of this," she sobbed.

Lance let her alone. He composed himself and opened the truck door. He walked back to where the dead bodies lay. Even before he turned on his flashlight, he could tell they were tossed off a truck as a maniacal trick to serve as speed bumps. He shined the light up the road. The dead were easily one hundred and fifty people strewn along the road. Lance walked further toward them. The odor off of them was not too offensive. They were recently killed. But then the smell of anything offensive was viewed in the perspective of Lance's own body odor. He saw an infant nestled under his mother's arm. Rigor mortis had set in before she and baby were loaded up and dumped on the road. Lance could not bring himself to shed another tear for these poor human beings. His heart could not fragment into any smaller pieces. He could not ascribe any sort of logic to such a dysfunctional level of logic—kill all of the Tutsis, and "all of our problems will be gone." In reference to Hutu government leaders who made that statement, Lance said, "No. You'd still be here."

***

Lance looked at his watch. It was July 16. One hundred days of genocide took the lives of nearly a million people, around twenty percent of the country's population. Besides the many guns and grenades the government could get their hands on, some 581,000 machetes were imported just for Hutus to hack to death their Tutsi neighbors. It was now over.

Lance and Tara rode with a U.N. Peacekeeping convoy. The morning sun was rising over the mountainous terrain. For once in a very long time, it was peaceful. Still, it was unsettling to see the death toll expressed as dead bodies left on the roads, in the streets, and in yards and homes—left where they dropped. Lance had to fight self-loathing for ever believing he was actually acclimating to this horror. It had gone on for so long. It was all he had come to know. It took all of his training and wit to survive. It was of some relief to learn that it was the Hutus' turn to flee. But to what end?

Lance rode up front. He knew there was a pile of clothing at one of the churches that could be washed and used for survivors. “It’s not far from here,” he said to the Canadian U.N. driver.

The morning glint of sunlight added to the headlights' ability to see further down the road. The church grounds were now visible. Lance could see the pile of clothes outside of the church itself. The U.N. driver turned up his nose in disgust. Lance excitedly jumped out of the truck and ran to the pile. He was finally able to offer something good to others.

Tara saw the breakdown of her friend and protector. The pile of clothing was still occupied by the dead within them. The pile was up to his shoulders. Tara came up to Lance to pull him away. “Lance, sweetie. We have to go. There’s nothing here.”

“I don’t understand. I was sure it was just clothing.” Lance moved around the pile, hoping to find even a tee-shirt that didn’t have a body in it. His eyes focused on a recently dead mother and her baby boy with his head under her shirt. He was nursing when they were killed. Lance took hold of the baby boy, perhaps half a year or so old. He would dignify the mother by placing the baby into her arms. The baby cried out. The cry was weak, drained nearly of life.

“Tara!” Lance scooped up the child in his arms and ran toward the U.N. vehicles.

“Oh, my God! It’s still alive!” Tara yelled. The U.N. troops scrambled.

“We need to get him hydrated. We need to get him to a Red Cross unit!”

“I’ll radio ahead,” said the U.N. driver.

***

The U.N. convoy pulled up to the tented area that had been set up by the Red Cross. It had proved to be a haven for Lance and Tara more than once. Lance hurried with the infant to the triage tent. “Dr. Maxwell! Quick! I need you.”

“Lance, is that you? In here.” Dr. Maxwell called out from inside of the tent. The tent was enclosed on three sides and with an open flap in the front. “I found a baby boy.” He placed the infant in her arms. Laura Maxwell was a short, Midwest American woman of bountiful energy. She examined the boy.

“Lance,” she said, looking up at him sorrowfully, “he’s dead.”

“What? No! I found him.”

“Lance. It’s time to come home.” Lance turned around. It was Jeffrey Ralston, with Josh, David, and Graham. Ralston looked at the stain-clothed, scraggly bearded, and putrid smelling man of whom he could not be more proud. It was time to clean up and go home. It was time to heal.

Chapter 64

Megiddo, Israel

32°34′44″N, 35°10′50″E

July 19, 1994

"I carried two extra magazines with me. I had four rounds left. I killed over forty men and sabotaged as much as possible. It just wasn't enough," Lance lamented.

"Yes, Lance, I understand. But I need you to compartmentalize it like you do everything else. It is your gift," Ralston replied.

"My gift?"

"I never told you this, but I had the eager misfortune to go into Cambodia, and I saw the killing fields, the mass graves, the half-starved people. Calling Pol Pot the Hitler of Cambodia was no exaggeration. I wanted to fight against what I saw. That's when I joined the CIA, leaving my commission in the Navy."

"Did you see the people beat and killed—hunted down like animals?

"No, Lance, I did not."

"Danny, when you liberated Dachau, did you see the Holocaust in action?"

"No, Lance, only the aftermath. That was enough," Danny said with a sigh.

"You need to go back to school. That is best for you." Ralston stated.

"I'll have to retake my classes for this lost semester."

"That should be fine. I'll pay as I have all along."

"And I have a new aircraft design I'd like to build. I call it the Sparrowhawk." Ralston's ears perked up. "It's a tandem bi-wing aircraft, which doesn't exist other than in my mind."

"Naturally," Ralston said flatly.

"I want to take a G. E. T-Fifty-Eight engine and adapt it for jet aircraft. But with an added refinement. I want to turn it into a twin-spool medium bypass turbofan engine."

"Lance," Ralston said, annoyed. "We don't need a jet aircraft with some unproven engine system from junkyard parts just so you can tinker."

Lance preferred his dream of Ralston's unilateral acceptance and praise better.

"Lance, if this is what you want to do, you have my support," Danny voiced.

"All right, Lance," Ralston relented. "As you wish. In between classes, build your jet engine thing-a-ma-bobby—and your Fastglass."

Chapter 65

Mt. Igman, Bosnia
43°44′24″N, 18°09′00″E

December 12, 1995

"I need you" were the words Ralston spoke that set things into motion. Before long, Lance found himself making three jumps out of a perfectly good airplane. It had been a number of years since his last jump. His cold-weather training with Graham was to be put to use.

Lance boarded a CIA Gulfstream jet at Megiddo Airport minutes after his third jump put him safely back on the ground. The aircraft then headed northwest toward Italy.

Hours later, Lance boarded a *Black Ops* C-130 cargo plane at Aviano Air Force Base and headed southeast toward the Balkans. The *Dayton Peace Accord* was to be signed any day, but some warring factions still carried on fighting over the shredded remains of Yugoslavia. Lance was missing his finals once again over the same madness—genocide.

The backend of the C-130 opened up. Lance gave a wave with his white-gloved hand and moved his white canvas cargo sack out the back first, which dragged him out once the fifteen-foot cord went taut. He deployed his rectangular ram-air parachute once clear of the aircraft. He looked up at the white canopy and settled in for a slow ride several miles forward where the Black Ops aircraft could not politically go.

It was late afternoon and getting dark early. Hopefully, his glide down just past the ridge of Mt. Igman would be with no observance. He didn't need action. This was a rescue mission, and the only enemy should be the cold.

Lance executed a half turn and glided more steeply into a small clearing of trees. The cargo sack hit first, and then Lance touched down. He immediately freed himself of his parachute, rolled it up, and put it in his cargo sack, leaving no trace.

Mt. Igman was just below five thousand feet at its peak. Lance stepped his way carefully through the snowcapped mountain. He saw the ski jump platforms beyond a ridge of trees. He kept his cautious foot-by-foot motion toward them.

Lance was hit with a snowball. Seconds later, gunfire broke out.

***

"Has Lance checked in yet?" Ralston asked, pacing up and down the Black Ops aircraft. He hated the NATO-imposed boundaries of the No-Fly-Zone, given how he was concerned, overly so, when it came to Lance. But, there were four others dependent on him. The radio operator called out to Lance. "Desert Wine, this is Grapevine, over—" Nothing.

Finally, a crackle on the radio offered some hope. Oddly, they heard humming, and then a *rat-ta-tat* sound one makes with a snare drum. Someone was singing: "*Here I stand, thrown from the sky. Pushed out of a plane and left to die. Oh—be careful what you say—they should have sent—a Green Beret...*"

Ralston forced his hand over the radio operator's hand, hitting the mic button. "Will you quit with the frivolity and focus on the mission?"

"Relax, Grapevine. I was jumped by four Serbs—militia, most likely. I scared them off. I'm near the ski jump area. I'm making my way over now."

"Do you see your objective?"

"No. Wait. Yeah. Amazingly enough, I do. I'll contact you shortly. Desert Wine out."

***

At the base of the massive ski jump, it was three hundred steps up the ramp or *inrun* to the platform. The inrun had about a thirty-five-degree angle on it. Lance had to climb up about one hundred steps, a third of the way up. He stepped over the rail and knocked on the JetRanger helicopter door. "Hello." He opened the left door. "Good afternoon, gents. Or early evening if you prefer." The helicopter sat eschewed inside of the ramp.

"Who are you?" the man in the pilot's seat asked. He was barely moving.

"I'm here to help," Lance replied kindly.

"Look," the pilot grumbled in pain. "Before the elements got the best of me, I checked the engine. The combustion chamber took several rounds. That's why I had to set it down. The tail rotor was shot up some too. The control linkage is very stiff."

"Yes, just as you reported. How are the others?"

"Bad. We're all bad. Hypothermia and probably some frostbite now."

"Here." Lance pulled out several hot packs. "Start putting them in your clothes and your shoes." Lance tore off the plastic wrappers and gave them to the pilot.

"My right foot took a bullet. I'll need some help with my boots."

Lance nodded. "Understood. I'll give you morphine once I get you warmed up."

It was bitterly cold. Lance was still cooling down, but he had been huffing and puffing since his feet hit snow. He opened the door to the passenger compartment. He saw three men all bundled up on the bench seat. "Are you men stable?"

“None of us have long if we don’t get warm,” the blond-haired man said. A burly black man sat in the middle with blood on his right thigh. The man on the left waved faintly.

“Here. Start putting these in your clothes and your shoes if you can. I’ll help you if you need it. I have some hot coffee in a thermos and some protein bars. You’re going to be alright.”

Lance helped them with getting warm. He had light thermal blankets with him, making them as comfortable as he could. They were doing better.

Lance stepped up on the footrest on the backend of the helicopter and opened up the engine compartment. The combustion chamber was literally shot up. With tools in hand, he began taking off the wire to the igniter and the fuel injector line, freeing them from the old combustor. The combustor was attached to the backend of the engine by thirty small nuts and bolts.

It took an hour and a half to free every last small bolt with finger dexterity operating nominally in this level of cold. A powerful head strap light pushed back the surrounding night. Finally, he freed the combustion chamber from the back end of the engine and from the compressed air tubes that fed the combustor. He looked inside the engine and could see the first turbine. He reached in and spun it. It looked fine. No damage. He settled in his mind that it would take several more hours to reassemble the engine.

Those expected hours later, the engine was back together. Lance stuffed his cargo sack into the luggage compartment. He looked behind to the east to catch the first amber ray of the morning sun. At least he would be able to see where he was going. He climbed into the left front seat. “Well, mates, let’s see if it works.” Lance turned on the master switch overhead.

“If this works, it will be one of the most amazing things I ever saw,” the pilot said.

“No, you landing this thing on a ski jump has to take the gold.”

“Name’s Sam, by the way. I was aiming for the lower part of the run. The sticky tail rotor wouldn’t let me hover and turn, so I had to do a running landing, and the ramp was here.”

“How did you know about this place?”

“I was stationed here during the Eighty-Four Winter Olympics.”

“Understood.”

The engine began its long whine to life. At 13% r.p.m. Lance lit the engine, and the deep throaty sound of combustion gave the four men hope for the first time in two days. The anti-torque pedals were not moving. It was a problem that would plague all of Lance’s efforts. The helicopter could not be steered in a hover or slow flight. The fuselage would want to spin opposite of the main rotor's rotation.

"You're going to have the same problem I had coming in," Sam said.

"Well, what better place to do a running takeoff than on a ski slope?"

"If you can. We have about a hundred feet in front of us."

"Okay, here goes. Everyone hold on." Lance rolled in full power. He slid the helicopter as fast he could down the ramp. Like many a ski jumper before it, the helicopter flew off the ramp's end at thirty-knots indicated airspeed. They needed sixty. The pedals were vibrating madly as the tail rotor was out of balance from its damage. The tail boom wanted to swing to the left. Lance tried to correct it by control inputs to the left, but it was straining. It was like two opposing forces trying to do the tango. Then the aircraft smoothed out. They had enough forward airspeed. Lance climbed. They were already high from the start, but he needed more altitude. They headed due west.

Lance kept the helicopter at 105 knots indicated, with a reduced power setting, which moved them decently and lowered the vibration on the tail rotor. The last thing he wanted was for the vibration to get so bad that it tore off the tail boom.

Lance took out his sat phone. He plugged his headset into it. "Grapevine, this is Desert Wine, come in, over."

"Desert Wine, this is Grapevine. Go ahead."

"Grapevine, we're airborne with four friends."

"Desert Wine—" Lance smiled at the cheers he could hear in the background. "Proceed to your destination."

"Roger that, Grapevine. Have medics standing by. E.T.A. to the coast is roughly forty-five minutes from now, and we will be making a running landing."

"Understood, Desert Wine. All will be waiting when you get here. Grapevine out."

Lance was glad that he didn't have to deal with people on the ground. He didn't want or need another crazy genocide to go through. Rwanda was terrible enough for several lifetimes.

"It's a beautiful country," Sam said. Lance noticed a bit more color in his face.

"Yes, I can see."

"I mean the people."

"I get you, Sam. Maybe they should have stayed Yugos."

The helicopter proved its mettle by holding together as they transversed the sandy shore for open water. Lance dropped down to three thousand feet. They were past any reprisals and had now only to find a spot in the vast Adriatic Sea. He redirected the helicopter on a southerly course.

"You know we either hit Italy or splash in the ocean," Sam said.

"I'm planning on neither," Lance replied.

Twenty minutes crept by Sam reckoned. The coastline was barely visible. His concerns were allayed when a U.S. Navy Huey Helicopter pulled alongside them. The co-pilot motioned for them to follow.

Shortly, a sliver in the ocean could be seen. The sliver was surrounded by other smaller slivers that spread out over a few miles of ocean. It was the Sixth Fleet of the U.S. Navy. This was gladsome to Lance. The vibration on the pedals had made his feet sore. He reduced power and lowered the speed to seventy knots, which eased his mind concerning that worrisome tail rotor.

The slivers were all recognizable naval vessels; destroyers, cruisers, munitions ships, and the flagship of the fleet, the aircraft carrier U.S.S. America. Lance lowered his altitude to one thousand feet and maintained seventy knots.

Lance was close now. He lowered the collective pitch control and began a slow descent. He kept control smooth and steady. The helicopter was now just two hundred feet high and about a quarter-mile aft of the carrier.

Lance brought the helicopter from above the ocean to over the black rubber asphalt that paved the carrier's deck. He lowered the helicopter, pulling gently back on the cyclic stick until the skids touched the spray foamed deck. He was down. He rolled off the throttle. There was still enough torque to whip his view to the right as the helicopter spun and skidded sideways to a halt.

Several yellow, blue, and green shirts rushed toward the helicopter. Air crewmen and medical personnel with gurneys hurried in to remove Sam and the others. Lance still had to let the engine cool down. He saw a very pleased Jeffrey Ralston standing in front of him. Lance felt uncomfortably warm in his white winter gear and needed to cool down himself. He rolled the throttle closed and shut down. He reached up overhead and pulled the rotor brake handle. The main rotor came to a stop.

Ralston came around to the door. "Well done, Lance."

Lieutenant Commander Scott Ensor picked up on the name as he was helped out of the helicopter. Lance Rio had come a long way.

"This is now my second taste of genocide," Lance said, stepping out of the aircraft.

"Operation Cocktail. You were wondering about the mission. They were to locate and record everything from mass graves and other illegal ventures against humanity. Sam is ours. And then we had a Navy SEAL, an FBI forensic specialist, and a friend from MI-Six. They hit pay dirt. Slobodan Milošević is in Paris right now signing the Dayton Peace Agreement."

"He should be in the Hague right now."

"Soon enough."

"You know, Jeffrey, all that needed to be done was to divide up the land into four pieces, and everyone go their separate way. Problem solved."

"The world doesn't work that way."

"I would *make it* work that way."

"Well, you can't. And you have finals to get back to."

Chapter 66

Kigali, Rwanda

July 18, 1996

The Dassault Falcon 50 was on short final for Runway 28. Lance, flying co-pilot on this leg of the trip, brought the three thrust levers back to idle as he held the flare for touchdown. Once down, he engaged the single thrust reverse lever. The bizjet slowed.

"My plane," Manfred Steiger called out as he moved the small wheel tiller to steer the aircraft onto the taxiway. Lance hoped that in the two years since he was last in Rwanda, its dark spectre had lightened. He still had dreams, dark and terrible.

The Onyx Aviation bizjet was directed to parking. They shut down. The eight-year-old aircraft was the fourth acquisition for Onyx Aviation Services. It had been some time since Lance and Manny flew together. Lance looked back as they walked from the plane. "Hey, Manny."

"I know. We're the same type of plane shot down that started the genocide. Or the excuse."

They shook off the thought.

"It still spooks me, *Plain*."

"Oh, you missed that about us. Very well. I understand, *Peanut*."

Out front of the terminal, the once touted M&M flight crew stepped into a taxi.

They arrived at the U.S. Embassy's main gate. The air had a calm to it. Still, Lance's defenses were on a certain level of alert. Lance would see about their accommodations.

Lance walked in with his bag strapped across his shoulder. He found the office of David Reed and entered. Tara was packing indecisively various items into boxes.

"Hello," Lance said kindly.

"I didn't think they would be sending you back here," she said.

"It's a calmer time now."

"For who?"

"Tara," Lance said entreatingly. He put down his bag and took his friend, her tears falling in his comfortable embrace. "What's this all about?"

"David and I have been reassigned. That's all."

"That's all?"

"What is there to say? He's back to Washington. I'm going back to Langley. Am I so uninteresting, Lance, that he needs to have mistresses scattered about?"

"You are as beautiful and as ever interesting, well, as ever."

"Thanks, sweetie, but my husband should be saying such things to me. I won't let him touch me. I don't know if he'll be bringing home AIDS or worse."

"I'm so sorry, Tara." Lance sat down across from her.

"You're a good friend, Lance. You always have been."

"How much time will you need? I can fly you out of here now if you want, and I'll come back for him later."

"Are you kidding? I have a lot of mess still to go through before I'm ready."

"I guess I'll be here for a few days. Maybe I can go up and see the mountain gorillas this time and enjoy the scenery."

Tara stood poised and proper. "Come, I'll take you to your rooms."

Lance did see Mr. Reed come the morning. The meeting was short. The Reed's had personal investments in Rwanda's coffee business down in the Maraba area, thus the delay.

Lance enjoyed the scenery out in the forest. He and Manny watched along with the tour group the famous silverback mountain gorillas in their natural habitat. He smiled at the antics of the six hundred-pound animals. This was a perk, a moment to forget human troubles and be one with nature. He thought it funny how mankind fought against itself in the concrete jungles of the world, only to get back to nature in some fashion.

The tour guide addressed the group that final pictures were to wrap up in a few minutes and that they would retreat as quietly as they approached these magnificent animals. It was a wonderful day.

The drive back was as peaceful as the drive to the tour agency's place of business. Lance realized that he didn't even pack a gun. It was nice. Friendly. Renewing.

They arrived back at the embassy compound.

Lance left Manny in his room and went cheerfully to his in the guest quarters. A cup of tea and a shower were in order.

There was a knock at his door, far too quiet for him to hear in the bathroom. The lock was released, and the doorknob turned slowly. The door opened, only inches at first and then enough to allow passage.

Lance was dressed in his favorite linen causal dress trousers. He checked his appearance in the mirror. He looked forward to a less somber dinner with Tara. He grabbed his shirt as he went back into the room.

Tara was leaning up against the door. She was dressed in a white bathrobe.

"Tara, what are you doing here? How did you get in here?"

"You think I can't still pick a lock?"

"This is wrong."

"Why, Lance? Are you going to tell me it's not appropriate?"

"To start with."

"Same old honest spy." She moved away from the door, her steps careful and deliberate, her stride smooth and knowing.

"Tara, you need to leave."

"No, Lance. Our time has come, and it's past due."

"No. Tara, please, listen to me." His grappling convictions only drove her closer.

"Shh…it's okay," she whispered, putting her finger to his lips. She dropped his shirt to the floor. "This is our time. Just let it happen." She smiled. Her hands slowly pulled the robe tie apart. She was in no hurry. She would enjoy him throughout the night.

"No!" Lance grabbed her hands and yanked the robe tie taut. Tara flew sideways, landing against the bed on the floor. He was grieved he may have hurt her, given two years ago, he risked his life countlessly to save her from harm.

He grabbed his shirt and put it on, wrapping it as tight as he could around himself. He sat on the wooden desk chair. He was shaking. Slowly, he composed himself.

"Tara, I have become many things. But, one thing I will never be—is an adulterer!"

"Oh, Lance," she said, her tears and shame strengthening.

"Tara. I will always care about you. But, not like this. You had no right." His anger flared. "You had no right!" He stood, turning from her. "You both will be ready to go by morning. Please leave."

***

The mood was somber between Tara and her husband and between them and Lance. Lance loaded the last of their baggage and waved for them to exit the vehicle.

All of the shades were drawn on the aircraft's windows. "Manny, would you please see to Mrs. Reed's comfort?" David Reed looked to board, but Lance stopped him. "Mr. Reed, I have some new marching orders for you."

Lance waved for the vehicle to go. The driver waved and drove away.

"Yeah, what is it?" Reed asked with his hands impatiently on his hips.

Lance stepped away from the door. Reed followed. All Reed saw was a quick flick of Lance's hand. Reed froze up in pain, dropping to his knees. He struggled to take in a breath. Lance knelt beside him.

"Very simply, either you divorce Tara, setting her free to find someone that will be loving and faithful to her. Or you honor your marriage to her. I leave that choice with you. However, if you continue to hurt her—I will take exception.

Clear?" There was no answer but the look of bitter disgust. Lance's teeth clenched. "I said, clear?"

"Clear. We're clear."

"Good." Lance helped Reed to his feet. "It should be a pleasant flight."

The Onyx jet taxied forward, revealing the Onyx Lear 45 brought in during Lance's sleepless night once Ralston understood the situation. It would take him home.

Chapter 67

Haifa, Israel

August 11, 1996

It was hard to believe Lance was thirty-eight years old, and in all this time, the basics of life and happiness still eluded him. With his baby face, Lance still looked a very confident twenty-five years old, depending on whom you asked.

Katya came up to him at the Technion cafeteria. "So, why are you not continuing with your degree?"

"I'm going to San Diego next month for a while," Lance replied.

"How long will you be gone?"

"Six months or so. Don't worry. I'll stay in touch."

"Could I come out to see you? I hear San Diego is a beautiful city."

"It's very nice. And we'll see."

There was a skewed emotional content to their friendship. Katya moved it closer on her terms. She seemed eager to see him, yet there was something that impeded her from drawing fully close to him or any man. She was a good woman, and she deserved better than the legacy left her by her father.

Chapter 68

El Cajon, California

32°42′54″N, 116°57′36″W

September 28, 1996

Eric Pitts waved goodbye to Gina and the kids as he drove him and Lance from the house to Gillespie Field airport. The two hangars he leased served the purpose of the growing kit plane world. The kit plane world was not just a world, but now an industry. Hundreds of kits from true glass that's fast, to slow and cheap had flooded the international marketplace. Computer science rallied to the burgeoning kit plane market with aeronautical engineering software. The pricey software installed on Eric's laptop had greater computing prowess than NASA's Cray computers of just a decade ago. Peripherally, much new equipment lined the walls, shelves, and lockers of the hangars. Two long tables, smooth and clean, were at the ready. With companies like Aircraft Spruce & Specialty Co., laying hold of the needed and specific type of parts for kit plane designing and building made it easier to fabricate a dream. Today was their day—finally!

The first step in creating a prototype kit plane was lightly gluing several polystyrene foam cores or blocks together to make a full-size block—for the fuselage as Lance and Eric had done with the Shadowhawk and as Lance had done with Wes Gent many years before.

This time a high-tech milling company made the plywood templates. It saved time and gave unmatched precision. The templates came in three pieces that were joined as a single piece and then attached to each side of the block. The templates were numbered as before.

It was time to start carving. It had been a while for both men, but they were eager. At the No. 1 mark, the hot wire cutter began its slice into the polystyrene foam. The voltage was good, with no drag, providing a clean cut. "One," Lance called out. "Two," Lance called out. "Three," Lance called out. Eric matched his pace of moving the hot wire cutter frame in sync. Soon they were past the 30 mark and then the 40 mark. Two hours later, they finished the top of the fuselage. A new aircraft had begun taking shape.

This phase of the operation, the carving out shapes in foam, was called making a "plug." When completed and in the form desired, the plug was fiberglassed with epoxy resin and then sanded micro smooth. From there, a master mold was made. The mold was then coated with a releasing agent, and the composite material, be it fiberglass, carbon fiber, or Kevlar cloth, was placed inside of the mold. This was called a "lay-up." Finally, the epoxy-coated fabric would be vacuum bagged, where all of the air would be removed and then baked in an oven at 250° F.

To bake under pressure, Lance and Eric found and turned an old fuel tanker trailer that once hauled gasoline from refinery to gas station into a poor man's autoclave. It was heated by propane and could be pressurized to 125 psi. Heat and pressure made for superior parts.

At day's end, they had a profile shape of the Sparrowhawk. "You're sure you want to kick it up a notch?" Eric questioned.

"Positive," Lance affirmed.

"Well, when we get this baby airborne, you won't do something stupid like get yourself killed, will you?"

"Special, isn't it obvious by now that the greatest peril to my life is always when I'm on the ground?"

***

Katya sat in a chair in her Haifa apartment that overlooked the Mediterranean. It was November, and the climate was cooling. The view always refreshed her no matter the time of year.

Sergei Volkov, a St. Petersburg Russian, sat opposite her. He grew up together with Katya. He was tall and lean with a scar down his left cheek. Sergei's surname Volkov meant wolf. Since Ganandy's death, Sergei had become known as "The Wolf" in the Russian underworld. He ruthlessly lived up to the hype. He was in the Spetsnaz, the Russian Special Forces, for a time, yet this visit made him nervous. He knew Katya hated her father, but not why. His feelings for her had resurfaced within minutes of entering her home. Still, she was standoffish in their conversation.

"There is not much left, but there is one common factor in the destruction of your father's business," Sergei said.

Katya thought it amusing that Sergei called her father's crime syndicate a business as if he manufactured something useful. "What is this?" she asked flatly.

"Not what. It is who. Here, this is a picture I found of him. Your friend, Lance Rio. We thought he was dead."

"No, he is very much alive." She looked at the worn photo of Lance.

"He is an unusually dangerous man, Katya. He had a wife in Germany. Your father placed a price on her head and his."

"And he retaliated? What did you expect?"

"He is clever, this devil. He swept through the whole Bratva and destroyed it and others. If I was not elsewhere, I would have been swept away with the rest. I believe you are next."

"Why would he want to do me harm?"

"He swore complete death to every living thing that was your father's. You are the last of his focus."

Katya looked scornfully at Sergei. "You men are so evil."

"This man is. And this has to be avenged. We go to San Diego."

***

It was Sunday. Eric was with his family. Lance was at the hangar. Three months in, they had molds. The molds produced skins for the fuselage and wings. Spars and ribs were built for the wings and control surfaces. The lower half of the fuselage was together and rested on padded sawhorses. Despite Ralston's grumblings over so radical a design, he was in town to check on their progress.

The Sparrowhawk's unique wing system required more thought than estimated to work out the bugs. But, the full-span flap panel that attached to a control surface worked perfectly. Lance would let Ralston see it in action over trying to explain it to him.

Lance was finished for the day, the air was still warm for this time of year, but that was the desert. But the desert turned cold at night this time of year. Lance pulled off his dust mask and dropped his coveralls. He washed as much dust off of him as possible this side of a shower.

"Now, I find you," Katya said.

"Katya! What are you doing here?" Lance asked excitedly. "I know I'm a dirty mess, but come here." He hugged her. It warmed her, and then it unnerved her. He affected her like no other man. Even with the knowledge of his past and purpose, she didn't realize that her arms were around him.

"Katya. Why didn't you tell me you were coming?"

"I spoke to you a week ago, but I wanted to see this San Diego. So, I surprise you."

"Where are you staying? When did you get here?"

"I am staying in the city of San Diego near the water. I came here two days ago. I wanted my jetlag to finish first."

"I think you'll have a few more days of that. But come, I'll meet you for dinner."

She gave him her particulars. He took her face gently in his hands and kissed her forehead. "I have missed you." Lance left the shop excited. Katya left the shop, confused.

It wasn't long before Lance was home, in the shower and back out the door, leaving Eric and Gina betwixt. Something told Eric that Lance had let his guard down. He knew about Katya from Israel and that Lance took her old man and syndicate down, but her suddenly showing up had red flag warning written all over it. Eric grabbed his cell phone.

"Jeffrey, it's Eric. That Russian girl that Lance knows from Israel is here."

"What? Are you sure?" Ralston questioned.

"Yes. Lance is on his way to meet her for dinner. He just left a few minutes ago."

"Listen. Get your firearm. I will have a team out to you ASAP. Pack lightly and plan to spend a few days away."

Eric thought of his wife and his ten and twelve-year-old. They were in danger. He had his Beretta in his back pocket within seconds of hanging up.

Lance drove into town.

The night was clear and cool along North Harbor Drive, which ran along the famed wharf of downtown San Diego, where several ships of different vintage lay berthed. The Star of India, the only still sailable ironclad three-mast sailing ship in the world, floated motionless along the pier where she was moored.

A hand reached up from under the watery surface, grasping hold of a mooring line that hung from the stern of the ship. The man pulled himself up from the water with little disturbance. He remained motionless as a couple walked past the pier. Scott Ensor smoothly transitioned himself from the stern onto the deck, toward the front mast. He climbed the webbed ropes up to where they attached to the mast. "Navy in place," he radioed.

Katya was happy but unsure of how to register her feelings toward Lance by the way he held her hand as they strolled down along the water's edge. It was quiet and charming, magical, and intriguing. Their dinner together was so enjoyable. Lance didn't find it within himself to wait any longer. He stopped and took Katya into his arms. "I love being with you." He moved his hand to her face and caressed her neck. He pulled her to him. Katya could feel the warmth and energy of Lance the moment his lips touched hers. She instinctively responded. His embrace, his kiss moved her to a new level of acceptance. His lips pushed deeper into hers. She hit her threshold. For the first time in her life, she wished it would have stayed submerged, but she was drowning. She pushed away from Lance. He now understood.

"Katya, who hurt you? Tell me."

"Why do you say this to me?"

"Because you have no reason to fear love from me, and you do. I suspect with any man. Who hurt you? Was it your father?" Lance watched a shiver rattle her body. Her honey-brown eyes widened with incrimination, her face thinning in color. She was discovered. Her hidden burden was exposed. Her shame made public. "So, we can add incest to your father's list of crimes. I don't care. He's gone, and we're here. Katya, listen to me. You can overcome this. I will help you."

"I can never be. I've tried," she cried.

Lance could only imagine the trauma Ganandy put his daughter through. It caused him to feel a new sense of loathing for the deceased crime boss. "Katya, don't let your father rule your life anymore. He's gone. You're free of him."

"Is that why you killed him? Because he tried to kill you and your wife?"

"Your father was a vicious, cruel, and evil man," Lance said bitterly. "But, I am free of him. Just as you are, if you want to be."

Lance's intuition kicked in too late. Katya pulled a small semi-automatic pistol from her purse. Lance recognized the Russian *Malysh OT-21*. "You want to kill me, Katya?"

A silhouette moved closer. It was a man wielding a silencer-equipped Makarov. "You have done well, Katya. I have him now," Sergei said, stepping forward.

"Sergei Volkov," Lance said, smiling thinly.

"Yes, the only one you missed."

"They say if you don't get all cancer, it comes back."

"And I am back." Lance raised his hands. "Put your hands down. Put them in your pockets."

"Tell me, Sergei, you plan on making points by killing me?"

"Something like that."

"Well, I knew it wasn't about Katya. You just used her to get to me."

"Shut up! You don't think I know what you are doing?"

"She'll never love you, Sergei. You'll have to force yourself on her like her father."

"I said to shut up!"

"You wouldn't force yourself on me, Sergei, would you?" Katya asked. A snarled smile wrapped around Sergei's face. His left hand found its way around Katya's pistol and removed it from her insecure grasp. He raised his arm, aiming at Lance.

"Goodbye, Katya," Lance said, tensing up. Sergei flinched, Lance spun to the side. Sergei groped the air and dropped to the ground. Lance ran to Katya. "Don't shoot!"

"Don't shoot!" Ensor said over his mic.

Lance held Katya as her legs buckled. "No! Katya!"

Her weakened hand caressed Lance's cheek. "I choose you," she said as she dropped from the living.

"I said don't shoot," Ensor growled into his mic.

"It's dealt with," the dark voice replied.

Ensor came down from his perch and slipped back into the water from where he came.

Lance disappeared. That part of him that was functioning logically knew a cleanup crew would be less than a minute away. He slipped away down a dark side street.

Lance drove the short way up Interstate 5 until he hit Highway 8 and headed east, back the few miles to El Cajon and home.

Lance pulled up into the driveway and took a breath. He wiped his eyes.
He got out and hurried to the front door. His key was barely in the lock when the doorknob was ripped out of his hands. The door flung open with Eric holding his Beretta on him. The gun dropped, and so did Lance's gaze. He saw his two suitcases at the door. "Sorry, Lance, but get out."

"Eric. You don't know what happened."

"Don't care. You're dynamite to be around. Can't have you risking my family. So just go. Sorry if I missed something. I'll have it forwarded to you back to Israel or wherever you are, but take your bags and go."

Lance had no fight left in him. Eric was right. Lance drew trouble wherever he went. He could not live or love without it being taken away from him and without the risk of death to those around him. He took his two bags and left.

Chapter 69

Dessau, Germany

December 15, 1996

It had been many months since Lance last came to his other home. Dessau was no longer a city lost in the old East German dictatorship but a thriving city in a unified Germany. It made sense to build a hangar at the airport. It also made sense to build a small upstairs apartment for overnight stays.

Lance rose early, ready to enjoy his first cup of tea. He had made friends with a cab driver that shuttled him back and forth into town. The small upstairs sanctuary sheltered him from the outside cold and world.

The *Computer-Numerical-Control* or CNC *milling machine* was at work, carving out the inner workings of his mind. He might have a new and exciting engine, but no Sparrowhawk to put it in. It was one crisis at a time. Lance came downstairs to check on the CNC machine's progress.

"You must tell me how you managed to get lost, including your jet, given it's not an easy thing to hide." Lance didn't jerk too much at the sound of Ralston's voice. Ralston came around the wing of the Citation toward Lance. "Is this where you've been for the last week?"

"I've been working. And Dessau has become a wonderful place since the end of the Soviet era. But, sometimes the end of an era isn't the end of an era."

"Did you love her?"

"I knew her for three years, Jeffrey." The depth of Lance's voice was gone.

"Then, you were more than friends?"

"No. Her father ruined that for her. With any man. You know what they say, incest is best—it's all relative."

"Stop that talk," Ralston scolded.

"Sorry."

"Lance. I need to know where you are with things."

Lance waved Ralston forward to the large clear plastic window of the milling machine. Ralston watched the 5-axis, computer-controlled unit cut into a solid piece of titanium alloy that had now milled eight of the nineteen fan blades that would make up the front fan of the proposed jet engine.

"Even in my despair, Jeffrey, I keep working. I—progress." Lance shrugged. "I won't have a plane to put it in, though."

"I'll see that you do. When you finish up here, go back to Israel."

"If that's what you want." Lance took pause. "Jeffrey, did you show her dignity?"

"Yes, we did. She's back home. I'll show you where."

"Thank you."

Ralston did not know what to do for Lance. He had suffered too much heartache. He did not know if living for a machine would help heal or not. It was one reason why he let Lance get overly ambitious with this project. He was never one to hamper creativity. However, a broken spirit could topple everything.

Chapter 70

Jerusalem

December 25, 1996

For a large portion of the world, many would wake to hurry down to a tree and open presents. Lance had a turbine engine resting on a folded drop cloth on the kitchen table. There was light snow outside, so he worked inside and was glad Danny wasn't around to see his Ruth Street house turned into a workshop.

Yet, Danny came through the front door. He saw a four-foot-long-wooden crate labeled: Dakota Air Parts, Inc., Fargo, North Dakota, USA. "I guess Santa was here."

He noticed that two Bibles, Vine's Expository Dictionary and the books: The Non-Christian Cross, by J. D. Parsons and The Two Babylons, by Alexander Hislop, were laid out on the coffee table. He picked up the book by Parsons. It was his first edition of 1896. He put the century-old book back on the table.

"Lance."

"In here, Danny."

Danny walked curiously into the kitchen to find his young charge. "You have a helicopter engine on my kitchen table."

"As soon as I separate the power turbine and transmission from the front part of the engine core, I will have a turbojet engine."

"You are quite the tinkerer. However, this is my kitchen. And why all the reference material laying out?"

"Research."

"Yes, I must remember your overly forensic approach to everything."

"That's because the truth is so well hidden right there in plain sight. As I told you, I won't be held captive by the lie—by anyone ever again."

"I appreciate your passion, as always, but my kitchen."

Lance cleared the table an hour later.

Lance and Danny sat and ate ham sandwiches for lunch. "I see you have gone to our favorite Russian deli for your pork needs."

"It gives me a chance to keep my Russian up."

"I am concerned about you, my boy."

"I know I'm tweaking a bit. But, look at it in the bigger scheme of things. It's Christmas, and as usual, they're fighting at the so-called holy sites. Me, I'm here and at peace. And it's not even his birthday."

"You've reasoned this out as well?"

"I have now. It's a Roman pagan thing. Winter solstice and all that. I also figured that if Jesus was thirty-three and a half when he was executed, on a *stauros* mind you, had he lived, he would have turned thirty-four around early October, counting six months back from Passover."

"Yes, your gift for reasoning out the seemingly obvious."

"Not everything."

"Such as?"

"Noah's flood. How? Where did all that water come from to drown the earth? I mean, that's plausible."

"A master of meteorological aviation, and you haven't figured it out? I am shocked. Grab a Bible from the other room and turn to the first page."

Lance retrieved a Bible from the living room. "You mean, Genesis one-one?"

"Yes, Genesis one-one."

Lance maneuvered the book to its beginning. "Okay. 'In the beginning, God created the heavens and the earth.'" He looked up, grinning. "I've heard this one before."

"Everyone has. Keep reading."

"'And the earth was waste and void, and darkness was upon the face of the deep, and the Spirit of God moved upon the face of the waters.'"

"The English word *spirit* is from the Latin word *spiritus*, meaning *breath*. The original Hebrew word you already know is *ru'ach*. Also meaning breath. But, in the truest sense of the word, it's God's active force. His power, His self-generated energy. Or his Holy Spirit directed to accomplish something."

"I know. It's not a living being. Every time you break down a lie, the truth is something simple."

"Usually. Keep reading and especially note verse six," Danny instructed.

"'And God said, Let there be a firmament in the midst of the waters and let it divide the waters from the waters.' Footnote…" Lance looked down the page for footnote 2. "Hebrew meaning *expanse*. What's an expanse?"

"Simple. Waters below as in the oceans. Water covered the very surface of the earth."

"I gather then there are waters above?"

"Exactly! The expanse."

"Which is?"

"Bear in mind that many people, over a very long period, have convoluted what is a very simple understanding."

"Yeah, I get that. It's a chronic problem."

"John Calvin stated in fifteen-fifty-four that they were clouds."

"Clouds cannot hold that amount of water to flood the earth, Danny."

"I only said that John Calvin called the expanse clouds. Think higher. Add to that the mammoth display at the St. Petersburg museum you enjoyed visiting. It's all tied together. Think it through."

"Well, the sun always hits the equator no matter the time of year. That's a given. Warm air rises along the curvature of the earth, where it cools at the poles and circulates back down again. But, how does the mammoth come into play?"

"Reason it out. You're doing better than most."

"Okay. An inordinate amount of water presumably had to come from somewhere. It didn't come from outer space." Lance's eyes lit up. "Water vapor? No! It can't be."

"How can you say no to what is obviously yes?"

"You're saying the expanse is the Thermosphere?"

"You tell me?"

"It's the largest section of the atmosphere, and it's practically in outer space. And it's hot! Admittedly, it could hold a vast amount of water vapor. So you're saying God condensed this water vapor into rain and flooded the earth?"

"It's the most reasonable explanation. If you recall that the mammoth was plucked from the icy muck in Siberia at the turn of the century. Still undigested in its stomach was the buttercup flower, which only grows in moderate climates."

"So, the expanse was like a water canopy that gave the greenhouse effect to the poles. That would explain why fern fossils have been found in the arctic. Logically, when the water canopy was ripped away, the poles froze and quickly. But that mammoth, like others they've found in Siberia, are attributed to the Ice Age. To the movement of shifting continents."

"My boy, that mammoth was found with food still in its mouth. It died in mid-chew."

Danny got up from the table and turned his interests toward cleaning up his house.

***

Eleven large wooden crates sat stacked before Lance. They were collectively the Sparrowhawk.

Danny and Lance popped open the final crate. Danny felt that he was uncovering the black shell of a giant prehistoric beetle. He trusted that Lance knew their proper sequence of assembly. "What is the first step?"

"Well, I need to turn the barn here into a workshop," Lance said, scanning the barn interior.

"We don't use it for anything but storage these days. So it is yours."

"I will need tools, equipment, and supplies. And I'll need help."

"Will, an old man, serve as help?"

"Danny, I would be delighted to have your help." The small white pig grunted his support as well. "Yes. And you too, Alfonso."

Lance's mind went immediately unencumbered. He would pour a concrete slab and shape up the old barn to set up his shop. The area just outside could be paved to join it to the long road that ran to the other side of the kibbutz. He smiled. That long road could serve as a runway!

It was the middle-end of April. He still had to finish this semester at Technion. By June, he hoped to be up and running.

Chapter 71

Miami, Florida

June 30, 1997

Death was habitual for coming without warning. That is outside of armed conflict. In that arena, there was no ambiguity about why death happened. It was purposed. Yet, it still came as a shock, a suspension of disbelief that a companion was gone.

There was great agony inside of Lance as he gently rocked Sybil Gent. She clutched him tighter in hopes that her feelings of loss could somehow be secured to something tangible, and she could step away pain-free. It was hard to fathom that Wes was gone. A stroke two years earlier had set him up for his eventual, untimely death. Lance had planned to visit him and Sybil over the coming summer.

Lance found it hard to sit through the eulogy and hear that death was nothing more than a portal, a means of travel to another realm, instead of the insidious, diabolical, and heartless enemy of man that it was. It took his beloved mentor and friend.

Danny said to Lance. "You wanted to speak out, didn't you?"

"It's what comforts them. What good would it have done to say different?"

Danny had asked to travel with Lance to support him. Lance was grateful. Danny saw firsthand the love he had for this man back in America and the positive effect he had on him. It also allowed Danny to get a stronger sense of Lance's beginnings.

Lance drove into the old mobile home park he once shared with his first wife, Keri, now seemingly eons ago. His old mobile home was still there but had fallen into disrepair. It was his past, and he felt no attachment to it, though some sentiment.

Lance drove to Opa-locka airport with Danny. Some of Lance's revisited history was pointed to outside a wire fence. His hangar that once housed his MU-2, he poignantly stated in detail much of the pivotal events that would send him on the path to intelligence work as a career—unknown to him at the time.

It was down Interstate 95 to the end of the Florida mainland that the rental car took Lance from his past to past his beginning.

The drive over the Jew Fish Bridge and a turn here and a turn there told Danny that Lance knew it as if he never left. They were in famed Key Largo. Lance turned onto another street. It was now a slow drive down where he stopped in front of the house he once called home. It was someone else's home now. Someone else parked their car there. He looked to the other side, to the home of the Drakes. Someone was home.

Lance drove off. "You really can't go home, can you?"

"Part of your heart will always be here, my boy. And that's okay."

"I feel like I'm always running because I keep getting chased off."

"Perhaps. But you have moved forward. That's the important thing."

Danny was content to know Lance all the more fully now. He was ready for their drive down to Key West.

***

Though Lance sat serenely on the balcony overlooking the ocean with his feet up on the railing, he was not. He was in sober contemplation. There was much beyond his capability in understanding and execution. He found it crippling. Acceptance of earthly limitation only frustrated him. If only he could push beyond the confines of flesh and blood, beyond the slow pace of understanding in incremental layers, he might have a better grasp of the universe and his role in it. The hotel only offered him one such source for answers outside of the phone directory.

He heard the door open to the hotel room. Danny had gone on another round of sightseeing. He wanted to go back and see Hemingway's home down on Whitehead Street. Danny recounted to Lance that after the war, in 1946, he visited Key West and, in a rare moment, had a brief run-in with Hemingway himself. The door seemed to take longer for one person to come through, but perhaps Danny had more souvenirs with this latest sortie out amongst the gift shops.

"Lance," Danny called.

"Out here, Danny."

Danny came through the patio door. He saw that Lance had in his lap the Gideon Society's contribution to hotel nightstands everywhere. The hotel's stationery and pen were on the small table next to him with several pages of notes inscribed.

"You look troubled, my boy."

"Well, I went looking for it." Lance closed the Bible.

"From skimming through a few pages?"

"From the first six chapters."

"Yes, Genesis is an interesting series of events."

"It's an interesting series of firsts."

"And what did you discover?"

"To start with, the Creative Days are in correct order. As it would have had to happen. There were no incestuous deities behaving badly or slicing open the belly of god A, from jealous god B, whose spilled intestines thus became the universe. None of that. Each creative period or day was in the proper scientific order for the Earth to become inhabitable."

"And you thought you would find different?"

"I didn't know what I would find, Danny. I never read it before."

"I guess we did skip around since you first came. What else did you learn?"

"I see Adam and Eve were to be fruitful and fill the earth. So there was to be plenty of sex—which leaves me encouraged. And then there was, of course—the first lie. This Satan—what does his name mean, by the way?"

"Resister. Adversary. Opposer."

"Makes sense. Well, Satan became the first lawyer."

"Oh, Lance," Danny said, chuckling. "I know of Satan being called Devil, meaning slanderer. Serpent, meaning deceiver. Manslayer, referencing when he began. And the Father of the Lie."

"See! Lawyer! Think about it. How did he dupe Eve? Lawyer's tactics. Didn't he say: 'Is it really so? Or isn't it true?' Strategic questions designed to sow doubt—exactly what lawyers do. Tactically, Satan didn't challenge the Creator's power. Oh, no. He knew better. Far more insidiously, he challenged his right to rule by inserting a new legal precedent: self-determination. Independence by rebellion. By the creation, no less."

"You deduced all of this?"

"It's all right here. The rebellion part was a no-brainer."

"Some would argue we are better off."

Lance erected himself. "Danny, perfection was theirs to lose! And did! How is that better? Our cells should continue to regenerate indefinitely. That's our design. They don't. Our brains should operate vastly superior to what they do. They don't."

"If you are going to say that we only use ten percent of our brains, that is a myth. We use the whole brain."

"I know that no part of the brain lies dormant. I mean in potential. We couldn't fill our brains to capacity if we lived to a trillion years. We average seventy-six."

"Fair enough. However, that is not our reality."

"What if it was? I get that Adam joined Eve in eating the rebel fruit because he didn't want to lose her, his companion, after living alone for so long as the only one of his kind. How he must have trembled, fully knowing the consequences of her actions. Instead of trusting the Creator, he panicked. And *panic-equals-death*. In the end, he lost her anyway."

"And if this is all allegory? Or just a metaphor?"

"I didn't find Eden mythical or a metaphor. I've flown a hundred times over two of the four rivers mentioned here that flowed through Eden. The Hid'de·kel or Tigris, and the Euphrates. It was just a place on Earth. Man had to have a start somewhere. I assume that the same grass, plants, and trees there are everywhere, or varieties thereof. Whether this is all true or not, it's no stretch that mankind operates in complete misalignment in everything he does. You know, like our first rental car. We seem to never get anything right. That has been our history. And that's not allegorical."

Danny sighed. "Oh, the way you think sometimes."

"Why, what did I say?"

"Misalignment. *Chat·ta'th,*" Danny said in Hebrew.

"That means to miss or miss something."

"You would know it better by the word *sin.*"

"Like in sinners, sinners repent? That sin?"

"Yes, that sin. It means to miss the mark."

"You mean like in perfection?"

"Technically. It does run deeper than that. But misalignment or out of alignment with God's will and purposes, besides our physical disparity."

"Yet, I read there is hope."

"Lance, do not do this. Such hope is not our reality."

"So, you've said. But what if it will be? When God pronounced a death sentence on the three of them, as he should have, he also said he would produce a seed. And so would Satan."

"I believe it says enmity between the woman and Satan."

"It's not Eve. She was done. Sentenced. I'm thinking the woman is symbolic of some new feature that God had now introduced. It's clear there will be conflict between these two rival factions. Satan's seed would bruise God's seed in the heel. I gather Jesus being put to death. But, because he's supposed to be resurrected, the wound or bruising isn't permanent."

"And you don't find that metaphoric?"

"No. Symbolic, or more accurately representational. It seems fair to say that if man never sinned, missed the mark, rebelled—whatever, there would have never been any need for Jesus to come to earth and die for our sins and all that. But what I found really interesting is that Satan gets a bruising in the head, which signifies a fatal wound. So this rebellion has a time limit. I like that. I bet everything I read further on hinges off this verse fifteen."

Danny shook his head. "Fascinating."

"And these seeds are obviously people. Us most likely."

"Tell me. Whose seed do you think you are?"

"It should be obvious, Danny."

"I'm happy you found Jesus and all, Lance, but we do have work to do," Ralston said, stepping through the patio doors.

"I haven't found Jesus, Jeffrey. At least not six chapters in."

"Have you considered it's all allegory?"

"Didn't you hear what I just said about lawyers? And you're a Harvard one."

"Whatever. Do you know what yesterday was? Were you paying attention?"

"Yes, Jeffrey, in spite of my grieving. The Chinese got Hong Kong back yesterday. This short-sightedness of man is what I've just been talking about."

"Glad to hear that you're topical."

"I am. In fact, something else I discovered you'll want to hear."

Lance opened up the Gideon publication. He read: "Chapter six. Verse one. 'And it came to pass when men began to multiply on the face of the earth and daughters were born to them. That the sons of God saw the daughters of men that they were fair; and they took them wives of all which they chose.'" Lance closed the Bible. "What I just read is the first documented alien invasion of our planet."

"Oh, Lance," Ralston said with a sigh, his hands now impatiently on his hips.

"Can you tell me with full certainty this did not happen, Jeffrey?"

"No. I cannot. However, you are blinding yourself to a few facts."

"Blinded, am I? Here's a fact. We humans can only see with the aid of white light—a very narrow part of the electromagnetic spectrum. There's more going on right in front of your kisser, Jeffrey, than you can shake a stick at."

"All right, Lance. How will I find this interesting?"

"If this is true, which would explain a lot, mind you, these super beings, at least to us, took the form of men and came to earth for some nooky."

"And why would they do that?"

"I don't know, Jeffrey. Maybe because they are beings of pure energy, pre-matter, and all that, and thus—have no genitalia. Thus the switch to life forms that do."

"Stay out of the realm of fantasy."

"Fantasy? Sure, we're all quick to believe in *Trelane*, but not these beings?"

"Who's Trelane? And where's the part that's supposed to interest me?"

"He just told you, Jeffrey," Danny said stiffly.

"Continue. But make your point," Ralston said with a wave of his hand.

"Jeffrey, Moses wrote the book of Genesis. Moses is also a name brand in Islam."

"True. But would you be interested to know that Moses didn't write the Torah, the first five books of the Bible?"

"Leave it to you to play devil's advocate."

"He is referring to the Documentary Theory," Danny offered.

"They say that about Shakespeare. There are always those."

"It will be something else you will no doubt research to death," Danny added.

"Later," Ralston said. "You were making a point about Moses."

"Moses, or *Musa,* is mentioned in the Quran more than any other individual. His life is narrated and recounted more than any other prophet. Moses or Musa said that these sons of God, these super life forms came to earth and took all the beautiful women they wanted—for sex."

"You lost me."

"Oh lord," Lance said, rolling his eyes. "Jeffrey, don't you get it? All of these nut-jobby-jihadist believe that seventy-two virgins are waiting to have sex with them in heaven if they only blow up something or someone. I just read to you where Musa says to the contrary."

"Maybe Musa got it wrong. It's been known to happen."

"Are you telling me that Moses, a prophet of God, lied?"

"All right, Lance." Ralston seated himself. Lance had his attention.

Chapter 72

Jerusalem

August 31, 1997

The phone rang. "I suppose you've seen the news?" Ralston's said.

"I have," Lance answered.

"What are you doing?"

"Reading my Bible. Danny left me a modern English version here when I got in yesterday. As a gift. No thees and thous."

"How soon will the Sparrowhawk be flying, given no further distractions?"

"I need more help."

"I know it's a sad day, Lance. The world lost its princess. But there's nothing you or I can do about it. Just our jobs. Get back up to Megiddo and continue your work."

"I don't have a landing gear. I can't fly it off its sawhorses."

"Leave it with me."

"I'll speak with you later, Jeffrey." Lance hung up the phone. He continued to be glued to the television, not unlike hundreds of millions of people from around the world.

***

The original barn served nicely as Lance's workshop/hangar. Strategically it was the building closest to the ranch house, about three hundred feet away. Where cattle once stood on dirt and straw, a concrete floor spanned the interior. The barn was thirty meters long and over half as wide. The old barn doors were replaced with steel-reinforced sliding doors.

The Sparrowhawk fuselage stood half-assembled, resting on three sawhorses. The four wings were completed and nestled in their cradles.

Lance loaded the magazine into the semi-automatic pistol. It was a new firearm he acquired over the summer. He took aim, viewing his target down the sights of the Glock-20, and put all fifteen, ten-millimeter rounds within an inch of one another on the target at the other end of the barn. When he finished, as was his discipline, he removed the magazine, cycled the chamber, and put the gun down on the small table in front of him. A widening slice of light cut in front of him. Danny stood at the parted doors. Lance removed his ear-muffs.

Danny approached Lance casually. "I just came to tell you that your landing gear and other parts have arrived."

"Really? Cool."

"And Jeffrey has also provided some help for you to finish."

"Who?"

An imposing silhouette filled the gap between the barn doors. And it humbly remained there. It would not enter unless asked. Lance languished for a moment and then walked ahead of Danny to the door. The man found himself fidgeting with his fingers.

"You're family, Lance, and I treated you like you wasn't. We've been brothers, whether in arms, or just because, but we always been brothers," Eric Pitts confessed.

"You know I would put my life between anything bad and your family a hundred times over, don't you? Which they were never in any danger."

"I do. And I hope you can forgive me. I threw you to the curb. I panicked."

"And what does panic equal?"

"Death."

Lance took pause. He looked at Danny. "Danny, would you show our guest to his room? He must be tired from his travels."

"As you wish, Lance. Eric, would you please go back up to the house. I'll be there in a moment."

"Sure, Danny." As Eric stood back from the barn door, Alfonso Pig rushed in, now that it was quiet. "Hey, you have a pig. In Israel."

"We do." Lance bent down to pet Alfonso. "A very loyal animal."

Eric had nothing else to say and left for the house.

"Lance, you need to make your peace."

"I had peace a moment ago."

"He is your friend. You two are brothers."

"Brothers? Let me tell you something, Danny. Roger was my one true brother. And he's dead. But he always told me to watch out for anyone calling you brother."

"I'm sorry you feel that way. Does that include me?"

"Would you ever betray me?"

"You know the answer to that. I will attend to my guest."

Danny took a painful look back at the barn. Lance was one of the most warm-hearted people he had ever known and yet could be one of the most cold-blooded, almost reptilian. Several rapid-fire shots rang out. Alfonso Pig ran out of the barn, squealing in protest. The shots ended. The barn went silent. Lance marched out of the barn and up the short path to the house.

Lance caught sight of Eric and Danny at the front door. Alfonso, seeing his master, scurried back down. Eric looked up. Lance looked harder. He would take whatever verbal bashing Lance had to give.

"Special!" Lance yelled out, holding his arms open. Eric hurried his large, tired frame off the porch and down to meet Lance, wrapping his arms around him. The two men had tears.

Danny smiled. He remembered Lance sharing with him the Genesis account of Jacob and Esau. Of two brothers overcoming their controversy and reuniting.

***

Thrust exceeded drag. Lift exceeded weight. With rotation at 90 knots indicated airspeed, the homebuilt jet engine powered the Sparrowhawk smoothly into the sky. As the landing gear had been the final issue with the aircraft, Lance saw no reason to leave it dangling even if this was its maiden flight. Lance had the blood of an aviation pioneer. Upon receiving its electrical command, the main gear pulled inward and then swung forward, up into the belly of the fuselage with the doors covering over them. At 130 knots, which came quickly, Lance retracted the flaps and was at 230 knots by the end of the runway.

"Well, I'll be." Ralston tilted his head upward to follow the small jet. Now, he felt safe to contemplate the aircraft's permutations.

"Don't tell me that we didn't do ourselves proud, Jeffrey," Eric Pitts said boisterously.

At one-thousand feet, Lance pulled the thrust lever back to where the aircraft moved through the air at 230 knots indicated. It was a good speed to test the sparrowhawk. He made a gentle turn to the left. It was smooth. Everything felt stable.

As he paralleled the Megiddo Airport runway, he could see Ralston, Special, and Danny down below where he left them next to the truck and flatbed trailer.

Ralston studied the Sparrowhawk as it flew by across the field. He still couldn't get over the seemingly radical design of two sets of wings. Each wing had small downturned winglets. The nose section was sharp but somewhat wedged-shaped. He wished Lance would get the *Lotus Esprit* sports car out of his mind when it came to designing. It was painted in a series of striking shades of blue that ranged from lighter blue tones to medium dark blue on the belly, with a stripe down the middle in vintage Pan Am blue. Ralston had envisioned some sort of camouflage, but Lance disliked drab colors. The Sparrowhawk would hide well enough amongst the sky and clouds.

The Sparrowhawk had a blended body design, where the wings at the root gradually widened and flowed into the contours of the fuselage. This ran the length of the fuselage to form sharp leading edge strakes toward the nose and nearly squared ends by the engine exhaust nozzle that served as split-flap speed brakes. It was clean and sharp in appearance. Lance made sure that was well pointed out to Ralston. It had a tapered bottom air intake. In front of the air intake, there was an angular divot on the belly of the aircraft.

"What is that indentation on the belly, just in front of the air intake?" Ralston asked.

"That's Lance's thing," Eric said with a chuckle.

"What do you mean?"

"Jeffrey, this bird is meant to break mach one."

"You're joking."

"No, sir. She's meant to kick it up a notch!"

"Oh my," Ralston said. He had to rethink his earlier permutations.

Lance put the Sparrowhawk through tougher maneuvers, always keeping in mind to respond to any unexpected hiccups. So far, none had presented itself. He hit the power, increasing speed to 350 knots indicated, to get a sense of its pickup and stability. Everything continued as expected, so he kicked it up a notch.

The Sparrowhawk shot by the runway at a quick clip and then raced toward the sun. Lance keyed the mic. "Special. Four hundred and forty-five knots on this last pass."

Eric squeezed the radio mic with the joy of a proud father. "Hey, Lance! You looked great on that last pass. Awesome!" He tempered his enthusiasm and let the technical side of his being take over. "You've been at it for about an hour. Why not bring her in, and let's have a look-see?"

"Roger. Returning to base."

This was a truly auspicious moment in Ralston's career. He had a new tool. Nothing in a long time so impressed him.

Lance turned around with a sharp ninety-degree bank and felt the g-forces build up quickly to seven-plus before he relaxed the controls and rolled back to straight and level flight. The aircraft handled all high-g maneuvers as expected. There was nothing overreaching about the machine. Lance found himself one with it by the time he was heading for landing.

Lance moved the flap lever to the first notch: T/O. The flap panel of the FLAP-TRACT-SYSTEM slid back and dropped to 12 degrees, extending itself by nine-inches of travel from the trailing edge of each wing. Lance then moved the flap lever to the second notch flap setting: LANDING. The flap panel canted down to 25 degrees. The full-span elevators on the front pair of wings and the full-span ailerons on the rear set of wings moved within the air stream to keep attitude control. The hybrid flap system was similar to a "flaperon" system used on the F-16 but was truly unique to the Sparrowhawk.

Ninety knots indicated seemed to be the magic number. It proved to be a safe rotation speed and a landing speed with full flaps and gear down. The aircraft demonstrated that it would stall at sixty-six knots indicated with full flaps.

The landing gear dropped and locked. Eric followed with binoculars. He was rooting for Lance from takeoff to the aircraft's first landing. He had a solid chunk of his life tied up in its success.

The Sparrowhawk came over the threshold. The landing was a bit bumpy, but Lance knew that he would get better at it by the next test flight.

"Right on!" came Eric Pitts' gritty, muffled exclamation.

Lance applied the speed brakes and the wheel brakes that had proved to work well when he did high-speed taxi tests the day before. And then it dawned on him. There was one test left to do. Now that he knew that the plane was safe and stable, he had to do it. He came to a stop. He still had two-thirds of the runway in front of him.

Eric was puzzled, now concerned. He radioed. "Lance, everything okay?"

"Yes. But there's one thing more. I need you to clock me."

"What?"

"Clock me."

"Oh, okay. I get you." Eric pulled off his wristwatch and set the stopwatch feature on it.

"Let me know when you are ready," Lance radioed back.

"I'm good. Let her rip!"

Lance focused on the instruments, the runway, and himself. He brought the thrust lever all the way forward. The engine spooled up to its max of 3,244 pounds of static thrust. He released his feet against the brake pedals. The Sparrowhawk lunged forward in rapid acceleration.

Eric Pitts watched closely as the nose gear and then the mains came off of the runway. He hit the button on his watch.

The Sparrowhawk arched upward into a steep climb. It continued to accelerate.

"Incredible," Ralston mumbled.

"Thirty seconds, Lance. Keep her going," Eric said, watching his watch and watching the ever-ascending Sparrowhawk chase rarefied air.

Eric keyed the mic. "Lance, five seconds, four seconds, three seconds, two seconds, one. Mark."

"Special, keep it going," Lance exclaimed. The radio went quiet. "And—now! What's the time?"

"Lance, seventy-seven seconds. How many feet?"

"Twenty-three thousand," Lance radioed.

"Unbelievable," Ralston said, shaking his head. "Tell him to land."

"Lance, good buddy. Bring her on home. I can't even see you."

"Just passing twenty-five thousand feet now."

Lance rolled the aircraft up into a loop and flew upside down, back the way he came. He could see the small sliver of asphalt that he would be landing on in a moment. He also noticed he would be over Ramat David Airbase if he didn't drop down immediately. Danny had cleared the use of this airspace with his people. Still, he didn't want to have a couple of Israeli F-16s scrambled just to pop up and say "Hi" either.

Lance felt uncomfortable being upside down for so long as the blood pooled to his head. He pulled back on the control stick until the aircraft was dropping straight down. Speed built quickly—very quickly. The negative g's were growing. He hadn't operated in the realm of extreme aerobatics for a long time and had to get used to it again.

Lance pulled the thrust lever back to idle. Before long, he was in a six hundred-mile-per-hour dive and accelerating. He engaged the speed brakes. The aircraft slowed modestly. At seven thousand feet, he pulled back on the control stick. The g-forces increased as the nose of the jet came up. Five g's, six g's, seven g's, eight g's of gravitational force built up. And then something overcame him. He added full power. It was a moment when everything he was, everything he had worked to become, every creative and daring aspect of his life culminated into a singularity—all for this moment in time.

The pragmatic, careful, and calculating nature of Jeffrey Ralston returned to him as the briefly overly enthralled spectator diminished. "Wait a minute. Lance is an excellent pilot, but he has no supersonic flight experience."

The three men watched as a blue whisper darted across their path. There was no sound. And then it was gone. A rapid pounding—hitting twice shook the very air that they breathed. Ralston, like Danny and Eric, hunkered down at the heavy crackle. Ralston realized his concern was now answered in dramatic fashion. Lance just went supersonic.

Lance maneuvered the thirty-foot aircraft back down to the behavior of slow flight. He was on a half-mile final to Runway 9. He put in the first notch of flaps. He continued to slow to approach speed with the second notch of flaps. He held it at 90 knots indicated. The landing gear came down and locked.

The aircraft held sure over the numbers. Thrust was retarded to idle. The Sparrowhawk settled with a moderate nose high flare as the main landing gear made gentle contact with the runway. The speed brakes flipped open, wheel brakes were applied, and the newly christened kit plane turned off the active and taxied back to where it began the day's adventure.

He rolled up parallel with Eric, Ralston, and Danny and shut down. A few seconds later, he raised the canopy and released his safety harness.

Eric shot from the pack and hurried up to Lance. "Son—that was some fine job of flying. Hey, I gotta jump in the back and go for a spin."

Ralston and Danny moved quickly toward Lance. Ralston stood as if he was giving an ovation. The physical presence of achievement brought back the giddy spectator.

***

Lance startled to consciousness. It was just after six in the morning, and there was no point trying to go back to sleep. His mind was already wound up and racing.

Lance turned on the electric kettle in the small kitchenette inside the barn. Minutes later, he walked around the Sparrowhawk like a proud parent, sipping his tea.

He took one of the bench stools and parked it behind the exhaust nozzle of the aircraft, and stared inside it. Answers were staring back at him that he just couldn't decipher—yet. Creativity was like nature. It took its time.

"Bashiq," Ralston said softly.

"Sorry?"

"Bashiq. Loosely translated Sparrowhawk." Ralston bent over to look inside of the thrust-emitting end of the kit plane. "Waiting for an epiphany?"

"A Rolls-Royce engineer once told me it was possible I had come up with new turbine technology."

"But?"

"He doubted it."

"Why?"

"If anyone were to come up with new engine technology, it would be them."

"Never mind him," Ralston said, annoyed. "You proved them wrong."

"No. This isn't new technology. Clever maybe, but not new." Lance broke his gaze and looked up at Ralston. He was clean-shaven and dressed. "Are you leaving?"

"Duty calls. But I wanted to spend a little time with you before I do."

"But you didn't get your ride yet."

"After the first hundred hours. I trust that you built a safe machine, but I need to head back to Langley."

"Don't worry. I'm being careful. My pride is in check."

"Which comes before the crash. I guess you've read that in Proverbs."

"If that's where it is. I'm still in Deuteronomy."

"Since you're all keen on donning the mantles of a scholar, maybe you should study the Quran."

"The Bible, at least the Torah, precedes the Quran by over two millennia. Regardless of what the Jawist, Elohists, and the Priest Codex people would have you believe."

"I gather that you read up on the Documentary Theory."

"Did you know that a team of researchers at my old alma mater did a linguistic analysis of Genesis?" Ralston felt a strong urge to correct Lance as he had not graduated from Technion but sought the better of it. "They fed in some twenty thousand words, and the computer spit out an eighty-two percent probability of the stylistic fingerprint of a sole writer. Let's call him Moses."

"Anyway."

"The basis of the theory is the different titles for God, such as *`Elo·him'*, *`Adonai* and *`El Shad·dai*. See, this is why you have to watch scholars. People go by different titles all the time. If I said the king of rock and roll, you would know who I meant. Just like Elvis the Pelvis. They are different titles for different attributes to the same person."

"They could come from separate authors."

"True, but more likely uttered by the same author to describe a different attribute of the same object—that being the point. If I said, he's witty, creative, playful, focused, or aggressive; they are just different observable attributes of the same person."

"Instead of Yahweh, the name of God. I get it."

"It's not Yahweh. For one thing, there's no W sound in Hebrew, just like in German. So it would have to be *Yah-vey* or *Yah-vah*. In fact, within the divine name is *Hav-vah. To be* or *to become*. I wouldn't have appreciated this until I learned to speak German and be reminded that all language is based on existence or *to be*. So the divine name literally means: *He Cause to Become*, which would be very indicative of the Creator. The other thing is that Hebrew is triliteral in structure."

"Because Semitic languages are of a three consonant root."

"Exactly. The pronunciation would be closer to *Ye-ho-veh* or *Ye-ho-vah*."

"You seem to have it all worked out."

"No. It's been with struggles. I throw a few Jehovahs around, and Danny acts like I'm pelting him with pebbles. Yet, the divine name is contained in everyday names like Elijah, Jonathan, Joshua, and Benjamin."

"It has to do with a superstition."

"It has to do with a lie."

"Lance, while everyone hates to be lied to, they're more comfortable living the lie."

"So I've seen. However, this is not reflected in the Law Code. Did you know there were six hundred other laws besides the Ten Commandments?

"Six hundred and thirteen in total, including the Big Ten. Our laws are based on Judeo-Christian teachings."

"Based? No. Our laws are Roman. They pale in comparison. If ever there was a perfect law for imperfect people, this was it. For fifteen centuries, there were no amendments, no interpretations, and most importantly—lawyer proof. No spin. They were too emphatic."

"You would prefer to carry on with animal sacrifices before the altar and all that?"

"Hey, barbeque! It served its purpose. But I was thinking more toward the laws that governed behavior. Did you know that the Law commanded you to love your fellow as yourself?"

"No, I did not. Nice thought, though."

"It wasn't a thought, Jeffrey. It was the law."

"You cannot make people love one another, Lance. As a lawyer, as an intelligence officer, I assure you, you cannot force love of neighbor."

"You're telling me you can't see the problem-solving application here?"

"As I said, nice thought. Devotion fades over time. And what one generation agrees to, the next usually does not."

"Yes. People have a habit of trading gold for lead. Case in point, the Jubilee. Are you familiar with it?"

"A little. I know every fifty years the Israelites had a Jubilee."

"And every seventh. Say that a man had to sell himself into slavery to pay off a debt. Come the seventh year—he was free. His debt cleared—simple logic. When people go into debt, the nation goes into debt. The Jubilee kept the nation from becoming a two-class system. The very rich and the very poor. It kept the national economy sound. It kept greed under control. Property values didn't spike as the seventh or fiftieth year came around. They lowered. It strengthened the individual, thus the nation. There's a great lesson here."

"We have debt forgiveness, Lance."

"Not like this. A man got his land back come the seventh or fiftieth year. Those that owned it in the interim made a profit. It was a win-win."

"We have what fits the modern world. We have the S.E.C."

"The S.E.C. might send a man to prison, yet it can never make the victim whole. The Jubilee undid the damage, reset everything."

“Lance, ancient man like modern man has always had greed and poverty, starvation, bloodshed, and war. And the easiest way around any law is simply to ignore it.”

“You’re right, Jeffrey. And it’s all quite clear to me now. Maybe we don’t mean to be; it’s just the seed we are.”

Chapter 73

Dessau, Germany

April 9, 1998

The maternal nurturing of necessity that gave birth to invention could pull Lance out of a funk like nothing else. Manfred Steiger sat very thrilled in the back seat of the Sparrowhawk. Manny had flown up from Munich for a ride. Lance had brought the nimble, experimental category aircraft up to forty-five thousand feet, where it purred along at Mach .95 on seventy gallons of JET-A fuel per hour. At 627 miles per hour, the Sparrowhawk was safe for three hours of cruise flight. The M & M express was back in action, even if just for a joy ride. Lance missed working with Manny. He had little to do with the operations of Onyx Aviation Services of late.

"So, when are we going to go supersonic?" Manny asked with some impatience.

"We can't do it unless I go into a dive and build up speed. Not enough oomph—engine wise, I'm afraid. Yet!"

Lance had logged nearly two hours total supersonic time in the Sparrowhawk's one hundred and eighty-six hours of total flying existence. He hit speeds over eight hundred miles per hour. The aircraft was capable of more. Lance had become one with his creation, and he now knew how to improve upon it. He had many ideas still to bring into the realm of pliable reality.

Lance considered his position out over the Baltic Sea. "Ah, what the heck."

"What is, what the heck?" Manny said, forcing himself to sit up as straight as possible within the reclined seat and five-point safety harness.

Lance called air traffic control for a rapid descent. Manny felt light in the seat instantly as he watched his thrust lever jump forward and their altitude plummet simultaneously. Quickly, very quickly, Manny watched on his electronic flight instrumentation panel the airspeed indicator jump past Mach 1. The German coast came up surprisingly fast. The vertical speed indicator stabled its display readout at a twenty-two thousand foot per minute drop.

"You're going supersonic, Manny!"

It was exciting for Manfred Steiger to experience faster than sound travel. Everything rushed up at him quicker than he could immediately process. He saw Mach 1.3 readout on the airspeed indicator with a ground speed passing 750 knots per hour and increasing. The jet continued to drop out of the sky until Lance leveled off at five thousand feet and pulled the thrust lever back to idle. It was a three-minute thrill ride into the supersonic.

"Any longer, and we might overshoot Germany," Lance said, smiling.

"Are you a buzz bomber?" came the excited voice of German Air Traffic Control.

Lance keyed his mic. "Negative. I'm an experimental aircraft out having fun."

"Oh, you rich boys with your toys," the controller radioed with a small laugh. It wasn't exactly true, Lance thought, but it served his cover I.D.

"You're now a Super Duper, Manny."

"Is that what you are calling us now?"

"Hey, to me, you'll always be Plain."

"Well, Peanut, how fast did we go? I am asking whilst I wait for my tummy to catch up."

Lance chuckled. "Mach one point four. Eight hundred four knots or around nine hundred twenty-five miles per hour. We hit a new speed record."

"If you can add an afterburner, then you will have something."

"That's the plan."

Lance was cleared to traverse into German airspace.

The Sparrowhawk continued to drop in speed and altitude. "Okay, Manny, your plane." Lance took his hands off the controls.

Manny held the controls steady at one hundred thirty knots as Lance set the flap lever to the first notch. Manny felt the mild buffet of the wings, increasing their ability to generate more lift. The aircraft slowed. Manny had no forward view to speak of from the back, but his side view was quite good. He turned the jet to fly downwind for Runway 9.

"You're doing very well, Manny." Lance moved the flap lever to the LANDING position. "Hold it at ninety knots. You'll need more control input with full flaps, but you'll see it works fine."

Manny rolled left onto their base turn and then onto final. Lance noticed a Cessna Caravan parked next to Manny's Cessna 172 at the hangar.

Lance could see that they were just a little to the right of the center of the runway. "Just a tap on the left rudder." The Sparrowhawk centered perfectly. "Good."

Eric Pitts stepped out of the Caravan's door. He then moved out from under the large wing quickly when he heard the sound of an approaching jet aircraft. He had a good view of the Sparrowhawk. The aircraft never ceased to thrill him.

A wave of burnt copper hair flowed out past the same door. A woman stepped out and then stood to the side of Eric.

Over the runway and past the numbers, Manny moved the thrust lever back to idle. The nose came up just a bit higher for the flare. Manny held it. The mains touched down, and then the nose gear contacted the asphalt. Speed breaks flipped up. Manny pushed on the toe brakes and. He felt a tug of resistance to forward motion. They slowed and came to the end of the runway. The runway also served as the only taxiway.

"Okay. My plane," Lance said.

The Sparrowhawk backtracked down mid-length to the only off-ramp and past a few other privately owned hangars. A few people stood along the taxiway and waved. They always smiled that wistful look, understandably. The Sparrowhawk came to the last hangar on the right where it shut down. Lance unlatched his canopy and gave it a push upward. Lance, free of his restraints, lifted himself up, placed his foot on the fold-out step and then stood on the tarmac.

Manny, still seated, was enjoying the moment a little longer. His hand exited the confines of the aircraft and shook Lance's hand. "It's like heroin, isn't it?"

Lance looked into the sterling blue eyes. "I believe so."

Eric and the woman approached. "Hey, Lance," Eric called out.

"I'm glad to see you made it up here, okay," Lance said as he gave a hug to the big man.

The woman smiled. Her face was mostly covered by a headscarf, not with unsimilar glamour of Grace Kelly. Large sunglasses covered what was left. The rest was hidden under heavy makeup, though the woman was quite attractive.

"Well, I've had to fly in worse and being shot at." Eric turned to the woman. "Lance, this is my niece, Beverly de Havilland."

"Oh," Lance said, poorly disguising his surprise. "Well, Beverly, welcome."

"I know I wasn't expected, but thank you," she said. Her voice was sweet but with that certain lilt of a tomboy. She was statuesque, nearly as tall as Lance. She hesitated but then removed her sunglasses. The late afternoon sunlight turned her eyes from captivating pure crystal gray to mesmerizing light amethyst.

"She's my sister Carla's oldest," Eric added.

"It's nice to meet you." Lance extended his hand. Her hand was warm, rather firm when she gripped his. Lance took his hand back and waved it toward Manny. "This is my friend Manfred Steiger. Manny."

"Yes, I know. We've met."

"Oh. Okay. Right," Lance said awkwardly. Then he straightened himself very prim and proper. "Well, please come and shake the dust of travel off your feet."

"I'll bring you up to speed, Lance, over a beer. But we have our goodies to unload before it gets dark."

"That's fine, Eric. Let me put the Sparrowhawk away, and then we can park the Caravan inside too."

Beverly looked over the experimental aircraft with a coy look of intrigue. This man Lance Rio also intrigued her.

An hour later, Lance waved as Manny rocked his wings of the skyward bound Cessna. It had been a good day. The night might be another issue. Lance followed his friend's departure for a moment longer and then headed back to the hangar.

Lance entered through the swing-out man door located off to the side of the main hanger doors and locked it. He went upstairs.

"Okay," Lance said, seating himself at the peninsula counter that was the only indication of separation between the kitchen and the small living room. "Was ist los?"

"What? Oh, yeah. What's up?" Eric said, a bit off-kilter. "Well, Beverly, since she was a kid, always looked up to me. She followed me into the Navy when she turned eighteen."

"Okay," Lance said neutrally.

"I was in for ten years. I'm an A and P and worked on F-fourteens and eighteens and for a while on Navy Hueys. We come from a flying family, I guess you know. I soloed at sixteen and got my private the day I turned seventeen. I have almost nine hundred hours with some multi-engine time," Beverly stated.

"So, how long have you been with the Agency?"

"How did you know that?"

"On occasion, I'm very intuitive," Lance replied.

"He is very intuitive," Eric said, nodding somewhat in Lance's direction.

"Then yes, I followed Uncle Eric into the CIA. I was looking for a change. Something to get me off a ship and into people, places, and things."

Lance grinned wryly. "So, you were looking for a new noun."

"You're a sharp one, aren't you?" Her eyes remained lit up to where Lance had to arch back a bit to break his gaze.

"So, what brings you here?"

"I've spent the last two years in the Middle East. I worked in the U.A.E. for a jet charter company."

"Is the business run by the agency?"

"No. But I was a plant. I ran the maintenance operations for both sites, though I was domiciled in Qatar. I'm fluent in Arabic."

"What's the name of the business?"

"Tiger Gulf Jet Services Limited. It's a U.K. company."

"It's an M.I.-Six front."

"How do you know that?"

"I helped set it up a few years ago. I have a good friend in British Intelligence. Anyway, continue."

"As you would know then, I met a lot of Middle East aristocracy. I caught the eye of a certain Saudi prince. You know they grow them like weeds over there."

"Yes, like V.P.'s in a company—everybody and their dog."

"He wanted me to come work for him."

"Just work?"

Beverly scowled. "What do you think? I'm a white girl with—"

"Hey! You watch your mouth, little girly!" Eric said tersely. "Lance was only asking out of concern."

She softened, remembering she was a guest and tempered her tone. "Sorry, uncle." She worked her crystal gray eyes back up to meet Lance's. "The Agency said yes, I said no. I told the prince that I'm a California country girl who wouldn't do well in a harem."

"Who was the Saudi?"

"Prince Khaled Mohammed bin-Aziz."

"Al-Saud?"

"Yes. That's him. You know him?"

"Of him."

"Well—"

"And—what the prince wants the prince gets?"

"Yes," was all she could muster.

"He abducted her, Lance. My little girly." Eric said as if his next move would be to look for a gun. "That boy stepped on the wrong toes. He just don't know it yet."

"How long ago was this?"

"I was shanghaied four months ago. They got me out a week ago. Your friend Manfred was one of the pilots that flew me out once the extraction team came in and got me."

"I know that Jeffrey will be speaking to you about it, Lance. Bev was able to gather some interesting intel on this guy. She did her job."

"Okay. What are your orders at the moment?"

Beverly looked down. There was some shame. Then she removed her scarf. There was no mistaking the luminescence of deep purple visible under the heavy makeup. Lance stood and came before Beverly. He moved his hand up to her face. He lightly touched her cheek. She trembled. Her hands reached up to grab his, her soft gray eyes pleading. Lance brought up his other hand to take hold of hers.

"You are safe here, Beverly. No one will hurt you."

***

From Dessau to Israel was approximately eighteen-hundred statute miles. Lance should have been happier now that with Eric's help and design input, the exhaust nozzle was no longer a solid ring or tube but was now broken up into six semi-circular ports, with each wrapped around by bypass air. It made for a much quieter aircraft. A quieter aircraft meant better odds of survival when it would soon come to sneaking into and out of places—*persona non grata.*

Lance was glad, at inception, that he fully adopted a glass cockpit. LCD screens replaced all dials and gauges. The "steam gauges" were gone before the Sparrowhawk ever left the drawing board. Now GPS moving maps and other digital reference amenities presented themselves to Lance with second by second updating. Lance took a refreshing look down at the azure waters of the Mediterranean Sea below. Seeing the beauty of the earth without having to see foolish human interaction was reaffirming to his spirit.

"Well, what Eric did, which was a surprise, was that he had the new exhaust nozzle TBC'd," Lance said.

"Naturally, you'll explain," Ralston voiced through the left ear cup of Lance's headset.

"Thermo Barrier Coating. It's a ceramic coating that is applied by plasma vapor deposition. It's similar to how they vaporize aluminum, and the vapor then sticks to plastic moving off of a roll, which is used to make candy bar wrappers, bags for potato chips, and so on.

"Okay, I get it."

"If we applied it to the other turbine section parts, we could run the engine hotter by about another two hundred degrees or so."

"Is that Celsius or Fahrenheit?"

"Jeffrey, do I ever fail to transpose idioms?"

"Don't forget I operated for years in the lands of metric before you."

"Duly noted. And since I have you on the horn, I think I have figured out the next generation afterburner."

"Really! And—"

"It'll work. Eric agrees. In fact, we're talking supercruise possibilities."

"And how will or does it work?" Lance could hear in the silence the deputy director's wheels turning.

"Similarly to a traditional system, but it should maybe be ten or twelve times more efficient comparatively. I'll read you in on it later."

"All right, Lance. Do what you do. You've proven yourself."

"Eric will need to get back to California soon. And then there is Beverly."

"Oh, I understand that you both worked well together. And that she jumped right in and assisted you."

"Yup, she jumped right in, all right."

"Keep her as long as you need her."

Lance felt fingertips touch his shoulder. It was a woman's touch. "Can I give you a ring in about an hour or so? When I'm on the ground."

"That will be fine. Speak then."

Lance clicked off communication with Ralston, which joined the left ear cup back in sync with the right.

"Are you done with your secret communiqué with Deputy Director Ralston?" Beverly asked.

"Yes."

"So, will I still be serving under you?"

"Well, I wouldn't put it that way."

"However you want to put it, lover."

***

The Sparrowhawk circled over Megiddo Airport, but to Beverly's surprise, they flew around a large mound and then northward. Lance set up the landing procedure to land. She was sure they were going to land on the road. The road connected to a ranch house with a red barn near it.

She heard the distinctive sound that the flaps system made when they're extending. First to the takeoff setting and then a moment later as the kit plane slowed further to the landing setting. The tumbled roar of rushing air coming up inside from underneath and the sound of hydraulics told her that the landing gear was lowering.

The Sparrowhawk touched down and slowed to a fast taxi. Lance made the turn in the road and headed for the barn. She saw her Uncle push the barn doors apart. Lance taxied inside, bringing the aircraft to a halt with a mild jerk. After a cooldown, the engine began its slow whine to stasis.

Lance raised his canopy. Beverly took the cue and raised hers.

Eric came around to her. "Well, Bev, what'da ya' think? Pretty cool, huh?"

"Awesome!" was her reply.

Eric hadn't seen a smile like that on her in a long time.

"I'll put things away while you two go up. I'll be up shortly," Lance said.

Lance connected a tow bar to the nose gear and carefully wheeled the aircraft around to face the outside. Beverly was a distraction but a helpful one. She knew her way around sophisticated aircraft. Possibly, she knew her way around men better. To put it in aviation terms: Lance was an afterburner—Beverly, a thrust reverser. He wasn't going anywhere.

Lance didn't notice that twenty minutes had gone by until his many thoughts were scattered by a squealing Alfonso Pig rushing into the barn. Alfonso brushed up against his master. Lance knelt down to hug his pet. "How are you, boy?"

"Now I've seen everything," Beverly said.

Alfonso rushed back to her. "He likes you," Lance noted.

"I've raised a pig or two," she said. "Are you coming in?"

"Soon. Are you settled?"

"Yes. So, where are you going to stay?"

"In here."

"You can't stay with me?" she said, moving closer to Lance.

"That would be inappropriate, Beverly," Lance said flatly.

"O, come on, lover."

"Would you not call me that, please?"

"But we are. You're not going to say it was a mistake? Maybe in the shower."

"You picked the lock to the bathroom. You invaded my space. And the incident got shampoo in my eyes—when you struck!"

Her hands found their way on his chest and wrapped around him. Her lips, soft and gentle, moved in and cornered any thought of escape. "I still hear no complaining."

"Beverly. Bev. Bev," he managed to say as her lips covered his. He took her in his arms and kissed her passionately.

"Where can we go?" she whispered.

"Nowhere. The pig will squeal."

His lips pushed back into hers. Her kiss, her touch, brought warmth into him as it did two weeks earlier in Germany. But logic forced its darkened hand between reason and passion. He stood back but did not let go of her. "A mistake? Let's call it a lapse in judgment, on my part."

"Really?"

"You ambushed a very lonely man. And got soap in his eyes."

"It's just sex."

"No. Sex is communication. It's emotional nourishment. Just sex, as you put it, has crippled nations."

"Wow. I guess you put me straight." She brushed her lips up against his as she turned and strolled out. Alfonso strolled out with her.

"Traitor," Lance muffled. His life was now complicated.

Lance removed his bag from behind the rear seat of the Sparrowhawk, and after slinging it over his shoulder, he closed the canopy. Lunch sounded right. It wasn't too many steps before Eric met him at the barn doors. He had that knowing, goofy grin on his face.

"You, dog, you!" The bag rolled off Lance's shoulder. He had no more strength. "I knew you would be good for each other!"

"So, this is a conspiracy?"

"Look, you can't be doing this business for that much longer. We can set up a sweet business back home. The kit plane world beckons. And you'll have a good woman, and I know she will have a good man. See perfect! I know you, little buddy. She's already fallen for you."

As Lance and Eric walked back up to the house, he didn't quite know how to process this immediate relationship. Knowing Beverly less than two weeks and having been intimate with her was usually a recipe for disaster. He would eat lunch and then take Alfonso for a walk and try to clear his head.

Chapter 74

Gibraltar

36°08′00″N, 05°21′00″W

August 10, 1998

"That's so weird," Beverly said as she watched automobiles, bicycles, and pedestrians move across Winston Churchill Drive, which also crossed the runway of Gibraltar International Airport. "They say this is one of the most dangerous airports in the world."

"Not at all. It's all very charming," Lance said. He watched her watching the people below. She kept her gaze for only a moment longer as the Citation flew parallel to the runway below on their downwind course. "Not to worry, they'll be closing off the road shortly."

Beverly put in another notch of flaps. Lance placed his hands on top of his knees. This was her landing. Her flying with Lance turned out to be the right medicine to get her back out in the field. They had been inseparable since. They were a healing to each other.

"Gear down," Lance called. He moved the landing gear lever down. A moment later, he called: "Gear down and locked."

She turned the aircraft smoothly to make a right base turn and then again to the right for a turn onto final. She was lined up with Runway 27 and now on short final. The warm blue tones of the ocean below gave way to a short stretch of sand and then asphalt. The Citation held itself aloft until power was cut and then settled gently onto Gibraltar soil. Beverly snapped in the thrust reversers and applied the brakes. The aircraft slowed to taxi clear of the active. The Citation was waved to a stop on the tarmac.

Lance watched as Beverly went through the shutdown procedure. The engines spooled down, and quiet ensued. "Well done," Lance said to his giddy co-pilot.

Beverly noticed that the main road was opened back up again with cars, vans, and pedestrians crossing the runway so nonchalantly.

Lance got up from his seat and went back into the cabin. He looked at his two passengers. "Well, Mr. and Mrs. Remberg, we're here." Lance opened up the door, dropped the step, and then stood outside.

A car drove up. Simon and Erika were an elderly German couple from England, set to enjoy their holiday. They were also the poster couple for the success of Lance's cover I.D. as a corporate pilot. Simon joined the Nazi party at age nineteen and later was a Stasi officer. Lance caught his East German accent layered under a Munich accent. When Lance made a light comment of

Simon sounding much like an Ostler, it sent an almost imperceptible shudder through the man. Naturally, Lance played it off as nothing. Simon denied it, but it was enough for Ralston to initiate an inquiry, and it paid off handsomely. For Simon and Erika to keep their current life, they had to tell the CIA everything less the Israelis be notified. They cooperated. Of course, they never knew of Lance's involvement.

Lance and Beverly trolled their suitcases behind them as they strolled to the terminal. He took her hand and kissed it. He was proud of her. But then, he was caught up in a whirlwind that was Beverly de Havilland. And he wanted to be no other place on earth.

Evening came. Beverly looked stunning. She wore a medium-light blue summer dress and white sandals. He found her sense of shoes pragmatic as well as elegant. The heels were not too high, with a wide base for stability.

She took her seat, escorted in place by the maître d' as another waiter seated Lance at their table. The maître d' spoke, but all Lance could hear was the silent sparkle of her pure gray eyes as shimmers of amethyst danced in them from the candle on the table. "A moment, gentlemen, if you please," Lance requested.

"Certainly, Señor Rio. And it is nice to see you again," the maître d' said. With a bow, he left the two of them.

"Should I be impressed?" she asked.

"That I'm a well-traveled man? No. It comes with the territory." He leaned in. "That I'm the happiest I've been in an extraordinary length of time? Yes."

"That sounds more of a responsibility than a compliment."

"If you take it that way. You didn't have to care about me."

"You're not a hard man to care about."

"We're past caring, Beverly."

"Now, don't you go falling in love with me." Lance noticed that the sparkle in her eyes dimmed. They were eyes that reflected uneasiness. They shifted a bit too much as one would if escape was now in mind. Lance turned away, looking at the flickering candle instead.

"Love is quite honestly the last thing on my mind." Lance took his wine glass. "I am enjoying the companionship, though." It was the first time in his life he now recognized himself as a liar.

Dinner was as enjoyable as the ambiance of the light sea breeze and crashing waves in the background suggested. They even managed light banter and laughter. Lance wasn't much of a dancer, but he took her for a spin on the dance floor to a slow-paced but intensely romantic Spanish song. The way she held him as they embraced and twirled on their feet gave him new hope that she would not shield off deeper feelings.

At their table, she watched the shimmers of candlelight reflect off the two black mirrors that held their gaze on her. It had always captivated her from the first time she saw him genuinely smile. "I get that I should be bracing for another romp in the sack."

"You mean more lovemaking?"

"Sex, lovemaking, I'm there with you. However, you want to spell it. I just don't want to complicate things. For now, lover, I'm yours."

"And if I don't want this to end?"

"Right now, it's wonderful. But, I don't know where this is going to lead." Beverly took a drink of her wine. "That's why the one thing I am very faithful about is taking the Pill. So you don't have to worry there. As long as we're together—sex away."

"That's not very Catholic of you."

"Hey, they were wrong about Galileo. They're wrong about this."

"Then I guess this is the way it will be." Lance took his wine glass and sipped down the remainder of the soulful liquid.

Beverly put her napkin on her plate. "Come on, let's go for a walk."

Lance and Beverly walked along the road, listening to the gentle crash of waves with each rolling set pursuing higher ground up the shore. Beverly broke off her hold from Lance, kicked off her sandals, ran down to the beach, and tempted wetted fate. "Come on down!"

Lance kicked off his sandals, rolled up his trouser legs, and strolled down to the beach.

Beverly ran ahead of an incoming wave right into the arms of Lance. His embrace was sudden, deliberate. She looked into the dark, fathomless eyes that never failed to sparkle when he looked at her. "Lance."

"Yes."

"What are you thinking?"

"Stuff."

"What kind of stuff?"

"You and me stuff."

"Did anyone ever tell you that you are a very precocious man?"

"Not that particular word."

"Well, they should." A thinning layer of ocean swept over their feet. The cool bubbling sea foam invigorated Beverly. "Let's go skinny-dipping."

Lance stepped back, taking her by the hand, and pulled her again to him. "I'm all for the skinny."

"I thought so," Beverly said. She followed the man she chose to be with up the beach.

Moonlight filtered its way into their room, where he could see some sparkle in her amethyst eyes. She could see his smile. Then she felt the warmth of his lips upon hers.

"Bev," Lance said in a whispered tone that surrounded her.

"Yes."

"The one thing I'm not is a liar."

"About what?"

"That I am very much in love with you."

Morning came.

Breakfast was enjoyed as they sat on the balcony that overlooked the Mediterranean Ocean. Lance tried to read the newspaper. He noted the date. 11 August 1998. He enjoyed it as a morning ritual whenever he could have a newspaper handy.

"So, you really love me?"

"Is that so strange to understand?" Lance replied without looking away from the paper.

"Well, I've heard it before."

"Well, probably not outside of being in the throes of passion."

"You be nice," she said, plucking a grape from the fruit tray that sat in the middle of their table. "Maybe it's just infatuation." She thought a moment. "But not with you."

"I don't rush into such things."

"So, now you want to marry me?"

"Marriage is what men and women do. You know the birds and the bees. Fruits and vegetables."

"You know you are a very precocious man," she said, pointing.

"In spite of turning forty today?"

"You don't look it."

"Don't count on me acting it."

"At least not in bed."

"Anywhere. As long as you're happy to be with me."

"I told you you're an easy man to fall for. But, I don't want to complicate what we have."

"And what do we have?"

"Great sex for one. We have adventure and excitement. Face it, lover, we make a great team."

"You just proved my point."

"Oh, I did, didn't I?"

"Beverly, let me put it this way," Lance said, taking hold of her hand. "I'm in love with you for all of the right reasons."

"Just like that?"

"Honest, mature love is not complicated. I hope you will come to recognize that." Lance went back to reading his newspaper.

***

Driving in Gibraltar was a bit of an enigma. While all the street markings were British, along with texture and feel, it was the opposite of driving in the U.K. Here, the steering wheel and controls were on the left side of the car, while you drove on the right side of the road. It was known to throw off many a British tourist being so familiar with unfamiliarity.

Lance drove southward along Sir Herbert Road around the coast of Gibraltar. As the entire landmass of Gibraltar was roughly three square miles, it didn't take long to get anywhere. Beverly followed the long steep ridge that gave Gibraltar its notoriety with her camera.

As they came around the tip of the peninsula and then drove northward on the now congested western side of the Rock, they pulled into a parking lot. Beverly saw a descending cable car. "Oh, we're going up on a cable car."

"We are."

Lance strapped on his backpack, and they went to the cable car station.

Lance enjoyed following the contours of the ground below as the terrain changed with elevation. The cable car rolled past the mid-station bridge and continued upward to the "Top of the Rock."

They arrived at the top. "Oh, look, monkeys," Beverly said enthusiastically of Gibraltar's celebrity residents, the Barbary Macaques. They were a tailless species of money that inhabited the upper part of the Rock.

The cable car came to a stop, where near thirty people disembarked. Beverly was quick to take out her camera and capture one of the smaller rock apes jumping on a German woman.

"They're so cute," she said. Lance took her in tow and led her southward. "Where are we going?"

"To the Bat Cave," Lance directed.

"They don't have bats in there, do they?"

"Bats? No. Batty people? As soon as we get there."

"You be nice," she said, hooking her arm in through his.

Beverly saw the large white sign over the entranceway to St. Michael's Cave. "I read that there are over thirty miles of tunnels up here. If we get lost, we can do it."

"Behave, you."

"Where's your sense of adventure." Lance swatted her on her rear. "Oh, so it's S and M, is it?" she said with a wiggle.

"If you mean Slap and Maneuver, yes, right this way."

"The brochure says that it was believed St. Michael's Cave was bottomless."

"That ties into the belief that you entered into the Gates of Hades from here."

"It's like we're going on the Indiana Jones Adventure ride at Disneyland."

The *Cathedral Cave* was the largest of the chambers. It was set up as a hospital during World War II, though never used as such. Due to the cavern's natural acoustics, it had since been converted into an auditorium, complete with a stage and seating for over four hundred people. Lance had always thought it would be nice to catch a concert here someday.

Beverly gazed over the entire chamber, noting the otherworldly stalactites that hung down in various geometric shapes and sizes that over time had dripped down to form the rising stalagmites. Some formations were translucent, giving life to the thought that perhaps hidden alien powers were contained within embedded crystals. He could tell that Beverly was in awe of the place. Lance was, too, though this was his third visit.

"Where the lights are hitting, it looks like it's covered in pure gold. That's so cool," Beverly said.

"It's amazing what rainwater has created." Lance then realized he was happy to be sharing this visit with someone this time. He put his arm around Beverly's waist.

"Imagine if they started breaking off and dropping on us."

"Then we'd need Indiana Jones to come to the rescue."

"That's your job," she insisted.

They both dropped their sunglasses back on when the bright noon sun hit them upon exiting St. Michael's Cave. Lance led Beverly to their left and down a pathway to the south.

The traveling duo came into the Jew's Gate area. An old concrete battery that once supported an artillery gun now held the *Pillars of Hercules*. The bronze monument heralded the idea in antiquity that the Strait of Gibraltar was the literal end of the Earth. Lance escorted Beverly up the steps onto the landing and stood before the beautifully sculpted twin fluted columns wrapped loosely with scrolls that supported a large monolith with a circular plaque in its center. The plaque said: The Ancient World.

"You're kind of like Hercules," Beverly stated.

"I don't have his strength, unfortunately, but my tasks are aplenty." Lance gazed over to the conservationist's building that looked after the plant and wildlife. To the left of the building lay the first step on their next journey. "Ready?"

"Yup! Where next?"

Lance looked at the series of steps that led up into the thicket. "Next, we climb the *Mediterranean Steps*."

"How much walking are you planning on us doing today?"

"We're hiking, remember? About ten kilometers."

"Six miles?"

"We've walked about four kilometers of that already."

"Well, I know who will be too tuckered out this evening." Lance grinned. "Seriously? You act like this is our honeymoon," she protested.

Lance held Beverly's hand as they strode south around the top. As they climbed, they could see the hazy mist of the Moroccan coastline less than ten miles in the distance. The vistas would only grow more breathtaking as they climbed the stone steps hewn out of the limestone that lay intermixed with dirt and rocky trails. The steps were cut by the military during World War II so that a runner could be sent to communicate between the many artillery battery stations. They continued upward.

"Man, this is like mountain climbing," Beverly said with some complaint.

"Hiking, Bev. It's like hiking. It's just a trail with the occasional steps." Lance reached back and pulled her up to him. "One small step…"

Beverly pounded one foot in front of another. She was grateful that she was in decent shape and that there was the occasional rope railing to aid in the upward climb. Lance always kept an eye on her. His grasp wasn't just a hand up. It was the way he held her hand. Sometimes with a kiss on it. Perhaps it was the way a man who truly loves a woman holds it. She shrugged off the idea. Relationships weren't meant to last forever. Not that she ever saw. Could her life with Lance be any different? Some incompatible element always crept in. She didn't understand why. But it always did.

The climb was tough and had a small element of risk, but it was breathtaking. Lance stopped at a flat spot before another set of steep steps along the trail. Beverly dropped her body soundly on the lone bench. Lance removed the backpack and took out two bottles of water.

"Lance, may I ask you something?"

"Of course."

"Why do you think most relationships don't work? You know, last."

"Selfishness primarily."

"You say that for everything."

"What kind of explanation are you looking for?"

"I don't know. Something else."

"There is nothing else, Beverly. All the ills of our world are based on selfishness."

"Sorry, I asked."

"Don't feel that way. I'm being honest and accurate with you. Do you want me to give you some high-sounding, half-witted philosophical answer?"

"No, I suppose not."

"Then trust what I say."

They reached the top of the trail, the final push up many steps with the fenced-off military area just above them. Beverly looked back down the winding path of immeasurable steps along the cliff face. It reminded her of the Great Wall of China. Lance sat on a large rock and beckoned Beverly to sit with him. He wrapped his arms around her. "We made it," Lance said proudly.

"Now what?"

"We walk back."

"Back down the steps?"

"No. We take the pathway back to the cable car station. We can get a bite to eat and then head to the northern defenses."

"Okay. Let's go." Lance resisted her standing, pulling her back as he leaned back. His fingers gently moved her head back to the left, where his lips were waiting to meet her's. She felt his wanting and his passion. But then something else in a nurturing way that had her hand caressing his hair. She pulled back and looked at him. "I get it now." She kissed him and stood, holding out her hand.

Beverly was on her second bottle of water as they enjoyed a sandwich at the café. The intrepid duo then made their way along the northern spine of the Rock.

They stood on the concrete pad of the Princess Anne Battery. Their trek to the farthest points north gave the vistas below the sheer cliffs of the entry into the central part of town and the runway. Beverly could see Lance's jet down on the tarmac. To her left lay the moles or piers that gave a pathway for the seafarer to reach land. A cruise ship lay berthed along the north mole, and she could see passengers walking in crowded groups to waiting buses. She then noticed two large yachts berthed along the detached moles. There was no way to land except by boat. She saw a small boat speed away from the vessel in front.

"Lance, may I use your binoculars?" Lance pulled off his backpack, pulled out the small pair of binoculars, and gave them to her. She scanned. At the same time, Lance noticed three men get out of a black car. They walked around his Citation, inspecting it, much too closely for his comfort.

"Here, let me see them." He took the small binoculars and quickly brought the three men into focus. They were well-dressed Arab men. Lance turned to Beverly. She was as white as a sheet. "What's wrong?"

"We have to get out of here, Lance. Now!"

Lance zoomed in on the cruise ship. Then zoomed in on the two yachts. His attention was drawn to the second yacht. Along the upper deck was the sword of Allah in gold. The angle was tough, but he could see the name of the vessel: *Crescent Sheikh*. It was the yacht of the Saudi prince that had abducted Beverly eight months ago.

"Right. Let's get out of here." Lance dropped the binoculars into his backpack. Two Saudi men with guns drawn stood behind them. Lance put on the backpack and raised his hands. "His highness, Prince Khaled Mohammed bin-Aziz Al Saud requires your presence," the man said, speaking in a manner that suggested a cordial invitation. The gun suggested otherwise.

"I'm not going back there," Beverly yelled. She was losing it.

Lance had to act fast. "Hey! I don't know what this is all bloody about, but we are tourists on holiday. So, I suggest you just leave us alone."

"We know who you are, Mr. Rio. You will come with us," the man said insistently.

"Who are you?" Lance insisted.

"His name is Hasan. The other is Razak," Beverly said. They were large men with the look of capability. Lance sized them up. How they moved, what drew their attention, and the level of meanness in them. They were factors.

"You cannot just abduct people. Ursula, what is this?"

"Ursula?" Hasan said, laughing. "Is that what she has told you her name is?"

"You listen here," Lance said, shaking his finger at Hasan. Hasan focused a second too long on the shaking finger, laughing at the audacity of this Lance Rio. Lance had Hasan's hand twisted, his index finger broken while pulling the nine-millimeter's trigger with an immediate shot to Razak's chest. Lance secured the gun in his hand, sending Hasan off the battery mount with a kick.

"Here." Lance gave Beverly the gun. Lance took Razak's gun.

Beverly stepped down to a groaning Hasan. "It's like the last time you perverts tried to rape me." She put two in his chest. Lance understood.

Lance saw three other Saudi men run toward them. "Come on!"

Lance took Beverly by the hand and ran for the trees to their right. It was their only option. Behind them was a straight twelve hundred foot drop. They saw three Saudi nationals inspect their fallen comrades. Lance hit the speed dial on his cell phone.

"Bob's your uncle," Lance said as soon as Ralston answered. Lance used an odd, humorous British expression for his immediate need of British help.

"Lance. What's wrong?" Ralston said.

"G.I.P."

"Saudi Secret Service?" Ralston thought that the General Intelligence Presidency seemed a stretch, but he trusted Lance's instincts over the absurd.

A moment later: "Lance, my dear fellow, are you there?" came the concerned voice of Sir Trevor Rees. Gratefully, thankfully, he now had the upper echelon of both the CIA and MI-6 on the phone.

"Yes, Trev, I'm here," Lance said wearily.

"Good to hear your voice. Now listen. Get back down toward Amelia's Battery. There is an old tunnel entrance there that connects to the old World War Two Tunnels. You need to get to what is called Willis's Gallery. If you can get there and get through the old metal gate, I can get you back down the Rock back into town. I've alerted our people there."

"I'm listening. Wait! Hang on. We need to move. Beverly, stay calm and focused."

"I am."

"That's my girl." He smiled at her. She reverted to her training.

They darted across the road. They were spotted. Two cars sped down to the parking area by the Upper Gallery exhibit. "Not good," Lance mumbled.

They ran back around to an isolated gallery with an old rusted metal gate. The gate was installed in the late 1800s and looked it. Lance whipped off his backpack and reached inside. He pulled out a serrated wire, wrapped it around the lock bolt, and then slid a plastic handle through the loop on each end. He moved it back and forth vigorously, cutting through the rusted bolt quickly.

"I wondered if you had any neat spy gadgets with you."

"Always." Lance pried the gate back enough to get them through. He pulled the gate back closed. They hurried into the blackness. It would take a minute for their eyes to adjust. Beverly held onto Lance's hand and followed in sync.

"Lance. Can you hear me?" came Trevor's voice.

"Yes, Trevor, I can still hear you. Jeffrey."

"I'm here, Lance," came the consoling voice of his mentor.

"Lance, we'll lose you in the tunnel. So, what you must do is follow the tunnel to the end, which will put you at another old iron gate. Go through it and keep going."

"Understood. I'll call once we get to the other side."

The small flashlight illuminated a set of iron bars just ahead. Lance made quick work of its lock as before.

They stepped back into sunshine. Lance redialed. "We're through. We're outside."

"Well done, Lance!" exclaimed Trevor.

They were by the old wall next to the ruins of the Moorish Castle Estate. Lance helped Beverly over the wall, and then he jumped up and over it. They headed down the hill via a footpath of concrete steps.

Beverly and Lance continued down the road until a car stopped. With relief, they were British tourists.

"Can we give you a lift?" the cheerful driver said. He was with his teenage son that seemed less enthusiastic about their travels.

"Oh, that would be great, mate," Lance said. He seated Beverly in the back and jumped upfront. They felt a measure of safety, especially when a car with four Saudi nationals, Lance was sure, squeaked by them on their way to the top.

"Thanks, mate," Lance said. He and Beverly stepped out and headed for a taxi. They were back in the car park. A smiling Arab man approached.

"Hello, Lance Rio and Beverly de Havilland. Bob's your uncle. Right this way, you two. I'm Yousef, MI-Six. But call me Joey." He was a pleasant fellow, Lance thought. Most importantly, he was there to help.

Joey turned onto Devil's Tower Road, which gave Lance a chance to view his plane through binoculars. "Not to worry, Lance. We had our officials chase off those goons and check it for any tampering."

Joey pulled up to the Caleta Hotel lobby area. "I'll be back in about an hour."

***

They were back in their room, long serviced by the maids. Beverly seemed shy to undress in front of Lance and went into the bathroom. He heard the door being locked and the shower turned on. He would respect her feelings and shower privately after her.

***

Lance took his seat in the Citation. Beverly took hers. After the preflight startup procedure was completed, Lance lit off engine No. 2, followed by engine No. 1. They were cleared to taxi.

They turned around to go to the beginning of the runway when a black Mercedes-Benz saloon pulled out from the line of cars and walking crowd to intercept them. Lance added power, pushing the jet slowly through the crowd, waving his hand for them to get out of the way. He accepted a few flip-offs that came from incensed pedestrians. One man slammed his hand down on the left wingtip as it passed through them, followed by a musical interlude of horn honking from the halted line of vehicles.

"Gulf-Bravo-Bravo clear for immediate takeoff," came the clearance from the tower. Lance moved the thrust levers forward to create some distance from the irate passersby, and then he hit full power. There was no flight plan. The moment that the mains left the runway and sovereign Gibraltar soil, there would be no trace of the flight having ever taken place.

Chapter 75

Megiddo, Israel

August 15, 1998

Lance woke as he had the last four mornings—alone. He was back in his bed at the ranch house with Beverly in the guest room. The incident in Gibraltar had scared her badly. The clock read just after 6 a.m.

Lance traipsed quietly from his room to the kitchen, only to be intercepted by Alfonso Pig. He followed to the side of his ubiquitous master. Lance could swear that Alfonso was tiptoeing until he realized that this was the natural gait of a pig.

Lance found his tea stash and stood over the teapot to catch it before it whistled. Breakfast could wait. He and Alfonso headed outside.

Lance had finished his tea on the walk to the barn, but he held the empty cup like an engine nacelle hanging from a wing. He took several glances inside the cup. He reasoned that the secret to true fuel atomization lay within the empty vessel.

Lance stood in front of the Sparrowhawk, sipping a new cup of tea. Like a faithful thoroughbred that waited for his master's return, the Sparrowhawk only needed to be let loose. "You know, Alfonso, you're due for a ride." Lance saw his backpack that rested on the workbench since his return. He thought he should unpack it.

Lance looked at the empty second cup. It then came to him, a new concept in turbine engine combustion. More specifically, it was the combustor itself. It would be similar in design to a typical annular or ring style combustor but altogether different. He took his cell phone from its holster. A moment later: "Hello," came the voice of Eric Pitts.

"Special."

"Hey, Lance."

"I think I figured out a way of making a new generation combustor. I mean, we are talking about really driving up the heat," Lance said.

"And I assume we generate this heat upfront and then cool it down before it hits the high-pressure turbine."

"Naturally, but I'm talking about six thousand degrees Fahrenheit. Maybe more."

"Wow! You do mean hot. Okay. Do the creative thing you do, and we'll put it together. I could pop over there maybe next month. How's it going with you and Bev?"

"She's still a bit shaken. I don't know what she's feeling about being in any neck of the woods where Khaled is."

"Give it time."

"I just know I don't want to lose her."

"You won't, buddy," Eric said warmly.

Alfonso grunted. "I'll call you later." Lance could smell the coffee. He heard a giggle at his nose wrinkling up. His beaming eyes locked in on Beverly. "Did you sleep well?"

"Better. But, I miss waking up next to you," Beverly said, strolling up to Lance. "Good morning, Alfonso." Beverly put her cup down on the bench and then wrapped her arms around Lance. Lance held her, rocking her gently.

"What would you like to do today? We can take the Sparrowhawk out for a spin if you want. Or whatever you want."

"Do you always have to be so wonderful?" Beverly mourned.

"When I'm with you."

"Stop it!" came her plea with a tear.

"Okay. It's stopped." Lance let go of her. "I don't want you upset. Today is a good day."

***

Beverly's flight had been called. It was nearing the 1:10 a.m. departure time. Lance and Beverly had an enjoyable dinner in Tel Aviv before journeying to the Airport. It was by Danny's connections that Lance would be able to see Beverly off at the gate.

"I've trained you well, and you should pass your tests easily. Next time I see you, you will have your ATP, with a jet type rating."

"Thank you for that. For everything."

"When you come back, we will talk."

"Yes. It will be time for that talk."

"First things, first." Lance noticed her fellow passengers lining up in the queue. "I will miss you. Terribly so."

"Me too. You've been one of the best things to ever happen to me."

She held Lance in suspension with a final kiss goodbye. It would be a long month before they were reunited. Lance waved a final goodbye as Beverly moved past the ticket agent and into the jet bridge portal. He would watch her plane depart before leaving for Ruth Street in Jerusalem and some sleep.

***

With Lance's life and work schedule, a Saturday morning lie-in would have been just another day, but today was different. It was early October, and it had been more than a month. He would be traveling down to Tel Aviv to pick up

Beverly and reengage his life with her's. He looked at the royal blue velvet ring box on his nightstand. It would stay in the drawer for a couple of days until the moment was right. He let Danny know his intentions a week ago. Lance even thought of Alfonso being the ring bearer.

Lance came out of his room with Alfonso, feeling well-rested. When he turned the corner into the kitchen, he saw Danny and then Ralston.

"Jeffrey."

"Lance, sit down, please," Ralston said.

With a look of dread, Lance sat at the table. "She's not coming, is she?"

"No," Ralston said. He found it difficult like never before to deliver bad news. "She's at Langley at the moment. I want you to take some time off."

"And go where, Jeffrey?" Visibly shaken, Lance rose from his chair.

"I'll be here, Lance. When you're ready."

"Thank you, Jeffrey." Lance walked out the front door. Alfonso followed. Ralston watched Lance and his pet head down the trail to the barn. Then Lance dropped to his knees, trembling. Ralston arched back, groaning.

"Danny. Please, keep an eye on him as you have all of these years."

"As always, Jeffrey."

Lance took the third attempted call from Eric Pitts. "Lance, I am so sorry. I didn't know till now. After she got her Citation rating, I thought she would be coming back to you. I chewed her out royally, let me tell you what. I don't even want to know her right now."

"I know you meant well, Special. And I love you for it. It's my fault for not listening. Apparently, it was just sex."

Chapter 76

Langley, Virginia

October 12, 1998

Jeffrey Ralston took his chair. He expected a knock at his door any minute. The briefing would be on time, jetlag notwithstanding. He called them all from their overseas assignments for this Monday morning meeting.

Joshua Wilson, David Nance, and Mike Castro sat in front of Ralston's desk as they had for the past fourteen years.

"Lance's assertion that Khaled is part of Saudi intelligence seems to be valid. It would give him greater access to things. It looks like he used those resources to find Beverly de Havilland. Unfortunately, she's not the only abductee. There have been others," Ralston addressed.

"Are you saying that the prince is a serial rapist?" asked Mike Castro.

"Predator. Let's just say that our narcissistic prince is trouble. There is this girl, all of seventeen, a rebellious youth that partied her way into being abducted one night. The problem is that she's the daughter of Moshe Samelson. Ring any bells?" Ralston watched his men's eyes widen.

"The head of operations for the Mossad? Are you kidding me? This fool will start World War Three!" shouted Josh Wilson.

"So we carefully build an environment where we can take out the prince if need be."

"What about Lance?" asked David Nance.

"Right now, he's working on some new-fangled afterburner system that he and Eric have developed for the Sparrowhawk. I want that to be his focus for now."

Chapter 77

Megiddo, Israel

November 1, 1998

Eric Pitts held onto Alfonso Pig. As it turned out, Alfonso loved to fly. He also got to spend three days in Germany at the Dessau hanger. He was a curious pig. Behind Eric's seat, nestled in with their bags, was a new combustor for a new generation of afterburner. Lance was insistent within himself that he turn his ideas into reality.

"See, little guy. Not only are there pigs in Israel. They can fly," Eric said. Alfonso climbed onto the rear instrument panel, stretched forward, and gave Lance a nuzzle with his snoot. Lance reached back with his hand and rubbed the flat nose and then his head.

Lance dropped the gear after the second notch of flaps became set. He held the established 90 knots indicated over the fence and settled down on the long road that continued to serve as his runway.

Inside, the Sparrowhawk was wheeled around, now facing the barn doors. By all rights, the Sparrowhawk was now an established kit plane. They could reproduce the same model over and over again. As an airshow performer, it would stand alone.

An hour later, Lance and Eric were the equivalent of being scrubbed in with coveralls and gloves on. They were going to perform an enginectomy (Lance's word), starting with its removal from the aircraft.

Two hours later, the engine rested on its engine stand. Their custom six-port exhaust system was removed in favor of a newly designed afterburner combustor system. "This should revolutionize, well, everything!" Eric said.

"Now, if the parts you made back home fit nicely, then we have a new system." Lance was hopeful. Eric brought the double-walled nozzle and held it against the combustor, the heart of the system.

"Lance, how is this thing supposed to work?" asked Danny, who entered the barn with their lunch. "I know the typical systems and how they work, but you're anything but typical."

"Ain't he, though?" Eric chimed.

Lance frowned. "Anyway, the Sparrowhawk was designed with some wiggle room for growth in its systems. Basically, we are channeling some of the bypass air and all of the ram air into this new afterburner combustor, which will rocket out of this new nozzle that looks like, well, like a rocket nozzle. "It will allow us to supercruise, supersonically."

"You will have this together today?"

"Oh, no. There's another week's worth of work here."

Lance and Eric worked into the night, which came early this time of year.

"Let's call it a night, Lancey-boy. I'm beat."

"Okay, Special. We made a decent start today."

The night was cool but calm. Eric liked it here in Megiddo. It was out in the country. He came in from the kitchen with a bottle of kosher beer that he had developed a taste for recently. He came up to Lance, who sat as he often did with his Bible in his lap and the yellow note pad next to him, ready to write.

"Still at it, I see," Eric said. Lance looked troubled. "What's wrong?"

"Special, this is how it should be."

"How what should be?

"Earth. Our civilization. Human society."

"Okay." Eric dropped his large frame into the plush leather recliner next to Lance. Danny came into the room and sat opposite them in his wooden rocking chair.

"Here, let me read it to you. Sixty-fifth chapter of Isaiah. 'And they will certainly build houses and have occupancy; and they will certainly plant vineyards and eat their fruitage—.'"

"Sounds good to me so far."

"'They will not build and someone else have occupancy; they will not plant, and someone else do the eating. They will not toil for nothing, nor will they bring to birth for disturbance.'" Lance looked up. "This is how it should be."

"Well, that's a nice snapshot of Heaven."

"It's not Heaven. The Israelites never entertained the idea or belief of life in Heaven."

"I happen to know that Jews believe they're going to Heaven."

"Not originally."

"Dude, you're talking about a completely whole new set of dynamics to our world. And that just ain't gonna happen."

"Has to."

"You get real on this, little buddy."

"I am. If it's true, I just read you God's intent."

"Lance, you would have to get rid of the structure of—governments, the corporate world, religion..."

"Sounds good to me so far."

"Danny, tell him," Eric pleaded. "Lance. I know you're into this Bible, Middle East thing and all. Don't get me wrong. I'd love my own vineyard and no one causing me disturbance. But, it just ain't gonna happen."

"Why so certain?"

"Little buddy—you'll need more than what you got. What, you think you can zoom around in the Sparrowhawk and right the wrongs of this world? You better plan on putting a phaser in it instead of the mini-gun we're planning. I think you're getting a bit gung-ho with all of this Old Testament and New Testament stuff."

"No such thing as the Old and New Testament."

"Excuse me? Danny, tell him."

"He is correct, Eric. Technically," Danny said.

"They weren't testaments, Eric. They were covenants. You know, an agreement, or contract," Lance added.

"Danny. You're the scholar around here. What's he saying?" Eric snarled.

"What Lance is referring to, Eric, is that the Latin Vulgate influenced the King James Version of the Bible. The Latin word *testamentum* was used in Second Corinthians, instead of the actual Greek word *Di·a·the'kes* that is correctly rendered *covenant*."

"You mean he's right?"

"Yes, I'm right. Think of the Bible more correctly as the Hebrew Scriptures and the Christian Greek Scriptures."

"Well, you believe what you want to believe."

"No. I will believe what is true."

"Your truth!"

"No! *Thee* truth! Quit getting your ears tickled! Discover for yourself."

"Look, Lance."

"No, you look, Eric. Your ignorance is not mine."

"Whatever," Eric said, bouncing to his feet and pounding his way out the front door.

"Lance!" Danny admonished. "Knowledge puffs up—Love builds up."

Lance stared at Danny. Then dropped his head, hopped up, and went out after Eric.

As temperatures and tempers cooled, Eric stood on the porch and gazed out at the heavens. He was nursing another bottle of beer. Danny came out. "Where's Lance?"

"In the barn. You know, Danny, sometimes that boy scares me. In a way, we have unlimited resources and just enough know-how to be really dangerous. We ain't on some crusade. I've learned better. Between you and me, the best thing Lance could do is retire."

***

As it often does in aviation, results were the sum total of setbacks. The new afterburner system would increase efficiency by at least a factor of ten over existing afterburning jet engines. Instead of running the fuel tanks dry in twelve minutes or so, their afterburner system would run the Sparrowhawk's fuel tank dry in just over one hundred twenty minutes, or two hours.

Lance turned to a heading of 290° so they would shoot out past Haifa and over the ocean.

Eric entered information into the laptop that was tied into the nervous system of the aircraft. "Ready?"

"Ready," Lance responded.

"Okay. Let it happen, ship's captain."

Lance called out. "In five, four, three, two, one, mark." Lance moved the single thrust lever forward to the detent stop. He pulled a small catch, a lever built into the handle just for this hoped-for moment, and moved the thrust lever forward. A muffled roar came from the back and a slight jolt. A continuous push on the back of their seats let them know they were accelerating rapidly. "Mach one," Lance called out.

"Roger that. I'm reading steady in the green."

"Mach one-point-two, now three. Mach one-point-four, one-point-five."

"Roger that. Skin temps are coming up as expected. Time to take her up. I figure we're running over eighteen hundred pounds of thrust off the afterburner right now."

"Roger that," Lance said, pulling back on the side stick.

They climbed quickly. The divot or ramp door underneath was fully open. Ram air rushed in and compressed, giving the afterburning system all the puff it needed. Lance leveled off at sixty thousand feet. Lance and Eric marveled at the blue and white-lined curvature of the earth. "Now, this is God's country," Eric said.

"It's stunning up here," Lance added. "Okay, we are accelerating again. Mach one-point-two, three, mach one-point-four, five." The airspeed indicator kept climbing. "Mach one-point-eight."

The airspeed indicator settled at Mach 1.8.

"Okay. Are you ready for some numbers?"

"Ready."

"We're at sixty thousand feet. Outside air temp is minus sixty-nine-point-seven degrees Fahrenheit. That's a little Americana thrown in, so you don't forget. In Celsius, we're minus fifty-six-point-five degrees. At Mach one-point-eight, we're traveling at one thousand thirty-two nautical miles per hour—or—one thousand one hundred eighty-eight statute miles per hour. We're covering nineteen-point-eight miles a minute. Fuel flow—six hundred twenty-one-point-one. Just under ninety-three gallons an hour. We're like the SR-Seventy One,

Lance. We're a ramjet engine now. We're more efficient at supersonic than at subsonic cruise. Way cool, dude! And we're a friggin' kit plane!"

Lance had an inner peace come over him. He was validated. No one could tell him no. Nor would he be told what was possible. His evidence was empirical.

The Sparrowhawk continued on its northwest trajectory. "Hey, we just hit twelve hundred nautical miles per hour and rising. She still has more to give," Lance said. The aircraft was going to hit mach two. It was seconds away from that milestone.

"Lance, take it out of supersonic!" Eric cried out. Lance dropped the thrust lever to idle. He noticed on his instrument panel, the Sparrowhawk's outside skin temperature was at 193.2° C. "We're cooking the skin at three hundred eighty degrees Fahrenheit. Too much friction. We need to cool her down before we risk catastrophic failure here."

"Okay. We're slowing." Lance reached up and touched the canopy. He could feel the heat warming through the transparency. It would soften and deform under the tremendous outside pressures.

"You know what this means?"

"Yup. If we want to stay up here in the kitchen, we need to handle the heat."

Chapter 78

El Cajon, California

March 9, 1999

Lance and Eric had their fix down to a science to solve the heat issues of the Sparrowhawk, which required some irreverent orthodoxy.

By early afternoon, they had pulled new wing skins out of the former fuel tanker turned autoclave. The new wing skins, a bit larger, were first, two layers of ceramic cloth bonded ceramic adhesive. This shell was then bonded with high heat-tolerant epoxy resin to six layers of carbon fiber cloth. Using vapor deposition, a thin layer of ceramic film was applied to the surface.

Testing the new wing skin by applying 600°F of heat on the outer surface resulted in only 287° Fahrenheit net temperature migrating through the wing skin. The Sparrowhawk would feel a third of that temperature at supercruise. Everything internal and structural would be safe.

The fuselage was just an empty shell. The exterior paint was removed and buffed lightly down to the carbon fiber surface and etched. The same system of protection was then applied.

Cotronics, Inc., a ceramic adhesive manufacturer, was a bit surprised their product was being used this way. Ceramic adhesives were a newer technology designed to handle insane temperatures from 1,200° up to 4,000° Fahrenheit. But it dried hard and could crack. So, a new adhesive was formulated with some flex to it for aerospace applications.

These new technology applications gave the boys the idea of designing a high supersonic or even a hypersonic aircraft. Perhaps one day, creating their own spaceplane and enter the X-Prize. The X-Prize contest would award ten million dollars to the first people outside of any governmental organization that could build a reusable spacecraft. Fly it up to an altitude of 100 kilometers, or 62 miles, defined as the "edge of space," and return safely. Then repeat the flight within two weeks. It was a thought and a grin.

The Sparrowhawk was now suited to its higher calling. The task of putting every single thing back into the aircraft lay before them. The best place in the world to test the Sparrowhawk was just north, where they could put her through her paces unencumbered. Their day was coming.

***

No place on earth was so well equipped by nature to do flight testing than the Mojave Desert. The new and improved Sparrowhawk handled its high skin temperatures with little fanfare at Mach 2.04. The nose, windscreen, and leading edges of the wings ran hotter than the rest of an aircraft flying sustained supersonic.

"So, why do you run hotter for the same speed as the Concorde?" Ralston asked.

"Because the Concorde is two-hundred and two-feet long and sleeker ratio wise," Lance replied.

"Makes sense." Ralston looked through the double-walled glass laminate canopy and marveled at the curvature of the world beyond him. He could see the stars above him, though not as brightly as at night. Then he wasn't that far below the eternal night of space. At least that's how it felt.

"Eric and I have decided that for safety's sake, we should only cruise at no more than eleven hundred miles an hour."

"That's statute miles, I take it?"

"Yes. I figured it would be clearer than saying Mach one-point-seven."

"It is." Ralston was satisfied with all of the testing that he felt safe to take his first flight finally. "Very well. I hereby dub thee fully operational."

Lance made a smooth but fairly steep U-turn. The one hundred eighty degree turn would have them skirt part of Nevada before they could line up on Runway 30 back at Mojave Airport in California, still one hundred forty miles away—about six minutes from now.

The landing was uneventful. Turning off of the active, Lance spotted Scaled Composites. This was Burt Rutan's place, Hangar 78. Burt was the father of the modern kit plane development and movement. Rutan, though, had moved on to newer horizons. He was funded to develop a spaceplane to compete in the X-Prize. Would he do it? Time would tell. But then, it started Lance daydreaming on new things as they taxied back.

Lance shut down in front of the hangar he and Eric rented. The main cabin door rotated down from the Gulfstream jet next to them in anticipation of Ralston boarding shortly. Ralston stepped out of the Sparrowhawk. "Well done, Lance. Pack up and head back to Israel."

Chapter 79

Above Israel

August 31, 1999

Lance had about a three-second burst of ammo left. He came around again on the target and blasted what was left of the old pickup truck. Many an Israeli fighter pilot had preceded him in aerial combat training on that old truck. The new prototype M-134 Minigun, now designated the M-140LA (for Larger Ammunition), spun its six barrels and depleted the last 150 rounds of .338 *Lapua Magnum* ammunition. The kit aircraft now lived up to its namesake. It was a small but deadly predatory bird.

With the push of a button, Lance ordered the Gatling gun to rise back up from the "Talon's position" into the aircraft's nose. It was on an electrically driven chassis that also housed a camera so Lance could see what he was firing at on his LCD color instrument display screen. It was FLIR capable. The *Forward-Looking-Infra-Red* camera would let him see the bullets fly to their target in the black of night without tracers. It was about stealth. Quiet in—quiet out.

Lance flipped the Sparrowhawk around on its side and pulled 9 g's positive to egress the training area and head back up north to home. "Talon One, you are clear of the area and safe to resume course heading three-five-zero," came the voice of Israeli military air control.

The Sparrowhawk seemed to want to please Lance. It handled all of its changes in design with style and flair. And it was fair to say that Lance was now one with his aircraft.

Chapter 80

London

January 1, 2000

The cloudy, overcast midnight sky reflected the fireworks to the point that Lance swore he was in the "Battle of Britain."

"BOB, you say," Graham Rye said, downing the last of the bourbon from his tumbler.

A minute earlier, it was still 1999, and all was quiet on the front. They could faintly hear Big Ben begin its cycle of dongs that harkened in a new year, which aligned one's thinking to the fact that it was also a new decade, a new century, and the start of a new millennium, all simultaneously inaugurated with the first stroke of midnight.

Graham was very festive, while the other members of his team were more laid back. Most went quiet and enjoyed the splash of lights bouncing off of the clouds. Lance wanted to travel to Greenwich to the Old Royal Observatory and stand on the Prime Meridian Line that marked 0° longitude. Graham talked him out of it, stating that the trains and such will be full of drunken wallies, whereas here, the drunken wallies were self-contained and, for the most part, harmless. Graham made sure that Lance had a stiff drink of his choice at the ready. Lance settled on a pomegranate martini. He would have preferred it be a crushed ice, slushy drink but took it on the rocks. Graham knew his friend was not that festive. Lance told him of the conclusion to his life and world with Beverly de Havilland. Graham knew that pain. They sat away from the others. "So, what are you going to do now that you put a Tommy gun in your ladybird?"

"I don't know. Evil persists."

"True. But, how much longer do you want to do the spy thingy?"

"Dunno. There's a part of me that wants to see if I can still do some real good."

"Noble. Very noble. I give you that. But—"

"I have more technology to develop, G. I'm only now on the cusp of some very important things. And I need the resources that Uncle Jeffrey provides."

"Yeah, but you have funds of your own. Over the years, I know we've liberated a few bucks from those sinister in heart that didn't need the cash any longer. And you work with low overhead."

"Perhaps you're right. Maybe this will be my last year. Maybe I'll find a good woman somewhere and settle down."

"And live where?"

"Good question, matey. I don't know. Maybe go back to the U.S. Eric would love me to move out to San Diego and put together our kit plane business."

"What kind of planes would you manufacture?"

"Probably something simple. In the two to three hundred knot speed range."

"Could you stand it? I mean building aircraft that are less than your full potential."

"Well, Dr. Siggy. A two hundred and thirty miles per hour aircraft can be great fun for the whole family."

"An estate wagon with wings," Graham added.

"It's funny that you should say that. When I got my private license, my flight examiner told me that the Cessna one-seventy-two I was flying was a station wagon with wings."

"There you go."

"Except my wings are always rated for twelve g's."

"So noted," Graham said, raising his glass to Lance.

Lance watched Danny, who under persuasion came with him to London, go to the door. Danny shook hands with the man as if they were old friends. Danny's countenance was sympathetic. Lance found it odd that he expected a visitor. Then Lance recognized the man. Moshe Samelson looked disheveled. He was dressed in suit and tie. The former Israeli Defense Force general, now Director of Operations for the Mossad, took on a presence of determination. He and Danny approached Lance and Graham.

"We're going to work, aren't we?" Graham muttered.

"Lance, this is Moshe Samelson," Danny introduced. "The one that has let you work so freely back home."

Lance extended his hand. "Sir. It is a pleasure to meet you finally."

Samelson took hold of Lance's hand with both of his. He pleaded. "As a son of Israel, Lance, I beg you, bring my daughter back to me."

Chapter 81

Jeddah, Saudi Arabia
21°32′36″N, 39°10′22″E

January 21, 2000

Lance sat in the pilot's seat of the Onyx Aviation Services Learjet 45. Manfred Steiger sat in the co-pilot's seat. They waited for Mike Castro, who donned the mantles of a Saudi businessman. Lance squeezed out of his seat and stood outside of the door.

A limo pulled up. Mike Castro, in a fifteen hundred dollar suit, stepped out and immediately boarded the aircraft. Lance stepped in and closed the door.

The past week in Jeddah allowed Lance to learn the lay of the land. He even traveled down to Mecca and the *Masjid al-Haram* mosque and had a glimpse of the *Kaaba*, the holiest site in Islam. He gazed upon the remaining fragments of the *Black Stone* housed inside of a silver frame on the eastern corner of the cuboid-shaped structure.

Mike Castro spent time in Jameel Square, the heart of the business district in Jeddah.

"Well, I learned that the prince was in his office, two floors up from where I did my business. He'll be here until after the Hajj. But the small talk is that the prince does love his delicacies. If you know what I mean."

"I just wish there was a way we could be introduced. I have nothing in common with the man," Lance said with some frustration.

"Actually, Lance, there is a way. You just won't like it."

Chapter 82

Titusville, Florida

28°35′28″N, 80°49′12″W

May 19, 2000

Lance's Citation jet seemed small, tiny for the first time in his life. It was even claustrophobic. "It's good to see you, Lance," Beverly de Havilland said. Lance continued with no reply. "Well, say something."

"I'm here to listen," Lance said flatly.

"You're here to facilitate the mission," Ralston said from the co-pilot's seat.

"Fine." Lance sat opposite Beverly in the main cabin. "Then this is strictly business."

"No. I am giving you two the chance to say your piece, and then we get on with the mission," Ralston said as he slid the two cockpit door halves shut.

"Lance," Beverly said, taking his hands into hers. "I'm sorry how things worked out."

"Doesn't matter. I won't see you ever again after this."

"Lance, I tried to be where you are."

"You tried," Lance snarled. "You'll never know love. True love. Because you'll keep searching for it from those like you. It will elude you. Don't believe me? You will." The aircraft shook. "What the—" Lance slid the cockpit doors open. "What's going on?"

"Look," Ralston said, pointing. A young man stood back on a small aircraft tug after winching the nose wheel up in the bucket. Lance opened the cabin door and jumped outside, noting the new Gulfstream G-IV bizjet parked next to him. It was large and impressive. Lance marched up to the front of his aircraft. "Hey, what are you doing?"

"I have orders to move your plane over to another spot," the young man said.

"By whom?"

The young man nodded toward the Gulfstream. "The guys in the G-Four, you know, like their space."

"Oh, really? You have two seconds to detach the tug from my plane." Lance's insistency won out. The young man decoupled the bucket from the nose wheel, backed up, and drove the electric tug back to the hangar.

Lance came around back to the cabin door and poked his head inside. "Looks like I'm going to get my introduction after all. We won't need Bev. So, Bev, have a nice life and all that. But never, ever contact me ever again. Ta."

"Oh, Lance, don't do anything stupid," Ralston said.

"Me?" Lance pushed himself from his aircraft.

He marched up to a well-dressed Saudi having just come around the front of the Gulfstream. "Who do you people think you are? This is America!" Lance shouted. "You'll move my plane over my dead body. So back off, chump!"

"You will move your aircraft by demand of his highness," the Saudi man ordered.

"Well, your highness is my lowness."

"Infidel!"

Lance didn't want to use a racial epithet to elicit a reaction, so he modified it. "Look, sand mucus. Don't be calling me names."

He figured the man heard what he wanted to hear. He did. Lance felt the back of the man's hand. It stung a bit. Lance blazed a trail of strikes on the man's face and body. He kicked the man in the side of his left knee. The man buckled, reaching for his gun. Lance took hold of it and his opponent's hand and spun him to the ground—hard! He was out. Lance saw a second pair of feet drop to the ground from the Gulfstream door. As he hurried around the nose of the aircraft, Lance discharged a round into his leg. He flopped to the ground. Lance took his gun as he came around the left side of the jet and trotted up the airstairs.

He came in swinging the gun fore and aft.

"Mr. Rio. Come in," said a voice from behind the curtain.

Lance moved the curtain away. He could see the Saudi prince sitting down to his lunch with his chef, he supposed, standing next to him. A third bodyguard pointed a gun toward Lance.

"Tell your man to drop his gun, or I'll shoot him too." The prince spoke in Arabic. Nicely, Lance understood. The bodyguard holstered his gun and stood at the ready with his hands folded.

"There's no further need for violence, Mr. Rio. Come, sit, and join me." Lance came nearer. The prince gestured. Lance took a seat opposite him at his table that held a banquet fit for a king. The prince was tall and smiled an epicurean's smile. "I am Prince Khaled Mohammed bin-Aziz al-Saud."

"You obviously know who I am."

"Yes, my dear Lance, I do. You have no middle name I have noted."

"Perhaps I should borrow one of yours."

"Ah-ha!" the prince shouted. "A man clever in tongue as he is with his hands. So before I make a formal complaint with your government about the CIA's reckless behavior, I could rightfully have you shot as you are on Saudi soil. But do share some lunch with me."

"Huh? CIA? I had to learn to be this way when people point a gun at you in my business."

"And what is your business, Mr. Rio?"

"I gather you've heard of Onyx Aviation Services?"

"I have."

"I own it. Well, with an eccentric old uncle, whom I've only met twice."

"Yes, I know. So, you deny being a spy."

"Yeah! Look. You can't imagine the weirdoes I've shuttled across the sky. I could tell you stories."

"You killed two of my men and badly injured several others."

Lance took the napkin before him and wiped his bleeding lip. It left a bloodstain on the napkin. He replaced it on the table. The prince unfavorably took note. "Then don't point guns at me. But this begs the question, why are you stalking me?"

"No, not you per se. I was here to see the Space Shuttle Atlantis launch this morning. But, I am interested in the girl you were with."

"She was just a fling. A flake, really. But if you will excuse me, sir, I have a flight to get underway." Lance stood. "And while you might be on Saudi soil inside of here. I'm afraid you're grounded on American soil for now."

"Oh, how so?"

Lance put two shots through one of the oval windows. "Good day, your highness."

Chapter 83

Megiddo, Israel

June 4, 2000

"'You, O king, happened to be beholding, and look! a certain immense image. That image, which was large and the brightness of which was extraordinary, was standing in front of you, and its appearance was dreadful. As regards that image, its head was of good gold, its breasts and its arms were of silver, its belly and its thighs were of copper, its legs were of iron, its feet were partly of iron and partly of molded clay,'" Lance read.

"You are reading from the book of Daniel. I can tell," Danny said, taking his seat in his rocking chair opposite Lance.

"The second chapter, but follow me on this, Danny. Daniel is interpreting a dream that King Nebuchadnezzar, the ruler of the then known world, had." Lance found his place. "'You kept on looking until a *stone* was cut out not by hands and struck the image on its feet of iron and of molded clay and crushed them. At that time, the iron, the molded clay, the copper, the silver, and the gold were, all together, *crushed* and became like the chaff from the summer threshing floor, and the wind carried them away so that *no trace* at all was found of them. And as for the stone that struck the image, it became a large mountain and filled the whole earth.'"

"And you find this somehow ominous?"

"If true. Yeah! Please note." Lance found his place. "He says to Nebuchadnezzar at the end of verse thirty-eight—'you yourself are the head of gold. And after you, there will rise another kingdom inferior to you; and another kingdom, a third one, of copper, that will rule over the whole earth. And as for the fourth kingdom, it will prove to be strong like iron. Forasmuch as iron is crushing and grinding everything else, so, like iron that shatters, it will crush and shatter even all these.'" Lance looked up. "The iron, this has to be Rome. No doubt about it."

"It is. The copper is Greece, and the silver is Medo-Persia."

"Then, are we the feet?"

"You mean the feet of iron mixed with clay? What makes you ask that?"

"This is what." Lance found his place once more. "'And whereas you beheld the feet and the toes to be partly of molded clay of a potter and partly of iron, the kingdom itself will prove to be divided, but somewhat of the hardness of iron will prove to be in it, forasmuch as you beheld the iron mixed with moist clay. And as for the toes of the feet being partly of iron and partly of molded clay, the kingdom will partly prove to be strong and will partly prove to be fragile.'"

"I still don't understand your point, Lance."

"Seriously, Danny? Then note." Lance read: "'Whereas you beheld iron mixed with moist clay, they will come to be mixed with the offspring of mankind; but they will not prove to be sticking together, this one to that one, just as iron is not mixing with molded clay.'" Lance looked squarely at Danny. "This fits the United States political and social scene like nothing else I have ever read."

"Lance, you must stop going off on these tangents."

Lance drew an immediate look of annoyance. "A tangent is a straight line. That's the only way I am traveling with this. When I was nine, my school abruptly sent all of us home in the middle of class."

"Why, what happened?"

"Martin Luther King was assassinated. Nineteen-sixty-eight. I remember the race riots that swept the U.S. I remember all the war protests quite well. And now the U.S. is so polarized politically and socially—nothing is mixing with anything anymore."

"This can be said of many nations."

"True. Except, they aren't the current world power on earth."

"Lance, you're putting too much stock in all of this. All this prophecy business may sound good, but it's just words written a long time ago."

"Is it? What I just read has come true. And it may be fair to say it continues to come true."

"Lance, I don't have the energy for this."

"Why would you say that? If people understood the legacy that Nimrod left mankind, with Babylon being the original home of the manmade god."

"They don't care to. They don't want to. They just want their ears tickled."

"I don't understand your attitude of late."

"Because you take all of this too far. There is nothing to learn from the past that will affect our present circumstances. I had hoped in the beginning. But continuous disappointment cured me of that. You will see."

"I'm never disappointed by taking in knowledge, Danny."

"You will come to the same conclusion. I assure you."

"This is why I didn't tell you on a trip to Iraq last month, I hired a car and drove down to Babylon. Do you know what I found? Nothing. Just ruins."

"Did not you read it would be a desolate waste forever?"

"Yeah, but I didn't believe it. It was the capital of the entire world! The famed Hanging Gardens and all that. Many ancient cities have been destroyed and rebuilt. Rome was razed to the ground and rebuilt. London. San Francisco in more modern times. Look at Hiroshima? And it was nuked! They're always rebuilt. But no, not Babylon. Why? I finally saw the reconstructed Ishtar Gate on my last trip to Berlin. It was awesome! So don't dampen my spirit, Danny. Support me."

Danny softened. "Then, forgive me. Please, continue."

Lance found his place once again. "Verse forty-four says: 'And in the days of those kings the God of heaven will set up a kingdom that will never be brought to ruin. And the kingdom itself will not be passed on to any other people. It will crush and put an end to all these kingdoms, and it itself will stand to times indefinite; forasmuch as you beheld that out of the mountain a stone was cut-not-by-hands and that it crushed the iron, the copper, the molded clay, the silver, and the gold. The grand God himself has made known to the king what is to occur after this. And the dream is reliable, and the interpretation of it is trustworthy.'" Lance shut the book. "Did I just read about Armageddon? The real Armageddon."

"Oh, Lance. You asked questions scholars still argue over."

"I'm not interested in arguing, Danny. That's pointless. I'm interested in knowing the truth."

"This is what I say, my boy. You have been blessed with gifts from God. Use them to vanquish evil in the world. This is what has led you to me in the first place. This—I believe."

"The stone was cut out but not by human hands, Danny. It became a kingdom, or, a better word, government, that replaces our human governments. And it rules to time indefinite. That ain't us."

"Lance, be like Moses. He acted as the Staff of God, but it was not by his hand that he accomplished what he did."

"Can a human be the Stone?"

Danny gazed intently at Lance. "Lance. Be the Stone."

Chapter 84

Aden, Yemen
12°48′00″N, 45°02′00″E

October 12, 2000

The U.S.S. Cole had pulled into the Yemeni port earlier to begin refueling. Its four thirsty turbine engines needed to be fed for it to continue as mission capable. It was 11:18 a.m. local time, and crewmembers were lining up in the galley.

A small boat had pulled up alongside the port hull, near the galley area of the ship. It had unnerved several security members on board to allow the craft to approach with no system of warning them off. The Rules of Engagement did not allow them to fire upon the small two-manned boat.

The two men said their peace to Allah and ignited the several hundred pounds of explosives nestled between them.

The name of *al-Qaeda* "The Base" would loom as bright as its logo's full yellow moon. It could rightly be said that this was the prelude to the "War on Terror."

Chapter 85

Dessau, Germany

January 1, 2001

Lance unwrapped a solid copper and exotic alloy disc from its packaging. The disc was twenty-two inches in diameter and an inch thick. "We'll see, laser boy," Lance said in memory of his transportation and argument with laser specialist Professor Anton Krexa more than a dozen years ago.

Lance thought for a moment about the New Year's party at Graham's home in London he had turned down. It was just one minute past midnight, London time. He missed being with his friend, but his work took priority. In the months ahead, the Sparrowhawk would have a new engine. It would be more powerful, more fuel-efficient, and quieter still. His visions propelled him in design and purpose. Lance also was set to incorporate a new bearing design. The bearings in this new engine would be oil-free, suspending its rotating parts on a thin film of air. Lance visited *Mohawk Innovative Technology, Inc.*, or MiTi, in New York, who were the pioneers of this new type of bearing. What Lance wanted from them did not exist, but, like other companies he had dealt with, they rose to the challenge.

Lance packed the disc away for now. He tried not to think of the ominous task that lay ahead. Back in San Diego, Eric would be working on the flesh to Lance's skeleton. The framework was always first. Here in Dessau, Germany, was that start. California was the completion.

***

The last three months in California hit highs and lows in the realm of success.

"Okay, we hit a snag," Eric Pitts said.

"We'll make it work. If we're not precise, we're persistent," Lance replied.

"I didn't go back to school myself to fail now. And given we built this one from scratch, we were bound to hit a snag or two."

Ralston waltzed in. His attention was drawn to the long workbench. He noticed that the front fan of the new engine was different from any he had seen before. He tilted it up. He could see that it was a *blisk*, a single milled piece, but an inner ring separated part of the fan blade that then extended outward to an outer ring.

"You made a shrouded front fan?" Ralston queried.

"New concept, Jeffrey," Lance said. "Twenty large-sweep fan blades for bypass air. But a new inner high-compression design right up front."

"Fascinating. How did you come up with this?"

"The engines on my Mits. The radial compressor is up front. So I thought that we should do the same here. Why start the compression part of the engine further back? It's just wasting space. Except this design compresses the air differently." Ralston noted the inner blades had a very different geometry to them. "All told, we should be getting a thirty-three to one compression ratio, with an increased efficiency of about the same."

"Fascinating," Ralston repeated. He then noted the MU-2 nestled in the corner was without its engines. Two different looking engines rested on cradles under each wing.

"We pulled them after their first three hundred hours for a complete inspection. Our proof of concept works," Eric said. "They'll go back on after we get this baby into the Sparrowhawk."

Ralston picked up one of the axial compressor wheels. It, too, was a blisk and shrouded. It was the same for the three turbine wheels. He noted again that within the front and the back of each shroud, or rim, was a modified air bearing. He understood that once the engine spooled up, each blade assembly would be separated from one another by the same thin film of air as the main bearings, all spinning in near-frictionless harmony. "Wave of the future once again."

"If we were at liberty to tell anyone about it," Lance remarked.

"Yes. It's all still very hush-hush. Just think of all that you do as a testbed for the future," Ralston said.

Jeffrey watched the assembly, even handing out parts and tools as required. The hub of the engine seemed to be where the combustor was housed. Everything was assembled forward and rearward from this point. He handed Lance the smaller of the three turbine wheel assemblies. He noted it was ceramic coated. He was intrigued to learn that the turbine blades were effectively cooled from bypass air coming from the front fan alone. Typically, the turbine section was cooled with power-robbing bleed air from the engine's compressor section. This engine was different.

"This cooling system will have a legacy behind it one day, Jeffrey," Lance added.

"Yes, the potential is widespread in possibilities. But, before we sell your wares to the big boys, I would like to see the agency set up with its own mini air force. I think we are getting there. We have drones, but to have a small air force of, say, Sparrowhawks, or better. I assume better is coming?"

"Yes. The *Echo Jet*."

The next day, Ralston watched the engine spool up and light off. He looked past the cradled engine coming to life before him. He saw it advancing his purposes, things beyond what Lance Rio would ever care to ponder.

Lance watched the Turbine Inlet Temperature hit 1,370° C on the digital readout. That meant that the high-pressure turbine was handling the 2,500° F blast furnace. For such a small engine, it was a milestone. The new air-cooling system was working as designed. Lance reflected that it would move him that much closer to his own set of purposes, things beyond what Jeffrey Ralston would ever care to ponder.

Chapter 86

San Francisco, California
37°47′00″N, 122°25′00″W

September 11, 2001

Lance treated this Tuesday morning like it was a Sunday sleep-in. All he knew was that he did not want to leave the deep sleep world for the groggy world of awake, but his cell phone would not stop ringing. He had a cheerful, melodic ring tone, and yet he still found it annoying. He grabbed his phone. "Hello."

"Lance," Ralston said.

"Yes."

"Turn on your TV and watch the news."

Lance sat up, turned on his light, took the remote, and turned on the TV. He noted it was 7:30 and settled the channel on the Good Morning America news show. He was stunned. It only took a few seconds to see one of the World Trade Center towers billowing smoke about a quarter of the way down from the top.

"What's going on, Jeffrey?"

"You are seeing for yourself. A passenger jet flew into the tower you see in front of you."

"An accident?"

"One might think so, except you are probably watching Tower Two."

"What?"

"Yes. Both towers were hit with passenger jets flown right into them. A third jet crashed short of its intended target, and a fourth passenger jet slammed into the Pentagon."

"Where do you want me?" Lance sprang out of bed.

"Israel. Unfortunately, the airspace over the U.S. is now closed down."

Lance watched the TV screen as he threw his travel bag on the bed. His mini-vacation was over. And then he watched the South Tower blowing out dust, smoke, and rubble collapse upon itself.

Lance would watch the Northern Tower collapse in minutes to come. The world just entered into a new era of chaos.

"Jeffrey."

"Yes, Lance."

"There's no denying it now. Looks like she's in heat again."

"Who's in heat?"

"Are you in your office?"

"Yes."

"Look on the wall. The bitch."

Chapter 87

Megiddo, Israel

October 5, 2001

It could well be said that no intelligence agency supportive of the United States sat on its hands. From the CIA to the FBI, from MI-6 to Interpol, no one slept. Everything was stepped up, moved forward, and pursued. The question of why was important, but not as important as who. Who were the players? The reason why was apparent. The mandate of Islam was *submission*. That's what the name meant. It was not unlike Christendom in the Middle Ages that demanded similar submission—forcibly. There had to be a connection that Lance, in his studies, could exploit. He hoped.

Lance had the Sparrowhawk fueled and ready for his next mission. He was loading a blend of armor-piercing and incendiary rounds into the 1500 round capacity magazine. Eight times so far, he launched from Israel, flew to Afghanistan, strafe al Qaeda and Taliban targets, refueled, and flew home. It had its effectiveness, but it wasn't near the knockdown punch he wanted.

Lance's mobile phone rang. "Shalom, Jeffrey."

"Lance. We have a change of plan, which is still being formulated. Scrap the current mission. Prince Khaled has his two Gulfstream G-Fours fueled and ready to depart to Caracas, Venezuela, for an OPEC meeting. In fact, they're airborne. We know that the Samelson girl is traveling with him, but the other aircraft has certain identified terrorists on board. I want you to splash the second jet. It's time to put the fear of God in this man. I'm working out refueling points for you as we speak. It will be either in Chad or Niger and then a final refueling at Freetown, Sierra Leone. That is before you hit the Atlantic."

"Hit is such an uncomfortable word."

"You know what I mean." Ralston seemed in no mood for levity. "Maybe a thousand miles out, knock the second jet out of the sky and then return home. It will send the warm greeting I'm intending to al Qaeda."

"What about the prince?"

"We figure he will wet himself for now."

"Why not roll that fear into something I can use?"

"How so?"

***

Ralston arched back sharply in his chair at Langley. "Lance, are you out of your mind? Do you know what the logistics are involved in what you are proposing?"

"Jeffrey, just get me to our facility in Nassau, where I can leave the Sparrowhawk. I'll get the forty-five airborne ASAP."

***

Lance flew at supercruise on an intercept course. He made it to the first refuel stop well into Niger, which meant hand-pumping Jet-A out of four 55-gallon drums one at a time to top up the 240-gallon fuel tank. This powered him to the African west coast, where he landed at Freetown-Lungi International Airport in Sierra Leone. Once he left the African coast, it wasn't long before he flew apprehensively into the void of the mid-Atlantic. Prince Khaled's two G-IVs fuel-stopped an hour earlier at Freetown and now had the range to make it to Caracas nonstop, whereas Lance was hoping to bum a ride.

The Sparrowhawk supercruised at sixty-two thousand feet. Lance saw two blips on the right instrument screen. They were Prince Khaled's jets. One of the blips flashed in red—his target. The tracker placed on the aircraft was doing its job.

Radar told Lance he was now just fifty miles out. He moved the thrust lever out of afterburner mode. A moderate sensation of losing speed was felt. He could no longer out fly the impending night behind him. With the thrust lever moved to idle, he descended. "Jeffrey," Lance radioed.

"I'm here, Lance. I'm watching your signal on my computer screen. You're looking good. Right on target. Plus, further arrangements, crazy as they are, are in play."

"Well, my window is getting smaller by the minute out here."

"If necessary, you can make it to Ascension Island."

"Barely this far out. It's spooky out here."

"Focus on the mission."

"You know I'm only forty-three."

"You look twenty-three. And often act it."

"I'm surprised you didn't say childish."

"I was thinking it."

"Well, if you don't want to hear a tantrum, *Bumble Bee* better show up."

"You'll be fine. I'm standing by."

The Sparrowhawk leveled off at forty thousand feet and crept up behind its prey. The other was right above at forty-two thousand feet.

"Target acquired."

Lance followed from behind. He put a small burst inside the tailpipe of the starboard engine. Catastrophic engine failure dragged the bizjet back. Immediately the Sparrowhawk climbed, where it depleted every round of ammunition into the second jet.

Prince Khaled rushed up to the cockpit. He braced himself as the two pilots fought to regain control and steady the aircraft. Khaled saw fiery debris cascade down in front of them. The captain turned sharply to miss the debris field. There was nothing left of the other aircraft, and now they were crippled. The prince moved back to his seat, wondering if he only had seconds more to live. The Gulfstream continued to lower in altitude, where the single running engine would be more effective.

Lance headed the namesake bird of prey northwest at its typical 1,100 miles per hour supercruise speed setting, where he just overtook the encroaching night once again.

He took a moment once all things settled down for him and looked heavenward upon the celestial hosts that painted the night sky. You could see so many more stars at these heights. He felt divinely surrounded.

"Bumble Bee, this is Stinger. Over," Lance radioed. He waited. He found himself reflecting on the idea of ditching at sea again with no reply.

"Stinger, this is Bumble Bee. Over."

"Bumble Bee, glad to hear your voice," Lance said, relieved.

"Stinger, did you get lost out here?"

"I'm just about where I am supposed to be lat and long wise."

"Stinger, then let's get together in say ten."

"Roger that, Bumble Bee. See you in ten."

A young airman had hoped to be gone on leave to a week's worth of fishing hours ago when he was wrangled on board, last minute. The twenty-four-year-old cargo master had hoped to see more action in his fifth year in the U.S. Air Force. Yet, what he was about to do defied reason, but then this was the military. He was securely rigged, clothed in cold weather gear, and carrying supplemental oxygen. His crewman, equipped similar, let out some cable and opened the rear cargo doors. Frigid Atlantic air stirred around him. He took the long hook in his gloved hands and pushed himself out toward the back of the ramp. From out of nowhere came a nose wheel. He kept the small picture in mind until he hooked it and scurried backwards to see the Sparrowhawk being winched in toward him. The main gear rolled up on the ramp. It was a good catch.

After three minutes, Lance shut down the engine and signaled to be winched inside. The doors of the C-17 closed. It would take time to pressurize the cargo hold, so they had supplemental oxygen ready for Lance.

The C-17 increased speed and hustled to the Bahamas, where another part of the apparatus was enroute. The young airman was finally involved in a real black ops mission. There was a single pallet of four 55-gallon drums of Jet-A waiting to be pumped.

Two hours, thirty minutes later, the C-17 slowed again to open its doors and lower its ramp. Lance began the starting procedure. The C-17 pitched up, and the Sparrowhawk rolled out of the aircraft.

The Sparrowhawk was now under its own power. The gear retracted. Lance watched the doors and ramp of his host close, but not before seeing the airman wave. Being a Black Ops flight, he couldn't tell anyone about the one that got away.

***

Lance arrived at Caracas International Airport. He was amazed that Khaled flew his crippled aircraft to Venezuela instead of landing at an airport on the Brazilian coast. Perhaps in fear, he felt that there would be more sympathy for him in an OPEC nation and be less vulnerable in the cover of darkness.

Lance stood in his uniform. He opened the door for his two passengers to exit the Onyx Learjet 45. They appeared to be businessmen but were CIA. Lance put on the brave face of an exhausted charter pilot, which was not a stretch. This nonstop poetry in motion—plot and plan wise left a lot of people worn out. The time between Lance stepping out of his Learjet and the prince's damaged G-IV's arrival was a short eleven minutes.

The G-IV parked to the left of the Onyx Lear 45. It was easy for Lance to walk near the prince's aircraft and look amazed at the destroyed engine. He saw the prince do a double-take from the window. Bodyguards in front and behind the prince soon surrounded Lance. "Lance! Lance Rio!" Khaled shouted.

"Your highness," Lance said, bewildered. "This is your aircraft? I heard the NOTAM about an aircraft in distress but didn't know this was you."

"Saboteurs and thugs are behind this."

"Is it an OPEC thing?"

"Why do you ask this?"

"Because that's why I'm here. I flew in two businessmen from Munich. I just landed."

"There are forces out to get me," the paranoid prince stated.

"I don't understand."

"I am not safe here. Only in Jeddah. You must fly me from here."

"Prince Khaled, I can't just leave my clients here."

"I will pay you for your time. And for you to make other arrangements for your clients. Please. We must go."

"Certainly, the authorities can protect you."

"No. This is the best way before new plots can be formed against me."

"I don't see how I can," Lance said.

"I will pay you one hundred thousand American dollars. Right now."

"A hundred grand? Seriously?"

Prince Khaled snapped his fingers. The bodyguard from the rear stepped forward with an attaché case. He opened it and presented it to the prince, who then waved his hand toward Lance. Lance looked upon row after row of neatly stacked twenty dollar bills. "You always carry around this much cash?"

"I always keep petty cash with me."

"Oh. Right. A moment please."

Lance walked back to the Learjet and poked his head inside. Manny Steiger was stretched out in a mid-row seat. "Ready for a turnaround? To Jeddah?"

"Seriously?" Manny frowned.

"Yeah. I'll take the first leg."

The prince grew impatient. He could see what looked like Lance arguing with his employee. "Lance. It is imperative that we go!"

Lance stepped back from the aircraft and walked back to Khaled. "Okay. You have a deal. We need to refuel and have a bite. It will take around two hours."

"That will be acceptable." Khaled waved. The attaché case was closed and handed to Lance. The prince and bodyguards moved in unison back to his jet.

Nearly two hours later, Lance stepped away from the Lear 45 and waved for the prince to come. Six people came toward Lance. Two were women, both tightly wrapped. "Whoa. Whoa. Your highness, I can only take you and one other. I am using the extra fuel tank for us to get back over the Atlantic safely."

"All right," Khaled said, flustered. "You will take myself and Yousef, my most trusted."

"Then climb aboard," Lance said as he let out a yawn.

"Just stay awake," Khaled said.

"It's been a very long day, your highness. And now it's going to be a long night. I even had a cup of coffee."

Lance recognized one of the young women as the Samelson girl. There were people on the ground set to extract her by morning and send her home. Hopefully, the party girl had learned her lesson, and World War III was now averted.

The Learjet 45 lined up with the runway. Takeoff power was set. The jet sped down the runway. At *Vr*, Lance rotated the aircraft into the night sky. They would fly to Natal, Brazil. There they would refuel and then head back over the Atlantic to Freetown, Sierra Leone, Africa. From there, it would be across Africa to the country of Chad for refueling and then finally to Jeddah, Saudi Arabia—and sleep!

***

Lance woke to the gentle rocking of the yacht. He looked at his watch and figured he cranked out about nine hours of sleep and remembered he was aboard the Crescent Sheik. He dressed and made his way back to the stern of the ship. He made it a point to study every nook and cranny he could. The walls were of teak wood with gold-lined trim, and the carpet was dark green. The seating was in white leather.

He saw Manny enjoying breakfast with their host. "Ah, Lance Rio, come and enjoy breakfast with us, for soon we must depart," Khaled said. "A final favor from you, if you will? I've ordered us back to shore."

The prince was dressed in a business suit covered by a *thawb* or Arabic robe with an *agal* or Arabic headdress. He looked official.

"Good morning, your highness. What favor?" Lance took a seat.

"Due to the horrific nature of events two days ago, the king has summoned me to Riyadh over the matter. I would ask you to take me, and then you may depart with my gratitude."

"As you wish, your highness."

"Ah, splendid. You will eat and refresh yourselves, and then we will be off." The prince looked around and then at Lance. "So, what do you think of my vessel, the Crescent Sheik?"

"She's magnificent." Lance resisted the idea of telling the prince the name sounded like a brand of condom.

"I am particularly proud of her. I spend as much time on her as possible. The sea gives you so much freedom. I imagine the same freedom you experience in the air." The prince noticed that Manny finished his meal. "If I am not being too rude, Mr. Steiger, perhaps I may have a moment privately with Lance."

"Yes. Certainly, your highness." Manny rose and excused himself.

Yousef placed a plate in front of Lance. "Thank you, Yousef."

Yousef smiled. He had a worn feel to his movements and an earthy, pungent smell about him, like a farm animal. This was of interest though off-putting.

"Yousef is my most loyal servant. I love him like a younger brother."

"Yes, I sense he means a lot to you."

"You intrigue me, Lance Rio. I have not come across a man like you. You are dangerous but not a military man. You operate in intrigue, but you are not a spy."

"I just fly planes, your highness."

"But, you are thoughtful and loyal. And you are quick on your feet when need be. I want you to be my personal pilot and bodyguard."

"That's a very kind offer, your highness, but I must decline." Lance noticed a twitch in the prince's expression. "Onyx takes up most of my time."

“I will buy it, and you will come fly for me.”

“I’m simply too independent for that, your highness. Please understand. But, perhaps Onyx Aviation Services could be of service to you. I fly a fast single-pilot operated jet. If you just want me exclusively.”

“I will respect your decision, man of intrigue. But, I may call, and you must come.”

Chapter 88

Megiddo, Israel

October 20, 2001

It had been a quiet day for learning. Lance sat semi-reclined in his chair that faced the bookshelf in the living room. Danny had been out for most of the day but found Lance sitting with his Bible, surprisingly with a copy of the Quran, his notepad, and two reference books sitting open on the side table as he entered.

"Well, my boy, you look admirably ensconced in research."

"I am. The connection I had hoped to find, I think, I have found regarding the children of Abraham. Or put another way—the Middle East conflict."

Danny grinned, put his bags down, and took his chair opposite Lance.

"What did you find?"

"It does step on many toes."

"This subject always does. But tell me."

"The priestly class was to be a separate function from the political class—as specified under the Law of Moses. Separation of church and state, if you will. However, come down to the time of the Maccabees and the Jewish revolt of One-Sixty-Six B.C.E. when they ousted the Syrian Greeks and took back control of Israel, you now also had a definitive blending of priestly and political elements for the first time, which was a big no-no. And should always be a big no-no."

"If you are talking about the Pharisees and Sadducees coming on the scene around this time, this is true. And they came to wield great power."

"Abusive power. Along with the Herods, they became part of a hard diabolical dynasty with scandals that rivaled the Caesars and the Borgias."

"And you blame them?"

"*Am ha'aretz*, Danny. A contemptuous term. But not originally. Nonetheless, they treated the people—like—dirt! No wonder Christ laid into them like he did."

"I understand, Lance. But if you look to equate them with now…"

"Look at the pattern, Danny. It hasn't changed. What do you think the bishops of Rome were? Especially during the Middle Ages. Pharisees with a cross. Look at how they treated the people. The Inquisition. What do you think these Imams were and are? Pharisees with—well, a bad attitude. Hateful. It's just a continuation of that same corruption of the Pharisees. But now I know where it started. You cannot deny their influence even down to this day."

"So you blame us?"

"Us? Who's us? Danny, no group is inherently loyal or faithful. It's always down to the individual. And such things go back even further. Unplug the Jude Dudes—" This brought a small chuckle from Danny. "And plugin, I don't know—the Australians. Whomever! It doesn't matter. The result would still be the same. Why do you think much of so-called faith has been forced by the sword? Traditions of men."

"And what do you think you can do?"

"The Pharisees and Sadducees never had a right to exist under the Law. But then they were appointed by Rome and embraced Greek philosophies over the Law of Moses. The Law they were supposed to teach, represent, and uphold."

"You might be taking this all too far."

"You keep saying that. You said to be the Stone."

"I meant within reason. Otherwise, you will find life very troublesome."

"Danny, all I've ever known is troublesome."

"It would take great power to change the world and bring about peace. Don't be naive."

"I'm not. But you forget. The Stone's *first* priority is to crush!"

Chapter 89

Dessau, Germany

December 7, 2001

Being a jet pilot could send you across several time zones in a single day, but at this time of year, it was the weather zones that got to Lance. Outside of the hangar, it was freezing with moderate snowing. Five hours earlier, Lance was flying back from mildly temperate Greece in his Citation. He could watch the changes to the earth below as he flew northward from Mediterranean mild to snow-covered Europe. He had the gas heaters going inside of the hangar to take the chill out of the air. He would be spending some time here until called elsewhere. He had not spoken to Jeffrey Ralston in over a week.

There was talk on German radio about today being December seventh, the sixtieth anniversary of the attack on Pearl Harbor.

Lance maneuvered himself around his jet to a long table. Lance slipped the heavy copper disc onto the shaft of a new apparatus and nestled it inside one half of the housing. He slid on the other half of the housing. Carefully he placed the first of nine wedge-shaped brackets around the apparatus that held the two halves together. Care was exercised as each bracket contained neodymium alloy super magnets. With over eight hundred pounds of magnetic attractive force per bracket, keeping fingers clear was a must.

Turning on an electric motor, the homopolar generator was operational. The *homopolar generator* was the first device ever created to produce electrical power, invented by Michael Faraday in 1831. Lance's hero, Nicola Tesla, had improved upon the original design, and Lance believed he had improved upon his. What drew scientific and military minds to the simple *homo* or *same* polarity D.C. generator, was that it produced extremely high amperage. There was a large disc built that produced two million amperes. That was what Lance was after, mega-amperage! But in a far smaller package.

The disc rotated to its target speed of 8,000 r.p.m. Cutting magnetic lines of force, the disc generated a staggering 666,492 amperes. Impressive, but not enough. The experiment was a success but not practical for application. Some design changes came to mind to increase magnetic compression. The digital readout caught his attention. 666, a "*man's number*" caused a shallow grin.

He shut down the experiment, resigning himself that it would be at least two months before he could resume his experiments. Then it dawned on him. He reflected on the time while living in Hawaii, his father had taken him to the Pearl Harbor memorial atop the sunken battleship U.S.S. Arizona. Like his parents and all victims of war, whether hot or cold, it needed to end. "Perhaps soon."

Lance's thoughts were pulled from the past with the ringing of his phone.

"Lance. I need you. You must come!"

"What is the problem, your highness?"

"You must come."

"Come to Jeddah?"

"Yes. Come to Jeddah. I will be waiting for you."

The Citation jet was airborne for only two minutes before Ralston called in. "I will be in Jeddah by tonight," Lance said. "I need to take care of something first in Munich."

"That will be fine, Lance. We've been working diligently on spooking the good prince, and now he's reached out to you. You know what to do."

***

Prince Khaled was amazed that Lance did not have a co-pilot when he first arrived in Jeddah. Lance explained that this aircraft was designed for single-pilot operation. It pleased the prince to have such privacy.

Lance flew the prince, with Yosef and two bodyguards, to four stops in Saudi Arabia, up to Syria, back down to Jeddah and then to Pakistan, a stop in India and down to Singapore and finally to Jakarta, Indonesia.

"This is our final stop, my dear Lance. And tonight you can have a good night's rest. I shan't keep you going much longer. We have made much progress in my charities, and I am thankful for you shuttling me around. I have enjoyed it," Khaled said.

"That's fine, your highness. I always wanted to come to Jakarta."

The limo pulled up to a high-rise office building. The prince and Lance stepped out of the vehicle with the others and headed through the revolving doors.

Inside a marble-lined foyer and reception area, Lance studied the security. He followed Khaled into the elevator while the others stayed. The eighteenth floor was selected.

Stepping into the non-descript corridor, Lance followed Khaled to the office three doors down. The small plaque said: CCCF. Lance took quick note of the contact switch inside of the top of the doorjamb as he entered. Khaled turned off the alarm. Lance caught two of the four keys pressed and took note from where the prince's fingers came. He would be able to disarm the alarm within three tries.

Lance walked in a large circle to examine the small reception area. He saw no motion detectors. There were four opaque glass doors that barred entry into those offices. They might be security protected by the alarm system as well.

Khaled entered what Lance figured was his private office. He followed. Lance saw no hint of an alarm system on the glass door.

Inside was a handsome rosewood desk and a computer monitor on it. Khaled sat in his chair. "We do a lot of charitable work from this office complex for this part of the world. We cannot forget the needs of our brothers here." Lance reminded himself that Indonesia held the largest Muslim population in the world, except it was not a Muslim state. Yet, al-Qaeda was just as dangerous here.

Khaled typed on the keyboard. "I run my businesses concurrently alongside it. This is what pays for our ability to do such charity." Khaled struck the keyboard seven times.

"What does CCCF stand for?" Lance asked casually, strolling around the office.

"The Crescent Circle Charitable Foundation."

"I see." This was a place of interest. All Islamic charity organizations were. Was it a front for terrorism as many such charities had been found to be? Lance was going to find out.

***

Khaled had enjoyed his expensively prohibited wine, which Lance was able to add a small sedative to aid his sleep. After dinner at the hotel, Lance made his way out of the lobby in a simple disguise, jumped into a black saloon, and sped away. Mike Castro drove the car.

They went back to the office building that Lance had visited earlier. Mike had the clearance issue to board the elevators already in hand.

On the eighteenth floor and down the corridor, Lance picked the lock and entered. Then worked the alarm and disabled it in two tries. He moved across the reception area to Khaled's office and picked the lock.

Mike Castro moved around the desk to Khaled's chair and powered up the computer. Within four tries, Mike had broken through the encryption. He was in. There was a list of banks that supported CCCF. Only one was known to be started by the prince himself: CRESCENT COMMERCIAL BANK & TRUST, established in 1984. "Will you look at this? There's an account with the Vatican Bank. That's spooky."

"Why should that surprise anyone?" Lance offered.

As quietly as they entered, they left. Lance would go back to his hotel and sleep rather peacefully. The success of a mission always lulled him into a deeper sleep. It was as if he could mentally sign it off and leave it behind. He would be flying Khaled back to Jeddah tomorrow. It would be many refueling stops along the way. At least there was something new for the boys back at Langley to chew on. Khaled was a silent partner in the expansion of Sharia Law to Osama Bin Laden's verbose outspokenness. Al Qaeda was front page in the news and took center stage in the intelligence community. Lance thought about his experiments and the need to get back to Germany.

Chapter 90

Dessau, Germany

April 8, 2002

A new copper disc, twenty-four inches in diameter, spun at 12,000 r.p.m. Everything was scaled up.

Lance was tired, having worked through most of the night. Even so, he was energized along with his generator. The digital readout showed the disc producing 1.1 million amperes. "Cool! Now we're weapons-grade."

A heavy cable of dozens of strands of the same copper alloy as the disc sent the deadly current through it and into the latest design in supercapacitors. A green light told him his experiment was ready for action.

Lance had moved the Citation outside. He wore a Nomex suit for protection. At the other end of the hanger, a one-inch thick large steel plate rested on a stand. Behind it was another steel plate to act as a safety buffer.

He moved behind a meter-long metal barrel with handles at the back end, mounted on a tripod. Short, hollow, plasma charged cables ran from it to the capacitors. The apparatus was part microwave emitter and part reflector. Lance set a high-speed camera in motion, one of the newer, very pricey digital cameras that were becoming all the rage.

Lance aimed the emitter to the center of the steel plate target with a laser and then turned the variable aperture on the front of the barrel to what he thought would produce a small three-inch diameter beam.

It was 6:03 a.m. Lance lowered his welder's hood. He pulled the red trigger. In a millionth of a second, the robust capacitor discharged its electrical fury through the emitter. In turn, the emitter carried the compressed energy through the air sixty feet to target. The room lit up. Lance could feel the surge of heat. He heard mini thunder and the snap, crackle, and pop of vaporizing metal. And then a rush of cold air hit him. The micro-second experiment was over. Lance lifted his hood. The beam of compressed linear lightning vaporized most of the first target, ate away much of the safety steel plate behind it, and burned a six-foot hole in the corrugated steel wall of the hangar.

"Oh, no!" Lance shouted in panic. He ran up to the hole and looked outward into town. He had to hide what he could. No one could know. He had to dismantle the weapon. Yes, it was now a weapon.

So far, no one showed up from town. Fortunately, no one was on the airport grounds either. With a sigh of relief, Lance put away his new toy and brought the Citation back inside. His spy mind ran to the next logical step. He started up the CNC machine and let it continue its work on the turbine blisk assembly, now nearly milled to usefulness.

Lance felt the strain in his back. His great day for experimentation turned into a dreaded Monday. He had to get hold of the company that built the hangar. They were a bit up north near Berlin. Since this was a prefab metal structure, he calculated that only four pieces needed replacing. He would pay out of his pocket and settled on using cash. He couldn't let Jeffrey know. And he needed another place to run his experiments. Lance went upstairs to get their phone number. Even with the promise of extra cash, the crew would not show up until Thursday.

***

Anxiously, Thursday came!

Lance evaded the question of what happened by merely saying: "I rather not talk about it." The repair ran the course of the day, and then everything was seemingly back to normal.

Lance continued to feel anxious. He needed to relax. How could he? He was playing with high-energy fire. More research was required. It also dawned on him that the Sparrowhawk had no weapons bay. One would be needed. A means to control and better direct the beam was critical. The plasma beam was negatively charged and shot to the positively charged metal plates as purposed. However, the plasma beam sprayed and scattered, as shown by the high-speed camera footage. And, of course, it went to ground. The energy blast, like a real lightning bolt, would go to ground. That's why lightning bolts didn't do more damage than they did. The energy was quickly absorbed by the earth itself. This was a major hurdle to solve. The easiest of these to solve was a new aircraft. Lance hit the speed dial on his handy. It rang.

"Hello," Eric Pitts answered.

"Special."

"Hey, Lance! I was just thinking about you. How's the Sparrowhawk doing?"

"Good. But it's time to put the Echo Jet on paper."

Chapter 91

Megiddo, Israel

August 11, 2002

"I never see you, my boy, but rarely now," Danny said.

"I just have a lot on right now, Danny," Lance said as he turned back to the steel slab table. It was a new apparatus Danny had not seen before.

"What does this do?"

"Hang on, I'll tell you in a minute." Lance turned on the machine. Motors came to life. A 30 mm, thick molten slab of material was extruded from the front end of the machine. The white-hot heat quickly turned to red and then to a dull yellow. Lance hesitated for a few seconds and then grabbed it with his bare hands.

"Lance, be careful!"

"It's alright, Danny." Lance pulled what looked like a sheet of white polystyrene foam core material from the machine.

"This is for the new aircraft?" Danny cautiously touched it. It was barely warm.

"Yes, but it's not Styrofoam. It's ceramic foam. Flexible ceramic foam."

"So this is like the Space Shuttle tiles?"

"Except it's much stronger and now flexible."

"How did you solve the inherent rigidity problem?"

"You would think it would be three years at Technion, studying material sciences, but, no. It was an answer on Jeopardy.

"The American TV game show?"

"What is, yes? But now that it works, I'll pack this up and ship it to San Diego."

"But you were just there. You will burn yourself out at this pace."

"Danny, I'm forty-four today, and my time to do what needs to be done is reduced. Let me finish up, and then we'll have dinner. You can tell me about your trip back home to New Jersey."

Danny left Lance to his work. He walked out of the one-time barn and thought of simpler times. It was true. Lance was getting older, though he still looked younger than his years. Danny, on the other hand, was eighty years old. Time had withered away for the onetime Mossad co-founder and farmer.

Lance braced his foot on the bottom of the meter-wide ceramic foam sheet that stood taller than him. He bent it against his knee. He added more force with his hands. The material flexed slightly more. He applied more pressure. Now, he could hear tinny micro snaps propagating. Then the ceramic foam sheet snapped! The material exceeded his hopes by bending better than two inches. This was a milestone and a game-changer. The Echo Jet would not be restrained by heat issues like the Sparrowhawk. It would fly much faster than its sibling. It would have no equal on earth or above.

***

"I think we are headed for war, Lance. They're talking regime change," Eric Pitts said as he held a newly cooled sheet of ceramic foam. "I like this new gizmo, by the way. But you want this bird to be fly-by-wire and then a VTOL. Why does it have to hover? We're not military here."

"Because we're special, Special. Special operations. Outside of that, we're pioneers. We're moving aviation forward." Lance drank the rest of his morning tea and then stared inside the cup.

"Have your epiphany yet?" Eric asked as he placed the ceramic sheet inside of the mold.

"I think so," Lance said blankly. "High-speed siphon pressure. See, the answer is always simple."

Eric stopped. "Okay. Write it down. We need to focus on what we're doing." He wanted to blast Lance for always inventing, yet the last thing he wanted to do was stymie him. However, they were doing something never before done in aircraft building. "Come on then, let's suit up and form this next piece inside of the mold."

A new fabricator in San Diego built them a sort of flamethrower that could heat up the ceramic core material. As the ceramic sheet softened, Lance and Eric pushed the sheet with the steel flat plate pole of the same apparatus, working it quickly into the heatproof mold. The mold had thousands of holes that applied vacuum pressure, pulling the sheet tightly into it. When formed, it would then go into an identically shaped standard mold for the wet layup process. The Echo Jet would exist. Perhaps in time for war. Eric worried for Lance.

***

"So, you are back in Megiddo," Ralston said over the phone.

"Yes. Today is my first full day of jetlag. Right in the face."

"Khaled has been deemed a threat to national security."

"And you would like me to carry out the order?"

"When and where we'll discuss. It needs to be particularly ignominious, I would prefer. Soon it will be time for the hajj, and he doesn't leave Jeddah before then."

"Then, the hajj will be the place. He will die at Mecca."

Chapter 92

Mecca, Saudi Arabia

21°25′00″N, 39°49″00″E

February 8, 2003

It was a logistical nightmare, controlled chaos that planners of the annual event hoped to achieve with the *Hajj*, the Islamic pilgrimage of two million Muslims converging to a single spot on the map.

Lance had observed it as the Muslim Olympics, where faith and finance somehow worked in concert, along with long-suffering and much fatigue. Like the Olympics, the hajj was good for local business. There was everything from food to jewelry to be sold.

The near three months since the order came, Lance had to study with diligence to become a Muslim. It was highly encouraged that Muslims traveling to Mecca come in groups for the five-day quest of purification. Lance was teamed up with MI-6 agent, Whaled "Wally" al Kahtani, a British-born Saudi, who worked with Lance to get him into shape for the journey. Wally made sure Lance understood that the mission was embedded within the journey itself. He needed to have the right mindset, given the crush of people he had to flow and ebb around.

"The prince is up ahead with his entourage. You will know him by his green inner dress as he wears his *ihram*," Wally said. The ihram was the attire, a two-piece white cloth that a man dressed himself in for the hajj. Lance wore his ihram and blended in with the rest.

The *tawaf*—the circling, had begun. Seven counter-clockwise turns around the black-draped Kaaba that was the center of focus. Lance and Wally moved as close as possible to the center, where the prince and his group were. It would be a long and arduous event. It was already hard on the feet. Those who came here may have taken vacation time, but this was no vacation. It was a contemplative focus on one's spirituality. Lance appreciated that aspect of it.

The third tawaf around the Kaaba was not the charm. Lance and Wally had to reset their gait from a medium stride to that of a penguin.

Come the fourth and fifth trip around the Kaaba, they got closer, even close enough for Lance to hear Khaled shout out: "Allahu Akbar!"

"Yeah, God is great," Lance said sourly.

"Don't lose heart, my friend," Wally affirmed.

Lance tried to shake the kinks out of his legs and yet not lose his stride and have someone immediately step on the back of his naked heel again in the simple sandals he wore. "We need to push our way over, Wally. It's now or never."

He forced his way over the chanting and soulful fellow marchers. Lance could see the silver rim on the upcoming corner of the Kaaba that housed the sacred black stone. Some believed it to be a meteorite that came to have religious significance. It was a target for Lance.

Khaled pushed his way over to kiss the black stone, placing his head inside. Lance pushed forward and aimed the simple ring on his finger that would drop him dead in seconds, only to find himself tossed about by the ever-pushing populace. A shove by a dozen people pushed Lance into Khaled, pushing Khaled out of the way and smacking Lance's face into the black stone. It cut his lips. He missed! An elderly man took Lance's face in his hands and said in Arabic: "He has kissed the stone!" Lance felt several pats on the back. The hands slipped from his face as the wave of people carried the joyful man away.

Wally pulled Lance forward, back into the swirling rhythm of the tawaf. "Oh, my friend, you have done something that most true believers will never get to do."

Lance frowned. "So I have. Lucky me."

"Wipe your lips. And let us make the final tawaf. You are doing very well. This is my fourth hajj, and I haven't been blessed to kiss the stone."

"I missed, Wally. I almost had him."

"We can try again when we go to Mina."

"Mina? No, I'm done. The mission's scrubbed."

"Hardly. We can try in the next phase of the hajj. But first, we must offer two Rakaat prayers. And then we must run inside of the Masjid al-Haram, inside of the mosque."

"I don't think I like you right now. I know my feet don't."

"Yes, I know. You can throw some of my stones at Satan."

Inside of the mosque, multitudes hurried in step more than ran between the hills of Safa and Marwah, which reenacted the frantic running of Hagar looking for water for Ishmael, Abraham's firstborn. As the crowd swelled inside the mosque, the pace became slower as the faithful moved back and forth between two green pillars. "You know how this is the world's largest mosque," Lance said.

"Yes," Wally acknowledged.

"It—ain't big enough."

The journey by tired foot the next day was being addressed by Lance to Wally. Wally countered: "Endure Lance. It's a short walk to Mina and our tent. Only six kilometers. Tomorrow we journey fourteen kilometers to Mount Arafat and pray for forgiveness."

Wally traveled in style. Lance gave him that. While they, like all men, wore the ihram to denote equality, the tents with catered food and air conditioning spoke otherwise. Their tent even had a mattress on the ground. Lance planned to rest and then recite prayers. It was good practice to polish his Arabic.

The next day, Day 3 of the hajj saw their journey take them nearly nine miles south to Mount Arafat, where Mohammed was said to give his last sermon in 632 C.E.

"Lance, we are at the Hill of Forgiveness. This is also the place where tradition holds that God forgave Adam and Eve two hundred years after their expulsion from the Garden of Eden."

"That doesn't make sense, Wally."

"Why do you say that?"

"Because Adam and Eve were both warned of the consequences of eating from that one tree. God said if they disobeyed, they would surely die. There would be no forgiveness. They didn't make a mistake that we weak, imperfect humans make. They made a deliberate choice. We suffer because of them down to this day. To say any different would make God—a liar. That he doesn't mean what he says. And what about Moses, or Musa, Wally. He recorded the affair. Is he a liar too?"

"Whoa, Lance. I see your point, but this is the belief in Islam."

"Forgive me then. I meant no disrespect. Let's go find Khaled."

They found Khaled's group listening to Imam Abdul Al-Badr rant and rave politely given where they were. This Imam was not only on Lance's radar but in his sights. He was known to have sent several young men already to their deaths in suicide missions. It was not known if he had a hand in 9-11, but it was known that Khaled was financing this man through his so-called charitable foundations. Lance deemed he had two targets now. Lance was right regarding the Imam's pedigree. He did have a bad, even nasty, attitude—that of a Pharisee.

The night before they left the plains of Arafat and traveled back along their elongated circuitous course back up to the plains of Mina to Muzdalifah, Lance had to think up a new plan that would make the prince's death an embarrassing, shameful one. During the night, he came up with a scheme that caused him to pray for forgiveness to a God he only knew on paper.

Come morning. Lance woke achy and grumpy. Sleeping out of doors, on the ground, in the open air, was the last straw. This was a mission, not a pilgrimage, and it was a matter of enduring failure.

Whaled was up and already collecting pebbles. It was both mission and pilgrimage for him. Lance at least appreciated some of the modern allowances during the hajj. They could leave this area and get a meal. Lance reflected on having pizza at the mall next to the Masjid Al-Haram Mosque. They would be traveling the four miles or so back up to Mina for tomorrow's activity: throwing stones at the devil. At least he would be sleeping on a mattress tonight.

Ramy al-Jamarāt, the throwing of stones to defy the devil, was the action end of the hajj and one that Lance felt a reinvigorated self-presence. He threw his first lot of seven pebbles at the pillar, an obelisk not so dissimilar in appearance from the Washington monument. The pillar was symbolic of Satan the Devil.

"Wally, do you know what the names Satan and devil mean?" Lance asked as he cast his final stone of seven.

"Not in Hebrew," Wally answered as he threw his last stone of the day.

"It should mean the same in any language. Satan means resister. Or one who rebels. Devil means slanderer. One who lies about another."

"Makes sense," Wally said. "Tomorrow, we throw seven more stones at this pillar and the other two that represent each place that Satan tempted Abraham not to sacrifice his son, Ishmael, as opposed to Isaac. I say this out of respect for you, Lance, as you live in the land of the People of the Book." That was a kind way and somewhat code for Wally not to utter the word Israel or the word Bible. They were, after all, in the Kingdom. "And on the third day, we throw seven stones times three again, where we visit the other two pillars."

"Which is why we gathered forty-nine stones in all. What I'd really like is a rock, so if I see Khaled, maybe I can bing him in the head. It would be a far kinder end than what I dreamt up the other night. Sad to say."

"Then it is fortuitous that you are here resisting the Resistor."

Lance thought in actuality if he resisted anything, or did he just play along? Though Islam was not his religion, some of the things he experienced here gave pause to the course his life had taken. He threw one more stone.

"What are you doing? Only seven stones."

"Call it one for good measure."

It was finally the fifth day of the hajj. Exhaustion had spread to all pilgrims and those that supported the event. Lance and Wally did, find Khaled and his group about twenty rows in front of them. Lance did throw a rock that stunned Khaled, but no fatal blow.

For now, it was again the walk, the tawaf around the Kaaba once more before calling his journey over. Lance, could say that he did the hajj from start to finish. It would always be a special event in his life.

Chapter 93

El Cajon, California

March 23, 2003

"So where's home, Lance?" Eric Pitts said directly.

"Why such a loaded question? It's everywhere. Dude, I'm still jetlagged. I've been on the flipping go since Mecca."

"Oh, the places you go, Lancey-boy. That's okay. But, one day I want you to call here home. After this bird, we don't need no super-duper supersonic super machines. We can put together kits we can mass-produce and give people a nice aircraft that will be fun and safe to fly. I want you to promise me we will be doing just that in the near future."

Lance stopped working. He looked Eric squarely in the eyes. "If I should survive what's ahead. After that, I'll call it quits. We can build kit planes to your heart's content. Maybe include that supersonic four-seater."

"With that swing-wing design, you wanted for the Echo Jet?"

"We'll call it the—" Lance re-envisioned an earlier sketch of a fixed main wing that swept forward somewhat and then a pivoting outer wing. "— *Mantis*."

"Okay, I like that. That sounds cool. It's a deal." They shook on it.

The Echo Jet was taking shape. It looked like a beefier version of the Sparrowhawk. It was nine feet longer at forty feet in length and five inches wider. Still, it was a bit sleeker with a new twin-tail design. Lance wanted an X tail design. Eric said no. Regardless, it was a prototype like no other, designed to handle the heat and stress of multi-Mach airspeeds. There was one option left open for Lance, though begrudged by Eric. The ability to make the Echo Jet a true VTOL—*Vertical Takeoff* and *Landing* aircraft. Soon it would be time to put all the pieces together, start her up—and let her fly.

Eric was happy as the day wore on that Lance was with him. War raged in Iraq for the second time in modern history. It was good to have him home.

Chapter 94

Monte Carlo, Monaco

43°44′23″N, 07°25′38″E

June 1, 2003

Lance took his spot that overlooked the harbor. Though race cars or formula one race cars specifically were not his interest, watching them speed around the blocked off streets in a two-mile run, eighty-seven times, was for a point in time—breathtaking.

As the sun settled on the villa-lined principality, Lance moved down to the harbor and boarded a forty-foot cabin cruiser. It was berthed across from the Crescent Sheik. Prince Khaled made the yearly pilgrimage that catered to his epicurean sense of philosophy.

The CIA had found its way to Yousef, Khaled's most trusted manservant, and turned him. Greener pastures were promised to Yousef on the other side of the hill. He need only to cooperate. Desperately, he agreed.

Lance was overly agitated and found it hard to settle down. "You're late," Ralston said sternly.

"I needed a moment," Lance growled.

"You threw up again? Get over it. This is your op."

"I can't watch that stuff anymore. Perverts."

"It's nothing we haven't done a couple dozen times before, Lance. We aren't dealing with the delightful. We deal with the depraved. Nor do we deal with saints. We deal with the sadistic. Let it go. It's all going to plan. Plan B, that is. Now suit up."

It looked to be going right. Two members of the security team always remained onboard the Crescent Sheik. They dropped, each catching a silenced bullet. A dark figure moved in and put the dead men in the water. The bodies floated for a moment and then were plucked under.

Minutes later, Lance surfaced from the still water of the harbor. A hand reached out to him from the stern.

Onboard, Lance doffed the thin, dry suit and donned the black hood of an al Qaeda terrorist. Lance, code name: *Fish*, helped Roman Sanders, code name: *Rover*, prepare. Rover went up to the bridge. Fish went below deck.

Khaled had a change of mind in satisfying his closet passions in the usual sex villa he frequented incognito when in town. So, Plan B was quickly set in motion.

Yousef stood in front of the double teak doors leading to Khaled's bedroom suite. Lance came from behind him. Yousef turned, trembling. "I am about to be free?"

Lance spoke in gruff Arabic but consolingly. "You are soon to be liberated and start a new life." He saw that Yousef was carrying a suitcase. "No travel bags. Only the clothes on your back. Go, put everything back as it was. You must leave this old life completely. Trust us. You must be calm to greet Khaled when he comes." Lance held up his drysuit. "After, put this on and swim to the small flashing green light. You are nearly free. Now go." Lance patted Yousef on the shoulders as he passed him. He could well imagine the physical abuse that Khaled had put him through over the years.

Lance entered. He set up and hid two small digital cameras that caught the bed from different views. "How does the feed look, Mother?"

"Fish, the feed is good," Ralston said, code name: *Mother*. "All we need are the participants who are making their way now."

Lance could hear Khaled tell his two accompanying bodyguards to go up top. A tall, very blonde man wearing a white dinner jacket entered. He looked around. He noticed the two crossed swords mounted above the headboard.

"A beautiful bedroom," the man said. He sounded Scandinavian.

"You make it all the more beautiful, you lovely man," Khaled said.

Lance winced as he observed on a small wrist-mounted flat screen monitor. Given what he had witnessed at the sex villa earlier, Plan A was all for naught. Lance reached for his Glock-17, 9-mil. His left hand screwed on the suppressor. He would end this. Letting it go on longer would not embarrass the Saudi royal family to any higher degree and expose Khaled's hypocrisy.

Lance sprung open the closet door and aimed at the blonde man, now sitting up in bed.

"Lance, wait!" the blonde man whispered intensely.

Lance found himself the one now trembling with every permutation of thought possible. "David?"

"Yes, Lance, it's me," said David Nance. "Our guy baled. I'm back up."

"No. Please, not you. I can't do this anymore."

Lance's hurried steps down the corridor came to a stop. Rover stood in his way. "You intend on stopping me, Roman?"

"No, Lance. But are you going to let that evil man go? Or are you going to put a stop to everything he stands for? This is your Op. You tell me."

Lance didn't have time to wrestle with his conscience, now screaming at him. "Fine. But, we wrap it up now."

"No! We stick to the plan! All of it!" yelled Mother through their earpieces. Both Lance and Sanders had to rub their ears.

Lance stared at David. Khaled was still in the bathroom with the door closed. "How long do you—"

"We'll discuss it later," David said. "Now shoot me."

"Darling, I shan't be but a moment longer," Khaled called out.

"Ew!" Lance said, snarling up.

"Never mind, ews and icks! Focus!" Mother demanded.

Khaled came out in smiles. His heart sank when he saw the blonde man lying dead in a pool of blood. Lance stepped out in front of him. "*Liwat*!" he shouted in Arabic, taking aim.

"Do you know who I am?" Khaled shouted back in Arabic. "I am Prince Khaled Mohammed bin-Aziz al-Saud. How dare you enter my private quarters!"

"Beautiful. He just identified himself. Mother should be pleased," Sanders said.

"Mother would have been more pleased if we had them in the act," Ralston replied.

"No matter. It's dealt with."

Sanders was right. He heard the muffled thwack of two shots. And the sound of a body hitting the floor. He then looked at his wrist-mounted monitor. Lance took a sword from above the headboard. Khaled was on his back, still alive. The sword was lined up with Khaled's neck.

"Allahu, Akbar!" came the shout. Khaled paid according to Sharia Law.

***

Danny Sharon watched from the porch as Lance connected the electric tug and backed the Sparrowhawk into the barn. Danny sensed that things were not right since Lance returned from the mission in Monte Carlo.

Lance nestled the homebuilt bird of prey into its shelter. He removed his bag and closed the back canopy. He caught movement behind him. "David!"

"I came to visit. I've always had an open invitation up here at the ranch."

"Yes. Yes, of course, you have." Lance looked shamefully at David. "I'm done with those types of missions."

"What does Jeffrey say about that?"

"You mean did. He yelled profusely. And I hung up on him."

"That explains his lousy mood of late. But, look, Lance, I'm disturbed that you're disturbed. I don't want my sexuality to come between us."

Lance winced. "Yeah, but you never came off that way. Or shoved it in my face. And I never saw you in bed before about to do gay."

"So, that's it? We're not friends anymore?"

Lance put his bag down. "I've been in this business twenty years now."

"Wow. Has it been that long? Yeah, I guess so."

"Remember when I was just a contract pilot for the Agency—and scared? Jeffrey sent you to help me. You said not to worry. You were my new big brother. I'm still very grateful to you for that, David."

"So we're bros?"

"Yes, we're bros."

"But you're not happy with me. Do you think by choice I decided to be gay? Come on. Do you think that I would choose a lifestyle that has so much prejudice and condemnation to it? Why would I want to put myself through that? Hey! God made me this way."

"No, David. God did not make you this way. You are a product of human imperfection, as the rest of us."

"So you are saying is that I just gave in and accepted it? I chose this lifestyle?"

"You did. Not how you were born. But the other."

"You are so wrong, and I never figured you for a homophobe."

"I have no fear of homosexuals, David. You're confusing fear with acceptance."

"What does it matter? I'm going to burn in hell anyway, right?"

Lance sighed. "No, David. You're not going to burn in hell."

"The Bible doesn't say kill the gays and let them burn in hell?"

"No," Lance said with a small grin. "It doesn't."

"Yeah, I bet."

Lance grew annoyed. "You listen. Do you imagine thousands of years ago there were no gay people here in Israel?"

"I never thought about it."

"Now you are. Do you imagine that when parents noticed their sons or daughters lacking interest in the opposite sex as they grew older, it unnerved them, given the exacting nature of the Mosaic Law? You better believe it did."

"You mean the death penalty? Say it."

"Yes, for committing homosexual *acts*, it carried immediate execution."

"And of course, you don't find that just a bit too harsh?"

"At first. Naturally. But then I looked at it from a perspective other than my own."

"Yeah, whose?"

"Guess."

"Oh."

"What I came to realize is it's about family, David. The family unit and the imperative nature of preserving it. That's why adultery carried the same punishment. The family. The foundation of civilization."

"Well, things are different today. I'll probably get married one day—to a man—and sorry, but you'll just have to accept it."

"Okay."

"Yeah, I bet okay."

"David, what do you want from me? I'm no judge of you."

"Then accept me."

"When have I not?"

"Then accept this as the wave of the future."

"No. It's the wave of the past."

"Oh, I get it. This is about Sodom and Gomorrah. Nobody knows if those cities really ever existed."

"If you dig deep enough, they usually turn up. But I was thinking more like ancient Greece or Rome. Gay marriage is nothing new. Heck, Nero was reported to have married two men. Danny has a copy of this lesbian love letter written around three hundred B.C. in ancient *Koine Greek*. It's quite poetic. Same-sex people cohabited openly back then too."

"Be that as it may, I'm dealing with the here and now."

"And expecting a difference? I see."

"Do you have to sound so glib?"

"David, those empires imploded because the family unit died. Now, being honest, how does it look today? You know, in the here and now?"

"I'm not oblivious. I see the mess and where it's heading."

"Then, in reality, aren't you being just a bit old-fashioned."

"Funny," David snarled. "Because of a few parallels?"

"Identical repeat. But then I saw our current swing start back in the late sixties."

"Oh, come on. You were just a kid."

"Yet, I saw the changes. Look. I saw Two Thousand and One when I had just turned ten in Nineteen-sixty-eight and got it."

"Man, no one got that movie!" Lance smiled and waited. David calmed somewhat apologetically. "But, I know what you mean. So where do we go from here?"

"Well, firstly, you will come in and shake the dust of travel off of your feet. And tomorrow, I'll take you to hell."

"Excuse me?"

"Don't worry. I doubt if you'll have the same reaction I did."

David clued in. "Because of that priest from way back when?"

"Which only you and Danny know about."

"Don't worry. Your confidence continues to be well placed."

"I know." Lance trembled sorrowfully. "I just know the thought of losing my friend has been too much to bear." Touched, David held his arms outstretched, his head cocked. Lance grinned. "Okay. Now you look gay."

"Yeah, whatever. These are the same arms that held you when you cried your eyes out over Beverly."

Lance did not know how long there would be those arms to hug him. He wrapped his arms around his friend, not wanting to let go.

***

Jeffrey Ralston had come over the years to feel a bit unnerved at times when he took his chair in his office at CIA headquarters. Here, he had full resources available. But distance was still distance. He had been with the Agency too long to ignore personal problems with those under him. Just a month ago, he ordered a case officer home from an operation because he knew a divorce was looming. The officer needed to be home with his family. He made it so.

Mike Castro, Joshua Wilson, and David Nance sat before Ralston. "As always, I'm glad to see all of you back here again, safe and sound." Ralston turned to Mike Castro. "I will be looking forward to your report, Mike, and for that matter you as well, Joshua, with the situation on the ground in Iraq since the war ended." Ralston took pause. "But, my worry is with Lance. David, you were last with him."

"We had a great week together. We cleared the air. Lance voiced his concerns, well, as only Lance can do."

Ralston rolled his eyes. "Yes. No doubt. He has great love for you, David. For all of us. We've been his only family if you think about it." Ralston sighed. "He's out past the stars sometimes, which reminds me. Who the hell is Trelane?"

The three men looked dumbfounded.

"Trelane, Trelane," David said. "Oh! He's a character from the original Star Trek. He's a super being that took the form of a human and can turn energy into matter at will. Some think he was the precursor to the character Q on Star Trek: The Next Generation, who was also a super being that could manipulate matter at will and materialize a human body."

"I guess it makes sense. Anyway, how is his mind?" Ralston asked.

"He still has a lot of fight in him. That's for sure. But, I think he's done, Jeffrey," David offered.

"Done?" Ralston sat up. "There's still so much for him to do. However, he'll be traveling back to San Diego soon to complete the Echo Jet. It'll give him a break for a while. Now that Khaled is neutralized, there is still Imam Abdul al-Badr to focus on. And I want to know him."

***

"I've finished, Danny," Lance said. He closed his Bible and sat it on the end table, finishing his notes on a yellow tablet. His sixth.

"Well done, my boy," Danny said, taking his rocking chair opposite Lance. "And…"

"And I'm still perplexed, complexed, and suplexed."

Danny chuckled. "Most recently?"

"The Four Horsemen for one."

"Ah, of the Apocalypse."

"One of these Rough Riders was given a long sword to take *peace* away from the Earth. Followed by the *disease* horsey and the *starvation* horsey."

"Do you believe what you read was inspired?"

Lance shrugged aimlessly. "How—do you—ignore the knowledge, all the truths, exposed lies that years of study and research have given you? True enough, there is no peace. Especially not since Nineteen-fourteen, when these horsemen seem to have started their ride."

"My usual curiosity."

"World War One was supposed to be the war that ended all wars. Right? Instead, it began the bloodiest period in human history. These horsemen fit that reality perfectly."

"I still believe you are meant for greater things than being a spy."

"Please don't tell me a politician."

"Oh! No, nothing so redactive as that."

"Then how do I fight this long sword?"

Danny thought. Then he smiled. "Rock—Paper—Scissors."

"I don't follow."

"Rock crushes scissors. Or another way to look at it, stone crushes sword."

"Be the Stone?"

"My boy, be what you were called to be. Be the Stone!"

Chapter 95

Gillespie Airfield: El Cajon, California

November 21, 2003

The Echo Jet stood on its landing gear. The fuselage was painted in similar blue tones, dark and medium, like that of the Sparrowhawk. The ceramic-based paint was designed for high heat applications. The four wings were painted and ready for installation.

Ralston looked pleased. "Is there any reason why the Echo Jet should not be flying by year's end?"

"None," Lance replied.

"Good." What stood before Ralston was the equivalent of the SR-71 Blackbird. Possibly he dared think the new F-35. Notwithstanding its sophistication, the Echo Jet was still a kit plane. The kit plane industry had been leading innovation in general aviation for over a decade. Perhaps here, the same was true.

***

Ralston had an al-Qaeda target just outside of a large training camp that bordered both the foot of the Noshaq Mountain and Hindu Kush mountain range and the desert in the northeastern territories of Afghanistan. It was also close to the border with Pakistan. It was somewhat isolated, thus ideal for training recruits and the pep talks that kept them on their murderous course. The camp was first discovered by the British SAS in early 2002, about six months into the campaign, to fight al-Qaeda and Taliban forces in the region.

Lance looked at his instruments. He brought up the digital page of the top view outline of the Echo Jet. Outside skin temperatures registered over 400° F. The nose and front windscreen were hitting temps over 700° F., flying at Mach 3.3., at 80,000 feet. Inside the canopy, however, it was mildly warm against the palm of his hand. Much better. He cruised at the same speeds and altitude that the SR-71 Blackbird typically operated above the earth's surface.

Lance could see Mount Noshaq in the distance as the early sun rose in the east. He mused that Noshaq was over fifty thousand feet below him, which gave him a shudder as to what he had accomplished. It was time to take the aircraft out of hyper-drive and slow down to subsonic. He brought the afterburner thrust lever back to off, and then he pulled the main engine thrust lever back to idle. There was a firm sensation of loss of speed though it would still take time to slow down below Mach 1. At the extreme speeds he was traveling, it was relatively easy to overshoot a destination. The Echo Jet commanded a whole new set of respect for its prowess. His experience gained from the Sparrowhawk prepared him for the Echo Jet.

"Are you nearing your position yet?" Ralston voiced over his headset.

"Soon," Lance said.

"Our Special Operations Group will be feeding you intel directly. You will be taking out both al-Qaeda and Taliban forces."

"I remember them before they were Taliban. When we fought the Russians together."

"That was a different world ago. You can thank Dr. Abdul Al-Badr for funding and inspiring these guys."

"I did offer the cure."

"What? Oh yes. Well, I think more than Moses is needed here."

"Destroying the lie that fuels this madness can be more damaging than destroying a camp, Jeffrey."

"Echo, this is Ant Hill, over."

"Hold on, Jeffrey. Ant Hill, this is Echo, over."

"Echo, be advised that bad guys are mounting up for early morning raid. Are you ready to ruin their day?"

"Roger, Ant Hill. I'm a few minutes away. Stand by, Jeffrey."

"Understood. Standing by."

Lance engaged his optical equipment and zoomed in to his target below. He saw five vehicles traveling in tandem along a dirt road. They were small pickup trucks. He could see each truck bed packed with Taliban holding up their AK-47s. He turned on the weapons system master switch. He came low over the dirt road. He followed the dust trail. Lance kept bleeding off speed until he could set the first notch of flaps and slow down. He snuck up behind the targets. He was too close, and it was too late for the Taliban soldiers that caught sight of him. He fired, pushing slightly on the right rudder pedal and then on the left to create a spray pattern. He emptied all 2,000 .50 calibre rounds from the latest version of the six-barrel Minigun, the M-150. He added power for the first time in half an hour, leaving behind a burning end to his prey.

Chapter 96

Jeddah, Saudi Arabia

June 7, 2004

Khalid Mohammed Al-Wahidi, or Lance Rio, was a relative of Jamil Mohammed Al-Wahidi or Mike Castro. Lance and Mike rose again from their bow with a hundred other men in the mosque before Dr. Abdul Al-Badr.

"We are besieged by the Infidel," Dr. Badr shouted. "They dare step foot on holy ground. Our reward is to hurt them as our brothers did in New York. Our reward is in Heaven."

"Lying Pharisee," Lance growled quietly.

The service was over. Lance had befriended the good doctor by several modest donations that led to several private meetings. Lance took the initiative to hug the Saudi clergyman and plant a small bug on him.

Lance and Mike had pizza delivered to their apartment. They listened in on the receiver. Dr. Badr continued his diatribe about Westerners and Zionists. Notably, he had five newly selected recruits for suicide bombings.

"This guy is one evil dude," Mike said.

"We need an angle on him," Lance said, pushing his food away.

"I know. We'll find one."

Dr. Badr dismissed his staff. He was alone. He dialed on a cell phone. Lance did not understand the greeting Dr. Badr gave over the phone. It wasn't Arabic. "Wait. Is that a Pushtun dialect I am hearing?"

"No. No. It's Farsi," Mike said. "This guy is speaking Farsi."

Lance smiled. "The good doctor is Persian."

"Looks like we have our angle," Mike added.

It was no secret that Iran looked to exploit terrorism, using Muslim fanatics from neighboring countries while keeping their fingernails clean. You never heard of an Iranian suicide bomber. Iran, being predominately of the *Shiite* faction of Islam, hated by nature the predominately *Sunni* faction in Saudi Arabia.

"What is he saying?"

"He will be flying to Tehran in the morning."

"And so will we," Lance confirmed.

***

The game of musical spies at Jeddah International proved to be straightforward and successful. Badr was spotted going into a water closet and coming out as someone else. Lance had him pegged. Badr would be tailed to his place of origin—Iran.

Mike and Lance were on the same flight along with half a dozen other operatives on their first leg of the journey to Dubai, where travel visas would be waiting, and then on to Tehran.

***

Lance strolled through the Tehran International Airport terminal to the exit, sporting dirty blond hair, blue-gray eyes with his luggage in hand. He slid into the back of a waiting car. He was in the land of the *Supreme Leader*, where the game with Muslims was played differently.

A three-car team, which Lance was riding in car one, moved into position to tail the black Mercedes-Benz saloon that drove east from the airport. Shortly, the car Lance was in split off from behind the luxury sedan, and another car came in behind it. It was safe to believe that the man known as Dr. Badr did not know he was being tailed.

Twenty minutes later, Lance's car came within three vehicles behind the black sedan.

"We are heading to Mellat Park," the driver said. There were no names given. Lance knew the young man, perhaps all of thirty, was part of the underground to topple the current Islamic régime in favor of a secular state. Since the fall of the Shah of Iran in 1979, Ayatollah Khomeini took power and became the supreme leader of Iran, instituting *velayat-e faqih*, or "Islamic Rule." His successor, Ayatollah Khamenei, mirrored his directive. The very rigid Islamic state did, as a matter of course, round up those sympathetic to the former Shah's régime and execute them. Thousands died. Thus, Khomeini had fully imposed absolute authority. Their lives were never to be the same. His philosophy was to be spread to all Muslims and be exported in the form of new revolutions within the Islamic world. Iran was funding Gaza in their attempts to drive out the Israelis. Lance would never let that happen on his watch.

The third car in the tailing operation came right behind the black sedan. They both turned onto Taheri Street. The car Lance rode in turned left and drove parallel to the park and then turned right and came around the other way. By then, the others had landed their fish. They now knew from which condominium building this man resided.

Lance got a good look at the driver in the third car. She was a woman. She wore a hijab that became compulsory under the new Islamic rule, something not disclosed at the time of women's support for the new régime. Now the women of Iran were stuck with it. Not trusting in nobles, nor the son of earthling man, came to mind. Then his thoughts drifted back to the Echo Jet and what he could authoritatively implement on his own.

"She is my wife," the driver said. "You can call me Reza. We will know which unit this man lives in by tomorrow. And then you can come to know him."

Two days later, intel had informed that this man had visited the Ministry of Intelligence and National Security building not far from his condo. Lance came up to the rather elegant stone-white building that had twelve floors to it. He entered the lobby, made his way to the elevator, and stepped out on the fifth floor.

Lance scanned the door for any electric or electromagnetic signal. There was one at the upper left-hand side. Lance slid in the thin magnetic strip and picked the lock. He was inside. He looked for any sign of motion detection. He saw none. The reflective shine of sunlight on the marble floors guided him toward the living room. Another door led to what was the man's office. A desk faced Lance. He came around it. He turned on the computer and picked the locks to the drawers, and began going through them. "I'm in. He has a desktop computer that's powering up." He plugged in an encryption-busting flash drive.

"Understood. Standing by," came the voice of Mike Castro.

Lance let the flash drive do its work. In the meantime, he took many pictures with a tiny digital camera. It was the latest in spyware. Much of what he photographed was in Farsi, but some pages of English now surfaced. And then, there was a picture of him closing the door to his Citation jet. Lance felt a great wave of angst flush through him. He also saw pictures of what he assumed to be an American, perhaps a businessman. The next photo was disturbing. It showed the Iranian spy and the American businessman handing AK-47's to a group of Arab men. Lance figured they were Hezbollah or Hamas who operated freely north of Iran. These groups were empowered in Gaza, within Israel, and in Lebanon, and significantly in Syria. More arms, more killing with money being made over it. Lance found another picture of him, but with Beverly. The photo looked to be taken when they were in Gibraltar. Lance felt sadness and hurt in his heart. Whatever this man was up to, Lance had somehow fit into the equation.

Lance removed the flash drive from the computer and turned it off. He replaced the photos and documents and locked the drawer.

Lance made his way to the front door and looked out of the peephole. He saw figures standing just to the side of the door. Quietly, he moved back and went to the glass sliding door and out on the balcony. "What's wrong?" Mike asked.

"Unfriendlies waiting for me in the corridor." Lance hopped over the railing and lowered himself and dropped a foot or so down to the balcony's railing below him. He repeated the movements until he was safely on the ground. Mike shook his head. A quick casual stride across the street, and he was in the car. They drove off.

Later, after Lance forced himself to eat, given his startling revelations and incoherent intrigue, he took Reza aside. "Listen, I need an honest translation of some of this stuff I recovered. Will you translate for me privately?"

"Yes. I will help you."

"After my friend leaves tomorrow. My life may well be in your hands, Reza."

Mike Castro left Reza's home come morning and was taken to the airport for a flight back to Dubai and then a British Airways flight to London.

Lance looked at his watch. It bugged him that the readout was a bit harder to see. He put his laptop up on the table and waved for Reza to sit by his side. "Okay, Reza, please tell me what it says. All of it. And then tonight, I will take you and Afshan out to dinner."

The dinner conversation was all about the wonders of Iran that a tourist would enjoy seeing and experiencing. There were many. The political and religious elements were at the heart of the problem that hindered most from enjoying what a country like Iran had to offer. The meal was enjoyable. It settled Lance down enough to appreciate the genuine concern from Reza and Afshan. More importantly, in Lance's mind was their safety. They were young to carry such a burden of toppling a régime. He thought of his device that could throw linear lightning bolts if he could only make it work.

At home with Reza and Afshan, Lance spent time going over more of what he discovered. They did not understand all of it but knew that Lance had been betrayed.

***

Lance was back home in Megiddo.

"Danny, please tell me you would never betray me."

"My boy, what has brought such a question?"

"I've always operated anonymously. Well, mostly. Now I am known by this Persian."

***

There were new visitors to the kibbutz, which always unnerved him if he had to take the Sparrowhawk out. He kept the Echo Jet in the same hanger as his Citation at Megiddo Airport. While they were somewhat isolated, Danny's farmland was still a place where people came to be one with nature. Fortunately, they were on the other side of the property.

Lance was set to paint the new barn, starting with an oil-based primer to seal the wood thoroughly. Danny trusted Lance's knowledge and former expertise of his onetime occupation. Lance worked alongside several people from the U.S. and the U.K. and a French couple who recently joined the kibbutz. This is how they chose to spend their vacation time. Lance orchestrated his eager team of six behind paint rollers on long poles.

"That's it, rather than soaking up the sun on some beach. I want to paint," a familiar voice said.

"Hey, Graham, you made it!" Lance shouted. Lance pulled off his glove and shook Graham Rye's hand. "And we're priming. A great paint job starts with good solid priming."

"Paint won't do as well?"

"The primer is specifically designed to soak in and seal the pores, so the paint has a thicker film on top. *The primer goes to ground*."

"Goes to what?"

"That's the answer. *Primer goes to ground*!" Lance had his revelation. This was the answer to *baraq*, the Hebrew word for lightning.

"Mate, you're not making sense," Graham said.

"No, G. I'm making perfect sense. I get it now." Lance put down his paint roller and walked away from the guests. "I may be in big trouble. Someone I work with has outed me. I think it's Jeffrey. I don't know how and I don't know why."

"No, mate. I don't see it. He's gone too many extra miles for you."

"Then why does an Iranian spy whom I thought was a Saudi cleric have photos of me?"

"What? Okay. I'm here now. Let's go see what's up."

Lance drove his Mazda pickup back to the house with Graham following in his rental car. He had a group of people that cared about him and would help get to the bottom of the mystery.

***

Lance made a major decision on this trip to Dessau. He had emptied the seats in the cabin of the Citation to make room for the *Baraq* device, the tentative name for his death ray weapon.

"So, this is it?" Danny asked.

"This is it," Lance said as he boxed up the parts and moved them inside the jet.

"Perhaps you will fulfill some prophetic value after all. History at least," Danny offered.

"As it has been said, prophecy is just history written in advance."

"I am honored that you have taken me into your confidence, Lance, but tell me, what do you hope to see it accomplish?"

"Unity. Peace. One thing about first-century Christianity is that it truly was an international brotherhood. And it was achieved within a few decades despite the opposition of the Roman Empire. And others. There's been nothing to equal that phenomenon to date. And there needs to be."

"A tall order, my boy."

"Not if you can turn any opposition into ash."

"You make me nervous with this talk. But making it happen is another story."

"Now that I know what to do, you're going to see this stone—rock—and roll."

***

Lance thought about this place called Megiddo and how it was the root word for Armageddon. Its record of decisive battles that shaped world history was not wasted on him. Lance embraced its significance.

He was ready to demonstrate. It didn't matter that he turned forty-six years old on this eleventh day of August. He worked through the negative thoughts of running out of time.

Lance unhooked the small trailer from his pickup and left it at the end of the road that served as his runway. The trailer held four—one-meter square plates of thick steel. He drove back to the barn where Danny stood, looking apprehensive at the alien device mounted on another trailer. Lance hitched it up and drove it partway down, so the two trailers were four hundred meters apart.

The sun was setting. The kibbutz was void of guests at present. Those few that lived on the land were in their homes, at the other end.

The newest disc, at thirty inches in diameter, produced just over 2.5 million amperes of power. Eighteen brackets ran the circumference of the housing. He charged two String supercapacitors, his design, up with five million amps at the ready. "These two modules are ionizers. This one will deliver a medium-strong negative ion beam. This other module will deliver a much stronger positive ion beam."

"Why can't you just use the positive ion beam since the baraq beam, as you call it, is negatively charged?"

"Simple. The first beam being negative will dope the target. Whatever the target may be. The stronger positive ion beam will be attracted to that beam or negatively ionized target. It will act as the actual primer. It will seal the ground, or I should say the target surface. When the main beam is discharged, it will be attracted to the positive primer beam. What should happen is that the main beam's energy should stay on the surface and not go to ground."

Their conversation lessened as it went dark. Lance turned on the system. He targeted the steel plates down the road. The laser's red dot proved the microwave-plasma emitter, i.e., gun barrel, was correctly aligned. "Lower your hood, Danny. We're about to unleash two point five gigawatts of energy."

Lance started the high-speed digital camera rolling. There was another digital camera, fifty feet from the target already running. Lance lowered his welder's hood. He pushed the RED button. The small computer circuit responded by discharging the high voltage negatively charged particles along the microwave beam. A half-second later, the computer released the high voltage positively charged particles along the same linear beam. They could both see an intense electric flash as the two dissimilar electrically charged particles embraced. Another half-second later, in that anticipated one-millionth of a second, the computer triggered the plasma gas switch and emptied every bursting electron into the emitter. The three-inch diameter superheated linear bolt shot down just feet above the road and slammed into the steel plates. The flash was enormous. A mini-wave of thunder was created, hitting Lance and Danny. Lance lifted his hood. Danny did, likewise. They saw a few flames at the target site.

"Let's go see the results." They jumped into the truck and drove down the road.

At the target site, the acrid smell of burnt steel and tires was quite strong. Virtually nothing was left of the steel plates or the trailer that supported them. Even in the oncoming darkness, an eerie charcoaled presence of the steel plates and trailer were seen on the melted asphalt road, not unlike a nuclear shadow.

"Danny, what have I done?"

"Oh, my boy. You have done a great and fear-inspiring thing."

Lance felt his stomach knot up. He knew he was playing with fire from God.

Chapter 97

Gillespie Field: El Cajon, California

September 30, 2004

"You know I've been working like a dog?" Eric Pitts stated as he pushed.

"We're doing things in record time," Lance replied as he steered the tow bar.

"Well, the wife and the kids are coming down on me about me living here."

"It will calm down now." They stopped. The Echo Jet was inside the hanger.

Lance would be here for a couple of months or so to install the new VTOL fan system. The results were many arguments over the phone with Eric, who finally backed down and agreed on the new front fan system. Just as he went along with the new fuel injection system that required a new combustor that also needed new changes to the engine. It was hard enough to engineer the clamshell doors that closed to deflect the engine exhaust for VTOL flight mode.

Eric was overwhelmed. It was just after midnight. Come the morning, he and Lance would begin the engine removal, modification, and reinstallation project. The new engine mod would extend range and speed to scary!

The single-piece, three-tiered front fan was a marvel of engineering, or so now Eric claimed.

Ralston entered somewhat bright and bubbly in the afternoon. "And what do we have here?" He took note of the front fan that Eric and Lance held in their hands as the two slid it onto the front of the engine and bolted it in place.

"The outer or third tier is comprised of seventy-two blades that blow the air forward instead of backwards, for vertical lift," Lance answered.

"That's very clever." Ralston studied the outer ring of blades. He could see that the inner and second-tier blades moved the air back through the engine while the short, outer blades were angled forward. "Doesn't this put a lot of unnecessary drag on the engine?"

"No. The chamber that feeds air to the VTOL fan is kept in near-vacuum until the rear air intake doors open. Think of it as *On-Demand* VTOL like the Harrier Jet. And it saves space. Real estate is valuable in an aircraft. Remember, aviation is about compromises."

"So are a lot of other things," Ralston said knowingly. Lance noticed.

Night fell, and work stopped for the day.

***

Ralston took a sip of wine. He and Lance were seated away from others in Ralston's favorite restaurant in downtown San Diego.

"My anonymity is my life, Jeffrey. Every time I'm outed, I always suffer immeasurably."

"What do you know that I don't?"

"What do you know about a certain Senator Darrell Manning?"

"Of the House Intelligence Committee?

"Yes," Lance said flatly.

"You suspect him in some sort of leak."

"Has he ever been to one of your barbeques?"

"Now, you suspect me?"

"Did you sell me out for some political expediency?"

"What?" Ralston bounced in his seat. "Listen, buster, you have no idea of what I have gone through over you. I have funded your projects. And I have always been there for you. You have a lot of nerve, Lance."

"All right, Jeffrey. This Iranian spy, HesAm Ali Tehrani. Who is he? HesAm, by the way, means a *sharp sword*. I'm getting really sick and tired of all these long sharp swords aimed my way."

"Your point?"

"How did he come to have photos of me?"

"Why didn't Mike bring them home with him?"

"Trust. Tehrani also had photos of the good Senator involved in an arms deal?"

"Yes, there is a trust issue here."

"Exactly. Whom can I trust? I can't operate with this over my head."

"You plan to put down a sitting U.S. senator?"

"I will prove to be a long sharp sword of my own. There's been enough selling out of operatives lately by politicians."

"Finish your work here. Leave the rest to me."

Chapter 98

Côte d'lvoire, Africa

06°51′00″N, 05°18′00″W

January 26, 2005

Lance thought that the title "Jewel of West Africa," as the Ivory Coast was sometimes called, was wasted on Cote d'Ivoire, owing to the fact that the Blood Diamond trade emanated from there. It was true that the region, especially the neighboring countries, were steeped in civil war, usually one right after another. Côte d'Ivoire was the largest exporter of cocoa in the world. Lance thought: "Make chocolate—not war!"

Lance observed the Antonov An-32 parked on a long, tree-hidden dirt strip. Now that it was empty, it was being loaded with bundles of coffee. Coffee was also an export. Except, the majority of what this cargo flight just imported was death. The *Forces Nouvelles*, rebel forces that controlled a big part of the north, were still trading blood or conflict diamonds for weapons.

It was disconcerting to see Karl Frick walk out of the back end of the aircraft, down the ramp, and up to a waiting vehicle. He shook hands with an emerging figure of large stature. The big man moved away from the black SUV with a swagger, not unlike John Wayne. Lance had learned much about him in the months since the Mossad kindly revealed who he was. Lance viewed him as an enemy of the state—and humanity. With Senator Manning being a former case officer in the CIA, flying with Air America for a time in Vietnam before turning to politics, this man was groomed for corruption. Both men took seats into the SUV and drove off.

The twin-engine, high wing transport aircraft started its number two engine, followed by number one. Lance hurried back into the thicket and down an old path for nearly a mile that led to a small clearing.

The Echo Jet stood there awaiting its master. Lance pulled down the retractable step and leaped up and over into the cockpit until his feet rested on the rudder pedals. He strapped himself in and waited.

A few minutes later, he saw the An-32 stepping heavenward in the distance, its gear still retracting.

It was time for action. Lance shut the canopy. The engine spooled up to idle. With a push from his thumb on the side-stick controller, the fly-by-wire system obeyed his command. Two rear rectangular exhaust nozzles popped out and rotated downward as clamshell doors closed off the main exhaust nozzle. Three ramp doors popped up toward the middle back of the fuselage. At the same time, two nozzles underneath the middle of the aircraft opened up. Thrust was added. The aircraft rose nearly silent as the last bell and whistle to go into the Echo Jet was engaged. The electronic noise-canceling system, based on aviation headset technology, quieted sound waves with *anti-sound*. What looked like somewhat flattened megaphone speakers within the nozzles bathed engine thrust noise with sound waves 180° out of phase, canceling out most of its noise footprint. The Echo Jet left no echo.

Once high enough, forward flight began with a push on the side-stick controller. The fly-by-wire system rotated the rear exhaust nozzles slowly rearward. At one hundred twenty knots, the rear exhaust nozzles were fully aft. Another push with his thumb and the VTOL system tucked itself back into the fuselage. The transition time was seven seconds to full forward flight.

The Echo Jet came near to the An-32 as it climbed through eighteen thousand feet. Lance thought of its plunder it carried back to Russia in coffee, cocoa, and diamonds, where it left weapons in trade.

Lance dropped below the aircraft, turning on the weapons system master switch. The mini-gun lowered to the "Talon" position. His first shots caught the left-wing on fire. He emptied two short bursts into the right-wing, catching it on fire. He created some space between him and the burning turboprop. The right half of the bomb bay doors obeyed a command to open and launch a missile. Lance watched it shoot out from underneath him and seconds later slam into the conflict-enabling aircraft. The wings bent and folded, causing the aircraft to tumble before exploding in a twirling ball of fire. The loss of all that cocoa saddened lance.

Lance found himself over the ocean, flying in large gentle circles until his radar and sight caught the ascending bizjet. Lance concluded that Manning and Frick were all smiles, thinking they had just cleaned up financially.

The Echo Jet closed in. Lance sighed heavily. He moved his thumb away from the fire button and turned toward the more crucial part of this mission.

The Echo Jet slowed in hover mode until he spotted the two canvas-covered military trucks that had taken the weapons off of the now-deceased Russian transport.

The kit plane came low over the dirt road. Lance targeted the rear truck. He fired. The kit plane version of a Hellfire missile rammed itself into the back of the truck. It exploded. He launched his last two missiles into the front truck. It was done. The continuation of conflict was denied, to a point, for now.

***

"How do you feel?" Danny asked, taking his chair opposite Lance.

"Well, the Hog Snout missile works great. But this piecemeal killing isn't the way. The affairs of this earth need to be settled once and for all, Danny."

"How would you feel meeting with some friends that share your thoughts?"

"Nervous."

"They are the ones that will be nervous. I'm nervous, yet I know and love you."

"Who are they?"

"They are necessarily associated with the U.N., but not in its uselessness. You want peace, my boy? They are the ones to help. Allow me to set up a meeting."

"Tell me something, Danny. Jeffrey had something on you all these years. What was it? Did you try to destroy the Al-Aqsa Mosque and the Dome of the Rock?"

"He had nothing on me, as you put it, but during the Six-Day War, Harold Ralston was here. When we retook the Old City, it was our chance. He stopped us." Danny paused, sighing. "It is still unfinished business."

"He knew it would bring greater war. Perhaps globally."

"Not with your weapon. I have fought four major wars in my time. Three of them here, for this land. It is enough. Maybe, as you say, settle the affairs of man, once and for all."

***

The Chewy-Jewie Pizza Parlor, along King George Street, was a yearling compared to the other food establishments. An ex-pat Italian-Jew from Brooklyn, New York, by the name of Phil, ran the parlor. The New York-style pizza was a hit with the crowd. Lance had enjoyed eating there more than once when he was in Jerusalem.

Lance and Danny sat in the Land Rover for three straight hours.

"We are four for four, Danny. Today should be attempt number five. Soon."

"Yes, your friend Tehrani must be in great angst over these failed attempts."

"Getting somebody prepped to commit suicide and murder in the same throw isn't the easiest thing in the world to do."

"No, it must be inculcated deeply in mind and heart over time."

"Yeah, brainwashed." Lance looked at his watch.

A somewhat dinged-up white sedan pulled up along the street, about eight car lengths away from the pizza parlor. What looked to be an eighteen to twenty-year-old man stepped out onto the sidewalk. He moved reluctantly, even stopping to turn around. Lance could see movement inside the car of others waving him on. "I think this is it."

Danny, pumped by the scenario, kept an even stride with Lance as they crossed the street. Lance's trained eye could tell the young man carried more weight than usual for his thin frame.

The young Palestinian man entered the pizza parlor. Lance and Danny entered through the glass door and took their position in the order line in front of him. There were fourteen people inside. Lance observed the young man looking around. Danny turned to face Lance. Lance noted his button-sized chemical sensor, nodding ever so slightly that this was their man. Danny nodded for Lance to move for a clear shot. Instead, Lance spoke in Arabic: "I don't understand why there is a conflict between Musa and Mohammed." Danny's jaw tightened. This was foolish. The shout of "Allahu Akbar" had to be near. "Nowhere in the Holy Quran does it mention seventy-two virgins waiting in Heaven."

Danny was not happy. He would push Lance out of the way for the shot. "I don't get your question," Danny replied in Arabic. He played along for the moment.

"Musa said that the angels came down from Heaven to earth to take the beautiful women to lie down with them. So, if there is no romance in Heaven, why are we taught that we get the virgins when we go to Heaven? I don't understand."

"Perhaps Musa is mistaken," Danny thought appropriate to say.

"He is a prophet of God! Do God's prophets lie? No! They do not. I hold the great prophet in the highest regard. I think this is a teaching of men. It blasphemes against the Holy Quran!"

"You must calm down."

"I don't like the idea of young men blowing themselves up, while those that sit back and laugh at the slaughter—go *untested* themselves. This is the coward's way. Did the great Saladin use such cowardly tactics? No! He rode with his troops straight into battle and took Jerusalem back from the Crusaders. If he were here, he would look at these suicide attackers as cowards. No honor. No Heaven. I am certain."

The young man rocked in place for a second and then marched out the door.

"You took a tremendous chance with all of our lives," Danny scolded.

"Did I?"

Lance and Danny moved outside along the street. They spotted the young man nearly to the car that brought him. The young man yelled at those in the car. The car started and pulled from its parking place as the young man dove through the opened rear window. Lance pulled Danny down in front of a parked car. The explosion was sharp and rattling. Then it was quiet. Soon the noise of investigation and curiosity would occupy this avenue of eateries.

Danny stood. "Only you would have this situation." Danny walked back up the street.

They drove to the parking lot and walked into the Jewish Quarter to Ezra's home. Danny rang the bell. Ezra answered the door. He saw Lance. "Why is this man here?"

"Were there any killed in the explosion?" Danny asked poignantly.

"Just the four Palestinian terrorists. Most of the explosion was contained within their vehicle. Fortunately, the lights were red, and no traffic was moving. They failed."

"Then, you must thank this man for stopping them."

Ezra stepped back and opened his door.

Lance saw three long-bearded rabbis sitting at a wood plank table. They smiled. Lance thought of them as the three wise monkeys of Japanese lore for some reason. See no evil—hear no evil—speak no evil.

"Gentlemen," Lance said.

"Are you still Christian, boy?" Ezra spouted.

"No, but an hour ago, I was a Muslim." The three rabbis chuckled. "You know Ezzie, I've read and studied the Bible from cover to cover."

"There is no one time read, and you are done. It is continuous. It is your whole life," Ezra snapped.

"I didn't go at it like it was a dime store novel. I read, researched, and meditated on what I learned for years."

"You are closest to a Christian. So you are Christian."

"Ezzie, quit being such a schmekel."

"Go back to your triune god."

"There wouldn't be a trinity if you weren't so stupid about using the divine name!"

Ezra lunged forward, pointing. "Blasphemer!"

Lance lunged forward. "Yeah, well—Jehovah! Jehovah! Jehovah!"

"Ah!" Ezra growled, covering his ear.

Lance stood erect, grinning, his indignation lessening. "They always fall for their superstitions."

"You will burn—"

"Ezra! Enough!" Danny shouted. "Or I will shoot you myself."

"Sorry, Danny. But this stupid Pharisee pushes like he always does, and this time I had to go all Monty Python on his—."

"Lance, please!"

"—Bum. Let's go with bum," Lance said, softening his gritted mien.

"Yes, let's."

Lance realized Danny just saved him from that rare but colorfully expressed tirade, which he would have found distasteful.

The three rabbis chuckled.

"Mr. Rio, it is a pleasure to finally meet you. I am Rabbi Benjamin Tuckman."

"I am Rabbi Bernie Fineman."

"And I am Rabbi Bradley Zuckerman."

The three B's, Lance thought. He nodded graciously. "My apologies, gentlemen."

The dinner was modest in conversation until Ezra rocked in his chair and fell forward. Tuckman caught him and pushed him back against his chair.

"Not to worry, Mr. Rio. We spike his wine when we need to talk in confidentiality."

"Interesting cover I.D."

"One of many," said Fineman.

"We are all formerly active Mossad like Daniel here and serve in the U.N. Security Council. The U.N., as it is, will never bring peace. I believe you know this," Tuckman stated.

"I do," Lance acknowledged.

"This is what we ask of you. With your apparatus—free us of Islam. Free the world. Whatever you need, whatever the cost," Tuckman pleaded. "We don't seek power. We just want peace. We all have had our fill of violence. I want what's left of my children to know a peaceful Israel and a peaceful world. I don't think we ask for so much."

"You don't, sir," Lance said tenderly.

"Whatever the cost, Mr. Rio. Hear us. Whatever the cost," Bernie Fineman added.

"Even if the cost is the necessary destruction of this city?"

Their eyes widened. Lance observed intently.

"How can you destroy our way of life?" Fineman begged. "You love this land!"

"Islam is our mortal enemy! Not here in our ancestral home." Tuckman shouted.

"No," Lance said emphatically, "It is not. Babylon has always been your arch enemy. You forget. And I mean by its influence, which has permeated all religion, all politics, and all thought. But, Islam will go the way of Babylon, just as the Temple Mount has."

"What do you mean?" Zuckerman asked.

"No third temple. None was ever required. You need to prepare your hearts and minds that the reign of the Pharisees is over. Which is what came back to bite you in the first place."

"This is madness!" Tuckman cried.

Lance sighed, rolling his eyes toward Danny. "I don't have time for this. I won't sit here and argue over the interpretation of a stop sign."

"Benny! Silence!" Danny counseled. "Listen to him. He is our only hope."

Chapter 99

Gillespie Field: El Cajon, California

April 30, 2005

"Okay. What else?" Eric Pitts said. Ralston stood poised to listen.

"It is a new type of engine. Well, it's based on an old theme," Lance said.

"And that is?"

"Steam. It's a steam engine. A turbo-steam-engine."

"What?" Ralston said. "You want to sit around and wait while the water boils?"

Eric winched. "Yeah, Lance, even with a flash boiler, you're looking at…"

"Oh, such small minds. No, Eric. No, Jeffrey. Instantaneous steam."

"Okay, Lance. Your crazies tend to work out," Eric said.

"Think of a turbo-steam-rocket engine."

"Focus on what we have here before you go running off to Mars," Ralston admonished.

Lance frowned his way over to the workbench. On it was three pieces that made up yet another new combustor. Ralston noticed that twelve protruding cone-shaped slots ran the diameter of the combustor ring. "I still have to TIG weld it together, but I wanted to show it to you in its separate components first. This is the middle ring. The AJACS system will send in fully vaporized fuel mixed with air. This piece, the inner combustor ring ramps up the combustion temperature to around six-thousand six-hundred degrees, as before. But the high-pressure turbine will now handle two-thousand-eight-hundred degrees. Our best design yet. We expect to see another twenty percent increase in fuel efficiency. The Echo Jet will have a range well past three thousand miles. That is in high-medium supercruise. About Mach two point seven."

Ralston looked over at the Echo Jet. "How much longer will you need to be here?"

"At least two more weeks."

"That's fine. I'll see you tonight." Ralston walked out.

"Tell me, Lance. Do you have any more inventions up your sleeve? Or are we done?" Eric asked, somewhat frustrated.

"The steam engine."

"Will you forget the steam thingy for now?"

"You asked. But there is one more notion I have. The T.D.E."

"The what?"

"T.D.E. The Turbo-Disc-Engine."

"Seriously?"

"Inspired by the Wankel engine, but this has one, maybe two moving parts. It spins. Like a disc. Hence, a disc engine. And will run on one hundred octane low-lead aviation gasoline. Maybe even supreme autogas."

"Finally! A simpler engine." Eric wrapped his arms around Lance. "Finally! A gas-powered, smog-producing engine. Nice and simple." Lance frowned. "Okay, I'm sure we can make it green somehow. Can we use the AJACS fuel injection system on it?"

"It would be perfect for this engine."

"That's what I've been waiting to hear. Well, get me some drawings so I can shoot it into the computer and start the engineering on it."

"I've already done the preliminary design work on my computer."

"Okay, the big question is when can you quit, and we start our kit plane company?"

"When the world changes for the better."

"You know that will never happen."

"It will, Special. And sooner than you think."

***

It had been years since Lance last attended the famous Jeffrey Ralston Fourth of July barbeque. He caught bits and pieces of gossip and mild political intrigue in his mingling, which generally he found boorish, but now it held his interest. Guests were arriving throughout the afternoon. Lance got to see some old friends from the CIA of long ago. He stuffed himself with ribs as usual.

The guests had all gone except Mike Castro, David Nance, and Josh Wilson. Lance enjoyed only a few sips of wine when Maggie Ralston stepped outside. It was just past nine p.m. "Lance, I need you to go into Jeffrey's study."

"Okay. I'll be in in a minute."

Lance entered the study. "There's the little son of a bitch that's caused me so much trouble," bellowed Senator Darrell Manning.

"What's going on, Jeffrey?" Lance asked, studying his environment. Karl Frick glared at him. He sat in front of Jeffrey's desk. Manning stood, pointing.

"You don't think I know about your little escapades, Mr. Rio? Well, I do."

"I operate within the charter of my assignments."

"And Jeffrey operates within his limits, as overseen by me."

"Not just you alone."

"You want this to be a pissing contest, boy?"

"What do you want, Senator?"

Mike, David, and Josh stood behind Lance.

"Let me put it this way. You better find yourself, one damn good lawyer. You have illegally interfered with special operations."

"Maybe we should have Tehrani here since he's part of this. Did the CIA train him? You—back in the day?" Manning scrunched his face up tighter. "Figures."

"He's been working with us," Manning said.

"With a side business of plotting suicide bombings. With your blessings, Senator? The Israelis won't be too happy to learn about this. Anti-Semitism is so unbecoming."

"We'll see how smug you are when you are up on the charge of treason. And it'll stick!"

"Lance," Ralston said. "Listen to me. I will get you a top-notch attorney. One of ours."

"Plan on doling out a couple hundred grand while you're at it. For starters." Manning smiled cruelly. "I'll see you in Leavenworth."

"While I appreciate that Cessna is based in Kansas, I'll pass."

"Don't get cute with me, boy. You're in a heap of trouble."

"Boy? And if anyone has any explaining to do, it's you."

"Lance," Ralston said. "They will tie this around your neck. That's how it works."

"Tell me, Jeffrey, when I stopped that kid from blowing up the pizza parlor on Tehrani's hit list, am I in trouble for that as well?"

"I'll find a way to hang that on you too," Manning pointed.

"You have too much power, Senator. Corrupt power. That will end. Jeffrey, you let this man come into your home, knowing full well that he has engaged in illegal activity and threaten me?"

"His hands are tied, boy."

"I see. I'm the scapegoat." Lance considered that Manning was part of the fifteen-member U.S. Senate Select Committee on Intelligence. Given that he shook up Manning's world, Manning would have the means and access to locate him, in this case through Ralston. Jeffrey would have to come clean, or his career would be in jeopardy and his head on the block.

"And I want his jet, jet plane, whatever the hell it is, confiscated," Manning yelled.

"You should have kept your dog on his leash, Jeffrey," Frick added.

"Karl, it's been eighteen years. You're not still holding a grudge?" Lance said smugly.

"Yeah, you make jokes. You put me in diabetic shock and busted me up. Broke my jaw."

"You hit me first. From behind."

"But I'll be there to see you hang."

“I want this man neutralized from any further activity,” Manning growled. The big man stopped in front of Lance and poked him in the chest. “Get your lawyer. I’ll be seeing you before a senate hearing come next week.”

Lance thought immediately how the system would work in the senator’s favor no matter what he reported to the committee. They would side with their own. That’s how it worked. He would be locked into the very legal system that he hated. It was his enemy.

“Jeffrey, you know how we’re a nation of laws?”

“Yes, Lance. I do.”

“We’re just not a nation of justice.”

“Move.” The senator pushed past Lance. Lance turned and grabbed him by the underside of his right arm and squeezed.

“Lance, no!” Ralston jumped up. Lance raised his right hand and struck Manning open palm in the chest. He let go. Manning stumbled back, clutching his chest. He fell backwards on the floor. Lance spun around, kicking Frick out of his chair. Mike, David, and Josh wrestled Lance to the floor.

“Lance, stop it!” David yelled.

Lance struggled for a moment. Mostly reflex. Then he went motionless. “I’m calm, David. You can let go.”

“Let him up,” Ralston ordered. They came off Lance and helped him up. Lance stepped near the expired senator and shrugged. “Those black hearts just don’t hold up like they used to. I’d go with a heart attack.”

Lance enjoyed the rib fest at the Ralston’s. It would be his last.

Chapter 100

Megiddo

September 11, 2005

It was a quiet Sunday morning, before dawn. However, Lance was amped. The Echo Jet was amped, meaning the four supercapacitors secured within her belly were fully charged. A new emitter design featured a variable focus aperture. It was too long to mount vertically in the weapons bay. So, Lance built a servo-driven chassis to rotate it down. Nonetheless, it was tight.

Lance had been making a daily flight over Afghanistan for the last week. He saw the desert dune come to life without their ever taking notice of him.

"You have trepidation?" Danny said.

"Shouldn't I? Otherwise, I'm just another psycho. I feel like Paul Tibbets, just before he climbed into the Enola Gay."

Danny nodded. "It's no small thing, my boy. Time to go."

***

Lance kept the Echo Jet to only mach 2.5 and for only thirty minutes.

The sun rose from its night's sleep and crept slowly over the horizon. Lance took a moment to enjoy the warming shades of impending daylight and bask in the morning glow of a new day—a hopeful day. A very dedicated day. Near the Iranian border, as he approached Afghanistan, Lance pulled the power back to idle. From seventy-seven thousand feet, it would still be a speedy descent to target.

Lance brought the Echo Jet down to one thousand feet and engaged the belly camera once the aircraft stabilized in hover mode. He zoomed in. The emerging sun still hadn't cast light over the deep shadows of the dune. There were an estimated seven hundred below. Some were moving around, and others were still lying asleep on their blankets. "It's like a terrorist's love in," he quipped.

Lance opened the left bay door, lowered the emitter, and set the aperture to its widest opening. The dune was roughly three hundred feet in diameter.

A man by the name of Amir was just waking. He wasn't sure, but he thought he saw a fleck up in the sky. It was a spy plane, a drone. He yelled out.

Lance could see the scatter of people below. It didn't matter. He closed his eyes and squeezed the trigger.

Amir jumped up as millions of ants invaded his body from within the warm blue glow before a yellow-white light stunned him. He went blind with only a small sense of remarkable heat, searing his thoughts out of existence.

It was done. Lance looked below. He slid the aircraft to the right of the target. He saw a plume of white heat form into a fire tornado from the molten mass below. It wouldn't reach him, but it unnerved him enough to slide over.

It was time to go. Fuel was being consumed, and he had three countries to cut back across before reaching home. Lance moved the Echo Jet out of hover mode and transitioned to forward flight.

Lance relaxed a little on the ride home.

"Lance. What have you done?" came the voice of Jeffrey Ralston over his headset. This could not be. There was no sat phone link-up turned on. Lance rechecked it.

"Hello."

"I'm here, Lance. Tell me what you have done?"

"I must be dreaming." There was no way he was hearing Ralston. The airwaves were silent—nothing registered on the instrument panel.

"Lance."

"Jeffrey, if this is really you—say so!"

"Lance, talk to me. What have you done?"

Lance engaged the voice. "I have just taken the first bold step to realizing a better earth."

"And how do you plan to accomplish this?"

"By replicating this action on a global scale. Call it Armageddon."

"Just like that?"

"Nothing of this magnitude is ever just like that."

"And what will you do?"

"First, I will drop the Empire State Building."

"Why would you do that?"

"How else can I get all of congress in the same building—at the same time?"

"And do what, Lance?"

"Lawmakers are always the weakest link in any government and the most willing to compromise integrity. Partly, they cannot help it. It's bred into them as lawyers. You know the type, Jeffrey, repackagers of truth. Not the type I want leading me. So, now, necessity is laid upon me."

"Burn them down, you mean. And then what, move on to the White House?"

"Street etiquette, Jeffrey. The Stone is set to strike the feet of iron and clay first. Then Wall Street. Their gold and their silver will not buy them their lives. It will be similar with the U.K."

"And make the United States and the United Kingdom the laughing stocks of the world?"

"When the Anglo-American world power is obliterated, crushed before the eyes of the world, no one will be laughing. When everyone is caught off guard, I'll burn down the Kaaba during the hajj. Vaporize it off the face of the earth. And then a quick jaunt over to Riyadh. The same will hold true for Iran. And then when everyone thinks I am correcting matters in the Middle East—the Kremlin. Every—last—vestige of the Soviet spectre will finally be gone—no more trouble from them. Then on to China and North Korea with their goose-stepping troops so proudly on display. I'll burn down a hundred thousand of them in a couple of seconds. They will look invincible no more. Across the globe, I will efface evil and corruption. There will be nowhere to hide. The effect? People will, for the first time in history, see that crime and corruption do not pay. Brutally so. And therein a basis for hope."

"And you will accomplish this with just the Echo Jet."

"No-no. I will have a new aircraft with many, many times this power. Beautifully, its damage will be permanent. Religion—that harlot with its blood-stained hands will cease to exist. All governments of earth will be crushed—pulverized to harmless chaff. Just as prophesized."

"All in the name of justice?"

"Oh! Beyond justice, Jeffrey. Moral excellence! All the different forms of government and economic strategies that have ever existed on this earth have failed to provide true peace and security. They always have and always will."

"So, you plan on implementing some sort of Utopian society?"

"A lazy, self-absorbed society? Hardly. I plan to go back to the beginning. The way it was intended. Ask yourself, how did our Creator plan for us to live on this planet? Did he mean for us to compete against one another based on some minerals we dig out of the ground? Or did he mean for us to cooperate and build human society together so that we all get to benefit from our hard work? Not just a few. Did he mean for us to rule over one another, subjugating the many under the thumb of a few? I think given our bloody history, the answer is clear." Lance paused. "We will tear down and dismantle our cities and spread out with each family having a share of land."

"You plan on turning mankind into farmers?"

"It's called self-reliance. Ever hear of it? Besides, people will be less likely to spoil the earth if they have to actually work to care for it. And naturally, starvation will end, which is manmade, to begin with. And no homelessness."

"So you plan on us spending our days raising crops and canning food?"

"Guess who is going to be Secretary of Canning?"

"Glad to know I'll be around."

"You're the best man I know for the job, though you will carry no such title."

"I see. So, no industry? You plan on killing that off too?"

"Greedy, repressive commercialism? With joy. Industry? Not at all. Quite the reciprocal. But we will make what we need. No one will slave his life away in a factory. We will have city centers to service each community. The main point is that a man will not build and someone else occupy. A man will finally see good for all his hard work and be home with his family. So no, Jeffrey, no Utopian society."

"Lance, you cannot do this!"

"Hey! It's God-ordained!"

"People won't want it."

"Jeffrey, do you hear yourself? People get used to prison. What do you think will happen when all the massive levels of stress pour off of them? Debt. Traffic. Pollution, to name a few—gone! You don't think people might somehow get used to that?"

"There will be those that oppose you. They will fight you."

"With—what? Solomon wrote that a wise king sifts out the wicked. This is what I have been doing for some time. I plan to introduce a single, simple, understandable global Law. No loopholes. Straightforward. Emphatic. Because all mankind will be able to experience the blessings of what I purpose, the Law will be something tangible. They will want to embrace it."

"Lawyers will find a way around it. Have you figured that one out?"

"Asked and answered. No lawyers. I will never allow the corrupt legal systems of this world to bring any more harm to people—ever! I will burn it down. Besides, no one man will ever have any power greater than that of a county clerk."

"There will be disputes."

"That goes without saying. But the disputing parties will be asked this one question that the whole Law will hang upon. Did you show *love of neighbor*? That will cut through to the heart of the situation. Life and death may hang in the balance of how that question is answered."

"All you are doing is forcing your ideologies by the sword."

"Am I? After a time when things settle and are peaceful, I planned to offer people the choice to go back to this ugly gridlocked world. Or continue to prosper in our peaceful new world."

"There will be those."

"Solomon also wrote when the wicked rise to power, a man hides himself. But when they perish, the righteous increase. What do you think their answer will be?"

"I still don't see it."

"There will be no longer any Harvard or Oxford. The same high standard of knowledge will be taught everywhere. What a man learns in Arkansas, another man will learn the exact same thing in Africa or Australia. It will be the same shared universal knowledge. As an added refinement, I will see to it that all, especially our children, will learn of the failure of this system and why we will never want to go back to it. Or face the ravages of man dominating man to his injury all over again."

"What will be the incentive if you don't have a currency? I assume by what you are saying you plan to have a moneyless society."

"Seriously, Jeffrey? The same resources exist whether you have a couple of twenties in your pocket or not. Everyone digs. Everyone works. Everyone benefits. People want to be happy and content and use their full potential. Something that's just not possible now."

"So you plan on making us all one big happy family?"

"Isn't that what we want at the end of the day?"

"And all will bow down to Lord Lance!"

"No, Jeffrey. Only a fool seeks fame for himself. I will guide humble mankind from the shadows."

"You're not being realistic."

"I see. You think I should continue to support your little democratic experiment? For that to work requires our elected officials to act selflessly, and the people they represent also act selflessly. Ain't gonna happen."

"Lance, listen to me!"

"No! No! You had your chance. And-you-blew-it! Now, it will be taken from you!" Lance spoke no further.

Chapter 101

The Red Sea

27°17′02″N, 34°11′05″E

September 15, 2005

The powerboat came to a wake-producing halt when its twin engines were cut back to idle, where it bobbed for a few seconds before settling. The sun was setting, and the calm of night approached. Roman Sanders set up for his target still five miles away.

The target was a sixty-five-foot cabin-cruiser pushing its way northward.

The powerboat was still. "Are we close enough?" Lance asked.

"Don't worry, kid. I never miss anything at or under a thousand yards." The cruiser veered to the right to enter into the Strait of Tiran. "Yup. They're heading to Sharm el-Sheikh. Probably for a little gambling," Sanders said.

"It is Egypt's French Rivera."

"And an easy way for him to get in and out of Israel. He set up shop in Gaza some time ago. Time to tie off your name from his. Let him come up into range. And then make your call."

Lance dialed the cell number. "Hello," the voice of Tehrani said.

"HesAm Ali Tehrani," Lance said coldly.

"Who is this?"

"Lance Rio, here."

"Ah, Mr. Rio. You have found me." There was some trepidation in his voice.

"Mr. Tehrani, I find myself in the intolerable position of being known by you."

"So you did break into my home. Where do we go from here, Mr. Rio?"

"We need to meet."

"Are you familiar with Sharm el-Sheikh?"

"I am." Lance viewed Tehrani standing on the rear of the cruiser with his cell phone to his ear. Sanders was poised for the shot.

"Meet me there tomorrow." The call was ended.

Lance waited for the shot. The wake from a passing yacht upset Sanders' rhythm. "No good. Lost the shot."

"We will have another opportunity tomorrow."

"Negative. I've never failed on a mission before. Tonight, Tehrani—is dealt with."

Lance had in mind the terror attack two months earlier in Sharm el-Sheikh, aimed at the Egyptian tourist industry where eighty-eight people were killed. It was time to say goodbye to Tehrani. Lance powered up the twin engines. "I don't want to be the one that breaks your perfect record, Roman."

Lance, quickly, with a wide margin, passed Tehrani's cruiser and steered his way into Naama Bay, the heart of the resort area. In the 1980's it was little more than a fishing village, but due to the excellent scuba diving, it grew into the trendy resort it is today. It was sad Lance thought that Tehrani, who came to enjoy the spot, was probably behind the terror attack.

An hour later, Lance had anchored the powerboat a short distance from the southern pier. He could hear party after party; music and dance lined the street along the beach.

The cruiser flowed into the nightlife lit bay and slowed to line up with the pier. Lance wanted to make the shot. He was good, very good, but he needed great. He needed Sanders.

Sanders corrected and settled his weapon for his part and for his legacy. "Make the call, Lance. We're good to go." Lance dialed.

"Hello," Tehrani answered.

"Rio, here." Lance viewed Tehrani in shades of green light, drinking champagne out on the stern.

"I did not expect you so soon. I haven't made the proper arrangements."

"I'm here now." Lance watched Tehrani pull the glass from his lips. "I hope the champagne was good." Before Tehrani could move to the right or left, Sanders caught him just behind the left eye.

"It's dealt with. Make the call."

Lance dialed. In Tehrani's condo, the name of Lance Rio with fire would draw back into the shadows of anonymity.

Chapter 102

Megiddo, Israel

September 17, 2005

Lance was content. He finished prepping his flight bag. Soon, Ralston and other observers would be coming to the house, and then they would drive the three miles to Megiddo Airport and board his Citation jet. Lance would be flying them to Afghanistan, to the site that he obliterated six days earlier. He looked forward to seeing his handiwork. The buzz was that al-Qaeda was stunned to have so many of its soldiers dead. They were still mystified by what means western powers used to kill so many so suddenly. It put fear into them for the first time in a long time.

A white van pulled up out front. "Lance, they are here," Danny said. "I trust all is secure."

Ralston entered. He was dressed in beige clothing, set for an excursion into the desert.

Within the hour, the Citation headed skyward with a turn toward the east.

***

Lance made a normal landing into Bagram Airfield, Afghanistan. Once clear of runway 03, he taxied to the tarmac and shut down. The airbase sat nearly 5,000 feet above sea level. As with most of Afghanistan, the mountainous country was above 4,000 feet.

Lance was loaded into the middle Humvee of a three-vehicle caravan. Like any airman who had ever rained down destruction, he had never seen the up-close damage of his actions. He would today. He had his scientific curiosity. He wasn't comfortable with its discovery so soon, however.

They headed to where the foot of the mountains, valley floor, and sand all met. Lance recognized one of the observers. The man was on the damaged helicopter in Bosnia he repaired and flew out. He heard Ralston call him "Captain." No matter. This was their show for now.

They arrived at the onetime training camp. Josh Wilson took the lead. He ran a Geiger counter as he approached the edge of the dune. The results turned up negative. He looked down upon the two hundred meter circle of sand. "It's—it's unlike anything I have ever seen."

"What do you mean?" Ralston asked. He came to Josh's side, stopping only to look at the bottom of his shoe and finding glass fragments embedded in the soles. Ralston looked down upon the sand-dusted crater. Charcoaled smears that once were human beings fanned out some distance from what Ralston deemed the epicenter. The cataclysmic event welded whatever was living to the dune.

"I'm going down, Jeffrey," Josh said. He began his sidestepping downward into the sand when his feet came out from under him as the sand gave way upon the slick surface underneath. Josh slid down, yelling, leaving a bloody trail from his leg.

"Secure a rope and bring a medical kit," Ralston ordered.

This startled Lance. There should be no drama. The drama was over. This was assessment. Lance hopped out of the Humvee.

Captain Scott Ensor steadied himself with the rope slipping on the way down. "It's glass," Ensor yelled. "It's all glass."

"What do you mean, Captain?" Ralston asked.

"I mean that something melted the sand. Turned it all to glass. What wasn't vaporized, that is. You sure someone didn't set off a nuke in here?"

"Quite sure, Captain," Ralston replied.

As Lance stood above, his countenance faded from confident to astonished. He beheld the eerie, alien world of his own creation.

"Come down here, Lance," Ralston ordered.

Lance, carefully as the others before him, stepped down the crystallized path to the bottom. He could feel the crunch of broken and fused sand beneath his feet. There were some blinding reflections of glass being revealed from just under the sand. "Josh, are you okay?"

"Yeah. But be careful, Lance. There's a lot of sharp edges down here."

"That's good advice for everyone," Ralston announced.

Lance moved outward toward the rear of the dune. The observers, which included David Nance and Mike Castro, followed by Graham Rye and Trevor Rees, began pushing on a few charcoaled remains.

"Ew, that's nasty," David said, turning up his nose.

Ensor came up next to Lance. "Look at that. What's left of these guys are burnt to a crisp." He turned to Lance. "Thank you for saving my life, by the way."

"What? Oh, you're welcome," Lance replied.

Ensor moved to another carbonized figure. He pushed his foot through what he believed to be the man's ribcage. The acrid, rotting smell of death soon permeated the area. The decayed odor flowed into Lance's nostrils and caused him to gag. He shot back from the corpse. "Hey, you okay, Lance?"

"Yeah. It just got to me. That's all."

Ralston came up to Lance and Ensor. He saw death shadows painted against the rock formation of the dune that rose up into the foot of the mountain. The heat blast traveling outward had seared these men and burned their silhouettes around their bodies on the rock behind them.

Lance turned and fast stepped away from them. He couldn't escape it. Ralston chased after Lance. "What is it?"

"This is all wrong, Jeffrey," Lance said, gagging again.

"Quit that!" Ralston gagged himself. The smell was growing in intensity. He turned around. "Everyone. Quit disturbing the remains." He turned back to Lance. "What's wrong?"

"This!"

"It's certainly not pleasant," Ralston said as he moved past Lance. "Come here and help me." Lance turned and threw up. It started a chain reaction with everyone.

Ralston wiped his mouth. "My God!" He saw a man with his face partially burned off, revealing his seared musculature around the cheek and jaw. He looked as if he had materialized inside of solid glass. It flowed in him and around him. Lance stared at the man. His mouth was open, forever encapsulating his final scream.

Lance stepped back. "What have I done?" he said quietly. He turned and vomited again. He staggered back to the rope, clutching his stomach.

"Lance! Come back here!" Ralston yelled.

"Oh, what have I done? Dear God. What have I done?" Lance mumbled as he ascended the rope. Ralston came after him.

Lance sat back in the Humvee and tried to calm himself. His heart was racing, sweat pouring from him, as did tears. "Lance!" Ralston marched up to him. "What was that all about?"

"Don't you get it, Jeffrey? I'm not the Stone!"

Chapter 103

Gibraltar

October 23, 2005

The Echo Jet leveled off at fourteen thousand feet. Lance was just past the island of Malta to the north. He was flying subsonic at just over four hundred knots. The Echo Jet, which looked to have broken the SR-71's top speed with better than 2,500 miles per hour—was making her final flight.

Stalwart determination was for the moment containing a cringing heart. This was a go-no-go decision, and it needed to be made now as Lance entered the Strait of Gibraltar with open ocean just beyond. The sun was setting in the west—the direction of flight.

Earlier, Lance dismantled the disc-generator and took a grinder to it, and cut it up. Piece by piece, it was stuffed into the backseat and luggage compartment, along with twenty-five pounds of high explosives.

Lance slowed the aircraft down to 200 knots indicated and engaged the autopilot. He looked at the VTOL button. He would never press it again. He hesitated but then committed to action, seating his goggles around his eyes. With a hand on each handle, he pushed the canopy latches past OPEN to Emergency Release and popped the top. It flew up, tumbling back. He clicked the digital timer to ON and freed himself of his restraints. He held onto the small backpack that stayed nestled in his bosom. He hit the autopilot disengage button and shoved the side-stick controller forward. The aircraft nosed over as he jumped up as high as he could go. He was clear of the Echo Jet and in freefall. He opened his parachute. After the snap up and in an established glide, he turned back once to see the Echo Jet coming back up to its set altitude. There was sorrow. His legacy would be buried where no man could find it deep in the Atlantic. Lance had a measure of relief in that he would not see it happen.

Sentiment cost him the three hundred extra feet needed to hit the beach. He would land in the surf. He could hear the waves echo from shore.

The cool water quickly enveloped him. His hands felt for the buckles. He freed himself before the tangled lines could wrap around him. He surfaced and began the few strokes to shallower water. It wasn't long before he was walking in the surf.

Lance came to rest on the beach. He stood up, took a deep breath, letting it out with a sigh. He worked off the wet jumpsuit and stowed it in his backpack. Still, in wet clothes, he headed away from the surf.

Sand turned to gravel and gravel into asphalt as he stepped onto the road. He walked north along Keightley Way, dialing his cell phone. "Hallo," Manfred Steiger answered.

"Manny, I need you to come get me."

"Where are you?"

"Gibraltar. Can you come in the morning?"

"All of the planes will be out."

"Can you come now?"

"Ja. I can come in a couple of hours. Are you okay?"

"A little wet, but okay."

***

Lance finally found his reading glasses. He found the exercise of trying to remember where he laid something that he seldom needed as beyond a chore. He had faced the fact that his eyes had lost the acuity of his youth.

Danny came to sit as he always did before Lance. "Are you sure that you did the right thing, Lance?"

"No. But yes."

"Tuckman and the others aren't taking this very well."

"I figured."

"We are asking your help with some flying duties, though."

"That's fine. I'm about done with all of this anyway."

"And then you will go home?"

"Israel is my home. Here, with you and Alfonso Pig." Alfonso snorted at the hearing of his name and then rested his head back down.

"Eric still wants you to come to California?"

"Yes."

"What about the Sparrowhawk? Do you plan on keeping it here?"

"That's up to Jeffrey. It would still make a great kit plane, and we have the molds to make more."

"Then, a day at a time, my boy. A day at a time," Danny concluded.

Chapter 104

Port Sudan International Airport, Sudan

19°26′01″N, 37°14′03″

January 12, 2006

The sun was getting low over the small airport that serviced the city, a few miles to the north. Port Sudan was a place where Lance spent some vacation time in the past. It was a lovely city with all of the amenities to make one relax. He sat in his Citation jet sat at the end of Runway 35. Lance thought about the hajj going on just across the Red Sea from where he sat. It was the final day of the pilgrimage. He frowned and wondered how many lost their lives this year from being trampled. He remembered his raw heels from his sojourn around the Kaaba.

A dusty beige blip on Lance's radar screen—his eyes caught the small jeep working its way down to meet him. This was the third flight he did for Danny and his friends, the three B's. It was a continued favor, nay, it was a concession to his pulling out of taking over the world. In truth, and despite seeing the results of his handiwork in Afghanistan, Lance did give afterthought about at least using the Echo Jet to destroy as many warlords, drug lords, and some landlords as possible. He couldn't in the end. It was no longer in him.

The three men in the jeep pulled alongside the jet. They would be able to conduct business uninterrupted by the seldom-used airport.

Lance stepped out of the aircraft. "Gentlemen. This seems a bit extreme meeting here, but I understand that private negotiations are going well."

"It is, Mr. Rio," the man said. He was about Lance's height, bald, with pale blue eyes. They were hard eyes. He looked strong but gaunt and drawn in the face. He spoke with a Russian accent. He then raised a gun to Lance. "Do as I tell you, and all will be well. Take your tie off and open up your shirt. I want you relaxed."

Lance paused, but the wave of the man's gun got him moving. There were only four people in the world that knew where Lance would be. The taste of betrayal was in his mouth. He threw his tie into the aircraft. "The tower is going to want to know what's up."

"You told the tower you were having trouble and needed to shut down. We're the help," the Russian said.

"If you kill me, who will fly the aircraft?"

"I will. Now turn around and get back inside." As Lance turned to step inside, the Russian slugged him in the back of the head, knocking him forward. The Russian dragged him back by his shirt collar. Lance felt something fall inside. There was movement. He felt the sting. He pulled his shirt up and shook it. A yellow scorpion fell out. A deathstalker! He crushed it. Lance felt the burn of the injection site grow painful. He remembered his sting years ago. His body began tightening up. "There. Outside of a little anaphylaxis that should relax you."

"I need the anti-venom I carry onboard." Lance moved back to the doorway.

"Nyet!" The Russian jerked Lance back out and slugged him repeatedly in the face and body. Lance slumped to the ground.

Lance fought for clarity as the pain was intensifying. He noticed that the Russian had put his gun away. The other two men removed a canvas bag and carried a cylinder the size of a beer keg from the back of the jeep. It had some weight to it, but they managed it in through the door of the aircraft. Through blurriness and pain, Lance muscled himself up and jumped inside the door.

"Stop him!" the Russian shouted.

Lance sent his open palm up against the nose of the second man inside of the aircraft who tried to seize him. Lance struggled for the cockpit as the Russian caught hold of his feet. Lance fought the Russian and the effects of the ever-progressing venom. Through swollen and weeping eyes, he thrust himself forward until his hand felt the slot in the front of his seat. He pushed it, and his Walther PPK sprung out. Lance grabbed it as he was dragged back over the central console. He spun, putting a bullet into the Russian's forehead.

"The authorities will be down here when I call them, and you'll be in prison. Give me the anti-venom, and I will fly us out of here," Lance insisted.

"Okay," said the man in the back.

Lance eagerly pushed the hypodermic needle with its life-saving serum into his vein. As clarity came to him, he looked at the metal cylinder. "Is that what I think it is?"

"We are transporting it."

"Yeah, to Mecca. Deactivate it. Now!" Lance cocked the hammer back. The man pulled out a screwdriver and opened the panel. "Remove the detonator." The man complied. "How did you get your hands on a nuke?" The man set the small tube with the digital readout on it on the rear-facing seat in front of him. "How powerful is the bomb?"

"It will yield about one-half kiloton. It's not very big. It weighs forty-two kilograms."

"Thank you." Lance put two bullets into the man and shot his friend. Lance stepped outside. Still shaky, he grabbed the canvas bag off the back of the jeep. He moved back inside the aircraft. He closed the door and made his way back to the cockpit. He ached. His moments of lucidity were improving but gave his recuperation another hour.

He launched into the air and headed for Israel, a place he would no longer call home.

***

Lance threw up for a second time before stepping back into the Citation. He was badly weakened by the venom and his beating. He was still using the aircraft's supply of oxygen to facilitate his recovery. He continued to feel moments of delirium, and only shadows of what to do crossed his mind. Once cleared into Israeli airspace, he diverted, landing on the flat land of the Negev with the mountainous region behind him. He contemplated that he had three dead men and a small nuclear device on board. What to do? He was dozens of miles in any direction from any town. This was Bedouin country. His leather flight jacket, retrieved from the nose locker, kept him warmer, but the desert at night was freezing this time of year. He tested the bomb for radiation leakage with a small cell phone-sized Geiger counter. It read no detectable level of exposure. He treated the news as good.

Lance set the brake of the Citation with both engines running. The dead Russian sat in the pilot's seat. He needed to finish the final ploy in this game of death. He pushed the two thrust levers to full power and jumped out of the aircraft, shutting the door and locking it as it began skidding slightly in the loose dirt. He rolled underneath, shot out the brake line to the left main landing gear, and then rolled over and shot out the right brake line. The aircraft staggered until it chose a straight path past him. It traveled for what seemed forever along the desert soil until it finally became airborne. It didn't climb too high before it slammed into the rocky mountainous terrain ahead of it. He wished he didn't have to see his beloved aircraft destroyed. It was the end of everything.

Lance heaved the nearly one-hundred-pound small nuclear device over his shoulder in the canvas bag. He felt as if he carried the weight of the world once more. He walked northwest.

It was one of many stumbles in the night, but there was no choice but to press on. He thought about burying the bomb. It seemed too risky. He knew his mind wasn't clear. The ill-effects of venom, the cold of night, and the need for rest all rose to cloud his judgment. Lance picked himself up yet found no strength to haul the bag any further. He dragged it. He stopped. He needed to rest.

Lance woke to the penetrating chill of the desert night. It was nearing 4:30 in the morning. He slept better than an hour. He felt that he could soldier on and keep walking. It took two tries and a bit of a judo technique, but he managed to sling the canvas bag over his shoulder. He moved easier, slightly bent forward.

It was something to do with inertia. He didn't succumb to the desert cold or another scorpion but the entrapment of his thoughts. What happened to that young man who loved to fly and once faithfully loved a young woman? What happened to the innocence of starry-eyed youth that held promise? What did he exchange to combat the forces that took it all away? Lance thought of all that he had accomplished and the gains in knowledge he possessed. Yet, it could all be lost out here as of no account. He thought of human will and innovation. He summed it up as vanity and a striving after nothing more than wind.

Lance tumbled again with the honking of a car horn. The car came to a stop and backed up. "Man, what are you doing out here? I nearly hit you," the driver shouted.

"Where am I?" Lance asked.

"Highway Forty, north of Mitspe Ramon. I'm on my way to Midreshet Ben-Gurion." The driver's info made sense to Lance. He knew where he was. He must have covered a good fifteen miles somehow. "Man, what happened to you? You look like death."

"I feel about that way. I was stung by a scorpion. I must have been wandering."

"Here. Let me help you up," the driver said as he got Lance to his feet.

"My bag. It's heavy. It has expensive scientific equipment in it."

"Fine. We'll take that too. I'll get you some help once we get to the kibbutz." Lance was safe. He needed to get well and regain his strength. And then hold others accountable.

Chapter 105

Jerusalem, Israel

January 20, 2006

Lance woke, feeling for Alfonso, but it was just the second pillow. He would never see his beloved four-legged friend again. He rose and made his way to the bathroom. He still looked like death warmed over. His face, still bruised.

Lance went into the kitchen for his cup of tea. He would also eat.

Shortly, Lance went up to the attic, where he had stored the "device." It was safe from harm or use. He looked upon his guests, the three B's.

"Morning, gentlemen. Well, this is where it all ends. I knew you would never let me destroy Jerusalem. You would kill me first. Of course, I recognized you immediately as modern-day *Sicarii—dagger men*. Jewish assassins who killed Jews in political opposition, and sometimes the Romans. I guess it was something like the French Resistance. The tactic, clever and simple. Mingle in a crowd, especially during festivals, sneak up behind your enemy, pull out your trusty dagger from within the folds of your garments, stab, replace your dagger and then feign horror with the rest as the victim fell dead to the ground. And—usually done in broad daylight. Your predecessors were a primary force in the revolt against Rome. How'd that work out for you? And then they go and do a *Jim Jones* at Masada with about the same number of dead. Fanatical patriotism has never boded well for mankind. I never trusted you to believe this city could be rebuilt from its ashes later when peace came to earth. It would have been its last rebuilding. And oh, the archeological digs I had planned! Once the area was cleared." Lance shook with anger, glaring at them. "You would have me wipe out a billion people? As if all the evil in the world was contained in them. You fools!" Lance calmed stiffly. "But, now, here we are, where I will settle my account with you." Lance looked at the three helpless men tied and gagged to three secure chairs, where he had been keeping them for the past two days. He kept them drugged at night and wrapped in blankets. Outside of that, he felt no compassion for them. "Oh, I forgot one. I need Danny here to complete the set."

"I'm here, Lance," Danny said. He stood at the attic door. Lance whipped around, his pistol taking quick aim between Danny's eyes. Danny stepped forward.

Lance trembled. "We sure made a pretty poor showing, didn't we? Looks like I let a *man* chain me to another lie after all. Imagine me, the Stone, a stupid human. I am humiliated."

"Lance, listen to me."

"No! Never again!" his eyes welling up. "I loved you. Like father and brother. And you betrayed me!" Lance waved the gun to Danny's right. "Remember the child sacrifices just down the road? Were you set to dispatch me with no more feeling than them?

"In my heart," Danny said and then drew silence.

Lance waved the PPK his way. "I will kill them. Then I'll hand you my gun, and you can finish the job, right in my back—Dagger Man!"

"No, Lance," Ralston said, stepping in past Danny. Lance swung his gun at Ralston. "No more killing. No more betrayal. I know everything. About them, you, and the bomb."

"It's over behind the Nazi flag, if you were wondering."

"I was. But my immediate concern is you."

Lance trembled, and tears fell. "No need to bother about me, Jeffrey. It's all very simple, really. Either kill me—or send me home."

Ralston reached out and gently took the gun from Lance. "Time to go home, Lance."

Part 5

"A true companion is loving all the time
and is a brother that is born for when there is distress."
Solomon

Chapter 106

Florida Keys

February 20, 2006

Lance left his motel room and drove southbound, down U.S. Interstate 1. He didn't know where to go other than back to his roots—to Key Largo.

Lance came over the Jewfish Creek Bridge into town and snaked around to the streets that led him to his ancestral home.

He stopped. He took a sober look at the house of his youth. The memories flooded his senses, but he took it in stride. He turned to Roger's old house. He wondered if the Drakes were still there. He saw movement. He saw a spectre. It was Roger Drake looking out of the kitchen window. Before trepidation could set in, he was out of the rental car and hurrying up the driveway.

He knocked on the door. There was some shuffling inside. The door opened. It was a young man in his twenties. "May I help you?" he said. Lance looked carefully. He looked so much like his father. Lance felt emotions well up inside of him.

"Yes. Sorry. But, you look so much like your father. I was taken aback for a moment," Lance said apologetically.

"You knew my dad?"

"Yes, David. Your father was my best friend in the whole world. I used to live across the street." Lance pointed. "And we grew up together. My name is Lance Rio."

"Well, I don't go by David. I go by Anthony. And I was told that you got my dad killed."

"No. I would have taken any number of bullets for your father. May I inquire as to whom lives here now? Is your grandmother, grandfather still here?"

"No. They both died. I own the house now with my wife. Look. I need to go, but thank you for stopping by."

"Thank you for your time, Anthony. I appreciate you filling me in on the family. I will always have great love for them." Lance turned and stepped away from the door. Lance came to the realization, here was not home.

"Hey, wait!" Anthony Drake yelled out. He came around the car and extended his hand. Lance shook it. "Look, here's my card if you want to stay in touch."

"Thank you. I would like that very much. Perhaps we could have dinner in the future and catch up."

"I'd like that. I'd like to hear about my dad."

Lance was pleased to have a connection to his past with the young man. It made the drive down the Keys pleasurable. It was about time he had something to smile about.

Lance noticed a commuter plane taking off from Marathon Airport. He jerked the car off of the road and into the parking lot of the terminal. He sat for a time and then pulled back on the road, noting the final rows of hangers. He pulled off the road again. Several things snapped into mind and place. Lance believed he might have found home—Marathon.

Chapter 107

Gillespie Airfield: El Cajon, California

June 17, 2006

"Special, I'm here. I've been here," Lance said.

"Yeah, but not long enough. You still have that accent," Eric Pitts stated.

"And probably always will. Anyway, we have a new aircraft taking shape." Lance patted the upper fuselage.

"Well, as soon as your place is ready, you'll be gone again."

"Dude, look at what we did with me half a world away. This is a piece of cake. Marathon is where I need to be."

"Fine. You can be the east coast connection, I guess. As long as you're here for the building end of it, I guess I'll live. I wish we had use of that CNC machine. We could do our own milling instead of having to farm it out."

"I'll see what I can do. But, we're building as you wanted to build, so you should be chuff."

"Yeah, I'm chuff alright. So, what do we call this one? It's a four-seater version of the Shadowhawk."

"I was thinking of calling it the Strato-hawk, or maybe the Snork-hawk. Kidding. But, maybe something without the word hawk in it."

"We'll come up with something. You still plan on taking back the Mits?"

"In two weeks, when I go to inspect my new hangar. I've really missed her. We have a long history together."

"Yeah, you do. So do we."

Chapter 108

Washington, D.C.

July 4, 2006

"You've been in the service and the CIA for almost forty years. What do you think about your legacy, Roman?" asked Jeffrey Ralston.

"Not much," Sanders said. He felt free to speak with Ralston one on one, now that the barbeque was over and all of the guests had gone.

"I give it a great deal of thought. The one thing I want to do before I retire is nail Castro."

"It's been tried, Jeffrey. Shouldn't have been that hard, but that cat has had several sets of nine lives. You've never invited me here before. So what's on your mind?"

"You had a home in Havana, up in the hills, I understand."

"Yeah, it's still there. I take a trip in to see it every few years."

"Would you retire there?"

"It'd be nice."

"What if we put together a final shot at our legacies?"

Sanders sat back as intricacies formed in his mind. Then he leaned forward, taking a sip of his scotch. "I would need seed money. And give up my citizenship, short term, if I get you."

"I see we are on the same page."

"We need a solid plan."

"I have a solid plan. For some time, actually. A modified version of the old Operation: Mongoose."

"Then—you'll have your reason to invade. Consider it—dealt with."

"Then, the next time I see you, I'll have you shot—as a traitor."

"Something like that." Sanders stood, finishing his scotch. He grinned. "But let me get out the front door first."

Chapter 109

Marathon Airport

July 25, 2006

The MU-2 carried Lance at 360 knots, or 414 statute miles per hour. The new 750 s.h.p. engines, radically simple in their design, more than tripled the exhaust thrust. The unique first stage compressor acted as a mini turbofan though it swung a five-blade prop. The same prop design that once moved the ill-fated Shadowhawk through darkened Soviet-controlled skies. The aircraft could race toward the flight levels better than 3,000 feet per minute. Aerodynamically, small strakes protruded on both sides of the nose, just below the cockpit, to lighten the nose-heavy aircraft.

Lance landed on Runway 7, just shy of five hours—nonstop. He taxied back up to the beginning of the runway. There was a new hangar that sat back from the rest. Custom in every detail, though not readily observable. The heavy-gauge steel hanger was one hundred ten feet long and eighty feet wide. Lance shut down in front of the large sliding doors. He was home.

After he put the Mits away, he climbed upstairs to his apartment.

Inside was a well-appointed living room with an open kitchen design. A door each led to the bedroom and the bathroom. The granite countertops with stainless steel appliances added further to the room's appeal. A sofa was placed in front of a flat-screen TV that sat within a wall-to-wall bookcase. There were two windows on either side of the entrance door. Lance turned on the sconce lighting.

Come morning, Lance came downstairs and realized it was time to stock not only the fridge but the shop. The hangar was barren. He needed tools and machinery. It would be the order of the day. There was a knock on the hangar door at the far end. "I have the welcome wagon so soon?" Lance strolled to the other end, to the man-door, located within the last sliding door panel. He opened the door, swinging it inward. "Jeffrey."

"I was in the neighborhood."

"Really? Okay. Come in then, please," Lance said.

"So these are your new digs?" Ralston said, stepping inside. He saw that the MU-2 was back with its master. "I just wanted to check on you. I felt that I should give you time first."

"Thank you." Lance took pause. "I was going to release them, you know. And give them my gun. If you hadn't come when you did, you might not have recovered the bomb."

"Yes, I am aware of this."

"I told them as I tell you now. I will never kill again. Call it a vow."

"No, I would think not. Killing approximately seven hundred Taliban with your little homemade ray gun would put most off." Ralston caught a glimpse of capture. "Ever since you vaporized a hole in the wall of our hangar in Dessau, I have followed your progress with great interest."

Lance, standing in the middle of his cavernous hangar, felt pinned to the wall. He accepted the revelation. "You waited until now to say something?"

"Always when the time is right."

"Can we just say I was playing with some very big matches?"

"Yes, you were."

"What I said in the Echo Jet after I nuked the Taliban camp—that wasn't my imagination?"

"As I was flipping the bill with our friend, Dexter Turner, I made sure I could not be disconnected from the avionics and satphone link by you, but rather at my convenience. The same with our hanger in Dessau. Never forget your tradecraft."

"You didn't trust me."

"I trust you, implicitly. However, you have a tendency to go off on your little jihads. And that has never boded well for me."

"So, how far would I have gotten?"

"Would you have destroyed the boys up on the hill? Probably. The White House? Close. Wall Street? Tempting. Islam? Russia? China? With my blessings. Cuba, and many others? With my insistence." Ralston grinned. "Tell me, with your love of England, what would you have done with the royal family?"

"Ever see the play—The Queen and I?" Ralston grinned. "No matter. I am not the Stone."

Ralston headed to the staircase. "No, you're not. However, you had a rather interesting vision. I can't say you were entirely wrong."

"I wasn't any wrong. But you needn't worry."

"I'm not, Lance."

Ralston entered upstairs, perusing with a casual eye. "Not exactly Feng Shui, but looks cozy. Are you sure this is right for you?"

"For now."

"As you wish," Ralston said with another look around.

"What do you intend on doing with the Sparrowhawk?"

"I don't know yet. I may bring it here for safekeeping. I assume it would be safe here?

“I won’t go back to get it. And everything else is dead and buried in the Atlantic.”

“Yes, you’re thorough like that. Let’s go get some breakfast.”

It was a good visit. Lance told him that he and Eric Pitts were building a new four-seat canard kit plane. This sat well with Ralston. There would be no mach three-plus aircraft spitting out lightning bolts to lose sleep over. He also agreed to ship over the CNC milling machine from Germany. As a parting gift of sorts.

Lance stood inside of his cavernous hangar, all alone once again. He reminded himself of the old aviation adage: *There is nothing more useless than the runway behind you*. He would keep moving forward.

There was a knock at the man-door. “Boy, I’m popular today.”

He opened it to see two black SUVs parked in front of his hangar. They were pounding and vibrating madly. A young black woman, whose bling shook and swayed with her, stepped out of the lead vehicle and sauntered over to Lance. “You, Lance Rio?” the woman asked.

“May I help you?”

“Yeah. I’m L.A. Tonya. You know the rapper superstar.”

“Don’t know you. And I hate rap. Hate everything about it. And would you have your people turn down the noise? You’re disturbing everyone.”

“The sound’s the sound, baby.”

“Turn it down!”

Lance pushed the door. The woman stopped him. His hand took her by the wrist and moved her away. Four large black men jumped out of the vehicles. Something clicked inside of Lance that had laid dormant for half a year. She saw an aggressive stance and a man ready to attack.

“Easy, dude. I just wanted to see if you was for real. Tara Abbott is my auntie. She said that you could teach me to fly like nobody’s business now that you’re retired.”

“She did, did she? Well, I’m not flight instructing these days.”

“Why not? You know how.”

“I hate rap. I hate everything about it. I have seen too many ghettos to see that life celebrated in ear-busting music if you call what you do music.”

“Yeah, I call it music! And so do millions of others!”

“Well, there’s no accounting for bad taste. Now leave.”

“Sorry to have bothered you, sir. Forgive me.”

“Tell your aunt I say hello.” He had to ask. “How is she these days?”

“She’s remarried and semi-retired in Miami.”

“And what is your name? Your real name.”

“LaTonya Watts.”

"How old are you, LaTonya?"

"Twenty-seven."

"I gather you're successful."

"Yeah, I'm doing all right. But I always wanted to learn how to fly."

"Why me?"

"Auntie said it would be good for you. And I live in South Miami myself. You're not mad, are you?"

"Only at the noise. It destroys the hearing. And the message…"

"You really hate rap?"

"Rap is what you do—if you can't sing—and you ugly." Her bodyguards stiffened in offense. "Except you. You're quite pretty."

"Well, thank you."

Maybe it was time to re-engage with people and enjoy what he once loved to do. "Tell you what. Come back in six weeks, because I have a lot on and I'll teach you to fly. But I want commitment. You'll train to professional standards—*quietly!* Roger?"

"Roger!" Her arms wrapped around Lance as she jumped up and down, shaking him.

After they left, Lance took a walk up the ramp to the FBO in front of his hanger to get to know his neighbors and see about using one of their planes to teach LaTonya. It was a good first day in his new home.

Chapter 110

Havana, Cuba

December 1, 2006

Roman Sanders made his way along the pier. He smiled at being back home. He approached the handsome yacht and stepped aboard. A large, portly man with a well-trimmed beard emerged from the galley. He put the two drinks in his hands down and hugged Roman Sanders. "Roman. Finally, my old friend. Finally!"

"Ernesto. My oldest and dearest friend. It is good to see you again. Too many years."

"I was delighted to receive your communiqué but never thought I would see you myself back in Havana," Ernesto Cruz said as he handed Sanders his drink. "Rum Collins, as I recall."

"Yes," Sanders said as he took a seat on the plush leather sofa. "We just missed one another the last two times I was here. But, I'm here permanently now."

"I see." Cruz grimaced. "Have you been up past Papa's house?"

"Yes. It's my understanding that the house up past his is going to be on the market again. Soon."

"Then, we should take the boat out for a cruise and catch up."

"That would be a good idea," Sanders nodded.

As the yacht slowly powered its way out of Havana Harbor, Roman Sanders thought about the day his father took him and sped away from their hotel, pursued by Castro's army. He remembered vividly his father getting shot, falling out of the car, and dying in his small arms. It was Ernesto's family that took care of him. They were brothers. Now, he was back for more than revenge, but to correct larger matters still unresolved.

Chapter 111

Gillespie Airfield: El Cajon, California

March 3, 2007

"Okay, I'm stoked," Eric Pitts said. "Finally, dude, a sleek, beautiful aircraft with an old fashion propeller. Well, it's our high-tech version, but a propeller nonetheless. You still want to keep the name? I mean, we suffixed hawk onto everything we've built. Well, except for the Echo Jet. But we no speaky about that."

"It'll do," Lance replied.

"Okay, then. I dub thee the *Aerohawk*," Eric said, patting the fuselage and giving it a kiss. "You're official, girl."

Both men stood back and looked at the Aerohawk. She was a twenty-foot long, beautifully tapered canard-designed kit plane. "I've waited a long while for this, Lancey-boy!"

"I'm thrilled you're thrilled, Special."

"Finally!" Eric walked completely around the twenty-four-foot wingspan and then around the small front wing. He raised the pilot's side door and sat inside. "We just need an engine. Thee engine."

"The Turbo-Disc-Engine is nearly reality. Another month."

"Lance, you've been flipping the bill for everything. I've thrown in a good chunk, of course, but it's all been on you."

"It's okay."

"Yeah, but we're rolling right into our next hawk. And she's jet-powered. You gotta keep something for retirement."

"Well, you know what they say: If you want to make a little money in aviation—start out with a lot."

***

Lance had another blissful night's sleep back home in Marathon.

With each passing day, a degree of calm was added. And so were the pounds. Lance was tipping the scale thirty pounds heavier. Looser shorts did the trick and were his preferred attire. He was just another fat American, though he carried it well.

He sat in one of two folding patio chairs he bought and looked out through the open hangar doors. A lone figure stood at the doors. "Hey, Lance, you got a minute?" asked Floyd Hanson, Lance's neighbor up the ramp.

"Sure, Floyd, come in. Pull up a chair." Floyd did. "What's on your mind, sir?"

Floyd marveled for a moment at the MU-2's refinements. "You and your Mits. Charter business. We do some charter work, but what we need is a turboprop. I don't want to say yours is going to waste, but we could generate some new business with it. I have the clientele. And it's growing."

"I used to have a charter business back in the early eighties. But that was a long time ago. And with this very plane."

"Well, maybe it's time to start up again. I sure could use your help. I know you're all into kit planes and all…"

"Sport Aviation, they're calling it now."

"Oh, okay. Do you think we could work together? You fly, I pay you for your time and aircraft use, and I take a cut off the end. All straight up."

Lance reflected. He did help train LaTonya, and she got her PLL—Private Pilot's License. She was currently working on her instrument rating with Floyd when he couldn't be there. "Part one-thirty-five flying again? He paused. "Very well. But, no smoking in my aircraft."

"Everything you want will be respected. That's great, Lance. Thank you."

Lance was in that frame of mind to meet new people, and a few flights here and there would be good adventure. His days of derring-do were over with anyway.

***

Roman Sanders sat pleased, looking over the tranquil Mediterranean coastline of L'Esartit, Spain. Lunch was light but filling. He sat with Ernesto Cruz and two new pieces of the operation's puzzle. "I have the device in my custody," Sanders announced quietly.

"The one my brother built," Valeri Borsov said between bites. The short, burly Russian whose fifty years showed to be hard, exacting years despite his name meaning: "healthy" or "vigorous."

"We're in a new era, Valeri. If you want your twilight years to mean something, I need you fully on board. Redo the device."

"I will do this, Roman. I, too, miss Cuba. It beats driving cab in St. Petersburg."

"Nothing wrong with driving a cab," Sanders replied.

"But, it is a long drop from being KGB officer and before that a nuclear physicist. Like my brother, Valentin. May his death be avenged and with [illegible]ose. I hope the same for your brother Reza, Ashiq."

[illegible]vill," said Ashiq Mohammed Shah. The tall, distinguished Persian leaned [illegible]t will take some time, but you will have your missiles."

***

The charter service was a nice distraction for Lance, which often took him over Cuba. It wasn't the thought of being shot down as that wouldn't happen, per se, but it was the layers of memories. But, such memories were useless runway behind him.

Lance turned back to his passengers after he heard a shout. "Everything okay back there?" He could see that the bottle of champagne was nearly emptied between the three women giggling and laughing riotously.

"Just fine as we unwind," said Sonya Valdivia. She undid her seatbelt and came forward to catch Lance eye to eye. Her dark, shimmering eyes held Lance in a momentary trance. His first glimpse of her was with her chestnut hair folded over her right shoulder. She had perfect lips that were full and moderately wide that curled up on the ends.

"You should sit back and put your seatbelt back on."

"Yes, Captain."

Lance tried to be the dominant party, but her hand found its way around his neck, and then a soft full kiss took him to a place where there were no dimensions. Their lips parted. She was slow to let go. "Why did you do that?"

"To remind me," she mused.

"Of your amorous adventures with young men?"

"Boy toys! Can I sit up front with you?"

"Yes, just be careful of the controls." She took the right seat. "Here, put on the headset." Lance was still thinking of the kiss. He was sure that several plastic flutes of bubbly had something to do with her inhibition. For him, though, her kiss was sobering, down to his toes.

"It's a shame we can't just fly directly into Cuba and not have to go all the way to the Cayman Islands. Freaking Castro."

"I gather you're from Cuba originally, though you have an English spelling of your name?"

"True to both. I came to live with my brother Javier in Miami when I was sixteen. My parents are still there. My father used to own a large plantation before Castro took it for himself."

"I'm sorry."

"What about you?"

"I was born in San Francisco, a tradition since my father, but I spent my first few years somewhere in Havana. My father flew for Pan Am back then."

"Funny, you sound British or European."

"I lived overseas for most of my adult life. I'm only back to the U.S. since last year."

"Did you fly over there?"

"Yes. Charter work mostly."

"You must have seen and been everywhere."

"A few places."

"What do you girls do?"

"Seriously?" she said, somewhat indignant. "We're from Cabana TV. Anita is the six o'clock news anchor. Stephanie and I are the legal counsel for the station. You've never seen Cabana TV?"

"No, I'm sorry, I haven't."

"That's alright. I'll forgive you this time."

Lance held up his hand as the radio crackled to life. "Strap in. We're starting our descent." Sonya worked her way into the belt harness. She was impressed with the plane, all of the dials and gadgets—and the pilot.

Lance brought the MU-2 down on Runway 26. He was back in Grand Cayman after so many years. He was ushered to a spot on the tarmac where he shut down. "Okay, ladies, you have two hours before your flight to Havana."

"Thank you, Captain Rio," came the shouts of Anita Busquez and Stephanie Morgan. Anita was the alpha female of the three. At least, she thought. She was the TV star, and everything else, Lance surmised, ran in orbit around her.

"You should come with us," Anita stated.

"I think that's the champagne talking. I don't have a change of clothes."

"I don't plan to keep you in them anyway," Anita countered.

Lance turned to Sonya. "I imagine she's the consummate professional on the air."

Sonya shrugged. "Something like that. Hey! You should come with us. You haven't been there—since whenever you left."

"Thank you, but no. I would probably think only about my old home, and I've endured enough cardiac fractures for one lifetime."

"You have a way of putting things," she said with a curious smile. "It might bring you closure. Going back did for me the first time."

"I wouldn't even know where to look. I know the basic location, but not the street. It's somewhere in the Vedado district. I would know the house if I saw it. I used to study old photos of it. My dad especially would tell me about the house. It was a two-story colonial built in nineteen-sixteen, and it overlooked the ocean."

"You come, and I'll help you find it. I know my way around Havana."

"I thought you were all set to go boy crazy?"

"You're a boy."

***

The scent of tropical breezes overshadowed Lance's better judgment as he stepped off the Cayman Airways Boeing 737. He was in Cuba. The warm appeal of not doing it alone finally convinced him to step onboard.

Lance slept on the sofa in the girl's suite for the night.

He woke the next morning, accepting where he was, and looked forward to the day. He would see about accommodations for himself within the hotel after breakfast.

"Anybody up?" he said quietly. Not a stir. The girls were in two double beds. He didn't know how they planned to manage any romantic adventures. Then he didn't want to know. It was nearly 8:30. Lance rose and quietly went into the bathroom.

By nine a.m., the girls were up and in a beehive of activity. Lance felt a kind of kinship, like a big brother looking after his sisters.

Lance came downstairs to the lobby and arranged for a car. They were in the land of Chevy remix, so he went for a '57 Chevy—powered by a Russian *Lada* engine. Resourcefulness was a trademark of the Cuban people.

"I guess you two are going house hunting," Anita said.

"I wouldn't put it like that," Lance replied.

"You know what I mean. Well, Stephanie and I are going shopping. Sonya, give us a call later, and we can meet up for lunch."

"Okay. I'll call around one," Sonya confirmed.

Lance and Sonya drove back into the old part of town, into the Vedado area where homes once espoused wealth and pedigree. Now, they were marvelous crumbled relics of a bygone era. The logical step was to go to the end of Escobar Calle, or street closest to the water, and work back from there.

"We're looking for a white, colonial, two-story, with oak doors. The front porch has two columns in front. The back of the house will have a veranda that overlooks the ocean," Lance directed.

Sonya thought that Lance drove too fast up and down the streets. He was amazingly focused and too formal with her. "Lance, I'm getting hungry. And it's already two o'clock. We missed lunch with the girls."

"Let's just finish up this street." Lance stomped on the brakes as they passed two homes. Behind them on the adjacent street was a white two-story house that had a veranda. Lance picked up speed and turned the corner.

He came around and pulled up front. The faded white house stood silent in time. The twin columns in front were fractured and crumbly. Windows were broken, except some upstairs. "This is it. It matches the photos."

Sonya put her hand on his arm. "Are you sure, Lance?"

He smiled, nodding. "Yes. This was once my home. Will you go with me?"

There was a trustworthy charm to this man, and she was happy to help him find some solace. He walked with a certain trepidation, at which she hurried up the three steps and placed her hand within his. "It's okay. We'll do this together."

Her reassurance brought warmth to an insecure place within him. His smile told her so. This man truly appreciated her help and support. She found it refreshing. The door was locked, probably frozen over time. Lance looked around. "We can get in through a window. Can I lift you in through one?"

"Do we need to go in?"

"I may never get this opportunity again."

"Okay. Shoot me through." Lance found her to be a trooper. The front windowsill had broken glass pieces in it. That was a no-go.

"Let's try around back," Lance said as he took her by the hand.

The backdoor was opened. It had long been dried out and withered. They entered into the laundry room, which led into the kitchen, picked clean of its appliances and cabinetry. Lance scanned the yellowed white walls. With nothing more to tell him, he moved into the living room, ever holding onto Sonya's hand. It was barren like the kitchen. Not a single light fixture remained. Lance gently stepped onto the staircase landing and made his way up along the creaking steps.

Through the double doors was the master bedroom. Lance let go of Sonya and walked to the veranda. He opened the French doors with a couple of hard tugs and stepped out with one foot. It was spongy, and it creaked. "Lance, don't go out there. It doesn't sound safe."

"I'm not. Back in the states, this house would be condemned. Or have to be completely rebuilt."

"When did you leave here?"

"I was about three."

"About thirty or so years ago then." This caught Lance by surprise. She thought he was younger than he was. Okay.

"This was my parent's room. I was probably conceived right here."

"So, what are you saying to me, flyboy?"

"No, not that. But this is my beginning. Right here! This house!"

"I'm happy for you, Lance."

They moved along the landing to another bedroom. "This was my room," Lance said, equally moved. "Thank you."

Sonya took Lance by the hand and moved him from his room. "We can come back another time, but we need to meet up with the girls. At least you have some closure now."

***

Lance's thoughts harkened back to his home in Havana, but he also found the pulse of the city's nightlife engaging. "Put it behind you, Lance. We all have lost. At least we're alive and not in some gulag. Castro will get his one day. All of them will," Anita said. "So, tomorrow, we need to—shop!"

"I'm going to take Lance sightseeing," Sonya announced.

"That's a great idea. Let him see the Bacardi Building and a few other places. He'll enjoy that," Anita said with a wave of her hand.

Lance planned to secure a room of his own, but once again, against his better judgment, he stayed another night. He turned down an offer to snuggle up with Anita or Stephanie in their respective beds. He was glad that the girls enjoyed his company, but their self-proclaimed promiscuity unsettled him.

They all had a late morning start after a late-night became an early morning. Lance just caught the end of breakfast down in the dining room. He came back up to the room, only to find that Sonya and Stephanie were standing at the door.

"What's wrong?"

"Ah, we can't go," Stephanie said. Lance noticed the *Do Not Disturb* sign. "Anita is in there right now."

"What are you saying?" Lance asked, dismayed.

"She's—being serviced," Stephanie stated.

"You've got to be kidding me," Lance grumbled.

Sonya noticed Lance was genuinely upset. "Never mind, Lance."

Lance drove along with the rest of the mid-morning traffic. He turned onto Avenida de Bélgica. The coral-colored building, the tallest landmark in the city once upon a time, was easy to spot. It was the epitome of the art deco craze—of long ago. Everything in his life seemed—of long ago.

"Earth to Lance. Over," Sonya radioed.

"Oh, sorry."

"We're here. We can take a look around inside. They revamped it years ago and made it into an office building."

Lance's accumulated skills as a master spy were not wasted by dreary thoughts of the past. They picked up a tail. A small black car of Russian make had followed them for the last three blocks. Lance followed Sonya across the street to the front of the Bacardi building. The car doors opened. "Give me your camera."

"What?"

"Give me your camera. Now." She reached into her bag and fished out the camera. Lance held the digital camera at arm's length. "Smile." He flashed a picture of them hugging. "Follow me to the car." He took her by the hand. They crossed the street. "You are so beautiful!" he said loudly. She was shocked. He pulled her close and kissed her deeply. He heard the doors close and the engine start. The car drove past them. Lance felt her lips part as she pushed in closer to him. He pulled back from her. "I'm sorry. But it's the only thing I could think of. That car. Those men in the car were Federales. The state police."

"And you know this how?"

"When you've traveled as much as I have to repressed countries, you can smell them after a while. It's about watching your P's and Q's."

"So that was just a spy kiss?" she said, offended.

"We needed to dodge a bullet." Lance hoped he could dodge one now.

Sonya kept eyeing Lance on the way back. It turned out the adventure she was hoping to find had been with her all along.

"Do you plan on seeing your parents?" Lance asked, breaking the silence.

"Tomorrow. We'll leave early to avoid morning traffic."

"What do you mean 'we,' white man?"

"Funny. But you'll love them. Don't worry. I'm not taking you to 'meet my parents' meet my parents."

"I look forward to meeting them. By the way, do you know how to get to the Bay of Pigs?"

"Bahía de Cochinos. Yes, I've been there."

"Can we go?"

"Sure. When?"

"Now."

"Now?"

"Why not?"

"Okay. Turn around, and let's head to the highway."

Two and a half hours later, they were at the cove or upper part of the bay, at Playa Larga. It was beautiful. It reminded Lance why he chose the tropics as the place to retire. The area was thick with trees and fauna.

A few miles south of Playa Largo, Lance hit the brakes. The two cars in front of him skidded to a stop as a locomotive came out of nowhere, seemingly in a hurry. He recognized the aged M62 Russian-built engine. There were no railroad crossing signs, surprisingly. The tracks that crossed the road were still rusted from non-use. Interesting, he thought.

Traffic picked back up. Lance noticed an old faded, and worn concrete bunker not far from the road, mostly hidden behind jungle growth. The locomotive came from there. He pulled over. "Do you know what this area is?"

"No. I'm not familiar with it."

"Come on."

The old bunker was actually three bunkers nestled inside of a small cove that lined the shore. The three curved roof buildings had a concrete platform in front. This was where the railroad tracks ended. The concrete platform ran down the side that joined to a long wooden pier. The pier ran along the cove and ended out to the bay. Lance thought it odd. It smelled of intrigue. Then he dismissed it as another relic of the past.

They were soon following the single road south until Lance caught sight of a runway in typical disrepair. They were finally in Playa Girón. It was a beautiful location and the site of the final battle between Cuban forces and Cuban exiles in 1961. They would have lunch.

"Are you ready to head back?" Sonya asked.

"Yes. Thank you for taking me down here. Thank you for everything." He paused. "Listen. If you ever find yourself in trouble and can't get off the island, get word to me. I will come get you. Wait for me at those old bunkers. Our code name will be the *Farm*."

"You mean you will sneak in, get me and sneak out again. Just like that?"

"Just like that."

"Ooh, a man of mystery."

Lance drove north. He had a feel for the landscape and traffic routes now. It was getting near dinnertime, but he agreed to a final stop before they went back to the hotel.

Lance parked opposite the Bacardi Building. He waited in the car. Sonya had been inside for twenty minutes, and Lance was getting nervous, though it never showed. Finally, she came out with others as it was quitting time. He was relieved to see her. She came around the Chevy convertible and hopped in.

"Okay. We can go," Sonya said. Lance caught her smiling at him again. That, too, made him nervous. This may have shown.

Dinner with the girls was quiet, thankfully Lance thought. Instead of the rum-fueled vulgar exposition of Anita's and Stephanie's dalliances. Sonya, as it turned out, spent all her time with him. He still wondered why.

"Well, Stephanie and I are going to dance the night away. So don't wait up," Anita announced.

"It has been a long day," Lance said dryly.

"Somebody's a party-pooper," Anita stated with the last gulp of her drink. Her fourth. "You're in beautiful, marvelous Havana with three toxic sexy women, and what do you do? Nothing. We bought your airline ticket. We should get something out of the deal."

Lance put down his knife and fork; wiped his mouth. "If you will excuse me." He took his leave before he said something regrettably accurate. Sonya glared venomously at her two drunken colleagues.

"What?" Anita shrugged.

Sonya chased after Lance. "Hey! You promised me a walk along the Malecón."

In the soft orange glow of twilight and streetlights strung along the famed stone sea wall, Lance calmed. Sonya had her arm within his as they strolled amongst other couples, who frequently stopped to kiss, before walking on, hand in hand.

"Lance."

"Yes."

Sonya stopped. She faced him. "I want you to kiss me. Not a spy kiss. A real kiss."

"Sonya, you don't understand—" His words were silenced with a finger to his lips. She snuggled closer. She felt his uncertainty until her lips pushed it back, and they embraced. It was passionate. Tender. Moments went by.

"Come on, let's go." She took him by the hand.

"Go where?"

"Back to the hotel room."

He pulled his hand away. "No, that won't be happening."

"Why? I know you want to be with me."

"I am very grateful for your kindness, Sonya." He stepped away. She grabbed hold of him.

"Please don't go."

"But, you would have been better off chasing after your boy toys."

He turned from her, leaving a bewildered Sonya Valdivia standing alone on the Malecón.

Chapter 112

Marathon Airport

June 23, 2007

Lance enjoyed that he had a fully functional shop. He worked on things here, while Special worked on other parts in San Diego. With work completed on the Aerohawk, it was now time for the Aquahawk! He would patiently bring the jet-powered amphibian kit plane to life.

Eric's son just received his PPL and was working on his A & P. His enthusiasm and help to his father took much burden off of Lance, allowing him to complete his test pilot duties. As a result, the Aerohawk was now a newly certified experimental aircraft. The new Turbo-Disc-Engine was spinning out 377 shaft horsepower at 11,000 r.p.m. The water-cooled engine held much promise for the future of aviation and elsewhere.

The recently delivered CNC milling machine was busy cutting out a new front fan that would be finished by day's end. In the meantime, he had parts of the Aquahawk to build. If he wasn't truly happy, he was duly content.

Lance felt the draining of his finances by these projects. It forced him to take seriously Eric's demand that they "be ready" for *Oshkosh 2008*. They had a little over a year to get both aircraft perfected and ready to reproduce with the first deposit they may receive. Oshkosh was the granddaddy of all air shows on earth. Eric accepted readily that their joint company would be called *Aeronautical Dream Builders, Inc*. It had the right ring to it. Lance had not seen Eric as happy as he had now, despite the more advanced work they had accomplished. Aviation proved again to be a compromise. Eric had his propeller-driven aircraft in the Aerohawk, and Lance would have his jet-powered aircraft in the Aquahawk.

"Lance," Sonya said, walking up to the long table. Lance lowered his dust mask and pulled his earplugs.

"What are you doing here?"

"It's Saturday, and I thought I would drive down, now that I know where you are. I wanted to return the shirt you left behind."

"You needn't have bothered. Really."

"And I wanted to apologize for making you uncomfortable."

"People don't apologize for their speech or actions anymore."

"Will you just accept my apology?"

"Yes," he bemoaned.

"Good. You can take me to lunch."

"Can't. I have to finish my work here. I'm on a timer."

"What do you do here?"

"I build, or rather first design kit planes. You know planes that you build yourself."

"No, I was not aware that people did this."

"Well, they do. And by the thousands."

"Are they safe?"

"Well, nothing is idiot-proof, though I try. But a kit plane can usually shoot past production aircraft like they are standing still. My new prototype over there—" Lance pointed to the Aerohawk nestled under the left-wing of the MU-2, "is just as fast as my Mits. Well, the old version anyway."

"Wow. Can I help?"

"As you can see, I'm in the dusty phase of things. And I don't have coveralls that will fit you."

"As you wish. I just came to say hello and make peace."

"I appreciate the gesture, Sonya, but I figured on never seeing you again."

"Well, here I am! Anyway, I thought I would invite you to a barbeque party at my brother's house tomorrow. Unless you can't tear yourself away from your kit plane thingy."

"Sonya, why do you even want to see me again?"

"I like you. And it's only a barbeque."

"Then—you can pick me up at the airport."

"You can't drive up."

"Why drive when you can fly?"

***

Lance entered the old estate home. Sonya guided him from the foyer to the backyard.

"The house was built in nineteen-twenty, and my father bought it in nineteen-forty-nine. He used to love coming here from Cuba."

"I gather he hasn't been here since Castro took power."

"Correct. Again, blame Castro."

The house was large, the home a movie star from Hollywood's golden age would have own. It was modest for being palatial. Lance could tell it had been upgraded and remodeled over the years. Sonya waltzed Lance up to the man in front of the semi-circular grill island. He had a little extra size on Lance. He was graying at the temples but still held a thick black mane of hair.

"Lance, this is my brother Javier. This is Lance Rio."

"Pleasure to meet you," Lance said as he shook Javier's hand.

"So, you're the pilot that has my sister in a spin," Javier Valdivia mused.

"I would say I'm more of a novelty," Lance countered, grinning.

Lance found himself interwoven in conversation with the professional set, eight of them, whose dinner dialogue was ranged in topic. He had learned that Javier was a professor of psychology and sociology at the University of Miami. His wife Sandra was a stay-at-home mom with the youngest of three sons still there. Lance could see Sandra had trouble fitting in with conversation, but she was a kind woman and gracious host.

Eloise Coleman, an associate professor with Javier, with her partner Rosalyn, spoke rather boldly for Lance's taste. She was a conservative democrat, he figured, an erudite that sparked attention to her points of view. She targeted Lance. "Mr. Rio."

"Please, call me Lance. We've all been eating with our hands."

"Thoughtfully said. Lance, then, what is your position on gay marriage?"

"Sorry?"

"What is your position on gay marriage? And don't be shy."

"I have no stand on the matter."

"Of course you do."

"No, I don't. Really."

"Would you think us equal?"

Lance noticed all eyes were on him, with Sonya peering over the top of her wine glass. He sighed mildly. "In whose eyes do you refer to, Eloise? In mine? Some politician? God's?"

"In all eyes. Where do you stand on the issue?"

"I don't stand anywhere on the issue."

"That's not possible. Either you accept it, or you protest it," Eloise said persistently.

"I protest nothing. But no matter how hard you protest, being honest, you'll never be what I have been."

"And what is that, my good man?"

"A husband."

Sonya gasped and choked. She took several pats on the back, clawing verbally to speak. "You've been married before?"

"That should come as a surprise to you? Really? But, yes, twice."

"So why can I not be a husband to my wife, plumbing aside?" Eloise asked insistently.

"You're not a man. And for that you wouldn't understand, plumbing aside. In biblical Hebrew, for instance, the term: *'ish* denoted a married man." (Lance never cared for the other term for husband: *Ba'al*, which meant *master*. It was also an ancient pagan god that rightly deserved annihilation).

"You speak Hebrew?" Sonya asked, more annoyed than surprised.

"I once lived in Israel," Lance replied.

"Well, there's a lot to you, isn't there, sport?"

"Some think so."

"How do you spell eesh?"

"Aleph-Yod-Shin."

She glared at him. "In English."

Lance grinned. "I-S-H."

"That's *ish*. Figures. Married men usually are a bunch of little ishes."

"Given that woman was taken from man, a wife, *'ish·shah*, are a bunch of little ishes too."

Javier chuckled.

Eloise cleared her throat. "So, you don't accept my marriage?"

"It's not my standard, but it's your business."

"Well, you brought religion into it."

"No. I brought history into it."

"Fair enough. You're a scholar and not told us."

"No, I'm not a scholar."

"So, you believe that marriage should be between a man and a woman exclusively? You can say it."

"Oi," Lance said lightly. "Someone bring me a Bible if you would please."

"I'll go." Sonya hopped up. She moved into the house. In moments, she was back out handing it to Lance. "Is the Douay version okay?"

"It's a bible, isn't it? And technically, it's the *Douay-Rheims* Bible. From the two English colleges that were in France, back in the sixteen hundreds." She handed him the book. Lance declined possession. "No. You look it up for me."

"Okay. Not that I know where anything is," Sonya said, sitting poised.

"You're not going to quote Leviticus, are you?" Eloise questioned staunchly.

"Turn to Matthew chapter nineteen," Lance instructed. "More towards the back."

"Okay. I found Matthew." She flipped a few pages. "Chapter nineteen."

"Read from the beginning. I don't remember the exact verses."

Sonya read: "'And it came to pass when Jesus had ended these words, he departed from Galilee, and came into the coasts of Judea, beyond Jordan. And great multitudes followed him: and he healed them there. And there came to him the Pharisees tempting him, and saying: 'Is it lawful for a man to put away his wife for every cause?'" She stopped. "Okay, what's a Pharisee?"

"Bad guy."

"And what does he mean *put away* his wife?"

"Divorce her."

"Jerk."

"Just read."

She continued. "'Who answering, said to them: 'Have ye not read, that he who made man from the beginning, made them male and female?' And he said: 'For this cause shall a man leave father and mother, and shall cleave to his wife, and they two shall be in one flesh. Therefore now they are not two, but one flesh. What therefore God hath joined together, let no man put asunder.'" She stopped. "Okay. But if you are very independent?"

"Sonya, the fact that you are in any relationship, you forego some of that independence. By nature, you become, to a point, dependent. You count on one another. And that's fine."

"I understand what you are saying, Lance. I get it."

"Good. Now go to Genesis. Chapter Two."

Sonya scanned the book. "Read here? 'And the Lord God said: 'It is not good for man to be alone: let us make him a help like unto himself.' And the Lord God having formed out of the ground all the beasts of the earth, and all the fowls of the air, brought them to Adam to see what he would call them: for whatsoever Adam called any living creature the same is its name. And Adam called all the beasts by their names, and all the fowls of the air, and all the cattle of the field: but for Adam there was not found a helper like himself. Then the Lord God cast a deep sleep upon Adam: and when he was fast asleep, he took one of his ribs, and filled up flesh for it. And the Lord God built the rib which he took from Adam into a woman: and brought her to Adam. And Adam said: 'This now is bone of my bones, and flesh of my flesh; she shall be called woman, because she was taken out of man. Therefore a man shall leave father and mother, and shall cleave to his wife: and they shall be two in one flesh.'"

"Maybe if people better understood the roots of marriage, there wouldn't be so many putting away of spouses," Lance said.

"And what if I don't believe in the Adam and Eve story?" Eloise stated.

"Despite Genesis being the only realistic ancient narrative we have of our beginning, it doesn't change the meaning of the words or their application."

"But, you've been divorced twice. So how do you reconcile that?"

"I never said I was divorced twice. I said I was married twice."

"Whatever his status is, it's his business. We should respect that," Sonya addressed.

"Rightly so. Just as I am sure, Lance, that you respect our path." Eloise took Rosalyn's hand and held it up in a victory wave. "We've followed our heart."

"Eloise! Look out!" Lance said, snapping forward. "The heart is more treacherous than anything else. And is desperate. Who can know it?"

There was silence.

"Oh, my dear, Lance, you do have a way about you," Eloise said, chuckling.

"He certainly does," Sonya said, eyeing him.

"We have our differences of opinion, Lance. But I like you."

"I like you too, Eloise. I meant no offense."

"None taken. I did ask you for your opinion."

"I do believe what you believe matters."

"It can. It's all personal choice."

"Sometimes not." Lance took pause. "Consider that over a billion people believe that in a vision, Mohammed journeyed to Heaven from where the Al-Aqsa Mosque sits, next to the Dome of the Rock. Yet, there is no evidence, either historical or empirical, that he ever set foot in Jerusalem. And people die. A billion people believe that Peter was the first pope, the Bishop of Rome, yet there is no historical, biblical, or empirical evidence that he ever set foot in Rome. His missionary assignments were in Babylon or Mesopotamia. And people die. Millions believe that we evolved from non-living matter. Yet, after hundreds of millions of dollars spent well over a century, scientists have not been able to reproduce what so-called nothingness did. And people die."

"Who are you?" Sonya questioned.

It was late. Lance was bid to stay the night.

Lance came to the staircase when Javier popped his head out of his study. "Lance, would you come in here for a moment?"

Lance came into the study. He took a seat. Javier closed the door. "What's up?"

"Well, I thought we should talk. My little sister and I are very close, though she never listens to me. Especially in her choice of men."

"I've been nothing but respectful toward Sonya."

"I know. It shows. I know about her helping you find your old home in Cuba. I think that's great. And that you stood her up on the Malecón of all places." Javier chuckled.

"There's a first time for everything."

"So there is. But, she says you are a man of good character. I think so too. Your words were wasted on Eloise. But then she wasn't your real focus."

"I merely answered a question."

"So you did. I'm curious, Lance, how long did you live overseas?"

"About eighteen years."

"Intelligence work?

"Why would you draw that conclusion?"

"I was nearly recruited into the CIA. I've helped in efforts to thwart Castro at every turn. Or used to. I know that world very well."

"I'm retired now, Javier. Let's leave it at that."

"I'm just asking you not to hurt her."

"She found me."

Javier grinned. "Fair enough."

"And I'm the one always getting hurt. But tell me, this Cabana TV station she works for, is it like TV Marti?"

"An anti-Castro news station? Basically. As the station grew to reach more of Central and South America, Sonya was the one that brought in advertisers. Mostly air carriers and tourism, but some local advertisers too. It became a legitimate news station."

"I'm also thinking it's another CIA front, and she's been recruited as a courier."

"Against my wishes. I gather you observed this in Havana?"

"It was obvious."

"We'll keep this conversation between us," Javier said.

Lance rose and went to the door. He turned. "My first wife came from a troubled background, and there was no hope for us. But by her choice. My second wife was East German originally. A contract was placed on her by her former boyfriend, a Stasi double agent. I had to let her go, her and her two young daughters, my babies, for their safety. So only one divorce."

"What happened to the boyfriend?"

Lance smiled thinly. "Goodnight, Javier."

Sonya enjoyed making breakfast. Lance complimented her on her culinary skills. Mostly he thanked her for caring to do so.

She drove him back to the airport. She was still in awe of the oddly futuristic aircraft he walked around and sampled here and there in preflight. She stood at the gate, almost dutifully, watching his focused attention to detail. Finally, Lance took the right seat as he wanted to get used to flying as an instructor in the new aircraft. Lance reached over and inserted the key into the master switch lock and turned it to ON and then to RUN. Sonya listened to the unusual engine begin its slow whine to life. He held the starter button until 70 p.s.i. registered on the Intake Pressure gauge. It sounded like a turbine engine at startup and then for a moment like a piston engine. Once started, the engine had a throaty low wolf howl. She was missing him already. She was distraught. Lance noticed her. He was cleared to taxi. It pained him. He canceled his clearance and shut down the engine. He unstrapped himself, opened the door, and jumped out. He came around the aircraft and marched up and through the gate. She turned to face him, motionless. He took her into his arms and kissed her. She felt his powerful life presence envelop her.

"You confuse me," Sonya said, thoroughly bewildered, once more by this man.

"With the obvious?" Lance said, his smile both charming and reassuring. "If you truly care for me, Sonya Valdivia, then be my friend. A true friend."

"I understand," she said. "But, then, why did you kiss me?"

"To stir your imagination."

"Well, honey, that's not what you stirred."

***

Ernesto Cruz stood with Roman Sanders in the cab of the locomotive. The diesel-powered train pushed three coaches and a single boxcar on the end. It was now the second time that any train had traveled on the old rusted railway in over thirty years. It connected from the Australia train station, north of them, down to the Bay of Pigs. This stage of the operation took the greasing of many palms.

"Nothing like pocket capitalism, Ernesto, to get things done," Sanders said.

"Yes. More patience and I believe we will see our victory, Roman."

"One chess piece at a time."

The weathered coaches that were barely fit to carry passengers were from the old Hershey line when the Hershey Chocolate Company operated sugar cane fields in Cuba. The train ensemble creaked and rattled backwards around a curved section of track before crossing the road diagonally, into a final curve, then straightened up as they came to a jarring stop in front of the old concrete bunker platform.

The engineer steadied the old Russian workhorse. He looked at his watch. "Señor Sanders and Señor Cruz, I will have to get the train back to the plantation within an hour."

"That's fine, Jaime. Unhitch the boxcar, and you can take the train back. We'll do another run next week when you can pick up the boxcar."

Several men carrying welding gear, grinders, power saws, angle iron, and other steel pieces stepped into the old boxcar. The boxcar was to be readied for history.

***

It wasn't the number of loops that the Aerohawk did that upset Sonya, but the boy at the controls. "You think this is a bunch of aerobatics? I'm readying this for history," Lance said.

Sonya did as she did most weekends. She drove down to Marathon Airport to see Lance. She understood that he had his aircraft to get ready for display by next summer. She had learned a lot about the world and industry of kit aircraft. At times, it seemed his only pursuit. Perhaps it wasn't a fair assessment. In fairness, he took a lot of interest in her work. He had come to the TV station on several occasions to see her, almost snooping, she thought once or twice. He was the curious type. Sonya felt she could be open with Lance. It did bother her that she misjudged him. He was not a flyboy-playboy after all. Morality mattered heavily with him, yet when he kissed her, there was enjoyment and passion. This perplexed her. She never stayed overnight. He treated her very special. She understood he was building a solid friendship with her, but it was very fatiguing.

The Aerohawk made another unremarkable landing. Lance shut down in front of his hanger. He punched in a code on the remote, and the large doors slid open. They both exited the aircraft and stood in front of it.

"Ninety-two hours total time. The prototype is everything we had hoped it would be."

"I'm glad you're happy. But, why can't we do something else but be around planes?"

"Okay. Like what?"

"You know, boyfriend-girlfriend stuff. Something romantic."

"I thought dinner last night was of that setting."

"It was. And then you dumped me."

"I took you back to your motel room. I told you…"

"Yeah, I know. You don't want another Beverly scenario. All I say is lucky her."

"Oh yeah, lucky her. I'm sure she's still beaming. You keep making it about sex."

"I want to be made love to, Lance. So yes!"

"Who doesn't?"

"Then why all the moral pretense?"

"Pretense? Let me tell you something. I have found, and painfully so, that moral law is just as exacting as physical law and exists just as necessary."

She shook her head. "The way you put things sometimes."

"I'm back to arguing over the interpretation of a stop sign."

"What?"

"Never mind."

"Why, Lance?"

"Because—your way does not work. And I don't want it."

"Because I don't believe in bone of my bones, flesh of my flesh and all that?"

She watched Lance's eyes narrow in anger and then widen in sadness. "No. I shouldn't expect you to understand. Come, I'll take you back to your room now if you wish."

Lance moved his gaze from Sonya to the hanger. He stepped toward it. She put out her hand to stop him. "No, Lance," she said, trembling, her eyes tearing up. "You're right. I don't seem to understand what is probably very reasonable to you. And for that, I am sorry. You take care of yourself."

She kissed him on the cheek and left him alone—standing on the tarmac.

***

The Aquahawk stood proudly on its landing gear. The smooth tapered fuselage melded seamlessly in with its gleaming, air-slicing wings. The large but not too tall tail section housed the engine on top within a long nacelle. It was a work of art and science at its best.

Lance's cell phone rang. He sighed.

"Well, answer it this time," Eric Pitts said.

"Fine. Hello."

"Hi, Lance," Sonya said. "I was wondering if I can come by?"

"I'm in San Diego."

"Oh, I wish I had known."

"Why? It's been over a month. I figured you long gone."

"No, dude. Don't say that," Eric whispered, wincing. "Here, give me the phone. Hello, Sonya? Eric Pitts, here. How'ya doin' darlin'? I'm Lance's partner in crime. Say, if you feel adventurous, why don't you come out to San Diego for a visit and see how the other half lives? Lives with Lance, that is. Yeah, I get it. It's a long drive from Miami down to Marathon. I get you, darlin', because I have to try and build new high-concept aircraft with Lance over twenty-two hundred miles away. And before that, when he lived overseas, it was a life of jetlag."

"Here, give me the phone back," Lance snapped. "Hello. Look, Sonya, I'm forty-nine years old, okay. And I don't have a lot of time in which to do things."

"You're forty-nine?" her voice shot out over the phone.

"Yeah, and I still get pimples. I won't be back for at least another month."

"Will you let me know when you are back?"

"Sure. When I'm back." Lance ended the call.

Chapter 113

Miami

January 3, 2008

Lance figured that most of Miami was over its drunk three days into the New Year.

Lance entered the Cabana TV lobby. As he was known to several of Sonya's colleagues, he was allowed upstairs to the executive offices on the second floor. The spy in him wanted to eavesdrop on the goings-on of the third floor. He worried about Sonya being involved in courier work. That's how he started as a civilian, and it was problematic.

Lance came into the executive office suite, where each office was behind a wall of glass. Lance saw a flash of Sonya in her office. Her door was open. He heard a man's voice. "Come on, baby. Don't you miss me?"

"Eddie. Come on," Sonya said. "You know I'm too much woman for you."

"Yeah? Who satisfies you like I do? Come on, baby, let's do it. Right here."

"In my office?"

"It won't be the first time. Come on, Sonya. I know I'm making you hot."

"Maybe."

"It's been too long. You're done with that pilot guy, right?"

"Yeah, she's done with that pilot guy," Lance said, leaning against the door.

"Who are you?" Eddie puffed.

"The pilot guy, you idiot."

"What did you call me?" Eddie charged forward. Sonya stepped in front of him. Lance never moved. Eddie wasn't close enough yet.

"Not to worry, Eddie. She's all yours." Lance walked away amid calls to come back. Sonya chased after him.

Lance waited impatiently for the elevator.

"Now you wait just a minute," Sonya said, marching up to Lance. "Don't go assuming things. I have not gone behind your back. Eddie's my past. Long past."

"Sounds like he was just about to be your present."

"So, I led him on. That's because he doesn't listen. It's only harmless flirting."

"No such thing." Lance tapped the elevator button again. The elevator doors opened. He stepped in.

"No, Lance, no. I've been building something with you."

"Like this? You don't make me feel comfortable, Sonya."

"What do you want me to do?"

"Now? Nothing." He paused. "You know—I have no idea of what it's like for a woman to be faithful to me." He shrugged. "Not even once." With hurt, he said: "I imagine it's something quite special." The doors closed.

***

Lance did not want to be disturbed. This was part of the joy of living in a hangar, isolated from everything and everyone. It was just after nine a.m. He had run out of ice cream the night before, but to go get more was too much work. The pounding on the hangar door came again. "Alright, I'm coming, I'm coming." He came downstairs. He ignored the man-door and hit the remote, spreading open the big hangar doors by a few feet. "Sonya! What?"

"It's not Miss Valdivia, Lance," Ralston said. He knew about her—naturally.

"What can I do for you, Jeffrey?"

"That's not a very nice greeting."

"I'm sorry. It's good to see you."

"And you. However, I am merely here as a messenger."

"What's the message?"

Ralston waved his hand. Lance heard a car door open from outside. Ralston stepped aside. A feeble old man with a cane stood in Lance's doorway.

"Danny!"

"As you can see, I am worse for the wear. After eighty, every year is a bonus."

"Why are you here?"

"It was a difficult journey. But, I had to see you. And ask you for your forgiveness. If you can, I do beg it."

Lance stared at Danny. Emotion welled up inside of him. Betrayal seemed so standard in his life. "I had a long time ago," Lance thought he whispered.

"Oh, my boy, my dear, Lance." Danny held up his arms, kissed his adoptive son on the cheek, and embraced him with all his might. The tears fell.

Ralston was grateful for this moment. He worried about too much unhappiness in Lance's life. He wished he had moved to San Diego instead of isolating himself here. But fences were being mended here, in this moment.

"You must tell me all that you have been up to since your retirement. And then I must ask one more favor. I need you to come home." Danny smiled. "Alfonso has been asking about you."

***

Three days later, Sonya knocked on the hangar doors. There was no answer. She finally had to accept that she had lost Lance.

***

"I'm sorry to hear about Danny. He was a good man and a good friend to you," Eric Pitts said, guiding the Aerohawk with Lance via a tow bar connected to the nose gear into the hanger. "I think you're a better man for knowing him."

"I will miss him," Lance said fondly and sadly.

"And he left everything to you? The kibbutz and all?"

"Ezra fought me on the Ruth Street house. I figure that man will live to a hundred, so I just gave it to him."

"And how was Alfonso?"

"His happy snorting self. Bassam will look after him. I'll travel over from time to time to make sure things are copacetic."

They hunkered around the Aerohawk and removed the back cowling to expose the engine. It was still warm from its called upon service to power the Aerohawk back to California.

The Turbo-Disc-Engine continued to prove its worth. Given it was simple in concept made for less to go wrong. The power disc generated a lot of raw horsepower for a small engine. It was the engine to replace the piston engine as far as Eric personally was concerned.

"When you leave here, both aircraft should be ready to show," Eric said.

"Then, I'll be here for a while."

"Good. You know nobody looks after you like I do."

"I want to get back into shape. Get this fat off of me," Lance said with a look of displeasure.

"Hey, round is a shape," Eric said, patting his large midsection.

"I'm not going to be a victim, Special. Nor live alone. I'll find someone who wants me."

"Now, to be fair, Sonya wanted you. Probably still does."

"No. She's long-forgotten me in the sack with one of her boy toys."

"Well, Beverly's been asking about you."

"Oh, come on."

"Don't worry. I told her you found a real nice gal. Look, you forgave Anja for getting pregnant by that Stasi bastard. You forgave Danny. Heck, you forgave me!"

"Yeah, I'm one big marshmallow."

"You're not that gooey. Anyway, let's get to work."

Chapter 114

Istanbul, Turkey

41°00′49″N, 28°57′18″

July 3, 2008

A full moon shimmered peacefully upon the gentle waves of the Bosphorus. Its tranquil light would be the inspiration of many romantic notions this evening. It would also be the only calm of a political storm brewing thousands of miles away.

The old Soviet cargo ship *Lady Minsk* lay berthed along the busy pier. In the port of call office, the captain signed the manifesto. He took his paperwork and left.

From the rear deck, Valeri Borsov stood watching the captain heading for the gangplank. Ashiq Mohammed Shah came next to him. He admired the serenity of the first leg of their journey. "You can contact Roman. Tell him that our cargo is safely aboard," Shah said. Shah eyed another man behind him and turned. "Naser, go below and stay with the cargo until we are out to sea."

"Yes, sir." Naser obediently did so.

"Good," said Borsov. "We have straight shot to Havana. You will love Cuba. It is much different than Iran. Oh, the women."

"They both have dictators."

"Your problem, Ashiq, is that you go for the politics. It gives, how you say—the indigestion. Go for the money. Then buy your politics."

On the upper deck, above Shah and Borsov, stood a crewmember known as Alexei. He had been aboard since being loaded with cargo at its homeport of Odesa. The scruffy-bearded crewman observed for a moment and then went back inside. It was two weeks to Cuba, and he had time.

Within the hour, the Lady Minsk pulled by tugboats, soon set sail for Cuba.

***

The Lady Minsk cruised downward in the Atlantic. It would enter the Gulf of Mexico tomorrow. It was nearing the end of her journey to Cuba and beginning her role in history.

It was late afternoon when a JetRanger helicopter departed from Nassau, Bahamas, and headed out to sea, northeastward.

A little over an hour later, it dropped down on the cargo vessel. As it approached, it lined up with a row of stacked cargo containers strapped to the deck. The pilot maneuvered the chopper and planted its left landing skid firmly on top of a container. Roman Sanders stepped off with a knapsack. The helicopter moved sideways and, with a wave from Sanders, flew off. Sanders then climbed down and set himself solidly on the deck.

Captain Scott Ensor, known to the crew as Alexei, made his way along the side of the ship and stopped outside of Borsov's cabin. Looking through the porthole, he saw a man in with Borsov. When the man turned, he caught sight of Sanders. This was disturbing. What was the CIA up to? Ensor placed a small chip on the edge of the window. The digital ear picked up their voices. He recorded it.

"We're connected," said Borsov. Ensor could see him working a laptop computer with a satellite antenna attached to it. "Iran, Libya, Syria, and North Korea have all paid." The screen fluttered. "Ah, these satellite feeds…" The screen cleared. "Okay. Five million dollar transfer from Saudi Exchange Corp. to Minsk Enterprises, LLC. Our Saudi principals are in."

"Good. It took them long enough. They won't be able to explain their way out of this one this time," Sanders stated.

"The house of Saud will merely blame it on extremists. No matter, as long as we retire in Cuba with rum and women. Paradise, my dear Roman. Paradise."

"Borsov, you're pragmatic if nothing else. Well, lusty. Just make sure the paper trail, electronic and otherwise, is clean, clear, and distinct."

"Phase one, a kill radius of one kilometer. Phase two—global."

"Just remember I'm the one with a target on his back." Sanders went to the door.

"As it should be. That is why my job is to be K.G.B."

"K.G.B.? There is no K.G.B. anymore."

"I am K.G.B. *Keep'em Guessing Boys*," Borsov said, laughing a husky smoker's laugh.

"Russians," Sanders said as he left.

Ensor removed the digital ear and padded away.

The next day, Ensor went into the ship's lowest cargo hold. The only hold left to check. He began a systemic search, which would be the culmination of six months of undercover work. He took a pry bar and started with the closest crate, prying up the lid. The small LED flashlight illuminated the contents. It was negative. He carefully tapped the nails back down and secured the lid.

He stepped to the other side of the hold and pried up the lid just enough on another crate. He illuminated the inside, where he could see a dark olive green cylinder. His heart sank. It was a missile. He could see English letters and numbers on the side. More disturbing, he saw letters in Farsi, the language of Iran. Below that, he saw Korean letters. Given the crate's size, at around fifteen feet in length, he was looking at a disassembled Scud-B *Shahab*-1 short-range ballistic missile—headed to Cuba—from Iran. He took pictures. Then he removed a small detonator with a digital timer from his jacket. He stuck it into one of three bricks of plastic explosives. He stuck it underneath the straw matting and closed the lid. He noticed other crates near this one. There were five other crates of the same length. Six crates. Three missiles. He moved the flashlight around the rest of the cargo hold. He noticed a smaller crate had a hole chewed in it. He knelt. It looked like a beer keg. The thought amused him. The other thought worried him. He pulled out a pen and stuck it in the hole. It chirped lightly. "That psychopath has a bomb!"

There was nothing he could do about it. The sabotage was in, and a SEAL team could retrieve the device after the ship sank. He took his camera and focused. A huge rat lunged out at him. Ensor fell back, smacking his head. The rat ran up his leg and body. Ensor chopped at it, knocking it down. The cargo door swung open.

"What are you doing in here?" Borsov yelled in Russian. Ensor was startled now twice in seconds, yet he stayed in character.

"There are rats inside the boxes. I am stopping them," Ensor replied in Russian.

"What?"

Ensor grabbed the rat by the tail. "I have been chasing this monster through the other cargo holds, but now I got him," he said proudly. The stunned rat arched up, snapping its jaws.

"You are not a cat. This hold is off-limits. Now get out of here!"

Ensor took his catch out with him. He assailed several rows of steps back onto the main deck. He swung the rodent over the side. Looking at his watch, he had two hours before his five a.m. departure. He would get some sleep.

Ensor stood on the rear deck, watching the summer sun peak above the horizon, casting its morning glow upon the ocean waters below. It was time to signal the pickup crew. Ensor removed a small transmitter and pressed the single button three times. A moment went by, and then he got a steady green light. His ride was close. He zipped up his jacket. With both hands on the rail, he bent down.

"Don't—jump just yet," Sanders said. Ensor felt a shiver go down his spine. "Turn around, Captain." Ensor faced Sanders. The sight of him brought back all their bad blood. To the side of Sanders were Borsov and Shah. "Long time, Scotty."

"What are you up to, Roman?"

"You know this man?" Shah asked, unnerved.

"Known him since he was just a pup in the SEALs."

"Borsov, you fool, you allowed this American to infiltrate us," Shah said.

"Never mind! It's dealt with! You might have made it, but…"

"Now I'm not?"

"Nor are you going to scuttle my plans," Sanders said, holding the small detonator. Sanders watched the timer tick down to nearly zero. He threw it over the railing. It popped and sparked just behind Ensor. "This is as far as you go, Scotty." Sanders pumped three rounds into Ensor's chest, causing him to fall back over the railing and down into the sea below.

A Navy SEAL Mark V Special Operations Craft powered up. The eighty-two-foot-long boat soared through the waves and headed toward the last known location of the Lady Minsk. The ship did not sink as planned, and Captain Ensor was nowhere to be found.

In the distance, a weakened Ensor rose with a high wave as the Mark V SEAL boat dropped down. He could see the distant sliver and waved his arm best he could. His hand found the dye marker bottle tab. The bright lime green color surrounded him. A wave rolled him down and away, carrying his hopes of rescue with it. The SEAL boat was gone, headed back to Key West.

***

The futuristic hi-tech styling of pearlescence was reflected in the rolling waves. They were that low over the surface of the water. The Aerohawk then pulled up in a steep ascent, trading airspeed for altitude. In less than two minutes, Lance leveled off at five thousand feet.

"You should be impressed by now, Agent Marshall," Lance said, sitting right seat.

"I'm sure, Lance, these are fine for the kit plane enthusiast, but I'm not seeing it suitable for U.S. Customs work. I'm only here at the request of your friend Eric," replied I.C.E. official Andy Marshall.

"Really?" Lance dropped the nose and then snapped it back, loading up the g-forces. "Nine g's, Andy," Lance grunted. "Same as an F-Sixteen." Lance leveled and then turned the aircraft on its side, maintaining its altitude. "It takes six g's to keep a plane level on its side. You have nothing in your inventory that can match this aircraft. It is very fast, quiet, and very economical to operate. What more could you ask for?" Lance leveled the aircraft. He then noticed that Marshall had turned pale, with his color slowly returning.

"Okay. Okay. No more stunt flying. I still prefer metal planes," Marshall said.

"*Spam cans*? Sir, you're flying in *FASTGLASS*," Lance said proudly.

"Fast—what?

“Fastglass. Wave of the future, Andy. Here, you take the controls. Get a feel for it.”

“I still think this is nothing more than a flying surfboard,” Marshall said, taking the controls. He felt that if he were doing the flying, it would all calm down. Though the Customs agent wasn’t a pilot, he began enjoying himself. He made gentle turns. Lance saw that the kit plane was selling itself.

Lance made a scan of the instruments. He did a quick study of the moving map display. He took note of the small white airplane symbol on the screen that moved over a blue background with a red line that appeared, as they were very close to the Cuban ADIZ. The *Air-Defense-Identification- Zone*, generally set at twelve miles out from a country’s coastline, forbade crossing without permission—or risk being shot down.

Lance scanned outside the windows for any traffic. He lifted his sunglasses when he noticed a discoloration on the ocean surface about three miles ahead. “Andy, let me have the controls. My plane.” Lance slowed the aircraft down considerably.

“What’s wrong?”

“I don’t know yet,” Lance said as he flew along the imaginary red line.

“Keep this plane outside of their ADIZ,” Marshall said, studying the moving map.

“I am.” Lance could now see a bright green spot on the sea below. It was about a mile inside of the Cuban ADIZ. Lance felt forced to make a judgment call. The Aerohawk obeyed his command and dropped rapidly.

“What are you doing?”

“We need to investigate.”

“No, we don’t. I am telling you not to cross over into Cuban airspace.”

Lance continued downward, making a large semi-circle. The small white airplane symbol on the moving map crossed over the now flashing red ADIZ line. Lance brought the Aerohawk down to three hundred feet above the ocean surface and tracked toward the bright lime green spot. He slowed the aircraft further. He saw a man floating on the ocean surface. The man arched his arm in a wave. Lance circled again, dropping down to twenty feet above the sea and slowing to where he dropped 20° of flaps. The jacket the man was wearing had two reflective safety orange stripes that ran from the epaulets down the sleeves.

Ensor had a warmth of relief flush through him. It had been a struggle to keep up hope, but help had come. His beat and battered body would soon be resting on dry land. The sea was always home to a SEAL, where training and often solace took place, but it was not a place to recover. He watched the aircraft come around again, rocking his wings. Ensor waved again. A hard bump jarred him.

Lance saw the long silhouette hit the man and then circle again. "Hold on!" Lance came down lower and buzzed the tiger shark, followed by a tight high-g turn. He climbed and called in the distress on the radio.

Ensor was nervous and exhausted. He saw the fin break the surface. The fin dropped below the surface.

Lance came around again. It was all he could do. He was desperate to help.

The tiger shark hit Ensor from behind, lifting him out of the water, shaking him as Lance buzzed it. The aircraft scared off the shark again. But for how long? Marshall suppressed the need to vomit, which made Lance queasy. "Come on, Andy. Hold it together." Lance then saw several other silhouettes approaching the man in the water. "I have some bad news."

"No, we are out of here! Do you hear me? Or I will arrest you when we get back."

"That shark's buddies will be on him in about five minutes. We're going in."

"What?" Marshall yelled. "No way!"

"Don't worry. We'll float. We're a flying surfboard, remember?" Lance shut down the engine and feathered the prop. The aircraft slowed. The trick was to drop the plane as gently as possible, glide on the surface, and stop by the man.

A Cuban Navy Mil-8 "Hip" helicopter hurried into the action. Lance spotted it. He had a feeling of helplessness. He was gliding in without power, and the Cuban helicopter was nearly upon the man in the ocean.

The helicopter turned slightly to expose its left side. The large sliding door opened, revealing a turret-mounted PK 7.62 mm machine gun. It fired a single straight line that looked to hit the man in the water. A sizeable tiger shark lunged up out of the water fifty feet from Ensor, nearly cut in two. Now there was blood in the water.

"You're going to get us killed!" Marshall screamed. A line of bullets made its way to the Aerohawk.

"Turn the key! Turn the key!" Lance yelled. Marshall was dumbfounded. Lance reached over and turned the key to the RUN position to energize the engine system. He flipped on the fuel cutoff switch. The engine came to life as the invading swarm of bullets hit just behind Lance's seat, tearing it up.

The Cuban helicopter slowed to a hover over Ensor. The large, right-side door slid open. A crewman fitted himself into the sling and was lowered.

Lance came around behind the helicopter, adding full power. The engine drove up the airspeed quickly.

The crewman was halfway down to the ocean surface when he saw the sport plane coming at him. The Aerohawk came right under the helicopter and popped up in front of it.

The Cuban pilot overreacted to being startled and pulled back violently, rocking the big ship. The crewman down on the sling was rocked to and fro, swinging dangerously close to the whirling rotor blades.

Lance came around again. The big Mil helicopter turned to fire at Lance, but Lance banked sharply and disappeared. The crewman wanted up. The hoist began to rewind the cable that held him in the sling. Lance came up underneath again and popped up far too close this time. The Cuban pilot jerked the big "Hip" helicopter back. The crewman saw he would swing into the whirling rotors and grabbed the side of the door as he passed. His two feet were only two feet from the dicing blades. His crewmen pulled him inside. The helicopter abandoned its rescue attempt and flew away.

"Okay," Lance said with a sigh. "Back to our original plan."

"No! You take us home, or I'll shoot you!" Marshall pointed his service weapon at Lance. A roar and rocking startled them. "What was that?"

"Two Cuban MiG's. Hold on and put your gun away."

The two MiG-21s flew off in different directions.

Lance and Andy Marshall saw one MiG come straight at them. Lance caught sight of the other MiG behind them. He felt the air draft from behind his seat more acutely now. He saw the damage as he looked to keep the MiG behind him insight. He hit full power. With a quick look behind, he caught sight of the MiG firing a missile at him. He headed straight to the oncoming MiG. He had a tactic in this game of chicken—aerial judo.

The MiG in front fired its guns as Lance ascended sharply and barrel-rolled over him. The pursuing missile hit the oncoming MiG.

Ensor watched the action above. He kicked away from his spot as a chunk of burning aircraft fell toward him. A wing and piece of fuselage slammed into the water. Ensor saw a couple of sharks jump out of the water.

The second MiG pilot came around and lined up with the feisty kit planet. It had nothing to hide behind or to use defensively again. He would avenge his comrade.

The TCAS system that detected other aircraft in proximity to it showed a purple triangle on the screen behind the white airplane symbol and closing.

The MiG pilot had his lock on Lance. A gray blur caught his attention up and behind him. A U.S. Navy F-18 Hornet sat off to his left. He looked around and found another off of his right. The pilot of the first Hornet wagged his finger at him. Frustrated but duly warned, the MiG bugged out.

Lance saw the MiG shoot past him. He banked hard right to see behind him. The two Hornets shot by and then circled. He felt a massive drop in tension. His relief was furthered when he saw a U.S. Navy helicopter nearly to the man in the water. He turned his battered aircraft back toward Key West.

The naval helicopter hovered over Ensor. A rescue diver jumped into the ocean. He was safe. Though, his thoughts raced to the aircraft and the man behind the controls that risked his life to save him. He was grateful.

***

Lance was directed back to Naval Air Station Key West, Runway 3. After landing, he taxied back to where he first picked up Agent Marshall.

"Well, that was quite the demo ride," Lance said. He opened his door and worked his left leg over the control stick and out of the aircraft. He came around and opened up the left side door for Marshall. "Come on, Andy. It's over. That man is safe, and I can repair the damage to my aircraft in time for my airshow coming up."

Lance helped him out of the aircraft. Lance shut the door. Several armed Navy personnel rushed outside. Marshall doubled up his fist and hit Lance on the back of the neck, dropping him to the asphalt. Marshall whipped out his gun and held it on Lance. "You are so under arrest. You crazy, maniac!" Marshall looked at the security people. "Cuff him and put him in a cell."

The bunk in Lance's cell was less than comfortable for untold hours.

"My-my-my," Ralston said. Lance woke. "So much for your retirement."

"I understand you two know one another," Marshall said.

"Lance Rio. The only man to ever give me jetlag in the same time zone."

"You spooks are way too out there for me," Marshall said. "Don't ever come knocking on my door again, Rio. We're done. Guess he's your problem now, Mr. Ralston."

"Come on, problem child. I'll take you home."

It was falling to early evening. Lance convinced Ralston to fly with him in the Aerohawk so it would be back home in Marathon. Reluctantly, Ralston agreed.

***

Lance opened the hangar doors remotely and taxied the Aerohawk inside.

Thirty minutes later, two black SUVs pulled up and parked outside. Their doors opened too late. Sonya had maneuvered past them and ran inside of the hangar. "Lance!" Sonya yelled. She wrapped her arms around him. "Are you all right? Are you okay?"

"Sonya, what are you doing here?"

"When I saw the news, I knew it had to be you."

“Not even married, and she’s picking you up on radar. Interesting,” Ralston mused.

“Castro closed down all airspace over Cuba. My flight was canceled,” she said.

“Yes, Lance. You created an international incident. I will leave you now.”

“I had to try and save a man’s life, Jeffrey.”

“You did. You can rest well on that. I’ll see you soon.” Ralston strolled through the hangar doors. The two SUVs a moment later drove off.

“Why did you come here?”

“I told you. My flight was canceled.”

“I don’t know anything about your flight. You should’ve just gone home.”

“But I’m here with you now.”

“I don’t have time for this. I have to start repairs on my plane.”

“Can’t I stay and help?”

“Help?” he asked wearily. “I rather you didn’t.”

“But you need help.”

Lance walked off, rolling his eyes. She noticed that he lost weight and looked quite buff. No, she wasn’t leaving.

Chapter 115

Bethesda, Maryland
39°00′06″N, 77°05′41″W

July 23, 2008

Captain Scott Ensor lay in a hospital bed. He wasn't so drugged that his mind raced with relevant facts of a nuclear conspiracy that jolted him to consciousness. It hurt to move. He suffered cracked ribs and bruising. Between being shot in the chest, rammed, and chewed on by a large shark, he was okay with the damage. His Kevlar-lined jacket stopped penetration of both tooth and bullet.

A naval officer entered the hospital entrance. He was in his summer whites and carried a black briefcase. The gold-plated name tag said: Lt. Cmdr. M. Geary. The tall blond man walked with a natural smile. The man was in his forties but moved with a younger man's energy and grace. He took the elevator to the fourth floor.

He strode past Room 407 amongst the nurses and medical staff. He ducked inside a closet at the end of the corridor. He had a key. Moments later, Geary stepped out of the closet and went down the hallway to the men's room. He was dressed in an orderly's white top and lab coat.

Geary moved back down the corridor and into Room 407.

Ensor stirred. "Who's there?"

"Good morning, Captain. How do you feel?" Geary asked.

"Less like a bus hit me and more like a car."

"Good, sir. I'm glad to hear you are improving." Geary opened up the blinds, letting the new day in the room. He pulled out a syringe. "The doctor ordered something to keep you relaxed and sleeping. Sleep is usually the best healer." Geary took hold of Ensor's I.V. line and swabbed the injection port with alcohol. Ensor focused uncomfortably on the needle. He looked down at the orderly's trousers. Something was wrong. They were too crisp. The orderly emptied the syringe and then capped it. He placed it back inside his pocket.

"Would you straighten my pillow?" Ensor asked.

"Certainly. Anything to make you feel more comfortable." Geary leaned in. Ensor slugged him on the side of the jaw. The man dropped long enough for Ensor to grab him around the neck, swing his leg out from under the covers and pin him up in the bed with him. Ensor grabbed the I.V. line, ripped it out of his arm and pushed the end into the orderly's mouth, and held him as he struggled. It didn't take long. The flinching calmed. The grasping hands softened and went lax. Low, barely audible wisps of air exhaled. Then silence. Ensor relaxed his hold. He backed out of his bed while pulling the orderly into it. Ensor placed the covers over him. He went into the bathroom.

Admiral Arthur Raymond Mayfield, one of the first African-Americans to reach the rank, felt the arthritic after-effects of his former SEAL days as he pushed himself up the steps prim and proper to the hospital entrance as a member of the admiralty should.

The admiral came into Room 407. He thought he saw Ensor in the bed until he came out of the bathroom. "We have a situation here, I see. This soon," Mayfield said, noticing that Ensor was clean-shaven, though his hair still quite long.

"Well, sir, I haven't spent six months undercover to end it in a hospital bed."

"Any idea who he is?"

"One of Sanders' I'd say."

"What I have learned from the CIA is that it seems our marine major has strayed from the faith. So, if this is some kind of conspiracy, we need to know. If he's sold out to terrorists, we need to know."

"I want to continue what I started, sir."

"You look like hell."

"Feel like hell. I'm good to go."

Mayfield looked at the dead man. "How did you know?"

"Wrong trousers."

Mayfield pulled back the covers. He noticed the lab coat, scrubs top, and summer white trousers. "Fantastic." He put a small gym bag on the bed and opened it. He pulled out a pair of khaki cargo pants, a shirt, shoes, socks, and a jacket.

"Do you know who the pilot was?" Ensor asked as he took to dressing himself.

"Yes. A Mr. Lance Rio."

"What? I know this guy. He's CIA."

"We have no record of him with the Agency. He lives down in Marathon, in a hanger."

"Admiral, he's CIA."

"Well, this continues to get more interesting," the admiral said. "Scotty, I'll help you all I can, but you'll be on your own for the most part until I know who to trust. You be careful."

Chapter 116

Marathon Airport

July 24, 2008

Eric Pitts stood looking at his baby, his prize aircraft, in disbelief. Lance had gutted it of seats, interior trim, and the two rear side windows before Eric journeyed east with the Aquahawk. "You're supposed to be retired!"

"I know," Lance said as he towed the Aquahawk inside. The hangar was getting crowded. Lance put the Aquahawk next to Miss Solitaire.

"Lance, Oshkosh is only four days away, and we have no aircraft to show!"

"We'll repair it in time. Maybe a day late, but I figure you can still go ahead in the Mits as planned, and I'll bring up the Aerohawk. Come on, let's go upstairs."

Lance pulled the last piece of Eric's luggage from the back of the Aquahawk. They headed for the stairs.

Sonya stepped out on the landing. "Hi, Eric. Welcome to Hanger del Rio," she said graciously. Eric took a good look at her. He was pleased.

"Hey, darlin'," Eric said, smiling. He leaned in toward Lance. "Son, I am going to imbue upon you as much misery as possible for the next three days."

"I know," Lance said in surrender.

Lance had Eric and Sonya sit at the counter on the bar stools. He put their dinner plates in front of them. "We'll have to work out sleeping arrangements."

"As long as I get the air mattress. I sleep good on that thing," Eric chimed.

"Where do I sleep?" Sonya asked.

"You can sleep on the sofa. Or in the Mits in a sleeping bag," Lance offered. "I sleep in my bed."

Sonya went to speak but took a bite of food instead. Then: "You know, Lance, I think you could do with a hobby other than planes. Something to relax you."

"You mean like Yoga?"

"Exactly. Or martial arts," Sonya said enthusiastically.

"Is she kidding?" Eric grinned. Lance looked at him sternly. "Gotcha. Never mind."

"You mean like judo or something," Lance offered.

"Or Tai Chi. I've been doing Krav Maga for a few months. You could join me."

"Israeli martial arts, no less," Lance mused.

"Yeah, I guess you would know about it living in Israel."

"I'm—familiar with it."

“Or Kabbalah. I’ve been looking into that.”

“Jewish mysticism. Sonya, have you ever heard of the Mosaic Law?”

“Nope.”

“It’s the law of Moses. You know, the Ten Commandments, plus a few others thrown in. It governed the affairs of ancient Israel for a number of years.”

“Really? I didn’t know about that part.”

“Well, if Moses were here and caught you practicing Kabbalah, he would look for a sword, most likely, and then hack you to bits,” he said roughly, followed by a smile.

“Why?” she protested.

“Because spiritism carried an automatic death sentence.”

“Fine,” pouting as she went to the refrigerator. She sighed upon opening the door. “Lance, why do you keep so much chocolate in the fridge?”

“Well. There’s an old Klingon-Swiss proverb that says—*Revenge like chocolate is a dish best served cold.*”

“Funny.”

Eric chuckled, being keenly observant.

Sonya came downstairs wearing a pair of Lance’s coveralls all rolled up. She looked adorable. Lance turned to focus on his work. It would keep the torment in his mind to a lower level than he was currently experiencing.

“I’m ready to help,” she said.

“Darlin’,” Eric said, “first, we need to put a hat and mask on you.”

Throughout the day, Sonya aided the boys. Eric found pleasure in her willingness to help and learn. She realized she was in the company of masters of what they did. She would soon pull away to go make lunch upstairs. She was excited that she helped Eric replace one of the shot-up rear side windows that he had to scramble to get ordered from their window vendor. It cost them quite a bit extra to get them as soon as they did. But the aircraft was coming back online quicker than Eric had hoped. The bullet holes were being patched excellently by Lance. Eric’s heart was not sinking so fast by the end of their sixteen-hour workday.

***

Scott Ensor waited just outside Washington D.C. There was a knock at his motel door. He held the gun in his right hand and stood to the side of the door. “It’s Ray.” Ensor opened the door. The admiral stepped inside, carrying a *Skyroll* garment bag slung over his shoulder. “I have some more cash for you and a Canadian Visa card, which you’ll need in Cuba. Take this garment bag. Sorry, it’s not a backpack. But, it’s one of my special versions. It has all you’ll need, and it's carry-on. If you find Sanders in Cuba, put him down. Stop this madness. It should be like cutting the head off the snake."

"Understood, sir," Ensor said, taking the garment bag. He now looked like a tourist on a private holiday.

"I'll meet you down in Miami in a couple of days, just in case. From here on out, call me Lionel," Mayfield said, handing Ensor a piece of paper. "Memorize this address. It's Sanders' old house. Castro's finance minister, Miguel Ricardo del Toro, lives there. Word, or better yet, legend has it that del Toro shot and killed Sanders' father. Of interest to us is that his wife Sophia del Toro, who's about twenty years younger, wants out of Cuba. We know that overseas money has been coming into Cuba through del Toro."

"Fidel wouldn't like to hear about that."

"No, he wouldn't. But, she could be an asset. Find her. Also, I plan to have your old SEAL team on standby at Gitmo. Whatever it takes. Stay safe, Scotty."

The admiral rented Ensor a car that carried him on the I-95 south to Florida and down to Miami, the first leg of the journey. He was healing but still suffered pain. Nonetheless, he had a mission to complete. He had never failed before and refused to now.

***

Lance towed out the MU-2 from the hangar. It was time for Eric to leave for Oshkosh.

The Aerohawk looked beautiful again, though a couple of minor divots showed through the white pearlescence paint. The filling of bullet holes was a bit rushed. The aircraft was still masked off where the burgundy-red and blue striping was touched up.

Lance had removed the two rear-facing seats on the Mits to make room for the plastic containers full of paraphernalia for the booth they rented at Oshkosh. Sonya carried out the last container, handing it to Lance. "Go upstairs and see what's keeping Special," Lance asked.

"Why do you call him that?"

"Because he is. I'll tell you about a kit plane called the *Pitts Special*, later."

"It already makes sense. I'll go check on him." Lance packed the container inside and then turned, watching Sonya hoof it upstairs.

"Baby, I want to do this," Eric voiced over his cell phone. "Yes, I'll butt my nose in just this one last time. Look, the ticket is already printing."

"Eric," Sonya called as she came into the apartment.

"Look, she just came in. I only have a minute. Yeah, love you too. See you tonight." Eric hung up. "Sonya, I need to ask you something."

"Okay, Eric," she said, coming closer.

"Do you love Lance? Flat out—yes or no?"

"Yes," she said with a tension-relieving sigh.

"Okay, good. I thought you did. Lance is my best friend. I love that man more than most of my natural family." Eric took the collection of papers from the printer and stapled them together, and then folded it. "This is a ticket to Oshkosh. I got you the most direct flight out of Miami I could. It leaves August second. That gives you four days in Cuba and time to get back here. If you want this, that is."

"I do, but I don't think Lance does."

"He loves you, Sony-girl. But, he's had a rough past."

"He won't open up about it. Other than, well, you know."

"Yeah, I know. And that's her loss. I'm in your corner now. I'll be there for you. Just don't hurt my boy."

"I won't. I think we can be a healing to one another."

"That's good. Just be the best thing ever to happen to him—'cept me." Eric grinned. Sonya giggled.

Eric had a lot of flying to do today to be up at Oshkosh by early evening. With the Mits' greater range and speed, he should be fine, Lance thought. He still had to park, open up the plastic containers and dress up the booth. Eric would also show off his landing gear, control stick, and throttle quadrant business for the kit plane market, which was doing quite well on its own.

Eric and Sonya came downstairs. "You ready?" Lance asked.

"Ready. Let's do it," Eric said.

Lance and Sonya followed the MU-2 out and watched as Eric lined Miss Solitaire up on the runway. They saw Eric wave. Full power was added. In seconds, the powerful engines drove the aircraft down the runway and up into the air. Sonya took hold of Lance's hand as they walked back to the hangar. It made Lance uncomfortable, and yet it nourished him.

"You have something on your mind?" Lance asked.

She stopped. "Lance, my father didn't get me out of Cuba by his contacts. He was no longer influential. I got out on my back. I got a bad case of V.D. that burned out my reproductive organs. I just didn't know it until it was too late. I didn't just lose my virginity to an uncaring man. He took my ability away to have children. What that did to me—I—and now I'm forty." Lance found his hands caressing the hand he held. She saw genuine empathy for her in his eyes. "I don't know what has shaped you. But in amongst all of the evil still out there, is there a place for you and me?"

"You don't see things as I need you to."

"I have come to appreciate your fidelity. And I will never ask you to betray that. I have been the same as the day I met you."

"Really?"

"Really," she said warmly. "Which means I'm chomping at the bit here!"

The airport stood quiet. A car passed by, noting a man embracing a woman out in the middle of the tarmac.

***

Miguel Ricardo del Toro paced along the Malecón. The former general and trusted aid to Fidel Castro took frequent looks over his shoulder. The unsettling news he faced distracted him from what hotel pathway he walked in secret. He looked for the wrought iron gate. He found it and hurried to it.

Gilberto, a man in his forties, studied the old general. "General. Come in here," he said. Del Toro came inside of the wrought iron gate. Gilberto closed it behind him.

"Why am I here?" Del Toro demanded.

"The letter you received explained that a man has isolated your activities aside from the government's. Castro would not be pleased."

"Who sent it?"

"The son of Julian Sanders."

"I do not know of a Julian Sanders."

"Think back general to the beginning of the Revolution. This man Sanders was a casino owner. Here, in this hotel. It had a different name back then. You killed him. His son is seeking revenge."

Del Toro took a sober look at where he stood. "What can I do?"

"Remember."

"There was the boy. Roman. He—." Del Toro touched his nose, remembering. "He, he is the one that wants revenge?"

"Sí. And I believe he will take it."

"When Gilberto? When?"

"Now," Gilberto said, stepping to the side. Del Toro arched back violently and then slumped to the ground.

Ernesto Cruz's yacht, about one thousand yards offshore, started its engines and cruised away.

***

The Aerohawk transitioned through the Girón corridor. The aircraft buffeted heavily over the rocky terrain, pitching up two hundred feet and then dropping three hundred feet. Lance caught Sonya *genuflecting*. "Our Father who art in heaven, hallowed be thy name. Thy kingdom come. Thy will be done on earth as it is in heaven," she murmured, grasping hold of the edge of her seat.

"That won't help you."

"I just prayed to God."

"You just prayed to God to keep his name holy or sanctified. You neither know God nor his name and the meaning behind it. You also prayed for his kingdom or government to come and replace earth's existing governments. That being his will. So you just prayed for nothing related to your fears."

She glared at him. "Then teach me."

The turbulent air settled. Lance wished he had kept his big mouth shut. With every plot and plan to say goodbye, there came a new invitation for her to remain in his life.

The Aerohawk flew past Cuba and back over open water toward Grand Cayman. It wasn't long before the experimental aircraft was lined up with the runway and then taxiing to the tarmac, where it shut down.

After the stop through customs, they were directed to the terminal.

Lance stood before Sonya as far as he could go. It was ticketed passengers only. "Sonya, it's time to say goodbye. I think it best. I appreciate your help over these past few days, but our lives just aren't in sync."

He expected her to react harshly. She didn't.

She nodded. "I understand. Thank you for caring."

Lance kissed her on the cheek. "I will always care about you. Be well."

Sonya wasn't far through the line when she smiled. Her car was back at his hangar. And she would see him at Oshkosh. This type of conspiracy was turning out to be fun!

Lance waited until she was shuffled out to the tarmac and heading to her plane, his emptiness growing. He felt a sharp poke in his back. His mind raced! *Sicarii!* It settled on much farther in the past.

"I remember you. You kill my brother," the man said.

"Rojas!" Lance whispered.

"Good. You remember. I looked for you for a very long time, but you disappeared until I find you fighting Cuban fighter jets. They don't name you, but I pay good to know this brave and daring pilot. I know one day I find you."

"What do you want?"

"My revenge."

"That was a long time ago. Your brother shot and killed my brother."

"What do I care? Now, in there." Rojas pushed Lance toward the men's restroom.

Lance hesitated at the door. Rojas pushed him through. Lance turned to face Rojas. "Miguel, I'm not a part of this anymore. I just want to be left alone."

"Oh, I am going to leave you alone." Rojas flashed a grin. Lance felt a surge coarse through him. He looked Rojas in the eyes. He studied the trademark stiletto knife in his hand and how he held it.

There was flushing in one of the stalls. A man came out. "Get back in there!" Rojas yelled, waving the knife. The man broke free of his static pose and jumped back inside the stall, shutting the door and locking it.

"Don't do this, Miguel," Lance warned.

"Don't beg. Die like a man." Rojas moved closer. He lunged a half step, which put him close enough. Lance's foot caught the butt of the knife and drove it up from Rojas' hand into the ceiling. Rojas grabbed his injured hand. He grinned. He lunged at Lance. The base of Lance's palm caught Rojas in the nose, driving his head back and his legs up over his head. He dropped onto the back of his neck. Lance heard the crack. The body shivered for a moment and then lay without movement. Rojas' eyes opened. They were panicked eyes in a motionless body.

"All I wanted was to be left alone. Away from all you people."

Lance was shaken, but no retirement could dampen his ability to assess and focus. Calmly, he rejoined the rest of the public in the terminal as if nothing ever happened.

Sonya had already begun counting down the days until she would see Lance again. She took her seat next to the window. Three rows back, Ensor fastened his seatbelt. He looked out of the window and looked to relax for the brief flight to Cuba.

***

Lance came down the ladder over the insistent knocking on the hanger doors. He kept them locked given yesterday's events. "Lance, open up," Ralston ordered.

"Coming, Jeffrey." Lance opened the man-door. Ralston stepped inside. Lance closed and locked it.

"Well, for one who is supposed to be retired—you're rather active." Ralston strolled around the tables and work area. "Rojas is dead. You needn't worry. I have people on the situation."

"I didn't kill him."

"You broke his neck clean."

"It was an accident."

Ralston grinned. "Not the way I trained you."

"I don't want this anymore, Jeffrey."

"So you've said."

Lance stepped back over to the Aquahawk. Ralston came around to the other side of the aircraft. Lance patted it. "Definitely—Fastglass."

"Yes, I always thought it a cute nickname."

"You might also find it cute that this bird has bomb bay doors."

"You want to drop bombs?"

"No. Life rafts."

"Of course. What else would one drop?"

"And you know what else? All of our intrigues throughout the millennia, meaning that of man, have amounted to nothing in the end."

Lance climbed back up the ladder to the engine nacelle and closed the access panel, locking it.

"Why so certain?"

"Senseless—Human—Interference—and—Tactics."

"And what's that?"

"Well, Jeffrey. If you caught the acronym…" Lance reached inside of the engine nacelle and spun the fan blades. "That's what keeps hitting the fan."

Chapter 117

Havana, Cuba

July 30, 2008

Captain Ensor stood at the edge of his bed and unfurled the Skyroll garment bag from the center cylinder. He unzipped the flap at the end of the cylinder and removed his toiletry bag. Further inside the cylinder, he removed the divider, and from that, he opened the cover and removed the frame of a Glock 26 subcompact semi-automatic pistol. Inside of his toiletry bag, he held his electric shaver, removed the bottom of it, and pulled out the empty ten-around magazine. He turned on the shaver just to make sure it still worked. On the garment bag, he parted the handle's edge and worked the gun's slide out from it. It was quickly mated to the frame. Then Ensor opened a pack of AA batteries. He unraveled the wrapper, revealing a nine-millimeter bullet. He unwrapped nine more. Shortly, the magazine was loaded and inserted into the frame. He now had a means of defense.

Ensor drove in style. Nothing in his mind spelled out Americana more than driving a classic Chevy car, even in Communist Cuba. He believed that the Chevy would rule here once again.

The Chevy toured its way around the road that led up into the hills. Ensor slowed down to nearly a stop to catch a glimpse of one of his favorite author's home. He wondered for a moment what it would have been like back in the day when Hemingway lived there. His sentiment satisfied, he drove on.

A few houses further up, he found his target: the old Sanders' home. Ensor reflected on how much time had spanned since Fidel Castro took power. It was just four months shy of fifty years. He drove past the house. His cell phone rang. "Hello."

"It's Lionel. Castro's finance minister is dead. Our major got him. Damn impressive shot."

"I'm at the house now. I'll stop in and say hi." The phone went silent. Ensor got quietly out of the car and placed the Glock in his waistband.

From up the street, a car came and braked hard in the driveway. Two men got out. Ensor came around and behind them. He saw the partially reflected image of a woman looking out of the large window in the front of the old stucco house. The two men pulled pistols and shot at it. The window fractured but didn't break. The two men realized their futility and ran for the front door. Ensor pursued.

The first man kicked in the front door, and they both ran in. Ensor heard shots fired. He came to the door. He heard one man say, "Gilberto, aqui."

Ensor entered quietly. He found his way to the front room and came up behind the gunmen. They turned. Ensor instinctively commanded the baby Glock to defend him, dropping one. The other ran to the back of the house, returning fire. Ensor moved back into the foyer, firing twice. He wounded the gunman who ran, dropping a laptop. The woman lay on the ground bleeding. She was in shock, gasping, trying to reach out to Ensor, who knelt by her side. "I'll get help. Are you Sophia?"

"Sí. Finca—Finca," Sophia del Toro said as she reached with her right hand toward the laptop. Ensor now noticed it. The laptop had two bullet holes through the screen.

"Let me get you help." Her hand came to his cheek. She smiled and expired. The car in the driveway started abruptly and sped out in reverse. It took off down the street. Ensor closed her eyes. They were lovely eyes. She was a beautiful woman, even in her sixties. It was all a shame. Ensor stood and recovered the laptop. He closed the door behind him.

He drove past the house slowly, feeling regret for the woman. "So what is Finca?" Lionel asked over the phone.

"I don't know." A few houses down, he saw the Hemingway house again. "Wait. Yes, I do. Finca Vigia is the name of Hemingway's old place. I'm looking right at it."

"What's your plan?"

"Coffee."

As Ensor drove down the hill, he could make out Havana Harbor. He saw an explosion aboard a cargo ship. It was the Lady Minsk, which he located earlier in the day. He pulled over and grabbed a compact pair of binoculars. The ship was already listing to the port side. He could see crewmen jumping overboard. The Cuban government would blame the U.S. for terrorism. Instinct and experience told him this was just part of Roman Sanders' plan. Ensor needed that cup of coffee.

Ensor parked and went into an Internet Café. Like most things with global reach, they were for tourists only and off-limits to most of the Cuban citizenry. Nonetheless, this was also a place for opportunistic citizenry.

Ensor purchased an Internet card, plugged a phone line into the laptop, sat at a table, and played with it. He stood up. "I think I need another coffee," he said. He got his coffee and stepped outside.

He waited a very patient ten minutes. A teenage boy in long strides walked out with the laptop. "Hey, kid! You can keep the laptop. I just need what's on it." The startled kid stopped. He didn't know whether or not to run. "You don't need to run. You can have it."

"I can have it? Really?"

"Sí. Just help me hack it. I need a screen. Deal?"

"Deal," the young man said, extending his hand. "Come with me."

Ensor followed the teenager through the streets. He was glad the kid spoke reasonable English. He followed the kid into an alleyway and then into a small detached garage behind a block of apartments. He unlocked a padlock and opened the rickety corrugated steel door.

Inside, Ensor could smell decades of grease and grime. The place lit up marginally when a single light bulb hanging from a wire revealed the interior. There was an old car that looked abandoned for years. Much of its body was spotted with rust.

"I am Diego," the teenager said.

"Scotty. Call me Scotty."

"Okay, Señor Scotty. Give me a moment." Diego went behind a few old barrels. He removed a wooden box. He had an old monitor and a CPU unit that was missing its side panels. No doubt cannibalized from other parts. He plugged an extension cord into a wall outlet. "I know it does not look like the new computers you have in the United States, but I get to upgrade it with the help of my cousin in Miami." Behind them was an old warped shelf. He pulled down a small cigar box and opened it. He removed a cable and plugged it into the laptop, and connected it to the monitor. The screen came to visual life.

"Great," Ensor said. He could now see what was on the laptop. "The password should be 'Finca Vigia."

"Ah, Papa's house," Diego said with some enthusiasm. All these years later, Hemingway was still held in high esteem.

"Well, you look like you know what you are doing."

"The security protocols are very predictable in this country. And yours," Diego said with a wink. The HOME page for BANCO DE CUBA appeared. "Ca-Rumba!"

"It's okay. It's okay."

"You are trying to break into the bank?"

"No, just his."

"Whose?"

"Finance Minister del Toro."

"Oh. Then, Señor Scotty, you have come to the right place." Diego grinned. This was exciting.

"Can you send an email from here?"

"Sí. To anywhere in the world. The State cannot keep us from the outside world anymore."

"Just make sure you wipe the hard drive clean after you download it."

"Yes, I will. I can put this on a floppy disc for you."

"Yeah, I guess that will have to do. Shame you couldn't download it to my phone."

"You have one of the new smartphones?"

"Yes," Ensor said, pulling it out.

"I can help you." Diego pulled out another cable and adaptor and plugged it into Ensor's phone and then into the computer. Ensor never questioned the art of resourcefulness from the seemingly unlikely.

Ensor pulled out some cash. "Here. You earned it." He would read the contents of del Toro's accounts on the journey home.

***

In-flight, Ensor studied money transfers from Iran, Syria, Libya, North Korea, and Saudi Arabia to BANCO DE CUBA via Minsk Enterprises, LLC. Some of it was making sense. He further put two and two together. He thought of the small nuke he discovered and the missiles to launch it. Was Sanders' plot to launch the nuke onto American soil? Why? The five payees were from countries that sponsored terrorism. He was glad to be on his way to see the admiral.

***

Ensor sat in the same rental car he left at Miami International Airport. He remembered when he first met Sanders; Sanders called Cuba home and hated Fidel Castro with a passion. Ensor had an idea. There were phone numbers listed outside of the bank's main listings. He dialed. A woman's voice came on the line. He hung up. He dialed again. Another woman answered the phone. He moved his thumb to the END button. He entered the third number. "Hola," a man's voice said. It was Sanders' voice. He would know it anywhere. He hung up. He dialed the admiral's cell.

"Lionel, I need to transfer the funds from this account at the Banco de Cuba into a secure account."

"How much?" the admiral asked.

"Twenty-five mil."

"What? Okay, Scotty, you've done well."

"Is there any political event coming up? I need to know. And get the team ready. I'll need them somewhere in this."

"Done. I'm ready for the account number. What do you plan to do with the money?"

"Bait. I found Sanders. He'll have to come to me. Here's the number."

***

Ensor showered and retaped his rib cage. Then he sat on the edge of his bed in the motel room. His cell rang, finally, three hours later. "The money's been transferred to a Cayman account," the admiral said.

"Good. I'll give Sanders the good news. Hold on, sir. I'm about to stir a hornet's nest."

Ensor ended his call. He dialed Sanders.

"Hola," Sanders said.

"Roman, how are you?"

"Who is this?"

"Scott Ensor."

"Scotty. You're not dead. That's very unlike me. It'll be a headshot next time."

"You may want to wait on that. I've got your money. All twenty-five million of it."

"I see," Sanders said roughly. "So, you were the man at del Toro's place."

"Your old casa, I believe."

"Something like that." Sanders paused. "What do you want, Scotty?"

"Like you, a comfy retirement."

"You're not retired."

"I am now."

"I will find you, Scotty. I promise you."

"I know you will. And I'm going to help you. Meet me in Miami this time tomorrow. I'll let you know where."

"Lance Rio. He's the one that found you floating with the sharks. Shame."

"You know him?" Ensor asked casually.

"I worked with him many a time. It's just like Lance to be big-hearted and try to save someone else even at his own risk. He in this with you?"

"Never met the man."

"Uh-huh. See you in Miami, Scotty. Don't be late."

Ensor dialed nervously. "Lionel. There's a problem. I need to know where Lance Rio is."

***

Sanders turned to Ernesto. "Lance Rio. A great Op. He's supposed to be retired. Turns out he has our money. He's working with a navy captain, ex-SEAL, named Scott Ensor, who's supposed to be dead. I need to know what's making Lance tick these days."

"Does he have family?"

"No. No one. Quite the loner. Like me, I guess."

“We can shake the tree and see what drops,” Ernesto said. “We’ve come too far now, Roman.” The large man sat back quietly.

Chapter 118

Wittman Regional Airport, Oshkosh, Wisconsin
43°59′04″N, 88°33′25″W

July 31, 2008

Lance made what he called the *Skittles Approach*, as large colored dots located fifteen hundred feet apart on the runways aided controllers to sequence aircraft safely but efficiently. From the Aerohawk, he could see the sprawling specs of mass humanity down below, interwoven between aircraft of every type possible and row upon row of tents by the thousands.

Of the hundreds of thousands of people below and of the ones that ventured by their display booth, he hoped that Eric kept them intrigued enough until he taxied up with the goods. This would be historically the first time in a long time that a new aircraft had a genuinely new engine to power it. He felt a rush of excitement as he lined up to land at the world's largest airshow and aircraft fly-in. This was the granddaddy of them all, and it felt good to be here!

He was cleared to land Runway 18R, past the blue dot, and given a "well done" by the tower for touching down right on the pink dot as instructed.

He was given a progressive by ground control to taxi to his booth. He could see Eric waving. The distinctive howl that the engine made drew attention. These first few minutes on display were auspicious.

Eric ran up to the aircraft and opened the door for Lance. "Hey, Lancey-boy, you made it! We've been getting a lot of interest. Come on. You must be tired."

"No, I'm fine. It was a good flight."

It didn't take long for people to circle the Aerohawk like schools of fish. Both doors were opened up for cockpit and cabin viewing. Lance sat in the booth in a lounge chair. Fatigue caught up to him, and he was out.

***

Sonya wrangled the line inside of the terminal at the airport. She wanted to stay with her parents longer, but she was on a mission to be with Lance. She found her man, and that was that.

Sonya marched through the terminal and took her place in line.

"Miss Valdivia, may I talk with you?" Roman Sanders asked. He was with Gilberto.

"Who are you?"

"I'm here to get you out of here."

"Did Lance send you?"

"Yes. It's not safe, and we have to get you out by other means."

"But, my flight is in an hour."

"State security will have you in custody in half an hour."

"Are you taking me to the Farm?"

"Exactly," Sanders said without missing a beat. "Once we're on our way, I'll let Lance know where you are."

"So he's coming to get me?"

"That is the plan," Sanders confirmed.

***

Lance meandered around from display to display. He didn't find anything new, but the atmosphere was exciting enough. He joined in long lines to see many of the static displays strewn about, whether they were aircraft or the latest in avionics. He went from booth to booth. He took a walk through a U.S. Air Force C-17 that reminded him of his mid-air piggyback ride with the Sparrowhawk. As he walked out of the tail section, he thought of Sonya. He found himself missing her. Terribly so. He had to face it. He needed her. She was the missing element in his life. He certainly had put her through her paces, and she absorbed it all and kept coming back. She was a trooper! She was a keeper.

Lance caught the sign above the booth: AERONAUTICAL DREAM BUILDERS. He marched right up to Eric. "Special. I am going to marry Sonya. I have made up my mind."

Eric grinned. "I know. I've always known you were, little buddy. Just sit tight. Stay here. Cover for me while I go see someone," Eric said, walking off with a lilt in his step.

Eric trotted down to the skywriters' camp. He came up to a beautifully restored Stearman bi-plane and its owner. "Hey, Billy, it's on. In about an hour from now."

"Sure thing, Eric. Happy to add my part."

That hour later, Lance watched a red and gold colored Stearman rumble over the runway with a wing walker on top. Of all the derring-do that he had ever done, he didn't see himself ever tempted to do that.

"Hi, Lance."

Lance dropped his gaze. "Captain." Lance noticed that Ensor was casually dressed. His hair was long, and he was unshaven.

"Looks like I owe you again," Ensor said.

"Looks like it's becoming a habit."

"A good habit. Anyway, can we talk? It's important."

"Sure."

"I, rather we talk on the move."

Lance turned to Eric. "Eric, I need to talk with this man. I'll be back."

"Everything okay?"

"We're at Air Venture Two-Thousand and Eight. Everything's A-Okay," Lance beamed.

The two men left the booth. They mingled their way through a crowd and then set off on their own.

"What's on your mind, Captain?"

"First, call me Scotty. Secondly, Roman Sanders."

"What about him? I haven't seen him in couple-three years now."

"He's turned traitor, Lance. There's a kill order on him. He's working with terrorists against the United States."

"No. No way. We were never close, but I know this man. He hates Communists, dictators and enjoys terrorizing terrorists. Trust me."

"Well, he's being funded by them."

"To do what?"

"That I cannot say."

"Then I don't know how I can help you. As I said, I haven't seen Roman in some time. I'm glad you're okay, Captain, Scotty, but please leave me out of this. All of it."

Lance strolled by one of the tents, where people stood, crowded around a stage. He peeked in. He saw Burt Rutan himself and Sir Richard Branson on stage, each holding microphones. They spoke of space tourism. Lance thought that if he brought his steam engine technology to reality, coupled with his ceramic foam advancements, he and Eric could build a spacecraft of their own. The Spacehawk? He chuckled. Never mind, he thought. They were building simple aircraft, respectively, like the Aerohawk and the Aquahawk. He didn't have the money to do more advanced work. He had to save the rest of his nest egg for his life with Sonya. Outside of his profits from Onyx Aviation, there was no other source of income.

Lance caught sight of their booth and made a slow beeline for it. LaTonya Watts had fans huddle around her. "L.A. Tonya's in the house," he heard her say. He appreciated her endorsement of the company, but the press was starting to show up. It unnerved him. He caught Eric's eye. Eric nodded for him to keep on walking. Lance got lost in the crowd.

Later, Eric paced while on his cell. He was perturbed. Lance came up to him. "I am so sorry, Lance. She was supposed to be here. Gina went to pick her up."

"Who, LaTonya? She's here."

"No. Sonya."

"Sonya?" Lance heard the deep rumble of two Stearman bi-planes roll down from the sky and loop upwards. The red smoke came on. And then off. The planes looped up again, and the red smoke came on again, this time completing the sky-born heart. The other Stearman came low over the runway. The wing walker unfurled a banner. It said: SONYA WILL YOU MARRY ME?" A roar of applause broke out over the airport grounds.

Lance looked around, stunned. No Sonya. Nothing. "Oh, Eric."

"Lance, don't hate me. Something went wrong."

"What happened?"

Ensor wandered around all he could. He grabbed his cell phone. "Lionel. I think we need to read him in. He can handle it. And we may need his help."

"Very well. I still have our people good to go," Mayfield said.

"I'll call you back." Ensor hurried back to Lance, a quarter-mile away.

The crowds around the Aerohawk had thinned considerably. It was lunchtime, and the lines at the food vendor booths multiplied with each passing minute. A man moved past the booth and went inside the tent. He smiled at Eric.

"Perhaps you could tell me about this Aerohawk. It looks fast."

"Oh, it is," Eric stated.

"Do you have any brochures on it?"

"Sure do." Eric turned his attention from the man. "Just one second."

Roman Sanders chopped Eric on the back of the neck, sending the big man crashing to the ground.

"Eric, where are you?" Lance came into the tent. Sanders drew a bead on him, waving him further inside with his gun. "Roman. What is this? What are you doing here?"

"The price of betrayal."

"Who betrayed you?"

"You did."

"I haven't done a thing! I've been out of it. You had to know that."

"I thought so, but I want my money back."

"What money?"

"Don't insult my intelligence. You and your buddy Ensor tried to pull a fast one."

"Roman, sorry, but I don't know anything about any money."

"Drop it, Sanders!" Ensor said, rushing in. "I want to shoot you as is."

"And I'll shoot Lance," Sanders replied.

"I still get you." Ensor held his aim. Sanders threw his gun down. Lance rushed over to Eric.

"He'll be okay," Sanders said. "By the way, Lance, I've got Sonya." There was no hesitation. Lance brought a solid punch on Sanders' jaw knocking him off his feet. Sanders slowly sat up. "And here I thought, Lance, you'd gone soft."

"Where is she, Roman? I won't ask again." Sanders knew that look when Lance was about to get deadly.

"Truth is, she got away. Something about a Farm. Your new hideout? You give me my money back. Transfer it all back, and we're good."

"He doesn't have your money," Ensor smirked. "I do. He never did. Lance hasn't got a clue about any of this, Roman."

Sanders gritted his teeth. His whole plan, set to follow a deadline, was unraveling before his eyes. "Oh, Scotty. Very clever."

"Lance, where is this farm?" Ensor asked.

"Cuba. Bay of Pigs. There's an old abandoned set of bunkers there inside of a small cove. I need to go get Sonya."

"I can have a SEAL team go in and get her."

"Yet, if I don't show up, she dies," Sanders smirked.

"You hurt her…"

"That depends on you." Sanders shifted.

"That will be enough of that," Ralston said, entering the tent with Josh Wilson. "We'll take custody of Roman."

"That's okay, Jeffrey. I always have a backup plan," Sanders said, whipping his wrist. The small tube gun jutted out. He grasped it and aimed it at Lance.

"Lance, watch out!" Ralston jumped in the way, knocking Lance down as the weapon discharged its single, determining round. Ralston jerked, twisting and dropping to his knees. Sanders rolled, just missing a bullet by Ensor. Sanders had his backup pistol in hand as he fired, narrowly missing Ensor. He fired again, hitting Josh Wilson. He charged through the injured and ran out of the tent.

"Jeffrey!" Lance grabbed hold of Ralston. He took the shot to the left of his abdomen. "We'll get help." He turned to Josh Wilson. "Josh, are you hurt?"

"I'm okay, Lance. My jacket is Kevlar lined. Hurts like a mother, though."

"We need to get help for Jeffrey. Where's the captain?"

Sanders turned long enough to see that Ensor had a clear shot lined up at him. Sanders fired three shots into the air. The crowd stampeded in multiple directions. Ensor lost the shot and Sanders.

Sanders ran up to a man who was about to get into his pickup truck and yanked him out, knocking him in the head with his gun. Sanders drove off. A security car chased after him. He caught a glimpse of Ensor taking aim. The bullet was deflected by the cab, but it struck. Sanders' head bobbed back. He felt lightheaded and touched the right side of his face. There was blood. It was a flesh wound. He laughed.

Ensor lost him again.

Sanders tossed out a flat hand grenade. It exploded in front of the pursuing security car, disabling it. Sanders lined up the truck and jumped out onto the grass as it slammed into a row of parked aircraft. The mayhem had the crowds not knowing which way to run. Sanders got lost again in the panic and smoke.

A pilot was ready to mount his Pitts Special S-2. He wondered what the commotion was on the other side of the field. Sanders put his gun between his eyes. "Fly me out of here now, or I will shoot you in the face." Sanders motioned the pilot to take the front seat. He quickly took the rear seat. The Pitts heaved and sputtered to life. "Get moving."

"I don't have a clearance."

"Here's your clearance," Sanders said, pushing his gun up against the back of the pilot's head.

"I tell you I can't go," the pilot insisted. Sanders looked around the cockpit. He saw the throttle and pushed it forward.

"Now, move out!" Sanders barked.

The Pitts cut across the field and took off on the taxiway despite orders from the control tower to halt.

The crowd below thought it just another aerial demonstration. Sanders was gone.

"You're supposed to be retired, dude," Eric said, rubbing his neck.

"Yeah, I know. Look, I have to go get Sonya."

"Where is she?"

"Cuba. At the Farm. You two take care of Jeffrey." Lance stood. "The ambulance is here."

"You be careful," Josh added.

"I will."

Lance strapped into the Aerohawk. He engaged the starter and spun up the engine. The aircraft made a fast taxi across the grass to the nearest taxiway.

Lance was granted an emergency departure. The Aerohawk climbed quickly. He had half tanks of fuel and plotted where he would land to refuel. His next stop after that was Marathon. Base and home.

Ensor made his way back to the Aeronautical Dream Builders tent. He noticed that their aircraft was gone. "Eric, where is Lance?"

"Gone."

"Where? Please, I need to know. I can help him. One Navy man to another."

"He's been gone about an hour. He's on his way back to Marathon."

"He's planning to get his girl?"

"Yeah. Look. He knows what he's doing." Eric's head still hurt, but he was coming to the fact that danger continued to follow Lance. "But, if you can help him..."

"I will. I promise."

***

Lance had taken the Aerohawk up high to twenty-two thousand feet, where he would get better speed and range. He donned supplemental oxygen at fourteen thousand feet to sustain him. The engine was turning max out. Every mile and every minute counted.

***

Lance could see the lights of Miami in the distance as the sun was dipping lower over the horizon. He knew that there was a big rally for the Republicans today. In association with the rally, there was the Cuban Democratic Front. They were a new political organization that came out of nowhere. The president was set to make an appearance, he recalled. It didn't matter. Only Sonya mattered.

Lance turned away from the Miami area and set up for his approach into Marathon.

Lance shut down the Aerohawk. He would give himself forty minutes to ready the Aquahawk and himself. A quick shower was in order. He donned the dark two-tone sporty gray flight suit he wore on many a sortie.

Lance wrangled on his shoulder holster and placed his Glock-20 securely inside it. He hoped it would not be necessary. He packed the silencer that went with it. His vow of non-lethal action came to mind. He still didn't know how to process Miguel Rojas. The Colombian drug lord was alive when he left him. It sponsored the thought of his taser gloves. He grabbed the leather-clad electric eels and charger that went with them.

Lance came downstairs and put his bag and armaments inside of the Aquahawk. "You're a hard man to pin down," Ensor said. Lance jumped and spun around.

"Gees! Where did you come from?"

"I caught an F-Eighteen from Oshkosh down to Key West and drove up here. I came to help you. You need help to get your girl. Let me help you."

"I appreciate it, but please stay out of my road," Lance said, placing his fingers into his gloves.

"I can't let you go," Ensor said.

"You have no choice, Captain, and please lock up." Lance moved to the left of the Aquahawk to board as Ensor stepped in front of him. Lance moved his arms, knowing that Ensor would raise his. Lance grabbed Ensor around the left arm. The right glove discharged its high voltage through Ensor's body. He seized up. Lance slung Ensor over his shoulder and placed him in one of the MU-2's seats sitting on the hanger floor. "Forgive me, Captain, but she is my heart, and I must rescue my heart. Please lock up."

Out on the tarmac, with the hanger doors sliding closed, Lance pushed his foot into the step and heaved himself up and into the Aquahawk, sliding into his seat. The master came on. Soon digital information on the three screens appeared. His left hand found itself on the thrust lever, and his thumb wrapped around the end to push the slightly recessed starter button. He depressed the red button for three seconds and released it. The FADEC computer system took over and monitored startup. At 15% RPM, he squeezed a tab underneath the thrust lever handle and moved the lever an inch forward from OFF to the IDLE detent position. A moment later, he heard the deep throaty sound of combustion. The small turbofan engine spooled up to life. He turned on his taxi and running lights. He radioed the tower for an immediate departure. It was granted.

Lance lined up with center markings on the runway. He closed the canopy, securing it. It was three hundred and seventy-five miles to Grand Cayman. His journey would take about forty minutes. He saw two speeding patrol cars with their lights flashing. The tower called and denied takeoff. Lance hit the thrust lever and was off. He saw the two vehicles try and cut him off, but he had takeoff speed and pulled back on the side-stick controller. The fly-by-wire system obeyed his command and transitioned the amphibious aircraft to flight mode.

Ensor rushed out of the man-door and past the hanger to see the two Navy patrol cars. He caught the Aquahawk climbing, guessing about six thousand feet a minute. No one would catch him now.

Chapter 119

Playa Girón, Cuba

August 3, 2008

Lance dropped down to below one hundred feet as he approached the inlet to the Bay of Pigs. It was just before five a.m. with minimal sunlight highlighting coastal features. To his right, as he flew north, the coast was mostly all beach. On the left were the Zapata wetlands. He continued into the bay.

He lowered the full-span flaps and the retractable step underneath the fuselage of the Aquahawk. The step served mostly for breaking suction from the water on takeoff. He entered ground effect at sixty-five knots indicated. He cut power, held it as long as possible, and set down on the calm water.

The rudder trim tab also served as a rudder in the water. He scanned the area with binoculars. There was no sign of Sonya or any other soul. He decided to guide the Aquahawk toward the cove. The inner, semi-enclosed part of the cove was more of a lagoon. Built inside of the lagoon was a large concrete boat ramp. It went up the bank and connected to the bunker area. It looked all the more intriguing seeing it from the bayside.

Lance shut down the engine. He maneuvered the Aquahawk inside the lagoon and up to the long pier with the onboard electric jet drive. It was slow but quiet. The main pier stood about six feet above the water. Below that, a thirty-foot-long dock floated on the water. He lifted the canopy, stood, ready to tie off the aircraft when he saw his heart. "Sonya!" he called quietly. He was relieved. She smiled. His smile went flat when Sanders walked up behind her.

"What are the odds, Lance, that your new hideout is also my new temporary base of operations? At any rate, welcome to the Farm. Or should I say Bahia de Cochinos?"

"Yeah, Bay of Pigs."

"Now-now. And do me a favor. Park your aircraft up here."

Lance hesitated. Nothing new in the way of a plan came to mind. He engaged the starter. The ramp looked large enough to launch amphibious assault craft once upon a time. He lowered the landing gear, powered the Aquahawk up the ramp, turned left, and then turned left again onto the concrete platform, next to the bunker. He shut down the engine. His eyes and thoughts were on the straight shot in front of him. It looked a good five hundred feet to the end of the pier. All he needed was thrust to escape.

Lance stepped out of the aircraft. Sanders approached Lance with two armed guards, taking his Glock from his shoulder holster. He eyed the aircraft. "Oh, we boys with our toys."

Lance looked at Sonya. "Are you all right?" She broke free and ran, wrapping her arms around him.

"Both of you come with me. I need to put you on ice for a while," Sanders ordered.

Lance and Sonya were escorted inside of the first bunker. It was dark and dank inside with only newly fashioned fluorescent lighting, offering moderate illumination, powered by several car batteries. A generator could be heard in the back of the building. It was mostly empty, except for six long wooden crates and some cots placed along the wall.

They came up to a metal door. Gilberto opened it and turned on the small ceiling light. It was a storeroom originally. Now it was their jail cell. A metal cot was inside and a rusted metal chair. "I have to figure out what to do with you two," Sanders said.

"Well, we could start with better accommodations. I could go into town for a few knickknacks," Lance quipped.

"Oh, Lance," Sanders grinned, "how I could have used you on this one."

"Okay. What do you need?"

"More than I know you would be willing to do. That's the problem."

"What are you up to, Roman?"

"Just taking back what's mine. That's all. Don't do anything foolish." Sanders closed and locked the door behind him.

"Are you okay?" Lance said, taking Sonya by the shoulders.

"I'm scared, but now that I'm with you, well, I'm still scared." Lance tested the cot. "What are you doing?"

"I could use some rest. I was up early to plot your escape."

"And we see how well that went."

"Hey, and ouch." Lance held out his hand. "Come here." Sonya took his hand and nestled down next to him.

"I finally get you into bed, and it has to on this."

"Should we survive, you will."

"You mean that? I mean, if you still want to marry me, the answer is yes."

"Shouldn't you wait to be asked?"

"You did." She sprang up and grabbed a small photo of the wing walker holding the banner that asked for her hand. She cuddled back against Lance on the cot. He studied the picture.

"Roman." Lance let it go. It was done. "Rest for now." He went off to sleep. She found Lance's breathing to be very stable, rhythmic, and soothing. She closed her eyes and soon drifted off to a place where they could be safe together.

Lance held Sonya's hand as they were escorted back out to the lagoon. The day had gone to twilight.

A yacht was berthed at the end of the pier. Ernesto Cruz came walking along the pier with Sanders. Cruz studied Lance for a moment. He said: "Not long after the Bay of Pigs invasion, Castro built this facility out of paranoia, only to abandon it a few years later. Thus, it is fitting that this is the place of the new revolution."

"Now, Lance, we need to talk." Sanders slugged Lance, dropping him. Lance pushed up instinctively to fight, but Sanders kicked him and pounded him a few more times. Sanders signaled Gilberto to throw a switch on a control box next to a plastic bucket. A pair of underwater lights came on. "Get up." Sanders placed his hand on Lance's chest and pushed toward the edge of the pier. "There are several dedicated questions I need to ask you—after you've been primed." Sanders pushed Lance backwards. Lance fell into the lagoon. When he surfaced, the first ladle full of chum was tossed on him. Lance dunked back under to wash the smelly, oily fish guts and blood off of him. When he surfaced, he could see the reddish glow dispersed around him.

"Really, Roman? You need to go this far?"

"I have a beautiful plan and operation, Lance. That you and Scott Ensor have nearly ruined. There's a bigger picture here."

"I told you, and he told you, I have nothing to do with this. Wake up, man!"

"I want to believe you, Lance. And for the most part, I do, but this is not how things work out in my experience. I can't indict the other principals in this without the money."

"What money?" Sanders tossed another scoop on Lance. "Roman, you maniac! This will accomplish nothing. I only came for Sonya."

"Okay, Lance. Tell me, who else came with you? What's the plan?"

"I'm alone, Roman. I told you. Sorry, but it's that simple." Lance angled himself to swim forward.

Sanders fired a swath of bullets across Lance's intended path. "Just—keep—treading!"

Lance felt, for the first time since retirement, the desire for lethal response.

Sanders turned to Gilberto. "Keep him treading." Sanders took hold of Sonya and pulled her around the front of the bunker. Cruz followed.

Lance worked to conserve energy, but he hurt, and his burning arms and legs had long gone tired. He didn't realize by instinct he was swimming to the ramp until a spray of bullets reminded him to stop and keep treading. His flight suit felt like it was clad in iron. Its weight was taking its toll. At times, he would hold his breath just to relax and float. It didn't register that the compound's exterior lights were on and that night encircled him.

Sanders and Cruz marched Sonya back out to the pier. "Well, Lance. I'd say you're now properly primed."

"There's nothing more to tell you," Lance uttered between breaths.

Sonya's attention was drawn to the entrance of the lagoon. She heard splashing. "Get him out of the water!"

Sanders caught sight of the fin heading directly to Lance. At that moment, one of the underwater lights burned out. Sanders drew his gun. He scanned laterally and into the water, but it was too dark to see clearly.

"Lance! Lookout!" Sonya screamed. Lance turned around, but it was too late. The large tiger shark was on him. It dropped below the surface and dragged Lance underneath. There was a moment of thrashing and then silence.

Sonya broke free of Cruz's grasp and struck him in the face. She ran at full rage to Sanders. He grabbed her arms and shook her. "Knock it off, or you'll be next."

Cruz wiped his face. "I'm sorry, my dear, that you were made an unwilling part of this." He looked at Gilberto. "Take her back to the cell."

Lance had both hands tearing the flesh of the shark's nose in his counterattack. Its mouth was at his abdomen, but its teeth were on his right ankle. He was being pulled down below this shark by another shark. But they weren't teeth. It was a man's hand. He could barely see in the murky water. He felt something attack his face. It pushed its way into his mouth. He felt compressed air blow in and fill his lungs. There were no bubbles that escaped with his exhale. He took another secure breath. He felt something cover his face. It was a facemask. He put it on and cleared the water out of it. His vision cleared. He could see a man helping him. It was Ensor. Lance calmed. There was a black rope tied around the shark that Ensor held onto to guide the dead shark. Ensor also had a black rope tied around his waist. He tugged on it. Lance and the shark were pulled with the captain further down into the depths.

Sanders paced along the pier, looking for any sign of movement. His gun swung to and fro. There was nothing. He relented. It was dealt with.

Lance saw other divers. They were all wearing rebreather scuba gear and sitting inside of two flat black S.D.V. mini-subs. They were Navy SEALs! He was safe. He would follow their lead. Ensor took off the rope and tied it to the back of one of their subs. It towed the mighty fish away. Lance held onto Ensor, who held onto a handle on the other sub. It powered up and moved along the bottom slowly. Lance knew they were headed out of the lagoon. His thoughts raced back to Sonya. He would return for her.

Lance washed up on the beach like a piece of driftwood. He was finally on dry land. He laid on his back and rested. "Come on, Lance. You're alright," Ensor said.

"You weren't the one treading water for the last two hours with a cracked rib."

"Believe me, I can identify. We'll tape you up. You're a tough cookie."

"Resilient, Captain. I've always considered myself resilient."

Then, the six-man SEAL team emerged from the sea. They were in a well-covered spot of mangroves. Lance knew he could rest for a while in safety.

"Where did you get that Trojan shark?"

"You like that, huh? It kept bugging us and was on its way in to see you."

"That has to be a first."

"Second, actually."

"Well, thank you at any rate."

"The way I see it, Lance, I still owe you. And like I said, I'm here to help you, brother." Ensor turned to the SEAL team leader. "Sharkey."

"Aye, sir," Lieutenant Rick "Sharkey" Machado said.

"We get some rest, and then I'm going to take our resilient friend here on a short scouting party. No matter what, you have your orders."

"Aye, sir. We're good to go."

"I always thought that was a Marine phrase," Lance said curiously.

Ensor grinned. "We own the Marines."

Lance grinned himself. He was glad they were not in a bar.

Lance slept four of the five hours allocated to him. Soon, he and Ensor were quick-footing it the near mile back up the coast, walking along the highway road. It was just before three in the morning. Lance hoped this time the element of surprise was on his side.

The two men stepped over the railroad tracks and crouched behind a bush. There was a single guard out front. Ensor watched Lance push a button on the back of the metal band that decorated the black leather gloves near the cuff. "Taser gloves? Is that what you zapped me with?"

"You like that, huh? Two-hundred thousand volts run along wires in the stitching and out these small metal prongs on the first and third fingers."

They heard rumbling and heavy metal clanging. A train was coming. The locomotive rolling in reverse pushed three passenger cars and a boxcar at the end, stopping in front of the bunkers. Sanders' guards proceeded out of the bunker, wheeling out components into the boxcar that Ensor recognized as the Iranian Scud-B Shahab 1 missile he found on board the Lady Minsk. The boxcar was their launch platform. It wasn't hard to figure out that the small nuclear device Ensor discovered would be included in the assembly.

"Come on," Ensor said.

They sneaked around to the ramp. At the Aquahawk, Lance reached inside and pulled out his trusty Walther PPK with its silencer.

"Captain, I will never kill again, though I have a gun in my hand. Which means that my blood and Sonya's is on your hands. Am I clear?"

Ensor's expression deflated. "Yeah. We're clear, Lance."

Their awkwardness was redirected.

"It's not that I miss," Sanders voiced from behind.

"We just make poor targets," Ensor replied.

"Must be. Where's the rest of your team, Scotty?"

"You know I haven't led a team since being promoted to captain."

"I know you're not alone."

"Don't you think you would've been cut down by now if there was a team here?"

"Maybe. Let's go."

Inside the bunker, Ensor was reunited with the six wooden crates he found on the ship. Yet, only one missile was being assembled. "You know, Roman revolutions never quite work out the way they're planned," Ensor offered.

"True. Revolutions have become more of a hobby nowadays than a cause. Have a seat."

Lance and Ensor had several wrappings of nylon rope bind their hands behind their backs. They sat on one of the empty crates, currently helpless. Borsov strolled in, followed by Shah. "Everything is ready." He sneered at Ensor. "It is my friend that thinks he is a cat."

"You should have left well enough alone, Captain," Shah said.

"And you are villain number?" Lance asked smugly.

"There are no villains here. Only heroes. They made today possible," Sanders touted.

"No, Roman, you're terrorists," Ensor said venomously.

"We're terrorizing nobody, Scotty. Well, maybe the Cubans a bit. We're simply—starting a little war. Shouldn't last for more than a couple of hours or so. Should all be home by dinner. I will be anyway."

"The rally," Lance said. "The rally in Miami today. For the Cuban Democratic Front."

"We call it the C.D.F. I thought I was going to have trouble starting an organization to reform Cuba, but to my surprise, an office, a few computers, food, with some seed money, and it took on a life of its own. I still never get over the blatant naïveté of people, especially college kids. I believe there may be twenty thousand people in attendance today," Sanders added.

"And the president is set to give a speech," Ensor confirmed.

"I do believe that's what has been scheduled."

"Roman, you really plan to nuke the rally?" Ensor said, bewildered.

"What?" Lance said, perking up. "You have a nuclear device?"

"One kiloton, to be exact," Borsov said somewhat proudly.

Lance's mouth went dry. "You fire a missile from here, and they'll track it."

"I think that's the idea, Lance." Ensor looked Sanders squarely in the eyes. "You're really going to do this?"

"I really am."

"Just to get your house up on the hills back?"

"For a start."

"You'll kill a lot of innocent people," Lance said.

"No such thing as innocent people, Lance. I told you that," Sanders scolded.

"You still don't have the money. There's no paper trail," Ensor said.

"There is no money per se, but there is still a very distinct paper trail. The money you took was put into a Cayman Island account. We've done our homework. The trail will still lead back to our principals. For our compensation, we plan to take one of Castro's accounts once the Banco de Cuba is in our control. I always have a backup plan, Scotty." Sanders turned to the others. "Let's go." He looked at Naser. "Keep an eye on them, and most importantly, keep your distance."

Naser sat in a chair facing Lance and Ensor. His gun flinched every time Lance or Ensor stirred. They were wiggling uncomfortably after sitting on wood for the last two hours. "They must be on the yacht," Lance whispered.

"Silence!" Naser growled. "You American devils will die, and Allah will bless me."

"Your hatred will never be blessed," Lance said flatly.

"Don't waste your words on this moron," Ensor replied.

"What? What is this you are saying about me?" Naser scrambled off his chair, waving his gun. He came up to Lance and backhanded him. It hurt. "Come! Say something else to me!"

"I didn't say anything to you in the first place. He did."

"Say something else."

"Okay, your breath stinks."

Naser breathed in Lance's face. "How do you like this?"

Lance leaned as far away from him as he could. "I don't."

"Hey! Moron!" Ensor shouted. Naser turned slightly. Lance rammed his head into the side of Naser's head, knocking it over to Ensor, who swung his head and connected to the other side of Naser's head, knocking it back to Lance as Lance hit it back to Ensor who gave it another bash. Naser dropped.

The two men wobbled where they sat. "I can still hear the crowd yelling—olé!" Ensor remarked, forcing his head to clear. "You okay, Lance?"

"Duh, yeah, Howard—I like to box," Lance replied in a nasally Bronx accent.

"You're alright, Rio," Ensor said, chuckling.

"You keep saying that. Oh, my head. My face." Lance reached down to the back of his right shoe and pushed. A small flat ceramic knife slid out. Lance cut his ropes. He was free. "Here, turn around." He quickly knifed through the ropes that bound Ensor.

"Come on. We're stopping this," Ensor stated.

Ensor took Naser's gun. They bound and gagged their captor behind the crate. Finding a toolbox, they rummaged through, finding a cordless screw gun, a set of screwdrivers, pliers, and a couple of flashlights. They took the toolbox with them.

They stepped out carefully from the bunker, crossed the fifteen feet of the platform, and slid open the boxcar side door by just enough to get inside. They slid it closed.

With flashlights on, they saw the missile perched on a makeshift launching cradle. It had a large hydraulic piston underneath to raise it up into firing position. Shining their lights around the boxcar, they saw that the roof and sides were rigged with hydraulic pistons to fall open for the missile to launch.

"Interesting," Ensor said. They both went to the front of the missile and began removing screws. There was a small metal control panel on the launcher.

"How much time do we have?"

"Not much," Ensor sighed.

Lance removed the final screw that held the nose section in place. The nose was free. Lance unplugged an electrical cable, and both men sat the nose cone down. Lance needed more light, but he was familiar with the weapon and how it held a payload. He removed more screws.

"The bomb is free. We can remove it," Lance said, lifting. They got the beer keg-sized device on the floor of the boxcar. Lance studied it. "I know this bomb."

"How?"

"I schlepped it halfway across the Negev desert." He shook his head. "Jeffrey," he growled.

"Never mind now. Go get your girl."

Lance slid open the door. Dawn was breaking. He slipped back into the bunker.

Ensor tapped on the missile casing. He could hear a dull echo inside. The fuel tanks were not full. The missile would not have the range to reach Miami. It would detonate over the Gulf of Mexico. It was now clear. The Mid-East money accounts, the two other missiles in the bunker left for discovery. This was a political sting operation. It would bring down the Castro régime, North Korea, and possibly break the back of Islam. It was a nuclear-powered crusade. Sanders was no traitor. He was playing a part. Ensor shook off the thought of acceptance. He could not let this escalate any further. He turned his attention to the control panel. It was a manual setup. The coordinates were probably set, but its steering was dead without the nose cone and navigation computer. There was an old chipped knob that set a mechanical timer. Ensor took the cordless screwdriver and opened the panel cover. It was jury-rigged, with a remotely-controlled servo keeping the timer wheel from moving. It was simple and practical. He gave Borsov that. Ensor turned the knob from the twenty-minute mark to one minute. There was a shudder in the boxcar. The train was coming to life. He heard others outside.

"I'm going up to the cab, and we can go to the launch site," Sanders said.

Lance came to the bunker's jail cell. He heard Sonya fighting. "Get away from me!"

Lance ripped the door open. Gilberto reached for his Ak-47 leaning up against the wall. Lance ran and jumped under the cot. He reached up and grabbed Gilberto by his crotch as the glove discharged. Lance held on like a pit bull as Gilberto screamed and bounced Lance and the cot up and down before collapsing. Lance pulled himself up. He sat on the cot, rubbing the back of his head and then his knees. Sonya reached for him. Her left hand caressed him, as her right hand rattled the handcuffs as the chain went taut. "Sorry. I don't bounce back like I used to. Where's the key?"

"In his shirt pocket," she said.

Lance found the key and released her. She fell into his arms. "Are you okay? He didn't hurt you?"

"No. You came in like Zorro. Just in the nick of time."

Lance grinned, bemused. He handcuffed Gilberto to the cot. "Stay by me and do exactly what I say."

"You lead, I'll follow," she said eagerly.

Lance stopped and kissed her. "But, always by my side."

Sanders climbed into the cab of the locomotive. "Okay, Jamie, let's go."

“Today, I must have the train back by noon, Señor Sanders.”

“It won’t be a consideration by then. Let’s go.”

“Wait,” Borsov said, climbing aboard. “I’m the one with the remote.”

Ensor felt the train shake. He rolled the bomb to the door and slid it open. The train was moving. He rolled it out onto the platform. He ran back and pulled the servo arm off with one of the pliers. The timer began its countdown. Ensor jumped out of the boxcar. He tried picking up the bomb, but it was pulling on his broken ribs.

Lance came out from the bunker with Sonya.

“Lance, take an end.”

Sanders watched as the train went slowly around the long curve of the track. His eyes widened when he saw the boxcar flay open. “No! It’s not supposed to launch yet.”

Sanders saw that the nose cone was off the missile. He watched in gritted horror as the rocket motor sparked to life and came to full thrust, pushing its way off the launcher and ramming into the first passenger car, tearing its way through the second and then into the third. Borsov and Sanders jumped out of the cab. What was left of the missile slammed into the locomotive with a tremendous explosion. The smell of burnt diesel fuel was in the air.

Lance and Ensor carried the bomb around the platform to the Aquahawk. Sonya saw Cruz and Shah on the yacht. They pulled their guns. “Lance!”

Lance saw two small wakes from out in the bay speed toward the yacht. The yacht arched up in its center from the shock wave, engulfing Cruz and Shah in flames.

Two of Sanders’ men aimed at Lance and Ensor. They were cut down by two shots. The SEALs were somewhere around and in action.

Sharkey and two SEALs came up to Ensor. “Captain, the compound’s been secured. We have air support on the way just in case.” Sharkey and Ensor looked over the device.

“The detonator was housed on this end, but there’s a radio receiver on top of it now,” Lance said, noting two L.E.D. lights.

“This could be trouble,” Ensor added. One of the lights flashed.

“Trouble, Captain?” Borsov said. They turned to see the burnt and tattered man limp toward them. The SEALs trained their weapons on him.

“Easy boys,” Ensor commanded.

“If you shoot, my finger comes off the trigger. It detonates in five seconds. Nothing can stop it. This is *my* backup plan.” They noted his fingers around the handheld remote transmitter. “Maybe I am generous. I give you one minute. Or I give you ten minutes.” Borsov turned a knob. “I am giving you now twenty minutes just to be sporting. But, where can you run in twenty-minutes?" He laughed.

A single shot sent Borsov to the ground and the remote out of his hand. Sanders stepped forward and grabbed the remote. It started a count down from 20:00. Sanders was burnt and bleeding. He staggered, oozing life with each step.

"The answer is nowhere." Sanders dropped to his knees. Ensor moved in closer. Sanders raised his gun at Ensor. "You though, Scotty. You're mine." He couldn't hold the gun up.

"Sorry, Roman, but this is far as you go." Ensor put a single shot into Sanders. He fell back. Ensor took his gun and the remote. "Okay, people, we need a plan."

"Lance, what are we going to do?" Sonya begged.

"Ah—ah—the Aquahawk!"

"How?"

"Bomb bay doors. They should be wide enough."

Lance popped the rear canopy open on the Aquahawk, working furiously to remove the back seat. Ensor grabbed the seat as Lance handed it to him. Lance pulled a floor panel, exposing the two belly doors. "We can fly it out over open water and drop it into the sea."

"Agreed," Ensor affirmed. "I'll steady it for you, Lance, until you're ready to drop it."

"Okay. Let's do it." Lance hopped out and stepped up into the front. Ensor jumped into the back and took hold of the bomb, straddling it on his hands and knees. He could see that the bomb did rest on split doors. He put on his headset and closed and locked the canopy. Lance turned on the master. Life came to the instrument panel. After a few quick procedures, he engaged the starter button and lit the engine. The engine spun up quickly. Lance strapped in and put on his headset. "Can you hear me, Captain?" Lance said.

"Loud and clear." Ensor took the remote and looked at the readout: 17:22 and counting down. "Okay, Lance. We're running out of time. Let's go."

Lance saw the worry on Sonya's face. He would come back to her. He gave her a confident thumbs up. Lance lowered the flaps to takeoff position. "Hold on, Captain, we may not have enough runway ahead of us."

"Understood. I'm good to go!"

Lance looked ahead. He held the toe brakes down and brought up full power. When the engine gave all it could, he bent his feet back off the brakes. The Aquahawk lunged forward, quickly picking up speed. In seconds he was off the concrete platform and bouncing on the wooden pier. The edge came too quickly. There was not enough speed. He hit the landing gear lever up as they flew off the end of the pier at 55 knots indicated. The nose dropped down. Lance resisted pulling the control stick back too sharply, though the water was rushing up to meet him. The jet settled in ground-effect long enough to build up speed.

"Okay, we have flying speed." Lance pulled up sharply to gain altitude. He headed out over the Zapata wetlands and then turned to the south.

"Easy, Lance. It's bad enough if this thing leaks, but easy on my boys."

"You'll love your three-eyed kids all the same. How much time is left?"

"Fifteen minutes, thirty-five seconds. Give it all you got!"

Lance continued southbound.

Two MiG-23 fighters pulled up to the left side of Lance. He felt deflated. It was all he needed. They were signaling to land. Lance shook his head no.

Ensor looked up. "Great. Tell them that we have a nuke about to go off."

Lance keyed his mic. "Havana Control. We have a nuclear device that is about to go off. Please give us space."

"Negative, you must land now, or you will be shot down," Havana Control replied.

"Well, so much for diplomacy," Lance said. "Hold on."

"Ever since I met you," Ensor sighed.

Lance rolled the Aquahawk hard to the left, nearly hitting into first the MiG jet. The MiG pilot's knee-jerk reaction almost caused him to slam into his wingman. They were shaken and scattered long enough for Lance to dive the Aquahawk and turn around.

Sonya saw the Aquahawk dart by overhead. "What is he doing?"

"He's being chased," Sharkey said. He saw the two MiGs fly over around two thousand feet.

Ensor heard beeping. "What's that?"

"Radar detector. They're trying to lock on. But we're not that radar friendly," Lance said as he headed to the more mountainous area in front of him. Lance dove the aircraft, pulling up in a nine g turn to the left. He could hear Ensor's hard groan.

A missile shot by and hit the hillside. Lance grimaced. He followed the hilly terrain and into a canyon. Lance turned the Aquahawk on its side, pulling eight g's to maintain level flight as he hugged the canyon wall. Ensor struggled to look up. All he could see was an earth wall whipping by. They were so close. A gust nearly blew them into the wall. His life was firmly entrusted to the man in the pilot's seat once again.

The canyon walls ended. Lance rolled level and then dived. He pulled up sharply into a ten plus g loop. He felt the blood drain from his face. His eyes pull back into their sockets. The completion of the first loop put him inverted.

The two MiGs flew by. He came over the top and then rolled level into another dive and then flew out of the canyon.

"That one hurt," Ensor groaned.

"You're still conscious? Wow."

"What was that maneuver?"

"What else—a Cuban Eight."

Lance saw a large cloud mass, ten fluffy miles of it. He aimed for it. "How much time is left?"

"Less than eight minutes. I'll give you a two-minute warning."

Lance entered the clouds at just over five thousand feet and continued climbing. The small aircraft was showing impressive speeds well past five hundred miles per hour. At eight thousand feet, he broke through the cloud layer. He kept the canopy just above the clouds.

From the other end of the cloud layer, Lance caught two sets of fins coming at him. He braced for impact—growling. He then held his breath as the two MiGs shot by buffeting the Aquahawk.

"What was that?" Ensor said, fighting to keep the bomb stable.

"You don't want to know."

"Lance. We have to drop this bomb. We just have over four minutes."

"Okay. Hold on. I'm heading back out to sea."

Time and events seemed timeless, though the reality was that maneuvers, climbs, dives were happening in multiples and groups of rapidly passing seconds. Racing through the sky at over eight hundred feet per second demanded split-second attention. Lance put the Aquahawk in a dive and turned left to exit the clouds on a southwesterly direction.

The Aquahawk flashed below the clouds, passing six hundred miles per hour. Lance brought it low, just one hundred feet above the ocean surface. They were outside of the Cuban ADIZ and in international waters. "Captain, I'm going to open the bay doors. Watch yourself."

As the aircraft slowed, the radar detector sounded off. "They've locked onto us! We didn't make it!" Lance waited for the illegal missile to strike them. He would go the same way as his parents. Another missile on an intersecting course collided with the Cuban missile. The flash and rumble erupted behind them. Lance was confused. Now the two MiGs bugged out.

Lance felt a presence. He looked up to his left and his right. Two F-18s stationed themselves on each side of him. "Commander Rio," came the voice over the radio. "You have an escort by the United States Navy. Drop your bomb, sir, and bug out." Lance felt a relief that soaked through his body.

Lance brought the slowed aircraft down to forty feet above the water.

“Lance, just coming up on two minutes.”

“Okay, stand clear. I’m opening the doors.” Electric latches retracted. Small hydraulic pistons pushed downward. The bay doors opened. “Bombs away.”

“Lance, it’s stuck! The bomb won’t go through.”

“What? Ah, okay. Hold on.”

Lance climbed and then dived. Coming back down quickly to the water, he pulled up sharply, loading the aircraft with high g forces. Ensor pushed as hard as he could. With his last straining efforts, the bomb eased downward. It popped through—and so did he. His head popped through his grasping arms, knocking off his headset. Ensor was able to grab hold of the rudder pedals. The Aquahawk shivered from side to side. Lance felt the rudder pedals moving against his feet. “Captain,” he called. There was no reply. Lance turned around the best he could. He removed the right ear cup from his head. He could hear screaming.

“Lance! Lance!”

Lance got it. Lance climbed again. He dropped the nose into a sharp dive. Ensor’s body flew back inside of the aircraft, where his back hit the top of the canopy. Lance rolled inverted and closed the bay doors. Lance then rolled upright and climbed under full power. They were out of there!

Chapter 120

Marathon Airport

August 11, 2008

"You don't look it, you know," Sonya said.

"That doesn't change the fact—I'm fifty today," Lance pouted.

"With a lot of puppy still left in him. And you're here with me."

"That part I'm grateful for."

"Rest now," she said. Lance still showed signs of bruising and pain. He fell asleep on the sofa. She could only imagine the troubles this man had seen in life. She recalled how vividly he told her of the ocean below lighting up like a giant aquarium. He could see vast schools of fish and coral reef formations until that same light turned into a blinding pool of fire that blew up into a six hundred-foot-high column of water. The man she knew as Roman Sanders was blamed for the incident. The word "rogue" was used often to describe the man and the plot. Oddly, it opened a marginal amount of dialog between Cuba and the United States.

Lance came back into a semi-conscious state. She stroked his forehead.

"Lance."

"Yes."

"Do you still want to marry me?"

Lance sat up slowly. He looked concerned. "Are you sure you want to be with me?"

"Come with me." She took Lance by the hands and pulled him off the sofa.

They came downstairs. Sonya opened the door of the Mits and sat on the bench seat. Lance looked puzzled. "Well? Take your seat, Captain." Lance worked his way into the pilot's seat. "Buckle up." Lance did just so, strapping himself in. Sonya swung around to the right rear-facing seat as with their first encounter.

"Now what?"

She put her arm around his neck and gently pulled him to her. It was like their first kiss. It took him dimensionally elsewhere. She pulled away slowly. "I'm sure."

"When?"

"Now."

"Do you mind if I heal up first?"

"You're sturdy enough." There was a knock at the man-door that echoed around the hanger. "Besides, it's not good for the man to continue alone." Sonya filed out of the aircraft.

Moments later, Sonya plopped back inside to the right rear seat. Ensor stepped inside and sat on the bench seat. He was clean-cut, befitting a naval officer. "Well, this is cozy."

"Captain," Lance said, surprised.

"You have to start calling me Scotty, Lance."

"Okay, Scotty. What brings you here?"

"Well, while the politicians wrangle with what happened, I wanted you to have this."

Ensor handed up a large envelope that Sonya took and passed to Lance. He opened it, reading its contents. Lance's jaw dropped. "Twenty-five million dollars! Me?"

"Yup," Ensor said, grinning. "It came from the countries that sponsored Sanders little caper. Jeffrey Ralston agreed to shelter it in one of your old Cayman Island accounts. We both felt it was safer there. Personally, I want to see what else you'll come up with. I hear talk of space. So, take what you need. Come on. Let's go have dinner."

Chapter 121

Miami, Florida

December 28, 2008

Sonya took a few moments away from her husband and brother. The call on her cell phone connected. "Hi, Eric. How's the best man doing?"

"Hey, darlin', how you doin'?" Eric Pitts replied.

"We're fine. In fact, we're great. We had a great honeymoon in England, Germany, and Israel. I got to meet everyone, especially Alfonso Pig."

"Yeah, you can't help but love that walking set of baby-backs." Eric took pause. "Everything okay with you newlyweds?"

"I've never been happier, and I seem to keep Lance smiling."

"I'm sure you do. So, what's up?"

"You know we have access to this slush fund. How about building the Mantis?"

"Wow. Moving back into the supersonic arena again. I don't know. We were barely able to do what we did."

"But you did it."

"Yeah, but it took over a dozen others—and keep it all secret. It took its toll. Believe me."

"Lance needs it."

"Yeah, that mind of his. Well, you'd have to spend a lot of time out here."

"I don't mind."

"I guess that would get you out of that bat cave you been living in."

"I don't mind that either. As long as I am with Lance. Look. We have this thing to go to in a few days."

"How ya' feeling about that?"

"Nervous. But, I guess the world moves on."

"That's a good way to look at it. Remember, the runway behind you is useless. I tell you what. Go do your thing and then come out soon, and we'll talk about the Mantis project."

"It's a deal."

"Okay, darlin', speak soon." She hung up.

Sonya eyed her husband laughing with her brother, Javier, as she came outside. Lance caught sight of her. Their eyes met and sparkled. Mrs. Rio hooked her arm in with Mr. Rio's, taking her place by his side. Maybe that was all that mattered.

Chapter 122

Havana, Cuba

January 1, 2009

It was fifty years to the day that Dr. Fidel Alejandro Castro Ruz took power in Cuba. The seizure had caused many life-changing events in Cuba and around the world. Many had died. Many found rebirth inside and outside of the country. Lance and Sonya were two such survivors. Their lives culminated in interaction with one another—as one flesh.

It was late in the afternoon, in addition to a long wait. Fidel Castro, a shell of the man he once was, came out to greet Lance and Sonya. His brother Raul Castro walked by his side. To the Cuban leaders, they were just a couple of hapless individuals that got involved in a conspiracy and had the presence of mind to prove victorious.

Their meeting was brief. There was a lot of celebration in the city today and across the island. Their valor had at least gained them welcomed travel to their ancestral home whenever they desired. Lance escorted Sonya outside the building.

"Are you okay?" She asked, concerned.

"I was going to ask you the same," he replied.

"I'm fine, as long as I am with you. The runway behind us sort of thing."

Lance grinned. "Yes." He took her hands in his. "And we treasure what's before us."

The last of the day melded into twilight, as once before, with the famed old wall lit up along its path. "I believe I still owe you that walk along the Malecón," Lance said.

Lance recognized the spot where they both once stood. He stopped to her bewilderment.

"Okay, I hate it when I don't understand you," Sonya protested. "Why do you want to remember this exact spot?"

"Because, here, my wife, in spite of everything—is where I fell in love with you." His arms wrapped around her, pulling her close, vowing within himself to never let go.

For Lance Rio and all who had come in and out of his life—another moment in time had come full circle. And with that, he was finally at peace.

EPILOGUE

Marathon Airport

December 21, 2012

Eric Pitts put his arm around a very anxious Sonya Rio. Ensor stood confident while Jeffrey Ralston found himself pacing a few steps here and there. With others present, heavy with anticipation, they waited down on the hanger floor by a radio. “Mantis to base, over,” Lance radioed.

“Mantis, this is base. Go ahead,” Eric radioed back.

“Base, she’s performing beautifully. I’m taking her into supersonic.”

***

Lance moved the two afterburner levers forward on the center console. He looked outside and watched the smaller left fore wing rotate back from the main forward-swept wing, in concert with the right-wing, knowing that it was slicing even cleaner through the air.

The Mantis fully raked back for supersonic travel, delivered Mach 2.5 at sixty-two thousand feet. The permutations of this new sweet four-seater were unknown at this exact moment in time. But, to Lance Rio, if the truth be told, it was just another kit plane—*FASTGLASS*!

About the Author

Tony Tiscareno lives in the San Francisco Bay Area, with England being his second home for half of his life. He is of Mexican-Scottish heritage.

A professionally-trained screenplay writer, coupled with his love of all things aviation, science, and history—biblical and secular, has led him to write this, his first novel with the exploration of these themes.